# A Short Introduction to Anneliese

A NOVEL

James Elkins

un

THE UNNAMED PRESS
LOS ANGELES, CA

Five Strange Languages

1 *Stories, like Illnesses*
2 *A Short Introduction to Anneliese*
3 *Weak in Comparison to Dreams*
4 *Ghosts Are*
5 *An Inventory of the Dead*

AN UNNAMED PRESS BOOK



Published in North America by the Unnamed Press.

www.unnamedpress.com

Unnamed Press, and the colophon, are registered trademarks of Unnamed Media LLC.

Hardcover ISBN: 978-1-961884-43-4
EBook ISBN: 978-1-961884-44-1
LCCN: 2025933924



Cover design and typeset by Jaya Nicely

Manufactured in the United States of America by Sheridan

Distributed by Publishers Group West
First Edition

# Contents

## Part I

1 A Quiet Dinner .......... 1
2 Movies and Resorts .......... 27
3 The Peaceful Blue Jura Mountains .......... 53
4 A Walk to the Ruheplatz .......... 91
5 The Bucket List .......... 118

## Part II

6 The Thirteen Theories .......... 157
7 Anneliese's Summer Reading .......... 204
8 The Gray Notebooks .......... 322
9 In a Year We May All be Gone .......... 358
10 In Slow Steps, Toward .......... 366

Notes .......... 485

Author's note on the music .......... 573

# A Short Introduction to Anneliese

We're each of us enigmas to ourselves, that's despite what Socrates thought about living the examined life. He said, The unexamined life is not worth living, but he should have said, Examine your life if you'd like, if it'll make you feel better. If it'll convince you you're clever and profound, by all means go ahead, try to figure out your life, puzzle out your mother, plumb your doubts and desires. But look at me, Socrates should have said, I claim to know who I am, but all I really know is I'm about to drink poison.

# PART I

# 1

## A QUIET DINNER

**ON WEDNESDAY,** February 5, less than three minutes before the first time I met Anneliese, I was fully dressed, fast asleep, face down on a starched bleached hotel bed sheet. The phone rang with an awful rasp. A quiet voice on the other end said, Samuel Emmer? We're in the lobby, anytime you're ready.

The dinner, which I'd forgotten, was with an old friend of Catherine's named Anneliese Glur. She is in Frankfurt, Catherine had said, and you have an overnight there, so why don't you two meet? I checked my face in the mirror without registering much of anything except the presence of a head, and bolted downstairs.

Anneliese was tall but bowed. She greeted me with a loud Aha! and shook my hand harshly.

Her companion was a full foot shorter than her, elegant but brittle looking. His eyes were bleary and he seemed tired, as if he were about to say good night.

Glad to meet you at last, she said. Hope you don't mind I brought along my brother Paul. Actually he insisted.

They had made a reservation in the hotel restaurant, so dinner was only ten steps away. We were seated at a table overlooking the river. Three swans came into view, straining in the shiny black water.

It's been ages since I've seen Catherine, she said, maybe two years?

She looked in Paul's direction, but her gaze missed him and rested momentarily, and with visible disapproval, on a bright red pen in the server's apron. Paul nodded as if he had actually been asked whether it had been two years, and smiled as if to say, This is how it is.

I ordered sparkling water, and soon the evening was underway: a monologue from Anneliese, covering her acquaintance with Catherine, their years in England, Catherine's sudden departure, her own return to Switzerland, the little summer house she and Paul rented in a forest near the Basel-Mulhouse-Freiburg airport, how lovely it was and yet how remarkably infested with spiders, how their cousin's daughter Luzia loved it there, despite her allergies—and then Anneliese asked if I noticed the odd way the swans on the river outside were trying to stay in place despite the swift current.

Why do they do that? she said. It's hopeless.

Maybe there's something to eat just under the water.

No, Paul. The river is too deep, they can't reach anything down there.

The three swans were borne steadily backwards until they went out of sight.

Last summer, Anneliese continued, Luzia broke the second toe on her right foot.

Sorry to hear that, I said.

She stubbed it on a half-buried plank that turned out to be part of a collapsed shed. Our neighbor Adelheid Wyrsch had let the shed fall apart, creating a minefield of rusted nails. I told her she needed to clean it up, but she wouldn't, she kept saying it was on her own property, and I kept saying that was okay, we didn't mind walking on her property. After that she mainly stayed in her house. She developed a habit of pulling her curtain aside just a fraction of a centimeter, undoubtedly to spy on us. Paul couldn't see it, but I could, I could see her little eye there in the shadow, so I put up a sign, STOP SPYING ON US ADELHEID WYRSCH YOU BITCH, and after that she always hurried from her front door to her car holding a newspaper in front of her face, and then the neighbors on the other side asked if we might perhaps take the sign down, so I had to put up another sign facing their house saying GOOD MORNING WHOEVER YOU ARE

MIND YOUR OWN BUSINESS, and so they moved a cabinet in front of their window, and after that it was peaceful, even though I still couldn't get any work done on account of the spiders.

Sorry to hear that, I said.

Most of the year, Anneliese said, Paul and I live in Basel with Luzia and our uncle Hans in a large leaky building, where I am proud to say I know no one, because I never talk to anyone in the entry or the stairwell, even when they say hello in an apparently pleasant and innocent way, because you never know just how boring people can be. Interesting people are rare, Samuel. They keep to themselves. Uninteresting people outnumber interesting ones and swarm over them like moths. It's dangerous to say hello back to anyone, because then they might regale you with incomprehensible gossip or boring reminiscences or pointless anecdotes or vacuous boasts or preening self-assessments. Or they'll list their miraculous children or their illustrious ancestors, or even their legion of lovers, or worse, they'll tell you about their unimaginative travels, their favorite films or music or food or sports or pets or hobbies, they'll start telling you about jigsaw puzzles or stamp collecting, for god's sake, and if you say you're not interested, they'll try to entertain you by showing off their waggling ears or flaring nostrils or oscillating eyes or invertible eyelids or trick joints or musical knuckles or their prehensile tongue, and if you say, Please stop, only children find those things entertaining, then they'll take you aside even though there is no one around and recite their calcified grievances regarding other people who live in the building, and if you tell them you just don't care and you try to walk away, they'll launch into disturbing confessions about their sweaty feet or excessive salivation or bleeding gums or nauseating hernias or scabs or scars or warts or moles or corns, or their personal plumbing problems and intimate accidents and slipped disks and swollen glands and collapsed lungs, their lungs that simply collapsed for no reason, causing them excruciating pain and a creeping sensation of cold pooling blood inside their chests, and if you don't stop them right there, it'll get worse, they'll tell you about their sudden blackouts, their psychotic fantasies, their recurring blinding headaches and terrifying violent hallucinations, and then you will hear all about their invisible companion named Eiklar, whose body is made of bark, and if you try to push them away, they'll grab your arm and pull you even closer and whisper in your ear about the really troubling difficulty they are having with neighbors, certain neighbors who won't talk to perfectly harmless friendly people who only want to say hello, and what's to be done about that, and what's going to have to be done right away about that, and how those unsociable people need to sell their apartment and move to some isolated cabin in the forest near the Basel-Mulhouse-Freiburg airport where they can spend their days swatting spiders, and so you see, Samuel, it's best to keep silent. People are like ants, Samuel, they bite or sting, if ants sting, otherwise they just bite, as I repeatedly experienced over my many years of uninterrupted service to the University of Basel, which by the way, despite all its inconceivably stupid fiscal decisions and its nerve-wrackingly incompetent administration, all of which amount to a more or less devastating emotional and intellectual experience for the faculty, or at least for me, has nevertheless managed, once again, to secure a Swiss National Science Foundation grant as a Center of Excellence in the Biological Sciences, which leads me, and this, of course, or so I assume, will be no surprise to you, to be able, indeed quite pleased, to invite you to come to visit for at least a semester and perhaps as long as a year.

Thanks, I said. But I don't think that's for me.

You can't invite him, Lysi, Paul said. You don't work there anymore.

As long as a year, she said again.

We were silent a moment.

So, I said, you're in Frankfurt for a visit?

Paul shook his head.

I understand it's hard to decide, Anneliese said. Life pulls us in different directions. Luzia is a good example of such an incapacity to reach a clear decision. She showed an early penchant for science and then she surprised us by announcing she wouldn't go to university because she'd decided either to be a ballerina or an actress, imagine, a ballerina or an actress, the two most clichéd notions it is possible for a young girl to have, but what can you do? So we praised her, even though we didn't mean it, but then just when we reconciled ourselves to supporting an unsuccessful unmarried girl for an indeterminate number of years while she spiraled into depression and self-loathing, Luzia announced she was going to apply to be a retail salesperson at Manor Basel Department Store, even though that store has nothing to recommend it except apparently a cashier who works there, whom Luzia said is very handsome and always looks sad when he hands you the receipt, but as soon as she'd announced that, Luzia had another idea. She said her true passion was to be a licensed upholsterer. Now I have no idea where she got that notion, and in fact it turns out there is no such thing as a licensed upholsterer, but that didn't matter because then she changed her mind again and said she wanted to be a petroleum engineer, probably because she saw an advertisement on television showing a woman in a yellow hard hat pointing at an oil well; and then she wanted to be an auditor for government agencies, even though she could not specify which government agencies, or even clearly define what an auditor does; and then a nurse anesthetist, even though she was incapable of describing even the most basic elements of that profession, short of saying anesthetists use what she called "gas masks"; and each time she announced one of these capricious notions, Paul said something like, "Oh, that's a wonderful choice!" or, "Oh, how interesting, how promising!" or, "Oh, good idea, Luzi!" but still Luzia didn't settle on anything, she just went on and on, announcing even more ridiculous ideas. She wanted to be a family psychological counselor, she said, and then a police prosecutor assigned to domestic disputes in the St. Alban neighborhood, that's where we live, so Luzia was making fun of us, because sometimes Paul and I disagree on certain subjects, like for example whether Luzia means anything she says, or if Luzia has ever been sincere even once in her life, but Paul and I never actually argue, so it is preposterous to think anyone would call the police to stop us from arguing, we are perfectly reasonable people, or at least I am, Luzia was just being malicious, making fun of us, and then she said she wanted to be a protocol enforcer for domestic restraint orders in the St. Alban neighborhood, and at that point Paul, even you knew she was making fun of us, because you had told her that your office was managing a case brought by an adopted child against its parents, because that is what Paul's office specializes in, *Erwachsenenschutzrecht,* adults' rights, and Paul had just told her about a case involving a protocol enforcer and a domestic restraint order, and Luzia had simply stolen his story and used it against us. Such unbelievable preposterous rude nonsense, as if the police would ever need to be involved in our domestic issues, and through all this, Paul, you kept praising her, "Oh, wonderful idea, Luzi!" you said, "Oh, Luzi, that would be great!" although after a while your praise seemed, shall we say, lukewarm, until finally I said, "Please! It is perfectly clear Luzia is being insincere, she is being fundamentally disrespectful, she is making these things up. She is making fun of us, she is being aggressively dishonest, she is condescending to us, and in fact she is lying at our faces." You see, Samuel, Luzia was bone idle, she had no intention whatsoever of doing anything except freeloading off us into the hazy future when we would be reduced to signing our pension checks over to her in exchange for our dinners, she was just pulling our levers, she was pressing our buttons, she was pressing on our buttons. It's a stupid expression, you don't push a button, you button a button, well, I guess we're talking about emotional buttons, so maybe you press those, but no, it doesn't make any sense, it must be wrong. It is a typical example of how awful language is. I have a whole theory about that, which—

The waiter appeared.

Anneliese didn't even look at the menu. She told the waiter she wanted sirloin and salad, nothing but sirloin and salad, no sauce on the sirloin, no dressing on the salad, any kind of salad, it didn't matter, but no dressing, and no side dishes, no vegetables, no appetizer, and above all no garnishes, no cute little sprigs of parsley, no whimsical sprinkle of oregano, and for that she would pay anything they wanted, provided they did not tell her what the price would be, or offer different sizes of sirloin, or other cuts of meat, or ask how she wanted her steak cooked, salt was okay, but she did not want to be offered pepper on her steak, the waiter was not to come at her with an enormous pepper grinder, and she did not want to be visited halfway through the meal with some awful question like, How is everything tasting? or, Can I get that out of your way? and she did not want dessert, and she would not change her mind about not wanting dessert, and she did not want the waiter to slip the dessert menu onto the table with a sly smile, she wanted nothing but sirloin steak and salad, and the waiter was not to hover over her as if she was an orchid, and not to watch her discreetly from some corner as if she was a princess. The waiter was to serve her and go away.

He kept silent, watching her. After a moment Paul and I ordered, and when the waiter was out of range she resumed.

Language, Anneliese said. I have a theory about that. It is like when the only suit in your closet is a badly fitted, dumb-looking suit that you should have thrown away years ago. Like this one I am wearing now. But you have to wear the suit, you have no choice.

It looks lovely, I said.

Of course it doesn't, she replied. And language is like that. It is awful, it's ridiculous, it makes us all look stupid. But we're cowards, we don't speak up, we praise language all the time.

We do?

Oh, language, that's what we say, Oh, language, you're so flexible, so beautiful. Ah, the great poets, ooh, Vergil, eee, Milton, aah, Goethe, but if you just stop for a moment, Shakespeare, I forgot him, wow Shakespeare, he is amazing, but if you just stop and consider how shabby language is, Rilke too, I forgot Rilke. Oh my oh my Rilke, so swoony, so deep and dreamy... so we praise language all the time, but if you stop for just one minute, you see how embarrassing language is. You're just ashamed to be seen in public using language, but you have no choice, you have to go on saying things like, She pushed on our buttons. It's horrible, but you struggle on, twisting and turning in your tight, badly tailored Language Suit with its 1970s style super-wide lapels and big shiny plastic buttons, language buttons, buttons you have to push on. Language is not the beautiful miracle that makes us human, blah blah. Language is ill-suited, there, see? I am forced to make a joke out of my own idea, I have to wear the ill-fitted suit. Language has forced me to make fun of myself, my idea is wrapped around me like this suit.

She squirmed as if she was struggling in a straitjacket.

This is my ill-fitted suit for English. I also have an uncomfortable polyester suit for my Swiss German, a bolero with porcupine quills for Spanish, a stained silk dress for French, and for Latin I have a suit made of leather armor with ostrich feathers. Ha ha. So Samuel, if you think language is beautiful and elegant and sublime and the very condition of our awareness of our supposedly miraculous lives then you are fooling yourself. It's true that a couple of people used language well, but that just proves my point. For everyone else, for the billions of us who have to live with language, it's like wearing humiliating, grotesque, clown-like clothing. It's—

I think that's enough for now, Paul said softly.

Thank you Paul, you're right. Where was I? So one day Luzia came downstairs for her free breakfast, first of her three free meals of the day, and as she was about to tell us her latest lie, I said, "No! This is it, time's up. No more nonsense. We are your loving guardians, yes, but we are not patsies, I am not a buffoon, I am not a waggle doll, do not treat me as a punching bottle, stop pressing onto my buttons. Go back to your room. You have twenty-four hours to decide what you really want, otherwise no more free food." Well, she ran away crying, and then *Ka-wumm!* as if by magic, an hour later she came back to breakfast all dressed for business and said she was going to get application materials for the Swiss International Law School, she was going to be a lawyer like Paul even if law school was, as I immediately pointed out to her, crushingly achingly mind-numbingly boring, even if law is a profession best suited, oh my god, suited again, what can I do, anyway a profession best suited for people with drastically limited mental capacities, sorry Paul, but that's true isn't it? Is it? Never mind, sorry, anyway I told Luzia she was right to do it because she would have a stable life, and, as I also pointed out to her, she would be able to attract the affections of the handsome boy who works as a cashier in the Manor Basel Department Store. That made her especially angry for some reason, but she did go and apply, and she was accepted, of course, because she's brilliant, and now she's a typical miserable student in law school. That is how my ward resolved her life. May we all be so lucky, may we all be so determined, may we all put our noses onto the grindstone of life and grind our noses down until they are curved plates of bone.

She scratched her nose, pondering what she'd said, and then she launched back in, saying Luzia's struggle to find a profession was similar to my own struggle to decide whether to accept her offer, even though actually, she said, I had been given only two choices, the semester residency and the generous year-long residency, whereas Luzia had at least claimed to be pondering many choices, and also the parallel wasn't exact because I had never, or so she assumed, seriously considered becoming a ballerina or an actress, although she did not mean to presume, because such things happen all the time and they are perfectly ordinary, but probably I hadn't thought of taking a job in a third-rate department store just to chat up a handsome cashier who seemed sad and lonely but probably just had indigestion, although if I ever had a desire to do such a thing that would also be okay, but she, Anneliese, hadn't really thought I might like boys or even cashiers, at least until just now, and really she hadn't thought it at all, even just now, because she had only meant to make a parallel between Luzia's incapacity to choose and my own stubborn lack of commitment. She hadn't intended to imply anything about me, a person whom she hardly knew, well, actually, didn't know, but just to say everyone struggles.

I wasn't struggling, I said. I'm really just not the right person to visit a university. It's been years since I've even been in one.

She can't invite you anyway, Paul said.

She turned her head in his direction and again missed seeing him. This time her gaze swept up and across the stuccoed ceiling and out the window, where it settled slowly on the water like a fly-fisherman's cast.

Everyone struggles, she said. I struggle with our ward, with my work, and all the time with language, even though no one seems to share my concern about language and even though I have to admit I use language a fair amount.

Our appetizers and entrées appeared all at once, along with two large plates for Anneliese, one with nothing but a steak, the other with assorted greens. The waiter put down an extra bottle of water and slipped a dessert menu under my plate. Anneliese cut a lump of steak, and then she continued while she chewed.

You know what they say, she told me, if you have your health, you have everything. That's an old maxim, or a saying. Actually it's a cliché. Or maybe it's even a proverb, well, not a proverb, those are from the Old Testament, proverbs are precepts, not maxims. A wise person is not rude, she does not waste other people's time, a wise person is considerate, all sorts of nonsense like that, those are proverbs. I read the Book of Proverbs, they are almost all wrong. A wise person keeps her own counsel, it says, a wise person seeks counsel, those are both ridiculous. If people are wise then they tell other people what to do. A wise person speaks slowly, that's another one, it doesn't sound right either, a wise person is calm, well I was calm when I first started reading the Book of Proverbs. A wise person knows that to good and true love fear is forever affixed, well that is just creepy, and some proverbs are nonsense, like, a wise person is a ring in a pig's nose, or, a wise person does not poke the fire with a sword, or, a wise person gathers acorns and keeps them in a lovely muslin bag, why are those things proverbs? And why are they even in the Bible? But so Samuel, if you have your health you have everything, that is not a proverb or a precept, it's probably just a maxim or a cliché, what matters is that it's true, but also, on the other hand, if you don't have your health, all right then you may still have everything else, because the opposite of a thing is not its converse, so if you do not have your health you may have lots of other things, or wait, it's because the opposite is not the inverse, because if you don't have everything then it may not be true that you do not have your health, or no, wait, it's the converse of a statement that is not its opposite, but not the other way around, or the negative may be the converse, or the negative is the reverse but not the inverse. I can never remember those logical relations, those principles of logic or laws of logic, or wait, are they principles or axioms? Maybe they're just rules of logic, or even conventions, anyway one of them says that the opposite or converse or inverse or reverse of a thing may not be the negative of that thing, or whatever. I don't care, I really don't care, I really do not care, actually I do care but not right now. At the moment I'm only just trying to say that if you have your health you have everything, and if do not have your health, you may have everything else, but you have less than everything, which I guess means something, but in my experience the world always tends downward to its worst possible condition, so if you do not have your health, I think in fact you have nothing.

That could be true, I said. I'm lucky that way, so far.

She filled her mouth with greens and steak.

It's been a hard year for me, I said. Maybe Catherine told you? Back in the spring my wife Adela left, and then in August, Fina went off to college.

Sorry to hear, Paul said. Fina is your only child?

Yes, I said, and now my job description's changed. I think you know that Catherine put me on a committee, that's why I'm in Frankfurt. This year hasn't been easy. It would be nice just to have a day or two to relax.

I know what you mean, Paul said.

Sorry, I said, I don't mean to complain. The committee I'm on, this new job, has changed a lot of things for me.

Catherine didn't tell me anything, Anneliese said, but if you don't have your health I think you have nothing, you are nothing. Since you do have your health, you possibly have something. But if you do not have your health, and I mean mental and bodily health, if you do not keep a tight tight grip on your health, then you have nothing, you are no longer anything, you are nothing.

A busboy leaned in to refresh the water glasses.

You are just waiting to die, she said, looking at the busboy.

He froze. She swatted him away.

In fact no one who is over thirty has their health. I have a healthy appetite, but on the other hand I am not entirely, wholly, perfectly well. I have certain medical problems.

How about we don't go into those? Paul asked.

First of all, I have scabs, and—

Please, Lysi, no.

Fine, okay. But I am very much preoccupied with matters of health and wellness, Samuel, and that is itself a pathological condition, a species of hypochondria if you will. In fact I am not sick, but I am not well. Perhaps I am sickly. I am haunted by memories of health, because I no longer experience health, I simply think about it, the way you might think about the smell of a rose. I dream about my youth like any older person does. Just this afternoon when we were preparing to come meet you I was standing in front of my psyche mirror, bandaging my scabs, and I thought, Anni, you can never be beautiful again, you are weak, you are falling apart, but you know, it's not that bad. You were a beautiful young woman once, you saw yourself in this very mirror. You have your memories, you remember when you were young and lovely. You know what health was, you remember what beauty was. You've experienced those things, you were lucky in life. For a moment I felt embarrassed. But then I realized how dark the world actually is. I was not actually seeing what I used to look like, and I wasn't feeling what my health used to feel like, I was only thinking about them. In the same way, when I think of a rose I don't actually smell it. I mean you may recall the smell of a rose. I don't. I can't remember the smell of a rose. That's because I don't like the smell of roses, I may never have smelled them, well, that can't be true exactly, but I may not have smelled one for my entire adult life, because why would I, I don't like them, at least I think I don't, I can't remember when I might have smelled one, so I have no examples in mind when I think of smelling roses. I suppose it's true that I may actually like the smell of roses, but I have no intention of ever finding out, because I would undoubtedly relive the unpleasant experience of smelling a rose, and I would be ashamed that I hadn't trusted myself enough to continue believing that I do not like the smell of roses. But Samuel, maybe you know what roses smell like?

To me they smell like clean sheets.

Roses do not smell like sheets, and if they did, no one would buy them except people who don't like the smell of roses, except that if roses actually did smell like sheets people wouldn't know what roses smelled like, so they wouldn't bother buying them at all, they would just buy more bed sheets. So actually, and this is my real point, no one remembers the smell of roses, because memory is fake. People say, Oh, you smell like a rose, Well, thank you darling! You smell pretty nice yourself. Do I really smell like a rose? Well, how the hell would I know? I have absolutely no idea what it is like to smell a rose. When I think about the smell of a rose, my mind presents me with a color postcard of a rose, with the words I am a Rose, Fragrant, Lovely, & Sweet printed in some stupid floral script, and I just want to vomit, just retch all over that little postcard. Memory actually does not exist. I have a theory about that too, it is like my theory of language, but not as pleasant.

Paul groaned, then flinched.

Well, I said, I can remember when I was young and healthy.

Well, of course you can't, she replied. When a person is young and healthy, they don't think about their health, and that just is health, that is what health is, it is a thing that is, it does not know about itself, it does not ask itself questions, it doesn't diagnose itself, there is nothing to cure, nothing to improve, nothing to know or feel, nothing to think about, because real health is literally and exactly the complete absence of thoughts about health.

I suppose that's true, I said. I don't remember how I thought about my health or even really my body when I was very little. But I do recall things. I remember running and playing, especially in the forest behind our house. There was a very deep lake nearby, and we used to look down into it and wonder what would happen if—

Later in life, she continued, every memory you have about health is like an anesthetic, it masks the pain of realizing you are not healthy. It is like a neurotoxin, it paralyzes your mind, preventing you from understanding that you do not actually remember what it felt like to be healthy. So my memory says to me, Anni, you were healthy last year, remember? And I say, Well, no, I don't. And my memory says, Anni, dear, don't get upset. Just think back, it was only last year. So I try to picture it, this so-called health I had. And what happens? Nothing. I remember I did not feel pain. Exactly! my memory says. See? You do know! But I do not know. All I know is that I didn't suffer. I didn't yet know what it was going to be like when I got a year older. Look, I say to my memory, You're so smart, you tell me. What was that state I was in last year, when I didn't have these symptoms, these conditions that Paul won't let me talk about? Well now, Anni, my memory says, that was health. That was nothing! I say to my memory. Nothing! A vacuum, an absence. I push my memory in the chest with my finger, I poke it hard, like this!

She jabbed her index finger into my collar bone.

I say to my memory, Are you actually trying to tell me that was health? When I felt nothing? Well, gosh, I guess I am, my memory says. Okay, memory, Anneliese yelled, thundering and waving her arms, that is just about enough. We are done here. This conversation is over!

She scowled. Paul swirled the wine in his glass, suggesting a perfect balance of mild fascination and hopeless boredom.[1]

There was a pause, like one of those uncanny moments in a storm when the winds cancel themselves and everything holds its breath. Outside, four more swans were swimming against the current. They drifted toward the bank, then away out into the river toward the far side, then back, like anchored ferryboats, always crossing, but never landing.

Then the monologue began again.

After you smell your rose, she said, or when you no longer have a sickeningly perfect body, like I once had, after your period of delightful experiences is finished, that is when this pain starts up. Because then you realize, I mean I realize, I mean I already have realized, that those experiences are gone. What I have is reams of miles of streaming hopes and dreams and thoughts about what I might have touched or smelled, tasted, nibbled, or kissed in my past, but those things are gone. They are gone, they are gone, they are gone.

Not completely, I said. You can still tell me about them.

That is absolutely no solace whatsoever. It is the opposite of comfort, it is a handful of salt that you are rubbing into the pus-filled sore where my memory used to be.

Hmm, I said, that's gross.

I can never know what real health was like, she said, because my feeble brain cannot bring it back to me.

In another way, I said, that's what's wonderful about childhood. Those memories are weightless. Like the air inside the forest, I used to love that. Or the sound of bees in the fields. That's how I recall Watkins Glen, where I played when I was a child.

Lovely, Paul said.

Just the feeling of looking down into the dark of the lake, or up into the sky—

Say I lose my cat, Anneliese said. A cat that I have loved for many years. Say one day the cat just vanishes. No one understands why things like that happen. I mean, this is an illustration, I don't actually have a cat. Actually I don't like cats, I despise them. They are heartless, loveless, and sneaky, and they're so primitive, with their little egg-size brains and their stupid tiny teeth. I would never, we would never, would we, Paul? we would never own a cat.

A nearly imperceptible shadow formed in the middle of Paul's forehead. He was taking mental notes. Perhaps he was tracing her story back to some encounter they'd had with a cat.

The cat is not an optimal example, she continued, I regret I mentioned it, but the point is that if the cat I supposedly loved for all those years has gone, and I want to have a cat, I mean I don't, I wouldn't, but if I did, if I do, then I can, it's easy. I get one, just like the one that vanished, and I put it on the sofa, and then if I want to see the cat I just look at it, and I say, There, you stupid cat, there you are. Memories do not work like that. Memories are like people who died, you can't just bring their corpses back and put them on the sofa next to you. The whole subject of memory is unutterably sad. You still believe you have memories. That is very sweet, but it will not last. For better or worse, and probably worse, or definitely worse, and these days I think much worse, I can't say the same about myself.

Can we talk about something else? Paul asked.

Oh, well, I suppose we have all the usual problems, Anneliese said. My work, Paul's job, our ward who is apparently planning her entire life so she can impress a department store clerk, and then the car accident—

You were the offending party, Paul said.

Yes, I admit that, and we also have the usual men's and women's problems, but I won't tell you about those unless you ask me, because some of the things that happen—

Slowly, Lysi.

She closed her eyes, put down her silverware, and placed her hands on her lap.

I only wanted to say, all these things have added up, and many of them are personal matters after all, but the worst by far has been caring for our uncle Hans. That man has presented us with a very difficult situation, about which really the less said, etcetera, but still, it has been one of those time sinks, those energy saps, which are corrosive to everything bright and positive and productive, to the point where my own work, which has come a very long way since I started, over twenty years ago, when Catherine and I were working in England, before she left the life of science, like you did, and by the way heaven only knows how you get up in the morning, what possible interest can there be in making sure people in Guelph, Ontario, of all places, have healthy drinking water, I mean did you just wake up one morning like Tom Stockmann and think, Oh my god, the poor people of Guelph, Ontario might be drinking water with unacceptable levels of fecal bacteria! I need to quit my career immediately and move to Guelph, Ontario, even though I don't even know where it is, and take a job that goes absolutely nowhere and pays almost nothing and has no glamor or status or even any discernible interest, and stay there for the rest of my life taking samples of drinking water to protect people from fecal bacteria, heaven forbid some innocent Canadian child might become indisposed!

Actually, I said, waste water is more Catherine's job. She works in the Harris Plant. I'm on the other end, which is purification. It's a natural extension of things I did before. And Canada is a nice country, it might remind you of—

Was it Catherine who convinced you to move there?

No, I said, Adela and I were looking for a place in Canada on account of her visa problems.

So did Catherine tell you it would be good to give up on your career and move to rural Canada, like she did?

Actually we met her in Guelph. We didn't know her before that.

Maybe she wanted to have someone suffer along with her. She would do a thing like that, if there is one thing Catherine can do it's make people miserable, but still I absolutely cannot understand how either of you drag yourself into work each morning.

Anneliese, I said, I don't really know you, but let's just say there's more to the picture than you're seeing.

Okay, fine. So back to Catherine. When she and I did that work, even though if the truth be told, and if push came to shove, which it does all the time, she didn't really do the work, the crucial work, the work that opened up the field of uncultivable organisms, so it wouldn't strictly speaking be right to say she pioneered anything, not exactly, anyway, not without some very, very careful qualifications, which I have no intention of going into just now, but I could, or someone could, or someone should, and sooner or later someone will, someone has to describe, accurately and without prejudice, exactly what Catherine's role was in those years when the study of uncultivable organisms was just starting up. But what really matters in the end, and it just sounds so horribly selfish to say it, but here it is, I mean why not be honest, especially with everything I have been through, what is the point of being nice, for example regarding Catherine's so-called contributions in those years, paper after paper stealing my work, what is the point of finessing, bending and scraping and avoiding the truth, or, well, okay, let's just say lying, what's the sense of lying when everything's changed? Catherine's given up the field and gone to work in your provincial water treatment plant in Guelph, Ontario, so what's the point of being polite, when I am falling to pieces, when I can't even remember my exceptionally beautiful scabless body, when all of that has been erased and I am not even dead yet, not quite dead, because that is how I feel, no longer fully alive but also not quite dead, sorry, I lost track of my sentence, so but anyway why should I not say, openly and clearly, that the problem is our uncle Hans?

She raised my glass to take a sip, but the wine didn't quite reach her lips. On a second try she took a big gulp and swallowed a mouthful of air. Then she replaced my glass and leaned forward on her elbows.

What matters to me, she said, in my own selfish way, is that my research, the work of my own little life, which I choose to do supposedly for fame but in actuality only for myself, to keep me as sane as possible, to give me a sense of purpose while I battle on through these outrageous and embarrassing illnesses, whose end could not possibly be any clearer, while I try with decreasing success each year to convince myself that I have at least some control over my thoughts, that my life is more than the sum of my pitiful little shakes and sweats, what counts is that the work I do, which actually is fundamental, in a way that I cannot explain to you right at this moment, that my work is very nearly ruined, because of Hans, about whom, etcetera, but let's just say he has become such an issue, that he has, well, he has stopped my work dead on its tracks.

She put her hands on the table. Her eyes rose slowly to the ceiling as if she was following an escaped balloon. She stared at the stucco decorations, looking here and there, her head wobbling slightly as she traced the curlicue designs around the edges of the ceiling.[2]

It's really so sad, Paul said quietly. It's dementia.

Oh Anneliese, I said, I'm so sorry!

Not her, Paul, said. Our uncle. We think he has forgotten most of his life.

She took a forkful of salad. Apparently she knew it was Paul's turn.

Every day after lunch, he told me, our uncle walks down to his old grammar school, where he was a student seventy years ago. He likes to sit on a bench in front of the school, facing out into a field. At first Lysi and I did not know why he went there, and then I remembered. When I was a little boy, I went to the same grammar school, and there was a playground out in front, in the place where Hans likes to sit. Many years ago, they moved the playground to the back. There were seesaws and little metal horses for the youngest children, and a big swing set for the older ones. You had to be brave to use that one.

Paul's voice was soft. I became aware of the sounds of silverware, and other diners speaking quietly.[3]

I was afraid to go on the high swings, he continued, but I used to watch the bigger children. I guessed that Hans also remembered the old playground, or even one that was there before it. I asked if he was thinking of the playground, and he said, "Yes, it was right here." Last year he used to go out every day after lunch to sit on the bench, looking out at the field in front of the school, but in his mind's eye he saw the playground. "Was there a swing set?" I asked him. "Swings, and a *Wippe*," he said, a seesaw. "Did you ride on that?" I asked, and he said, "We held hands across and tried to stay on."

That's sweet, I said.

I stole a glance at Anneliese. She was still examining the ceiling. She looked like a clown after a show, deflated and a bit lost. Apparently listening didn't suit her.

After Hans sat a while in front of the grammar school, Paul continued, he used to walk farther down the hill to the sports stadium, where he played as a student in the *Hochschule*, fifty or sixty years ago.

How old is he? I asked.

Eighty-two.

Eighty-three, Anneliese corrected. Born in 1937. Overdue for symptoms of senility.

He sat in the seats of the stadium, Paul said. Sometimes it was closed and on those days he stood at the wire fence. He must have remembered his great triumphs there. Our mother used to tell us he had been a star athlete.

I asked him what he was seeing when he watched the field, and he said, "Lausanne," or "Grasshopper Zürich," those were sports teams back then. Lysi and I don't remember him ever talking about sports. He knows we wouldn't recognize the names of the players or the famous matches. After he was finished looking at the stadium he used to walk to the Ruheplatz park, it's a large park at the edge of the city. We don't know for sure, but I think he must have walked there with his first wife, Marlene, the woman who would become his first wife. We never knew her. Our mother told us Hans and Marlene once had an apartment there, at the end of that park. When Lysi and I were children we hardly ever went to that neighborhood. I asked Hans if the park reminded him of Marlene, but he didn't answer. He used to go every day and sit on a bench at the far end of the park near the St. Judas Thaddäus church.

Anneliese picked at the linen tablecloth with the tip of her knife.

I asked him once, she said. "Why do you go to that park? There is a nicer one up the Bottmingen Road, or you could go to the Merian gardens, they are exquisite even in winter. Why do you go to that park where there's no view and no cafés and you have to walk so far to get back home? Why do you go to that bench in the corner of the park, where there's nothing to see but the road and some buildings? Why won't you tell us about your first wife? What did Marlene look like? How tall was she? What color hair did she have? What did she do, where was she from, what was she like, did she have brothers or sisters, how long were you married, what happened in the end? Did she leave you or did you leave her?" He didn't answer me, but not because he was thinking about Marlene, that's all in your head, Paul, you confused him with questions. He didn't answer because there was nothing in his head.

She held up a fold of the tablecloth and punctured it with her knife.

Lysi, please, Paul said. It's my turn. If I may continue. For a year or so, that was Hans's walk. Each time exactly the same route. The missing playground, for ten minutes. The sports stadium, for ten or twenty minutes. Then down to the park and across to the St. Judas Thaddäus church. He stayed there longer, sometimes a half hour. Then back to our house along the main street. He rarely spoke. Some days it was cold, other times it rained or snowed. He didn't seem to notice. When I walked with him I kept his arm in mine, but I often felt alone. You see, Samuel, I had no idea what he was thinking. I couldn't see the world through his eyes. It's like he was walking by himself and I was his shadow. Or we were both shadows, thinking of our own separate memories and our different lives. When I let go of his arm he didn't seem to notice. A couple months ago I just stopped going with him.

Paul held the rim of his plate with his left hand.

Two weeks ago, he continued, Hans went for his walk as usual, but he didn't show up for dinner. We went out to look for him. We followed his route, but we couldn't find him. Luzia helped, and she called some of her friends. Two of our neighbors also joined in the search.

Four, Anneliese said.

We went in different directions, back and forth along his route. We searched for an hour or more, and finally, when it was nearly dark, one of our neighbors found him under some trees behind the stadium. The neighbor called me, and when I got there I saw Hans on the ground. He said, "Paul, I am lost." He had been crying. I sat down next to him. There were six or seven of us standing or sitting on the grass with him.

Nine, Anneliese said.

She was pushing the tip of her knife into the weave of the tablecloth and pulling threads up into loops.

It was getting dark, Paul said. We all waited. For a long time we couldn't get him to stand up. When we tried to pick him up he went limp and shook his head. "Lost," he said. "I am lost." Eventually he let us stand him up and we led him home.

On the way back, Anneliese said, I kept asking him, "What were you doing? What were you thinking? What is wrong with you? Why didn't you call for help? What were you looking for? How did you get there? Who is the President of the Federal Council? What animal looks like a horse but has stripes? What season is it when leaves turn colors?" Then I took him by the shoulders and shook him, that was to test for spinal injury, and that's when he slapped me. It wasn't very hard, it didn't hurt at all, so I said, "Are you feeling weak? Is your arm paralyzed? Are you dizzy? You look dizzy. Are you lightheaded? Do you feel like vomiting? Do you want to sit down again?" Then I administered a standard cognitive capacity test. I told him

I was going to name ten objects, and he had to remember them. "Okay," I said, "here we go. Remember what they are because I am going to ask you about them in a minute. Ready? Ball. Bull. Bar. Pan. Jar. Pin. Pen. Fan. Bill. Bell. Remember those. Here they are again. Ball. Bull. Bar. Pan. Jar. Pin. Pan. No, not pan. Pen. Fan. Bill. Bell." I told him it would be easier if he remembered all the B's first. Ball. Bull. Bar. Bill. Bell. "Just concentrate," I said. "Ball. Bull. Bar. Bill. Bell. And then remember the three that start with P, there are only three, I am sure you can remember three things. Pan. Pin. Pen. Pan. Pin. Pen. Pan. Pin. Pen."

Let me, Paul said. The next day we went to a doctor, and he told us Hans was exhibiting typical Alzheimer's behavior.

He didn't answer, Anneliese said. I even told him to think of a sentence that could help him remember the ten words. Put the pen and the pin in the pan. Let's plan to put the pin in the pan with the pen. Please place your pen pin in the pan. Pin the plan of the pen to the pan. I must have repeated the ten words a hundred times on the way home. He just kept shaking his head.

Lysi, please. The doctor said that the reason Hans is silent is that he has already forgotten many things. The doctor told us Hans went on his walks because he wanted to remember three things in particular, the grammar school playground, the football stadium, and his first love. According to the doctor, the route to the grammar school, the stadium, and the park might be all he can remember. They might be the only things he has left. The doctor's idea is that Hans cried because he had forgotten how to do his walk. He was following the same route every day because he was trying hard to remember, not to forget, just those three things: playground, sports victories, first wife. He was reminding himself, again and again, so that even if he forgot everyone else, even if he forgot both of us, he would still have those three memories. The daily walk helped him do that. But then the world got dimmer, the doctor said, and his route became harder to follow.

We don't know any of that, Anneliese said. He might have just been walking out of habit.

It does sound like he was remembering things, I said.

He was, Paul replied. He made it to the stadium that day, but when he left he forgot how to get to the park, or perhaps he forgot the park completely and didn't know where to go next. So he kept walking, hoping to see something familiar, and ended up under those trees behind the stadium.

We don't know that, Anneliese said.

She had picked a hole the size of a bottlecap in the tablecloth.

We know, Paul replied, so quietly I almost missed it, and then, to me: I agree with the doctor, I think Hans's memories are nearly gone. His only comfort was his routine, his walk. And then on that day he lost his way. When that happened he lost everything. We knew he'd been forgetting things, one after the other, for years, but when I heard the doctor's diagnosis I realized how sick he has become. The doctor said it was likely that whole decades of his life have dropped out of his mind. When we were talking to the doctor, I remembered that four or five years ago Hans had stopped mentioning his second wife, Emmy, that's Luzia's grandmother, who died twenty-five years ago. They had been married over twenty years, so it hadn't occurred to me that he might have forgotten her. When we got back from the doctor's office I asked Hans about Emmy, and it seemed as if he couldn't remember her. He just said, "Yes, Emmy." Then two days ago he forgot who Luzia is. He was annoyed to see a strange girl in the house. We said to him, "This is Luzia, your only grandchild," and then he remembered.

Oh no, I said.

He probably knows he is going to forget us all. I think the most important person in his life was his first wife Marlene, the one who has been gone so long, the one we never met. That's why he cried, that's why he wouldn't get up. He knew he had forgotten the most important thing in his life, and he couldn't remember what it was.

Paul pursed his lips. He needed to talk, but he also needed to rest.

The waiter was looking at the hole Anneliese had torn in the tablecloth. She put the butter dish over it and pressed her hands flat over her knife as if she was trying to calm a small animal.

He still goes for his walks, Paul said, but since that day I always go with him. We haven't been back to the park. I could take him there, but the doctor said that if he sees the Ruheplatz park and the church, and he can't remember why he wanted to see them, he may have a permanent breakdown. This week we've just gone to the playground. When he's finished looking at the field he offers me his arm and I lead him home.[4]

I feel sorry for you, Paul, Anneliese said, but then she shot me a look that meant, this whole business is such a pain.

The doctor told us we should stop him from walking by himself, Paul said. He predicts that soon Hans won't remember anything, and he'll just be left with a compulsion to get out.

That's all it ever was, Anneliese said.

The doctor also told us that for his own good we should keep Hans at home. He said sometimes you can stop Alzheimer's patients from wandering by using a door chain, because it's too much of a puzzle for them. I can't bring myself to do that. He wants so badly to see the playground, and I don't want to deny him. He has so little left and he is trying so hard to keep it.

I'm really sorry, I said. It can't be easy. Maybe you could get a carer to help?

I'd just love to help him keep whatever memories he has.

That sounds right, I said. My mother didn't suffer the way your uncle is, she didn't forget things, but she also had a first marriage, to a man who died. My brothers and I never knew him. He was her great secret. One time she told me she loved him more than—

Well, Anneliese said, putting her napkin over her entire meal as if it was a corpse, it has been a pleasure. I hope I have not been too voluble. Paul says I have a tendency to be voluble. I believe I know what that means, I mean, okay, I know what the word "voluble" means, what I mean is that I know why he chooses the word "voluble." Wait a minute. Check! Check! Waiter! Check!

Her screams startled people at the other tables. The waiter ran behind a counter to prepare the bill.

So why does Paul select the word "voluble"? He complains about my manner of talking, my style of talking, if you can say that, if you can call it that—it sounds grandiose, Ah, there's Professor Doctor Anneliese Glur, she speaks in a grand style, she has a great grand style of speech. Perhaps Paul is right. The main thing is, he thinks I offend people, or I put people out, or I put people away, or no, I push them off, I disturb people by talking in this so-called "voluble" manner. But Paul is wrong. "Voluble" is wrong, it's the wrong word.

The waiter rushed over to Anneliese with the check.

No! She yelled, pointing at me, Give it to him! What Paul should object to is not my voluble talking but very simply the volume of my talking, by which I do not mean loudness of sound but rather cubic volume of speech. My thoughts come in spurts and floods, my talking may or may not be voluble, whatever Paul thinks he means by that, but it definitely has volume, it is volumetric—Paul, that is a better word, make a note of that—and so people sometimes find me hard to listen to, or rather hard to attend to, or to engage to, I mean with, or listen to, or hear, they find me hard to hear, that's a stupid expression, isn't it, because everyone can hear me, and there are even some people, well, one person in particular, who actually finds me hard to stand, he can't stand to hear me talk, and that's also a stupid expression, because it implies the person needs to sit down when I talk, anyway I know this particular person can't stand, as he says, to hear me talk, I know this because I had the misfortune of seeing this person almost every day when I worked at the university. He operated the elevator in the science building, and he insisted on repeating that he could not stand to listen to me. "For god's sake," he said, "Dr. Glur, come to the point! Please just come to the point! I just can't hear this! I can't stand to hear this! Oh god oh god oh god when will you stop?" That sort of thing. But no amount of begging can force me to produce a period when I do not wish to produce a period, because I need to develop the volumetric requirements of my thought in order to be satisfied with what I have said, despite what that man thinks—he is, after all, an elevator operator, surely a profession that is unlikely to attract a person who ever thinks of an idea that takes longer than one minute to articulate—whereas I have five decades of experience calibrating the relation between the volume of my own verbal ejaculations and the volume that most people expect, which is just a few cubic centimeters of talk as opposed to my liters of verbal volume, and as a result I am exquisitely sensitive to people's feelings, I have glottal antennae for this sort of thing, and therefore, and this is my point, I am quite sure, even without asking you, that you understand me very well, you would be capable of receiving my liters of verbal volumetrics far better than that addled person who operates the elevator, you could swallow and ingest my verbal volumetrics without any discomfort, I know that you are fundamentally sympathetic, capable of being more than an acquaintance, more than a friend of a friend, which is technically all you are at the moment, so even though you have rejected the university's offer of a residency, which was a very generous offer given that you haven't worked in a university or published anything in a number of years—

And neither have you, Paul said.

And given that your only real expertise is the purification of drinking water, the elimination of amoebas and fecal bacteria from drinking water, which is, if you do not mind my saying so, an almost stupefyingly uninteresting subject, but you come with Catherine's highest recommendation, she told me I should meet you, but anyway to tell you the truth the offer isn't a very good one, because the university wouldn't pay you very much—

She can't pay you anything, Paul said.

And let's just say my colleagues are not the most delightful people the world has ever produced, they didn't make god sit back on his haunches and say, Now that was a good day's work, I made Sybille Kröller, that's quite an accomplishment, I created Spadella Wurmel, she's awfully special, and let's just say Basel isn't the cutesy poster that the Swiss government fervently hopes it is, and besides, the water in Basel tastes funny, you'd know all about that, Samuel, you'd be able to tell me why it tastes funny, although I already know why, it's because the pharmaceutical companies, Evolva, Polyphor, and the others, they urinate unspeakable chemicals into our water supply, but anyway, even aside from the university's offer, which you were either wise enough or rude enough to reject, aside from that I know from a lifetime of experience judging the effect of my so-called "voluble" way of speaking, or I almost know, I am nearly certain, that Catherine is right, you have the capacity to understand me, and the goals and purposes of my life and work, not just adequately but deeply.

She fell silent.

I kind of doubt it, I said.

They both rose. It seemed the evening was over. I paid the check and we walked out to the foyer. I thought of saying something sympathetic to Paul, but the two of them were silent as they got their coats. I gave Anneliese a hug goodbye, and on the way out Paul caught my eye and it seemed for an instant as if he shook his head in warning.

Back up in the hotel room I lay on my bed in the dark. People were walking along the waterfront. When they passed under my window their conversations became suddenly loud, clanging in several languages. Even the current in the river sounded sharp, like broken glass. The swans had gone, beaten back by the current.

I went into the bathroom and splashed my face with cold water. The splash sounded loud and unpleasant. I adjusted the tap until a stream of warm water ran quietly through my fingers.

# 2

## MOVIES AND RESORTS

**AFTER THAT EVENING** I didn't hear from Anneliese for nearly a month. She called one night when I was in a hotel in Knoxville.

Ah, thank goodness, she said, without saying hello, thank heavens. I am so fortunate I reached you. I got your number from your secretary, Mrs. Rosie Hirondel, and I found her number on the Guelph City website, where the Municipal Water Department is inconveniently listed under "Other Services." I must say she was less than forthcoming. I told her I wanted to call you, but she said she is not permitted to give out personal numbers of employees of the Municipal Water Department, so I said, "Mrs. Hirondel, while I cannot assure you I am a close friend of Samuel Emmer's, I am indeed an acquaintance, and as you yourself know I met him in Frankfurt, you know this because you yourself sent me the name of his hotel and the time of the dinner, and you did that because you were ordered to by Dr. Catherine Sounder, and so, Mrs. Hirondel, if you would stop and think about this for one minute, you would realize that if Dr. Emmer had any objections to receiving my phone call, he would have told you. He would have said, 'Mrs. Hirondel, from this moment on I instruct you to never give out my number, on general principles—which, by the way, I refuse to tell you—especially to Anneliese Glur, despite the fact that she is clearly a friend or at least an acquaintance of mine, and if you do I will have to report you to your Director,' whomsoever that may be, I mean, you know of course, but I am trying to tell you, Mrs. Hirondel, this is what Samuel would say, I don't know the name of your Director, or if that person is even called Director, but Samuel has clearly not told you any such thing, and therefore, if you are rational, which I am really beginning to doubt, you have no choice but to give me his personal number immediately!" Well, Samuel, she hung up on me, can you believe it? She is impertinent, incompetent, block-headed, stubborn, and awful, this Mrs. Hirondel, she is a horrible employee. I am sure you know this, and you are probably already collecting evidence that will help you to fire her, so if you would like me to send a letter describing what she did to me, I would be more than happy to write it, I would do it immediately, I would send it by courier to your personal, home address.

She's actually Miss Hirondel, I said, and she's perfectly nice.

So I called her back right away, and told her I was once an eminent Professor at the University of Basel, a genuinely close friend of Catherine's, and a fairly good friend of yours, that's what I said, I hope you don't mind, it seemed accurate enough for the purpose I had in my hand, and she was clearly frightened. She knew her job was in the line, or in line, her job was online, no, not online, her job was on a line, and she gave me your hotel phone number immediately, and then, can you believe it, she hung up again! But aside from Mrs. Hirondel's incredible rudeness, it was actually relatively easy to get your number, in comparison with how difficult it would be here in Switzerland. You know that North American institutions are so much more accommodating in that particular way than our European ones. We don't like to give out information like phone numbers and email addresses because heaven only knows who might be bothering us, I mean, it's as if we think the world is full of people who do nothing but say to themselves, How can I bother those awful academics? Who can I call or write just out of the blue? What inane, misinformed question can I ask? You know, Samuel, I read somewhere, I can't remember where, an essay by a major scientist—I mean, someone really important, like Stephen Hawking or maybe E.O. Wilson, or someone of that caliber or that status or that level of prestige or that degree of fame—anyway this person, I think it was a man, but whoever it was, I think it was Wilson, actually, no, it wasn't, it was that person who worked with Hawking, what was his name? Barker, no, Penrose. Penrose, how could I forget him? Penrose said that most of his time was devoted to answering questions posed by what he called "lay people," really ignorant questions, like, I have discovered a flaw in the Pythagorean equation and I believe all of mathematics will topple, or, I have discovered and proved the existence of a new element using just my home chemistry kit, or, I can prove indisputably that Darwin did not believe his own theories, but presented them as an elaborate, lifelong practical joke to get revenge on his parents, who had pushed him into natural history and whom he secretly despised, not just in the ordinary way people dislike their parents, but in a deep, horrible, intense way, he hated them so ferociously that he dedicated his entire life to ruining their old age, and I can prove that indisputably with a letter I found in which a friend of his says Darwin didn't like the way his mother cooked beef stew, or, I have proven conclusively, using the simplest arithmetic, that E is not equal to $mc^2$, but is just a tiny tiny bit greater than $mc^2$, and I can demonstrate that with a simple wood-burning stove, a calendar, and a spirit level, or, You will be amazed when you read this, and you will probably wish to quit your job, but I have irrefutable evidence that I wrote the very book that made you famous, but I wrote it forty years ago when I was six years old, and the only reason I have not come forward earlier, aside from my native modesty, is that I was, as you can no doubt infer, a child genius, and I wrote the book in an obscure dialect of Old West Norse as written by Þjóðólfr of Hvinir, and because my life has been filled with so many prodigious accomplishments, including the mastery of twenty-one languages and the invention of two more grammatically and lexically complete languages, one of which was used by the eminent director so-and-so to portray an alien language spoken by the people of a distant galaxy in the year twenty-five million AD in the blockbuster film, what was it called, which grossed five hundred million dollars not including secondary markets and merchandising, netting me over twelve hundred dollars, which I mention as token of the exceptional power of my intellect, because of accomplishments like that I had understandably set that one manuscript, which I did not believe had any particular value in the enormously greater scheme of my bewilderingly large life, to one side, and that my mastery of that obscure dialect of Old West Norse had to be refreshed before I could present this manuscript to the world, but now I am afraid you will be going down in flames, because this manuscript contains all your ideas, but expressed so much more accurately, eloquently, and provocatively than you could ever hope to do, using delightful expressions and turns of phrase used only in that particular obscure dialect, and it is dated a full thirty years before your own supposedly original publication, so you're going down in flames, you bastard, you're a typical narrow-minded academic with a grossly inflated sense of yourself and I will take special delight in crushing your pretentious face into the dirt of oblivion, no one will remember you, ha ha, ha ha, etcetera, well, Samuel, I'm sure you know that kind of person, so Penrose said that most of his time was taken up with people like that, lay people, even more than he could devote to his own research, and so he decided to go off the grid, as it were, not by unplugging, but simply by declaring, once and for all, that he would no longer answer any emails, letters, or phone calls from people he did not know, and even that he would never again answer a question from anyone in the audience of one of his lectures, starting immediately, at that moment, with me, of all people, he refused to answer my completely reasonable question, which I had asked very clearly and succinctly in under half an hour, and which he had then "answered" by declaring in public, that starting at that exact moment, the moment I finished asking my question, actually, I had not quite finished it, but there were several people in the audience making so much noise that I could not quite get to the end of my question, although I almost got there, but starting from the exact moment that I stopped talking, mainly, by the way, just to make sure I was safe, because there was an especially loud person right behind me chanting, "Sit down! Shut up! Sit down! Shut up!" but at the exact moment I fell silent Penrose declared not only that he would not answer what he called my "so-called question," but that he would, from that precise moment on, and as a matter of principle, never again answer a question, an email, or a letter from someone he did not know and never again take a phone call from someone he did not know, as long as he lived, and that is good example of the reason why European websites tend not to give much information about people, well wait, I don't mean we are all besieged by lunatics like Penrose, or, I mean, like the people Penrose mentioned, I mean the other people, not me, but, and... sorry, I lost the thread of my argument a bit there, oh this was my point, because we feel as if we might be besieged, we think we might be bothered by cranks and crazies, we think that if we give our phone numbers and emails crazy fans will start appearing, and even worse, some of them will not only be hopelessly ignorant lay people, as we know they are, but also actually malicious, some of them will come to our offices, and follow us to our homes, and stand outside our kitchen windows while we are eating breakfast with our husbands, if we have husbands, happily and innocently eating breakfast with our husbands, I mean, we'd be eating breakfast, each one of us, in her own house, with her one husband, not that I have many husbands, actually I don't have a husband at all, but so the stalker would be standing in the flower bed, right there in the front yard, waiting patiently for me to finish my coffee, and then he would come and knock at the door and produce two books, one in an obscure dialect of Old West Norse, and the other his own translation of that book, entitled *Authoritative Compendium and Concordance of the Original (And Brilliant) Ideas Later Shamelessly Stolen by "Doctor" Anneliese Glur, Newly Translated by the Author Himself from Old West Norse,* and that would only be the beginning of the horror that would then ensue, because horror always "ensues," that's what horror does, it "ensues," and okay, but all this is really just a fantasy. We wish there were people out there who cared about us, who read our research, who want to write to us and speak with us and maybe, in the end, even follow us around, we almost wish there were stalkers out there, not that we want real stalkers, and not even zany people with preposterous ignorant theories, but that in our fantasies we certainly want to be read and praised and deferentially questioned and even followed around a little, because that would mean we matter. So in my judgment, all the secrecy in European websites has to do with our need to have people care about us, so when one person actually wants to contact another, for a perfectly legitimate and non-insane purpose, such as mine today, then it can be needlessly, gratingly difficult, it can be frustratingly, annoyingly impossible, there can be all kinds of obstacles, like for example if you tried to find my email on my institution's website, you would first have to negotiate a series of menus and options, and then, when you finally found my page, you would see a picture of me, nearly unrecognizable because it was taken so many years ago, along with a brief summary of my so-called "research interests," including only the very oldest material, which I presented at the time of my *Habilitationsschrift,* I am sure you know what that is, Samuel, and no contact information whatsoever, but I can't change anything on the website without sending a petition to Sybille Kröller, she's the chair of the department, and I absolutely, categorically refuse to do that because she is nothing short of a monster. I am glad I am no longer working there, because she has stewed a little hell in the department, my former colleagues are floating haplessly in it like sweating potatoes in a pot of soup, well, potatoes don't sweat when they're in a soup, I suppose, or maybe they do but you don't see it, but you know what I mean, she is devious in the extreme, self-regarding to an excruciating degree, and power-mad in a wildly crazy manner, to the point where she has thought up plots that would make Machiavelli dizzy, they would make Sherlock Holmes scratch his head like a dunce, they would have Agatha Christie spinning in her chair like a demented pensioner, to the point where she, I mean the chair of the department, should be arrested, except that she is far too intelligent to ever let herself say anything that could be actionable, she could out-Freud Freud, she could run rings round Lacan, there isn't a person I know who could get inside that head of hers and survive long enough to figure out how to escape. She has tried for years to get me out of my office, even though as a former full-time permanent employee of the university, despite the unusual circumstances of my termination and the ongoing litigation, which brought us to Frankfurt, I am absolutely entitled to my office, and the lobby, stairwells, hallways, and restrooms of the building, and even the elevator, although I would never go into the elevator again because I might meet that man who used to get down on his knees and say, "For god's sake, Dr. Glur, I can't stand it anymore, please just be quiet, please let us just ride five floors in glorious perfect silence, just once, please just once," and so on, that person would just never shut up, but anyway the campus police have told Sybille many times that I have access to my office and the public areas of the building, including the elevator, but she has fought me for years, because, well, I don't know exactly why, but I think what she really wants is to make it seem as if the faculty are unhinged, not just me, although I am clearly her principal target, but all of the faculty, that they're somehow all unhinged, which doesn't seem likely if you consider it, but if anyone can persuade people of such a thing she can, and personally, I think she is doing this not only so she can be seen as the savior of the department, not only so she can be celebrated as the whistle blower of Swiss science, but mainly, really, she does it because she is psychotically impelled to destroy people, that is, if there is actually any person behind those swollen overheated eyes and that unspeakable "I am your very best friend ever but I would kill you in the time a mosquito takes to flap its nasty little wings" smile, a horrible wrinkled death rictus of a smile, that look in her eyes that says, I would take a nibble of both your eyeballs if I could get away with it, and then I'd be the first one there with the miraculous poultice that would heal your ghastly wounds and restore your sight, provided of course someone is around to see me administer the poultice so I could take the credit, because otherwise I'd let you scream and writhe and take blind swings at me while I picked my teeth, she can't stop her relentless campaigns of utter destruction, she is crazy like those insects whose brains are taken over by fungal parasites, like dogs in the last hours of rabies, like people ranting in straightjackets, like, sorry… where was I? I just meant to say that I can't change the department website, but I don't want to anyway, because I don't want "lay people" writing me with ignorant claims, endlessly bothering me with dimwitted questions, following me around and standing out in my garden waving their hands to attract my attention, holding up books supposedly containing astonishing proofs of the unoriginality of my own work, which I had forgotten because I wrote it so many years ago, no, wait, that's the other story.

I heard a gulp on the other end of the line, as she drank too much of something, then coughed, then gagged.[5]

So, she continued, that is why, if you go to the trouble of finding my page on the official website, you won't see my email, much less my phone number. But I found your contact information very easily, not just because that moron Mrs. Hirondel is so easily frightened and—

It's Rosie Hirondel, and she is not a moron.

She is untrustworthy. She gave me your personal phone number after only a minute of polite conversation, so how honest could she possibly be? In my opinion she is unreliable, and quite possibly devious, she is the kind of person who would give away any kind of secret, she might even sell secrets, she—

I don't think the Department of Water Management in Guelph has any secrets.

Okay, fine. And so Samuel, my dear friend, is it a bad time to be calling? I hope not. I'm sure it isn't. How could it be? It's ten-thirty in the evening where you are, in Knoxville, Tennessee, and I doubt there is anything to do there. You finished your work at the zoo yesterday, ha ha, I bet you didn't know I knew about that! I can't imagine what you did today. What could anyone possibly do in Knoxville? Here it's a lovely night, very quiet, four-thirty in the morning, one of my favorite times of day, second only to the early evening, that is an especially civilized time of day, when people settle down with their drinks and watch a movie and pretend everything is fine, well, normal people do that, at least I imagine normal people do that, Paul and I certainly don't do any such thing, we have never wasted our evenings that way, and actually, now that I think of it, I don't know if people do sit down in front of their televisions and watch movies. I think they don't, I think they just say they do so other people think they are normal, I bet most people do exactly what I do: after dinner I go to my study. Paul cleans up the kitchen and then sits with Hans, at least I assume he does that, actually, now that I think of it, I have no idea if that's true either, because like most people, immediately after dinner I go straight to my study and close the door. On the rare occasions when I do attempt to watch movies, for example when Paul asks me again and again to spend an evening with the two of them, when he asks me consistently and politely for a number of days in a row without missing any days, because that would show me his request was more than a whim, and when he asks without becoming anxious, because that would reveal he has other motives and that he is just saying he would like to sit in the front room and watch a movie, whereas actually he wants to talk about something, for example some new problem he says has discovered with me, so but when he asks calmly, politely, and consistently for a number of days in succession, then I go into the living room and Paul selects a film and we watch, or rather he watches, and Hans stares into space, and I try to tell Paul about the work I have been doing, and he keeps nodding and pointing to the television and putting his finger to his lips, on those evenings I realize just how horrible it is to sit and watch a film. Movies are awful. Just think about it. First you see the name of the famous director and the famous actors, Anthony Perkins, Janet Leigh, that's okay, but the names just go on and on, I am forced to watch an endless parade of meaningless names. Why should I care who designed the sets, or put up the lights, or smeared make-up on the actors? But the names just keep coming and eventually I am thrown back down onto my own resources, I have to find a way to entertain myself. I have no idea what that means, by the way, thrown back on my resources. Did someone push me down? And what were my resources doing on the floor? Anyway I am thrown away onto my resources, even though it is a film, and I am supposed to be entertained, so I try to amuse myself by reading the lists of names. I am told Mort Mills is in the movie. Why should I care Mort Mills is in the movie? Do I need to know this Mort Mills? Is Mort Mills one of our great actors? Is that a name to remember, Mort Mills? Why should I have to think about this Mort Mills person? The film is not called *Psycho: The Amazing Adventures of Mort Mills*. So why should I have to see his name? And it is a funny name, Mort Mills, I wonder what Mort stands for, is it Mortgage? Or Mortician? I don't care, and the only reason I even think about Mort Mills is that I have nothing better to do, the director has not given me a choice, I have to keep reading, I have to keep seeing these pitiful attempts to publicize jobs that should have been done quietly and without complaining. Apparently Hollywood is filled with small-minded people with inflated ideas about themselves, like Mrs. Hirondel, people who should just do their jobs in sullen silence.

Rosie is a very caring person, I said. Her brother runs a farm outside Guelph, and she goes out to help with his son, who has epilepsy. Her uncle—

Okay, fine. But then next I am told that the film is Copyright ©1960 by Shamley Productions, what is the point of that? I mean, would someone steal the film if it wasn't labeled "Copyright ©1960 by Shamley Productions"? Of course not, it's just that Shamley Productions wants their name in the film, well, if I ran a company named Shamley Productions, I would be embarrassed, I would keep my name off the film, and by the way, why do they say "copyright" and then put the symbol for copyright right after it, because the word "copyright" means exactly the same as the symbol for copyright, so why print both of them, was the director so scared that someone would steal his film? Did the director think there are master criminals out there who want to steal his film, and when they see "Copyright," they think, Great, I can steal this, but then they see the little copyright sign and they think, Oh no, I'd better not, this film is really protected, it is in a safe, it is in a Swiss vault, it is in a lead-lined panic room, it is in a Class 3 reactive powder geopolymer pore-free concrete military grade retaining wall safe, only a genius could steal this film, I may be arrested just for thinking about it, I'd better keep my distance, there will be other films I can steal, ones without that little symbol. And then I see that the man who was paid to type out all these names that I have been forced to read has put his own name in the film, there he is, Saul Bass, in charge of titles, Saul Bass designed the titles, it's another American name, like Mort Mills, Saul Bass. Good heavens, I say to Paul, "Saul Bass and Mort Mills, this is the worst nonsense, the worst. I'm going, I can't stand this any more," but he says, "It hasn't started yet," and I say, "It has," and he says, "Just sit still, Lysi, we've only just settled in, and you have your nice Mathilde Pêche liqueur," and I say, "How can you watch this?" But he just sips his red wine, and that means it's time for me to be quiet, but I can't, so I'm about to get up and leave, but just when I am about to jump up and run out, even though I have only recently arrived in the living room, and Paul is settled in with his red wine, and even though I have my Mathilde Pêche liqueur, which is my favorite, and even a plate of freshly baked *Schoggiweggli,* I love them even more, do you know Schoggiweggli? No? They are pastries with chocolate pieces, not like *pain au chocolat,* those are just grease flakes with bars of tasteless brown wax inside, and Schoggiweggli are definitely not like American chocolate chip cookies, those are pizza pies running with grease and sugar, no, Schoggiweggli are lickious, it means you want to lick them, or just nip at them while you sip your Mathilde Pêche liqueur, but still it's too much, and just at that moment when I cannot bear to be forced to sit and read lists of names of people I do not know and will never meet and do not care about and will forget almost instantly even if they have names that are so ridiculous they are actually memorable, like Mort Mills and Saul Bass, just when I am so insulted that I am about to take my Mathilde Pêche liqueur and go back to my study and promise myself never to agree to sit and watch another movie no matter how calmly and consistently and persistently Paul asks me, I see a scene of a city in the desert. There's a building under construction, and a crane beside it. The steel frame is nearly finished. I am interested in that, a little bit anyway, because I like to watch construction. I don't have any special training in building design, but I like to see what architects do, and I care in a general way about the look of the city. I often stop to interrogate construction workers in Basel. They are very secretive, they won't say anything about what they are building, and sometimes they even walk away when they see me approaching, but my questions are harmless, for example, How many toilets will this building have? Are you sure there are enough toilets? I counted the rooms, this is what I tell them, and I can guarantee you, there are not enough toilets in this building. But they won't answer, I suspect they know their buildings don't have enough toilets. So I am interested in the building under construction, a little anyway, but the camera is moving, it is panning to the right, the director wants me to see the city, but the camera doesn't go slowly enough for me to actually see the city or count the toilets in the buildings that are under construction. The camera keeps panning, and I see a taller building with a rotating sign on top of it. At first I can't read it, but as the camera sweeps by, the sign rotates, and then I can see Valley National Bank, with an eagle. At that moment the words PHOENIX, ARIZONA zoom into the screen from both sides. PHOENIX rushes in from the left, ARIZONA rushes in from the right, it's very distracting, and in the same instant the scene changes very slightly, but the next scene is almost exactly like the one before, and there is the bank again, this time larger and brighter, maybe I can get a better look at the eagle, but as soon as I spot it the camera keeps going right past it, and I am forced to look at more of the city. There are lots of lower buildings. I don't really want to look at those, but I have no choice. There are two larger buildings with no windows, I suppose they might be the backs of department stores, I see some American-style parking lots, but just then the words FRIDAY, DECEMBER THE ELEVENTH zoom into the screen from both sides, FRIDAY rushes in from the left, DECEMBER THE ELEVENTH rushes in from the right, it's very distracting, and at the same time the scene changes yet again, and again the new scene is nearly the same as the old scene, and again I have no idea why, and I see the same windowless buildings, but the camera keeps moving past them, it's infuriating, and then the words TWO FORTY-THREE P.M. zoom into the screen, this time they all rush in from the left, instead of half from the left and half from the right, and that is especially distracting. Okay, I know the film is a murder mystery, I was not born yesterday, but I really do not need to have meaningless facts shoved into my face, they don't make the film more exciting, they are just the director's way of saying, It's real, it's real life, but just because it's Friday doesn't make it more real, Friday isn't any more real than any other day, as far as I know, and two forty-three happens every afternoon, and also every night, and I didn't need the P.M. because the sun is shining, and I really doubt it's going to make any difference that it was December, not to mention the eleventh of December, and I wish the director would at least let me look at the city he has filmed in such an annoying fashion, and while I am thinking about all that, and wondering if the director is going to tell me the temperature and humidity too, the camera moves in toward an apartment building, closer and closer, and actually under a window shade and into a dark room. The blind is almost completely down, but the camera sneaks underneath it. That's fine, I like spying as much as anyone. It's dark. I see a chest of drawers, they're interesting, I wonder if anything is in them, but then I am not allowed to look, because the camera moves around the room, and there's a woman lying on a bed, she's looking up at a man who is standing there, but we're not allowed to see his face, instead we see the nightstand, it has a sandwich on it, and the sandwich is wrapped up, and yet it's lying on a wrapper, so it must have been double-wrapped, but who does that, I mean it's not an especially large sandwich, it's not the kind of big sloppy sandwich that might need to be double-wrapped, so what's the point? Maybe there were two sandwiches, and they ate one, but even if that is true, why did they fold up the wrapper for the first sandwich and put it underneath the second one? I mean think of it,

Samuel, why did they fold the wrapper for the first sandwich, and then put the second sandwich down right on top of it? By this time I am desperate to entertain myself, and I am willing to spend some time thinking about this, but I am not allowed to, because the camera is moving again. Behind the sandwiches there's a tray with a pitcher of water and two glasses. Next to them there's a bottle of soda and a cup of coffee, but neither one has been opened, so that's also a little interesting, because they ate one of the sandwiches, but they didn't drink anything, or maybe they just unwrapped the first wrapper of a double-wrapped sandwich and then gave up, but I am not allowed to look at that anymore, because the director is controlling my eyeballs. The camera cuts suddenly and I see the man, he's holding a towel and smiling at the woman. That's naughty, I mean what did he need that towel for? The woman is talking about how her boss has acid indigestion, and I really don't want to hear about that, why should I want to hear about the stomach complaints of someone I don't know? There is an old-fashioned fan mounted on the wall, I would rather look at that, but the man sits down on the bed, and the camera follows him down, and the fan goes out of sight. The scene goes on and on, and I am pulled from one thing to another, I see the couple on the bed, then I see her getting dressed, then him sitting down, then a close-up of her, then the two of then, then her by the mirror, then him by the window, then her, then him by the window, then her, then the two of them kissing, then him raising the blind, I know I'm supposed to be listening, but the view keeps changing, it is exasperating, I am forced to look at something I don't want to look at, and then I see her in a shot by herself, then him leaning on the window, and then the two of them again, it's so so irritating, but Paul just keeps saying he doesn't mind, "Shush," he says, but I can't, because it's so so distracting, I can't listen to what they're saying, I can't even entertain myself by looking around the room they're in, when are you ever in a room, ever in your life, and you can't just look around if you want to? That never happens, that is impossible. The camera keeps changing viewpoints, cutting from one person to another, back and forth, back and forth, there she is on the street, there she is in her car, there she is at a hotel, the director is forever telling me what I am permitted to look at, as if I am a child, as if I have not yet been given the license to rotate my own eyeballs in my own eye sockets, as soon as I see something it's gone, there she is in her hotel room, there she is at her desk, there she is in front of a mirror, there she is in the shower, there she is getting stabbed, then she's in the trunk of a car and we don't see her anymore. "That is actually a relief," I told Paul, "because at least we won't see her anymore," and Paul said, "You get worse every year." But really, Samuel, films are absolutely horrible. That is why I doubt very much that people sit contentedly in front of their televisions and watch films, although I admit I do not have any idea what people actually do in the evenings, and I have no idea where I got the notion that the period after dinner and before sleep is a civilized time of day, and I have no idea what that could even mean, or why anyone would want to be civilized if that is what civilized is, and so I retract everything I just said.

She took another gulp of whatever she was drinking.

I only wished to say, she told me, that Paul and I talked about the lovely evening we spent with you a couple of weeks ago. We both agreed it was wonderful to meet someone so sympathetic and understanding.

It was an unusual evening. And tell me how is Paul? He seemed very sad about your uncle.

He is, but that is his problem.

Last week I told Catherine we met, and she asked if we had come to an arrangement. I told her I didn't know what she meant.

I have no idea, Anneliese said. That is Catherine's problem.

And you're doing okay? You were concerned about your health. There's been a stomach flu going around Guelph, in addition to the usual viruses. Fina texted that they're all sick in her dorm.

I don't know this Fina.

Fina, my daughter.

Samuel, Anneliese said, I am delighted everyone you know is moderately sick, but of course I didn't call just to chat or to tell you it was a "lovely evening" or it was "wonderful" to meet someone so "sympathetic" and "understanding." And I really don't want to hear about stomach flus or acid indigestions. I have outlined for you my principal ideas about language and memory, I hope you remember them, they will be useful. Now listen.

There was a pause.

Okay. Where can I begin? Where can I even start? I am so tired this winter. Thank heavens I no longer work at the university. I still have nightmares about the classes I had to teach, in my dreams I give the same class a hundred times, a thousand times, as if I have lectured for centuries, until I became a desiccated mummy with a microphone nailed onto its chest, condemned for all eternity, because that's what they say, "for all eternity," not just eternity, it's always "all eternity," condemned to repeat the same lecture again and again, through hundreds and thousands of lifetimes, for all of full eternity, and it always has to be just the basic information, no thinking, only facts, because students don't want to think, they only want to learn names and numbers, what's known, what's real, what's true, what's reliable, science students just want to calculate. When I taught at the university the students needed to pass my examination, they wanted to graduate and get jobs, not just jobs of course but great jobs, the kind that involve massive amounts of money, which they could calculate, so they could say, "My net worth as of this evening, one minute after the markets closed, is precisely three gazillion Euros! I am happy at last, fuck that awful university and especially that demented Professor Glur with her endless complaining, she sounded like a pig, squealing about how empty our lives are, well, hey, we're done with her now, because now we're worth three gazillion Euros plus bonds plus options plus benefits plus perks plus packages plus sweeteners, well over three gazillion, maybe even pushing four, that would be heaven, but at any rate really securely at a bare minimum three, which is great, and definitely not down near two gazillion, that would be mortifying, that would be abject poverty of a kind that we actually don't remember anymore, even though that may seem implausible, since we're barely twenty-five years old, but still it seems eons since we became vertiginously rich, and now we're in the secure three gazillion range, and we are so done with Professor Glur's preaching and pontificating, no more speeches about how we're dimwits and we need to sit down and figure out who we are in life. We know who we are! We are invitation-only black metal credit card, endlessly perked ultra high net worth individuals!" That's what they'll say. Heaven forbid that any student would ever actually think. They only want to calculate, thinking seems old-fashioned to them, really useless, it's as if too much thinking is bad for you, it probably causes cancer, "Wait," they'd say, "that's not a joke, we really believe that thinking causes cancer, or at least thinking is basically bad for you, that's what we believe," that's what they'd say, that's what they probably think, even though of course they had to think even to realize that, but that is the kind of person we're talking about here, Samuel, a very typically superficial and mechanical, even motoric sort of person, I'm not sure if that's a word, motoric, anyway they'd say thinking is bad for you, actually bad, they'd say you can think for a few minutes if you need to figure out your average pre-tax cross-compiled projected semiannual restricted investment dividends, but when that calculation is complete you absolutely need to stop thinking, because heaven forbid you might ask yourself why, exactly, you need three gazillion Euros, heaven forbid you might look in the mirror one morning and ask yourself who you are, that would be really unpleasant, you might ask yourself what you're doing on the Earth, that would be spectacularly dangerous, you might ask yourself what is the point of your life, and then before you knew it you'd get sarcastic with yourself, you'd say, "Hey, Bub," because your name is probably Bub, or Bop, or Bulb, or something idiotic like that, "Hey, Blob," you'd say, "how have you managed to become so insanely self-satisfied when in fact you're living an utterly ordinary and almost completely meaningless life, anyway?" Then you'd see what you really are, and you'd look in that mirror and say, "Hey, Bleb, you pusillanimous runt, do you realize you have failed even to try to begin to figure out who you are?" And you'd start to feel all quaky, and you'd drop your ultra-lightweight Bluetooth toothbrush, and your lips would tremble, and the toothpaste foam would make you look like you're having a seizure, and your eyes would tear up, and you'd think, My god, my god, Professor Glier was right all along, my life is shit, I am nothing, nothing, Professor Glirr is a genius, a great woman, one of the world's great women, she walks among us, if that's the right expression. But this is all a fantasy, Samuel, because I don't have to be a genius to know that Blurp just stands there a minute, with cancerous existential despair eating away at his brain, which is nothing more than a damp brick of compressed Euro notes anyway, he looks at himself all trembly and weepy in the mirror and says, "Pull yourself together, Blemp, you have thee gazillion Euros, and Professor Glare has almost nothing left in her pension fund"—I'm not sure how Blub would know that, but let's say he does—"and that is totally pathetic, Professor Glüer is going down into the tubes, her retirement will be a mineshaft of misery, but my retirement will be astonishing, I'll just book an ultra-resort in Thailand and live there as long as I want for only two thousand Euros a day, Thailand is a pretty great place, and so easy to get to, there are so many resorts there, at many suitably high bracket price points, and so many lovely beaches, lots of fresh fish and fruit, an efficient service economy, it's really a perfect life for anyone in retirement," and to tell you the truth, Samuel, I thought of moving us all to Thailand, but then I thought, why would I want to go somewhere Blerp would go? I intend to stay right here where I am now, in my cold damp study in my leaky, dark prewar apartment here in Basel, where I can actually think, where I am not surrounded by those unsettling palm trees with the really long trunks that look like someone took a giraffe and put it on a rack and stretched it out until its neck was fifty feet long and rubbery and useless. Why would I want my bathroom to be impeccably clean each evening, with freshly folded towels on a silver tray, topped with jasmine and hibiscus blossoms, when I can have my stained unwashed towels embroidered with the words "Grand Hôtel Wehekopf"? Why would I want to be able to walk out onto my back porch and into the saffron-tinted Asian sunshine, why would I want to feel the warm sand under my feet, not scalding like in some cheap seaside resort, not stony like in some discount nature preserve, not shipped in like in those appalling resorts on the Black Sea, where the beaches are actually slime-colored clay and they bring in truck loads of so-called beach sand from quarries, which is abrasive and covered with powder that makes you sneeze, not like any of those, but soft sand, at once comfortingly warm and pleasingly cool, half-shaded by the odd rubbery shadows of the palm trees, quartz sand that squeaks under my feet and sparkles between my toes, soothing, like a dream of swimming in scintillating water, perfect and calming, why in the world would I want that? Why would I want to be able to get out of bed, walk ten steps and sink into my coral-colored heated indoor pool, or twenty steps and sink into my private infinity pool, or forty steps and sink into a refreshing saltwater pool with a view of the friendly seas of the

Malacca Strait, when I can walk only nine steps and sink into the ancient porcelain claw-foot tub that looks luxurious but is actually a torture device, because even in the summer it is ice cold, because the hot water always runs out, leaving me with a choice between sitting in four inches of scalding hot water with most of me exposed to the air, or sitting in a full tub of tepid water, getting colder every moment, until my entire body is electrified with cold and all I can do is look at the freezing tile floor that I am going to have to walk across to reach the corner behind the door, where there is a rack of frigid damp smelly Grand Hôtel Wehekopf towels? Why would I want to spend every evening watching the sun set over a crystalline sea, when I can enjoy the sight of four square meters of the side of the house across the alley, which is all I see from my bed, and contemplate how cheap they were to cover their house with lime-sand plaster, which is not suited to our climate in Basel, so that it cracked almost immediately, and has stains like mascara running out of the cracks, and pieces that have started to chip off, exposing the equally cheap green house wrap, which is also decaying, revealing the rotted wood underneath, like a gaping wound that just gets deeper and deeper, until eventually a hole will open into their house, and I will be able to see our neighbors walking around in their underwear, which is probably also stained and torn, with gaping holes that I can see right through? Why would I want an ever-changing menu of dishes prepared to my order, at any time I want, with any ingredients I request, served efficiently and cleared the moment I'm finished? Well, actually Paul does that for me, so okay. But then why would I want to have expert massages, performed in various national styles, given by handsome and beautiful masseurs and masseuses, when I can ask Paul to rub my shoulders for just thirty seconds a month as a token acknowledgment of the burning aches, racking pains, twinges, and spasms that trickle over me like fire ants? Why? Why would I want that?

I don't know. Do you?

Why would I want to be able to ride docile island ponies in the sand dunes, or drive the resort's complimentary Rolls Royces along the picturesque mountain roads, or be taken for helicopter rides to the base of stupendous waterfalls, when I can go along with Hans to see his depressing imaginary playground? Why would I want to live peacefully between sun and sand, like people have always been meant to live, without cares until the day of their death, when I can live with a brother who never lets me forget he exhausts himself at work in order to pay our rent, with a ward to fret about, with an uncle who is sinking into a tortured oblivion? Why would I want to live out my life in a place designed to make me forget the passing of time, with every day as quiet as the last, the same sun forever, changing kimonos and robes and evening wear for the season, which is always the gentlest summertime, the staff with their carefully expressionless faces placidly drifting down the latticed corridors, where I can feel I've lived a thousand painless thoughtless lives, where the world is a soft thing, bright, warm, and quiet, with no sense or stress, where I drift through my days without numbering or remembering them, singing to myself some lovely melody that no one knows, what in the world would make me want to live that life, when I can stay in my apartment with a tangle of worries buzzing around me like biting flies, pencil clutched in my hand, forever staring at the next blank page? Why? Why?

Maybe you should just tell me.

I am about to. So that is why when I taught I stuck to facts, I stopped telling the students what happens when a person actually dares to have a thought, I didn't tell them they were all just bags of meat, thinking would have shocked them into life, no, it was best to leave them to it, there is no way to make people understand things they aren't meant to understand, that's what Paul said once when he was pretending he cared about my work. He said, "I'm so sorry, Lysi, there just isn't a way to make me understand this, I wasn't made to understand these things, please, I'm sorry, I've tried, it's your work, I can't understand it, please, can I just go, I'm not able for it, please, I'll just go now, it all looks magnificent Lysi, now do you mind if I just go and check in with Hans, I'd like to go make my simple cookies and watch my simple movies, please let go of my arm," that's what he said, so I stopped telling my students that uncertainty is not an error to be corrected, that is what Burp would have said. But no. Uncertainty is like a rich soil, thought plants itself in uncertainty, uncertainty is what thought was made for, the only thing that stops thought is certainty, if it is possible to avoid certainty then it is possible to keep thinking forever, if I am uncertain about something, then eventually I am uncertain about everything, that is what Socrates taught us, didn't he, or was it Montaigne, or was it that other French guy, Pascal? No, it couldn't have been Pascal, or was it? Pascal, that's it, or no, wait, it was Montaigne of course. As soon as you begin to think, he said, you realize there are more things you aren't sure about, and they proliferate, and soon enough you become uncertain about everything, that's what Montaigne said, actually that sounds like Descartes. If you keep thinking, the world starts to look unfamiliar and barbaric, he said, you no longer like the things other people enjoy, rainbows for example, they begin to look unnecessary and garish, that's what Descartes said, sunsets look pompous, lovely spring days seem perfumy, snowfalls are childish, the old man in the moon looks sour and unpleasant. You no longer think cats are adorable once you see the hatred in their eyes, that's what Descartes said. Everything in life becomes unappealing and strange, you no longer understand anyone, it's as if everyone agreed to stop speaking languages that you know, they all talk in languages you do not understand, Mxyzptlk languages, you're surrounded by barbarians, the world around you becomes a vast frightening place built by idiots of certainty, captains of industry, titans of commerce, pillars of society, heroes of labor, pioneers of discovery, barbarians like Blorp, harbingers of change, giants of innovation, vanguards of progress, innovators of the future, visionaries of tomorrow, luminaries of innovation, sculptors of destiny, oracles of imagination, architects of utopia, gleaming sentinels of the impending mandatory enlightenment. Their cities are repellent, their magnificent buildings appear preposterous and misshapen, their cars look like metal tumors. Why do people like cars, anyway? They have round rubber feet, they are loud, smelly, and heavy, and they crash all the time. This is the effect of thinking, Samuel. You realize you are ringed in by barbarians like Blip, and it just gets worse, more of them are coming, Blips, Blerps, and Blorps, you are waiting for them, they are coming today, they are sailing from the opposing shore, they are massing on the Tartar steppe, they are swarming over the city walls, they are pouring into the city, night has fallen, they are everywhere, and then one day you wake up and your brother says, "Good morning, Lysi, guess what, I married a barbarian last night and we're going to have barbarian babies, isn't it wonderful?" He turns off the electric fence, throws open the gates and says, "We're all barbarians now, we love ignorance, violence, and money, we know what we know and we don't know anything else, and we don't doubt ourselves because why should we, we are swollen with idiocy!" and you say, "You're insane, close that gate," and he says, "How do you know I'm insane? What is sanity, anyway?" and you say, "This is my story, so I know," and he says, "Oh okay," but he doesn't close the gate.

There was a pause on the line.

Sorry, she continued, I am not entirely sure what that meant. I just wanted to say I keep my ideas to myself, I don't broadcast the fact that I dove into the well of thought. That's where I live, down in the well. This is what I need to tell you, what you need to know. I live in a well. I have gulped whole mouthfuls of the stinking water of thought, I am infected by doubt, I seethe with poisonous skepticism. Uncertainty is the water I drink, Samuel, it is stagnant and cold and has a curious taste. The well water is lovely, dark and deep. My feet don't touch the bottom. I call it the Nothing Sea. I tread water so I don't drown. Sometimes I hang on to the stone walls to rest. I have swum down to the bottom and felt around in the sludge, just to be sure the well is not bottomless. I discovered that the water in the well seeps up through the ground, through the muck at the bottom of the well. Some water comes from above, pure rain water, but not much, even in downpours hardly any rainwater falls into the well. The water comes up from below. It is filtered dark brown by the slime. It is soil water, soiled water. This is my life. People like Barf are right, thought does produce unease, that's why people don't like to think, that's why it is so hard to live down in a well.

Why not climb out?

What is there in the world? The well has the shape of my thought. But there's more, Samuel, because thinking needs unease, I need the chill water, I want the damp cold, my thought is dependent on anxiety, it loves uncertainty, there's an unhealthy kind of love down here in the well. Thought breeds uncertainty, and then thought breeds on uncertainty, thought becomes thick with desire when it sees uncertainty, it lets uncertainty breed on it, uncertainty impregnates thought, and then thought spawns more uncertainty, and then they all breed together and the result is discomfort,

discomfort is the child of uncertainty and thought, or maybe discomfort has two mothers, because unease was there too.

Sounds lovely.

People like Blimp imagine uncertainty is something you have to work through, like the puzzles in a murder mystery, where everyone gets agitated and thinks really hard until the detective solves the crime and the uncertainty vanishes and everyone is happy and mindless again. But no. Thinking continuously is like swimming day and night, forever, treading water, just barely keeping afloat, not hoping to climb out, just living in the well. I am afraid this sounds ridiculous. I was nervous when I knew it was time to tell you, but this is my life, Samuel. It is how I have found myself in the extraordinary position of thinking through the very foundations of our concepts of life, that is my work, it is about the deep philosophy of biology and life, following Aristotle, Oresme, and Uexküll, it is not just the usual what-makes-us-animal nonsense, but the very deepest layers. This is what I work on every day here in my study. It is where I have been led starting from the work Catherine and I did, following the path of uncertainty, always watching for signs of uncertainty, running away from whatever can be calculated, whatever can be easily known, looking for the path that has no signs, although I have to say, speaking of Catherine, that I could demonstrate in exhaustive detail, paper by paper, page by page and line by line and word by word, including every single word and not skipping any word, including even the smallest words, words like "the" and "a," I could demonstrate that every particle of those papers we co-authored on uncultivable organisms is actually mine: the ideas, the hypotheses, the experiments, the data, the statistics, the research, everything, it's all mine, she did not have one single original thought during the years we worked together, she was a puppet slave, she knew nothing, even after I taught her she knew nothing, because there is no way to make people understand things they aren't meant to understand, Paul said that and it's true, in Catherine's case, she just didn't understand.

She told me you're a good friend.

I am exaggerating, I don't know why I do that, she was a perfectly good collaborator, we worked very well together, she may not have understood everything, but that wasn't my point anyway, I wanted to say that those early studies on uncultivable organisms really opened my eyes. We were using new technology, metagenomic technology. I will explain it in simple words. We were sampling soil from farms around Iffley, that is where we lived. We found DNA from all the creatures that had ever had contact with the mud in those fields. We found cow DNA, of course, and traces of DNA from people, not just farmers but their ancestors, Roman, Celtic and pre-Celtic, and DNA from dogs, cats, ferrets, badgers, dozens of species of birds, rats, mice, shrews, and many other animals, even extinct ones, like mammoths and aurochs, and we found DNA of several hundred species of fungi, and of course protozoa, amoebas and bacteria, all the common things you find in the drinking water in Guelph, Ontario, and we found pieces of the DNA of toxic bacteria, including tetanus, anthrax, and botulism, and genetic material from viruses, all the common ones, and even rare and lethal ones, pieces of all their genetic material were there in the dirt in Iffley, in fact every gob of mud had fragments of all those creatures, it is amazing to think mud is like that, we say it's just mud, but what is mud if it has broken pieces of every creature that has ever stepped in it or spat onto it, or slimed around in it or died in it, so that was entertaining, but then, and this is what is so amazing, we started finding parts of the DNA of organisms no one had ever seen, microbes that cannot be cultured in the lab, uncultivable organisms, we found entire phyla of life, a dozen new kinds of viruses, eighteen new phyla of bacteria, that's eighteen, eighteen new phyla, completely new forms of life that had never been cultured. No one had ever grown them in a lab so no one knew they existed, but they were bacteria, so we named them, Urbacteria, Newbacteria, Proteobacteria, Parabacteria, we found so many we ran out of names, we named them after ourselves, Falkowbacteria, Sacherbacteria, Marybeckwithbacteria, Beffordbacteria, he was hopeless, but we named a phylum after him anyway, Curtisbacteria, Bohlenbacteria, Yanofsky-Vanderbaneggerbacteria, he works in a lab in Rotterdam, Kaiserbacteria, not Kaiser Wilhelm, William Kaiser, Bill, he is a biologist, Verabacteria, Adaorardorbacteria, he's Vera's husband, of course no one would name anything after me, so I had to do it myself, so there is now Anneliesebacteria and Glurbacteria, Teddibacteria, that is our ugly dog, and now there's Luzibacteria too, that one's named after Luzia, I thought it was cute, but when I told her all she said was, "Can I have something beautiful named after me?" and I said she was prejudiced, bacteria are handsome, and she said, "Would you marry one?" and I said "Humans can't marry bacteria," and she said, "Beggars can't be choosers," and I also named one Paulbacteria, he didn't like that, he thought it was an insult to have a bacterium named after him, but I told him it had already been accepted by the IBNC, the International Biological Nomenclature Committee, and it couldn't be changed. I said, "Paul, a bacterium is a noble ancient creature. You are now immortal, think of it that way, from now until basically forever people will use your name, at least if they happen to mention that kind of bacterium, which I guess won't be very often, probably actually never, but anyway think of it, Paulbacteria probably developed about a billion years ago, that's right! A billion, people are punies by comparison, we're a thousand times younger, we're nothing from their perspective, bacteria are the ancient ones of the Earth, they own the planet, not us, they wriggle among us, there are as many bacteria in each one of us as there are human cells, in fact, Paul," I told him, "each of your defecation events expels a hundred million bacteria, so after you have a defecation event, Paul, you temporarily have more human cells than bacteria, but not for long, because the bacteria multiply so fast, and if you're constipated," Paul often is constipated, it is a problem he has, "if you're constipated you have on the order of half a billion more bacterial cells in your body than you have human cells, so actually you're more bacterial than human, therefore having your name on a bacterium is a tremendous honor," and when I told him all that he seemed to calm down, or at least he was quiet. The discoveries we made were amazing, and I am not even mentioning all the fragments of DNA that were so strange we couldn't even classify them, so we called them viroids, satellites, particules, unconventional agents, unidentified vectors, intronparts, and so on, I'm only giving you these on the top of my head, I mean from off in my head, from off in the top of my head. This field, metagenomics of uncultivable organisms, which Catherine and I were working on, this field is still growing, and each time people find more uncultivable organisms, our place on the tree of life shrinks, so now we are almost invisible, literally, I printed the tree of life in poster size, and the branch for mammals is a twig, and *Homo sapiens* is not even visible on the poster because the writing is so small. We have vanished! We are specks in the scheme of life, and all around us life is thriving, we are infinitesimal flecks, bits, we're *klitzeklein,* just as bacteria are invisible specks inside us, so we are microscopic twigs on the tree of life, I can see that now, even though the analogy does not work, because I am not a twig, and I am not like a bacterium living inside some inconceivably enormous creature named Anneliese who is not even part of this analogy, it's confusing, but actually I can see it now with tremendous exemplary clarity, like the view from the Col de la Croix de Fer, where you can see everything, but it's all so far away that actually you can't see anything.

That's amazing, I said. You know, Catherine told me you were friends back in Oxford, but she never talks about her scientific interests, I mean outside of the work she does in the Harris Plant. None of us knows much about her. I remember she once told me, just casually, that she had lived in Kazakhstan for a year. And before that in Denmark, in a shipyard. I feel like I hardly know her, even though we've been friends for twenty years.

Anneliese put the phone down with a click. I heard her walk away. Then she came back and kept talking.

Where was I? Oh yes, this is what I meant to say. I know you understand me, as I said when we first met, even though you haven't been saying much of anything. I have been pursuing this work, which began back in England, I have been developing it for twenty years. I used to publish essays, but my work led me deeper, toward the analysis of life in general, the foundations of life and biology. I have been doing this work secretly. For twenty years I haven't published any of it, it has become my private work, I can't even tell Paul about it, I mean I do, but he keeps saying he doesn't understand, he calls it my secret work, and I keep saying it's not secret, and he keeps saying it's secret from him, and I keep saying no it's not, he could understand it if he wanted, and he keeps saying would I like to watch television. This is why I have been introducing myself to you, first with harmless entertaining stories about Luzia, movies, and resorts, and now with serious issues. However at the moment, Samuel, I think it is time for you to rest. I will call you tomorrow morning.

I'm checking out tomorrow. I have a plane to catch in Nashville.

I will call early. Samuel, I freely and openly admit I am exhausting and possibly boring, I openly and freely acknowledge that I am difficult to listen to or even to stand. But I need help. I have no idea if my theories are true, and even after I have written them down I sometimes have no idea what they mean. The work is tremendously difficult, I often have no sense of how to go forward, well, sort of I do, but really I don't, and I certainly have no idea how my research has gotten to this point where I can hardly understand it myself.

She was silent. I waited.

I wonder, she continued, if any of us ever know how we end up where we are. I guess we're little boats pitching on a choppy sea, floating off we know not where, drifting away we know not why, most of the time happy, bobbing in the water, bemused by the lovely weather or the salty waves or a passing seagull, smiling and joking, humming and singing, dozing and laughing, until at last our little boats tip over and we drown.

# 3

## THE PEACEFUL BLUE JURA MOUNTAINS

THE NEXT MORNING she called at six-thirty.

You know, she said, when you've been going through something truly horrible in your life, say a member of your family is very ill, she may actually be dying, it's the last thing you ever expected, and you've been spending your days at the hospital, driving there every morning, waiting in those airless reception areas, sitting for hours in her room, listening to the equipment beeping and the TV babbling and hearing panicked whispers and half-dead groans and piercing yelps, trying to take notes as the doctors talk their doctor nonsense, going every day three times a day to the same plastic laminate table in the hospital cafeteria, driving back home but not being able to sleep, going upstairs into her old room, the one she lived in until she got sick, seeing her favorite dresses still hanging in the closet, thoughts swirling and racing and yet hardly moving, all of that, and then one day while you're shopping you run into someone you haven't seen in a long time, and that person says, "Anneliese, how nice to to see you! Aren't we lucky with the weather?" Well, when that happens, you can't answer, you just cry, you don't know where to start, you just can't put that enormous experience into words...

Is Luzia sick? I asked.

Of course not, this is an illustration. I'm only saying I can't suddenly explain the work I've been doing as if it was a weather report. I have been preparing you for it. I know you will understand when the time comes. So as I was telling you yesterday, I have hurled myself into the well of thought. I spend my days at the bottom of the well, in the Nothing Sea. Myself my own dungeon. Milton said that. *Umnachtet,* made into night, that is what happened to Hölderlin. I have been down in the well for years now. I cannot sleep no matter how bone-tired I am, how weak and flimsy, because if I doze for even for one moment I'll drown. I need to keep thinking and moving, I can't stop, my thoughts have to keep circulating, I swirl my arms in the mucky water, I cannot let myself sleep. Actually, of course, I do sleep. I have a very comfortable bed, with an Eider mattress pad and gossamer pillows made by St. Genève, they are heaven, but never mind that, I live at the bottom of the well of doubt, in the putrid dark. I have to wait for months, until the very peak of summer, to see sunlight strike the top of the well shaft, just the top few feet, I never see the sun, just the light at the top of the well shaft, because at the latitude of Basel the sun is never directly overhead, in the well it is nearly dark even at midday, that is how it is with my work, there is very little light and I wait a long time for it. The air is sour. The stone walls are slick with the tracks of slugs, but this is where I live. Okay. Actually I work in my study, which is a bit dusty but nicely lit with large bay windows that look out onto a stone-walled courtyard where there's a small ornamental well decorated with flowers, that's what gave me the idea that I live in a well, actually I was quite comfortable when I thought up that idea, but you know even Saint Jerome had a nice cool cave with a fresh straw mattress and a little garden where he grew simple desert herbs and a selection of dates and figs. Beckett had his Aran sweaters and his Gucci bag and his soft suede Clark's Wallabees shoes. He wore his fancy clothes even when he was deep in some trash bin in his mind, so it doesn't matter, because my life really is a stinking well. I live at the bottom of a deep shaft, I see only a distant oculus of light. Every once in a while a bird goes by or a fly dives down to pester me. At night I see one star at a time. Occasionally I hear thunder, sometimes I feel rain, a drop or two at a time, my days are all the same, doubt, doubt, doubt, uncertainty, fear, cold, doubt, floating wasps and spiders, algal growth on my legs, unease, doubt, tingling in my feet, more doubt, flies, earthworms in the water, where do they come from, do they fall in from the top? Or is the bottom not as solid as it seems? Doubt, doubt, uncertainty, cramps, trembling, my arms are numbed from swirling in the water, I am frightened, Samuel, I am not calm, I admit that, I am telling you all this very honestly, I have never had an internal censor. Paul says I murdered my internal censor and hid the body, I told him that is ridiculous, where would I hide the body if I murder someone who is inside my own brain? But I am frightened. How could any sane person not be, in fact I hope my fear is evidence that I am sane, that's what Thomas Aquinas says, so I hope it's true, because only an insane person could live at the bottom of a well. Beckett spent his time on the Rue de l'Université in the 7th arrondissement, a fancy part of Paris. People stopped him and asked for autographs. Hölderlin was up in a tower, he had a lovely view. He had friends to visit him, Jaeggy, Bachmann, Benn, and Mayröcker. They all loved him. I am down in a well, it's much worse. I have not even mentioned the problems of evacuation, I am a closed ecosystem, I am reduced to drinking the nutritive waters of the well to survive, ingesting and excreting into my own private ocean, my thoughts circulate into my mouth, I swallow them, my thoughts, and then later out they flow out into the stagnant water, and then back into my mouth, my thought feeds on itself, well, actually I don't drink well water, Paul and Luzia cook me delicious meals, she makes traditional Swiss *Nusstorte,* that is a yummy caramelized nut-filled pastry, and he makes *Haselnusslebkuchen,* those were Hansel and Gretel's favorite cookies, Ossegg and Traxler proved that, and when Paul says we can afford it, we eat them with *Aargauer Edelblanc Likörwein,* that's a delicious sweet dessert wine, but none of that matters, because I am in the well, drinking the black water, in the day, at night, drinking and drinking, I drink it at dawn, I drink it in the day, I drink and drink it, this is what I choose, I will not give up, my life is absolutely devoted to my work. I do not want firm ground. I do not want to have a "nice time," I do not want to "take a break," as Paul says when he comes and shouts down into the well, I mean when he knocks on the door of my study, I do not want to "take it easy" or "relax" or "watch a lovely film like *Psycho*" or "just take a break for one fucking minute." This is my life, and I am absolutely dedicated to making something out of it. I live in the well. I do not need sunlight or fresh air, I do not need to eat anything except the earthworms and slugs that struggle in the well water, although I really do relish the lovely breakfasts Luzia and Paul make. He cooks me *oeufs en cocotte.* Do you know what they are? *Oeufs en cocotte* are like shirred eggs, do you know what those are? No? Shirred eggs are cooked in shirrers, *oeufs en cocotte* are cooked in ramekins. Do you know what ramekins are? Ramekins go in *bains-marie,* do you know what those are? It is really quite sad, apparently you have never had a well-cooked egg. *Oeufs en cocotte* are heaven, even though they are not my favorite, I prefer fresh croissants with butter, marmalade, or honey. And I very much appreciate hot chocolate for breakfast, I know it's not common, but if it is properly made, with Swiss chocolate, not Lindt, that is a godless international conglomerate, but actual Swiss chocolate like Cailler, it has a deep oak flavor, it is both rich and bitter, Paul takes just a square of Cailler chocolate and melts it in boiling water, and then he stirs in some simple syrup and crème fraîche, and sprinkles vanilla seeds on top. There is quite possibly nothing on earth as wonderful as my hot chocolate with a freshly baked croissant, and I mean fresh, one minute from the oven, made with real puff pastry, by hand, no machines, no shortcuts, two hundred and forty-three layers of pastry and butter, that is five folds into three layers, each one just six tenths of a millimeter thick, there may be nothing on earth as delicious as a croissant like that and a Cailler and crème fraîche hot chocolate, but you would have no idea about those things. You drink Cadbury's chocolate in Canada, Cadbury bars are just discolored oil sticks, we won't even talk about Hershey's and Nestlé's, those are pressed brown grease, and I have tried North American croissants, they are enormous gummy wads, eating them is like chewing kitchen sponges soaked in fat. I also have a penchant for *Apfelküchlein,* that's a deep fried apple cookie, and of course *Brunsli,* those are Swiss brownies, *Schwabenbrötli,* Swabian cookies, they're not Swiss but they are so delicious, and oh, I adore the old classic, peaches and cream, peaches from Cataluña, double cream from the Molkerei Hurschler, they use the very best milk from cows fifteen hundred meters up on the slopes of the Alps, and I add a dash of Mathilde Pêche liqueur, did I mention that? It's the best peach liqueur in the world, and a tiny tiny sprinkle of grated nutmeg. That is peaches and cream, that is heaven, it is just what I need before I hurtle back down into my hell of torture and despair. Paul says we have to stop buying Cailler chocolate and peaches from Cataluña, he says I have spent my pension and his salary isn't enough, he reminds me he has to save for Luzia's law school, but I can't think about those things, I can only think about my work. So you see, Samuel, I make fun of myself, a little, because I have to, my life is actually so strange and isolated that it would be hard to talk without making fun of it, I do it because I am embarrassed, when I tell you about my life and my mind it sounds like a pompous exaggeration, a farce, as if I am play acting a tragedy when actually I live a pampered privileged indolent irresponsible life, letting my own brother work to take care of me, behaving like an old baby, so I make fun of myself partly because it's embarrassing, but also because it is painful to talk about the state I am in. When I am in the well I am not a talking creature, I am like one of the slugs, swimming or writhing or drowning in the water, it is hard to tell. If you grab a slug and take a pair of tweezers and force its little mouth open, and say, "Speak!" then the poor creature makes small sounds out of its gummy mouth, and its brain gets twisted and electrified by the effort of speaking, and it emits a small slug yowl from the effort of talking, because ordinarily its mind is nothing but sticky goo, a goo inside its sticky head, and forcing it to talk ruins it, makes the slug insane, hurts it, that's how it feels when I talk about what my life is like, it hurts, and I just want to be dropped back into the well, into the Nothing Sea, because writing and writhing are all I can do.

Actually, I said, I can sympathize with what you're saying. This year, for me it's as if the world has crowded in. I'm not sleeping well. I guess for me life isn't a well or a boat, it's more like a trapezoidal room, a room leading to a long corridor that gets narrower and narrower. At the far end of the room there is a tiny space left for me, nothing but a chair and a standing lamp—

I don't understand that, sorry. Almost all rooms are rectangular, and ones that aren't are not particularly scary. Besides, rooms are provided with doors so you can leave. It is different with me. I am broken. I broke myself by thinking. Every time I have tried to reassemble myself, I've made things worse. There is no hope of assembling Runtzelken-Puntzelken, that's Humpty-Dumpty, you know we also call him Humpelken-Pumpelken, Runtzelkins-Puntzelkins, but it's all the same, he is a person who is delicate like an egg, and he breaks—Goggelmoggel, we also call him Goggelmoggel—he breaks into yolk, albumen, and shell chips. A mess. Goggelimoggeli. Schoggiweggli! *Vergessen Sie nicht die süßen Momente Ihrer Kindheit! Halten Sie diese Erinnerungen frisch mit einem Schoggiweggli – die perfekte Mischung aus weichem Brötchen und köstlicher Schokolade. Schoggiweggli! Aber warte mal, Anneliese... wenn du sie als Kind nicht mochtest, warum solltest du sie jetzt plötzlich mögen?*[6]

What?

Never mind. So when my life first started falling into pieces, I didn't notice. I'm not the world's most beautiful person, you may have noticed, but now that I have reached a certain age it isn't shocking, in fact it's expected, that little pieces of me fall off now and again. It didn't surprise me when a whole section of me worked loose, that is what happened with my skin condition, Paul wouldn't let me tell you about it, but you and I are scientists, I mean you used to be a scientist, so you won't mind.

Well actually, I'm packing up at the moment, I have a flight to catch in Nashville.

I know, don't worry. So I had a rash, it appeared just before a holiday to Abruzzo. I was delighted, because it meant I could stay home and work, but of course we went anyway, and while we were there blisters started to appear, at first they were like pimples, and then they filled with clear fluid. I knew something was very wrong, but the doctors in Pescara are idiots, and they sent me back to our rental apartment with a skin cream. I said, "Is this all I need?" and the doctor said, "Well, you don't have leprosy," and I said, "How do you know?" and he said, "The symptoms of leprosy are spots that are flat, faded, or lighter than the skin," and I said, "I have some of those," and he looked, but then he said, "We can't all be Francesca Ferrara," and I said, "Who?" and he said, "She is miss 'Miss degli Arbrëshe,'" and I said, "What?" and he said, "She's Arbëreshë, she speaks Arbërisht, she is miss 'Miss degli Arbrëshe' 2020," and I said, "Can I see your diploma?" and he just took me out to the front counter and showed me how to pay. Doctors everywhere, but especially, in my opinion, Italian doctors, are culturally abysmally ignorant. You can't talk to them about anything except sores and swabs, and even then, when you ask them entirely rudimentary questions, they reveal that they are incomprehensibly incompetent and stupefyingly uncaring, illiterate, and brutish. They think of patients as bruised cadavers with wads of money poking out of their mouths. So I went home with the skin cream, and of course it was useless, and soon the fluid in the blisters turned cloudy and they started to itch violently, and then they popped and the whole area between my belly and my crotch seeped and oozed, my little bubbly blisters were weeping, that's the medical term, *weinend*, and it is true, they were weeping, as if they were all sad, a whole heaven of sad little angel heads weeping cloudy tears, and finally, two weeks into our so-called vacation, the whole mass of pustulent skin crusted over and formed an enormous scab the size of a child's hand, except a really old child with rough gray skin, and the scab slowly detached itself from the tender pink skin underneath, and of course I couldn't resist peeling it away and breaking off loose pieces, and sometimes I tore the new skin underneath, producing blebs of blood, and during the last week of our so-called vacation I managed to rip most of the scab off, but I wasn't quite healed yet, because the new skin was very tender but also itched intensely so I lost even more sleep than when my groin had been a prickly mass of weeping sores, but after all life goes on, doesn't it, and as long as we're alive our bodies try to heal themselves, and so I healed at last, even though I'm not much to look at in a swimsuit.

That's a relief. But maybe we can continue this conversation after I get back home?

My rash was only the first of an avalanche of illnesses I have contracted since the horrible so-called vacation to Abruzzo. Swollen joints, shooting pains in my hips, flatulence of course, well maybe that isn't an illness, but more properly an ailment or, in my case, even a condition, but anyway also tingling feet, dry eyes, and oh, yes, really chronic, awful indigestion, the kind where bubbles of acid burble up in your throat, then they burst in your windpipe while you're breathing, even in your mouth, and it feels all the time as if someone is boiling a pot of squirrel feet and vinegar in your stomach, it's horrible, as you know. Do you know? You don't know? So it's just me, but anyway all I mean is that *todos vamos al infierno,* we are all going to hell together, except that I won't make it in one piece because I am falling apart. Literally peeling and flaking. Once, I had pearlescent skin and rosy cheeks. My inguinal and perineal regions were beautiful, the skin there was smooth and soft, my pubic hairs grew in lush black curls, Willermus said that, he was my boyfriend in Gymnasium. But in Abruzzo a whole panel of my body, from my belly over to an inguinal tendon that is perilously close to my genital organs, a whole panel simply revolted and dropped away, and if the excrescence had spread farther down onto my genital organs, they would have... well, okay, that didn't happen, but as I speak to you tissues all over my body are weakening. My hypodermis is flabby, my papillary dermis is wrinkled, my epidermis is like paper. Now the latest thing, the latest in this parade of plagues and torments, the new thing, is crumbling nails, crumbly nails, crumbly, that's the only word for it, they crumble when I pick at them, the nails have become kind of cheesy, my glorious talons that I used to paint cherry red have contracted a kind of dry rot. It probably doesn't help that I live in a well, ha ha. But my nails used to be strong, I could pry up staples with them. Now what have I got? Pieces of fingernail just flake off, as if I were made of aged Parmigiano-Reggiano, the really dry kind. It doesn't make any sense, does it, I mean I am a rational person, I am a scientist for heaven's sake, I pride myself on my grasp of at least some of the fundamental conditions of our physical existence, especially of course in the biological sciences, even though my specialty is remote from medicine, but so it really does go without saying that I know about vitamin deficiencies, common fungal vectors, and the general properties of psoriasis and eczema, I am fairly well informed about each of those things, both on my own, and also by consultation with a more or less endless succession of doctors, and the conclusion is that my crumbly nails are not the result of any of the common causes of crumbling nails, but rather they are simply crumbling, whatever that means, they are just crumbling apart, like I am, it is as if I am a sand sculpture on a beach, and the wind is slowly abrading me, particle by particle, piece by piece, or grain, or flake, or chip, one chip of keratin at a time, flaking away, grain by grain, until, well... You may be wondering why I am using these mechanical terms, such as flake or panel or partition, when I am referring to my body, which has its own distinct nomenclature reaching back to the Egyptians, Indians, and Greeks. It is because that is how I feel. My life is not so much disintegrating as disassembling. I used to feel whole, in my body, my career, my mind, my family. Now each of those is coming apart. My body is the emblem of this disintegration, the visible sign, the outward symbol. The parts that fall off can be weighed and photographed, not that I'd do that, but I could.

Please don't bother.

Maybe I will! I could number them, measure each one, and photograph it, the way I once did with my mosquito bites, but that's another story. I believe that what is happening to my body is connected to the other parts of my life—and this is the point I want to make—so that when my body disassembles, so do my career, my mind, and my family. I know this sounds unscientific, perhaps even pitiful. I can't explain it to people here. My colleagues, I mean my former colleagues Sybille, Andrei, Walter, Spadella, Marcel Bieri, and Grettina, they are hopeless, and Ludwig Hassenpflug, I always forget him, because he is impossible to remember, my so-called friends and former colleagues are administrators, technocrats, capitalists, unimaginative middle class stuffed conservative cliché versions of the lives they see on television and read about in their glossy paperbacks. Paul and I had a dinner party recently for the rector and his wife. A simple, private dinner party for four, not counting Luzia and Hans who ate in the other room. That idiot Morschmulmig, he's the rector of the university, went on and on about how wonderful "our" university of Basel is, with its "spectacular and rising" world ranking, its "brilliant" faculty who are like "pressure cookers" whose lids just need to "fly off" and their "crazy creativity" will "fill the air" and we will "write our own ticket" and be at the "bleeding edge" of international research and reach "critical density" of "genius and innovation" and achieve an unprecedented concentration of "centers of excellence" that will "push the agenda" and "set the tone" for "decades to come" on account of our "perfectly tuned organization" that works with "binding synergy" and uses "tightly limited, rapid-action feedback loops" between "creators, disseminators, and facilitators" to produce "dynamic and self-correcting research" that is "fully internationally multi-directional" and situated "at the heart" of the "bases of production and manufacture" to produce an "unprecedented exponential upsurge in intellectual interest" in "our" university, resulting in a "dramatic," "surprising," "exhilarating," "spectacular," "propulsive" increase in “our” already “amazing” ranking among all universities of the world, as measured by the *Times Higher Education* world universities listing, “our” ranking of, wait for it, seventy-four. And when he said that, I told Paul, I could feel the blood vessels in my cheeks bursting with shame, literally bursting under the skin, producing one of my ecchymoses, my blood bruises, that’s how ashamed I was for him, my capillaries were actually perforating from the pressure of my embarrassment, I was so mortified for him, for his sake, and also for his horribly bloated wife, who was probably trying to grow a layer of fat around her body to protect herself from him, but mainly I was embarrassed for myself, for living a life that involved people like that rector and his bulbous wife. Maximillian Morschmulmig is so vacuous, so endless in his self-regard, so unctuous in his pathetic allegiance to his institution, which he believes is “astonishing” and “unique,” but which is actually just a university among many others, well down on the world listing, with seventy-three universities around the world ranked higher than it, I mean what aspiring student would look at the *Times Higher Education* listing and say, “Oh, wonderful, I think I’ll go to the seventy-fourth best university, that’s perfect for me because I am so mediocre”? As far as I can see my so-called friends and former colleagues don’t perceive anything about the world except their own reputations. They are hollow automata illuminated from within by their own self-regard. There is absolutely nothing in their minds except glowing cartoon images of themselves projected on the insides of their skulls for their perpetual admiration. When they sleep they probably dream about how people talk about them, or maybe they don’t dream at all, they just fall into a low-energy mode like a television when it’s turned off, and the little red light shows it’s still plugged in, or like a hibernating animal, slightly cold to the touch, just nominally alive. Actually I can’t understand how they dress themselves in the morning. I have seen them feeding themselves, and it’s monstrous, they sit hunched over and convey trembling spoonfuls of food to their mouths, they have a glazed expression when they eat, like they are defecating. I actually saw one of my former colleagues, Walter Stewens, giggling at a parrot. That is just how inane my former colleagues are. When you think about things, when you really question your life, then people you assumed were your friends just drop off the list, they become useless, their lack of sympathy is astounding, their lack of imagination is depressing, their lack of empathy is painful. They cannot be talked to anymore. So much for friends. So much for the people who were supposed to be understanding, who were supposed to accompany me through life, providing support and care. I am on my own.

Well, you have Paul.

Yes, and Luzia. But really I am on my own.

I can understand that. I have two brothers, but they don't have the capacity or the interest to be involved in my life. I used to think about that a lot. I mean I love them, or I loved them, but there wasn't really a connection.

Too bad. So if I begin with my body—

And also, Anneliese, I have co-workers, people like Catherine and Rosie, but less and less of a family. Last month I decided to do something about that. Catherine helped me. Do you mind if I tell you?

Actually, I do mind. Maybe later. So, if I begin with my body, and consider what has been happening to it, then it appears to me I am being disassembled. Something is taking parts and breaking them off of the whole, tearing me from myself as Marsyas the satyr said when he was skinned alive by Apollo, you know that story, his skin was cut from him while he was alive, just like my colleagues did to me, and Marsyas cried out, *Quid me mihi detrahis,* "Why are you taking me from myself?" This most intimate thing, my own body, which Willermus liked very much, he said it functioned very well, even though I was never an athlete, I didn't train for any of the popular sports, although I did play *Winkelschmerzel,* you know that game, where people crawl into the bottom of sleeping bags, and then the bags are rolled up tightly and tied around with rope and then pushed into the space under staircases and packed in with blankets so you twist and struggle and nearly suffocate? Do you? You don't? Too bad. Anyway, this body of mine recently broke its promise with me—because doesn't everyone think their body has promised to remain as healthy as possible?—my body broke that promise and divided itself into partitions, parts, sections, flakes. It gave itself permission—how else can I say it?—to disassemble. Several of those parts or portions have actually broken off. That is what happened with the platter of dried-up boils on my abdomen during the worst days of my Italian so-called vacation. A saucer-sized piece of me just slipped away, like a fried egg detaching itself from the pan.

Sounds pretty nauseating. But if you don't mind, I think it's time for me to check out.

Not yet. I know your schedule. Your untrained assistant Mrs. Hirondel told me when your flight departs. So the second dimension is my career. Please try to remember, as I speak, that four dimensions of my life are disassembling: my body, my career, my mind, my family. Just say it over to yourself, and you will be able to remember it. My career is also disassembling. Thanks to Sybille, and also, truth be told, to my own inability to collaborate with my fellow scientists—and I really have to say I am simply reporting this as a fact, I cannot explain why it has been so hard for me to attract and retain colleagues for collaborative research or multiply-authored articles, although it may have something to do with the fact that I snuck into their labs to correct their research, and probably also to certain personality traits I am supposed to have, which—

For example you don't care about the person you're talking to?

That is completely untrue.

And you don't listen?

Exactly right! So I have been unable to attract colleagues for collaborative research, although even now I cannot begin to understand why any potential collaborator would decline the opportunity to work with someone who understands his weaknesses, limitations, and prejudices as perfectly as I do, and is as willing to explain them, at length, in the name of honesty and collegiality—anyway because I cannot retain collaborators long enough to see any project into publication, my research record is dismal, it is broken. Snapped in half. The first half, full of promise. The second, nonexistent, or rather it consists principally of an enormous number of words spoken by me, in many professional settings, such as lectures, symposia, conferences, meetings, colloquia, seminars, and workshops, usually in a heated frame of mind, words which of course count for nothing, because not a single one of them has been written down and published. I cling to what remains, Samuel, like a spider hanging from an invisible thread, trying to reel itself up, but the thread keeps lengthening, dropping the spider onto the floor. Okay, I know how spiders work. I know their threads don't stretch, I know they can climb if they want, what I'm saying is arachnologically inaccurate, okay? But you see what I mean. My career is ruined, it has slid down the string that was supposed to pull it up, always up, into startling heights of fame and glory. It is falling, and that principle of continuous falling also applies to my standing in my field, my participation in our annual and regional conferences, the number of lecture invitations I have received, the number of downloads of my papers on the ResearchGate and Academia websites, my lack of success in finding new soft money for the coming funding cycles, the citations my work has attracted, as measured by both the *h* and the *g* indices, which our ruthless Swiss government uses to measure our standing—and regarding those indices, it bears saying that I once had one of the higher *g* indices in all of zoology, never lower than 118, a number so high that it attracted the notice and envy of Sybille Kröller and many other people, until, that is, it started plummeting, to its all-time low this morning of 7, a number that shows with cold accuracy that people are no longer citing my work, that they are actively turning away from it, that they're reading instead the work of my competitors, competitors, funny word, but accurate, they're the people I used to call colleagues or even friends, but now I attract only competitors, leeches, people who steal ideas from me, and people are even reading their work instead of mine, undoubtedly hoping to find something they can steal, because they're the sort of envious little-minded unimaginative people who read other people's work in order to find scraps they can steal, and it's easier to steal things that have already been stolen, because they're packaged, it's like laundering laundered money, by comparison with those people my actual competitors are titans, they're the ones who have ripped my career limb from limb, they're the ones whose gleaming teeth are beaded with gore from my eviscerated career, by comparison the little people who read the people who steal from me, they're like hyenas, timid but vicious, they hang back and then leap in and grab a strip of cartilage from my throat or a juicy balloon of fat from my intestine, and then they skitter back to their provincial colleges and peck away at their own horrid little publications, and of course they're careful to add some sniping comment about how the work they're stealing from is substandard, misguided, or wrongheaded, not to mention, they say, the work of Professor Anneliese Glur, who is named in a derogatory aside in footnote 52 of the paper they're stealing from, but it's not enough that the person they're stealing from notes Glur's work is useless and old-fashioned in footnote 52, no, these hyenas have to spit up all over the name of Anneliese Glur, they have to add their own little footnote, number 107, detailing exactly why the people they're stealing from underestimate how absolutely rudimentary Glur's errors are (it would be a separate question, they note, to ask why, exactly, these people they're stealing from are so circumspect about Glur's work, perhaps they owe her something, perhaps they're ex-students, perhaps they had certain inappropriate relationships with her, but we wouldn't want to speculate, they say, we're only noting that these people, the ones we're stealing from, are curiously gentle when it comes to Glur), how unwilling she has been to learn from even the most generous and positive criticism (which, they add, we have attempted on numerous occasions to offer to her, both informally and in seminars and other public settings, indeed going far out of our way to help her, but after a certain point, what can you do? I mean what can you do?), how Glur is substandard, misguided, and wrongheaded (words which, they say, now that we think of it, are a good test for honest legitimate scholarship that can face up to criticism and improve itself, work that's flexible and responsive to the contemporary global economy, work which is, well, not to put too fine a point on it, work which is like ours), and how, even though these hyenas are reluctant to say it, and even though it will take them away from their subject, it really is necessary, sadly, once again, to have to say how Glur's work is not only wrong (a common fault, we're only human), rambling (she wanders from point to point, doesn't she, and frankly, we don't understand much of it), and outdated (naturally, because she's what, sixty years old? seventy?), not only all that, but actively misleading (not just repeatedly wrong, but stubbornly, persistently wrong, as if Glur had a will to always get on the wrong side of each issue, always to misunderstand), and how sad it makes them to see the field dragged back into the nineteenth century (that's how far back Glur would set us, they say, but actually it can be demonstrated, by reference to her *h* and *g* indices, that no one reads her work anymore, in point of fact Glur's a thing of the past, no more useful to us now than a cuneiform tablet with instructions for counting donkeys), and with that they conclude their remarkably spiteful diatribe supposedly politely hidden in footnote 107, adding only that they don't at all mean to be critical, and nothing they have written should be taken as a critique in any sense, it is simply an assessment, it's all proper collegial and scholarly behavior, no one should be upset by it, certainly no scholar should begrudge the time it takes to thoroughly and patiently investigate all the errors and preposterous mistakes of another scholar, because it's for the good of everyone in the field, but all the same it is a tremendous relief that the Glur case is now closed and no scholar need ever consult the Glur texts or mention the Glur name again. That is how a lifetime of energetic, innovative thinking is finally squashed underfoot like a spider. And forgotten. Because when you crush a spider, you glance at what you've done, to make sure it's dead and it's not sticking to your shoe, but after that you walk away and never think of the spider again unless you're using it to illustrate some point, like I am now, and even then you only think of it for a moment, because it's kind of gross and weird to be thinking of a squashed spider, and after that it really is gone, like my name is gone, my reputation, my career, and everything I have done. You'll have to excuse me, Samuel. I have been speaking out of professional pride, and that is not only impolite and unpleasant, but more importantly it is a thing of the past. I didn't mean any of that about my work to be bragging, really I didn't. Once upon a time, I would have. I am not saying I'm a genius. All the empirical evidence is against it. I am a biologist, for heaven's sake, who used to work in a third-tier university in a second-tier first world country. I have a purpose in life, which is to investigate philosophic foundations of biological life. But so far that has been between me and my notebooks. As far as the world is concerned, in effect, in fact, I am one among hundreds. I'm like an acorn looking up at the oak tree and saying, That was me, I was big and imposing, not little and rounded, or, wait, I mean I am like the oak tree, looking down at my fallen acorn and saying, I made that, even though it's small, or, wait, no, not really either one of those. I have it now. I'm like an oak tree, struck by lightning, lying in charred panels and pieces all over the forest floor, my acorns scattered around, some burned but others nicely roasted. And a voice comes from the blasted stump and says, I was a great massive tree, and now I'm nearly nothing, but my oh my, I have to say some of those young acorns look quite tasty, or no, that's not right. Wait, I know: I am like the seven hydra heads, all chopped off, lying in the sand, howling and snapping in different directions, while my ruined body writhes around like seven headless snakes attached to the body of a lizard, or whatever a hydra is, I think the hydra actually is a snake, just that its neck divided into seven necks, but snakes don't have necks, so I don't really understand what its body was, but that's a good illustration of my career, because I am like the snapping heads, they see what's happened but they can't get back onto their necks. Or something like that. I am not sure about those metaphors, Samuel, but please pay attention, because this is where it gets complicated. The other two dimensions are mind and family. So who am I, or who is anyone, to say how well their mind hangs together? I may be somewhat effervescent. I get carried away sometimes and use up all the oxygen, as Paul says. Luzia just walks off, by the way, she is a clever child and for years I never even noticed when she did that. I have my so-called voluble or volumetric style of speaking, yes, but is my mind also fragmented? Am I several people? Is there one of me who calls people when they don't expect it, when they're in hotel rooms doing whatever people do in hotels—

Actually I'm leaving.

I don't mind, whatever you want to do in a hotel room is your own business, although probably the only thing to do in a hotel in Knoxville, Tennessee, is to leave as quickly as possible, but you may use up your life any way you wish, at least for now.

What is that supposed to mean?

Sorry, you distracted me with your interruption. So am I one person when I call people in their hotel rooms and talk on and on about my scabs without giving the least indication that I care at all about the person I am calling, and then am I a completely different person when I scribble in my notebooks? Am I one person when I work as a scientist in a lab, like I used to do, and another when I work by myself? Do I have multiple dissociative disorder, or multiple identity disorder, or maybe depersonalization disorder, or dissociative identity syndrome, or seven psyche syndrome? Do I have hydra head disorder, dismembered scholar disorder, or acorn disorder? I'm sorry, but I really don't think so. People have said I sometimes take a while to come to my point, especially that horrid elevator operator who still works in our building at the university, who begged and pleaded for me to finish, "Oh please just stop," he said, "stop, please stop, do please stop, and oh do please stop, you never stop, you just keep going, when do your sentences ever end? I can't stand to listen, please please please just come to the point," etcetera, he was very simply one of the world's rudest people, and aside from that he seemed to think I was the sort of clown who enjoyed hearing clownish parodies of herself, but I don't, I just don't, and I wished he would stop, I would have liked to say to him, "You just stop! I can't stand to listen to you saying, 'Oh please just stop, stop, please stop, do please stop, and oh do please stop, you never stop, you just keep going, when do your sentences ever end, I can't stand to listen, please please please just come to the point!' It isn't funny, it's hurtful, you horrible wormlike string of snot, you awful trailing thread of excrement, you weevil, you creeping centipede of a man, please please please just stop making fun of me," but I couldn't bring myself to say anything, because if I did he would parody me again, and that would be even worse, so I took my punishment, I never hooked my finger with its long crumbly nail into one of his nostrils and said, "I do come to my point! I am Professor Doctor Anneliese Glur! I am wild in my thinking, but it is the wildness of passion! Of invention! I feel things, I have convictions! If something hurts I say so, I don't cover it up, and besides, what appears to you as endless drivel is in fact rigorously logical beyond anything you can ever hope to understand. Actually I pursue syllogistically precise arguments at great length, with steely determination, unparalleled patience, and tremendous exactitude! I have thoughts you cannot begin to imagine, I am aware of every nuance of each word in every language that I have ever spoken, in fact I do not rant or improvise, I neither indulge in asides nor pause for irrelevant commentary, no, every single sound I utter is native to my innermost spirit, intent, and argument! By comparison with my book-length thoughts and their thousands of imbricated and enmeshed ideas, their intricately qualified positions and elaborately balanced judgments, by comparison with my arrays, lattices, and matrices of postulates, suggestions, and hypotheses, my expressive and often striking images, my articulate, judicious, and eloquent turns of phrase, my apparently careless asides, my strategically positioned repetitions, and even my occasional struggles with metaphors, analogies, prepositions, idioms, and other peculiarities of speech, every one of which is entirely intentional—by comparison with that unapproachably magnificent accomplishment of thought and speech your little 'Oh god oh god, I can't stand to listen, please please please just come to the point' is nothing, it is the splurting noise a camel makes when it hacks up its phlegm, it is a turtle's burp, it is the ploppy sound a fish makes when it excretes a bubble!" But no, I can't say that, because the elevator operator would inform Sybille, and she would run and tell Morschmulmig, and then I would be permanently banned from the only building on the university where I still have access, not that I need to go there, but it's amusing to walk down the hallways and see the shock on my former colleagues' faces. Walter's face turns from rubber to stone. Marcel turns from stone to rubber. Spadella turns from rubber to blubber. You know, Samuel, often when I get up in the morning it seems to me I am already talking. My thoughts continuously ramify and exfoliate, like a branching tree. My thoughts are arborescent, that is a magnificent word, isn't it, and it fits my mode of exposition perfectly. My ideas branch and divide like whirling brooks. I live like a baron in the trees of my thought, I nest up there, I build nests made of parentheses. Paul says that. "You keep opening parentheses," he says, "and just when I think you're finished another one opens, and another, and another, and so I get lost," that's what he says, and also things like, "It would take the patience of a hundred elephants to wait for you to finish a single thought," or, "Lysi, look, in all my life you have never once, not even one single solitary time, said anything in less than an hour, I mean my god, who can be expected to listen? Who? You give me horrible headaches, I become sick listening to you," those are things Paul says, I freely admit I am guilty of some of them, and I am aware that Paul is the most patient of people, and he is a good brother, at least up until my recent disassembly, but in this respect, in regard to the habit I have of being volumetric, he is absolutely and completely wrong, top to bottom, beginning to end, inside to out, because in fact even though I do nestle in the middle of my innermost parentheses, I am in here! I am armored by parentheses. I am expressing a large thought, and it means something. At least that is what I would have said up until a year or two ago, but now I am not so sure. These days I sometimes feel as if I just am my long sentences, they are me, I am nothing more than a tangle of thought threads, lacing and unlacing, disentangling and re-entangling, recirculating previously ingested thoughts, drinking my own well water, expelling it, drinking it again the next day. I feel I may be deeply confused. Not in control. Unstrung. Divided out into delays and asides. Disassembled. Internally multiply divided by parentheses, each one like a little curved knife, a miniature scimitar, cutting into my thought, dividing me from myself, severing my thoughts into slivers. I interrupt myself, like I am now, to remark on my own thoughts, I have reservations, and I have second thoughts about my reservations, like I do now, and asides about my second thoughts, I'm sure I'll have one of those in a moment. I am continuously slicing into myself, cutting away parts of my thought. My thought has been pared away from itself, like Marsyas's skin, the little parenthetical cuts are everywhere, not to mention the horizontal stabs of dashes, and the myriad little commas, each one like a *tourné* knife, slicing a little gash in my thoughts. So, have I orchestrated our conversations with truly intimidating control, or am I just in the process of ruining another day for you with my unending spray of thought mist? Did I plan every single thing I said to you since we first met, even back to my first few words about Adelheid Wyrsch and the minefield of rusted nails and splinters—and by the way I forgot to mention that later she slipped a letter under our door, saying the sign had to come down or she would submit a petition to one of the *Zivilkreisgerichte* of the Kanton Basel-Landschaft, the civil court—or should I admit I've been slightly confused at certain moments? I do admit I have been momentarily deflected by your attempts to engage me in normal conversation. Normal ideas throw me into a spew of confusion. I can't stop and think about the possibility that there might be other people. But I have not wasted a single moment of your time. I am running in order through the alphabet of my thought, I am performing an extraordinary introduction to an object that is too complex to describe. And yet—and yet I know, I can feel, that all this rationalizing and explaining is a lie. My mind is actually not in good shape. More and more I am aware of something else...

She faltered. I waited.

It's like at night, Samuel, when you watch a lightning storm. When the lightning flashes you see the shapes of enormous clouds that are invisible in the dark. You see them, and then they vanish. There are things in my mind that should not be there. There are partitions of my mind that have become detached, they have worked loose, they are hanging in the dark. I am at loose ends, whatever that is supposed to mean, probably something about loose shoelaces, but if so then it is not clear how a person can be at those loose ends, instead of just having loose ends, because if a person actually is a loose end, then what does the shoe represent? And who is wearing it? That whole metaphor is at loose ends. Anyway, my disastrous personality, which so few people can stomach—and I have to thank you, and believe me I will, even if it is only with a lovely dinner when we meet next time, because as Paul reminded me many times after our dinner, I cannot invite you to the university anymore, I am not exactly welcome there, I don't know why I invited you, I think I was just excited to finally meet you, I mean I don't suffer lapses, as far as I know, although I guess that if I did I wouldn't realize I had suffered lapses, unless someone like Paul reminded me, so it is a relief that he does not often remind me of things I get wrong, although he does tell me over and over that he cannot understand me, my work, or anything I say, so I guess those aren't especially good signs—anyway my somewhat challenging personality is only a veneer, it is not my authentic self. This problematic, apparently scattered, often exasperating personality that everyone sees, which has so many flaws, is actually the best lie my mind can make, the prettiest story about myself I can tell, in order to keep me hidden from myself, to hide what I really am. The other day I went for a dental checkup, and the dentist put a high-resolution video camera in my mouth and showed me, on a big television screen, how the teeth in the back of my mouth are cracked and collapsed, they are full of dark decay. They look like broken stones on a pier, covered with scum from the ocean. My dentist said, you see how things are. He said, these tooth ruins—that's my expression, I can't remember what he called them—these tooth ruins are seething with bacteria. Seething, that's also my word. Your teeth have been fracturing, he told me, and you have been swallowing pieces of them. Those are his words. Bacteria have been flooding out of these tooth ruins into your mouth, and you've been swallowing them, along with pieces of your teeth. Actually I made that one up. So far your system has tolerated it, that's what he said. But if we put fillings in here, we cap the teeth, then the bacteria will be driven down the nerve and into the jaw, and you will have tremendous pain, you will get an infection that will require expensive surgery. Expensive, that's his word. He told me he wanted to pull all my teeth out. I left the office and never went back. I am a biologist, after all. I don't mind bacteria. But my point is that when I saw those tooth ruins, I said to myself, This is what my mind is like. I have been eating pieces of my own mind, and now I am full of infection. I have been feeding off my own diseased thoughts. Word bacteria infest my mouth. That's what I've been eating, and I've been drinking my own excreted thoughts, diluted in the well water. I am a ruin, an infected ruin. My mind is like this. It is a frightening place, but... hold on. There's someone at the door.

There were indistinct voices in the background. Several people were talking. In the minute that followed, my mind returned to me like fresh air when you open a window. I waited for thoughts to appear, but then suddenly she was back on the phone.

Samuel, she said, I believe my mind is falling apart like my body, I mean in the same way as my body, I mean what happens to my body also happens in my mind. Think about it. It makes sense. My skin flakes and peels, so does my mind. My nails crumble, so does my mind. My pestiferous rash was a picture of my mind, engraved onto my body. I looked at it and saw my mind disintegrating. It wept, my rash, and then it came apart. My crumbling fingernails are faithful images of the wreckage of my mind. My tooth ruins are sculptures of infections in my mind, as if my jaw is an artist and it made a statue of my mind using tooth enamel and bacteria, and mounted it in my jaw for me to see. And my tooth ruins are also sculptures of my career, which is falling apart in the same way, poisoned by nasty colleagues and vindictive competitors. My rashes, my nails, and my teeth are faithful models of my disintegrating career and liquefying mind. Why not? Why shouldn't a person fall ill all at once, doesn't the body suffer along with the mind? Why shouldn't all the dimensions of a person react to the world together? So now comes family. It is the fourth of the dimensions, as you no doubt remember. It is simple, just repeat it to yourself: body, career, mind, family. You are married, right?

Was, I said, and then I added, am, because the divorce papers hadn't been drawn up.

Are?

Used to be.

Too bad. I never married. And neither did Paul. We did not live in the same house when he was in law school and I was studying science. But life brought us back together. He moved back to our family home in 1997, after our father died. At the time I was having certain difficulties at the university, and when I could no longer afford my own apartment, I also moved back. By then Hans's second wife had died and no one was in the house except him and Paul. For a number of years now we have been together, just like when we were children. Paul's job is only part time, so we are together a lot. Luzia visits us on weekends and sometimes she uses her old room to study. Our small family is what is left, and it is no longer a healthy bourgeois family with happy parents and sporting children and sunny grandparents and prancing dogs and piping birds and lurking cats. It is broken in a weird way. It's as if once upon a time our life was like a beautiful photograph showing a natural wood house, with the wood stained but not painted, you know the kind. Our life was like this beautiful photograph, and then someone glued it onto a piece of cardboard, put it in a special press, and punched it into jigsaw pieces. Then that person, whoever it was, although of course it could only have been me, but that's an entirely different problem, or maybe it's not, but anyway that person tumbled the pieces into a box, and labeled it *Anneliese's Beautiful Life, 3,000 Piece Jigsaw Puzzle Perfect for Hobbyists and Enthusiasts.* So what could I do? I took our life and spilled it out on a table. Now you should know I cannot assemble jigsaw puzzles, they drive me into distraction, they are an offensive against me, I dislike them intensely, I find them insulting, not because they show me a world in ruins, that's what I like about them, it's not that, it's because they show me that when the world does come apart, when it disassembles as we all know it will, it will split into cute rounded shapes. What could possibly be a more horrible end for our wonderful bewildering universe than to fall into baby-shaped pieces, I hate those nipple-like bulbs shaped like babies' heads. Each piece of a jigsaw puzzle looks like a plump infant. Sometimes the baby is headless, but it is always a baby. The edge pieces look like infants in baggy baby clothes. Well, actually the babyish nature of jigsaw puzzle pieces has nothing to do with this story. I only mentioned it because, actually I don't know why I mentioned it. But and so there I was, staring at the pieces and wishing I had my world back, as it appeared on the cover of the box, which showed the lovely house and the picture postcard mountains and a little bird on one of the gate posts, but all I had was this offensive pile of cardboard chips. And it was worse than that. Pieces were missing. I knew because I counted them, and there were exactly 2,591 pieces, but there should have been 3,000, so there were 409 pieces missing. And Samuel, wait, it was even worse than that, because I discovered the horrible person who disassembled my life—and by the way, I know that person was me, since this is my own illustration, and it perfectly fits the picture of my mind that I was explaining, in which my mind is split and divided and subdivided and yet I can see the whole pattern, I know where every piece belongs, but that is another story, or maybe it isn't—that horrible person actually threw in extra pieces, and I knew that because I was looking at the puzzle, wondering if I should even try to put it together, given that it was missing so many pieces, when I spotted a special piece. I thought, Oh! I know what that is, it's the little eye and the pink feathers on the breast of the little bird that perches on the finial of one of the gate posts at the end of the driveway by the beautiful garden in front of the lovely unpainted but tastefully stained house at the foot of the peaceful blue Jura mountains. And I thought, well, that's some sort of consolation, I'm not sure it helps, but what the hell. And then, not more than one minute later, I spotted another piece, a little eye and pink feathers of the same breast of the same bird that sits on the same finial of the same gate post at the end of the same driveway by the same beautiful garden in front of the exact same lovely unpainted but tastefully stained house at the foot of the peaceful blue Jura mountains. I looked at the picture on the box top, and there is only one bird, and it is in profile so it shows only one eye. So either the little eye and pink feathers on the second piece were from another copy of the puzzle, or the little eye and pink feathers on the second piece belonged to some other bird that sits on the finial of some other gate post at the end of some other driveway by some other beautiful garden in front of some other lovely unpainted but tastefully stained house at the foot of some other peaceful blue mountains somewhere else in the world, and that is a poetic thought, I think, don't you, Samuel? because it means there are many idyllic places in the world, with enough birds for each of them, but it is also awful, because it means those are not my mountains, those are not my houses, those are not my life, so what was that extra piece doing in the jigsaw puzzle box called *Anneliese's Beautiful Life*? And then something happened that made *Anneliese's Beautiful Life* even more horrible. I found a third piece with the little eye and the pink feathers. The eye in this third piece seemed just ever so slightly less bright than the eyes in the other two pieces. It looked glazed, as if the bird was older or it was tired or slightly farther away or a cloud had drifted overhead. At first I thought, Well, it's a large puzzle and there may be other birds hiding in the forest, maybe the trees are infested with birds, that would be natural and it might make the scene even more attractive. I looked at the box top to see if there were other birds hiding in the forest, but no, there was only one. Then I thought, Okay, maybe the bird only looks like a single bird but it's actually three birds lined up one behind the other, exactly one behind the other, not very likely but I was desperate, or maybe the whole puzzle was not what I thought it was, maybe it was a nightmare image disguised as a peaceful picture, and the bird was a little monster with three eyes. So I got out my Eschenbach folding pocket magnifier and looked very closely at the box top, but no, there was only one anatomically normal bird, in profile, with one little eye looking over at me, and at that moment I knew the problem was the puzzle itself, it was not a normal puzzle, but a hideous mess, in fact far worse than a picture-postcard scene of a lovely house with a monstrous three-eyed bird. It was a repulsive grotesque unsolvable puzzle that pretended to be a calm and harmless diversion, and that seemed fundamentally unfair, because the beautiful photograph was my story, and so was the idea of the jigsaw, and if you make up a story why can't you have the story work out the way you want?

There was a moment of silence.

Samuel?

I'm here.

So why can't you?

Sorry, I am not exactly sure what your point is.

Look, I made up this story to say our family was a lovely picture crammed with picturesque Swiss mountains that look like they have been scrubbed clean with toothbrushes, and then it disassembled itself like a jigsaw puzzle, but the story didn't work, did it, because my family doesn't have duplicate pieces, and we aren't missing any pieces, well, actually we are, so I guess that part is okay, but we're not missing 409 pieces, and what exactly do monster birds have to do with my family, not to mention interlocking babies, so the whole story fell to pieces, didn't it? So why can't my story work, considering I invented it? Well, of course I know. What is happening with my family is more profound than jigsaw puzzles, well, okay, fine, that is not saying much. But I have a deep understanding of profundity, I am after all a solitary scholar, what they used to call a pious, profound, and painful scholar, my work has gravity, even gravitas, that is an especially obnoxious sort of gravity, my work is full of trenchant and acute inquiries, searching theories, deep speculations, abstruse cogitations, and penetrating solutions, it is enriched by solemn pronouncements and strengthened by pleonastic axioms, I am afflicted with owlism, that is a sort of affected and pretentious wisdom, a dull and ridiculous pomposity, but it is only the outward placard of my actual nature, I am sorry this all sounds preposterous, but why shouldn't I tell you, how could I not tell you, why should I be coy, why should I act shy about my ideas as if I was a young girl out for her first dance, putting padding in my blouse but also undoing the top button, wanting you to look and then buttoning it up again, until even my mother says, "Oh for god's sake, just undo the damn button," why should I be like that at my age, I won't do it, I know with remorseless certainty that my work has great depths of meaning, deeper and truer than have occurred to other people, I work in uncompliant ignorance of doubt, an abyssal melancholy haunts the walls of my study, my theories involve unnatural fusions of unrelated species of thought, I am warmed by a deep contempt of my hoglike colleagues, I giggle when I see their books, I writhe to see my name mentioned in their condemned publications, my work is surrounded by high bulwarks of unpredictable learning and treacherous deep moats of turgid diffidence. I even sleep profoundly. After a day of work I fall into a bottomless chasm of oblivion, I am like a weary traveler buried in a sweet bed of flowers, like a little bee snoring in a poppy field, I continue on in a state of unmoving, mesmeric and annihilating silence, embalmed in a static peace, eyeless, mindless, my blood circulating so very slowly, for exactly four hours each night until four-thirty in the morning and then I jump up and rush back to my desk. I have been building my theories for decades now. I have created an enormous castle of theories with great walls and parapets, the turrets fly exotic theory flags with tassels and serrated edges, there are massive ramparts made of rude blocks of stony ideas, a great escutcheon above the portcullis with a shield per bend rayonny concepts of gules and vert, a fetid moat filled with liquid theories, a grand entrance hall hung with the banners of many conquered biologists and decorated with their stuffed heads mounted on armorial plaques—I gave them plastic eyes instead of glass eyes, it makes them look dimmer—and the castle is well guarded, there are concealed pits studded with vinegared pins, trapdoors opening into cisterns filled with verminous ideas, hidden troughs poured full of rancor, drops into dungeons littered with splintered invectives, my theories march day and night on the castellated battlements, I have stationed my theories everywhere, armed theories crouch in the crenels of my notched battlements, bloodshot theories lurk in my machicolations, ready with stones to throw at anyone who approaches, the acute eyes of my theories can be glimpsed in my arrowslit windows, they peer down from the spindle towers, dozens of them watch from the vertiginous stacked dormer windows high on the steep pitched rooves, warm round-faced theories glow in the rose windows, odd-looking theories press their faces into quatrefoil windows, I even have triplet theories in my three-light oriel widows, do I have to go on? I don't want to, my theories aren't actually some cartoonish Harry Potter castle, the point is I have experience in constructing theories, I have an understanding of the architecture of thought, so given all that, please tell me: Why can't I tell a simple story about jigsaw puzzles?

Maybe you get distracted?

It would be impossible for you to come up with an answer that is more wrong. I have never been distracted by anything.

You love giving long speeches?

Yes, but that is irrelevant. Don't be anxious, you will understand in a moment. The reason my story didn't work is because my family affects the way I think. I am preoccupied with Paul. He is especially frail because he has been working very long hours. I have only recently noticed this because I write all day, sometimes over fifteen hours a day! I have had tremendous days filled with ideas, I scribbled and scrawled and didn't notice when it was dinner time, and when I came out I wanted to tell Paul, but the dinner was all put away, and he was tired. He told me he couldn't listen. "Please no," he said, "Please not this evening." I told him anyway, because part of him listens even if he is cleaning the kitchen, looking out the window, or watching television. We are connected. It is mysterious, like the way particles in physics can be mysteriously entangled. If one remembers something the other forgets it, and you never know which one knows something until you ask, I mean you don't ask particles anything, they can't speak, but you probe them, and they can't resist the probing because they are very small and weak, or no, not that, maybe they like being probed, they're very little, you can't ask them, you can only probe them, I hope the probes are nice and soft, I don't know, I am not a physicist, but the idea is that as soon as a particle is probed it tells you how it is, well, it doesn't tell you, but it signals to you without words, like it smiles or waves its little hand, and at that exact instant the other particle changes. No matter if the two particles are near each other, or one is in a park and the other is in her study. If one signals it is positive, the other is instantly negative. Even though an instant before, the other particle didn't even know if it was positive or negative, but as soon as one particle signals it is feeling positive, the other suddenly realizes it's been feeling negative. I told Paul we are entangled like the little particles in physics, I told him how if someone probes me I might become happy, but he would be sad, but he wasn't really listening because he was having problems with the coffee press, the filter was lodged sideways in the press and the lid was stuck, and come to think of it maybe the reason he was having trouble with the coffee press was that I was experiencing a moment of exemplary lucidity—but okay, probably not. This is not good science, I know that you can't apply this sort of physics to people. Also Paul and I are quite large and do not like to be probed, or I don't, anyway. And please don't ask me why I am behaving as if I think subatomic particles have little hands, I don't exactly know why I added those details, and I certainly have no idea why probing made me think of people who are young or weak. I am simply speculating, I am using physics as a playful illustration, or actually as an allegory, no, that sounds pompous, I am using physics as an analogic yet emblematic heuristic illustration, and I told him that too, and he pulled really hard and the plunger popped out and the filter hit a cabinet and fell onto the floor, and coffee grounds splattered onto the counter and the tiles behind the sink, and I said, "See? See what I mean?" but he didn't answer. So I explained it all over again, and all he said was, "Sure, Lysi, yes, Lysi." He wanted to calm me down but he couldn't. You see, Samuel, my apparently self-absorbed platter, I mean patter, no, prattle, my banter? No, patter, or blather, yes, blather, why not blather, or *Plapper*, that is the German word, my plapper is intimately bound to an apparently unrelated skill, I am crazily sensitive to people who do not plapper. Such as Paul. I have a nearly incredible capacity to perfectly anticipate what such people intend to say, even though they may take a long time to find their words, like you do, and even though they typically only find a few words anyway, again like you—

Anneliese, I have to go.

Like that, see? Just a few words. For example Paul said to me, "I have an idea. Let's eat out tonight, because we haven't had a nice evening out in months. Can we go to that kebab place on the corner? We could even bring our food back and eat it here, in front of the television." I reminded him we had dinner with you not that long ago. "Right," he said, "we've been out once or twice in five or six years, can we please just go to the kebab stand on the corner?" And I said, "Ask me again tomorrow," and he said, "If you'd like," and he went off to his bedroom. That's all he said, "If you'd like," it wasn't even a sentence like "I see," and it didn't add anything to what I already knew, which was that he didn't really want to go out, or, here's another example, last week I said I was closing in at last on the end of my work, and okay, I admit that is not the first time I told him that, but he said, "That's it." Well, "that's it" is a sentence like "I see," but it isn't much of a sentence. I can read volumes of meaning into remnants of language like that. I know, for example, that when he said "that's it" he wanted to praise me, to let me know he supported me, well, he wouldn't put it that way, that is an American phrase, it makes it sound like the person can't walk, but if he really wanted to help me he should have said, "That's good!" or, "That's interesting, tell me more!" but he said, "That's it," because he wanted me to know he was not agreeing strongly, that he was barely agreeing at all, and in fact he probably hadn't been listening to what I was saying, so what he really meant was, "I'm here, Anneliese, I am your brother, I support you, and Luzia, and Hans, but I need to keep my distance, I need to make sure I don't use up too much of my dwindling energy trying to follow you or understand the things you say," that's what Paul wanted to signal to me with his whispered sentence, "that's it," and there is more, I can hear more in his sad little sentence, "that's it," because I knew he was deeply and perhaps irreparably exhausted, even damaged by my way of talking and thinking, and that his response, delivered with a minimum of enthusiasm and with just a shallow breath, "that's it," those two words, or three words, or let's say two and a half words, they were also a signal to himself, they were his way of saying to himself: I can go on, I can keep doing this. He needed to tell himself that because he has so little energy these days. His pathetic two-and-a-half word response was a way of humoring me and possibly also persuading me to be quiet, but it was mainly something he said to himself, and therefore its fuller meaning—and even this is by no means its full meaning, which would require a much longer phone call to explore—its fuller meaning was something like, "My dear sister, I am sorry. I wasn't really listening just now, because I feel secure enough in our relationship that I don't need to pay attention, but I know you need me to listen, so those two and a half words are my sign that I'm here, I am supporting you, and I could listen more carefully if you asked me again, but please don't, because it's been a long day, I haven't been eating well, and, although I don't think you have noticed, I have been getting up early, even before dawn, and sitting in the kitchen, I may be ill, but I want to keep giving you whatever I can. Those two and a half words, 'that's it,' are testimony for both of us that I am in the room with you, sharing your life, but they're a sign that I'm not really able to think along with you, because I am drained, weak almost to the point of collapse, and the little words, 'that's it,' those words remind me I am still going, hanging in there, I am your brother, and deep down you know this, because you know everything about me, because your mind is always boiling, you're always gasping and lurching, aching and howling, thrashing and wriggling, but through all of that you are also listening. You can hear my small voice and it comforts you," that is more of what Paul's little sentence meant, that is more like what Paul would have said to me. Only two and a half words, actually he says *das war's*, in German, and once or twice also *c'est ça*, that's it. They are nearly the same. *Das war's* is also two and a half words, and so is *c'est ça*. They are almost the shortest sentences you can speak. Yet I can hear what Paul means, and I can hear infinitesimal shifts in his tone each time he says those words in German or French. And that is enough. Yet Paul is still trying. Last week he bought himself some ludicrous salmon and carrot-colored shirts, tight polyester shirts with beryl-colored buttons. Maybe he wants to go dancing. I wonder if he wants to go dancing.

Well, Anneliese, that's interesting, and I'm sorry to hear about Paul, but my flight is coming up.

Please, you still have five minutes before you need to leave. So you see the parallels between my body, my career, my mind, and my family. I said four dimensions of my life are crumbling. Actually there are more. Actually there are seven.[7]

Oh no.

You have heard about two of the others, they are memory and language. Language is especially troublesome, and I have a few more things to tell you about it. I struggle all the time with language. I struggle against the preposterous laws of grammar, which, unlike all other laws in all other fields, were not written by any human, they were not written by anyone, think of it, Samuel, they were not written by Plato or Aristotle, they just spoke Greek, they didn't even realize what a weird language that is. And the laws of grammar were not written by some ancient blockhead like Hammurabi or Cyrus, all they wrote were laws about stealing people's cows. So why should we follow the laws of language like slaves, why do we need to toe on the line with prepositional phrases, appositional phrases, participial phrases, noun clauses, syntax, and tense, why? I agree with François Le Lionnais, language is an awful invention, full of constraints. I struggle with the awkward rules of verb tenses, for example in English there is past tense, but also past perfect tense, as if anyone's past is perfect, past imperfect tense, that is funny too, because whose past isn't imperfect, and there is pluperfect past tense, but no pluimperfect past tense, and there is past continuous tense, past discontinuous tense, relative past, absolute past, past progressive, historic past, why can't I just talk the way I want? Take you, Samuel, for example. You told me you were married, then you told me you are married, then you told me you were married. I am not an idiot, Samuel, I can see something is going on. I know you wanted to say, "I used to love my wife," let's call her Betty, "I used to love Betty." But those words, "used to," they would make it sound like you loved her over and over until you stopped, and that is not nice and maybe even rude. I cannot imagine Betty would be happy to hear that you told me you loved her over and over until you stopped. Maybe you were tired, or she said, "That's enough, thank you." Actually I think you meant, "I loved Betty, but I don't want to tell you how many times, because really, Anneliese, what happened between us is none of your business," or else you meant, "I loved Betty, but to tell you the truth I don't like thinking about exactly how many times, I just sort of loved her, but then I got tired and I had to stop." But the point is not what you and Betty did over and over again until she finally told you to stop. The words "used to" are a marginal modal verb, used only in the past discontinuous tense. Who thought that up, exactly? And when did that person live? Why didn't that person become instantly famous? Let's say she lived twenty thousand and seven years ago, and she was out herding sheep—

Anneliese, please, you told me your theory of language.

In late April in the Valle de Pineta in the shadow of Monte Perdido—

Can you tell me this later?

No. Please listen. That's where she was, although she didn't know that's where she was, because language wasn't completely built yet. Are we supposed to think she was out herding her sheep, hoping to find a way to tell everyone her delicate and refined sense of the life cycle of sheep, how they had once been acclimated to higher slopes but had become accustomed to richer grasses on the lower slopes, something like that, when suddenly she thought up the marginal modal verb-assisted past discontinuous tense that employs "used to," and she ran down off the mountain and burst into her farmstead and started talking in her new tense, "used to" this and "used to" that, and at first everyone shut their ears, because they couldn't understand her, because no one had ever thought of such a tense, and then someone asked her where her sheep were, and then someone else said, "Really, where are your sheep?" but then another person said "I used to think that if only I could say 'used to,' I would be able to express the way our sheep used to like the higher slopes, but then I got used to not being able to talk about that, because we had no modal verb-assisted past discontinuous tense!" And then someone in back stood up and said, "It's not such an accomplishment, because in order for her to have invented the marginal modal verb-assisted past discontinuous tense that employs 'used to,' she would have had to have been sitting on a mound of grass, looking at her sheep in the lower pasture, and then suddenly heard the words 'used to' in her head, well that's clearly nonsense, whereas she had, as we can deduce from her odd way of talking, actually probably only noticed the change after some long period of time that we can't really describe, which led her to the thought that the sheep had 'used to' graze on the higher slopes, and then, under the influence of thoughts we can't really describe, she experienced the shift to the lower slopes as having taken place during periods that we can't describe but which are now part of the discontinuous past, and that prompted her, finally, to articulate the change using her really odd and confusing new past discontinuous verb tense employing 'used to,' okay, but to simply sit on a tuft of grass and invent the marginal modal verb-assisted past discontinuous tense that employs 'used to'—which incidentally I think should be named 'nested perfect habitual conditional tense' in order to express the fact that the perfect tense, which we have known literally for thousands of years, is nested in the conditional tense—to just sit on a tuft of grass and do that she would have had to have had not only a deep understanding of the habitual movements of sheep, well so what, we all have that, but also an acute awareness of how those patterns might be reflected in new linguistic constructs with fancy names, we don't have that, because we are prehistoric, and besides, she would have had to have possessed the cognitive ability to distinguish between the immediate perception of change and the retrospective recognition of habit, and if she did, she certainly would have been able to consider the implications that her new verb tense is bound to have on the conventional understanding of past actions and states, including our own wobbly senses of ourselves, but there is no way she did all that, it is impossible, it is literally insane to imagine a prehistoric shepherdess with those sorts of historical, linguistic, reflective, analytic, pastoralist, and ovine capacities, so it just goes to show how amazing our sheep are, because without even speaking they have caused us to invent the nested perfect habitual conditional tense that employs 'used to.'" After that everyone was silent. "And by the way," the person continued, "I somewhat resent the notion that our language is somehow primitive, especially given the fact that ancient Indo-European languages often have more grammatical cases than modern ones, we have nominative, genitive, and accusative, but we also have ablative, locative, instrumental, and allative. There is nothing unsophisticated about our capacity to articulate our supposedly simple lives, as Steven Mithen would say." Well, of course no one understood that, but people saw how the new tense could help them to express infinitely subtle things they had all been hoping to articulate regarding the life cycles of sheep, and so her new tense became all the rage, and then it was just expected, and there was no other way to talk about the finer points of the life cycles of sheep, until, horrifyingly, everyone had to use the new tense no matter what they actually wanted to say, even if they weren't talking about sheep at all. Apparently prehistory was crowded with annoying people like that woman. Because of people like her, all of us have to continuously wrestle with language. I write, I am writing, that is present continuous tense, I was writing, past continuous tense, I have been writing, that is present perfect continuous tense, I have usually been writing, that should be a tense too—

That's five minutes, Anneliese. Time for me to go.

One and a half minutes left. I have discontinuously but repeatedly and tirelessly been writing, that should be a tense, or I may probably still be writing, I might pretty much definitely still be writing, I don't think I am writing any more, not normal writing, anyway, but I might not ever have intermittently not written, that should definitely be a tense. I will not ever have probably not been writing, I doubt I will have ever not been writing, I suppose it is likely that I have for a certain indefinable period not been writing, and yet I might always have intermittently or even continuously written, I have always been in an indefinite state between writing, being about to write, not having stopped writing, continuing to be about to write, and almost finishing writing, those aren't tenses, but why not? Also, who decided what gender things are? Who said spoons are masculine? They are masculine in German, and forks are feminine, and knives are neuter. Well, no one said it, that's who, no one, the whole whining squealing apparatus of language that we all live with is in fact not ours at all, and yet we have to keep trying to make sense, instinctively we fight to make sense. I do not want to say a comet is male, but in German, comets are male, that does not make any sense whatsoever, a comet is a uncanny thing that flies in the heavens, it is not a boy or a man, a comet does not have a penis or a beard, well, it sort of has a beard, but it doesn't have a penis, well, some comets do look somewhat like penises, but not really, in German a comet is male, he is a boy or a man. I think comets look like lovely girls with long silver hair, but my language forces me to say the comet is a male thing. That is wrong, it is perverse as Stéphane Mallarmé said, and also it is a kind of insanity, it is insane to be forced to say comets are male things. Le Lionnais wouldn't have minded, because he was French, and in French comet is *la comète*, feminine, it gets to be a girl with long silver hair, but in Swedish it is worse, comet is *komet*, it's in the so-called common gender, that means it has a gender, it is not neuter, it has a gender but it won't tell you what its gender is, it may be male or female or both, but why should a comet hide its gender, comets are already mysterious, and why do Swedish comets get to be more mysterious than other comets? Maybe I shouldn't say comets shouldn't have a gender, I mean it's their choice after all, not mine, I have no choice, ever since genders were invented in German I have to say comets are male, and I feel stupid saying it, especially if I say it when I am looking at a comet. That is just one example. Language is entirely made out of things that do not make sense, rules that are obviously and factually not sane, even though language is supposed to make sense, and actually language is what is supposed to make sense, in fact it is the only way we have of making sense, it gives us our idea of making sense, it has let me formulate thirteen theories about how my work may not make sense, I haven't told you those yet, but I will, and when I explain them I will use language that makes sense in order to make sense of them, and if we are not making sense while we think about sense then what hope do we have to even know what we mean, never mind saying what we mean, or meaning what we say, those are simple problems in comparison to knowing what we mean, sorry, I know I am not making sense, but that is because I cannot make sense, I assume you don't understand me, but I am making sense, wait, no, that is exactly wrong, you can understand me, but I am not making sense, because I cannot. I am *dysnoetos,* unintelligible. That is language. It was not invented by geniuses. It is a tacky badly fitted salmon and carrot-colored suit with beryl-colored buttons, it is uncomfortable, and it itches. And by the way, please do me the courtesy of not assuming that I repeat myself without knowing it, because everything I say is exquisitely carefully considered. I never forget anything I say, and if I repeat something it is because the person to whom I am talking needs to hear it again—and thanks to my unpleasant unending struggle with language I am a hawk-eyed observer of other people's language, the little sputters people call conversation, the sneezes they call wit, the awkward creaking structures they build when they set out to give speeches, the pitiful paltry words they speak when they finally get around to saying something, like you, the frail two-and-a-half word sentences they just barely manage to utter, like Paul, I can understand and interpret flaccid little sentences the way a fortune teller can look into the bottom of a teacup, at the scraps of leaves awash in lukewarm water, and tell a person's entire life and future, and so, Samuel, when I was talking about Paul, and you said you were sorry, you wanted to say you sympathize, or you can picture what I was saying, or that you understand me—well, I am the one who understands. I do not need to listen to other people because I nearly always already understand. I can now demonstrate that point, by telling you exactly what you have been intending to say, both about Paul and about my theories, and of course also about my timekeeping, but I will express your thoughts more eloquently than you would, adding explanations for things you aren't so clear about, perhaps also interpolating handy references to books you should have mentioned but haven't read, or places you would have named but haven't visited, and perhaps, if you'd like, also adding evocative illustrations of your principal ideas, described with sparkling details and painted in colorful tints, and concluding with a precise précis, drawing the consequences that you yourself hesitated to draw from your muddled ideas! Ha ha, sorry, just having fun. Seriously, though, I can tell you everything you would say if I gave you the chance, but I can express it all so much better. It will be a treat. You will marvel at your own thoughts unfurling and billowing, resplendent, like the flag of a new country flying for the first time, snapping in the clear air. So the first thing... oh wait, there's someone at the door again.

There were voices and music. Perhaps Luzia was having a party. Anneliese had probably been hiding in her study.

Sorry, she said. Why is the world so filled with impatient people? You are an excellent listener. I am grateful you listened to my ideas about my body, my career, my mind, and my family. Language is actually the sixth of the seven dimensions. The fifth is memory. I cannot talk about the seventh today. Memories are not only undependable, as everyone knows, they are not only sentimental pap, most sensible people admit that, but memories are empty, as I demonstrated at our dinner in Frankfurt, they are lies, as I proved using the example of the rose, but also, and this is the crux of the matter, the nib of the matter, the nub, the nib or the nub? This is the nut I have cracked, this is the nub I have nibbled! Memories are the way we stop ourselves, at all costs, from acknowledging that our past is gone. There are famous authorities, people with enormous cogitational capacity, who have studied memories for many years, Georges Sjilbour, Christa Vervliet, Willem von Leyden, Ed Slab, and they say memories are closer to us than our souls, Slab says that, they give us our thoughts and our minds, Vervliet says that, they present us with ourselves, that is Slab again. What would we be without memory? they ask. The most sensitive heart would lose the ability to show affection, grown men would go dry with despair, that's what Slab says. Existence would be nothing but a succession of meaningless moments, that's what Sjilbour says, there would be no way to know how much we love other people, that's what von Leyden says, we would be like cows, stranded in the idiotic present, all we would know is that our mouths are full of grass, that's what Nietzsche says. Well, guess what, I'd say to Georges Sjilbour, Christa Vervliet, Willem von Leyden, Ed Slab, and also Nietzsche, guess what, that is exactly what happens. You see, my ideas of memory and language have been getting more dire at the same time as my body, my mind, my family, and my career have been decomposing. Here is what I think: we need to believe we have memories, even if we have actually lost them, we need to keep thinking about our memories, even if it scars our minds just to recall them, because they are the lie that keeps us sane.

Actually I'd love to talk about that sometime.

Not now, you don't have time. So that is it, the end. This is a stupendous result for me, for my work. I am quite happy about it. Now you may be wondering why I called you today, so urgently, in your hotel, because it would have been normal, it would have been civilized, it would have been expected, or at least acceptable, or it would have been usual, or normative, that's it, normative, it would have been entirely normative if I had written you an email thanking you for dinner, because as Paul pointed out to me, you put the entire dinner on your hotel bill, even though, as I immediately pointed back out to him, your employer has no doubt reimbursed you, but he said I should at least send you an email, because, as he then pointed out, and as I instantly agreed, these days common courtesy is nearly, but not entirely—

Anneliese! I'm in a hurry.

Yes, you should have left twenty-three minutes ago. If you run you may make it. I only wanted to give you a small look, a glimpse, an aperçu, a taste of my concerns, because I have been thinking about our conversation in Frankfurt, and I feel that of all the people I know, you may be the one who can understand my work. I sincerely hope you are. Next month I am going to a conference in Montreal to try yet again to present my work, and I will visit you and Catherine in Guelph. Then I will be delighted to explain everything at proper length.

Will Paul come?

No, she said, and now good night.[8]

The line went dead.

I should have run out to get a taxi, but instead I opened a window and let the Tennessee air flow into the hotel room.

It was a quiet morning. A cloud of starlings formed and reformed itself over an empty field. For a moment it took the shape of a jigsaw puzzle piece, but before I could see it properly, the cloud twisted, and turned into a shape that has no name.

# 4

## A WALK TO THE RUHEPLATZ

I **WAS EARLY** for our dinner at the Yellow Hat Diner in Guelph, but Anneliese was already seated.

I am worse, she said, substantially worse than last month. At the moment my health is paper-thin.

You look fine, I lied.

No, she said. I am only out of the hospital two days. I am on the very point of collapse. I am a paper lantern with the candle blown out. I am a paper doll, fallen onto the road and waiting to be crushed. I am a paper napkin, someone has sneezed into it, and folded it, and then the fold has become ungummed, and the nasal mucus is on display.

She grinned, looking like a minor species of shark with some broken teeth.

Catherine has left, she said, but she will be back. We had an argument this morning. I met her here for breakfast and she insisted on bringing up her preposterous claims to priority in the research we did in England, claims which I then exhaustively refuted. Unfortunately both of us have prodigious memories, especially where our own publications are concerned. In point of fact we went through our publications one by one, fact by point, point by fact, stopping on the point of each fact, and every single time she had to concede. She had to admit that year after year, every idea was mine, every hypothesis, every experiment, each analysis, each result in every paper. As you might imagine she was not happy to discover that my command of facts and my interest in the truth and my stamina are so much stronger than hers. She didn't want to admit she was tiring of my examination of the points of each fact, she didn't want to say that she is no longer a scientist, that she can't understand the current problems and terminology of the field, and so as you can imagine she wasn't entirely happy and relaxed at the end of our breakfast, which was only a half hour ago because we argued continuously from eight in the morning until five-thirty this afternoon.

You had a nine and a half hour breakfast?

Yes, she said. I began with scrambled eggs, but they were watery, they actually sweated water onto the plate, so I ordered fried eggs, but the yolks were discolored and as hard as the rubber inside golf balls, so I had them taken back and ordered an omelet, but there were pieces of cold waxy cheese inside it, so they took that back, and they brought out soft-boiled eggs in the shell, but when I cracked them open the whites were not only runny, which is generally acceptable, but actually transparent, so at that point I became exasperated and I ordered everything on the breakfast menu. I told the waitress I could not be expected to continue ordering food and sending it back. "I am busy," I said, "this is a working breakfast. Apparently you can't cook scrambled eggs, fried eggs, omelets, or soft-boiled eggs, so just bring me everything else on this extensive and unappetizing menu, and I will find something I can eat." The waitress was very rude. She just stood there with her notepad out and her eyebrows raised. So I put down five hundred Canadian dollars, and I said, "I need to concentrate on my work. I feel confident that you can manage to cook at least one dish correctly, so please just bring me every single thing on the breakfast menu, one after another, except the four items I have already tried, do not bring me scrambled eggs, fried eggs, omelets of any kind, or boiled eggs, just bring me everything else, in order, from the top of the menu to the bottom, and do not speak to me again." The waitress said, "You are quite possibly the rudest person I have ever met," but she took the five hundred Canadian dollars, and as a consequence I ate, or at least tasted, sourdough toast, multigrain toast, a vile-smelling item called cinnamon raisin French toast, why do Americans love cinnamon so much, it has an unbearable stench, blueberry pancakes, which looked like the stomach contents of a moose, banana nut multigrain pancakes with cinnamon, cinnamon buttermilk pancakes with peach butter, they might as well just serve cinnamon paste in bowls, or bake cinnamon into great bricks their customers could lick, at that point by the way the cook was standing in the doorway to the kitchen with his arms crossed, glaring at me, California benedict, that has sriracha hollandaise and a slab of avocado as hard as a piece of balsa wood, an item called Lorraine scramble, which has peppered bacon, Gruyère cheese, caramelized onion, and charred scallions, I burped onto that one and the cook saw me, I thought he was going to run up to the table and mash my face into it, biscuits and gravy, corned beef hash, and a breakfast submarine sandwich featuring most of the ingredients from all the other dishes, heaped onto a foot-long baguette. The waitress asked if I would write a good review. I took her by both wrists and said, "You need to know I am not a food critic. I am actually insane. Just serve me and do not talk to me." After I said that to her there were no more interruptions, although as the morning went on I noticed the tables around us filled up with people who were watching us. Then I had a breakfast burrito with fried chicken, eggs, carrots, and cinnamon, which was quite possibly the single most nauseating thing I have ever tasted, a croque madame, which the cook had violently pressed into a flat oily plate, I felt sorry for the cook, he was probably infuriated and embarrassed by his inability to produce edible food, he watched me from the door to the kitchen, every time the waitress brought another dish he appeared at the door to the kitchen with his arms crossed. The waitress kept bringing the dishes and clearing the plates. I saw the staff looking at me and whispering. The cook bit the inside of his lip and vigorously scratched his forearm. Meats were last on the menu, so at the end I had sage sausage patties, American bacon, chorizo sausages, Canadian bacon, and veggie bacon, which was so tasteless I felt like pouring oil on my napkin and eating that instead, and finally a bagel with lox and sour cream, that was quite good, it had a side of cornichons and salted capers, I think the cook was proud and relieved that he had finally made one edible dish, it was really quite refreshing, and at that point it had been nearly nine hours and I was getting hungry again. I also drank twelve cups of coffee. Catherine said it was nice to see me eat. I believe she had a piece of toast. At the close of our breakfast she announced that she would be what she described as "slightly late" for her next "torture session." I think she'll be here in a few minutes. But back to me. The week before last I suffered a punctured lung, the most amazing thing. Who would ever think a lung could be punctured? It punctured itself, blew a hole like an old tire. I was just sitting at my desk, breathing in and out as I usually do, and then my entire chest felt as if it was full of ice water, and at the same time there was the most astonishing feeling of suffocation, because actually, as my doctor explained in the hospital—a very good hospital this time, by the way, the world-famous Universitätsspital Basel, ranked number fourteen in Europe—as the doctor explained to me, my entire chest cavity on the left side was filling with air, and my lung was lying on the bottom of that cavity like a deflated balloon. When the lung punctured it ripped from its lining in my thorax, so it was actually floating in a pool of blood inside my rib cage. The doctor said it was like a collapsed balloon in a swimming pool of blood and tissue fluid, whatever tissue fluid is. I said to him, "You're mixing your metaphors, why would a balloon be in a swimming pool filled with blood?" And he said, "Please don't shout, Mrs. Glur, it's not good for your deflated lung," so I used my weak, injured voice, because it was such a pleasure to see the look of concern on his face. "Actually," I said very quietly, "it is probably best if you don't even try to make up these supposedly helpful illustrations, people aren't idiots, we do not need to be coddled eggs, when people are sick or have experienced trauma they do not need to be confused and irritated with badly constructed analogies full of odd and violent images. It is possible you are a doctor but you have no imagination, no ability to picture things clearly or explain them cogently, and your balloon story is an embarrassing glimpse into your paltry mental life, which is apparently an unpleasant mixture of childish memories of balloons and fantasies of bloody swimming pools, combined with fragments of your medical education, all swirling around like tissue fluids, a truly horrifying mental life that I hope never to glimpse again. Also I would like to inform you that I am not Mrs. Glur, I have never met such a person even in my most squalid nightmares, I am Professor Doctor Glur *Universitate Oxoniensi emerita, basiliensis scientiae doctrix, collegii lectrix publica.*" It was a very productive conversation, and after that the doctor spoke very little. The main problem during the five days I spent at the Universitätsspital, aside from the horrible boredom of the place and the inhuman way that nurses continuously woke me at all hours of the night in order to ask questions like, "How are we today?" which is incidentally an unanswerable question in such circumstances because the temptation is to say, "How the hell do you think I am?" or, "I am in ungodly pain," or, "I wish I were dead but then again I wished that yesterday and the day before and the day before that, and I have wished it with a very special intensity every time I have seen you, you horrible grotesque gibbering harpy." Anyway the main problem at the Universitätsspital was that I could not cough, under no circumstance was I permitted to cough, even though my chest was fiercely itchy, and even though each time I inhaled, no matter how slowly and carefully I breathed, something inside would catch or tickle, so it was diabolical torture not to be able to cough, I wanted to take one of those long backscratchers and reach down my throat and scratch until I had scraped trenches in my throat lining, and also, because I couldn't cough properly, I was in immediate danger of infection, in fact my doctor told me that even a single mote of dust might ferry just five bacteria into my collapsed lung, and that would be enough to cause pneumonia and I would be dead within a week, that's what my doctor told me, and even though it was perfectly clear that I was supposed to think of five as an arbitrary number, five is also a strange arbitrary number, it isn't a few or a dozen, it is five, actually it is exactly five, and that worried me because it was unclear whether my doctor had read that somewhere, in which case he should have realized he needed to add at least a word or two of explanation, as you might expect between professionals, something like, Funny, isn't it, that number five, or, Yes, I'm glad it struck you, it struck me too. If he'd said things like that it would at least have given the impression he cared, even though we both knew he didn't, but it was unclear whether he'd actually read that number five, or if the number five just came into his head because he had five fingers on the hand he kept holding up to make me stop talking, or he'd had five patients die on him in the last month, or whether he was lying in order to sound knowledgeable, and if that was so, then he was a complete fraud, or, even worse, a fraud and a sadist, and he'd just invented the line about the five bacteria riding into my lungs on a single mote of dust because in his eyes I was some laughable hypochondriac with a minor complaint, at least in comparison to the five patients he had tried to treat that month who had died, but after that I thought about it for a day or two, because what else was there to do, and I concluded he probably made up the number five because he knew I would get much worse and might very well die, and he wanted to have a story he could repeat to the nurses, the hospital staff, and the medical board, he'd be able to tell them that he'd stood by my bed and told me that no more than five bacteria could kill me, but that I hadn't listened, I'd been a stubborn patient and I had caused my own death, and while he was going on about not coughing he was probably thinking, I have no idea what to do if that collapsed lung gets infected, why do I always draw difficult cases like this, I always panic when they call the code blue, I just run in and start making things up, and they're always the wrong things, I should have studied more in medical school, I'll be fired soon, I'll be put onto a pasture, I'll be assigned to some village where they can't even pronounce the word electrification, all because this patient's going to die and that will make six, six in one month. So Samuel, as I struggled to recuperate in the hospital, I was wracked by two paralyzing fears. I was horribly afraid of catching any kind of infection, because I knew that even though my doctor was an ignorant coward, it was still just barely possible there was some truth in what he said, that he had belched out a shard of truth along with the catarrh of his ignorant speeches, but also I was scared because coughing that could tear my delicate lung, the one the doctor had supposedly just repaired, although it felt as if he had just cut into my ribcage and thrown in a battery and some tape, anyway I was afraid that the supposedly repaired lung would once again rip away from the lining of my chest cavity, once again fill the cavity with blood and tissue fluid, and inevitably then I would cough even more, tearing the lung even further, until it had torn completely off, and then I would be fighting for my life and drowning in my own blood and tissue fluid.

She touched her left breast gingerly with the tips of three fingers.

In the end, she said, I recovered, sort of. But even though my lung was certified as "adequately reattached," and even though I have traveled here without incident, I feel that something catastrophic may happen at any moment. I can hardly be expected, under these circumstances, to be worrying about little things like the fact that in Montreal I was once again prevented from speaking, I was not allowed to complete my paper, in fact the microphone was actually taken from me. The man who took it said, "I am sorry, but we are out of time." I said, "I have a punctured lung," but no one heard me because the microphone had been handed to someone else. It doesn't matter, I no longer care, I can't be expected to be concerned about the remnants of my so-called academic career. We are all out of time, Samuel, each one of us. We are all on our way to the grave. I thought about that while I lay in the hospital bed trying not to cough. *Vamos al infierno de todos modos,* we will all be dead soon, and no one will remember any of us. We will be utterly and completely forgotten. *Omnes e memoria cademus,* we will all be forgotten, *fere e memoria elabimur dum vivimus,* we are nearly forgotten while we are still living, that's from Cicero, *etiam notissimi,* even the most famous of us. *Omnes una manet nox, et calcanda semel via leti,* that is Horace, I learned it in school. One night is waiting for us all, and everyone has to walk the path of death. I think that is the line, or wait, it's *quemque sola una manet nox,* just one night is waiting for each of us, *sed quomodo perveniamus nescimus,* we don't know how we will end up there, but we will, and we will all be forgotten. *Stat sua cuique dies.* We think our gravestones will last, and some of them will. But after a generation or two, no one will visit our graves, and in three generations no one will remember who we were, and that is true despite what we tell ourselves, that we are so important, that we have large families who will remember us, that we had many students and readers, those are all lies, our children will remember us of course, but our grandchildren won't think much about us, and please show me, anywhere in human history, the great-grandchild who ever visited its great-grandmother's grave, that is totally absurd and impossible to imagine, well, maybe it has happened, but you see what I mean, Luzia will visit my grave, I expect her to cry when she does, and when she has children she might bring them to my grave, that's common enough, but she might not bring them, and even if she does bring her children to my grave she'll probably only bring them once or twice, because I intend to be buried in the Roggwil cemetery, it is in the Oberaargau administrative district, in the Canton of Bern, where my mother is buried, we have been in the area for generations, it used to be called Rocchonuuillare, I wish it still was, that is a very seductive name and Roggwil is stupid and ugly, people there call it Roggu. Still, it's a nice cemetery, with carefully pruned trees and well-tended flowers. I have written special instructions that roses are to be kept away from my grave, I do not want to have roses near my corpse, if I do not like them now why would my corpse like them, anyway Luzia would have no reason to be out there, she'd have to make a special trip to show her children my grave, I mean it might happen, but it might not. She might tell her children some things about me, but you know how that goes, they would only really care because their mother did. And then what about the generation after Luzia's children? The generation of Luzia's children's children? They won't know about me. It is not likely Paul will ever marry or have children, despite the fact that he wants to go out dancing. That means that in one more generation after Luzia's children, no one in the entire world will know where I am buried. We will all be forgotten, we are nearly forgotten while we are still living, even the most famous of us, and to think I used to count myself among the more famous people in my field, but even the best-known people are more or less instantly forgotten when they die. *Soles occidere et redire possunt,* the sun can fall and rise, *nobis, cum semel occidit brevis lux,* but when our brief light has fallen, *nox est perpetua una dormienda,* we sleep forever. When I worked at the university we lost a colleague, Ferdinand Philipp Grimm. Before he died we all thought he was prominent and important and central to his field, Ferdinand Philipp Grimm, people all knew his work, but after only two years the department didn't get any more mail for him, and I checked and no one cited his work anymore, no one read it. I checked again about five years later, and I found that none of his essays were assigned in universities and his books were no longer in print. He has been entirely left behind by the world and soon no one will remember him any more, that is life, and I know this deep in my heart and also right here at this table, I know it all the time: I might as well be dead, because the moment I die, or a matter of months afterward, or at least within a couple of years after I have died, I will be utterly forgotten by my so-called colleagues, it will be as if I never existed, and the few people who remember me will think of me less and less often, until they forget me altogether. Paul and Luzia won't forget me as long as they live, that's true, unless they get dementia like Hans, but in the usual way of things they will think of me less each passing year, and when they die no one will miss me. For Luzia's children I'll just be a couple of stories. Anneliese spent her life in her study, Luzia will tell her children, she wasn't like a mother, she wasn't like me. Anneliese used to come out at dinnertime and talk about her work, she'll say, as if we could understand it, as if we were interested. Maybe she meant well, Luzia will tell her children, I'll never know. Someday, Samuel, Luzia's children might tell their children about me, but great-grandchildren don't care about their great-grandmothers, and their stories will be brutally simple, like, Your grandmother's guardian Anneliese was a scientist, or, Your grandmother Luzia grew up in a house with an eccentric scientist. Don't tell me that's being remembered, that's not being remembered, that's being forgotten, and after that, one more generation and I will be absolutely totally permanently forgotten. And don't tell me that libraries last forever. And don't tell me that many people are interested in genealogy, and family trees can be traced back dozens of generations. And don't start telling me about the internet, or about how digital information lasts forever. Do you think you are safe from oblivion because your name comes up after a search of 991 billion web pages? That actually is oblivion. And don't tell me Catherine said I am well known, she has motives for saying that. There are as many names as there are stars. No one cares. So realistically, let's say that in forty years or so, there will be no one alive on Earth who remembers me at all, and Samuel, you know something? I actually have it worse than that, because my body, my career, my mind, and my family are already falling apart, so I am not merely dying like everyone else, I am being forced to become angry and continuously upset, at my body, my family, and my career, which are failing, but even more at my mind itself, which is collapsed like a punctured balloon in a pool of blood and tissue fluid, and so...

The waitress had been standing beside us, pretending not to listen.

Welcome to the Yellow Hat, she said to me. Would you like some water or drinks while you wait for your friend?

We will not wait, Anneliese said. She snatched the dinner menu from the waitress and ordered the baby greens and blue cheese salad, the Thai satay chicken appetizer, the dry-cured sirloin with Béarnaise sauce, a side of anise potatoes, a side of garlic home fries, a side of rice, a side of white asparagus, a side of macaroni and cheese, a side of pearl onions and fennel, a side of pinto beans and bacon, a side of seared Brussels sprouts, and the hazelnut torte and double espresso for dessert, and then she stared darts at me while I slowly, and with some indecision, ordered pasta.

I really doubt I'll eat anything, she said to me. I would like to spend this meal with you, which may, and I don't mean to sound melodramatic, although this is necessarily melodramatic and even, I suppose, sentimental, this may actually be our last meal together, so I would like to spend it talking about life and death.

You're recovered, right?

No one recovers, *omnes una manet nox,* I thought I made that clear. Meanwhile my life in Basel ticks by, hour by hour. More and more Paul and I have to take care of Hans before we attend to ourselves. When he is not wandering around the apartment emptying drawers, moving clothing from one room to another, dragging chairs and tables back and forth between rooms, or trying to get out for his walk, when he is not mumbling or talking to people who aren't there, when he is not standing right outside my study door, silently, without moving, until finally I get so distracted and exasperated that I come out and threaten him with the broom, when he is not doing those things he watches television, or at least I should say he faces in the direction of the television and exhibits eye movements consistent with attending to television. Paul sits with him, and talks to him about what's on television, but Hans doesn't respond. I do not think he notices what's on television. I made a preliminary classification of his eye movements, to determine whether he is actually watching television. I pulled up a chair next to the TV and observed him. His eyes performed saccades in response to what was on the screen, he looked quickly and briefly at one or another thing, that is normal, but his eyes also drifted, as if he was following shapes moving in the air in front of him. The drifting movements swept left and right, from one corner of the room to another, and when his eyes drifted they did not stop or fixate on anything that I could see. His face got tense, he frowned like he was concentrating. Paul said Hans might see the swing set that used to be in his grammar school playground, or the stadium where he played in front of big crowds. Paul said he might be following a ball arcing through the air in the stadium. Paul also said he could be looking for his first wife Marlene. "She was the love of his life," Paul kept saying. "He is searching in the air for her." I said Hans's eyes were just moving randomly. "He has been using his eyes his entire life," I told Paul, "and now he no longer needs them, so they move by habit." While we talked Hans's eyes swept back and forth. "He has forgotten his eyes," I said, "he has forgotten how to use them to see things, how to close them when he is sleeping." Paul said that was an especially horrible thought and it was "perfectly clear" that Hans was thinking of places and people from his life, watching them pass back and forth before him, in his mind's eye, especially Marlene. Paul was entirely convinced he thinks mainly about her. I told Paul the only way to decide was to test him. "We can fit Hans with a bite bar and a forehead brace," I said, "we can strap on an eye tracker. We may have to use hand restraints to prevent him from pulling the eye tracker off. He may need to be lightly sedated. And if we do that," this is what I said to Paul, "we will discover that he is not thinking about anything."

Anneliese's salad and chicken appetizer arrived. She closed her eyes and turned away, as if she'd been offered a plate of warm garbage.

Recently, she continued, Hans has started speaking gibberish. He says random things, like, "I told you this isn't to do with that," or, "It was a yellow one," or, "If you jump, it is a long way down from the bridge to the river." Last week he said to both of us, "For heaven's sake, put your beautiful picture down." *Du musst dein schönes Bild ablegen,* you need to put your beautiful picture down. We talked about that one. Paul said he meant we needed to give up the beautiful picture we have of him. He said Hans was trying to tell us his mind is ruined. I said that was ridiculous, Hans's words are involuntary, they are dissociative speech, they no longer mean anything. That's what I said, but secretly I wondered. "Of course he means something," Paul said, "we just don't know what." When Hans said, "It was a yellow one," that reminded Paul that Hans liked a yellow dress that his second wife Emmy wore. He said Hans was remembering Emmy. I told him that was hopeful thinking. "Lots of things are yellow," I said. "Bananas, the sun, your teeth."

I thought Hans's mind was a mess, more like soup than like thinking, but actually it was hard for me to tell, because I can't even be sure what is happening in my own mind.

For a moment she sat quietly. Her face went slack and her eyes seemed to be pointing in two different directions.

The waitress, noticing the lull, came with her full order, including the dessert and coffee. Some plates overhung the edges of the table. My pasta was surrounded by Anneliese's food.

Suddenly she started up again at full volume.

Okay, she said. So last week I decided to go along with Paul and Hans on their walk. I wanted to see for myself what Hans did, where he looked, how his eyes tracked objects in his visual field when he was out on his walks. After breakfast he got anxious. He walked around the living room saying, "Where is that book I sent you?" and, "That package, I gave it to you, you signed for it, where is it?" He went to the front door a couple of times. Then he said, "I have to go, it's time to go." So we put on his winter coat and scarf, and his old-fashioned hat with its fur ear flaps. Paul and I pulled on our coats and gloves as well as we could while we managed him, because he is like a child, and as every parent knows it is not easy to dress yourself and your child while it's struggling. Paul kept saying, "Please put your hand in the glove," "Don't kick," "Be good," and Hans kept calling out, "Please, I have to go." Finally we were ready. It was very cold that morning, and our breaths all came out in clouds. I took Hans's hand to steady him, and Paul walked on the other side. We thought he was headed for the place the playground used to be. But when we got to the road that leads there, I felt his hard hand in mine—he has a bony grip, he's still very strong—and he pulled me toward a side street. Paul and I looked at each other, and we let him lead. It was a back route, a shortcut to the park. We went down a couple of steep lanes, where we don't usually go. I kept looking into Hans's eyes. He was staring straight ahead, at nothing, really. In a few minutes we emerged into the park, and he started walking in the direction of St. Judas Thaddäus. We crossed the park diagonally. He was in a hurry.

At that moment Catherine arrived.

She surveyed the table. Still hungry? she asked.

The waitress came back, and Catherine ordered a glass of red wine.

Anneliese doesn't eat, Catherine told me. Today she nibbled her dishes, one after another, for hours on end. She used her knife and fork to carve miniscule particles of food and place them delicately on the tip of her tongue, as if each dish was the purest poison. She might have eaten the equivalent of an egg. It's no wonder she's hungry. But when she's finished talking, then all of a sudden she eats like a maniac.

In Frankfurt she was chewing away, I said.

You know, Catherine, Anneliese said, even though I have conclusively demonstrated that when we worked in England in 1990, you stole every single one of my ideas, and even though I have to say I am sad, no, disappointed that you have done so little of your own work in the thirty years since then, and even though I am disappointed, no, actually baffled, that you chose such a completely unpromising and uninteresting job, a job that virtually no one cares about, in a real backwater, because this town is definitely a backwater, whatever a backwater is, although I guess it is part of a stream where the water no longer moves forward, as it must, naturally, but instead circulates around and around pointlessly, which is curious because you also study backwaters, your job is the cycling of water from sewage to purification and back into people's mouths, so your job is backwater, and your job is a backwater, and you work in a backwater, and even though I am baffled, or no, actually bewildered that you seem content in your mid-level position as the Biologics Supervisor at the Harris Water Treatment Plant in the municipal Department of Water Management in this little town in farmland Canada, that you seem to enjoy studying sewage and maintaining filters and settling tanks, which is, in metaphorical terms, quite appropriate for someone who went from the center of the currents of biology to a backwater, it makes sense that such a person would want to settle down and study settling tanks, places where there is no current whatsoever, but even though you have fallen so far behind in the scientific literature that it is no longer possible for us to have a professional-level conversation, and in fact, to be candid, it wasn't even possible for you to understand half of what I said this morning, yet despite all that of course I still consider us friends, close friends, great friends, great close friends. You think clearly about things that are not worth thinking about. I respect that. I have no idea if Samuel has that quality, because he is so timid. But I suspect he does, because you recommended him as your friend, and I have already been able to discuss several important questions with him.

Anneliese, Catherine said, I took the last hour to check my files.

She put some photocopies on top of the plates that covered the table.

The first paper we co-authored, Anneliese, was titled "Metagenomic Sampling of Soil in the Region of Boars' Hill, Iffley, Oxford, UK: Preliminary Findings." It does indeed contain the "seminal ideas of the study of uncultivable organisms," as you said fifteen times this morning. Here is the passage in question. We wrote: "We present documentation of >10k previously unrecorded partial genomes of viruses, archaea, and bacteria, representing possibly >18 candidate phyla previously unknown to science. On the basis of these samples we consider it probable that the numbers of new candidate phyla will continue to accelerate as computational methods improve, and we therefore propose the following equation: $E = 1/\log(ax + 1)$, where $ax$ is the aggregate number of candidate taxa, and $E$ the genetic contribution of multicellular species to the total tree of life."

Yes, Anneliese said, tapping the photocopy approvingly.

As you yourself said in our conversations this morning, Catherine continued, that result has stood the test of time. It is, as you pointed out ten times, a cornerstone of the field. You repeated the formula verbatim in seven subsequent publications, Glur 1993, 1997, 2001, 2002, 2002a, 2005, and 2009. In two of those, Glur 1993 and 1997, you mentioned our paper. In the others you cited your own earlier papers. That joint-authored paper of ours has been cited 2,351 times as of this afternoon at 4:50 P.M., although the peak of citations was in 1998, and the paper was only cited 2 times last year.

Anneliese began to eat, alternating between the chicken satay, the hazelnut torte, and my pasta.

I am aware, Catherine continued, as you also pointed out a dozen times today, that the equation $E = 1/\log(ax + 1)$ was often cited as Glur's Equation in the early 2000s. That is true. Today you also insisted eight times, some at great length, that you had discovered this formula, and that you are therefore the person who first made it known that the familiar species of animals and plants, that is, all of the Eukaryotes, actually comprise a vanishingly small portion of the total genetic diversity of the Earth, and that the fragments of DNA that people continue to discover everywhere, "on mountaintops, in glaciers, in ordinary garden soil, in drinking water, in thermal vents at the very deepest abysses of the ocean," as you put it in Glur 1993, somewhat inaccurately and with unnecessary histrionics, are evidence of our small place in the scheme of life. You also said, this morning, that the fragments of the DNA of uncultivable organisms are "fascinating," "compelling," "decisive," and even "romantic," because the organisms that the genetic material came from have often "never been successfully cultivated in laboratories, and, indeed, never even been observed." In Glur 1993 and again with insignificant variations in Glur 2002, you said that Glur's Equation is a principal part of the "second Copernican Revolution," as you called it, "demonstrating how insignificant *Homo sapiens* is in relation to the complexity and diversity of life."

That is all true, Anneliese said, waggling her empty wineglass at the waitress.

I then consulted our laboratory notebooks for the year 1990, Catherine said, and specifically for the months January to March 1990, when we were preparing for publication. On January 13, 1990, I wrote in my notebook: "We can quantify our results re: the diminishing percentage of Eukaryotes." One week later, January 20, I wrote in the same notebook: "A," that is you, Anneliese, "A does not believe quantification is possible." On February 7, 1990, after we had completed a draft of the Introduction and Methods portions of the paper, I wrote in the same notebook: "The data on the ratios of new candidate phyla to L," that is Leaton's phyla lists, is a "declining sequence, slash, possibly close to an inverse log relation." Note that, Anneliese. Two days later, I wrote the first recorded instance of the equation, $E = 1/\log(n + 1)$, and next to it I wrote, "A does not believe this." And finally, on March 21, 1990, I wrote in my notebook number 4: "A agrees my equation can go in the paper."

Please, Catherine, Anneliese said, I developed the equation in late 1989. You never understood it.

I was falsifying my notebook when I called the equation "my equation"? Catherine asked. When I wrote "A does not believe this"?

I have no access to your inner thoughts, Anneliese said, especially on those specific days twenty-nine years ago, so I should like to plead leniency.

Very well, Catherine replied, turning the page in her notebook. And in return I would like to surprise you. I also kept mimeograph copies of your lab notebooks. Perhaps you remember we shared our materials. Do you?

I do not, Anneliese said, but it doesn't surprise me.

In your own notebooks, which you lettered 1990A, 1990B, and 1990C, there are no entries regarding the equation until February 10, 1990, one day after I wrote "A does not believe this." On that day, you wrote in your own Notebook A, and I am translating from your German, "Catherine may be right about her equation." Her equation, Anneliese. Your handwriting. The next mention is in your own Notebook C, on March 4. You wrote: "Catherine's equation still seems wrong. Don't fully understand it yet." Catherine's equation. Your handwriting. And then there is this entry, five days later: "Catherine's equation is brilliant. It quantifies everything. Makes our project into real science. It is the best thing in our paper. I wish I could understand it. *Ich wünschte, ich könnte die Gleichung verstehen.*" Anneliese, I am the author of that equation.

Hmm, Anneliese said. She was eating voraciously, spearing food from different plates in succession. She took a bite of her torte, a swallow of coffee, and a Brussels sprout.

Catherine sat staring at her. Anneliese seemed unconcerned, but her hunger wasn't persuasive. She was playing at being busy, like an embarrassed child. Then she stopped.

Thank you, Catherine, she said, looking at her earnestly and, I thought, with gratitude.

In that case, Anneliese, Catherine replied, thank you for an entertaining nine and a half hour breakfast. I may not be successful, my current work may be unimportant, I may study backwaters in a backwater, I may not even be a biologist anymore. But you lie to yourself, and you don't realize it. You have lost the capacity to tell truth from fiction.

Anneliese held her wineglass up, as if she was toasting herself.

Catherine is right, Anneliese said to me. My mind is a compost heap. I keep thinking a diamond is somewhere under the raked leaves and orange rinds and celery snippets and mats of hair from the shower drain, but I can't find it, and meanwhile everything is fermenting, my compost is warm with bacteria. My mind is subsiding, cooking down into a useless mass. I am a *hapax legomenon,* a thing without precedent, without history or past, a thing dropped into the universe, *geworfen,* thrown into existence, tossed down onto a wasteland of metal and dirt, like a spider, or a gob of spit, something with no place in creation, alone, suffering, in isolation, in *Einsamkeit.*

She looked at Catherine, then at me, then at a woman who was eavesdropping at the next table. The woman turned away.

I am *solitarius, solivagant,* wandering alone in the world, like the man on Salas y Gómez island, do you know Adelbert von Chamisso? No? *Solivagant* is a wonderful word. Chamisso wrote a poem about one of the most isolated islands on Earth, Salas y Gómez. *Sol,* as in solitary, *solus, solitus,* and *vagant,* as in vague, or vagary, or vagabond, or valedictorian, or maybe not valedictorian, so *solivagant,* lost, alone in the world, that is what he felt when he stood on Salas y Gómez island and wrote his very romantic poem, and that is what I am.

You're not alone, Catherine said, you have a brother and family—

I guess I have my brother, yes. The two of us suffer together, not in *Einsamkeit* but in *Zweisamkeit,* each one of us is still alone but we know there is another who shares the same loneliness. We two comprise a *Zweisamkeit,* a twoaloneness, a loneliness of two people together.

You also have people who are willing to sit at restaurants with you and listen for nine and a half hours, and then come back for more. You are not exactly a gob of spit.

I am, she said. That is what happens to an organism when it no longer remembers its own life, when it has forgotten its own life and its place in the world.

You remembered to eat, Catherine said, even though it took a while.

I never thought I could forget the basic science that I did with you.

You didn't forget it, you lied.

Anneliese remained still, eyes toward the heavens. She looked like an old saint in one of those religious paintings, her eyes wide and slightly teary.

You see, Samuel, Anneliese said, how empty memories are. We are alone in the present, stranded like one of those songbirds that fly north from Libya, and they get lost, and instead of landing on the coast of Italy and refreshing themselves before they fly on toward the meadows and lakes of Switzerland and France, they lose their way, and when they finally see land it is the little island of Malta, and they are exhausted, nearly dead, lost, alone, starving, dizzy, if birds can get vertigo, I'm not sure, but they practically drop out of the sky from exhaustion and relief when they see the tiny island of Malta, and what happens? Do you know what happens? Gunfire! People shoot at them! People shoot them out of the sky. It's a sport in Malta, people shoot the poor exhausted half-dead African songbirds as they come down to land. The countryside in Malta is full of bird blinds, there are people who think it is fun to shoot tiny songbirds who are breathing their last few breaths, beautiful little yellow and blue songbirds that have flown so far over such great stretches of empty water, and just when they see a scrap of land, and gratefully stop flapping their aching wings and happily soar down toward the coast, just then, when they can barely see, because their eyes are dusted over from the relentless sun, and their throats are too dry to sing, and their lungs can barely bring another spoonful of breath into their battered little bodies, when they think, All I need to do is soar, just follow the air currents down, and I will land, and there will be a dry plant with some seeds to keep me alive until it rains, and then I'll tilt my little beak up to the sky and catch a drop or two of rain, that's all I need, and I'll live, well, just at that moment, they hear a tremendous roar and a blast, and the last thing they see is the flash of the guns from the hunters, and then their little bodies are ripped to shreds by lead pellets and they hurtle to the ground and they are dead. That is how much alone we are in the world. We believe we know who we are, the little songbird knows, at the genetic level, that it is a linnet, with its sweet rosy breast, or it's a serin, that's a heartbreakingly lovely yellow bird, or a greenfinch, or a hawfinch, or even a chaffinch, one of the most beautiful birds in the entire world, it has an understated palette of pale forest and meadow colors, it's not a garish parrot or a crass parakeet, with colors so bright they blind you. The chaffinch is exceptionally lovely, Samuel, I am sure you would appreciate it if you lived in Europe, where there are truly beautiful birds, not like the boorish American robin, it is like a bloated thug in comparison to our sweet little European robin, I admit the American robin lays miraculous cyan-colored eggs, but that does not mean it isn't a typical fat American thug, or what about the clownish North American bluejay or cardinal, they're like parts of the national flag, loud, vulgar, and stupid. Anyway the chaffinch was born in Libya, it doesn't know the word Libya, but instinctively, it does know. And it is trying to go to Ireland, it doesn't know that word either, but its eyes know, its body can feel the direction. And now the poor little chaffinch is nothing. One of its wings has been shot off, it's falling through the air, and in another few seconds it will hit the ground in Malta with a small puff of dust. It is alone in the world, like we all are. The hunters won't even bother to pick it up, they have many more to shoot. It'll just dry out in the sun. I'm not complaining, you know. My eyes are open. *Nunquam minus solus quam cum sola,* I'm never less alone than when I'm alone, which is always. I do not need memories, Samuel, *sola ipsa,* I alone, I am alone, *sub divo,* under the sky, like the dead songbird in Malta, *sola ipsa, sub divo,* under the wide sky, I am here, *sum ego sola, nemo me comprehendit,* I am the only one of my kind, no one understands me. I am even *dysnoetos,* I don't understand myself, well, Paul and I are the only two of our kind. *Dixi.*

God, Anneliese, you are so pompous, Catherine said.

I am a *busillis.*

And maudlin.

Possibly, Anneliese answered, using stalks of white asparagus to mop up her satay sauce. I am a baffling puzzle, *in diebus illis magnis plenae, indie busillis magnis plenae.*

Her head seemed unstable, like those plastic birds that wobble and tip their beaks in cups of water.

I will tell you both a beautiful story, she said. The magnificent Estonian biologist Jakob von Uexküll pointed out that ticks are among the simplest of the arthropods. Hard-shelled ticks, the ones he studied, they are blind. The larvae, the nymphs, and the adults, are all blind. They look like each other, too, the larvae, the nymphs, and the adults, it's strange, they all look alike but each stage has more legs than the one before it. They metamorphose, but they don't change shape like grubs, which become beetles, or like caterpillars, which become butterflies. Each time the ticks molt they come out looking the same, but with two more legs. Six, then eight, then ten. I don't know what to say about that. At any rate Uexküll says all they do in their life is climb a blade of grass and wait until they sense a specific chemical that is in the breath of warm-blooded animals, it's the only thing they can smell, that one chemical, oxalic acid, they can only smell that one chemical, but it is all they need, because when they smell it they leap, blindly, and hope to land on a warm-blooded animal.

Like you, Catherine said, springing on unsuspecting people like Samuel.

I am ignoring that. They can also sense warmth, and if they land on something warm, they bite. If the thing is not warm, they drop off, and creep along until they run into another blade of grass, and then climb, and wait to smell more oxalic acid. But if the thing the tick jumps onto is warm, it bites, and whatever comes into its mouth, it drinks. Then when it's full of blood it drops off.

Don't worry, Samuel, Catherine said, that will happen soon enough.

Then it molts and afterward there it is, slightly larger and with two more legs.

How many does she have now? Catherine said, looking under the table.

Catherine, please, this is actually an interesting story. So that's how life goes for the tick. People misunderstand ticks, that's what Uexküll said, they think ticks are simple, they have no sense of taste, they're blind, they can only smell one chemical, they have no social life, all they can do is climb, wait to smell oxalic acid, which by the way has no smell for humans, that's ironic, isn't it, or is it, anyway then all they do is leap into the void, hoping to land on the back of a rat or a badger or a deer, but people are wrong, Uexküll said, because from the tick's point of view, the oxalic acid in mammal breath may be a ravishing symphony of smells, who are we to judge, Uexküll said, what do we know, we don't know oxalic acid, that is for sure, for all we know it might smell as amazing as the bouquet from a bottle of 1965 Raymond Cheurlin Blanc de Blancs, Uexküll didn't say that, I'm the one who likes 1965 Raymond Cheurlin Blanc de Blancs, Paul says I like it a little too much, almost as much as my Mathilde Pêche liqueur, but Uexküll did say that even if ticks can't taste blood, the feeling of blood pumping out of a warm animal and swelling your stomach until it's larger than you are and your limbs and head protrude from your swollen stomach like the puckered mouth of a balloon, that feeling might be richer and more delicious than anything we can imagine, although it has occurred to me that Uexküll never tasted anything as divine as a 1965 Raymond Cheurlin Blanc de Blancs, he probably ate nothing but horrible Estonian food. The tick just jumps into a void, he said. That sounds obvious, I mean I can picture it, I don't think I have ever "jumped into a void," whatever that even means, no one jumps into voids, people jump off things onto the ground or they jump into the water, water is a kind of void because you can't always see what is beneath the surface, but of course water isn't a void, so it is almost safe to say no human knows what it is like to jump into a void, except maybe astronauts, and they have their own issues, and also I really don't think I have ever jumped into anything, I have jumped onto things, like the roof of my neighbor's porch when I rescued their cat Fritzl, and recently I jumped up onto a table, because Morschmulmig dared me to, we got in an argument about who, exactly, was a cartilaginous technocrat, unfit to make even the most trivial decision, unable to see beyond his own stubby snotted-up nose, incapable of a "leap of inspiration," as Morschmulmig said, or of leaping anywhere, that's what I said, I was making fun of the fact that he's got a big belly, and we ended up screaming at each other and I jumped up onto the table, just to show that in a literal sense I could perform such a feat, so if ticks, so when ticks, so if a tick, so when a tick jumps into the void, it might have a life-changing experience, entirely beyond our capacity to imagine, and besides, which one of us has ever "jumped into a void" in order to drink blood? Dracula maybe, but no human in their right mind in the real world has ever jumped into a void in order to bite an animal and drink its blood. People are wrong, Uexküll said, ticks may have very rich, subtle experiences, they might be profound creatures, maybe we're the ones who are superficial and stupid, well, Uexküll didn't say stupid, but our lives might be dull in comparison to the scintillating experiences of the hard-shelled tick, that's what he said, well, he didn't say scintillating, he said something like rich or subtle. The point here is we don't know how the tick experiences its world. In some dim way it might remember things, like, I smelled something, and jumped, and ended up on a frog, it was awful, frog blood is like puke, that's what the tick might think, Uexküll might have said that, I'm not sure, the frog example might be my own, but, and, Uexküll said, for all we know male ticks think about female ticks and vice versa, like I am sure you think about your wife, Samuel, you're married, aren't you? So you think about your wife, and probably you think sweet and complicated thoughts about your wife, because you love her, and you want to mate with her, I guess, and by the way, do you know how ticks mate? Do you? You don't? Okay, when a healthy, mature red-blooded male tick is fastened onto a rat or a deer or a badger, drinking blood, it tastes something funny in the blood, there are traces of the saliva, the salivas, of all the other ticks that are also feeding on the same animal, say it's a big badger, there might be dozens of blind hard-shelled ticks feeding on different parts of the badger, all of them males, and if I am a mature female tick, then my saliva has a special flavor, and the red-blooded male ticks taste traces of my female saliva in the badger's blood, mixed in with traces of the spit of the other male ticks, that might be a little unpleasant, like walking into one of those toilets in stadiums, where men go and piss into enormous troughs, and all the piss runs together and it must smell godawful, anyway, the spittle of that one mature female tick must come as a shock, like, Oh, my god! There's an attractive female tick drinking blood somewhere on this same badger! I've got to stop drinking and go find her! That's what the male tick "thinks," "thinks" in quotation marks, but that's what it experiences, Uexküll said, what an amazing way to find the person you love, it isn't easy to picture that, is it, imagine you're in a restaurant, and you're eating a cake, a chocolate cake, and all of a sudden you taste a trace of blood in it, really delicious blood, or the chocolate tastes like someone's sweat, but in a nice way, and you think, Oh my god, this food was made by a handsome virile chef, he must have sweated into it, or he cut himself and bled into the cake mix, I just have to go right away and find him, and mate with him! And you jump up and run back into the kitchen, I'm not sure if that's a very good illustration, but you see what I mean, so Uexküll said the taste of the female tick in the badger blood is exquisite and beautiful to the male ticks, it means love or, well, he didn't say that, he said something like the flavor stimulates the male tick, it gives the male tick's life meaning, it's what the father tick would tell its kids if it ever even knew it had kids, it would say, "Hey kids, this is what life's all about, when you are sucking on nice warm badger blood and your belly is distended like Morschmulmig's and the integument over your belly is becoming translucent, and the entire rest of your body looks like a nipple on the enormous swollen breast of your stomach, when your little limbs and head look like a tick sucking on a melon, ha ha, that's an existential tick joke, but seriously, kids, when you're sucking away on that badger, and you think you're in heaven, that's when you taste something else, and your spicules get engorged, you're feeling that special thrill, you're tasting the spit from the tick of your dreams, well, Speckle, my boy, you're a little young still, you only have six legs, you don't understand yet, but someday you will, your world will turn upside down, and well well, Splat, I can sense your spicules are pulsing, you have eight legs, you know what I'm talking about, there is something in the world more exciting than badger blood, and that's love, kids, heh heh."

Beautiful story, Catherine said. One of your better ones.

So, and, so there I am, a mature female tick, drinking blood mixed with many males' spittle, and I "think" or I "know" that soon I will be surrounded by male ticks who have stopped drinking, pulled their revolting barbed mouthparts out of the badger, and started clambering blindly through the forest of badger hairs to find me, and they will pile over me and mate with me over and over using their revolting barbed penises. I can hardly keep my mind on drinking, I am anxious, but also very happy. Well, I'm being whimsical, but only to make a serious point, that Uexküll said ticks may lead intricate and nuanced lives, so we should not look down onto them, we should stop disparaging at them.[9]

I don't think anyone spends time belittling ticks, Catherine said.

No, Anneliese said, my point is that Uexküll was wrong. Absolutely, completely wrong. Everything that I have just recounted is wrong, except for my whimsical story about the tick children, because whimsical stories can never be wrong, exactly, although they can certainly be wrongheaded, in the sense of misguided, misguided in the sense of poorly imagined, poorly imagined in the sense of insufficiently whimsical, or just plain boring and incomprehensible and tedious, well, other people's whimsical stories could be, I don't think mine are, but those questions of truth and fiction are quite difficult and I do not require them in order to make my point, which is this: Uexküll was wrong, a blind hard-shelled tick lives a sad little life. It can only taste a couple of chemicals, it can only smell one chemical. It can't think. It knows nothing. It has no memory, no family, no sense of itself. It is sad, pathetic, and lost. Like me. I do not live a full life. I live alone, I think and write. I rarely see another tick. At any moment I might leap up from my dinner and attempt to mate with the cook. He's been standing there with his arms crossed, in his stained t-shirt, for nearly ten hours, and that is not at all unattractive. I am like a tick that is struggling to think, to find its place in the world. I try to remember what it was like when I had only eight legs, or only six legs, or even when I was nothing more than an egg glued to the back of a badger. I struggle to understand what a badger is. What is a badger? It is a bulging warm forest of hairs, and it tastes like blood and tissue fluids, mingled with the spittle of many ticks. I struggle to understand myself and the world. But the struggle is hopeless, because I am nearly mindless. I cannot understand the world. My life is not the mysterious subtle symphony of gravity, heat, and oxalic acid that Uexküll hoped, he was a weird Estonian scientist, always trying to imagine the beautiful insides of mindless creatures' minds. I have no hope of understanding my life. If I ever had only eight legs I can no longer remember them. Are my eight back legs the old ones? Or are my back legs the oldest, and the eight in front are new? No matter how hard I try I can't remember having only eight legs. It does not mean I never had eight legs, it means I cannot remember. It would be just exactly like if I look at my two legs, here under the table, and I try to remember when I had four legs. I just cannot, I can't conceive it, I can't remember it. None of us can. We could sit here all day on our two legs each and try as hard as we can to remember when we had four legs, and we just couldn't.

When Anneliese starts counting her legs, Catherine whispered to me, it's time to leave.

Or wait, Anneliese said, what I just said is not right. The point is the tick can't remember, it can't figure anything out, can't find its place in the world, because it has no memory. My mind is just as weak. I have no memories, Samuel, none of us do. Our memories are fictions. You know Proust? You know the novel, where he remembers the pastry?

No, Catherine said.

I know you both know, I knew that you know, I mean I knew that you would know, because every cultured person, every educated person, basically anyone knows, I mean everyone knows about the madeleine, I'm sorry I even asked, although it was mainly a rhetorical question, but of course you know that too. Anyway. Proust spends a lot of time telling us what he remembers, but in fact he remembers nothing. In fact Proust is an idiot. Of course the pastry reminded him of pastries he had eaten as a child, that is no great accomplishment. But then, imagine, he sat at his perfumed desk and wrote his fragrant prose about memory and the forms and images of the past, of the dainty scallop-shell of pastry, so richly sensual under its severe, religious folds—that's what he says, he actually says that, he actually manages to be perverse about a cookie—and the way he delicately dunked it into his European lime-flower tisane, and how he raised just one teaspoon to his lips and took just a single sip... imagine, it was a demitasse spoonful of flower tea, with the tiniest softest crumble of the little pleated cake, god forbid he could have actually drunk the tea like a normal person, or just eaten a whole cake, they're only one bite anyway—and how the moment he swallowed his teaspoon with its half-dissolved crumble he felt the pleasure diminish, my god, he must have been a special little boy, and how, even though that memory had been dormant so many years, and the past was long gone and nothing seemed to remain of it, and although the people from that time were scattered and gone, even so, still, alone, and insubstantial, but with more vitality, persistence, and faithfulness, the smell and taste of the pastry and tea, which had remained poised for long long years, like souls, waiting and hoping for their moment, amid the ruins of the past, stood ready to remind him, and how, without faltering, they then brought, in the sip of tea, the vast structure of recollection, that is what Proust says, but in fact they brought nothing but those florid remembrances of memory, trellises of sentences atomized with the overscented cologne of time, hung with eloquently turned phrases, gracefully intertwined, bowers of garlanded sentences, linked each to the next like dancers holding a long braid of flowers, each stepping and twirling freely, and yet each holding the delicate strand of woven stems, sometimes pulling it taut and other times playing it out or spinning oh so elegantly around it as if it were a dancing partner, never breaking it and never letting go, continuing in their dance, around and around, embroidering and decorating the poor empty shell of a memory, never once stopping, because then they would notice that the writer had in fact remembered nothing except a teaspoon and a sodden fleck of pastry, and that the writer, desperate, desolate, disconsolate, knew that perfectly well, so he sat for days and then years until he had written those memories into existence, word by sensitive perfect word, because his past was gone, gone, gone, and even back in that misremembered moment he had nothing except a teaspoon that he had licked clean with his delicate little boy's tongue, and many years later, exhausted and enervated in his humidified study filigreed with incense, he had nothing to show for his years of diseased thinking but a book full of beautiful braided evasions. Is there a difference between Proust and a ten-legged tick? We are alone, stranded in the present. Nothing in our past can help us at all.[10]

Notice, Catherine said, she's already forgotten my proof. In an hour she'll be telling you how she invented the formula. Remember Chișinău, Samuel.

You are deliberately obtuse, Catherine, Anneliese said, you're trying to draw me, you're drawing me out from myself, you're making a drawing out of me, but I will not be a drawing. No one can make me into a drawing.

Catherine pushed back her chair. Well, she said, I find I'm not hungry, and I see Samuel at work, so I think I will go home now.

It was good to see you, Anneliese said, and then, when she had left, She is such a remarkable woman. She is right about everything. I have cared about her since we first met thirty years ago. But what a relief she is gone. It really does not matter who discovered that formula, because we are all like that poor little songbird, dying in the dust with the racket of rifles all around us, or like the tick, blind, lost, with no past, no future, its mouth full of blood and spittle, or like that Frenchman, on perfume life support. I have no illusions about that. And now Samuel, at last I can finish telling you about what has happened to my uncle. So Paul and I were hurrying across the park toward St. Judas Thaddäus. Hans was taking us straight there. Paul said he had never done that before. Some branches were down, and Hans walked right over them, stumbling and kicking them aside. In a minute we saw the church through the trees. He led us up to it, to the end of the park, and then he turned us aside. There was a bench there in the corner of the park. He pulled me, and we sat down next to him on the bench, me on one side, Paul on the other. This was his favorite bench last autumn, Paul told me. In front of the bench, across the street, was an old brick apartment house, next to the church. Hans just sat and looked. Paul lit a cigarette. Hans stared up at the apartment building. I got up and stood behind him, crouching down at his shoulder to try to see where he was looking. He was looking up to the third floor, on the left side of the building. Paul said he'd never noticed that. We followed the line of his sight. He was looking at the last window on the left. There was no one there. His face was tilted up, he was staring steadily at that one window on the third floor. I asked Paul if he knew what Marlene had looked like. "I have no idea," he said, "there are no photographs. But now I know what this window is. Once, a long time ago, after his second wife died, it would be about fifteen years ago, he told me a story. He said he and his first wife used to live in an apartment next to a church. He said they had a pet, a canary. They kept it in a cage on the windowsill. He said that every evening his wife would wait for him to come back from work. It was hard in those days, and he worked very late. His job was in a factory in Klybeck, and he walked back through the park. His wife said that she would wait and when the canary sang, she knew he was coming back. The canary saw him through the window, that's what his first wife told him."

# 5

# THE BUCKET LIST

SAMUEL! she yelled. Samuel! Thank you for calling. I hope you are well, and I hope your family is well, even though I am sorry to admit I can't remember your wife's name. I am not entirely certain, but I believe you have a wife. I think you do. But perhaps you don't.

Adela moved back to Bratislava, I said. I'm on my way to Basel at the moment, and I could see you there Saturday or Sunday.

I see. And how are the little ones? Wait, are there little ones?

Fina's not so little. She's gone to college in El Paso, in Texas.

There is no college there.

There is, it's called University of Texas at El Paso.

Of course there are no universities in Texas. And how is the baby? I believe you also have a baby? Do you have a baby?

Sorry. No baby.

Do you see how amazing that is? It is another sign I was right to select you. I am unmarried, you are separated. Neither of us has a normal family.[11]

It is pretty much normal to have a wife and daughter.

I bristle with rooster-like proudness that I am not in any way normal.

Fine. But what do you mean, you selected me?

And yet I appear normal.

Anneliese, what do you mean, you selected me?

Wait, I want to tell you how I appear to be normal, even though I am not. Samuel, if people knew the state of my body underneath my clothes, they would become alarmed and ask to leave. If they could read through my doctor's reports their mouths would go dry. If they saw what I looked like with my skirt pulled up they would wince and gulp. And that is just my body. My mind is in far worse condition. If people knew the work I have been doing they would become nervous and embarrassed. If they knew what I thought about all day long, they would get confused and upset. If they realized what I thought of them, they would be frightened and angry, and that is because when I meet people I compare them in my mind to various species of segmented marine worms. It is a useful way to classify people. You see, Samuel, some segmented marine worms have colorful stripes and spots, and that is how I think of people who imagine they are entertaining, I picture them as patterned worms writhing and performing various country dances. Harlequin worms, that's what Martin Frobenius Ledermüller called them. That way I don't have to listen to what they are saying, I can simply enjoy their ridiculous leaping and bouncing. I perceive their words as harsh squeaks, which complement their undulating dances. That is the first type of worm person. A second kind of worm has enormous gelatinous eyes that roll around loosely under flabby lids, they peer this way and that, their eyes stream with tears because because they never blink, that is how I picture people who envy everything, they are always agog, they think everyone has it better than them, and they are right, because they are worms. A third kind of worm is covered in a jacket of slime, the worm glistens with mucilage, those are the people who try to ingratiate themselves with everyone. When they hug you, you're left with a coating of sugary ooze. When I meet people like that I am impeccably polite. I pretend I am enjoying their company, but when it is time to hug goodbye I try to wave and walk away. If one succeeds in hugging me I turn my head to the side so my face doesn't get coated in candied slime, and then I immediately go home and scrub my skin vigorously. The fourth kind of worm has a rotary mouth like an electric floor polishing machine. That is how I picture people who attach themselves to people they meet and scour away all their thoughts until there is nothing left. Catherine is one of those worms, she attached herself to me and scraped away all my ideas and ate them. That is how I perceive Catherine, her mouth is round, and inside there are several rotating scouring heads made of large-gauge wire brushes. When I speak, my words go into her mouth and are rasped to shreds. I think a lubricant foam keeps the parts of her mouth in good operating condition and provides a detergent that aids in digestion. The fifth kind of worm has a toothless jaw with needles hidden in its gums that spring out and jab into its prey, like arrow worms, they have retractable grasping spines in their mouths, those are the people who think they are armed with lethal weapons but actually they only have little needles in their gums, and if you kiss them they spread their lips so their gums are exposed and the needles puncture your lips and poke onto your teeth, but those people are more irritating than anything else, and slightly alarming too, but definitely not dangerous, or maybe a little dangerous if you kiss them too much. The sixth kind of worm has a jaw that comes off its hinge so the mouth opens insanely wide, like bobbit worms, like goblin sharks, they try to eat animals twice their size, that is how I picture people who have huge ambition, they try to engulf everyone, but when they actually swallow someone they get horrible gastric pains and they end up vomiting the person back out, it's a mess and it can be mortifying for them. They should know it isn't that easy to swallow some people. I am pretty much indigestible myself, that's what Paul said about me, "No one can stomach you, you are totally indigestible," he said, and then he added, "You realize you are the one who eats people, right?" That surprised me, but I've noticed he is often correct, so maybe I really am that sixth type of worm. I definitely find people indigestible, and how would I know that if I hadn't tried to eat a few? The seventh kind of worm spends its life hiding in mud at the bottom of the ocean, those are like our cowardly Rektor Morschmulmig, he is a great friend of Paul's but I can't stand him, he is like the worms who live in burrows on the beach, sometimes you see their holes on tidal flats, with a spiral ziggurat of excreta next to each hole. I do not understand why those worms hide, why would any creature want to eat one of those worms, their stomachs are full of sand and muck, their bodies are jelly and rubber, they must taste vile, and if you actually did eat one it would keep squirming as it went down, but worms like Morschmulmig like to hide, and often the only thing you see is the worm's little hole and its neat little pyramid of poop. They are fundamentally squalid creatures, I just cannot stand Morschmulmig. He is also worm eight, they have swollen lips and tongues because they are always boasting. Lots of worms are like that, scale worms, blood worms, ribbon worms. People who are worm eight have puffy mouths and flabby jowls and muscular lips like stargazers, like bearded sea devils, do you know what those are? They are nightmares made by god and hidden under the ocean. Catherine is a good example of the ninth type of marine worm, an especially unpleasant sort of worm. It is common knowledge that some worms can spontaneously break up into segments. If you step on them they snap apart, and each segment is alive. That is how I think of people who seem to be there in the room with you, you think you're talking to them, but actually their heads are somewhere else, their heads are at home watching television, and you are talking to part of the belly or the tail. When we all met in Guelph, in the Yellow Hat Diner Catherine listened while I spent nine and a half hours disproving her claims about my work, but she wasn't actually there at the table. A few of her segments were missing. Some segments of her worm body were at home, maybe soaking in a nice bath, perhaps her rear segment was on the toilet, and her head segment was in the lab, looking up the old notebooks, scanning wildly with her spinning worm eyes, taking it all in, storing it up so she could come back for dinner and tell me I was wrong, so while we sat there blithely talking and sampling the bewildering Canadian food, it wasn't my old friend Catherine in front of me at all, or at least not all of her, it was a chair heaped with several worm segments, a knee, a belly, a foot—she is definitely an example of worm nine, an unusual sort of worm, and perhaps that is why we get along so well. Morschmulmig is also worm ten, they have translucent bodies that pulse with peristaltic contractions. You can see the clumps of food being forced along through their intestines, and you know how long it will take for the droppings to come out, those are people who live to eat, they do not think of anything except capturing more food, salivating, crushing, masticating, and swallowing, and then liquefying, digesting, compressing, dehydrating, and defecating. When Morschmulmig comes to our house for dinner he has a fine time gulping and slurping his food with his fluttering mouthparts, but all I can think about is the progress of the food through his intestines, the crowding of the food in his intestines, the food pushing onward through his intestines. His wife is different, I think she just absorbs nutrients directly into her fat. Morschmulmig knows he is a Rektor, so he has to behave himself, otherwise I am sure he would prefer to release his droplet turds onto our Carpathian carpet. Of course I cannot tell Morschmulmig what kinds of marine worms he is, because I also have to appear normal at all costs. When he looks at me he sees an ordinary person, once a lecturer and now an independent scholar. When he looks down at his plate with his bleary, badly focused worm eyes, he sees the usual lumps of food, tarnished silverware, and chipped glasses, the same as he sees at any of the faculty houses he visits. When he glances admiringly around our home, he sees the typical broken antique clock on the mantelpiece, the dusty worthless vases, and the obligatory photo wall with images of smiling people we used to care about. Paul and I keep an entirely ordinary house, even though it has a slight mold problem, the walls in the hallway are actually black and when I touch them, they are soft and spongy and the black stays on my fingertips and it is hard to wash off, but everyone has little house problems, right? We also have a small summer house up in the Walliser Alpen, you know everyone in Switzerland has a house in the mountains. That house is utterly and impeccably normal, a typical Alpine hut, a *Hütte,* a little *Alphütte,* that is what we call them, not like the house on the jigsaw puzzle, not like the little spider-infested house, the *Summerhüsli* near the Basel-Mulhouse-Freiburg airport, but a cute little Hütte, perched far up in the mountains, with an enormous overhanging roof, like they all have, and walls made of beautiful stripped logs, like everyone else's, and three old pine trees to give it shelter, not everyone has those, ours are really quite special, with their picturesque gnarled branches, I know our neighbors envy us, but our neighbors are worms with enormous gelatinous eyes, they are the second kind of worm, our neighbors, they have swollen gelatinous eyes that wobble on the ends of distended stalks, they think of nothing except what we have, anyway we have three magnificent and highly poetic ancient pine trees to keep our Hütte company on its lonesome high meadow, even though two of the trees have been cut down and the third one is actually dead, and the Hütte also has a single front window with bright green shutters and lemon-yellow window casings, and the whole tiny Hütte sits on a foundation of round boulders, just like they all do, except that our boulders are cracked, but we try not to think about that, because it means that someday when we are sitting at our supposedly delightfully small but actually painfully cramped table munching on our breakfast müesli, the room will suddenly go weightless and we will plummet thousands of meters into the valley below, blinking at each other as the droplets of milk and soggy müesli levitate around us, so we try not to think about that, we try to concentrate on our müesli and enjoy the picture-postcard view across the bluegreen Alpine valley to snow-capped peaks, it's really so idyllic, the cowbells echo and the church bells sound and the snow larks sing and the cool breeze whistles through the trees, or it would if we still had them, it is all so typical and cute that it makes me absolutely nauseous, I can't go anywhere near the Hütte, I haven't been there in years, I refuse to go, I will not sit there crunching on Swiss müesli, I don't even like Swiss müesli, in fact I hate Swiss müesli, everyone pretends it is healthy but it is actually made of powder-dry puffs of fruit and wheat flakes that taste like crusts of dust from under a piece of furniture, Swiss müesli is indigestible, so I refuse to go to our typical cute little Hütte anymore and that's why Paul made me buy a rowboat instead. My rowboat is also very typical, it has an enormous crack in the bottom that I have very successfully repaired with duct tape, except that it leaks. Of course, to the smeary eyes of a viscid person like Morschmulmig, my moldy house and my precarious Hütte and my unreliable boat are perfectly normal, and when Morschmulmig strains to focus his watery eyes on me, he sees a perfectly normal former employee. Like my house, I also have certain spots and discolorations, and my foundations are definitely crumbling. There is an enormous crack in my bottom, ha ha, and my teeth are chipped and discolored from decades spent grinding müesli, and in all those respects, too, I am entirely normal. And I have a family that appears normal. Here in Switzerland, the average household size is 3.4 people. We have four in ours. We are not related in the usual way, of course, Hans is my uncle and Luzia is his granddaughter, but that is what is left of our family, and the important thing is we appear close to normal, 4.0 instead of 3.4. But if I were in charge of the census, I would calculate it differently. Hans appears normal, like any elderly person who is nearly mute and unresponsive and will soon need a nurse. But as you know it is not that simple. Until last month

I thought he had no thoughts left, but then we discovered why he goes to the corner of the park across from the church, and now I see he is desperately trying to keep just one or two memories, out of his entire life. A dark fog is closing in, soon there will be nothing left for him to look at but meaningless shapes moving across the television screen. He is not a whole person anymore, he's not wholly a person, even though Paul fervently wishes that Hans can be an entire person again. I think Hans is a diminishing fraction of a person. The way I calculate it, he is approximately three-tenths of a person, and that number is shrinking every day. The other seven-tenths of him is gone. He does not remember it. Paul and I recall some of the missing seven-tenths, but if we added up everything we remember, which is of course impossible, but this is a mathematical fantasy, not a testable hypothesis, if we added our recollections together we might have one tenth of his life, after all it was his life, not ours, and even Paul doesn't know more than a fraction of it, like any daughter or any son, or I mean any nephew or niece, he doesn't really know much of Hans's life, Luzia certainly doesn't know me, by the way, she has absolutely no idea what I do or think, the only thing she knows is when to walk out of the room, and besides, it doesn't matter what Paul and I know about Hans, and it certainly doesn't matter that I don't understand Luzia, I mean how could I, the way she behaves, but that's not the point of my little mathematical fantasy, and incidentally of course I admit the fantasy is not actually mathematical in any interesting way, please don't bother to object about that, thank you, I mean thank you in advance, I don't know you well enough to be sure that you're not the sort of person who might interrupt me to make a point like that, but I certainly hope you aren't, because if you say, "Hey, Anneliese," and by the way I imagine you say "hey," because Canadians always say "hey," so if you say, "Hey, Anneliese, you can't add up memories like that, memory is complex, it's subtle, people aren't so simple. Memory is a profound subject that has fascinated generations of the greatest thinkers, like Vervliet and Slab. You really should know that, Anneliese," that's what you might say, even though I have already explained why it's not true, but maybe you are stubborn, or you just dislike mathematics, so perhaps you'll say, "Memory doesn't just fill up to a hundred percent like one of those annoying thermometers, or wait, not thermometers, bars, horizontal bars, moving horizontal bars, you know the ones I mean? They appear on your screen telling you something's filling up or emptying out or downloading or erasing or opening or closing, you know the ones? You must know them, everyone who has a computer has seen them a thousand times." If you interrupt me to ask a simple question about computers that you really should know—and by the way, they are called progress bars, everyone knows that—or for that matter if you interrupt me to tell me memory isn't simple and I can't calculate my uncle as a sum of fractions, then you would be right, but of course I know that perfectly well, as you can tell from the little imaginary speech you just gave, which was quite eloquent at the beginning, even though it was a bit ruined when you couldn't think of the term "progress bars," and so eventually you would realize that my calculation is only a fantasy, and it really wasn't worth the effort to interrupt me and tell me it's too simple. Paul and I actually know a tremendous amount about our uncle, some of which he has undoubtedly forgotten. We might even know more than one-tenth of his entire life, and now that he has forgotten so much, we are the repositories of significant information about his life, although I do not have the slightest idea what that means since we cannot return our deposited memories to the person who once owned them. Even if he came to us and demanded we tell him everything we know about him, even if he came at us with a gun and said, "I want my memories back, I don't know how you got them, and I don't know what they are, but I want them back, right away, so start talking, both of you," even then we could not return his memories to him, because he wouldn't recognize them, he wouldn't believe us when we said they were his memories. He'd become enraged, he'd wave the gun around like a cowboy, he'd say, "Those aren't my memories, don't you think I'd recognize my own life? What do you think I am, a patty? I am not your patty! You cannot make me into a patty!"

Patsy, I said.

What kind of a word is that? she shrieked. Patsy is a person.

So is Patty.

In that case Hans would say, "I am not Patsy! I am not any Patsy at all!" That's what he would yell. Okay? You are very sensitive about this Patsy person. Anyway we couldn't give him back his memories even if we wanted to, and if he pointed a gun at us we would be terrified, I have never had a gun pointed at me, and I would try my best to give his memories back to him. I'd say, "Look, you may not remember this now, but you were married twice, and you told us you really loved your first wife Marlene," but he wouldn't remember, and that would enrage him, he'd fire the gun into the ceiling and the plaster would come down on our heads, because that's what happens in movies. "I want my memories back," he'd yell, "I want them back this minute!" "Okay, okay," I'd say, "Maybe you remember this: you go for walks across town, to the park with the church," and then his face would change, because he'd remember that, and I'd say, "You walk across the park, to a place just opposite a certain apartment building, and sit on a park bench and look up at one of the windows," and he'd be transfixed, he'd remember, and I'd say, "You think about your first wife, don't you, how you two used to live there when you were young, in a cramped apartment with a canary in a cage in the window," and his face would cloud over, because he would know it was true, he would remember, he would see his first wife there in the window, and the bird cage on the sill, just the way he'd seen them when he walked through the park at dusk so many years ago, and he would realize that the one-third of him that is left no longer has a secure hold on that one most precious memory, about the years he worked in a factory and walked back across the park in the twilight, and how his first wife, the only person he ever truly loved, was up in that building in a corner apartment, making dinner in the darkening kitchen and waiting for the canary to sing, and he'd realize he would undoubtedly forget that story again in just a few more seconds, with no way to retrieve it until it came to him spontaneously, or maybe he wouldn't ever remember it again, he would just feel an urge to leave the apartment and go for a walk, or have a vague feeling of anticipation as he crossed the park, or a fleeting painful memory as he looked up at the building, not knowing why he was looking at that one window, or maybe he wouldn't remember his first wife at all until I happened to mention it again in some argument like the one we were having. He would know he had no hope of fixing the memory in his mind, he would realize that the next time he sat on that bench at the end of the park looking up at the apartment building he might see only an empty window, and it wouldn't be enough to remind him, he wouldn't know why he had come, and a dark despair would fall over him, and he would see that this exact moment, while the two of us were talking, might be the very last moment in his life that he would remember Marlene, and even now his picture of her was clouding over with the effort of keeping our argument in his mind, so he'd get angry again and fire the gun at our feet, and we'd jump up as if we could avoid the bullet, because that's what they do in movies. "You really do think I am Patty," he'd yell, "How could I possibly ever know who lived in that apartment?" And he'd point the gun right at us. "If you don't know who lived there," I'd say, "then why do you keep going to the park, to that one bench, and looking up at that building?" and his brows would pinch together and tremble like fighting spiders, and he'd say, "I sit on that bench because it faces away from your house," and I'd say, "You have already forgotten, haven't you?" and then he'd probably shoot me.

Do you think your uncle might actually shoot you?

Of course not. If I were him, I'd shoot us, because I would not be able to believe I wasn't me, that other people were me. I would not be able to believe that other people had parts of my mind, and one of them was even my niece, of all people. I mean me. If I was my uncle, I'd think, That woman, my niece, I mean me, that woman was never right in the head, she is such a Patsy, but what can you do? Still, I never imagined she would claim she is me, that she has my memories, even though she doesn't know anything about me. What kind of person says things like, "Okay, you've forgotten your first wife Marlene, we won't talk about her anymore, just forget I keep mentioning her, you've supposedly forgotten both your wives, it doesn't seem very likely, but okay, we'll let that slide, but look, you've even forgotten things that happened last summer, things you did last summer," things I couldn't remember, even though she said she'd just named them a minute ago, "But never mind," she'd say, "here's something you'll remember, surely you'll remember that your granddaughter Luzia is in love with a young man in the Manor Basel Department Store, she was talking about him at dinner last night, not years ago, not last summer, last night, she was going on and on about how handsome he was, and how sad, and how very handsome, and how lonely, and how exquisitely sad, and how delicately featured, and actually how terribly lonely, and yet how strikingly handsome, despite his pimple, my god I thought she would never stop, I'm sure you'll remember that, who could forget that drivel, that kind of endless self-absorbed nonsense, 'Oh he's so handsome in his Manor Basel jacket, his eyes are so deep and full of suffering, he must be lonely, see how languidly he scans the price tags, how beautifully he moves. Watch how seriously he blinks, now look at his ears! Aren't those the most beautiful pendant lobes you have ever seen, the teardrops of flesh that hang down, aren't they just adorable? See them, the little flaps of his ears, don't you want to give them a tug, maybe even a bite, and even the pimple, it's just a cute little pimple like a beauty mark,' and so on, just never stopping, surely you remember that, don't you? How could you not remember that?" And so on, never stopping, what kind of person says things like that? I know Luzia didn't say any of that because I would remember it, that's what Hans would think, I actually have an amazing memory, that's what Hans would think, so I have no choice, my niece is a menace, she is clearly insane, I have to shoot her, put her out of her misery, put me out of my misery, put us out of our misery, whatever, I'm not sure, but if I were Hans, I would spin the gun around my finger like they do in the movies, I'd look my niece up and down and say, "By gum, lady, you've been asking for this," and if he said that, I'd have no choice, I'd have to shoot him, put him out of his misery, put him out of my misery, whatever, I'm not sure, but I'd spin the gun around my finger like they do in the movies, I'd look him up and down and say, "By gum, feller, you've been asking for this."

Anneliese, you're going to shoot your uncle?

Samuel, please try to follow along. No one is shooting anyone. You could say Hans is dispersed. Some of him is intact in him, some is in me, some in Paul, there is a pathetic shred in Luzia, even though it doesn't amount to more than the thought that she has a crazy grandfather who is really really old and wrinkly, the fact is no matter how you calculate it most of my uncle is missing. He has forgotten so much, he's down to one-third of a person. If he had completely lost the memory of his first wife and the sports stadium and the playground, well then he'd be stuck in the present, and we could say, Never mind the past, what's gone is gone, you're with us now. But he forgets different parts of things and people from different years. Remember the breakup of the Soviet Union? I had a map, and when the Soviet Union broke up I used crayons to color in Ukraine, Lithuania, Estonia, Armenia, and the others, Kazakhstan, Kyrgyzstan, Tajikistan, what were the others? Turkmenistan, Ossetia, no, not that, Abkhazia, no, not that, Georgia! that's it, and the little one, Moldova, how could I forget Moldova, okay, okay, it doesn't matter, the point is Paul's uncle is not like Russia, because there is no clear border between him and things that are not him, he's more like that irrational border between the Netherlands and Belgium, it runs across streets and through people's houses, it splits their front doors in two, the border actually runs up the middle of one person's door, or those absolutely crazy places in India and Bangladesh near the border between them, where there are islands of Bangladesh inside India, not actual islands, I mean small territories, they don't call them islands, and, inside some of the islands of India inside Bangladesh there are even littler islands of Bangladesh, well, not islands in islands, that doesn't make sense, more like islands of Bangladesh in lakes of India in the land of Bangladesh, or lakes of Bangladesh in islands of India in the ocean of Bangladesh, I don't care, they're not lakes anyway, they're fields, and there is even one that is a small field of India in a field of Bangladesh in a field of India in the fields of Bangladesh, that is how crazy they are, just like there really is an island in a lake in Canada, and the lake is on an island in a lake on an island, but that is not exactly my point either, I am just trying to explain that Paul's uncle's mind is in pieces, part of him is there, but at the same time parts of the part are not. Paul can't even say to him, "Hans, you've forgotten so much, but you remember Anneliese and me, don't you? and you'll remember us as long as you live, won't you? because we are part of what you are, aren't we?" He can't even say that, because parts of people and things that Hans knew have gone missing, he probably remembers pieces of us, it's like he's walking in a field after an airplane crash, full of twisted chunks of metal, there are fires and sparks, things are smoldering, and all of a sudden he sees the tail of the plane with its logo, and he looks around furtively because he's afraid he will recognize some torn-off piece of a body.

That's a lovely image, Anneliese.

It's what we are like in Hans's eyes. We are severed feet and hands, *disjecta membra,* pieces of skin, half an identity card, a nose with a single eye attached to it. There is no way to put us together again. So my family of four is not actually 4.0 people. More like 3.3. And Luzia! She's not an adult yet, so she's not a 1.0 person, but it's worse than that, she's a teenager. You have several daughters, I'm sure you recognize the phenomenon. Teenage daughters are not people, properly speaking, they are problems. If I'm 1.0, I know I am not, but let's just say for the sake of this conversation that I am 1.0, full human, Paul is definitely 1.0, so let us posit that Paul and I together are the equivalent of two people, so 2.0, and let's say Hans is currently 0.3 of a person, then we total about 2.3 people, well then Luzia is not a number at all, she's an operation, she's like multiplication or differentiation. Or like the factorial function. You see I am trying to make my fantasy more mathematical. Luzia messes everything up, she operates on our nice little 2.3 family, she's like 2.3 to the minus 2.3, factorial, factorial, factorial, factorial!

$$2.3 + \left(\left(\left(\left(2.3^{-2.3}\right)!\right)!\right)!\right)!$$

She operates on the three of us and turns our family into something even less normal, a family of about 3.295 people. That's actually a good result, because we end up close to the official Swiss average of 3.4. Certainly our home life appears entirely normal. I have a nice normal house with a normal idiotic teenager, if she is a teenager, I think she is a teenager, and a normally demented older person and my house has normal mold and my boat has a normal split down down its bottom, and I have a normal split up my bottom, and if we all bail energetically the boat does not sink before we get to the fly-ridden island where we go to picnic for no reason whatsoever, except that Paul says normal families like to get out of the house once a year and drive to lakes and row leaky boats to flat mud islands and squat in damp grass and swat flies and drink warm wine and gnaw on crusts and chomp on cheese wedges and look back to the shore where there are perfectly nice restaurants with actual chairs and fresh bread and chilled wine and no flies, that is all normal, Paul says, well, actually he says, "Just be quiet for once in your life," but he doesn't mean it, he means it is all normal and that's why we do it. Luzia loves it too, by the way, she doesn't say so, but I can tell. Hans comes along because he has no choice. He just sits and lets the flies walk over him. So that is my family. We will not talk about them again. I do not permit the normal to intrude on my work.

I waited. There was a long silence. I heard a scratching sound, like she was filing her nails.[12]

So Samuel. I have introduced myself to you in the most entertaining way I can manage, and now that I have told you about my family and explained how I only appear normal, and that I am not, in any deeper sense, normal at all—as you may have guessed from my light-hearted stories about my mind, my lungs, my scabs, and the stone well where I live—now at last it is time to tell you about my work. I will begin with a story about my childhood, not because I need to, but because it's traditional to begin any large exposition, disquisition, or discourse or dissertation or whatever this is, actually it's just a short friendly introduction, it's traditional to open with a delightful preamble or preface or prolegomenon or prooemion recounting a simple story about the author's childhood. It is annoying, and actually completely unnecessary, but I will do it anyway because it is an effective strategy for capturing attention by revealing a glimpse of the endearing and promising youth of the person who will then go on to unfurl a lengthy and quite possibly tedious account of their dubious later life. When I was young, Samuel, I astounded my Latin tutor, well, "astounded" isn't quite right, I irritated my Latin tutor by demonstrating that Vergil made an error in the *Aeneid*. He did not attend to the motions of the moon. He has the crescent moon "like a little boat listing to the right," *luna crescens refert scaphulam / dextorse se inclinantem,* and then later he says it becomes a new moon, whereas the moon waxes from right to left, so a crescent "listing to the right" would continue to wax, not wane, and would become a full moon, not a new moon, proving Vergil never noticed the direction of the movement of light on the moon, whether the crescent moon grows to the right or to the left, and even though that may seem like a quibble, and not at all a flaw in such a masterpiece, actually, I told my tutor, it is a small but distinct symptom of an insidious problem, like that spot on your cheek, I told him, which could turn out to be cancerous, because Vergil did not notice nature in general, and his *Eclogues* and *Georgics*—which are, by the way, not at all similar in quality, one is sentimental rubbish in comparison to the other—are full of vague, indistinct, inaccurate, generalized, and unconvincing descriptions of trees, pastures, orchards, fields, hills, and streams, as they would be imagined by a person who lived his adult life in cities and never cared about actual farmers or real shepherds, who never noticed the seasons or observed the cycles of the moon. "So what is 'nature' in this so-called great poem?" I said to my tutor. "What is it, exactly? Is it anything?" "It is what Vergil makes it," my tutor said idiotically, and he covered the spot on his cheek with his finger. "It remains true," he said, "that 'Day is pushed out by day, and each new moon hastens to its death,' *Truditur dies die, novaeque pergunt interire lunae,*" he said. "No matter which way the moon darkens, left to right, or right to left, it still moves toward its death, just like we all do, don't we, you smart-ass kid?" That's what he said, more or less, and I replied, "That is undoubtedly true, Herr Speckstein," that was his name, Bernard-Louis Speckstein, my Latin tutor, he died years ago, "except for two things. First, that line you quoted is vague, because it doesn't specify in which direction one day pushes out the next, in which direction the moon darkens, and second, it is not by Vergil but by Horace, so it has nothing whatsoever to do with my objection, which was, not incidentally, very well balanced between an observation regarding a potentially insignificant error in the description of the natural world, and a generalized theorization bearing on a so-called great poet's capacity to observe and understand the fullness of the natural world in which we all find ourselves, a world that Vergil made his special subject in not one but two major works, especially because one of the two, that is the *Georgics,* is entirely about the natural world, so I hardly think quoting a couplet from Horace strengthens your case against me, if you even have a case, which I strongly suspect you don't, and by the way, that spot may actually be a melanoma." Herr Speckstein was quiet then, as he usually was after our discussions, because he knew he had lost, as he had many times before, and would many more times before I graduated from the Gymnasium, and also I think he was quiet because he suspected I might be right about his spot. Moments like that were the beginnings of my work, although I did not know it then. I was already constructing theories, already thinking, in an obscure and possibly belligerent way, about the very largest questions. I was already a scholar *in spe,* I was concerned with *natura naturans,* the nature of nature that creates itself, unseen by people like Vergil, they only see *natura naturata,* nature that is already made, a parade of clichés, they don't observe change, they don't see the logic of the world, they think nature is like a child's toy farm my father once gave me, which was advertised as "Complete with Farm Buildings, Farmer, Wife, Two Children, Horses, Pigs, Cows, Sheep, Chickens, Tractor, Plow, Harvester, Fencing, and Bags of Feed," all of them in pressed plastic, not one realistic in any way, the cows had plastic flanges projecting from them as if metal slabs had been lodged in their ribs and spines, the feedbags looked like mouse droppings, the farmer's wife's head was so small that she had no face, the sheep kept falling over, it was about as realistic as Vergil, I hated that toy farm, it was such an insult. I never forgave my father for giving it to me.

Do you have a theory about why he gave it to you?

That is not funny. But yes, I do, but no, I won't tell you. That concludes my story about my childhood, calculated to amuse and entrance you by giving just the briefest glimpse of my formation, the slightest sliver, the thinnest crescent toenail clipping of my earliest sense of myself. And now that you are lulled into a receptive frame of mind, it is time to explain my work, and above all the somewhat, or, well, no, deeply unsettling, or, well, really even terrifying, or maybe not terrifying, well, wait, yes, okay, actually deeply terrifying things my work implies about knowledge, reason, and history. I know what you're thinking. Not another theory, you're thinking, I'm going to be here all day, these theories of hers never end. Well, Samuel, this time unfortunately you are largely correct, in fact you are more correct than you know, in fact when you think you're going to be on the phone all day, you may be literally correct, but even so you are grossly underestimating the amount of time it will take for you to understand my work. You will need to devote an extraordinary amount of effort and dedication to the task. Your professional, familial, and social obligations must be carefully monitored. Your medical and health obligations, whatever they are, will have to be minimized. You won't have time for television, movies, or sporting events.

Do you have a television? Do you patronize movie theaters? Do you attend sporting events? Concerts, plays, opera? If so I am sorry, you will have to stop. Perhaps you can get refunds for your tickets. I have an exact plan laid out. You have to realize I have been working on this theory for twenty years, more if you take into account the miscellaneous early research that led up to it, including the formulas Catherine stole, even longer if you include all the notions I concocted during my early education, so, well, let's just say I have been working on it my entire professional life, even though I didn't know I was working on it until 1992. Philosophically speaking I suppose it is not possible to work on a project if you don't know that you're working on it. But once you have been working on a project for twenty years… why do I say twenty years, it is twenty-seven years, I am apparently unwilling to think about that enormous span of time, it is a frighteningly long time, no one works that long, and I can look back even further, because in a sense I have been working on this for forty years, even though I did not at first recognize what the subject was, even so, I was working in the direction of the theory, even though I didn't know it, I couldn't have told you where I was going, I was just going, but I must have been heading toward my theory, or at least in the general direction of my theory, because eventually I saw it, I don't know exactly when, certainly in 1992, but dimly before that, and so why not count the years when I didn't have any idea where I was going, think of Núñez de Balboa, he was hacking his way through the jungles in Panama looking for gold and pearls when he heard unexpected news: someone told him there was an Other Sea, that's what the person said, an Other Sea, other than the Atlantic, that's where the gold and pearls were, the person said, and so Núñez de Balboa pushed on, he fought everyone who lived in Panama, they were horrible ignorant people in his eyes, they were hiding their gold and pearls, he had some of them cut into pieces and eaten by his dogs, and the villagers fought back, he had his dogs chew on people and then he let them go as warnings, whatever it took, he just kept going, hacking his way meter by meter through the infuriating jungle, and then one day he climbed a mountain and cleared some trees and off in the distance he saw it, the Other Sea, the Pacific Ocean, the Peaceful Sea, the Water Hemisphere, the half of the entire Earth that is filled with water, the largest thing it is possible ever to discover on the Earth, limitless, awe-inspiring, blue in the distance, the jungle ended and the infinite expanse began, and he wept, you would too, and then he went down to the Other Sea, and claimed all of it, and hunted for gold and pearls, but he didn't find any, so he tortured lots of people and fed them to his dogs, okay, he wasn't an especially nice person, but the point is that when he started he had no idea there was an Other Sea, and yet he was heading toward it the whole time, that is why people say it was an expedition to find the Other Sea, it wasn't, yet it was, like my work, forty years ago I didn't know I was thinking about my theory, I wasn't, and yet I was. So it has been forty years. Most of my life! I don't especially like to think about that, it's not easy to think about it, because it means the theory is more than my career, more than my profession. It's my life, the writing is my life, it's whatever my life is in a larger sense, as they say, although I don't know exactly who says that, or what they mean by "a larger sense." That expression certainly doesn't mean a life like mine is larger than someone else's life, if anything it's smaller, it's shrunken, because I have missed so much. I don't watch television unless Paul forces me to, I refuse to go to movie theaters, films are torture, every scene in every film is torture, as I've told you, and the floors in theaters are sticky and after a while it becomes very boring to look at the architecture and the curtains. Also I have absolutely no interest whatsoever in attending large sporting events. I do not like to watch people shouting at balls. I do go to concerts, but I don't enjoy them, they make me very unhappy, all those people struggling with their instruments, pinching them, coddling them, kissing them, sucking on them, running their fingers all over them. Paul tried taking me to choral concerts, but I couldn't stand those either, all those open mouths, sometimes the singers' tongues tremble and their eyes roll shut, like it hurts to sing. I haven't traveled much, I've definitely never gone on an expedition, I haven't had a dog chew on anybody, although I can think of some people who deserve it. I don't have hobbies or skills or so-called outside interests, I'm not socially active, I avoid politics because that is just an ordinary form of mental illness, not an interesting one. I'm not larger than other people, I'm smaller, whatever my life means "in a larger sense," whatever people mean when they say that, for me it means my life is not an ordinary human life, the sort that I guess is shaped by children and love. By those standards my life is not a human life. I believe I have to say that, although I don't really want to because I love Paul and Luzia. I don't really love Hans, but maybe I do, because now I feel sorry for him, but I have to say it anyway: my life has not been a human life.[13]

Well, Catherine thinks you might be a tick.

She has known me a very long time, so there might be some truth in that. Okay, so four decades ago my theory was young, and like any infant it didn't know what it was, it wet itself and made funny burbling sounds, sometimes it spat in my face, it didn't mean to, but its mouth was full of mush and sometimes things just came out. As it grew up, my theory realized what it was. It tried as hard as it could to be the best theory it could, the deepest, the most intricate and surprising, the most handsome and dashing, the most seductive, the theory that would make people weak in the knees, or make them stand up and applaud, make them jump up and down, I don't really know how you jump down, by the way, I mean you jump up, right? and then you fall down, so it is not necessary to say someone jumps up and down, so okay, the theory would make people leap into the air and then fall down naturally by the force of gravity, and shout, "Amazing theory! Anneliese! Anneliese, that is an amazing theory!" That's what they'd yell when they saw what the theory was. Once they understood it, the attraction would be electric, it would be sexual, people who understood the theory would get excited, they'd get physically excited. Sorry, I don't know exactly what I'm saying at the moment. Paul calls my theory my secret work. I certainly don't tell the people at the university, and I don't like to talk about it at science conferences, well, actually I won't go to conferences any more, not after that experience in Canada, not after being yelled at by Penrose again, no one would go to conferences after that, and I certainly don't publish my work, I couldn't publish it even if I wanted to, there isn't any journal that would accept it. It would appear as raving, I realize that. An editor would read it and think, "Well, this person—what was her name again? Glur, Anneliese Glur, never heard of her, no, wait, I have heard of her, years ago, she published some promising things on uncultivable organisms, and then there was some scandal and she disappeared—anyway this person," the editor would think, "she has run herself into the ground, she's fallen into a rabbit's hole, she's stuck in a rabbit's hole, she has wedged herself face down, she has rammed herself into the hole of a rabbit. This material," the editor would think, "it's not wrong, exactly, but it's wrongheaded, it's not disorganized, there is sense to it, but it's muddled, anyone can just string together random thoughts and make them seem profound, I have seen so much of this kind of look-at-me-I'm-god's-gift kind of writing, it's loose, it's undisciplined, look at all those commas, it's just not that hard to do, I could do it myself, even though I gave up science and became an editor, I should never have done that, but now there's no going back, people who quit their professions make a big mistake"—not you, Samuel, although you did quit your job at the university, and that was a mistake, and then you took that job in Guelph, Ontario, that was also a mistake, but I am not talking about you, I just mean this editor would think that about other people, I mean the editor doesn't know you, how could he, I just made him up—but so the editor would read my submission and think, "This kind of thing isn't difficult, I could do it myself, maybe I should quit my job, stop reading other people's papers and start producing some of my own, if this is all it takes, I could do this, well, wait, I've never read about altruism in the context of memory, that's interesting, I've never seen metagenomics alongside a word like *phusis*, that's intriguing, but no, no, there's no connection, I don't see the links, I don't see the whole, the direction, the pattern, the reasoning, it's a jumble, it creates an effect of brilliance, but it's endless, it reads like an excerpt from a diary, it's exhausting, it's drivel. I bet this Glur person has written a lot more like this. In the end, how hard is it to string ideas together," he'd think, "to leap from one to the next as if there was no such thing as a conclusion, no such thing as a period, it seems meaningful, it appears skillful and well-informed, even plausible, but guess what, it isn't any of those things. Verbal diarrhea, that's what this is, effluent, there's no skill in pooping, everyone does it, and most people don't submit their poop to prestigious international journals like mine, so into the rubbish bin with you!" That's what the editor would think, he'd trash the essay, metaphorically of course, because it would be digital, he'd put it in the "recycle bin" but there'd be nothing to recycle, no loss, it'd be gone in a second with no second thoughts.

And yet the editor would be haunted. A week later he'd be reading someone else's paper, and he'd think, "Well, if this author had read Glur, he might have developed that thought..." and the editor would retrieve my paper from his "recycle bin" and look at it again, and again he'd think it was interesting but again he'd decide it was worthless, and he'd trash it again, into the "recycle bin," and this time he'd empty the trash, permanently delete it, erase it from his computer, because he'd be annoyed at himself for thinking my work had merit, and that would be that, or so he would think. He'd go on with his empty life, reading other people's papers, every once in a while wondering if he might go back to science and write some original papers himself, and have the career he'd first hoped for when he was a student, probably the same sorts of things you wonder about, Samuel, but he'd never do it, he'd keep his job as an editor, because they always do. He wouldn't think of me until many years later, when he was standing in front of his bookshelves, clearing them out, putting his books into boxes, getting ready to leave his office for good, and he'd pull out a book, and a whole bunch of papers would fall onto the floor, and he'd see a paper on altruism next to a paper on memory, and a paper on metagenomics next to a paper mentioning the Greek word *phusis*, and in a flash he'd see the connections, and he'd remember my paper, and he'd grasp his thinning hair in both fists, and he'd cry out in anguish, "I see! I see! Glur was a genius! A genius! Oh my god oh my god oh my god!" He'd realize that he had contributed to my oblivion, and he'd know it was too late, that I was probably dead, and he'd be right, I'd be dead by then, because this editor was quite dim, and it would've taken him his entire career finally to see that my work made sense. Of course I would have thought of him many times over the years, at first hopefully and with kind thoughts, when he might still have published my essay, and then with exasperation, and finally with a dull obstinate hatred that extended to his shriveled wife and cloddish son, and eventually even to his enfeebled grandchildren, who seemed to be stumbling about randomly in the playground where I used to go to observe them, I mean, where I would have gone, except I never submitted anything to that editor, I mean, he never existed, he's just an example, but still, I would have studied his family to determine how any human being could be so bewilderingly incompetent, blockish, oafish, doltish, mindless, brainless, and soulless, how anyone in his position could fail so utterly, so abysmally, so abyssally, how he could have failed to see the value of my work, anyway even if he had existed I wouldn't have sent him anything, he didn't deserve it, in fact I would have sent him letters explaining why I would never send anything to someone so spindly-minded, someone with the mental acumen of a roll of paper towels, no, I would have written him a series of letters explaining at length why he would never receive one of my essays, why he should just stop hoping he would ever receive one of my essays, I would write at length, each letter at least ten pages long, I would send a letter every month from the moment I first didn't send him one of my essays, to the moment I left for the hospital before I died, so when he cleared out his office he would absolutely have remembered me, in fact he would have had a special file of my letters, which his lawyer would have advised him to keep, and he would have opened the file, and consulted the index to my letters that I had thoughtfully provided, and he would have looked up "Today" in the index, and he would have turned to the appropriate letter, which I had written many years before, and he would have felt a feverish chill as he discovered my own account of that very moment, which I had predicted years earlier, in exactly the words I am using now, including his attempt to grasp his thinning hair, and his fishlike gulps, "Oh my god oh my god oh my god," including even a description of his feverish chill when he opened the file of my letters and saw that I had in fact predicted precisely what he was thinking, I had seen it all, I knew—well, wait, I suppose it wasn't too much of a surprise for him, since I invented him. I'm not sure what to say about that, I'm only trying to say I am glad he never existed, because I hated him. Anyway then he'd think, "I need to find Glur's papers, I need to edit them, I need to publish them, she has to be known, she is the Mendel of her generation, I have an obligation, it could make my life worthwhile, but no, really it's too late, let someone else do it, I have to get this office cleared out, Ferne is packing for the cruise, next week I'll be in Antalya, far away from my stale little office, I'll be lying on a beach chair at the resort, relaxing in the blazing Turkish sun, with green wrap-around sunglasses and a silly drink in my hand, and really to hell with this whole business." So Samuel, I know you are not relishing the idea of hearing my theories, but you know that some theories are actually wonderful, they are magnetically attractive. Who doesn't wish they had thought of $E = mc^2$? Such a small formula, so beautiful, so dangerous! And Euler's formula, $e^{i\pi} + 1 = 0$, I was in love with that when I was a student. It's like a person you love, but with the lumpy parts removed. And there's Freud, the idea of the unconscious, a sexy theory about sex. People's eyes get wide when they hear about it. Theories are like dark-eyed boys at the beach, or girls in red bikinis, or mysterious men in cafés who smoke cigarettes and read thick books and glower at everyone, or impossibly well-dressed women who walk elegantly but quickly, as if they are just passing through the ordinary world, theories are like powerful people who don't care what anyone thinks, their eyes shine with emotion, you look at them and think, I should have a life like that, but I don't, well I do, I mean I might, because my life's work is nearly completed. Soon, Samuel, I will be an object of desire. I have very little remaining to write. My theory is the only thing in my life bucket, my life bucket list, it's the last thing before I kick the bucket list. You know people say that expression, "kick the bucket list," it means you're going to hang yourself. You stand on a bucket, and when you're ready, you kick the bucket out and you strangle. I don't know what happens to the list.

It's kick the bucket, not kick the bucket list.

Where is the list, then?

That's different.

Anyway, those people are wrong. I found out they used to kill pigs by tying their back hooves onto the ceiling, they tied the pigs' legs to roof beams, or rafters, or they tied them to trusses, I guess those are made of beams or rafters, but so then at any rate some of those pieces of wood were called listing rafters, or listing buckets, or rafter listings, or bucket rafters, or, wait, bucket listings, that's what they were called, and when they stabbed the pigs in their carotid arteries the pigs kicked, and occasionally they kicked the bucket listings. So that was what people meant, they meant when you die horribly like a stabbed pig, you will struggle and squeal and you may kick your bucket listing. It doesn't mean you put a rope around your neck and stand on a bucket. And then I read in *The Dictionary of the Vulgar Tongue* that other people say the pig theory is not true, I mean people did call roof beams or trusses or rafter beams or roof rafters bucket listings, but that is not why people say "kick the bucket list," no, it's because of Catholic funerals. Catholics used to lay the dead person on a table, and the priest came and put a container of holy water just at the dead person's feet, so it looked like they were kicking the bucket with the list in it.

The list is different, you just kick the bucket.

Well, personally, whenever I feel like my ankles have been tied together and I have been strung upside down under a roof rafter listing, and someone has come into the room, upside down, and is walking toward me with a long knife sharpened on both sides, and he is about to insert it into my neck and open a sluice so my blood comes streaming out into a bucket, whenever I feel that way, I think: I won't wait, I will kick my own bucket, thank you very much. Anyone who is seriously ill, anyone who thinks they may be dying, thinks of suicide, it's natural. I think I would look exceptionally good stretched out on a long white table, dressed in an box-back coat and a felt Stetson, with shiny black straight lace shoes that pinch, well, it wouldn't really matter if they pinch, anyway my face powdered, my hair sprayed in place, my eyes glued shut, my mouth sewn closed on the inside so it would look like I just stopped talking, and my shiny shoes resting ever so lightly on the listing bucket. But seriously, it doesn't matter how a person looks when they're dead. All that matters is what's on the list that is in the bucket.

There is no bucket, I said. It's just a list.

People have all kinds of things on their lists. Luzia showed me. Americans love them. I want to skydive, they say, or I'd like to try a one-thousand-foot bungee jump. Or they say, I want to travel around the world, that's a recipe for misery, all those airports, all that diarrhea. Or Americans say, I want to learn French, Americans always want to learn French, they think if only they learned French they could lead a glamorous life, they could be a person of high culture, but the French are snotty, *morveux*, and their language isn't that beautiful, I speak French, it's full of *morveux* sounds, it's the language of snot and *snobisme*, it's not as bad as German, that is for certain, but it's nothing special, Italian is far more beautiful, and Romanian is even better, I think it is, anyway, although I haven't learned it, but I can't put that on my bucket list, I have no time to learn Romanian. Many people put losing weight on their bucket lists, they say, I need to get down to 140 kilos, if only I could get down to 140 kilos I would be happy, I would die happy if I were 139 kilos, that's about 300 pounds, I'd be Tinkerbell, I'd float on air if I were 139 kilos, Madame Morschmulmig probably thinks that, and maybe Rektor Morschmulmig does too, he probably thinks he could lose enough weight to jump up on a table like I can, Morschmulmig has an especially pitiful bucket listing. Once he told me he wants to steal something from a drugstore, and I said that was pitiful, and I asked what else was on his bucket listing, and he said, "I want to sneak into a concert," and I said, that is even worse, come on, tell me what you really want to do, and he said, "I want to fly in a tethered balloon, but I can't because I'm scared of heights, I'd lean over the side of the balloon and I'd lose my glasses, or I'd put my foot through the bottom of the wicker basket and then the floor would fall out and we'd all die, or a freak wind would come up and the tether would wrap around my neck and I'd strangle and my head would pop off, or the guy on the ground who holds the rope would be distracted by a video of a balloon disaster on his phone and the rope would go free and we'd rise and keep rising until there was no more oxygen and we'd all die, that has happened before, there are documented cases, or an eagle would try to land on the balloon and it would puncture, I saw a video of that once, the rip got suddenly larger and then the video got all shaky and you could hear everyone screaming, or the tether from another tethered balloon would get entangled with our tether and we'd spin around and around faster and faster and the two baskets would crash into each other and there would be a fireball, I haven't seen a video of that but I know it's what would happen, or I'd trip and stumble onto the burner and my shirt would go on fire and the tethered balloon pilot would reach for the fire extinguisher but it wouldn't be where it was supposed to be, where the law requires it to be, so he would try to put out my flames by patting me, and everyone would step back and hold their heads in their hands, and I would be horribly disfigured, those burner accidents happen every year in tethered balloons, but they keep them out of the newspapers, or a child would startle me and I'd jump overboard, or I'd see a plane on the horizon and I'd be sure it was heading straight for us and I'd jump, or there'd be a mouse in the basket with us and I'd jump, or someone would say in a loud voice, Jump! and I'd jump, because I'm naturally jumpy, it would be humiliating to die like that, with everyone looking over the edges of the wicker basket as I fell, saying, Why the hell did he do that? It was only a joke, My god he was jumpy, ha ha, but seriously, why do they let people like him go up in tethered balloons? They'd say all sorts of things to make themselves feel better as they watched me fall, getting smaller and smaller, heading right for the burnished pike at the top of a church steeple, which would at least be a spectacular gory death, and it would definitely go viral, but of course I'd miss the steeple and fall behind the church where they couldn't see me, and they'd all be disappointed. And so look," Morschmulmig told me, "I'm not going to go up in a tethered balloon, or do any of the other things on my list, I don't really want to do them anyway, please don't ask me again, Glur, I'm happy enough the way I am." Morschmulmig is a pusillanimous horrible mud-dwelling marine worm, worm numbers seven, eight, and ten, and he does not even deserve to have a bucket listing. He is craven, he is a bureaucrat. He is afraid of his own stapler. My point is these lists are wastes of time, I suppose that is why Americans like them. However, Samuel, and this is where I come to my point, I do have a list. Now listen and learn.

She paused.

Are you listening?

Of course. What else would I be doing?

My bucket listing has only one thing on it: my life's work. My theory, my writing. When that is finished I'll kick it off. Someday someone may hang me from a bucket listing and insert a double-edged knife into the soft tissue of my neck, or I may cough too hard and have an asphyxiation event involving blood and tissue fluids, it doesn't matter, what counts is that I have a list, and it has only one thing on it, my theory, my writing, and I will complete it, and then I will be finished. Luzia says I am a strange lady, but there is nothing wrong with being strange. Anyone who is not strange is just anyone.

You mean like me?

Wait, she said, I'm getting to you in a minute. So you may think I am nuts. I am a hard nut to crack, that is what Paul says. *Das Nüßlein beisset auf,* I tell him, bite my little nut. Paul says he can't bite my little nut, he says the nut is always hidden. But it's not, the work simply is what I am. I myself am the theory, I have become the theory, it's woven into me, it is woven in with what I am, sorry, I can't explain this very well, but after all it's not the kind of thing that can be explained, because my ideas have grown inside my sense of myself. Whatever that is. When I was an ordinary scientist, I did the usual sorts of work, thinking up experiments, building lab apparatus, collecting data, discovering that equation Catherine stole. Back then I was the young and promising and actually quite beautiful Doktor Anneliese Glur, and my theories were just a few sentences in my notebooks. But I want to be harsh and honest with myself. I have always had a propensity for theories, but I have never been able to actually write them, not normal ones, anyway, my theories bud, sprout, and burst, they exfoliate, and so in that sense also, my entire life has been dedicated to the gradual endless growth of this theory. I have a natural tendency—I mean it seems natural to me, meaning I don't have to think about it, not meaning that it's normal or even healthy, it undoubtedly isn't, in that sense it is a deeply unnatural tendency, this supposedly natural tendency I have, and yet its unnatural nature also seems entirely natural to me, not meaning that it's normal or even healthy, it undoubtedly isn't, this supposedly unnatural quality of my supposedly natural tendency, but meaning it seems inevitable that if I think I have a natural tendency, it is in fact unnatural—so I have a quite natural actually unnatural apparently natural tendency to worry about nature, naturally, I mean, whether natural things make sense, naturally. You know, Samuel, I do not always know exactly what I mean at the moment when I say it. I have realized that some things in the world just don't make sense, and I recognize the fact that I may be one of them. Some things in nature are just plain meaningless, like patterns left by waves on a beach, even when they spell out AG, my own initials, in curving fronds of seaweed, although I'll admit it was more like AO, or really FO, but then it happened again, only a week later, on the same stretch of beach on the Nordsee, and that time it was clearly AG, there were even periods, A.G., and the periods were made of round white seashells, imagine! The whole apparition made the hair stand up on my neck, and I didn't even know I had hair on my neck. When I ran back and told Paul about it, he said, "That's amazing," and I said, "Is there a lot of hair?" And he said, "I think it's sweet," and I felt the back of my neck, and it was fuzzy, and when I looked in a mirror in a mirror I saw the hairs were disgusting, they were long and white and wobbled like hairpins, so I went out again right away to a hairdresser. Some things are meaningless, but who knows what does not have meaning? Over the years, as my work developed, I was led into extremely complex problems. My theory did not become focused, it didn't compress down to a diamond like it did for Euler or Einstein, instead it kept getting bigger. I kept writing and writing, even though I never knew, I still don't know, I may never know, whether it all makes sense. Sometime around 1994 my work passed the point where it could be published as an essay, even if there had been an editor who could have understood it, but there wasn't, except the one I made up, and he wasn't much help, and then in 1996 it passed the point where I could sit someone down and explain it, I know because I tried, that was when my colleagues stopped answering their phones. Then around 2000 it passed the point where it could ever be published, even in multiple volumes, and now it has gone beyond the point where anyone with a career or a life or a bucket listing could ever read it. I have wondered many times if there is something wrong with my thinking, because my theory has not clarified itself into a single great idea like natural selection or a brilliant formula like $e^{i\varpi} + 1 = 0$, instead it keeps growing, it is an unlimited unnatural monster. I have not been thinking well, I have been thinking in a well, ha ha, actually I think I'm not well, and I am frightened to hear myself say that. I need to know if I am rational. Can this project of mine, this theory, this lifetime of writing, possibly make sense? If it doesn't make sense, if it is in fact not rational, then there is something wrong with me, because I have grown into the theory, I have spent so much time with it that I am not sure what I am without it. When I am in my study, like I am now, I feel crushed. The notebooks are literally heavier than I am. I decided I needed to find a reader, someone to read my manuscript. Paul agreed, or, well, actually he said, "Whatever you want, Lysi," but he was distracted because I had just shown him how unexpectedly youthful my neck looked without the hairs that had been disfiguring it. Of course Catherine can't read my work, because she would just steal all the rest of it. She suggested I ask you. She said you were perfect, she said your job was "ridiculously undemanding," that is what she said, that you had no career, you would never be promoted, you would never apply for any other job, and that you had no home life. I did some research to find out who you were, to see if you could read my work. And now I have a surprise, Samuel. In preparation for our first meeting in Frankfurt, I read all your professional publications.

I heard her shuffling her papers, or rather, my papers.

I obtained your publications thanks to your City Commissioner, Mr. Josh Salazar. I have read your early publications from when you were still an academic, three papers on amoebas found in drinking water. And I have read the four reports you wrote for the Municipal Water Department in Guelph from 2000 to 2006. You may find it useful to know that Mr. Salazar doesn't speak especially well of you. He said there were concerns about your work, and he invited me to send him a critical assessment.

More shuffling.

Hmm, she said. One moment, I am consulting my notes. Yes. Well, your way of writing is not linear. Neither is mine! But my writing has an overall, overarching, overgirding, I mean undergirding, hmm, well, I am not sure what undergirding is, it sounds like a kind of underwear, my writing has an overall, underpinning undercarriage of overarching structures underneath it. I talk in parentheses, my thoughts nest in parentheses, they nestle inside their nested parentheses. As Paul says, I open parentheses, one after another, ( ( (, and as time goes on, over a day or even, Paul says, over a lifetime, parentheses keep opening, ( ( (, but finally, in the end, they will all close, each one will snap shut with the power of a heavenly gate, ) ) ), ) ) ), and my points, all of them, from the smallest note to the largest theory, will be conclusively demonstrated and their cases definitively closed. That is what I tell Paul. Or used to. Last spring I thought of a new model. I told him my thoughts are like a rockslide, an avalanche. Stones hurtle through the air, I said, scraping and scratching against each other. "Right so far," he said. "Some rocks are pointed," I said, "some are rounded. There are blocks and shards, all of them careening, crashing, gaining speed as they fly down the mountain, my thoughts are like that," I said, "they are a chaos"—I swirled my arms around to illustrate—"but actually," I told him, "they are not just a chaos, because when they come thundering down into the valley they will fall, I am sure they will fall, I hope to heaven they will fall, they will fall together, into the shape of a house, like those American films of ranch houses in the desert swept away by atomic bomb tests, except run in reverse, from a chaos of radioactive dust back into the house from which it was exploded, my thoughts will fall together, that's what I hope," I said, "all the thoughts will assemble themselves and a great mansion will appear, perfectly finished, standing quiet under a serene sky: magnificent, a great edifice of thought, slightly pompous perhaps, but basically an object of awe, a miraculous construction, ornate, embellished with painted ceilings depicting clouds, naked people, and babies." I collapse, in German *ich breche zusammen,* it means I collapse, but in German it also says, I break together. I am breaking, I am breaking apart, but also together, I am multiply broken and disassembled, that is what I told Paul, but I am not sure he was listening, because he was on the phone. Whereas you, Samuel, in your three academic papers and your four reports for the Water Department, you demonstrate a wholly different way of thinking. You ponder and pause, your thoughts wander. You meander, you are like *Meandrina,* that's a genus of brain coral, have you ever seen those? They have convoluted gyri, like a brain, the coral looks like it thinks, but it doesn't. It is meandrine or meandrinoid, it seems to be pensive, it looks like it's intelligent, but it isn't, it's a coral. You are like that, I mean, you think, I guess, but your thinking meanders, like the convolutions of a brain coral. Your way of thinking is anguilliform, it is eel shaped. Anguilliform, one of the few great words of the English language. Your thoughts are not fractured like mine, they are anfractuous. Anfractuous, not such a great word, because it sounds like fractured but it means unfractured. Actually it's a fairly stupid word. Anguilliform is a much better word to describe you. Your writing and your thinking, and I imagine also your daily life, and I guess also your body, are eellike. Or wormlike. Actually I created a worm category just for you. You are the last worm, thirteen, and there is even an extra one, but I will not explain them to you now.[14] It makes sense that your professional specialty is protoplasmic flow, you write about plasms, endoplasm, plasmagel, plasmasol, you write about protoplasm in a language that is itself protoplasmic. You don't build thoughts, you ooze them, your thoughts squirm and ooze. It may seem I am exaggerating somewhat. Actually, all I ever do is exaggerate. It's a principle, a strategy for highlighting ideas that would otherwise be overlooked. But no, it is not an exaggeration to describe your writing in this way. I can defend everything I am saying by reading sentence by sentence through each one of your seven papers on amoebas and other microscopic creatures, examining every single sentence one after the other, just as I did for Catherine. We can do that later if you'd like. My own writing, Samuel, is entirely different. The avalanche of my thought is assembling itself. I hope it is all falling into place, every shard and fragment is finding its proper position. Tiny gleaming chips are flying onto the cheeks of Meissen shepherdesses on the grand Brèche du Benou marble mantelpiece in the royal salon just off the entrance of my generously proportioned mansion. Shards of wood, caught up in the avalanche, are flying in angled formations and settling into the cross-woven patterns of my Versailles parquet floors. Chips of ice are fusing into the ruffled feathers of the sculpted ice swan that floats in a salt-ice pool strewn with flash-frozen flowers in a silver salver in the middle of the Cuban mahogany dining table. Sorry, it's hard to stop. The point is I do not wander, despite what an inattentive person might think. My writing and speaking only seem to go off topic. Actually my thought has frightening logical clarity. My thought is *zetetic,* that is the highest standard of reasoning, it means my thought proceeds skeptically, carefully, step by step. My thinking has *pistis,* Samuel, it produces conviction, as Aristotle said. I employ the *elenctic hammer,* Socrates's sharpest tool, what Aristotle called the proof of undeniable connection. That means I examine everything I am given—every sentence, everything that is said, even in passing, even fragments and mumbles like yours or Paul's—and I determine what the speakers meant to say. I try to demonstrate, beyond any doubt and past any hope of recovery, that the statement or mumble in question is false, that the person who made it has no idea what it means, the person is in fact speaking nonsense, that is what Socrates showed, over and over, he proved that his fellow Athenians were confused, that they did not see clearly, they had no reliable knowledge of anything, they were inconsistent, they failed to understand their own lives, they misunderstood their own intentions and beliefs. That is the highest purpose of reason, the elenctic hammer. Socrates even applied it to his own speech. He determined without doubt or ambiguity that he himself did not have the slightest idea whether or not the elenctic hammer even worked. And yet he kept using it. He kept explaining to people why they did not make sense, and he kept insisting that he had no idea whether he was entitled to say that or not, because he had no idea whether he had found the best way to make sense or just a new way of pointlessly endlessly arguing. That is why Socrates was so annoying that he had to be forced to drink poison. Do you know how he spent his last evening in prison? He had a nice view of the Acropolis from his little stone cell, the ruin of it is still there in Athens, and did you know he spent that evening writing poems and composing music? Even though he had never done either thing and he was probably a terrible poet and a worse composer, he spent his last evening writing poems and composing music, because he knew with perfect certainty that he did not know how to find out whether or not he knew anything, so why not sing a stupid song or write some awful poetry? He was the wisest and most annoying person who ever lived. I operate the elenctic hammer with the full and complete knowledge that no one understands whether it works, I have it from the highest authority that no one knows whether it makes sense, I know this with *pistis,* and I use my certainty about the uncertainty of knowing what I am doing to pulverize opposing ideas with an unrelenting incremental zetetic force.

Anneliese, I can't really understand what you're saying.

That is not surprising. And so back to you. You are envious of your flowing and wandering microscopic creatures, you think like them and even desire to live like them. Psychoanalytically speaking you have a deep desire to be anencephalic or even acephalic, mindless or even headless. You wish you were as simple as an amoeba or a bacterium. As empty as water. You prefer mindless forms of life, it is an extreme form of the love for things other than people, as Waytz, Iyer, Young, Haidt, and Graham have demonstrated. You have unresolved unconscious ideations about returning to a protoplasmic state, which is exactly what Freud analyzed in *Beyond the Pleasure Principle,* Chapter 6. Your conscious mind carries on in daily life, you keep your job, probably because it is very nearly mindless anyway, and yet you are increasingly beleaguered by the desire not to think. Some deep part of you wants to lose awareness, to forget who you are. I deduced all this from your essays on amoebas and other protozoa in drinking water. For example in your first published paper, "On Previously Unknown Transport Mechanisms in Certain Amoebas: *Reticulomyxa filosa, Arachnula impatiens, Mastigamoeba longifilum,* and *M. aspera,*" a title, by the way, that would choke a rhinoceros, you wax eloquent about the way the creatures you study move. "The Impatient Spider amoeba *Arachnula impatiens,*" you write, "spreads its sticky netlike body in all directions, adhering to its prey as much as to itself"—that is evocative but not very scientific. "*Longifilum,*" you write, "makes its way softly and fluidly among the rotting vegetation, sliding past cells that boil with bacteria"—an entirely unnecessary description, which adds nothing to the paper's scientific content. Or in your second paper, "The Diminutive Nanoflagellate *Rhynchomonas nasuta* Grazes on the Eukaryotic Picoautotroph *Choricystis,*" an even worse title, by the way, you write, "This is a tiny creature, lost even in the world of water droplets," that's very poetic, although you ruin it by adding "and yet it can eat green algae, which apparently do not notice the minuscule injection of hydrolytic lipases that gently turn their interiors to a macromolecular mush." I don't even need to quote to you from your third professional paper, "A Supposition Regarding the Sexual Nature of *Vampyrella immaculata.*" It seems to be full of love for that particular amoeba. The three papers are about creatures that are largely ignored even within biology. I looked for citations of your papers, but there are none. I doubt anyone has read them since you published them. The amoebas you studied have no significance as pathogens, they aren't studied in labs, they have no ecological importance, they aren't even taxonomically significant. They aren't like *Naegleria,* the amoeba that gets into people's brains. They aren't like the *Entamoeba* that causes dysentery. They are odds and ends of creation. You are curious about overlooked creatures, you sympathize with animals no one else notices. You write as if microbiologists should drop what they are doing and culture the lovely *Vampyrella* or the tiny helpless *Rhynchomonas.* That's a typical small flagellate for heaven's sake. There are hundreds of species just like it. Eventually your desires will erupt into your conscious mind, and you will suffer an important life crisis, perhaps resulting in the end of your limited capacity for normative social behavior. You will find a way to meander like one of your amoebas, without thinking of the past or future, without knowing where you are or what you are. You are an *elucus,* Samuel, a drowsy dreamy person, not a *zetetic* person. And you are *grassatoris,* idle, someone who roams from place to place, *grassatoris,* a person who grazes, *elucus,* a person who dreams. After those three published papers you turned away from your obscure career as a biologist specialized in amoebas, a choice that at least might have resulted in some minor discoveries, and decided instead to become an expert on the amoebas that contaminate municipal water supplies. That change of topic certainly helped you get the dull job you now have, but, and this is more interesting, it was also a turn away from the difficult if unrewarding work of studying nearly unknown organisms, to the significantly less compelling study of relatively well-known organisms that affect public welfare. In short, a turn from curious private subjects to common ones. A turn apparently from interiority toward extroversion. And yet you, Samuel, are still private, unsocial, inverted, in fact I think more so now than ever.

My essays on drinking water show I'm inverted?

Every line speaks. You are inverted.

You mean introverted?

Inverted, introverted.

There's sexual inversion.

I will look into that.

Maybe you should, it might explain something.

Sorry, I am aware this is all a surprise, and it is unusual for recent acquaintances to present detailed analyses of each other, even if those recent acquaintances might later become good friends or even very good friends. You see, Samuel, I am like a person who works in a watch factory. Say my job is to assemble rotating bezel gaskets. I oil them with silicone grease, I tuck them up into the bezel groove, make sure they turn, see to it they are evenly balanced and well machined. At the coffee stand one day someone says, "You're so lucky you're working here, it's one of the few places left in the entire world where watch movements are still made by hand. You must be proud to be part of it," and I say, "Who are you?" and he says, "I'm Steffan, from the tourbillon line," and I say, "Where's that?" and he says, "Twenty feet behind you. I watch your back all day," and I say, "That is creepy, leave me alone," and he says, okay, wait, this isn't a good example. Here is a better one: I am like a fish. I swim around, minding my business, and also doing my business, because fish do their business right in the water, ever think of that? Anyway I'm swimming and evacuating and drinking and breathing and peeing and minding my own business, and another fish swims up and says, "Isn't this place paradise?" and I say, "Who are you?" and it says, "I am Stevie. I have been swimming right behind you all day, and you've been peeing the whole time." "Sorry," I say, and Stevie says, "It's fine with me. Listen, aren't the colors around here beautiful?" and I say, "I guess, but hey, I'm sorry you've been drinking my pee," and Stevie says, "It's all good," and I say, okay, wait, this isn't right either. Sorry, what I'm trying to say is that I don't know if my theorizing is admirable, because it's something I have to do. My thinking appears chaotic. I know that. In the end Paul agreed that my speeches are like avalanches, because they completely bury entire towns and everyone dies, that's what he said, I suppose that is accurate, although I don't think he meant it in a nice way, but he missed the idea that the overspilling cascade of rocks has a direction: it hurtles downhill, following a single channel, running faster and more tumultuously, but there is order inside it, he didn't see that. I told him the avalanche would come together at the bottom of the mountain, it would miraculously assemble itself into a magnificent house. My thinking is not like a normal avalanche. Those are a mess. In my case each spinning hurtling rock will find its exact place in the amazing edifice of my house, which is being built at the bottom of the slope by the avalanche itself.

Yes, you told me.

That is why I have numbered every thought I ever had, as you will learn next time we talk. Everything I have told you so far, from the first minutes of our conversation in Frankfurt, has been an introduction, a selective inventory, a preparatory or prefatory exercise, a propaedeutic inoculation to my way of thinking. It is Part I of what I need to tell you. Part II is coming soon. I never say anything accidentally. Every single thing I say is planned, everything, including three descriptions of avalanches, my incomplete inventory of worms, the Disney castle of my theories, my alarmingly simpleminded doctors, the various kinds of bucket listings, my descriptions of Hans, Paul, Luzia, Sybille Kröller, our ridiculous Rektor Morschmulmig, and even the editor who has, at least in my imagination, stubbornly refused to publish anything I sent him. I have made a selection of theories and stories as examples or models of my modes or styles and speeds or forms and kinds of argument. I have designed my stories to acclimate you to the way my thinking is enmeshed in an apparently random skein of divagations and digressions, parentheses and asides. I have contrasted my elenctic and even zetetic argumentation with your own anguilliform sort of thinking. Or meandrinoid, that's an even better word for you, because you wander in intricate ways best known only to yourself. I knew of course that it would attract your attention if I described your published papers, and I anticipated you would first be surprised, then offended, and later I hope convinced, by my hypotheses regarding your psychological makeup, your attraction to mindless creatures, and two things I haven't told you yet, your particular worm nature and your impending unmooring. And I designed, elaborated, and repeated the extended analogy of the avalanche that is chaotic and even lethal, as Paul says, but miraculously crashes into the shape of a beautiful mansion, palace, or chateau, with each little particle of rock finding its place in the edifice, careening down the mountainside and cementing itself perfectly into place, the little white pebbles shoveling themselves onto the garden paths, the toothlike slate chips flying up to the roof, cementing themselves into beautifully variegated tiles—I described this extremely unlikely sort of avalanche in order to indicate, because I cannot prove, but only hint, or rather hope, that my life's work may be an example of such an accumulation and synthesis, that it is tending toward a resplendent conclusion, that it might in fact be very near that conclusion. And I calculated everything I have said so that once you sense that my work and my thinking might actually be building toward a single perfect structure, then you should, if my introduction has been accurately tailored to your own interests, attention span, and range of knowledge, you should realize that Catherine was right, and you are the ideal reader for my work. I have studied and prepared extensively for our apparently informal and friendly conversations. I have also read documents that are available on your public record, your interactions with the law, yes, I know you were fined for illegal use of fireworks when you were fifteen, and you rode in a stolen car when you were seventeen, bad boy, and I know your addresses, from your childhood home in Watkins Glen, New York, to your present location in a condominium in Guelph.[15] I also know the price you paid for each place you have lived, and your mortgages, your car payments, your salary, your pension, your marriage license, your phone numbers and service providers, your social media, you don't seem to have many friends, do you?, your grades from grammar school to Colgate and Emory, your memberships in science organizations, now all lapsed, your subscriptions to science journals, now lapsed except the *Canadian Clean Water Journal,* my god that must be boring. I have determined you are capable of diagnosing my writing, most especially although perhaps unexpectedly because you have eely, or is that eelish, or eeloid, anyway eellike meandering thoughts, which you absorb from the puddle-like creatures you study. That is also what I concluded in the review of your work that I sent on to your supervisor, although I ended on a note of praise. "Mr. Josh Salazar," I wrote, "you may assume that I agree with your low assessment of Dr. Emmer. However I am able to say that he is as far above the pitiful duties of his job in your embarrassing little Municipal Water Department as a noble eagle is above the muddy land it surveys. You, Mr. Salazar, are a field rat in comparison to Dr. Emmer. You do nothing but scurry from one stinking burrow to another, squirreling away your feces or whatever it is rats do in their horrible tunnels, while Dr. Emmer soars above you, showing mercy, passing over your sad and frightened life like a cloud."

Please don't send that to him, I said.

Ha ha, you see I do have a sense of humor. I probably won't send it.

There was a long silence. I realized the conversation was over.[16]

She asked to meet in Basel on Sunday, after my work there was done.

Will Paul come along? I asked.

No, she said, our next meeting is important, Paul has to stay home.

# PART II

## 6

# THE THIRTEEN THEORIES

NOW, SHE SAID, planting herself in an upholstered chair in the dusky and nearly empty lounge of the Hotel Krafft, a voluminous winter coat billowing around and over her as if she were some ancient empress fallen on hard times, Now we can talk about serious things. Samuel, you are like an amoeba, or an eel, or worm thirteen. I guess you wish you could think more clearly, like a Greek philosopher or at least a somewhat less primitive marine animal.

Nice to see you again, I said. It's been a while.

Okay, hello. Actually, Samuel, I am jealous of your simple way of thinking. Oozing spilling thoughts can be relaxing, I guess, and wandering meandering thoughts may be sweet and dreamlike.

How are you? And how are Paul and Luzia? And Hans, is he doing okay?

Awful, same, same, and no. From now on, Samuel, our meetings will be more serious. You're going to have to stop speaking so much. I know you have good intentions, but please don't bother. Anyway you don't look well. I suspect you had a less than optimal experience yesterday at our local zoo. You see I am keeping careful watch on your schedule. But I don't have time to talk about your disastrous job. I want to continue explaining my ways of thinking. Your writing—the three articles you wrote when you were at university and your four reports on small creatures in drinking water—your writing leaks from one thought to another. You don't know where you're going next. You don't argue. Your mind squirms out of tight spots like a hagfish, that's a kind of jawless fish covered in slime. It has poorly developed eyes buried under its skin and a single nostril at the end of its snout. It removes its excess slime by knotting itself and pulling the knot from its head to its anus. That is probably good for its general health, I mean your general health. It is different with me, I am not a hagfish.

Well, you're rude, anyway.

I suppose so. Sorry. But Samuel, I have a serious issue. I have to understand how I think, whether I'm still rational, if I'm still making sense.

You are, sort of.

It's not funny. I am actually worried. It is hard for me to know which parts of me are not working right. Your anguilliform thinking should be perfect to infiltrate my work and show me what state I am in. You will be like one of your little *Naegleria* amoebas that worms its way into people's brains. I also think you will be perfect because you are so isolated from people. Catherine told me how you have been pushing away from your colleagues and even your family. She said you asked her for advice on how to cut down on friends and family, that really got my attention. I think Catherine is a good person to ask about that, because she is so antisocial. I am one of the few people who know about her life. But so I hope you can help me. Your allergic response to social life and your meandrinoid way of thinking should be perfect for me. You see, I tried to diagnose my own irrationality. I thought I could understand my apparently increasingly unhealthy mind using a part of it that is still sane. I made a careful inventory of all my ways of speaking and writing. I worked on that for months. I took nothing for granted, even apparently trivial things, like when I asked Paul to stop cooking me *oeufs en cocotte* every single morning forever, that was perhaps slightly rude but not irrational, although it was illogical because at that point he had not cooked *oeufs en cocotte* forever already, if he had I would surely have been completely insane after millions of years eating *oeufs en cocotte,* I would have been incapable of even imagining a day without *oeufs en cocotte,* I would have only been able to keep eating more *oeufs en cocotte,* because I would have known nothing in my endless life except eating *oeufs en cocotte,* it certainly felt that way, I just wish I would never hear those words *oeufs en cocotte* again, not to mention looking at yet another bowl of them, smelling the egg steam in my face, pretending to relish the lightly jelled albumen, trying to slurp down yet another spoonful of melted butter and egg water, I feel like I have had *oeufs en cocotte* every single morning forever, that's what I told Paul and it was unintentionally impolite, slightly exaggerated, technically illogical but nominally rational. When I studied my ways of thinking I considered everything: my logic and illogic, my rationality or irrationality, my grammar, that was difficult because sometimes I am not sure exactly what a sentence is, my choice of words, I am always careful to select words that are precise and yet as irritating as possible, my clarity, well, that is of course exemplary, my tone, I think that wobbles, veers, Paul says, careens, "you're careening again" he says, "you've run off the track again," he says, "there you go, Anni," he says, "you're off and running, no one can follow you now." Maybe I am wrong when I say he's always polite. Anyway also the form of my address, my deportment, I aim for clear and loud exposition at all times, and then my real intentions, my ultimate intentions, my unexamined intentions, my deliberately unexamined intentions, those are tricky, my inadvertently unintended intentions, those are easier, my unconscious intentions, Freud stopped there but I went on, I looked at my unconscious unintended intentions, technically those are impossible, my unconscious unintentionally repressed unintended intentions, my subconsciously unnoticed unconsciously repressed unintended intentions, my deeply repressed but entirely intended permanently unconscious unintended intentions, I examined myself relentlessly.[17]

It must have been exhausting.

Of course it was, there is no need to help me along by sympathizing. After a stupendous amount of work, I identified thirteen different illnesses in my own thoughts, thirteen problems in my thinking.[18]

Worms.

Not worms, problems. The worm list is different, even though it also has thirteen items in it, or actually fourteen, I'm not sure why that is. I will explain the thirteen illnesses of my thought to you now, one by one.

Great, I said.

This is not comedy, she replied. The worms are comedy, or well, they are coping. They distract me, they help me keep my temper. I guess that is already serious, but these thirteen illnesses are different. When I began my analysis of my ways of thinking and writing I suspected there might be some minor problems. I was aware of the fact that I am not as polite as I might be, and of course I was fully aware of my volumetric use of language. I had a hunch I am not as brilliant as Socrates, I had a suspicion about that because I usually fail to convince people of anything, even when I speak loudly and for a long time or until someone stops me. When I finish making a point and Paul says "That's it," he sounds tired, but that is okay, Socrates also exhausted people, even when he talked to great athletes they got tired, they had to sit down, Apoplexes wiped his brows, that is what Plato writes, after people talked to Socrates they went home and slept for days, that is what Plato says, Idiomentus slept for two days after he talked to Socrates, Plato says, and he dreamed he was on fire, even the great Ajax moved away from Athens and bought a bungalow on the beach. Socrates was famous because he never stopped arguing. When does he eat? people asked, When does he rest? Once, I came back into the kitchen after breakfast because I had forgotten to make a certain point, actually I hadn't forgotten, I simply wanted to clarify one of the points I had raised at breakfast, and there was Paul with his hands on the countertop, leaning over. I could see he was exhausted. When he heard me he flinched. It was quick, but I saw it. He flinched like you would if you saw a bee come flying at you, it only lasted a moment, but I saw it, and I realized he thinks of me like a pest, a kind of buzzing pest, like Socrates, that's the way people thought of Socrates, and I blushed with pride, you know people thought of Socrates as an *oistros,* a gadfly, and a *myops,* a pest, Socrates called himself that, he pestered people until they killed him, and people said he was *anopheles,* meaning useless or troublesome, like the *Anopheles* mosquito that carries malaria, so then I thought, maybe that's not so good either, but anyway probably to Paul my words are an annoying buzzing, an incomprehensible whining drone, and that's when I realized that he may not say "That's it" because he is too tired to respond, but because I no longer make sense. I was so excited by that discovery that I ran out of the room again, but then I ran back in and said, "Paul! I just realized something!" and he flinched again, and then right away he looked up and waited for me to keep talking, but then I realized what I had to do, so

I turned around and ran back to my study. I began my notes on the different ways I speak and write. I was pitiless with myself, remorseless and brutal, I was honest, unrelenting, and unremitting, I was a *myops* to myself, I kept attacking myself, I stung and bit myself repeatedly, incessantly. I was like a dance fly, a robber fly, a snipe fly, a stiletto fly, those are annoying little flies with ugly heads, they bite other flies, they sting them and chew on them.

Did Socrates bite himself?

My illustration may be slightly confused. I don't have time to stop and figure that out. Eventually I discovered that my thinking and talking do not have just one or two simple disorders, like your own protoplasmic peripatetic peristaltic thinking. I have contracted thirteen different diseases of thought, which have infected my talking, writing, and reasoning and rendered it very nearly impossible, I hope not entirely completely impossible, but virtually actually potentially impossible, for me to make sense at all. I imagine the thirteen diseases of my thinking as a ladder that has been lowered into the well where I live.

She glared at me like a teacher waiting for the attention of her dimmest pupil, and then held out her arms as if she was grasping the rails of a ladder.

There is standing water down there, she said, and the last rungs are hidden. The ladder begins at the lip of the well, the tops of the rails are in sunlight, but the rungs below are in shadow. The ladder has thirteen rungs. Each one is a disease of my reason. They lead down from daylight into the sour cold depths where I spend my time. The first diseases of my reason are harmless but irritating, like gnats, like hiccups, they are hiccups of logic, logic hiccups, not logical hiccups, hiccups in logic. The lower rungs are not so harmless, they are like tumors, or worse.

Her hands fell, without her noticing, into her lap.

These thirteen diseases in my thinking fall in an inexorable downward sluice away from normal sense. Away from light, reasoning, and logic, down into a morass of fetid thought burps, that is where I live now, this is where I am when I speak to you, *mi'ma'amakim,* do you know what that means? *Mi'ma'amakim keraticha hashem.* Never mind, I can't explain everything. You know, Samuel, my thought has tremendous peaks, my best thoughts reach colossal heights, all the way to a nearly transcendent transcendental *supre-*

*mum,* but my depths are deeper than my heights, my *infimum,* my lowest thoughts, are down there at the bottom of a cursed *chute,* at the end of a long *déchéance.* I think something in me wants to fall. I have an interest in decay, I want to see what is at the bottom of the well. *Mon désir de la déchéance et de la chute* are my best qualities, *même s'ils m'ont coûté ma propre perte.* Do you know what that is from? Never mind, you may find out eventually. I will now name the thirteen diseases of my thinking, one by one. Please pay attention. First is the Avalanche Theory. You have heard it before, so I will not repeat it, although I do not think you appreciate just how wonderful the house will be, how every droplet of mud and each tiny shard of rock in the tumultuous avalanche of my thinking will find its perfect place in the house they are miraculously assembling at the end of the valley. It is the only theory that has a happy outcome, although I am aware at every moment it is a fantasy. In the Avalanche Theory, no matter how ferocious things get, in the end the landslide of my thinking composes itself into a chateau of beautiful ideas. A chip spalled from the highest beetling cliff at the top of the mountain will tumble and spin for miles and then suddenly snap into the gilded Baroque picture frame of the enormous preposterous painting of me that will decorate the landing of the imperial staircase at the end of the remarkably well-proportioned grand hallway past the ample entrance and noble propylaeum. Another shard will fill a tiny gap—

I understand the theory, actually.

It will fill a tiny gap between the wet toes of a sculpted cherub who urinates into the fountain at the center of the entertaining and mysterious labyrinth hedge at the far end of the great reflecting pool. Another piece will complete the arc of the shackle of the Burg-Wächter industrial padlock that will secure the monumental wrought iron griffin-headed gates of the mansion, which are to prevent annoying people from visiting me while I am working. Also a rose-colored flake of rock will spin through the air, in through an open window, and then up my stone Renaissance triple-helix spiral staircase, into the master bedroom and onto the hand-carved rose marble frieze above the grand fireplace, where it will complete the tip of—

Really, I understand the Avalanche Theory. It's not especially rational, is it?

The flake will complete the tip of the parched tongue of the exquisitely carved bas-relief of the medieval borometz, that is my mythical animal, you have not heard of it before, so please don't interrupt me, I am in perfect control of my exposition. And I believe it is at least partly rational, but I don't want to talk about that right now. The borometz, the medieval Scythian lamb, symbolizes my life. It will be carved everywhere in my imaginary mansion. The borometz is a sheep, except that its umbilical cord is intact and attached to the ground beneath it, its umbilical cord is a kind of stem that links it to the earth, and as it grazes, the umbilical trunk becomes erect, it lifts the borometz off the ground until its legs dangle above the pasture, and the borometz stretches its neck down to graze, but can no longer reach the grass. It sticks out its tongue to get one last blade, and in the rose marble carving you will see the long tongue of the medieval Scythian borometz lamb straining downward, trying to lick up just one more tuft of grass, but the umbilical trunk keeps hardening and growing and the borometz rises above the pasture, and then it can no longer eat or drink, it gets weak and dizzy, its dewy eyes close, and in that way the borometz becomes a tree. Its wool mats into leaves, flowers sprout from it and they grow seeds, and the seeds become nuts, and before you know it, wait, do seeds grow into nuts? I think most nuts already are seeds, but not all seeds are nuts, because nuts are technically fruits, I mean they grow on trees, all nuts are fruits, or parts of fruits, I am not sure what kinds of seeds are not nuts, small ones I guess, wait, no, strawberries have tiny nuts on them, and besides, strawberries are not berries, they are fruits, but a nut is a kind of fruit, but most fruits are not nuts, and all fruits have seeds, but those seeds are not nuts, that is an example of the sort of seed that is not a nut, but no, the seeds that are nuts are also fruits, anyway the borometz tree grows nuts, they are borometz nuts, and at the end of the growing season the borometz tree sheds its nuts, they drop to the earth and sprout into lambs, and the little lambs graze the grass at their feet, but they cannot walk too far, because they are attached to the earth by little umbilical cords, and at first the little borometz lambs graze in circles, as far as their umbilici will let them go. They are like tethered dogs, they go around in circles. They innocently graze in the shade of the borometz tree without realizing it's their mother. The borometz symbolizes me because an umbilicus connects me to my writing, because my work is what keeps me alive, so the pasture is my work, and also the borometz symbolizes me because it is a mother to its lambs, even though it has nuts and an erection, but I try not to think about that, but at the same time my work is killing me, pushing me farther and farther away from solid ground, in which case the woody erect umbilical trunk is my work, getting stronger and pushing me out of my own life, and the pasture is people, because my work is lifting me away from them, and the borometz symbolizes me because I don't have much time left as a rational person, I am changing and becoming plantlike, but I never was rational because I was never a normal sheep, the kind without an umbilical cord that ties it to the ground. Actually, the borometz symbolizes me because I don't understand it and I assume it does not understand itself. I mean, how could it? How could a creature so unnatural understand itself, how could it ever hope to make sense of its life? When it is young it may think it is a lamb, that would be natural. Soon it senses something is wrong because it cannot walk freely around the pasture, and then it realizes it can no longer reach the pasture, and then it begins to starve, and all it can think about is stretching out its tongue to get one last blade of grass. It no longer has the energy to philosophize about what sort of creature it is. Once it becomes a tree it will probably not be able to think very clearly at all. Most trees do not think, but some do, I will tell you about that in three hours and two minutes. I think I may be most like a borometz sapling, because I am aware I should not have an umbilical cord, and I am often hungry.

Three hours and two minutes?

Approximately, depending on how quiet you are and how much additional explanation you require. That is about as well as I can explain why the borometz is my symbolic animal, and so anyway I will impress its likeness on every dish towel in the imaginary mansion of my work, which will emerge miraculously from the avalanche and dust of my notebooks. The avalanche is a defect in my thinking because thought is not supposed to be cataclysmically torrential and disarranged, even if every particle of it hopes and dreams it will find a place in a magnificent edifice of thought which however does not yet exist. Perhaps the borometz is the emblem of the Avalanche Theory, I think it would be nice if each of my thirteen theories has its own talismanic animal, don't you? But what do borometzes have to do with avalanches? If only I knew. You have also heard about the second defect in my thinking, the Disassembly Theory. Clearly my skin, my nails, and my left lung are disassembling. I have no idea what goes on inside my abdomen, but I imagine it's the same in there. Little slabs of liver probably slip off, blobs of kidney float into my bloodstream and get washed away. Have you ever held a liver in your hands? It's heavy but it's watery. It's easy to slice into pieces. My pancreas is like silken tofu, it isn't holding together, it's probably coming apart into slivers, I can feel them softly sliding, sliding softly in my omentum like snowflakes descending into mucilaginous darkness. I am losing tissue I used to have on my arms and thighs, the flesh there is becoming lumpy, my arms are lumpy, there is watery material between the lumps, it makes me shiver to feel the flesh under my upper arms, if I roll it between my fingers it feels like a down pillow that has gotten soaked and the feathers are stuck together in clumps. My wonderful silver hair keeps falling out. When I scratch my ears clouds of flakes fill the air. My entire body is like one of those Stalin-era apartment buildings where the concrete has become stained and cracked and detaches in chunks. The Disassembly Theory is not as entertaining as the Avalanche Theory, because if it is true then there will not be any mansion, nothing will come together. The Avalanche Theory is a mess but it is fun. I think I have a talent for interior design. There are seven parts to the Disassembly Theory, you know most of them already: body, career, mind, family, memory, language... I haven't told you the last one yet, you have so much to look forward to! All seven are all crumbling. I am not sure how I managed to make a theory of thirteen kinds of faulty reasoning when my mind is actually an example of the second of them. Also I am offended by the fact that the third dimension of the Disassembly Theory, that is my mind, actually contains all thirteen theories, because they are theories of how I think, which means I actually started my explanation inside the third dimension of the second level.

You lost me there.

It is simple. I suffer from thirteen kinds or levels of unreason, and probably each of them has seven dimensions. The second level contains all the dimensions, just as the third dimension includes all the levels.

You lost me again.

The thirteen levels expand from the third of the seven dimensions, which is also the third dimension of the Disassembly Theory. Okay? It is not especially rational, I know, and I should probably try to figure out how it happened, but I am comforted by the fact that it is not easy to think about your own thinking, because we are all by definition inside our thinking, I use my thinking to think about my thinking, I am my own *myops,* I try not to use my diseased thinking to diagnose my diseased thinking, but I cannot be sure I'm not using one of my thirteen diseases to diagnose the others. When I think about this I feel like a kangaroo looking for its navel. Is the navel in its pouch? Or is the pouch a kind of giant navel? Does the umbilicus go into the pouch? All mammals have navels, except Adam and Eve of course, so marsupials must have navels. But where are they? The borometz's umbilicus goes into the earth, that certainly doesn't make much sense. Maybe I have an issue with umbilici. Whenever I try to figure out how I made a theory of thirteen kinds of ruined logic when my own thinking is an example of the second one, or rather my thinking is an example of the third dimension of the second of the thirteen kinds, whenever I puzzle over this I start thinking about kangaroos. I should probably try to figure that out too. It seems clear the kangaroo is the talismanic animal of the Disassembly Theory, because the Disassembly Theory has a pouch and in the pouch there may be lots of other little theories, and some of them grow up, and they get to be bigger than their mother, so big they just tuck her away in their pouch. Or something like that.

Sure you're not confused about how babies work?

Please. You will have plenty of time to study the ladder. The third disease of my reasoning is called the Multiple Engastration Theory. This one is slightly disgusting, do you know about engastration? It is when you stuff one animal inside another one, for the purpose of having an especially delicious meal. This is how my thinking sometimes goes, I stuff perfectly nice ideas inside other ideas, I sew up little ideas inside bigger ones. A cook might put a songbird into the belly of a quail, that would be engastration, or a songbird into a quail into a chicken, or a songbird into a quail into a chicken into a duck, or a songbird into a quail into a chicken into a duck into a goose, or a songbird into a quail into a chicken into a duck into a goose into a turkey, or, here is one from a recipe I read, a cook might place a single caper into a small anchovy and stuff them into a large Greek olive and put that in the stomach cavity of a little garden warbler, stuffed into a bunting stuffed into a lark stuffed into a thrush stuffed into a quail stuffed into a lapwing stuffed into a plover, I always thought a lapwing was a plover, maybe it is supposed to be a golden lapwing or a northern lapwing, those are rare, you would have to pay people to go hunt one, maybe it is supposed to be a black-bellied plover or a golden plover, those are bigger, but not much, and what if you went to all the trouble and expense of having someone shoot a northern lapwing and it turned out to be too big to stuff into the golden plover, or if you had someone shoot a golden lapwing and it was too big to stuff into the golden plover, then what? The whole thing seems difficult and expensive, and some of those birds must be protected. I ate a lark once, it was horrible, tiny and greasy. Paul ordered a pair of rabbits, by the way, coated with full-strength mustard, cooked in a casserole with bacon, carrots, tomatoes, and spring onions, covered in button mushrooms and breadcrumbs, which I thought was much less appetizing, but when he saw the lark curled up in its little clay pot with its beak and its feet sticking up he left the restaurant and stood in the parking lot until I paid and came out, and then he drove me to a pharmacy and bought me a bottle of wintergreen mouthwash, anyway, some kind of plover stuffed into a partridge stuffed into a woodcock stuffed into a teal stuffed into a guinea fowl stuffed into a duck stuffed into a chicken stuffed into a pheasant stuffed into a goose stuffed into a turkey stuffed into a great bustard, do you know what a great bustard is? It is a very big bird, the only bigger birds you could stuff a bustard into would be cassowaries, emus, or ostriches, and that would make a single enormous multiply engastrated illegal expensive bird-forward dish, or how about lots of little auks into a seal, they do that in Greenland, or quail eggs into pigeons into a ram, they do that in Greece, or chicken sausage stuffed into a lamb belly packed in a mutton shoulder, they do that in Macedonia, or a capon into a baby pig, they do that in Portugal, or pigs' feet wrapped in pork intestine bags stuffed in a cow's stomach, they also do that in Portugal, or newly hatched chicks stuffed into the womb of a suckling pig, they also do that in Portugal, I don't know what is wrong with Portuguese people, or even quail eggs packed into a fish placed in a goose inserted into a sheep pushed inside a camel, I read that recipe in the *Milwaukee Journal Sentinel,* it was published in 1958, I don't know why people in the United States in 1958 were obsessed with stuffing things into camels, and I hope I never find out. But so this is how my mind sometimes works. I hide my simple clear ideas inside the bellies of bigger and often worse ideas. I put one idea inside another until my brain is packed with thoughts, each inside a larger one. Tiny tasty thoughts are hidden deep inside and gross charred thoughts are on the outside, and the whole thing exudes a nauseating odor, it drips with sickening juices that come from all the ideas crowded inside each other, you may even recognize this Multiple Engastration Theory from our previous conversations because you have been dining on it for some time, I have been introducing myself to you by slitting open each thought to get to the next one, and I can well imagine your impatience, how you wish you had a great saber-like knife to cut me open so you could see all the way inside, right to the choicest smallest morsel that began the entire process, but not so fast, that is not how the Multiple Engastration Theory works, it is an ongoing envelopment of thought, an onion forever growing new skins, and did you know engastration is also a natural process, that the body forms onion skins to protect itself from injuries? It happens in Charcot-Marie-Tooth disorder. A nerve swells, and to protect itself it grows a skin, and then it swells more under the new skin, and the skin grows a skin, skins keep growing around the nerve. I told my dentist that I have that disease, he said it is not a disease of the teeth, it is named after three people, and one of them was called Tooth, Howard Henry Tooth. I was embarrassed, so I left immediately and went to my doctor and told him I had Charcot-Marie-Tooth disorder, and he said, "Do you have hand pain or hand tremors?" I wasn't sure. "Or scratchy insoles? Do you have drop foot?" I was about to ask him what that was, but he was clearly uninterested in me, he only wanted to show off his knowledge of Charcot-Marie-Tooth disorder, so he kept asking questions. "Do you have chronic fatigue?" he asked. "Muscle atrophy? Curled toes? Grasping disorder? High arches? Do you at least have claw toes?" and when he was finally finished I said,

"Probably," and then I was embarrassed again and I left immediately. So the body engastrates itself, it forms new protective skins. There are also sclerosing inflammations of the bile ducts, I am almost certain I have those, but when I told my doctor, he said, "Do you have pain in the upper right part of your belly? Do you have a fever or chills? Have you been vomiting? Are you nauseous? Do you have clay-colored stools? Is your urine dark brown?" and I said, "Maybe," and he said, "Do you know about Munchausen's Syndrome?" and I said, "Do you know St. Anthony is the patron saint of condescension?" and he said, "Dr. Mrs. Glur, you do not have sclerosing inflammations of the bile ducts," and I was embarrassed again so I left immediately, and the body also protects itself by growing new skins in cases of neural fibrosis, and I think I have that also, because I have Lisch nodules in my eyes, they are very small, you can't see them in this light, but if we go outside and stand in the sun, and I stand very close to you, so our noses are almost touching, and you look into my eyes, you will see little nodules nestled among the colorful strands in my irises, like red berries on a vine, those are Lisch nodules, they are the sign of deep disturbances throughout my nervous system, each one is formed like a minuscule onion, tightly wrapped in many skins, except that if you peeled them my eyes would fill with blood. I tried to show my Lisch nodules to my ophthalmologist, but he said, "Just pop one of those breath mints in your mouth," and then he proceeded to blind me with that ridiculous machine they use to impress their patients, and when I could no longer see him at all he said, "You're fine, take the nurse's hand and she will lead you out," and the body also engastrates itself in cases of laminated periosteal formations where shells of bone form over fractures, I informed my doctor I have one of those in my thumb, and he took my thumb and wiggled it all around, and said, "We can test for this, Dr. Mrs. Glur, but the test is excruciatingly painful and takes six hours," and I said, "Ha ha," and he said, "You got me, Dr. Mrs. Glur," and I said, "You know, you are the nastiest person who has ever been given a medical degree, you have the empathy of a swarm of flies." Anyway, my body forms protective skins around its injuries, just as my mind encases thoughts one inside another. That is the Multiple Engastration Theory, it is a combination medical condition and recipe, and by the way, there is no talismanic animal for the Multiple Engastration

Theory, because the theory eats talismanic animals, it sews them up inside each other and cooks them into a single steaming heap of meat, so we will not need to talk about talismanic animals again. Kangaroos are especially annoying talismanic animals, because clearly they belong to the Engastration Theory and not the Disassembly Theory, and besides, I don't want to spend my time herding imaginary talismanic animals. The Multiple Engastration Theory is the third of my thirteen theories of the diseases of my reason, the third rung of the ladder leading down into the well, the ladder that starts in bright sunlight and goes step by step into the clammy darkness of the stinking standing water at the bottom of the well, where I live, mulling over the remnants of my thoughts, looking wistfully up toward the little circle of daylight so far above me. The fourth theory is the Jigsaw Puzzle Theory. You have heard a simple version of it, but there is more. By the way, Samuel, these first theories are a comical prelude. The Avalanche Theory is heartfelt and whimsical but unsound. I am fully aware no chateau will ever appear. The theory is rationally articulated but delusionally unrealistic. The Disassembly Theory is topologically amusing, but that's actually a very serious problem, it undermines everything, so I will ignore it. The Engastration Theory is lighthearted but ghoulish, it's mischievous but bloody. Things don't turn out well when you sew small animals into the body cavities of larger ones. The Jigsaw Puzzle Theory is the last entry in my comical prelude. It is also whimsical but in addition it is infuriating and disorienting. This is how it goes. Sometimes my thoughts are in bits like the pieces of a jigsaw puzzle, all scrambled up in the box. Then I'm a muddled mess, and I need to sort out my ideas, get them in order. I set all the thought pieces out in piles. Edge pieces here, blue sky pieces there, dark blue in another pile, they are probably watery thoughts, cloud pieces, those are cloudy thoughts, and so on. All the pieces of my thoughts in piles. Next I arrange each pile into rows. Then I pick up a blue sky piece and run it down a row of blue sky pieces, looking for a match. Usually I don't find one, but sometimes I do, and soon I have clumps of sky. Edge pieces are especially interesting, those are thoughts that seem to be at the end of my thinking, right at the border of my thinking, the edges of my thought, where my thinking stops, so naturally I am interested in them, I want to see how they connect.

I have an idea like that about puzzles, I said. I wanted to tell you before.

Samuel, everyone has jigsaw puzzle stories. Mine is infuriating and disorienting, and I very much doubt your story is anything more than a nostalgic anecdote about your childhood. We can't all drabble on about jigsaw puzzles. So in a while I have the whole rectangular frame, which is of course a huge disappointment, because my thinking cannot possibly have a perfect rectangular frame, but that's one of the reasons why people like jigsaw puzzles, they're so reassuring. Then I have a mass of dark blue, clearly a lake or a pond, and soon the picture of my whole thought starts to come into view—and that is when I notice there is a bird in the puzzle, it sits on the finial of a gate post at the entrance to a driveway by a beautiful garden in front of a lovely unpainted but tastefully stained house at the foot of the peaceful blue Jura mountains, that's the picture. The bird is the single beautiful piece, my most perfect thought, the centerpiece of my thinking. But as you know, in this case there are three identical pieces with the little eye and the pink feathers of the breast of the bird. It is infuriating, I become infuriated at the company, Lots-O-Fun Puzzles, well they are not, the puzzle seems to have been designed to enrage people, to make people feel ridiculous. I look at the box, and it says the painting was done by Gaspard Winckler and is called *Jura Mountain Landscape with a Single Gimpel.* A gimpel is a perfectly harmless rosy-breasted bird, but it is only a small detail in the painting, and why did the artist use that expression, *a single gimpel?* The title is perplexing, as if it was a joke aimed just at me. I became disoriented, I wasn't sure what to do. As I told you when I called you in Tennessee, I decided to count all the pieces. There are 2,591 thoughts in my mind, but there should be 3,000, so there are 409 thoughts missing, and some thoughts are duplicates of other thoughts, so I can never put my thoughts in order, I can never make the beautiful picture on the box lid. This is the fourth illness in my thinking, the Jigsaw Puzzle Theory. My thoughts are like the pieces of the exasperating badly made Lots-O-Fun Puzzle by Gaspard Winckler. The Lots-O-Fun Puzzle looked good in the store, it made me think I could spend a few pleasant evenings assembling a harmless picture of a house with a garden and a gate with a post and a bird, but that was just a ruse to show me how scrambled my thoughts are, the puzzle is a heartless demonstration of the chaos of my thinking, and the worst is the picture on the box, such a nice nostalgic painting of a house with a garden and a gate with a post with a finial and a bird, because not only can I never assemble that picture out of the absurdly mixed-up, repetitious, defective set of pieces, but I can never forget the picture of how my mind is supposed to look, the lovely property set amidst the peaceful blue Jura mountains, I can never have the mind that I have been promised by Gaspard Winckler and the sneering people at Lots-O-Fun Puzzles, never be pretty as a picture, never make full sense ever again, so I get angry and begin forcing pieces together, making a perverse forced-together picture by smashing thoughts into each other with my thumb until they sort of fit, even though some of the little tabs tear and even snap off, like babies' heads, but I actually enjoy that, I make a monstrous bird with three eyes, it is the imp of puzzle perversity. This is the Jigsaw Puzzle Theory, it describes how my thoughts just will not fit together, how I force them and end up making a violent frightening childish mess. The puzzle is my mind, the pieces are my thoughts, the beautiful picture on the box is like the idea we all have that our lives make sense. The Jigsaw Puzzle Theory has no cure. I cannot stop trying to force my thought pieces into a picture. At night I crush and mash thoughts together and stare at the picture on the box, I loathe that picture, it tortures and taunts me. *Jura Mountain Landscape with a Single Gimpel,* it's like everyone at Lots-O-Fun Puzzles is laughing at me, like the little bird with three eyes is sneering at me. The Jigsaw Puzzle Theory also has an Appendix, it is the only one that has an Appendix, each of the thirteen should have one, but for some reason only this one does. The Appendix is a question: Why doesn't everyone have this same problem? And the answer is: Because they never open the Lots-O-Fun Puzzle box. They just look at Winckler's lovely painting and imagine their lives are just like that. Most people have an idealistic picture of the way they think, they imagine they think in beautiful images. When people talk they just trade jigsaw puzzle boxes, "Here, check out my perfect house in the Jura mountains," "Oh that's lovely, and you can have a look at my glittering white beach house," "Gorgeous! and this is when we were married, that is my Handsome Doting Devoted Socially Responsible Husband in 3,000 pieces, and here's my Perfect Family that comes apart into 150,000 pieces."

It never occurs to people to actually open the boxes and look inside. If they did at first they would be delighted, "Oh my," they'd say, "What fun, let's assemble delightful pictures of our lives," and only later would they realize there are duplicate pieces and missing pieces, and at that point most people would just toss the puzzles out and never think of them again, but I cannot go back, there are 2,591 thoughts in my mind and they do not fit together, and yet there is also a perfect image to mock and infuriate me. The next time someone says to me, "Oh look at my perfect life, just like a painting," I will grab the Lots-O-Fun Puzzle box, open it and spill out the pieces, and I will start violently mashing them together until I have created a half-digested nightmare image. "Is your perfect life like this?" I'll say. "Like this?"

Okay, that is worse than my idea. You know most people think jigsaw puzzles are a relaxing hobby.

I already explained to you that I hate jigsaw puzzles, and I do not wish to be relaxed, and I hope I never develop a hobby. The Jigsaw Puzzle Theory is the end of the comical prelude. I hope you enjoyed it. Now we come to the unpleasant theories. The fifth one, Samuel, is the Unspooling Thoughts Theory. That is when my mind is like a spool with thread wound around it. The thread is neat and tightly wound, except for the loose end, because the thread has not been secured, it has not been pulled into that little notch they make in the spool, or is it a bobbin, I don't think bobbins have those little notches, but spools do, in the rim of the spool, there is a small cut there, in the edge of the rim of the top of the wooden spool, at an angle so the thread can go obliquely down into it, you are supposed to pull the loose end into the cut in order to secure the thread and keep it tightly wound on the spool, but I have not done that, because it's too finicky for me and I am impatient and my eyes aren't sharp enough and I don't dare feel for the cut because I might get cut by the cut, so the loose end of my thought hangs off the spool and when I pick up the spool to talk, my mind unspools. I discovered this fifth theory when I was looking back at my work of the last couple of years. When I write in my lab notebooks, I look at the page I've just written and the sentence that is forming, and I am generally optimistic, because I see my thought unspooling onto the page. It is a pleasure to see a single looping line moving across the page and making sense out of blank paper. I glance back at the paragraph before and remember my frame of mind when I wrote it, it was a little different, I was thinking of something else, I can't quite remember what led up to it, so I turn back to the page before, to see where the thread of my thought came from, and the page before is also filled with sentences, lovely continuous looping thoughts, but I don't like some of them. I wish I hadn't written a couple of them, they were badly formed, I remember I was just writing, as I do, hoping I would make sense, but things don't always work out the way you expect them to, do they? So then I become anxious, I keep turning back, page after page, I follow the thread of my thoughts backward until I come to the beginning of the notebook, which I started last spring. I am filled with pity and compassion for the confused person who wrote those pages, she was flailing, she didn't want to give up after so many years of work, but she had no idea where she was going, she just opened yet another notebook and began to write, and so I look around to find the notebook that came before, the one from last winter, and I see my study full of notebooks, dozens of them, actually over a hundred. It is dizzying, thinking of the thread of my handwriting unspooling over years of work, from one notebook to another, from some long-forgotten tangle, bravely and blindly moving on to the blank page. I return to the sentence I had just written. Those few lines are the end of the thread, but the beginning isn't visible, because the thread comes curling around the edge of the paper from the page before, and the one before that, my sentences are chained together like skydivers falling in formation, except without parachutes, all of them holding hands plummeting to their deaths, the thread leads back to the notebook from last winter, the sentences run back and back, they fill the notebooks that fill my study, thousands of pages, written over many years, my theory is really one long sentence, and here I am, very near the end of my long sentence, a sentence as long as most of my working life, and I see it unspooling toward me out of tangled confusions I had long forgotten. I am like a girl in some children's story who opens a closet and sees a red ribbon on the floor. She picks it up. It is attached to something in the back of the closet, but it's dark there and she can't see anything. She gives the ribbon a tug, but it seems to be tangled or tied to some object in the darkness. Suddenly it pulls back. She freezes. The ribbon pulls again, harder. There is something there in the dark. She takes a step forward, but no, no, that is a stupid story. Okay. I am like a doctor who is trying to pull a parasitic worm out of a patient. Its head is sticking out of a wet wound above the patient's heart. I have the end of the worm wound around a wooden tongue depressor, and I reel it in like a fisherman, but I can't pull it all out, and the patient is writhing. I wonder how long the worm might be. The worm is stretched tight around the tongue depressor, and I am afraid it may also be wound around the patient's heart. If I pull too hard the worm will break and the rest of it will be lost inside her body. I pull again, and the patient goes pale and her eyes roll up in her head. Hmm, that won't end well. Okay, here is a better story. I am like a little girl on a beach who sees a long seaweed thrown up by the ocean, a kelp, a giant kelp. She lifts it up, but it is heavy, its end is still in the sea, and she realizes it is living, it is still connected to its undersea roots. The seaweed goes down into the water, under the surf and deep down into the ocean, hundreds of feet, maybe miles. She grips the end of the kelp, the very last frond. It's salty and slippery. She looks out over the ocean. Her eyes are wide and empty. Then she walks into the sea, keeping her hands on the kelp as she goes. She will drown with her little hand on the kelp.

My god.

Sorry, that story is even worse. Okay, so I am like Norbert Casteret. He was climbing in the Pyrenees mountains in January 1925, making his way up a slope of boulders, and he stopped for a rest. He felt a warm breeze coming from behind him, and when he turned around he realized humid air was coming out of a small cleft between two boulders. He looked in but he couldn't see anything. Later he came back with a pry bar and a flashlight and he moved a boulder to one side and squeezed into the hole. It turned out to be a passageway, only two feet high, sloping gradually downward, and he crawled and pulled himself along it, hundreds of feet into the mountain, and finally he came to a room-sized cave chamber with a sloped floor, booming and whistling with the sound of warm air being forced through it, always a wonderful sign for a caver because it means large passages are ahead, and at the lowest point of the floor of this chamber there was a hole, like in a toilet, that is where the air was coming from, so he lay on his stomach and slid down toward the hole, and then went down into it, head first. The toilet hole went down and around, like a corkscrew, and got smaller and tighter. Casteret was like a worm inserting itself into something, it doesn't matter what, well okay, never mind the worm idea. The passage constricted. Blood rushed to Casteret's head. He was afraid he might get stuck there, head down in the corkscrew passage deep inside the mountain, but warm air was whistling in his face so he knew there was more cave ahead, and just when he thought he couldn't squeeze any farther, it opened out, and he saw nothing but darkness below him. He was upside down, pushing on the sides to keep himself from falling into empty space. He pointed his light down, but below him was nothing, it was pitch black. He couldn't see the bottom or even the walls. He was hanging from a hole in the ceiling of an enormous cave chamber. The air boomed and echoed. He fished out a coin and dropped it and counted the seconds, but he never heard it land. He was terrified. He squeezed and pushed his way backwards, back up into the corkscrew, head down, feet up, and then forced his way up into the cave chamber, then back along the long passageway and out onto the mountainside, and he never returned. He had followed the unspooling thought, and when it became genuinely frightening he gave up and turned back.

Well, he would have died.

Of course. Later he persuaded some people from his town to go explore the cave. The next year Pascale Ysaye went into the cave. He got to the place where Casteret had hung upside down, but then Ysaye lost his grip and fell into the darkness. Two years after that a crew of professional cavers went in with mountaineering equipment, and lowered themselves into the cave chamber. They found Ysaye's body. He had fallen 481 feet.

Who is Casteret?

Me.

So who dies?

Okay, she said, you are right, I am Ysaye and Casteret, both of them, and you are the professional team that will go and bring back the body. It is not a great analogy, but it's nicer than the others.

A bit.

Nicer than the little girl walking to the bottom of the sea.

Not really.

Okay, next is the sixth defect of my thinking, the Infected Mind Theory. That is when I feel my thinking is infected, as if something is alive inside my mind, like when you are in a pitch-black basement and you sense there is a spider next to you, hanging there in the darkness. You don't see the spider, but you know it is there. Just thinking about it makes you twitchy. It is probably an enormous spider. One of those spiders with heavy black bellies, or maybe one with a tiny white jellylike body and impossibly long legs that are reaching out to you. I can feel the spider in my mind. I have to breathe slowly and quietly, I need to think carefully, I must avoid certain thoughts, because the spider is a parasite in my mind, and it is watching me. It eats my thoughts, as soon as I have an idea it strikes, it injects poison into my mind, it siphons up my ideas and they go into its belly. Every day the parasite liquefies and drains more of my thoughts. Even the strongest ideas are sucked up and reduced to gastric juices. I become weaker, it is hard for me to work. Sometimes I stand there in the dark, in my mind, and the spider is also very still. I do not move, I cannot write, I try not to think. Maybe there are other spiders, perhaps there are many. I think the spiders have minds, there are other thinking creatures in my mind. I am no longer alone in my own mind. It's like the feeling I told you about, where lightning briefly illuminates enormous storm clouds, and then they vanish again into the darkness. I can't talk about this theory for very long, Samuel, because when I talk, I feel things in my mind are listening, they feed off of sense, and if I keep thinking, keep trying to make sense, they will inject more poison into my mind and slurp up my ideas and I will be a shell, like the shells that the spiders cast off when they molt, did you know spiders molt? They leave shells of themselves everywhere, sometimes it is hard to walk around inside my mind on account of all the spider shells underfoot. When they finish growing and become sexually mature, spiders stop molting, I mean real spiders. You are frowning.

I am wincing, this one is horrible.

I know that my mind has at least one adult, sexually mature spider in it, hanging in the darkness, and if I keep talking about it, the spider will suck up my last remaining thoughts and I will end up like a shell myself. Paul may not notice, but there won't be anything left inside, and then, but, well, now when I say this I absolutely realize that I am talking nonsense, people don't have spiders in their brains, but unfortunately that indicates that the Infected Mind Theory may be true, I may no longer be able to talk or write sensibly because the large, sexually mature spider that lives in my mind has siphoned away so many of my thoughts and made me so afraid of thinking new ones, like for example the thought that spiders in the mind are ridiculous, or the fact that I am not being very quiet at the moment, so if the theory is true I am attracting the spider's attention, perhaps it is quietly moving closer to me in the dark, gathering its legs around me, and yet nothing has happened, I am still talking, you are still listening, so the theory may not be true, either that or the spider is waiting, spiders are remarkably good at that. And by the way I am of course aware of the syndrome of thought withdrawal, *Gedankenentzug*, that is the psychiatric term, a psychiatrist would say this theory indicates I am suffering from *Gedankenentzug*, thought withdrawal, a delusion in which the patient believes her thoughts have gone somewhere else, but psychiatry is a baby science, it is only learning to babble, it drools its long words over everything, psychiatrists do not know anything about spiders, I doubt they have ever spent time in basements. I have. I doubt psychiatrists have consulted studies on the mass of spider shells produced by just a single generation of spiders. I have. I doubt they have considered that thought is not just withdrawn, it is liquefied and siphoned. A framed diploma printed in fake Gothic letters does not impress me. Bookshelves full of textbooks do not impress me. But if I look over the psychiatrist's shoulder and I see bookshelves with monographs on spiders, including special studies of their patience, the thickness of their shells, what they see out of each of their eight eyes, and their uses as metaphors of illness, that would get my attention. Anyway I don't want to say more about this theory. Each new thought I tell you makes me afraid, and maybe that is proof I can't trust my belief that there is no such thing as a mind full of large, quiet, sexually immature spiders, one very large sexually mature spider, and a floor full of spider shells, and, but... okay, so I will move on.

Well, that is disturbing.

From the moment I first sensed there were things in my mind that do not belong, I have been frightened.

What does it mean that just one of them is sexually mature?

I don't know, it's what I think. When I first became aware of the spiders, I wanted to run away, but I couldn't, because they are inside me. My first instinct was: Stay very still, don't move, and the things that are there in my mind won't see me, won't know I'm here. I stopped writing. I used to sit at my desk, in my study, with the door closed so Paul thought I was working. I stared at my hands. I tried to keep my thoughts quiet, so the things in my mind wouldn't bite. I didn't write anything down, because the spider would see it. I tried to keep my thoughts secret from myself, I looked away from them. I sat perfectly still, for hours, waiting for dinner. If you are in a dark basement and you are scared of something you think is down there with you, like for example a spider hanging from the ceiling right near your head, then at first you stay very still, it's instinct. You turn your eyes left and right, and you look up in case the spider is right above you. A minute passes. Or an hour, or a day. Eventually a door slams upstairs or a car passes by outside, and you realize you're just standing in a dark basement like an idiot. Why not just find the light or the stairs, and leave? There are always a few spiders in basements, it doesn't matter. We all have some things in our minds that aren't part of us, but for most people they are small and unimportant, like the frail harmless spiders that actually do live in basements. But not for me. Large things hang in my mind. That is the sixth theory, the Infected Mind Theory, and I could learn to live with it, if it was the only problem. But when the spiders move, when they twitch and vibrate and prod me with their hairy legs, then I realize I can't hide and the best thing to do is let my little frightened self shrink away, give her up, she is lost. The only thing left is to think like the large insistent parasites that occupy my mind, sympathize with them, see things from their point of view, take their side. Because there is no choice. I think you know how I feel, Samuel, because your intern in Guelph is fascinated by parasites.

How did you know that?

I may tell you later. So I picture myself as the sexually mature spider, big, healthy, with a spider-style pot belly. I look for the remaining signs of my life, Anneliese's life, so that I can digest her, liquefy and be done with her, excrete her and leave her on the floor with my cast-off shells.

That is awful, I said. You feel like that?

This is the seventh theory, the Encephalophagous Theory, the brain-eating theory, the opposite of the Infected Mind Theory. It is when I understand that the things in my mind other than me, that do not belong, are me. At first you may say, "Anneliese, this is seriously loopy, you are really losing me here," but you would be wrong, because first of all of course I do not think actual spiders are in my mind, and anyway I am not especially afraid of spiders, I mean not very many people like spiders, and those people have issues, but I am not phobic, I am only using spiders to illustrate the feeling that something is in my mind that is not me, it is a light-hearted illustration. The spiders are a joke.

That's a joke?

Not a ha-ha joke. The kind that helps when you feel dread. I know how I sound.

You sound frightened, actually.

Each theory has its mood. My Avalanche Theory is full of whimsy and wonder. My Disassembly Theory is delightfully hypochondriac. My Engastration Theory is stuffed with gluttony and gross anatomy, it's not my best moment. I get frustrated and infuriated thinking about jigsaw puzzles. The Unspooling Thoughts Theory fills me with pity and hopelessness. When I think about it I feel like I am walking down into the sea or falling into a deep darkness, I may drown or be lost in the dark. The Infected Mind theory reminds me of movies Paul made me watch. Spider movies put me in a twitchy mood, but somehow they are also sexy, I am not sure why. The Encephalophagous Theory is more like terror, or dread. Maybe the moods come first and the theories are stories I invent later to explain the moods. I get swept up in the moods of my theories, I dislike that fact but there is nothing I can do about it. The spiders are a joke, because they help me laugh about something much more serious. The idea that there is something in my mind along with me, which is not me, is almost intolerable, so it requires spider jokes, I can't think about it without spiders. I can't think that I may have to give myself up and become the things that are not me, I can't think like that, it's just not tolerable. Spiders are required. Whatever once was me, back when I was simple Anneliese Glur, a little girl, playing, Annabelle my mother used to call me, or when I was a beautiful young woman studying, Anni, that's what Willermus used to call me, whoever that person was has long ago stopped thinking. The part of my mind that was once my thinking self, my ordinary healthy I, the voice that thought and spoke, the one who felt sad or happy, she has been poisoned and wrapped in a cocoon, the way spiders wrap their paralyzed prey so they can eat them later. I don't know why they do that, by the way, why don't they eat their food when it's fresh? I guess spiders don't care how fresh their food is, or maybe flies taste good when their juices are rotted. Anyway I can no longer live in that poisoned state. Now I look at the prey with the eight unblinking black eyes of the predator, I regard the poisoned Anni as a remnant. At some point she fell silent. She had Cotard's syndrome, she thought her insides were missing, that's Cotard's syndrome, except she was right, they are missing. So I am something else, I am the parasite, *je est un autre,* that is the famous phrase, I am someone else, or *nous sommes autre chose,* we are something else, and we are encephalophagous, we eat brain matter. Whatever I once was no longer thinks. I am the engorged spider in my own mind, licking the last sickly tissues out of Anni's hollow body, siphoning up the few remaining thoughts. I am young and vigorous. When I write, I write as a parasite, I am the one who remains, and the thirteen theories I am telling you about are all written by the disease. All my notebooks should be signed, The Disease. I admit that a person with thirteen theories about her own irrationality is quite possibly not the world's most concrete solid sane personality, but speaking as a parasite, I am attracted to these thirteen theories, they are far better than the usual accounts people have about how they are not thinking right, such as, "I'm okay, just taking a day at a time," or, "Since my mother died I haven't been myself," or, "I used to hear voices, but my meds have quieted them down." Those experiences are simple by comparison. Reason is not an on-off switch, you do not go from Einstein at the age of twenty-six, when he just sat down and wrote out the structure of the universe, right into a yabbering marmoset, those are the stupidest monkeys, by the way, they have the smallest brains, marmosets have tiny heads, they are the monkeys least likely to come up with propositions about the nature of space and time. I like having thirteen theories because, you know, I have eight eyes and eight legs and, and a half-dozen spinnerets, so why not thirteen theories? Samuel, you are looking at me as if I have ten heads, please don't worry about spiders, I do not actually think I am an infestation of encephalophagous spiders, I am still a scientist of some sort, I hope. I am just trying to say something very difficult. My work has changed me fundamentally. I am doing my best. I am losing track of what I once was, and right now I feel I'm speaking with the voice of disease. I have been thinking in ways that are not ordinary, for lengths of time that are not ordinary, and this seventh theory is one of my tools for understanding what has happened to me. It is comforting, in an unhealthy way, to picture my older self as a poisoned carcass in a wrap of spider silk, because I don't have to worry about her any more. I think she was beautiful when I first spotted her, I am not sure, because even though I have eight eyes I don't see very well, and besides, it's dark in here. Anyway now she's a wrinkled skin in a cocoon. I am the parasites, we are healthy and dangerous! So that's it. If you do not mind, on to the next rung, the Flood Theory. Actually I won't tell you about that now. You will hear about it in twenty-eight minutes. Ninth is the Compost Theory. This is when my thoughts sink down together, they steep and rot in a warm mulch—

Anneliese, these are disturbing images.

They get worse. In the Compost Theory, I am compost.

But these are disturbing ideas. I'm sorry to ask, but have you been talking to anyone?

Paul says that sometimes. But psychiatric medicine is only a century old and it is practiced by teenagers. I have read too much to make me trust any twelve-year-old psychotherapist. I have read the *DSM,* all five editions, and the series *The Clinical Interview Using DSM,* volume 2, *The Difficult Patient,* and I've read Freud's *Collected Works* in 18 volumes, all of them, and the collected letters, and Fliess and Abraham and Binswanger and Ferenczi and Lampl-de Groot, and I've read Jung and Adler, and Rank, and Horney, and Sullivan, and I've read Lacan and Reich and Perls and Janov, Bass, Davis, Fromm, and the philosophers from Popper to Grünberg and Kusters, and the scientists from Eagleman to Solms, he makes great wine, by the way. I am like Francis Spiera, you will hear about him later. I have read everything,

I know all the arguments, no one can convince me, no one can comfort me. I know this does not sound likely, but you will understand later. So the ninth theory is the Compost Theory, I mentioned it when we were talking to Catherine. When I am compost nothing is clear or distinct, my thoughts smell rich and rotten, they stick together, cook down into humus, into mull, moder, and mor, those are kinds of humus, stages in the return to dirt. I no longer know if I am making sense or sentences or only sounds. I mean I know now, but I don't always. Right now I am rational, I think, because I have to be. But I have been subsiding for many years now, and recently more and more. Compost cannot understand itself. My thought is becoming a warm mass of fermenting bacteria and fungi. My ideas are entangled, like roots, like fungal hyphae. I can no longer form thoughts, sculpt or build ideas. I can only produce incomplete sentences, with defective grammar, words misspelled, deformed, scrambled around on the page. My thought emits sulfurous smells. There is no light on the page, my thinking dims and subsides. Mull is completed compost, tolerable to smell, useful to spread over gardens, but it is not the end. Mull compresses into moder, moder into mor, where the last remnants of living thought are extinguished. Even the bacteria are immobile and the soil is acidic and inert. That is where I am headed. It may be how the borometz feels when it turns into a plant. Its sheep thoughts become unclear, and by the way sheep thoughts are already very fuzzy, and they become even dimmer, like sheep's wool matted with mud. Grass no longer makes the borometz hungry, it doesn't notice the pasture, it turns to the sunshine and rain, it feels its nuts growing. It becomes a tree. Eventually it gets old, its leafy hair falls out, it is naked, or I mean it is bald, it is not naked because it has bark, bark is like clothing for a tree, and leaves are like hair, sort of. Anyway then it dies, its wood rots, its umbilicus trunk is hollowed by fungi, raccoons and bees live in it, soon it falls back onto the pasture, into the humus. My work becomes a clot, a packed mass of fermented waste. I used to have ideas, they were like the things you throw on compost piles like banana peels, eggshells, garters, old letters, leather shoes, I tossed them onto the compost of my notebooks and they deliquesced into gray-brown mull, they became dirt. Humus, mull, moder, mor. *Humus, humilis, humillumus.* I am a warm lump now, without much capacity to understand or observe myself. Midges land on me, a chicken picks at me, maggots tunnel through me. My thoughts are muddy, smeared and splotched. I am self-fermenting and self-lubricating, compost for purple fungus that will grow out of me. I think in gasses and sprays of fungal hyphae. I no longer have arguments or even words. I write pages and I look at them and I see clay. I am compacting, returning into substrate.

Well, at least this theory is peaceful?

It is. The Compost Theory is a way of letting go. When I experience my thinking like this, I no longer try to save myself, *non iam me ipsam servare nitor nec iam praeda sum nec praedator nec quidem in vita manere conor,* I am no longer prey or predator, I don't need to try to survive. *Cogitata non ut plerique homines fingo,* I can't build thoughts like most people, *quae iam mihi et madida et fragilia facta sunt,* my thoughts have become moist and friable, *sed lapidesque lignumque usitatarum cogitationum corruerunt atque putruerunt,* the stones and wood of ordinary thinking have crumbled and rotted. *Scribo clavas, folia, caenum in solo silvae. Cogitationes mihi muck vel mull vel moder. Quo propius aspicio quae scribo, eo minus video. Verba mihi argilla, calamus mihi trulla, atramentum mihi muck, argillaque diffunditur super paginas pugillarium meorum, tegoque paginas crusta fusca.* I write sticks, leaves, and dirt on the forest floor, my thoughts are muck and mull, or moder, the closer I look at what I write the less I see, my words are only clay, my pencil is a trowel, my ink is muck, clay spreads over the pages of my notebooks, I cover the pages with a brownish gray crust.

But Anneliese, you do write.

You are very sweet, and by that I mean naïve. No matter if I try to think or not, in the Compost Theory all I can produce is a tangle of vegetable fungus, that's what Darwin called humus, with spider shells, mites, nematodes, and myriads of bacteria, all glued in a matrix of lignin, phenols, waxes, silica, silt, minerals, eggshells, orange rinds, coffee grounds, and water, smeared across the pages of my notebooks like dirt, like shit.

And words. You write words.

Samuel, she replied, I cannot tell you how grateful I am that you are listening. But you are just learning. I know when my words are mud, my ink is excrement. This is still not the bottom, there are four rungs left. The tenth rung is the Surd Theory, not absurd, surd, it is a word mathematicians use for irrational numbers, it means that sometimes my thoughts are not whole, like 1, 2, 3, 4, and they are also not fractions, like 1/2, 1/4, 1/10, instead they are irrational, my thoughts are surds, $\sqrt{2}$, $\sqrt{3}$, $\sqrt[3]{\pi}$, my thoughts are no longer rational in the mathematical sense of the word, and so I am literally incapable of making rational sense, I am condemned to be irrational. No word I say is actually that word. Everything I say, including these thirteen levels, is actually nonsense. I may seem to be speaking in whole rational thoughts like 1, 2, 3, 4, body, career, mind, family, but I am really speaking in irrational approximations. Instead of 1, 2, 3, 4, I use $\sqrt[7]{2}$, $\sqrt[3]{7}$, $\sqrt[6]{731}$, and $\sqrt[9]{19{,}679}$, and if you calculate those, Samuel, you will find they are close to 1, 2, 3, and 4, but they are not 1, 2, 3, and 4. When I say "body" it is not body, when I say "mind" it is not mind. Understand? For example $\sqrt[6]{731}$ is not the number three. It is close, it's approximately 3.001. But that is not three, in fact it is nothing like three, because it never stops, it goes on forever, it is closer to 3.001370176672673045084064 3, it's easier to remember if you break it into sets of three numbers, like this, 300, 137, 017, 667, see how that helps to recite the number? So 267, 304, 508, 840, 643, that is how I remember it.

Okay, I see.

It goes on, 601, 415, 578, 713, 249, 078—

Okay, stop.

And then 809, 238, 212, 976, 033, 088, 057, 581—

Stop!

It never stops. Some surds are almost exactly the same as ordinary numbers. Instead of the number 5, I use $e^{\pi\sqrt{163}}$ minus 262 quadrillion, 537 trillion, 412 billion, 640 million, 768 thousand, seven hundred and thirty-nine. That is very, very close to the number five. On my best days, when I think of exceptionally clear ideas, I get excited, I think, At last! It's been so long! I have a rational scientific idea, a natural number kind of idea, like 1, 2, 3, 4, 5, 6, like body, career, mind, family, memory, language, but then I look again, and it's not 2, it's $\sqrt[3]{7}$, and it's not 5, it's $e^{\pi\sqrt{163}}$ minus 262,537,412,640,768,739. I am sure you can understand this even though you received a B- in algebra in high school, and another B in "Calculus and Applied Mathematics" in Colgate University, and a D+ in "Intro to Statistics," and by the way that was especially pitiful. The Surd Theory says: Give up, you no longer have distinct ideas like the simple natural numbers 1, 2, 3, 4, 5, or even like a banana peel or a leather shoe. You have surds. This is a horrible condition, thinking in surds, because I am infinitesimally near normal meaning, but I am deeply abnormal. It's the same with Luzia, since 2.3 to the minus 2.3, factorial, factorial, factorial, factorial is close to 1, but it is not 1.

$$\left(\left(\left(\left(2.3^{-2.3}\right)!\right)!\right)!\right)! \approx 1$$

She could make our family more normal if she was just 1.0, a normal person, but even if her function was

$$\left(\left(\left(\left(\left(\left(\left(\left(\left(\left(\left(\left(2.3^{-2.3}\right)!\right)!\right)!\right)!\right)!\right)!\right)!\right)!\right)!\right)!\right)!\right)!$$

she would still not be exactly 1. If she keeps going that way she will never, ever, be normal.

That surd $e^{\pi\sqrt{163}}$ - 262,537,412,640,768,739 will never be the number five, it is as far from five as it is possible to get, a universe away and yet infinitesimally close. My words sound like ordinary words, made of unremarkable sounds, but they are surds. My words are not normal, they are irrational, and so am I. Only slightly, but hopelessly. When I try to make sense, I am compelled to speak slightly irreparably wrong. Right behind my ordinary-sounding words are tremendously complex nonrepeating decimals. "Language has made it impossible for people to ever get to know each other," Fritz Mauthner said that, and it's true. That is the Surd Theory. My eleventh theory is the Despair Theory—

But actually, I said, you are using normal words.

They seem normal. You think you can find them in a dictionary, you can look up "my" and "eleventh" and "theory," and you find each word, except that you don't, because my words are not those words. They only sound like them, my words are counterfeit, camouflaged, they are elaborately made up so they look normal.

Actually they are normal words.

Three more rungs to go. I have a hard time talking about these last ones. I am sorry if they seem funny.

Not funny, really.

Samuel, I know what you're thinking. It's pretty clear that Anneliese is not sane, that's what you're saying to yourself, I should have seen it before, but now it's clear. There are bats in her bell tower, spiders in her brain, she is batty, she's bats, in fact she's bat-shit crazy, I love that expression, by the way, as if the feces of a bat are somehow insane, as if bats are inherently deranged and their droppings concentrate their mental illness and become violently and excessively crazy, as if the excrement produced by some animals is less sane than excrement produced by other animals, perhaps horses produce very sane manure, and human shit is slightly deranged, but bat feces are the worst, they are utterly psychotic, it's a nonsensical idea, but something sounds right about it. Anyway that's what you're thinking, she's a nut case, a borometz nut, nutty as a fruitcake, her elevator only goes to the thirteenth floor, her porch light's on but nobody's home, that's what you're thinking.

I'm not. I am just concerned.

Don't pretend. I could follow those first few theories, that's what you're saying to yourself, the first ones were odd but kind of fun, like she said, comical. I was feeling sympathetic, but this stuff about spiders, compost, and surds is too much, now I can see she really is a loony. Crazy as a loon, she is Looney Tunes, thirteen ways of looking at a loon, she's looney loops, you see I have looked all these up, you're thinking, When she finishes her speech I am out of here, that's how Canadians talk, Samuel, out of here, I'll go back to my ordinary witless job, at least it's sane, and I'll be sure to change my phone number and email, it is a pity, really, if only she was just eccentric, that would be fun, that's what I thought at first, I was interested in all the things she told me, the bucket list was entertaining, I liked the way she talked about movies, lots of it was boring, and I probably didn't understand why she was telling me some things, but no, she's deranged, it's actually sad. She's away with the fairies, lost her marbles, keys are gone and the shoes are too, rats in the attic, screws loose, *einen Vogel haben,* a bird's lodged in her head, well, that's a German saying, so you wouldn't know that one, or this one, *ich glaube ich spinne,* that is a truly great expression, one of the few good things in German, it means, I think I'm spinning, or, I think I'm insane, or, I think I spider, the expression itself is insane. You know, Samuel, I should make a note of that one, I can use it for the Encephalophagous Theory, but sorry—I was telling you what you are thinking, and I was about to say you are wrong, my insanity is not the simple bats rats birds and spiders type of craziness. If it was, I would just medicate myself and stay home. It is worse. I am perfectly capable of constructing complicated arguments involving multiple hypotheticals and several points of view, like this one I am building now, so when you sit there thinking, It's true, she speaks rationally enough from minute to minute, like she is now, even though it might not be the world's most rational thing to tell me at length what I am supposedly thinking, but okay, it is at least a rational speech, of some sort anyway, but she gets distracted by the smallest things, and some of her ideas are ridiculous, like the thirteen worms, and others are maudlin, like the well, and none is believable, they're concoctions, they are spun out of spider's silk, bats' wings, and thin air, and she's never rational for very long, she is always going off the rails, and she takes forever to make her points, I'd love to have a drink with that elevator operator, I think he's right, there is never an end in sight, first it was 4 theories, then 7, now it's 13, tomorrow it might be 38, or 102, or 259, or 626, or, oh, I don't remember the next number, there is a mathematical sequence, I have worked out a way to multiply my theories, but you don't know that, so you couldn't be thinking this part either, so anyway, Samuel, when you sit there thinking, Anneliese really is insane, she fulminates and complains, declaims and lectures, hectors and pontificates, monologizes and confesses, she just needs to keep talking, the whole thing is fascinating in an awful kind of way, well, Samuel, when you think these things, or when you think, I don't really know why I keep listening, maybe I'm weak-minded, or easily hypnotized, or I have nothing else to do, or my life is mainly empty and so I'm likely to listen to anyone, actually that one is pretty much true, or when you think, I don't know why I don't speak up more, I really should, someone needs to pin her down and put a towel in her mouth, she needs help, she's crying out for help, but who could argue with her, anyway? Apparently I can't, I should just tell her I'm sorry but I need to go, even if it's a lie, and fly back to my little Canadian farm town and get back to my stupefyingly boring routine, or Samuel, when you think, I wish she'd ask me about my family! My daughters, our baby, my job, what is wrong with her, anyway? Why can't she ask me about my health, my work, how could anyone have so little curiosity about someone they meet? Doesn't it occur to her that I might have something to add? Doesn't she see that I have my own ideas about lots of things, even jigsaw puzzles? Doesn't she notice I've started to really care about her, that I'm genuinely concerned about her, now that she's finally stopped lecturing and started telling me how she feels? Does she really have to keep interrupting me and telling me I'm wrong? Well, Samuel, when you think these things, when you ask these questions, does it ever occur to you that I do care, that is why I have gone to such trouble to research your life, your work, and your job. Does it occur to you that I have very little time, and I need to introduce my work, and then after that I might want to talk in a more normal way, and hear more about your childhood or why you were drawn to that lake, there was definitely something odd about that. But no, you just think, She really does have fundamental issues, way beyond my pay grade, she isn't reachable or curable, or you think, I really do feel sorry for her, but oh my is she hard to listen to, I never really know what she's talking about, half the time I'm lost, and to tell the truth a lot of the time she's boring, she's the most self-indulgent person I've ever met, self-involved, self-absorbed, she thinks she's Job, with her skin rash, she imagines herself sitting in compost like Job, by Biblical anguish and darkness beset, she complains bewails and bemoans, her rash burns and throbs, she is rippled with running sores, her mouth is full of bitter and arcane laments, her mind is a land of allusive gloom and thickest murk, the muddest thick that was ever heard dump, but you know? she seems to be doing okay, really, she has people taking care of her, cooking for her, for heaven's sake, she has her *oeufs en cocotte,* whatever that is, and her Mathilde Pêche liqueur, and her brother pays the rent and probably does the shopping, too, she doesn't seem to notice that, and she has a nice warm study with a view of a garden and a decorative well, she is privileged and pampered, she's an overeducated bourgeois Job, so give me a break, I just can't feel that sorry for her, well, when you think all that, Samuel, you are mistaking profundity for profusion, you are mistaking complexity for confusion, you are mistaking method for moder, and one small sign of how wrong you are is that I am at this very moment telling you what you think, verbatim, word for word, I am telling you exactly what you would be saying right now if I wasn't ruining your concentration by telling you what you are thinking of saying, if I stopped talking right now you would fill the silence with an exact continuation of everything I am saying, and that is, I believe, a very good sign, if not the best possible sign, that even though I am quite obviously distraught I make more sense than you suspect. You see, Samuel, I am not as oblivious as you suppose. Now you're thinking, She is terribly irritating, putting these words in my mouth, even though she is right, they are things I think, I did wonder who does the shopping, or at least they are things I would think if she would shut up and give me a chance, and she has made the whole thing even more irritating by mimicking some Canadian mannerisms I seem to have picked up, all of this without bothering to ask me what I actually believe, but why should she, since she's convinced she knows me so well, so yeah, and by the way that's another thing Canadians say, so yeah—she is a mess, she may not make it, but she might, she does seem to have an idea where she's going. It seems she has organized these speeches in advance. If I think back on the first things she said, when she was introducing herself, she was trying to entertain me but also show me who she was, more and more honestly, all those speeches about language and memory and bucket lists and normal life and mindless students and Asian hotels were well timed, now that I think of it, they were what she decided I could absorb at each moment, and I need to remember she knows about my job and even the zoos, which is weird and invasive but also kind of flattering, and she has read all my essays, which is definitely flattering, because as she knows, no one reads my work, and she has looked into my public record, that is troubling and quite possibly illegal, but still it's interesting and she hasn't threatened me or anything like that, and really, there is something tragic about her, pathetic and affecting, she really is an unusual person, I have never met anyone like her, maybe her theories sound unhinged because they are outside my ordinary Canadian experience. When you think all these things, Samuel, I know that you pause, and then you say to yourself, Okay, I guess I should give her the benefit of the doubt, at least for a while longer, she really seems to need my help, or at least she needs to talk, and after all I should wait and trust her because Catherine has known her for years, but no, what am I saying? She is seriously deranged and I need to figure out how to get away from her. That's what you are thinking, Samuel, you might as well admit it, well, actually you don't need to, I just admitted it for you, so now you're thinking, Okay, I give up, the best thing is to sit still and listen. Sometimes I'll nod like a simpleton and she'll think I'm agreeing with her, and when she finishes I'll go back to my room and call the desk and say No calls, No messages, I'm checking out in one hour, and I'll leave and she'll never see me again. I'll tell Rosie if she ever calls just hang up right away, don't say anything. She is certifiable, cuckoo for Cocoa Puffs, she's Fruit Loops, bananas, she's marshmallows, it's interesting how many children's foods are also expressions for insanity, anyway she's cooked her rabbit, I have no idea why that would mean a person is insane, if you cook your pet rabbit you are probably desperately poor and hungry, it's more sad than insane, but she's fried her slippers, slipped her handlers, she's doolally, she's yagablahblahboodleschmackablurble!

She smiled at me.

Well ha ha, she continued, but I can't spend all day joking. So my eleventh theory is the Despair Theory. You will hear about it in fifty-four minutes. It involves comets. You will think it is the worst of all. When you hear it you will become quite anxious for me, but there are still worse things. After it, there are two more rungs on the ladder that leads down into the very bottom of the well. The twelfth theory is the Non-Human Language Theory. I have been telling you how awkward and embarrassing language is, although I admit I enjoy a couple of words, like Humpelken-Pumpelken, encephalophagous, anguilliform, and *ich glaube ich spinne.* When you heard my theories about language, you thought, Well, okay, so no one knows who invented past tense, but that's all right, languages just develop naturally, it doesn't matter that we don't know who invented them, maybe they weren't even invented, maybe they grew without our knowing quite how, like babies. Why doesn't Anneliese calm down and just use language without worrying who invented it? Everyone else in the world does. Why does everything have to be invented by a genius? What about shitting, who invented that? Obviously not a genius, especially if our droppings are insane. So what's the big deal if no one invented the rules of language? Anneliese seems to be able to say whatever she wants anyway. Something's wrong with her, that's what you think, Samuel, I don't know what it is but it's complicated, she has some very unusual problems, well, gosh, I guess that's the whole point of what she's saying. Maybe if I just keep quiet and listen, and stop forcing her to tell me all the things I'm thinking, maybe I'll learn something. And so, Samuel, there is another possibility here, if you would just stop criticizing me for a moment. Of course someone invented the word "dog." I mean it is wildly improbable that words just came out of grunts—dog, tree, worm—those aren't grunts, they are inventions. Of course someone said "dog" for the first time, and of course that person is the inventor of the word "dog." But that was many generations ago and we have forgotten who it was. Probably no one rushed out and shook her hand and introduced her to everyone and said, "Everybody, meet Gag, she just invented the word 'dog,' she's a genius, let's throw a big party and carve her name in stone so everyone will remember her forever, never has the world seen a genius like her, she could name anything, even my cat, oh my god, I have just invented the word 'cat,' I want my name in stone too," okay, sorry, that was a stupid story. Back to my explanation. So thanks to some forgotten person we have the word "dog." Or *Hund,* or *chien,* etcetera. We do not have the slightest idea what the people who invented those words meant when they chose those sounds. For us the sounds are meaningless. Also no word for "dog" even looks like a dog. I checked, I looked up "dog" in dozens of languages, they all look like letters, well, I admit that an early version of the Chinese character for "dog" does look a little like a dog, or maybe a dog with an old TV antenna tied to its head, but you see what I mean. Everyone knows this, it is one of the dumbest things it is possible to know, but once you realize it, once you see that no one knows what the sounds in *Hund* mean, or in *Hond,* that's what they call them in Luxembourg, or in *gos* or *pas* or *klb* or *qen,* all the words for "dog" are meaningless sounds, and by the way linguists try not to think about this, they say the sounds of words are arbitrary, well, now they are, so but when you think about it then you suddenly see: languages are no longer human, they have no thought left in them. No one remembers what the sounds *d, o, g,* meant to the person who first said "dog." They used to mean something, but now they do not communicate any human meaning. You can get sentimental about the word "dog," because you have your cute little dog, when I was little Annabelle my dog was Knuddelbär, he was so cute, and now I have Teddi, he's not as cute, and I'm always telling him that, and so naturally I love the word *Hund* with a special squishy love, but *Hund* is still four meaningless letters, in German it sounds like the letter *H* and something else, *H und,* it could not be more senseless. "Dog" is an especially stupid sound. Even barking sounds intelligent in comparison to "dog." Words and grammar are prehistoric artifacts whose meaning has been forgotten. No one remembers who invented the past progressive, or what they meant by it, or why they needed it. It's just a prehistoric rule we obediently follow.

This doesn't sound as bad as those last few theories. You can still speak and write like everyone else.

You have to think about it. We have gotten used to our languages, we think they express our moods, we assume they fit our thoughts, we believe the words are ours, but actually languages are not ours. Almost every word in every language is either entirely meaningless sounds, like *Hund,* like dog, or else it's a half-hearted attempt to sound like something, like *meow* or *Miau* or *miaou,* that's French, or *nya,* that's Japanese, because in some languages people think the noise cats make begins with an *n,* but aside from meows and things like that every word in every language is meaningless. And all the rules for putting together these meaningless sounds were made by people who are long forgotten, for their own purposes and their own lives, which we have long forgotten.

But does that matter? Most people don't mind, right?

You have to think about it, then your spine will turn to ice. Grammar is like the labyrinthine law code of some ancient and despotic country. Or like a great palace built for aliens, where nothing fits, the chairs have spikes and the beds are the shape of forklifts. And yet this alien architecture is what we call home. All day, every day, we live with this inhuman architecture. It is the air our minds breathe, but it is not ours. Yet language turns to me and says, "Look, I am beautiful, you love me. Don't you recognize me?" Its eyes are swimming with tears. "I am your greatest and most profound creation," language says. "I am your heart. You love me, you know I am the only thing you have ever really loved. I am your innermost thoughts, I am you yourself." Except that it isn't. Its teary eyes are swimming with pupils. It isn't anything close to human. This is the Non-Human Language Theory. Language keeps trying to convince me the theory is not true. Language keeps telling me that it is human, that it's like me, that I love it, and sometimes I give in, we all have our weaknesses, language is handsome and strong, but it is dangerous when someone clings to you and says over and over, You love me, you love me. A person who behaves that way is likely to be crazy. "You love me, Anneliese, you love me, admit it. I am humanity's greatest gift to itself, everything about me is beautiful. You love me, even though you fight against me as hard as you can using every word you can think of, still you love me, don't you? In fact, Anni dear, you love me a lot," that's what language says to me, "because you never stop talking, do you, and you never stop writing, do you? Come closer, Anni darling, give us a kiss."

She held her arms out and closed her eyes.

Love is like that. You know your husband or wife is demented, but you love them, you're helpless. It's not abstract, it's a disaster. When we met, Samuel, I said language is like a bad suit, but the truth is we are all born in language coffins, and we have never been outside our coffins, so we have persuaded ourselves that coffins are a great gift. They fit us perfectly! we say. That's why language coffins have six sides, we say, look, they bulge out at the sides like we do, we can lie comfortably in them provided we don't struggle.

That's horrible, I said. But I don't feel like I'm in a coffin.

Our mouths are filled with language corpses.

Gross.

Thank you. By the way, I will apologize later if I got anything wrong about what you are thinking. I am just very worked up. I don't think you feel the Non-Human Language Theory, but your mouth and your mind are filled with language corpses, when you speak you choke on mummy shreds.

Every sentence you form is an animated corpse in your mouth. The laws of grammar were invented by people who are dust. Language isn't only a badly tailored suit, it is someone else's skin, and when you speak you wear it over your own skin, like the Aztecs did, and your smile is hidden behind its torn lips.

Okay, that's enough.

All right. Now the thirteenth theory is the Waves on the Beach Theory. I do not even like to say those words, waves on the beach, it is actually frightening to think about this last theory, even though it is the one that lives with me in the bilious water of the Nothing Sea. You say you don't mind that language is no longer human, but someday you'll be thinking about it, and all of a sudden you'll realize your mouth and your mind are filled with dead things that you will never understand, and you will be terrified, and you'll wish you had taken notes when I told you about the Non-Human Language Theory, but there is something worse. If I ask myself, Anneliese, why isn't anyone else concerned about how language is no longer human? Why doesn't Samuel care? He was so sympathetic when I talked about sexually mature spiders, and now his eyes have glazed over again, he looks like a dead tadpole. Well, the reason is that we can still use language, it helps us make sense of the world, so we forgive the fact that its passport is forged and it has conveniently forgotten its past. But what if language doesn't help us make sense of the world? Think of words as butterfly wings. So many lovely colors, such entrancing patterns. But what do they mean? What are they pictures of? Are the stripes and spots on butterfly wings like writing? They don't mean anything, well, the stripes might scare birds, but really, that is just the kind of idiotic observation that makes a scientist take out his pipe and puff away contentedly. And okay, some butterfly wings look like leaves or bark, but that is the sort of dumb observation that makes a scientist put away his pipe and take out a cigar. Most butterfly wings mean nothing. And please do not tell me they help each butterfly find its mate. All mice are brown, but they find their mates anyway. The wings of butterflies and moths are intricate pictures, and yet they mean nothing. Autumn leaves, too. They are beautiful, innumerable, striking against the cold blue sky, pencil yellow, butterfly orange, aorta red, but who are those colors for?

Trees don't see them. Squirrels are probably color blind. Do the colors make birds happy? Why do trees do it? Language is meaningless like that. When I go into a restaurant like the one here in the Krafft Hotel and I hear everyone politely talking, I see the pleasure of conversation in their eyes, and when I go into the university library I see the contented looks on people's faces as they welcome the words on each page. I have to leave, it makes me so sad. Language is like a flock of butterflies darting around a flower bed or a stand of autumn trees with all the colors in a child's set of crayons. All that color, all those patterns, they seem to be saying something, but they aren't. Language is not just inhuman, it is meaningless. People invented language, so the mind itself may actually be a natural form, not even a living thing like leaves or butterflies but something with no meaning whatsoever, like the patterns left by waves on a beach. "The sound that comes from human beings is called *kalām wa-alfāẓ*, 'speech' and 'words.' The sound that comes from water is called *dawīy*, 'roaring' or *kharīr*, 'rippling.' The sound that comes from minerals, stones, and wood is called *waqʿ*, 'thudding,' *ṭanīn*, 'clinking,' and *daqq*, 'grinding.' There is no difference." I read that in a tenth-century Arabic encyclopedia written by the Brethren of Purity, I won't tell you right now why I was reading it. Sometimes when a wave draws back it leaves scraps of seaweed, shells, and colored pebbles, and every once in a while those things form patterns, like when seaweed spelled my initials, it looked like the ocean had written A.G. Of course it hadn't, it was terrifying but it was also ridiculous, it was uncanny but also mortifying, as if nature had made a mistake, spoken by mistake. In the Waves on the Beach Theory, our thoughts are only patterns. We ponder and we puzzle, looking at our thoughts as if they were seaweed and shells scattered on a beach, trying to read their meaning. There are words in our minds, they seem heavy with significance, but in the end they are only patterns. *NIEMANDSROSE*, it says in tangles of seaweed. An amazing thing for seaweed to spell, clearly it's writing, it means something, in German it is "no one's rose," not a word, but close, very poetic. I am no one's rose, the seaweed says. Or, no one owns roses. Or, no one invented roses. Or, no one invented the word "rose." Or, I am a rose blooming for no one. Anneliese, the seaweed says, you bloom for no one. You are no one's rose. You live for no reason. I cried when I realized that. Then I thought, well, that's selfish, maybe it means people are like roses, we all bloom for no one. No one takes care of us. We are alone in the universe. I cried again when I thought of that. Then I pulled myself together. I realized the seaweed spelled *NIEMANDSBOSE,* or even *NIEMAMSMOSE,* or just *NIEMAMMZMOZM,* I wasn't sure, it didn't spell much of anything, really. It was just squiggles of seaweed, *NMZMZMZMZMZ.* If it had said *NIEMANDSROSE,* meaning we are roses that bloom for no one, that would have been heartbreaking, but instead it was embarrassing, because I had hallucinated the word in random swirls of seaweed. No one had sent a message, nature had not spoken. And then I realized: that is what our minds do, actually. We keep arranging and rearranging our ideas, but they never have meaning. We go down to the Nothing Sea, the nothing there to see. I walked home, and the patterns of seaweed were all around me, but they meant nothing, and the grasses on the dunes waved back and forth like people signaling, but that meant nothing, and the clouds linked in rows like old cursive handwriting, but that meant nothing, and then the stars formed bears and serpents, but those meant nothing, and later as the tide went out I heard the dark ocean retreat down the shingles of the beach, but that meant nothing, and I thought, well, obviously, I knew that, but then I thought, wait, my thoughts are the same, they swirl around in my mind and I keep hoping they have meaning, but they never do, they never can, no one's can, thinking is only arranging ideas so they seem to have meaning. Our minds form patterns, our writing is compositions of seaweed. I am like the froth inside the butterfly, the sap slinking along in the leaf. When I speak my mouth spits chitin. We hope there is meaning, because if there isn't, we are all like I was when I looked at the seaweed, pretending I could read it, pretending it was speaking. The Waves on the Beach Theory is intolerable, it means we spend our lives composing our words and thoughts, but we are not doing anything more meaningful than arranging stamps or flowers. Really there is no thought, there is only our waiting and watching.

So cheery.

It's not funny, she replied. So that's thirteen.[19]

Anneliese, I see how awful this is for you.

She sank farther down into her rumpled coat.

That is the ladder. Now it only remains for me to outline, in the same skeletal, rushed, and barely adequate manner, the form of my life's work, beginning with the first notes I took forty years ago, and how I cataloged them, and the manner in which I incorporated them into successive sets of notebooks. And I need to tell you about the writers I studied, because I studied people before me who embarked on massive projects, involving thousands of pages and millions of words, I did that because I needed to see how other people kept their work under control, how they made their work cohere, gave their thoughts structure and order, brought their books to a conclusion. Then I need to tell you how I plan to do the same, how long it will be before I kick the listing bucket, how I will transfer all the notebooks to you, how long it will take you to read them, and then what you will do after you read them. Unless you would like me to repeat the thirteen theories first. I can, but I will not include the eighth or the eleventh theory, because you are not ready for them yet. Would you like me to go over the others, one by one? No? No? Are you sure? Then I will assume you remember them perfectly. As you are beginning to see, my work takes a certain amount of time to explain, you might even think it is endless, I mean my explanation, not my work, the work is not endless, it has a beginning, although I can't remember it, and soon, I hope, it will have an ending. I see the look on your face. You're wondering if it's time to stop me. "Anneliese," you'll say, "I don't want to be rude, but actually your explanation does seem endless. Those were some really disturbing ideas you told me about. Don't you think we should talk about them? Aren't you curious what I think?" Well, I won't answer that, because I'll be thinking, That's what he keeps asking me, in my imagination, but he doesn't actually say much, and then you'll say, "I mean, is it really enough for me to just sit here and listen? I could be anyone, or no one. Why even talk to me? Is this how friendship works for you?"

That's not what I'm thinking, Anneliese. I am listening.

Samuel, this is your speech I am reporting to you. You are apparently mistaken in your understanding of my invented version of your notion of what you are thinking. If you do not mind my saying so, I think that imaginary speech you made a few minutes ago was quite good, although I doubt you are capable of making such a speech on your own. In fact, it was so good that I concede most of the points I imagined you made in my invented version of your speech. Despite your doubts, my explanation is composed and addressed specifically and only to you. It is planned, timed, and perfectly customized to your schedule, your narrow range of interests, and your faltering attention. For now it only requires you to listen. It is a question of friendship and trust. As you will see, I will want your thoughts, all of them, on these and many other points, but only after I have set out the conditions of my work. If I were a simple person this entire introduction would only take a minute, because my life's work would turn out to be something idiotic like a book about my dog, I would say to you, "Samuel, I have written a book about my beloved spaniel, her name is Spanielita, I call her my little Princess"—

I thought the dog's name was Teddi.

This is a parodic counterfactual imaginary response. Teddi is a nice dog even though he is ugly, and I would never use him to make a sarcastic point. "Samuel," I would say, "I have written a book about Spanielita, it's about her adventures with the sheepdog Sir Puddles who lives next door, when you read it you'll feel all warm inside, because that is how I feel when I think of my little Spanielita, she is the cuddly wuddly love of my life," and then I would show you the glossy cover of my book, depicting Spanielita inside a glowing heart, panting at the Eiffel Tower. But I am not a simple person, Samuel, and this is not a simple project. My apparently endless explanation is actually a miracle of concision. And, come to think of it, my individual thoughts are quite brief. Some are no more than a phrase or a single word. Ideas drop onto me like raindrops from a cloud. Little idea droplets. I never expect them. I have no idea how they appear in my mind. Like when you are out walking, and a raindrop strikes you, and you look up… but then you feel stupid, because what were you hoping to see? A little hole in the cloud that the raindrop fell out of? The next raindrop in line, falling down toward your head? Of course when you look up, you get a second drop right in your eye. So I do not stop to ask myself where my ideas come from. Perhaps you haven't noticed my tiny ideas, because these thought droplets or driblets or dewdrops are woven into the very fabric of what I say, sorry, that is pompous, and also it's a cliché, and also it doesn't make any sense, you don't weave droplets or driblets into fabrics, you weave threads, everything in a fabric is threads, even the little rabbit in the middle of the tapestry, because there's always a rabbit, I don't know why, oh wait, I remember, they represent chastity, or no, actually the opposite, they represent lechery, well, maybe not lechery, it's hard to imagine a lecherous rabbit.

She paused a moment, concentrating.

At any rate I know a better analogy: the Flood Theory, the eighth of my thirteen theories. My thinking is like a flooded river, Samuel, the kind you see on news videos. The droplets, drips, and dribbles have become a torrent, the river has overflowed its banks, it moves in great heaves and crashes, the water is clay-colored and dim like soapy dish water. It is full of branches, garbage, and pieces of wood. You see a car float by, and then a white truck. The truck is hit by the car, it's like a traffic accident. A whole house drifts downstream, with a dog balancing on the peak of the roof. The house snags on a tree that's still standing in the middle of the torrent, but the current turns the house and pushes it onward. You spot a couple of empty bottles, an air mattress, a telephone pole trailing wires, a single daisy resting lightly on the surface of the flood, an audio speaker, what else, a Styrofoam cup, a side table. Suddenly you see a head, a woman is gasping for air, there are books floating around her, and then she's gone. You shake your head, because what can you do? Then a motorboat, half sunk, prow up. The current flips it and it disappears. The river is rising, you have to step back and get on higher ground, otherwise the bank will crumble under your feet and you will be swept away.[20]

Was that you in the flood?

It's confusing, isn't it? I am the flood, so I guess I couldn't drown, but then again what do you do in floods except drown? I have flooded my banks, Samuel, I am forever going on, I am a mess and I'm picking up speed, that's what I hope, I want my thinking to carry everything along with it, I want to come tearing down off the mountains or wherever floodwater comes from, I guess from mountains, although it could also come from plains, really wet plains, floodplains, I'm not sure what those are, are floodplains plains where water goes when it floods, or are floodplains plains that are flooded with water? I mean are floodplains plains that sometimes flood, that sounds right, doesn't it, floodplains are floodable plains, but, or, are floodplains flooded plains, places where water goes after it has flooded some other places, like somewhere up in the mountains, and then it runs down onto the floodplains? I don't like the idea that my thinking starts out in any type of floodplains. Places like that are nasty, they have mosquitoes. I would rather say the water in my flooded thinking comes tearing straight down out of the mountains, it's meltwater, it's snowmelt, *Schmelzwasser*. I'm not sure what the difference is there, maybe meltwater comes from ice, but then it should be called icemelt, or melt ice, or ice meltwater, so people would know, anyway this water, whatever it is, cascades off cliffs thousands of feet high, it runs in rivulets through icefields, I don't know what those are either, but I am not about to stop and try to figure that out, although I suppose icefields could be snowfields that have frozen solid, or they could be formed when meltwater or icemelt or melt ice flows over cold ground, maybe especially cold floodplains, I'll have to think about that later, anyway this water comes racing down mountain ravines, gathers force and binds into a single tremendous torrent, it comes out of the mountains and sweeps through a town, like the Aare through Bern, for example, this is how I imagine it, this is how I imagine my thinking in the Flood Theory, the water of my thinking rushes into the houses, it breaks the doors open, smashes all the windows, goes through all the rooms, it pours into the basement, it even runs upstairs, it wants everything, it takes the photographs and paintings, leafs through all the books, pries open drawers and snatches secret diaries, carries everything with it, china, audio speakers, pillows, cats, people, lamps, bottles, silverware, wallpaper, it strips the thought off things, because it's a flood of thought, the Flood Theory is my favorite fantasy, its mood is crazy happiness, my thought carries everything out of the world and into the flood, that's what my flooded thinking is like, it's not droplets, it's glorious! Everything in the world is drenched in the flood of my thinking. It's also very romantic, all this destruction, but there's a problem, there's always a problem, isn't there, there's always some obstacle, you know how it is, you can be full of enthusiasm, you get very worked up about something, you really throw yourself into an idea, plunge right in, get carried away, get carried along in the current of your idea, your arms flail, your notebooks float all around you, your mouth is full of water, you're swimming for all you're worth, gasping, barely keeping afloat, it's wonderful, just the way thinking should be, but then there's always someone standing there on the bank looking at you in shock and sadness. That person takes a couple steps back so the bank doesn't collapse under her feet, and she watches you go by and she shakes her head, slowly, the way people do when they see something that's hopeless.

So I am drowning?

You might be. Floods are disorienting, you dream about drowning and you watch people drown and then you drown. So the person on the bank shakes her head, because she knows that eventually the flood will drain away and the sun will come out, and then guess what, there won't be anything left but junk. An ocean floor of muck. Like in the ninth theory, the Compost Theory. Trash, half-buried animals, ruined furniture, cars coated in mud, soiled clothes, even toilet paper, everything will be worthless, especially the toilet paper, that will be particularly useless, everything will have to be thrown away, that's what I am afraid of, I think my swollen flood-like thinking will drain away and my work will be revealed a muddy plain with useless broken things stuck in it. But I can't help it, I speak in a more or less continuous way, an endless way, I seldom stop, I mean why should I? Except every once in a while to breathe, and even then I breathe very quickly, I bet you hardly notice when I breathe, and there's a reason, it's because I have trained myself to breathe in the middle of sentences, not between sentences, because that would make it easier for people like you to interrupt me, so I have trained myself to breathe before prepositions, so for example I just said, "because that makes it easier for people like you to interrupt me, so I have trained myself to breathe before prepositions," when I said that I did not breathe in the middle, like this, "because that makes it easier for people like you to interrupt me, breath, so I have trained myself to breathe before prepositions," because then people like you could interrupt me right there in the middle of my thought, so instead I have trained myself to breathe before prepositions, like this, "because that makes it easier for people like you to interrupt me, so I have trained myself to breathe, breath, before prepositions," that way people miss their chance to interrupt me, and that is why Paul says, "For heaven's sake just take a breath," or, "Please just stop a minute and breathe," or, "For one blessed second, please, oh please, just stop, stop, oh god please stop," that sort of thing, or maybe I am confusing him with the elevator operator, but no, that person is vile, Paul is lovely, I think he means well, besides you also told me to stop, a few minutes ago you said, "Okay, stop," and then you said, "Okay, that's enough." Luzi doesn't say anything, she just walks away, she is the smartest one of all of us, but the point is that even though I do not customarily stop speaking except momentarily before selected prepositions, my speech is actually composed of small thoughts. Droplet ideas. But that is enough plapper. What matters is my work. It has become monstrous. My study is filled with notebooks. I mean that literally. When I stand in front of my desk I am shocked to see myself sitting there, up to my elbows in floodwater, the notebooks floating around me, waterlogged and swollen, in the wash of my hopeless ideas.

She surveyed the lounge with an alarmed expression, looking up and down the walls, and back and forth across the empty coffee table.[21]

# 7

## ANNELIESE'S SUMMER READING

**A COUPLE OF YEARS AGO,** she continued, I realized I needed to study how other people write long books, how they manage to give their books a shape, a pace, a satisfying ending, the kind of book you finish and say, "God, I can't believe I read all that, it took absolutely forever, parts were unbelievably tedious, but I am so glad I kept at it, it turns out the author wasn't just torturing me, I thought she was rambling, yet it turns out she had a plan, she knew what she was doing, and in the end it was an amazing experience, she's flawed of course but who isn't, her book holds together, it actually makes sense, and you know what? It is wildly imaginative, unsettling, hypnotic, and very peculiar, and by the way I will never, ever read it again." So I decided to read long books, and first I went to the library to read encyclopedias, because my notebooks are encyclopedic, and I thought maybe they are more like encyclopedias than normal books. I hoped that if I could find some good encyclopedias, really exciting ones, I could model my notebooks on them. My life's work would be an encyclopedia, with the volumes neatly arranged from A to Z. Encyclopedias are longer than the longest books, even very long books are scrawny by comparison with encyclopedias. The original encyclopedia was a French one in 10 volumes by someone named Louis Moréri, then there was another in 28 volumes. My edition of the *Encyclopædia Britannica* is 29 volumes, but it's too British for me. Pierer's *Universal Lexicon* is 34 volumes. There's an Arabic encyclopedia written by the Brethren of Purity, I mentioned it before, it is really only 52 Letters, and they added a Comprehensive Letter compressing all 52 into one long Letter, and then they compressed the Comprehensive Letter into a Condensed Comprehensive Letter, why did they do that? If you're going to write an encyclopedia, it should expand, not shrink. There's a Spanish encyclopedia with 119 volumes, and once there was a Chinese encyclopedia that was even longer, but there was only one copy of it, that's strange, isn't it, and then they lost it, except for part of one volume, I don't know how they managed to lose part of one volume, and when I read about that it occurred to me that maybe there never was a Chinese encyclopedia, or maybe it was actually short, or at least not as long as people say. I asked Arnulf Trausch about it, he is one of the useless librarians at the University of Basel, and he said the Chinese encyclopedia was 11,095 volumes long, and I told him I did not believe that, anyone can claim their book is 11,095 volumes long if they go and conveniently lose all of it except part of one volume. He said they didn't conveniently lose it, it was burned by French and German soldiers, and I told him that was convenient, and then he asked me why I wanted to read encyclopedias, and I said, "Just do your job," and he said, "Why don't you go and read Wikipedia, that will keep you busy," and I said, "Please be quiet for a moment, I am trying to decide what kind of worm you are," and he said, "Excuse me?" and I said, "I think you may be worm five, because you seem to have more gums than teeth, but maybe you are worm two, since you have large gelatinous eyes," and he said, "Professor Glur, will you please leave the library," and I was happy to, because he had reminded me that Wikipedia is bigger than any other encyclopedia. You can read all the articles in Wikipedia in alphabetical order, and if you do that they start long before the letter *a*, the first articles are actually on punctuation marks. The very first article is about the exclamation mark, and the next ones are about songs and popular bands.

!
!! (chess move, and a sound in the Juu language)
!!! (album)
!!! (American band)
!!!!!!! (Billie Eilish Invisalign track)

!!!Fuck You!!! (song)
!!!Fuck You!!! And Then Some (song)
!!! (Chk Chk Chk) (song)
!!Destroy-Oh-Boy!! (song)
!!Fuck you!! (song)

After those come lots of words that start with !, like "!Xóõ language," that is one of my favorite languages, the ! is a click sound, and then there is an article titled "!aaaH-aH ,yawA eM ekaT oT gnimoC er'yehT," which is "They're Coming To Take Me Away, Ha-Haaa!" written backwards, then words that start with a period, beginning with an article on the period, and then hundreds of words that start with %, then with &, then words that start with ', then with (, and so on. I was delighted, and I was just about to begin reading when I realized encyclopedias wouldn't help me because they have no form at all, they go idiotically from A to Z, or from "*!*" to "ZZZzz," which is an episode of the American television show *Outer Limits.* What could be stupider than to talk about everything? What happened to choice, balance, value, appraisal, judgment, consideration? I don't know why people write encyclopedias, what kind of people write them? What happened to order, reason, planning, organization, structure, form? Encyclopedias are like stamp collecting, Oh, wonderful, at last I have the 84¢ brown, now I have the entire set, look! No blank spaces in my cute little stamp album, isn't that satisfying? I feel very satisfied. It's not easy to get every stamp, you know. Okay, that's all good, but now what will I do with the rest of my life? Certainly for the foreseeable future, I will open my cute little stamp album most every day, and each time I'll sigh with contentment! But when I get tired of thinking about how pitiful it was when I only had two of the eighteen stamps in the series, how nervous I was when I was bidding on the 84¢ brown, how exquisite my 84¢ brown is, how beautifully centered and generously margined, how smug I was when Morschmulmig said he also collected German Democratic Republic ordinary issues of 1956-1959, but of course he didn't have the 84¢ brown, how unhappy he was when he saw my full set and admitted he only had the reissues, they are notoriously worthless, well, if I ever get tired of reliving those moments, then what? Then nothing, except of course I can recall the time I managed to get a copy of the infamous printing error on the 1¢ black, where the shirtless coal miner was engraved without his left nipple, a very scarce error, you'd think it would be hard to forget a nipple, I never forget nipples, I mean, if I was an artist I would never forget a nipple, I must have seen many nipples and I have forgotten all of them, I can't actually remember a single nipple except my own, is that normal? Anyway that is a stamp which I bought with only four months' salary, and immediately invited Morschmulmig to dinner, and set it out on a table, alongside an ordinary 1¢ black where the coal miner has his regular nipple, and of course along with the certificate of authenticity sent me by the Association of Philatelic Examiners, signed by Alexander Höhlentier, world-renowned authority on German Democratic Republic standard issues, which awarded my stamp one of its highest grades, Superb 98, and I watched with a gimlet eye as Morschmulmig's face slumped into a wormlike heap and his heart sank and mine rose like a happy worker in the GDR, although when the meal was over, and Morschmulmig had left, I couldn't think of anyone else who would be impressed and deflated by seeing my nippleless miner, and then I thought, okay, now my future really is empty. Encyclopedias are the same, they are the opposite of thinking, they actually stop people from thinking. You open one, like you open a stamp album, your mind gets all misty, you think the world is complete, all is in order, the 8¢ red showing the mother teaching Marxist principles right after the 6¢ purple depicting Soviet and German workers earnestly embracing, Aardvark before Albacore Tuna, Albacore Tuna before Albania, Albania before Albumen, that's nice, but do you actually read the article on Albumen? Of course not. Maybe that 6¢ purple isn't a Very Fine, maybe it's just Fine, the margins aren't as even as they could be, it should be replaced, that's what the stamp collector thinks. Just like encyclopedias, they can always be improved, they always need to be improved. You understand, Samuel, that I don't care about stamps at all, I'm just telling you how a stamp collector thinks, she gets concerned about quality, she decides everything should be Very Fine or above, many of the stamps in her collection are already Exceptional and a few are Superb, it's true, but maybe if I mortgaged the house again I could upgrade my entire collection—possibly the world's best collection of German Democratic Republic ordinary issues of 1956-1959—to Very

Fine or Exceptional. That would take years, thank goodness, the stamp collector thinks, and immediately she calls her bank. Or, if you are one of those obsessive people who write the entries in Wikipedia, you look up Albumen, and you can't find anything about it, only an entry on Albumin, that is a protein, and nothing on Albumen. You feel jittery, you panic. The world isn't complete, it isn't orderly, it probably isn't safe. Immediately you start writing. It's as if you have an outstanding collection of German Democratic Republic ordinary issues of 1956-1959, but you become enraged at yourself for being enraged at the enraging defects of your collection so you burn it. That would take about one minute, because stamps are very small. Wikipedia is crippled by the wooden mindset of the people who contribute to it. Why would anyone help write encyclopedias? What kind of mouselike person wants to spend her time writing an entry on Albumen, as if anyone would ever go to an encyclopedia to consult the entry on Albumen? Does such a person imagine someone sitting at breakfast, contemplating her perfect egg, with the whites nicely clouded but still nearly translucent, a really excellent egg, an *oeuf en cocotte,* not an ordinary indifferently cooked egg, raw or burnt or rubbery or greasy or runny or mucilaginous or scungilaginous or soupy or cold and clammy or stringy and gooey or the texture of warm phlegm, a person sitting admiring the milky turbid albumen of her perfectly cooked egg, and suddenly thinking, Oh my, I know so little about albumen, so very little. I am going to sit down and read a boring article about it right away. And does the person who is imagining this scene think, Oh my, what if there is no entry in the encyclopedia for Albumen, then what? Well, yes, that is exactly what she thinks. So she sits down right away and sets to work writing the entry on Albumen. Samuel, you think I am inventing this, but Wikipedia is enormous, the world must be full of people like that, people who cannot imagine anything else to do, they cannot think of anything else to think, clearly they prefer not to talk to their family, or maybe their family are all dead or they have run away, so these people spend their evenings crafting magnificent sentences like, "Albumen is the white portion of the common egg," and "Albumen is most commonly known as 'egg white,'" and "Egg white has many uses in edible food, for example meringues and mousses, and many other uses." And that is not the end of it, because for every person who feels lost because there is no entry on Albumen, and for every other person who sits up late writing their very best sentences about Albumen, there is a third person who wants to edit the article on Albumen, to make sure it is clear, orderly, error-free, and reasonably complete on its topic, and in addition well provided with properly formatted citations, and with no fancy adjectives or colorful turns of phrase (so that the prose is as dull as humanly possible), and with nothing subjective or biased (so that nothing is actually interesting), and above all with no original thoughts whatsoever (because Wikipedia is absolutely set against being original, it is utterly, systematically, publicly, officially opposed to contributing even a single new idea to the world). This third person reads the newly posted essay on Albumen, and she wants to mark it Citation Needed, Inappropriate Language, Possible Bias, Needs Revision, Possible Original Material, and if the essay is not improved right away, she wants to plant a little red flag on it, Flag for Deletion, because it is better to have no article on Albumen at all than to have one that is potentially misleading or contains a single morsel of original thought. But if it is hard to imagine a person who has a sudden desire to read an encyclopedia entry on Albumen, and if it is harder to picture a person who wants to write an entry on Albumen, then it is virtually impossible to understand a person who feels the need to police an essay on Albumen. What kind of nasty, lonely, cowardly person likes to needle the kind of sad, unimaginative, stamp collecting sort of person who writes the entry on Albumen, when all that person is trying to do is bring a small measure of calm to the skittish, unsteady, empty-headed person who feels a sudden need to learn about Albumen? What sort of appalling, sputtering, vicious, half-living person plumps her pillow and settles in for a good night's sleep knowing that fully 71 of the 80 sentences in the entry for Albumen have been marked Citation Needed, Inappropriate Language, Possible Bias, Needs Revision, Possible Original Material, and Flag for Deletion, most especially including the ungrammatical, repetitive, unbalanced, and entirely useless sentence, "Egg white has many uses in edible food, for example meringues and mousses, and many other uses"? I tried editing articles for a while, but I had to stop, because I was spending all day Flagging for Deletion, I Flagged everything, not just mistakes and missing citations, not just flabby sentences like that one about albumen, a sentence, by the way, which manages to say almost nothing and at the same time contains an infantile error, that expression "edible food," I mean what was that person thinking, and an unnecessary alliteration, "meringues and mousses," and a sickening rhyme, "mousses and many other uses," unbearable, isn't it? I literally could not sleep the entire night after I read that, "mousses and many other uses," anyway not just sentences like that, but entire articles, one after the other I Flagged them for Deletion, useless articles no one would ever need, especially biographical articles about supposedly important biologists who do not deserve to be remembered, and then another Editor noticed what I was doing, my Flags for Deletion were Flagged for Deletion, I was called into a Community Editor Forum, I was Advised, Admonished, and then Warned, and finally Temporarily Suspended, I was never permanently blocked, they don't do that, and I could still Appeal, but I was furious. What kind of sickly, neurologically defective, genetically compromised person spends her time policing the diligent, punctilious, dedicated people who are only trying to improve the articles that were written by the embarrassing, reclusive, socially crippled people who were only trying to help the poor, uncherished, vulnerable people who supposedly actually read articles on topics like albumen? So I looked up some of the Editors' identities, you are not supposed to be able to do that but of course you can, and I wrote to three of them and told them who I was, and as a result I was put on Indefinite Suspension for Behavior Inappropriate to Wikipedia Common Community Standards. I could still Appeal, but then I realized there is only one of me and an endless supply of obstinate Editors who want, more than anything else in life, more than reading a nice book or going to a movie, even more than finding out what happened to their families, although I doubt their families want to see them, even their mothers cover their mouths with handkerchiefs when they talk to them, their mothers must be heartily sick of hearing about Wikipedia, no, what these Editors want, more than anything, is to make Wikipedia accurate and complete, just in case some day, just maybe, someone will actually read the article on Albumen, or just in case some moronic new form of life arrives on Earth and is startled by albumen and needs to know what it is. So I stopped reading encyclopedias. I have seven reasons.

First, they are formless: they mindlessly follow the alphabet, they are captive to the completely arbitrary order of the alphabet. Second, there is no judgment in them. Third, they are formless because they have no judgment. Fourth—

Wait, what was that third one?

Every time I make a list, the third item causes trouble. The third reason is the first reason because of the second reason.

That doesn't really help.

Well, anyway, fourth, their readers are insipid and easily soothed. Fifth, so are their writers. Sixth, the editors are intolerable martinets. And seventh, I stopped reading because I was jealous. I want people to look at my bound notebooks all lined up on a shelf like a row of encyclopedias, each spine stamped with a nice asterism, and think, There it is, the whole world on one shelf, so attractive and intimidating. I hope my notebooks look like that, but now I know they are not encyclopedias. They are something more interesting. They have order but also disorder, they are comprehensive but they have gaps, nothing in them is moderate, nothing is policed. So I gave up on encyclopedias and started my search for long and complex books that could be models for my work. First I read the longest books in my own field, in biology.[22] I read Darwin, of course, his famous book is actually five volumes long. It turns out to be relentlessly unexciting, as if he hired a hundred bureaucrats from Brussels to rewrite it over and over and remove even the tiniest flake of interest, to ensure that no one would ever sit up and say, "Okay, at least that bit about tumbler-pigeons was interesting, it is curious that some pigeons tumble when they try to fly, so how exactly did that develop?" No one would ever have thought of teaching a pigeon to tumble, that's what Darwin says, but as soon as I read that I thought, I might have, if I was abysmally bored and surrounded by pigeons, the way I was feeling when I read that chapter, and then Darwin says probably no one even could have taught pigeons to tumble, and that is ignorant, people teach birds all sorts of things, they can talk, dance up and down, side to side, nod their heads yes, shake their heads no, windmill head, step up, sit on your shoulder, step down, moonwalk, climb a ladder, click their beaks, click their heels, cha-cha, ride a skateboard, wave hello with one wing, SOS with both wings, spin around, stop biting you, do the eagle pose, salute with one wing, say "yes ma'am!," wink at you, stop biting you, wings akimbo, stop biting you, hang upside down like a bat, drunk bird, go find some money, attack that child next door, stop your endless hopping, stop biting, go to sleep, statue bird, play dead, stop biting, fall onto the floor, play rotting bird with your beak open and your tongue out, of course you could teach a pigeon to tumble, and of course someone did, someone bored out of her mind like I was when I read Darwin. I wish I could have trained him to tumble, I would have taught him to tuck his hideous mangy beard between his knees and tumble down a cliff into the ocean. I wasted a month reading Darwin, that was like spending a month looking at a sink full of dishwater. I even read his last book, *The Formation of Vegetable Mould Through the Action of Worms*, it begins with the stirring line, "The share which worms have taken in the formation of the layer of vegetable mould, which covers the whole surface of the land in every moderately humid country, is the subject of the present volume," and I admit it is nice to know that "all the vegetable mould over the whole country has passed many times through, and will again pass many times through, the intestinal canals of worms," and it is heartwarming to read how he taught his two unfortunate sons William and Francis that earthworms are intelligent, and they act just like we would if we were sightless, legless, armless, and lived in vegetable mould, that is, they squirm a lot, and he ends his book, and his whole life's work, with a sweet reverie, looking over a grassy meadow in England, marveling how its irregularities have been smoothed by worms, as they inexorably and thoroughly passed the entire beautiful landscape through their bodies and excreted it in a more pleasing form. For me, meadows and rolling hills will be forever enhanced by my new awareness that they are soft sculptures of worm castings. And it is infinitely comforting to imagine the compost of my mind as rolling English hills. Darwin was a sort of clodpoll, I don't deny he was the greatest biologist, but he had an obstinate mud-like idiocy. I couldn't learn anything about structure and form from his books, although I did get some useful tips on composting. Then I tried to read the second-most famous book in biology, Buffon's *Natural History* in 44 volumes. Why is that book famous? Why is it a so-called classic of biology? "The wild boar is a magnificent animal," he writes, "he is immensely strong, but he is shy and eats only plants. He is sometimes to be seen by the light of the moon, delighting in a field of oats or barley, because he loves them more even than corn. He is content in his place in nature, and he produces happy grunts and puffs of abdominal gasses." I thought, okay, that is childish. And then Buffon tells me how to kill the wild boar. "And yet this peaceful monster can be savage. When you hunt him do not use hunting dogs trained on deer, because they will be sorely wounded. He will use his massive tusks to rip them open and you will have to leave them gasping and yelping in the field. As soon as you have killed him, raise the lower leg, reach in, and slice off his testicles, because their odor is so strong that in five hours they will spoil all the meat, and that would be a pity because great profits arise from the wild boar. Then you may light a pipe to perfume the air and guard against the steam of his innards. If he is young and healthy his flesh sells for double that of ox meat, his lard for more than double, and his blood, brains, and viscera are all good to eat and fetch competitive prices." It makes me sick thinking how much time I wasted reading Buffon, I read all 44 volumes, of course, because I read everything, it took me 23 days, I felt like he was leaning over my shoulder puffing his pipe and shaking his powdered wig until I was covered in wig dandruff, and then he sneezed and his snuff and snot went all over me, and then he laughed and his plywood teeth fell down my blouse, and that made him laugh even harder and his syphilis spot popped off and went in my eye, and then he started coughing and hacked a foam of boar lard onto my cheek, I couldn't stand it, I pushed the books away and read Linnaeus instead. I thought, This will be serious work, this is where I'll find a model for my notebooks. Linnaeus was the father of taxonomy, quite possibly more fundamental for my field even than Darwin. He wrote a very long book that arranges all living things in perfect order. Everyone uses his system, Kingdom, Class, Order, Genus, Species, but no one reads his book. When he first wrote it the book was thin, but he kept adding material, he had a collection of thousands of animals and plants that he kept in cardboard boxes, all labeled, in perfect order, and people sent him new animals and plants and rocks and shells and he labeled them all and put them in cardboard boxes and added their names to his book. In the end it was 10 volumes long, 6,257 pages, that is 503 pages on beetles, 49 pages on mosquitoes, 815 pages on vermin. I read them all. The pages on mosquitoes were excellent. But Linnaeus was a total waste of time. He made so many mistakes. I looked up worms, for example. There is a Class of Worms, which he calls Vermes. I wanted to see the most primitive worm so I could reassign Morschmulmig to the Lowest Possible Worm category. I looked in volume 10, Part VI, where Linnaeus puts worms. All my favorite worms are there. He divides the Class of Vermes into three Orders of Vermes, and he calls the third one Microcosmus, World of Little Worms, and he divides Microcosmus into several Families of Little Worms, and the last Family, the lowest one, is called Chaos, and he divides Chaos into four Genera: Proteus, that is the amoeba, then something he calls "Chaos fungorum feminum," the feminine fungus chaos, which he says is transsexual animal spores that turn vegetable and produce mushrooms, that is slime mold, he says it was discovered by the Baron von Münchhausen of all people, then something called "Furia infernalis," a tiny translucent worm that flies through the air and bites people who wade in swamps in Rear Bothnia in northern Finland, it actually burrows into the skin of people who have made the mistake of wading in swamps in Rear Bothnia, and it can only be drawn out of the skin with a poultice made of cheese curds, and then at the end of the list, there it was, the Lowest Possible Worm, the final worm in the entire world. The last thing God made, his least distinguished creation. The most degraded worm. A little sputum he hacked up after he made absolutely everything else. The Lowest Possible Worm gets a special category called Obscurae, Darknesses, mysteries within a chaos within the World of Little Worms, and I thought, great, this will be worm 14, Morschmulmig's Worm, and I see it is called "Spermatici vermiculi Leeuwenh.?," Sperm Worms discovered by Leeuwenhoeck, inventor of the microscope, with a question mark because Linnaeus wasn't sure, and I realized these are human sperm, first discovered by Leeuwenhoeck, which Linnaeus put at the very end of the category of worms, hiding them in a darkness in a chaos, probably because he was a man and he couldn't bear to think sperm are human, not worms, it was better to admit his body had creeping sperm worms inside it, because after all his body probably already had tapeworms, ringworms, and pinworms, it was better than admitting that the only thing men contribute to the world is squirming sperm, so he put the sperm worms as far away as he could, at the utter end of the animal kingdom, as far as possible from people. After the sperm worms there is nothing, they are the end of the universe of creation, the stain under the dregs beneath the residue of the sputum of creation, the hole in the bottom of the sea, and so the book ends, well almost, because the next page is titled Paradoxa, those are animals *in dubium vocatur,* they have been called into question, they are *forte ficta,* probably fictions, like satyrs and unicorns that Linnaeus couldn't quite believe were real. Paradoxa includes pelicans, because Linnaeus had never seen a live pelican, and he thought they looked monstrous, and for some reason people thought they pecked open their own breasts to feed their chicks with fresh blood, and opossums, Linnaeus had never seen them either, and he thought that when they were frightened their young climbed back into the womb where the nipples were located, and then there is the borometz, my emblem and favorite, an animal *in dubium vocatur,* like me! After that the book really does end. It's not a neat ending, not exactly conclusive. Transsexual fungus, sperm worms, pelicans, and the borometz. It doesn't look like creation was very well planned. For 6,256 pages everything is systematic in the *System of Nature,* but in the end it isn't, and in fact it quakes with errors. He puts sperm under worms, he puts whales under fish, he thinks a stork is a heron, a grebe is a loon, he thinks crystals are alive, he says they grow when salty male minerals impregnate female soil, and by the way I suppose that means male minerals have their own sperm worms, and he also thinks tapeworms have no heads and live forever, that's because back then everyone had tapeworms and the segments used to come out in the toilet, and everyone saw they were alive, but they had no heads, and that was just too much for some people, and another writer, Jonas Alströmer, said tapeworm segments in diarrhea were just excrescences of the inner film of the small intestine that had sloughed off, and they were not alive, but Linnaeus said Alströmer was wrong, the segments writhe in the toilet, he said, everyone sees them, they are clearly headless worms, Class Vermes, Order Cestoda, Genus Taenia, Species *Immortalis acephala,* Immortal Headless Tapeworms. Linnaeus jams everything into his maniacal system, he must have been an awful person.

Everything had to be classified into Kingdom, Class, Order, Genus, Species, I imagine he kept his family in cardboard boxes, one labeled Daughter, Descended from Wife and Self, another one Dog, deceased, pet of Daughter.

Actually Linnaeus sounds familiar, I said. He reminds me of my mother. She wanted to be a scientist. She classified everything, and in particular mushrooms—

Actually I am much more fanatical about organizing than Linnaeus, he was Swedish but I am Swiss German, we are far more compulsive. I don't know what your mother was, you can try telling me later if you need to. So I am attracted to long books because they have universes in them, they are *de omni re scibili,* on every conceivable subject as Pico della Mirandola said, *de omnibus rebus, et quibusdam aliis,* about everything and then some. Darwin, Buffon, and Linneaus wrote about everything they ever saw or even heard about, and by the way I realize Linnaeus was not just a fanatic, I understand that he is responsible for the analogic method in natural history, and I know he changed his mind about sperm worms, he decided they were lifeless things that float around in semen like wiggly drops of oil, at least he admitted they were human, and also I know he died horribly, his bladder, his tongue, and his "lower body parts" were all paralyzed, so I sympathize with him and I understand his work in its larger context, but I do not want my work to be an enormous collection of cardboard boxes. *System of Nature* is 6,257 pages of cardboard boxes, and one is wet because it's full of sperm worms. Actually the world is complicated. Systems are not that easy anymore. These days the long books in biology are not read by anyone. They are databases. Like *WormBase,* it's all about nematodes, of course I love it, but no one reads it because it's nothing but genetic code. The genes are all numbered in *WormBase,* you can look up gene 00006964 and you will discover that it is 10,263 base pairs long, and *WormBase* says the list of 10,263 starts out AGAAAATAAAACTCCGA... No human can read that kind of book. I tried, I fell asleep four times and I only read 581 base pairs of one gene out of 20,000 genes with 100,000,000 base pairs. I calculated that if I read *WormBase* eight hours a day it would take me two years and ten months and I would fall asleep 100,000 times. There are databases for the genetics of yeasts, there's *FlyWire* and *FlyBase* for flies, they have the complete fly brain, every single neuron, there is a database for Norway rats, for African clawed frogs, *GenBank* for viruses and bacteria, and of course the human genome project, millions of pages of genetic code, and the Global Biodiversity Information Facility, they are like Borges's infinite library, unreadable forever. Illiterate scientists program their computers to sample the databases so they can identify even more genes and put them into even larger databases. I realized there are no models in biology for what my work is, no books that are long and complex but still readable. If Linnaeus had written 6,000 pages on immortal headless toilet worms and just a couple of pages on cardboard boxes, he might have had an interesting book. Reading those books and looking at *WormBase* made me unhappy and unsure of myself, because I saw that I was not writing normal science. But then I had another idea. I turned to long books of history. I thought, Just because there are no interesting long books in biology doesn't mean I should give up, doesn't mean what I am doing is wrong.

But what are you doing?

I can't tell you that now. I need to explain what is wrong with long books written by other people, and then you will see why I needed to find a model for my work. So I decided to read the longest history books I could find. My work has history in it, the history of other people's errors, and my work is about the history of ideas of life, so it is a kind of history. I hoped I was writing a kind of history. I read Jules Michelet's *History of France* in 19 volumes, it is one of the most famous history books ever written. It's a pageant, a parade of French history, a triumphal march, it's full of temperance and beneficence, maleficence and concupiscence, it's swollen with overripe French pride. Michelet had no difficulty keeping his work in order because his story was so simple. He thought the Christian middle ages were abhorrent but the French people were innately good, and finally they triumphed, they invented the French Revolution, medieval France became secular, confused people turned rational, the French became magisterial and haughty, *hautain.* They embraced each other, they wept, they invented the forearm handshake, the *poignée de l'avant-bras,* they were proud and happy. That was our Revolution, they said, and on they marched with their forearms awkwardly clasped into the bright republican future, and I admit Michelet tells a great story, I wish

I had a simple story like that, or even a *gouttelette* of French blood in me, it would make me so complacent, but I don't, and I don't, and I'm not, and whatever my theory is, it isn't a crowd of French people waving flags and singing, so I went on and read Edward Gibbon's *Decline and Fall of the Roman Empire,* that's 12 volumes in my 1832 edition, 1,500,000 words, with 10,000 names of Romans and 12,000 names of places. I can remember about four of them. Supposedly it's the most accomplished book of history ever written, but it is a child in comparison to my notebooks, they are five times longer, and not only that but Gibbon's book is like a children's story because everyone knows what happened in the end: Rome fell, so Gibbon had no problem at all keeping to his theme, he just cast long shadows, in each volume the shadows are more sinister and the light is farther away, there is corruption and senseless killing, the great families are exterminated, the mighty and equitable empire of Augustus and Trajan is reduced to a distant memory, the feeble give way to the cruel, the timid to the inhuman, Rome groans beneath an unremitting tyranny, until the last godless spineless insecure emperor has his family killed in front of him while the Goths are approaching, good government is extinguished for another thousand years, and in the end there is Petrarch in the early Renaissance, standing among the ruins and wondering what became of the past. It is the world's longest obituary, the saddest and the greatest one ever written, but my work has no obituaries in it, except of course little headstones for all the scientists I don't like. So I stopped reading history. Either it's starry and full of *poignée de l'avant-bras* or it's about how the world sinks, law and culture are corrupted, one after another the sciences and arts are forgotten, until finally darkness and ignorance dance across the earth, and we all know that anyway, that's just how the world is, so why read about it?

Well, people talk about the lessons of history—

The only lesson in Michelet is that it's really good to be French, and the only lesson in Gibbon is that eventually nothing will be left of any culture except a person sitting on a block of marble and scratching his head or another person sitting at her desk wondering why she wasted two weeks reading such a long book about something so obvious. But they are both long books, like mine, so they made me jealous. I thought, Well, if my theory was that simple I could write it as a great parade or a pompous tragedy and things would be so much easier for me, and for you too. But it's not, so I went on. Next I read long books of medicine, because my work is about life, and doctors supposedly care about life. And that is where I found a genuinely complex long book, one that could be a guide for my own work. It is Robert Burton's *Anatomy of Melancholy,* only 1,509 pages long in the standard German translation. I assume you don't know it? Yes? No? Okay. It is a seventeenth-century medical treatise on depression, but really it is about bipolar disorder. It is magnificently disordered, like me. Burton would have loved that expression, bipolar, it would have sounded to him like a disorder caused by the North and South Poles, he would have called it something like The Disorder that makes a man feel he inhabits first the Northern, and then the Southern Pole, producing a double freezing effect, refrigerating his lungs, compressing and drying his brain, petrifying his liver, compacting his stool, ossifying his wooly calculi, that's what Burton would have said, causing his spleen to crystallize, spalling his eyes with a glassy ice, that's the way he wrote, polarizing his thoughts under malign astrological signs, producing clouded, unpleasant, and dire thoughts, causing him to think about glaciers, gross arctic bears, thick-lidded narwhals, the discarded cauls of infant mermaids, whatever, well, he wouldn't have said "whatever," that's a ridiculous modern word, but that's the way he wrote, as if he would never stop, just like me! Burton's mind set off on endless journeys, he would have been intrigued to be told he was bipolar, his imagination would have boarded ship to the iced regions of the Arctic and then spun southward toward the legendary Antipodes, and he would have loved the made-up words pharmaceutical companies use for their drugs, he would have appreciated Effexor, it sounds so Latinate, *effector, effectoris,* but also feminine, *effectrix,* it sounds like a person, That's Effectrix, my loyal assistant Effectrix, *ea pro me laborat,* and then there's Nootkatone, Evolva makes that, Burton could have said it comes from the exotic Nootka tree, brought at tremendous expense from the New World, and Pristiq, Prozac, Remeron, Sarafem, Fetzima, they would have sounded Arabic to him, he didn't read Arabic but he knew the Arabic philosophers, he would have imagined those drugs came from exotic places in the East, brought to Europe on camelback, and how about Trintelllix, Zoloft, and Zyprexa, he would have thought they were alchemical, conjured in dark cellars by bearded magi whose breaths are sour from drinking tinctures of mercury and chewing on arsenic stars. Trintelllix is the rarest of them all, Burton would have said, it is mystically spelled with three *l's,* Trintelllix, some say it was concocted by Hermes Trismegistus himself, the Thrice-kingly Hermes, his name artfully concealed in his concoction, Trintelllix, Trismegistus's most secret cure for melancholy, that is what Burton would have said, but I am making this up, I am just trying to show you how he thought. Burton must have talked for days on end, in that way I think he was actually worse than me. He knew he was not rational. Again like me. He was muddled and desperate. He wrote and rewrote his book, six times. He was trying to understand his own melancholy, his bipolar disorder. He knew the line in the Gospel of Luke, *medice, cura te ipsum,* doctor, please just cure yourself. Well, he was trying. The chapters are short, just a couple of pages each, and there are hundreds of them, nearly a thousand chapters in all. He gives his readers a hierarchical outline of the whole work, twelve pages long, with the different subjects arrayed in brackets.

{

{

{

It looks so systematic, so logical. First he announces he will treat the causes of melancholy, then the kinds, and last their cures. I thought I could do that with my own work, organize it into an outline. First the causes of my subject, which I haven't told you yet, then its kinds, then its cures. In Burton's book each subject bifurcates, trifurcates, quadrifurcates. Each Partition, that is what he called the principal parts of his book, each Partition has Sections, and each Section has Members, and each Member has Subsections. If you cut out the twelve pages of his outline and tape them together into a chart, I did that, then it is nine feet long. I spread it out on the floor of my study and I thought it looked wonderful, very hopeful.[23] But then I discovered that it isn't rational. In Partition 1, I will give you just one example, Section 2 is actually a small subheading of Section 1. That's not right, it's like Section 1 ate Section 2, and Section 2 is inside Section 1. So you don't read Section 1 and then Section 2, like in a rationally organized book. Instead you read Section 1, and then inside Section 1 you discover Section 2. And it turns out Section 3 is inside Section 2, like a dollhouse inside a dollhouse inside a dollhouse, or like quail eggs packed into a fish into a goose into a sheep into a camel. Some headings are divided into eight or nine subheadings, and it gets so complicated Burton forgets where he is in his own book. He neglects to label Member 2 under Section 1 in Partition 1, I mean he labels Member 1 and Member 3, sorry, just one more example, Member 1 and Member 3 are very clearly marked on the first page of his twelve-page, nine-foot-long table of contents, even though they are in small print, but he entirely forgets Member 2. I don't think anyone in all the four centuries since Burton has noticed that, but I did, I found Member 2 on page 138 of volume 1, so there it was, and when I checked the hierarchical outline, I verified he had put the description for Member 2 under Member 3, he had lost control of his own system, the whole thing was ruined right near the beginning.

Sorry, I'm trying, but I can't follow that.

It's simple, he put the description for Member 2 under Member 3. In Section 1, in Partition 1.

Okay.

And then, or at the same time, or maybe earlier, he forgot to label Member 2 in Section 1.

This is a model for you?

It is not an outline, it is a map of Burton's disordered mind, a diagram of his disarranged thinking. Still, I thought it was more promising than Linnaeus's cardboard boxes or an encyclopedia that goes from "*!* " to "ZZZzz." But then I noticed that it only gets worse, there's error after error, he forgets what he was talking about, he lumps categories that should be separated, he can't keep track of his thoughts, even in his short chapters. In the space of a page or two, he forgets his subject and starts talking about heaven knows what, how scholars are penniless, how clerics should be honest, how people used to put lotions on spears in order to cure wounds the spears had caused, how people used to eat fumadoes, whatever they were, smoked fish I guess, like in *fumabat,* or *fumare, fumado,* that was in order to be able to hold their alcohol better. Or how a pregnant mother looked at a dead body and it affected her unborn child, her baby was born looking like a corpse, and they called him Carcass Child, he tells us that, even though it has nothing to do with what he is supposed to be writing about, which is how older people are naturally melancholy and full of aches, sorrows, and pains, how they're churlish, and they sit there, suspicious of everyone, wayward, covetous, self-willed, and conceited, how they are braggarts, they admire themselves, they imagine they are noble and full of wisdom, but they are actually addled, they are wretches, solitary, struck down with grief, some of them are even witches and they "translate" themselves from place to place, that's what he says, they piss on rooftops, that is what old witches do, and then he tells us how people used to be more vigorous, but now everyone is weak. These days, he says, doctors can only take a thimble of blood from a patient, but it used to be that doctors could drain out six pounds of blood and their patients would still be happy and joke and dance. In one place he even stops and tells you how to defecate on a regular basis, because otherwise your face will become inflamed, you'll feel dull and cloudy, you'll get headaches, I thought that part would be useful for Paul, it's a problem he has, constipation, and then Burton recounts a story told by someone named Doctor Skenkius, he had a patient who was constipated for ten days, the man was grievously melancholy and his face was inflamed, he was a German merchant who had gone to the Nordeling Fair in Germany, which is actually the Nördlingen Stadtmauerfest, Town Wall festival, in Nördlingen, near Munich, it's held every couple of years, Paul and I have been there, it's great fun, it's a medieval festival, which is funny, because Burton lived in the seventeenth century and it hadn't been that long since the middle ages, maybe three centuries, but apparently even back in the seventeenth century people were nostalgic for the middle ages, anyway there is lots to eat and drink, and I can't imagine being constipated there, but this merchant was, until he went to see Doctor Skenkius, who gave him a philter, with a *ph,* not an *f,* that is, a potion or an elixir, an elixir is a drink made with alcohol, this one had mandrake root in it, because that was a popular diarrheal, or diarrheic, or diarrhoeal, or is it diarrhoeic, or diarrhoetic, I don't know how to get mandrake root anyway, so that wouldn't be any help for Paul, but anyway mandrake is a plant with lovely purple flowers and it has a root that sometimes, not very often, but occasionally, maybe rarely, looks like a person, not much, but a little, like a hairy tubby boy with fat arms and legs, and the philter or elixir cured the German merchant immediately, which I suppose means it gave him the runs, but Doctor Skenkius—it's an unusual name, isn't it, he also wrote about pleurisy, pleuropneumonia, pluralpneumonias, and plague—Skenkius had watched people "bleeding liberally," so he says, from the plague, so he wasn't really bothered by a constipated German businessman suddenly relieving himself at enormous volume. Skenkius says the result made the merchant "delighted" and he went on and ate his fill and drank two barrels' worth of beer. As you can imagine, Samuel, I became thoroughly frightened that I might be like Burton. I asked myself if I could learn from his system, if I could correct it and use it to organize my own work. His book has three Partitions, and as I said, each one is divided into Sections, Sections into Members, Members into Subsections. I modernized my copy, I changed Partitions into Roman numerals I, II, III, Sections into A, B, C, Members into (i), (ii), (iii), and Subsections into (a), (b), (c), that's the rational way to make an outline, which we were taught in school. An outline should alternate between Roman and Arabic numerals, and it should be uppercase first, and then lowercase. It should not be Partitions, Sections, Members, or any other fanciful terms. I put a line through every "Partition" and replaced it with I, II, III, and a line through every "Section," and replaced it with A, B, C, and line through every "Member," and replaced it with (i), (ii), (iii), and a line through every "Subsection," and replaced it with (a), (b), (c). And I corrected his engastrated headings so they were all rational and orderly. But my modernized outline didn't help, because in the last Partition, III, Burton actually switches the A, B, C's with the (i), (ii), (iii)'s, so that III divides into (i), (ii), (iii), (iv), and (v), instead of A, B, C, D, and E, that is completely wrong, you can't divide Roman numerals into Roman numerals, it ruins the entire idea of an outline, III should divide into A, B, C, not (i), (ii), (iii), and what's worse is he knew it and he didn't care. It would be as if someone says, "Listen while I count in twos, 2, 4, 6, 8, 10," and you say, "Thanks, I know how to do that," and he says, "Wait, 12, 14, 16, 18," and you say, "Everyone knows how to count by twos," and he says, "Wait, 20, 22, 24, 26, 80, 82, 84, 86," and you say, "You made a mistake," and he says, "I did not, that's how I count by twos," and you say, "That's not counting by twos," and he says, "It's how I count by twos," and you say, "Okay, what is 26 plus 2?" And he says, "80," and you say, "You're actually psychotic, aren't you?" And he says, "I guess so, but actually I have no choice but to conclude that you're the one who's psychotic," and you say, "Would you please leave now, because I don't want to talk to you anymore, I don't trust you, there's something fundamentally wrong with you," and he says, "Wait, I want to keep counting until I get to 202, because when I count by twos I always count until I reach 202," and you say, "Please don't, I don't want to listen," and he says, "Where was I? Oh yes, 86, 88, 90, 92, 94," and you say, "Please stop," and he just keeps going, "96, 98, 100, 102, 104, 106, 108, 110," you can't stop him but at least there are no errors, "112, 114, 116," and again you say, "Please stop," and he says, "Wait, 118, 120, 122," and you say, "Seriously, just stop," and he says, "Wait, here it comes, 124, 126, 180, 182, 184, 186, 188, 190, 192, 194, 196, 198, 200, 202, done," and you just walk away, and he yells after you, "I can also count by threes." What Burton does is like that. A scholar named Ruth A. Fox—that is a funny name, isn't it, Ruth A. Fox—she wrote an entire book about the "wrecked logic" of Burton's book, that's what she calls it, "wrecked logic." She thinks he mangled up his system because Partition III, the last part of the book, is about "indefinite" kinds of melancholy, dour melancholy, sour m., dreary m., pelting m., the Brethren of Purity called that last one *'ubūs mūḥish,* and 117 others, but especially it's about love m., the melancholy caused by love, and really, A. Fox says, Partition III is about faith, she says that is the ultimate kind of love. It really isn't Partition III, A. Fox says, it is the entire book. So the errors don't matter because they are overwhelmed by love and faith.

Okay, that sounds promising.

At first Burton says faith heals almost all wounds, including the wounds of science and the wounds of logic, faith heals melancholy, witchcraft, and constipation, at first he has faith in faith, love and faith, but then he notices faith heals everything except despair, despair is the worst, because people who despair can reason uncommonly well, no one can talk a person in despair back to health. He can't be persuaded, he can't be comforted, a person in despair has an unmoving *Unempfänglichkeit für tröstendes Zureden,* his condition is *an Geistesstörung grenzend,* on the edge of insanity, despair is *geistige Selbstzerstörung,* mental self-destruction. A person in despair, Burton says, is lost in the labyrinth of his own faulty faith, he has been mortally wounded by his own logic, he is bound for the grave. A. Fox thinks Burton realized his book couldn't cure him, she says he knew that, he knew he would not survive the writing of the book, she says he needed faith and love to heal his book, to heal himself of his own despair. But he knew he could not be healed. Burton was a vicar but he reasoned himself out of his own faith, he contracted the fatal illness of despair. He knew his book was ruined, there was no way to make it work. A. Fox says he eviscerated his own book, turned it inside out, cut the skin of his book and spilled its intestines out, I didn't make that up, that is what she says. And it is also what he says, right in the title of his book, which is actually called *Anatomy of Melancholy, Opened and Cut Up.* In Partition III, the last part of his book, where he was supposed to reveal how faith heals the wounds of logic and science, how it cures melancholy and even constipation, instead he anatomized his own *Anatomy,* dissected himself dissecting, demonstrated the organs of his own thinking, vivisected his heart and lungs, until finally there was too little of him left to lift the scalpel. When I read that I realized the Disassembly Theory isn't as lighthearted as I thought. Burton engastrated his ideas, and then he cut himself to pieces. He died by anatomizing himself, he saw his own thought cut open in front of him. He never finished the *Anatomy of Melancholy,* he revised it six times and republished it repeatedly, but that didn't help, the book could not cure him of his own melancholy, and afterward people say he killed himself.

Anneliese, are you thinking of that?

No one who thinks does not. Those who despair, Burton said, are like comets. They are round over most of their circumference, as heavenly bodies should be. They shine like shields, people in despair, Burton says, except they are punctured in one place, and out of that place spews their glittering viscera. Comets are mad where they spew but otherwise sane, they have diseased imaginations, comets do, Burton said, their blazing part is what everyone notices, people in despair write and speak in profusion, like me, they argue, they talk incessantly, their delusion is that they know the truth, well at least I don't have that problem, or maybe I do, they are convinced they understand faith and love and reason, I don't understand those things, but their knowledge is punctured by despair. The spewing hole propels them through the heavens, it spins them off toward oblivion, they become involved in perpetual night. They are the worst of the melancholics, they are far gone with melancholy, they are incurable. People in despair, Burton wrote, nothing can cure them, they know everything, but they are punctured like comets, they cannot be cured. Right in the middle of his book, six hundred pages into it, all of a sudden Burton writes, "Perhaps I am a comet, I flow helpless across the heavens, doubting, shining, rolling on my way toward oblivion, spitting the glistering viscera of my words behind me." That's what he writes, in the very middle of his book. I realized there is an orifice in Burton's book, a gaping hole, and his diseased imagination spews out of it. After that passage, he returns to his diagnoses. He knew his book was ruined by the open orifice of his despair. When he wrote, "The worst of all melancholics are people who despair," and when he wrote, "Perhaps I am a comet," it is hard to read those lines, because you can hear him struggling not to be the patient, to be once again the doctor. I understand that. As you remember, the Despair Theory is my eleventh theory. Burton was more frightened of despair than anything, more than illness, more than lack of faith, more than insanity. Comets are beautiful, he said, but they spin away into darkness. "Where will I go?" he asks. "What will happen to me?" Burton tries to recover his composure by telling stories. Burton tells the story of a sailor's wife named Hannah Allen. Her husband died "beyond the sea," and she went and lived with her aunt. She said she was strangled by her despair. She "ate poorly," Burton says, and she became so lean that one day her aunt saw the face of death on her. Every evening she said God hated her and she would strangle and die before morning. She said God had shot an arrow into her soul, and the venom of the arrow had drunk up her spirit, and made her choose strangling rather than life. Finally "in the night she rose from her bed," Burton says, "and out of the window broke her neck into the street," that's how he says it, "broke her neck into the street." I suppose like every reader before me, when I read that I thought of Burton himself, how people say he died by suicide, and I wondered: Did he think of himself when he wrote that sentence, and did the pain of thinking about it ruin his sentence? Out of the window she broke her neck into the street, it is a magnificent horrible expression. Then he tells a story about a man who fell off his horse into a river and died. He was suspected of suicide, which would mean his soul could not be saved, but a priest said Saint Augustine said a person can be forgiven *inter pontem et fontem,* between the bridge and the brook, in the moment they are falling, out of the world and into the river. Or out of the window and into the street. Burton says the man could have lived a full life in that moment between the bridge and the brook, he could have seen and felt and cherished that moment, breathed the air for the first time, an entire life in the air between the bridge and the book, because what is life other than an interval, an eternity in an instant, a brief period of falling, in the clear and quiet air, Burton says, between the bridge and the brook? And then just when I was wondering about that, how a life might be just a moment, but also an eternity, how the empty air under a bridge might have an entire life in it, how we all fall through life even when we think we aren't falling, Burton tells a bizarre story about an Irish man who was famous as a wit but was secretly in despair. He did everything in threes, he had three cups of tea every day, he called himself by three names, he wrote three books, the second had the number two in its title, the third had the number three, he had a great laugh, ha! ha! ha! three times, his wife said it was a good laugh, full of despair, and one day he took a razor and made three cuts in his wrist, and as he was dying he wrote a letter to his wife, goodbye, goodbye, goodbye. That story frightened me. The more I thought about that story the more frightened I became. I have no idea why he told that story, but it made me anxious about the number three, perhaps there is despair hidden in numbers. Then Burton says, I have recounted these stories of Hannah Allen, the man who fell off his horse—

That one is actually beautiful. Just the moment of falling.

Wait, because then he says, I have recounted those stories, and also the man who counted by threes, but they all pale beside the story of Francis

Spiera. He was a lawyer in Padua who felt he did not deserve to live. Burton says Spiera could not be comforted by any doctors, he means medical doctors and also doctors of the church, holy men, and philosophers. People told him he was melancholic, but he lectured them at length about melancholy, he knew all its symptoms, he showed why his case was worse, people said he was afflicted by black humor, plagued by *alysm*, burdened by *noia*, paralyzed by *desassossego*, but he knew all the illnesses, he repelled all the diagnoses. Spiera's case became famous, people from all across Europe came to see him, people wrote books about him. Huldrych Zwingli visited him, and Peter Canisius, the famous medical alchemist Paracelsus, the surgeon Ambroise Paré who had healed Captain Rat, the sad Hungarian philosopher Laszlo Földényi, Bernardo Soares, Count Taldegardo Francesco di Sales, Giordano Bruno, even the profound and quiet Montaigne visited Spiera. No one could dull the pains in Spiera's soul, because in despair a person can reason so much better than anyone around him. Spiera had demonic despair, that is what Kierkegaard called it, he defied all the doctors, he defended his misery brilliantly, endlessly, no one could keep up, he exhausted all the doctors, Burton says, he pleaded so perfectly against himself, he made the case against every cure, he spoke for days at a time, one by one the doctors abandoned him, but no one could convince him, Spiera exhausted them, one by one they left, and finally Spiera went home and desperately died, that's how Burton says it, he desperately died, meaning he died in desperation, meaning by suicide. Burton's book showed me myself, as if I had been cut open in the middle, opened up. I felt like these were the only stories I needed: Hannah Allen, who broke her neck into the street, the man who lived between the bridge and the brook, the Irish man who wrote three books and said goodbye three times, and Francis Spiera, who argued until he died, like Burton. I saw myself in all of them, but especially in Burton. "Who can heal a person who walks in a wildernesse of doubt," Burton says, "who roars for grief, who is all one wound, and yet can understand his wound, and all his doctors, and the wildernesse?" Read Spiera's story and "learn light quenching sense to fear," Burton says, learn how fear can ruin sense, read his story "so that others read not thee," so that people like me do not come across your desperate story in a book. When I read that, I thought, like many readers before me must have also thought, Burton saw he was like Spiera, unapproachably eloquent, able to argue against any solace, he must have known that no doctor could cure him, and that must have been painful to think about, and that is why people say Burton also went home and desperately died.

You can do things differently, you don't have to be like him.

I hope so. He lived four hundred years ago. He was a rector and a vicar, I think I know what those are, and an incumbent and a bachelor of divinity, I don't know what those are. There wasn't even science back then. He was one of nine children, I am one of two. He was English, he spent his entire life at Oxford, and I am a provincial Swiss German. Burton wrote a comedy, which he performed in front of the King of England, I have never done that, and the King hated it, because it was boring, and besides it had half-naked men in it, and also eight or ten kings, some of them also half-naked. I have never written a comedy, I cannot ever imagine doing such a stupid thing, and if I did, I would not perform it in front of the King of England, and if I did, I would be sure all the actors were fully dressed, and only three or four of them were kings, because there is almost nothing funny about a man's chest, at least I do not think so, and apparently some King of England agreed with me. In the end Burton was very different from me, except that we both attempted to write very long and complex books, we both made desperate attempts to organize our thoughts, we both got lost along the way, we both lived sedentary, solitary, private lives, as he says, although he also calls himself silent, and I am not exactly silent, but I am sedentary, solitary, and private, we both had ourselves and what he calls the Muses in the University as our only companions, although my Muses in the University are worms, and we have both certainly thought about dying in desperation, but that is common enough, especially among sedentary, solitary, and private people. Burton's doubts were serious, they corroded his thinking. Like the person who counts wrong by twos, except that he has no idea anything is going wrong. Dostoevsky's Underground Man was a simpleton by comparison. He said that if you claim 2 + 2 = 4, that is "simply insolence," he said 2 + 2 = 4 is a "piece of impertinence" and 2 + 2 = 5 is "very charming," but then he said 2 + 2 = 4 is also "excellent." The Underground Man knew perfectly well he was being perverse. The person who counts wrong by twos is much more interesting, he is not aware that he is doing anything wrong. You see every time he comes to a number that ends in 26, he skips to a number that ends in 80, so 22, 24, 26, 80, 82, 84, and 122, 124, 126, 180. And also, at the same time, he needs to count to 202 every time he counts by twos. That is an entirely different kind of irrationality, I think you will agree, Samuel. How is it possible to understand someone who counts in that way? He does two different irrational things, he counts wrong after numbers that end in 26, because he skips to numbers that end in 80, and also he always counts to 202, those are different irrational acts, I think, I mean from my point of view they are different levels of irrationality, they are not examples of the same kind of irrationality. The person's habit of skipping to numbers that end in 80, like when he counts 222, 224, 226, 280, 282, 284, 286, that is different from insisting on always counting at least to 202. And then there is the fact that he needs to count to explain himself, he can't just tell me how he counts, or explain why he counts that way, or what he is thinking when he counts that way, or how he can prove it is the right way to count. He has to count to explain it, and the counting is no explanation at all, it is just counting. He seems to know that, but for him counting is the same thing as explaining, just like a few minutes ago when you were annoyed at me for explaining my endless talking by pretending to talk endlessly. Maybe that is a third kind of insanity. The insanity of getting up to numbers that end in 26, like 126, 226, or 326, and then skipping to numbers that end in 80, that is different from the insanity of insisting that every time he counts he needs to go at least to 202, as if everything repeats after 202, or as if that is as high as he needs to go to convince someone, those are different from the insanity of not realizing he needs to demonstrate why this kind of counting is correct. So, Samuel, here is the question I ask myself, which applies to the dark things in Burton's book and the parts of my own work that are dark to me: I ask myself, Are these different insanities symptoms of one illness? Are they all signs of failing reason? Or are they different? Let's say I put this person's three insanities in a hierarchical outline, would they be all equal, like this?

{

{

{

Or would the second one be an example of the first, like this?

{ {

{

Or maybe the root-level insanity is the third one, the person's inability to explain himself, and the other two are just examples of it, like this.

{ { {

And let's say that this person can also reason about all this, he can explain it exactly like I'm explaining it to you, then he might say, Only despair can explain all this, only despair can account for these levels of unreason, only despair can encompass them all, like this.

# Despair { { { {

Maybe there is only one insanity in Burton, the insanity of despair, the insanity of the comet that festers like a sore, spewing infection and fever, but maybe there are different insanities, even thirteen of them, perhaps Burton is covered with insanities, like a constellation of poisonous stings over the surface of his mind. At one point he says, I have contracted a megalopsychia of the soul, my thoughts have leaked out of me and onto the pages of my *Anatomy,* and then right away he says, I have developed an excruciating micropsychia, my thoughts have been crumpled down into letters, lists, and diverse signs.

My god, Anneliese, this all sounds horrible.

What was wrong with him? Why did he ruin his twelve-page, nine-foot-long hierarchical table of contents? Why did he rewrite his book six times? Why did he break his book in half with those stories about despair? Why did his book fail to save him? He describes his book as a prison, an island, a labyrinth, a wilderness, he says he is like Bellerophon, you know who that was, don't you? Do you? You don't? Oh heavens, Kerényi said Bellerophon was the greatest of the heroes before Hercules, you know Kerényi, of course, Károly Kerényi? The Hungarian friend of Jung? You don't? Really? Oh dear. You know Jung, right? Don't tell me if you don't. Bellerophon's story is in Homer, Homer says Bellerophon's grandson Glaucus talked about his famous grandfather, whose own father, I mean Bellerophon's father, not Glaucus's father, I don't know what Glaucus's father's name was, but Bellerophon's father was also named Glaucus, but that's irrelevant. Kerényi says Burton says Homer says Glaucus says Bellerophon was lost in a wilderness, he wandered alone, Bellerophon "made a great moan" in the woods, he bellowed, maybe that's where the name Bellerophon comes from, bellowing in despair. He had once been a great hero, he found the Chimera, greatest of all the monsters, and killed it by forcing a big chunk of lead down its throat, but then he became proud, you know how it goes in these Greek legends, he challenged the gods, he tried to fly up to heaven on his horse Pegasus and of course he was flung down and landed in a thorn bush, that must have hurt, and he spent the rest of his life wandering in forests, blind, I guess the thorns blinded him, and lame, well, he did fall from heaven, so I guess that makes sense, so Burton says melancholy people are like Bellerophon, they have no companions left, they delight in forests and desert places, that's what he says, desert places means the places are deserted, not deserts, deserted, and melancholy people walk alone in orchards, Burton says, they linger in gardens, that's a lovely image, isn't it, like the romantic Prince Saurau wandering his grounds, Saurau, not Sauron, talking endlessly to whoever will walk with him, and then walking endlessly when no one is there, so aristocratic, so attractive, but it's not romantic, it's desperate. Burton says melancholy people prefer private walks, back lanes, they are fascinated by the confluence of waters, I am not sure what that means, perhaps melancholic people are hypnotized by places where two streams come together, I am not sure I have ever seen such a thing, well, I suppose I must have, but I can't remember any examples, and besides I don't see any connection between wandering in the forest and watching two streams flow together, that doesn't make any sense, but it's curious, isn't it? Especially if the person standing on the bank is blind, like Bellerophon, why would he want to stand near two rivers coming together? Surely they would sound just like one river. Still, melancholics love the place where two rivers meet and then continue together. It is fascinating, possibly. But not for me, I have no interest in that. Burton also says melancholics are attracted to standing waters, especially pools that are thick and ill-colored, what an outstanding word, ill-colored, melancholics like water that collects in canals and moats, where slimy fishes live, waters that are unwholesome, flecked with mites, waters that are mudded, unclean, and corrupt, he loves that word, it doesn't mean they disobey the law, it means ruined in body and spirit, corrupt, waters baked in the sun's heat, fermenting, foaming, with flies stuck to their foam, standing waters, you would know all about those sorts of waters, wouldn't you, Samuel, you love them too, don't you, you'd say they are full of amoebas, no one knew about amoebas when Burton was writing, he would have been attracted to them, he would have written dozens of pages about amoebas, amoebas are nothing but slime, exactly what melancholics desire, Burton says melancholics love rancid pools because they mirror the distemperatures of their minds, the water in those places is unfit, like the melancholic's mind, water like that cannot be used inwardly or outwardly, yet the melancholic recognizes his own corrupt and putrefied soul and he gazes at the muck water the way a healthy person may peer into a silvered mirror. Melancholics are black, he says, like stools, *al-sawdā',* black, and there is a pun in Arabic, *al-mirrah al-sawdā'* is melancholy, but *musawwadah* means draft or rough copy, so a melancholic can never write well or clearly, a melancholic writes prose like bile, clotted prose is melancholic, that is what Burton says Abū l-ʿAlā' al-Maʿarrī says in his petty and endless *Epistle of Forgiveness.* And melancholics are like Bellerophon, Burton says, they escape their friends, abhor all company, wander alone, long forgotten, through the forests, by stagnant pools, melancholy people sleep in hollow trees, they are vexed by their own black bile, they are afflicted by dromomania, an uncontrollable urge to wander, Bellerophon was the first dromomaniac, Burton says, he was swallowed up in melancholy, Burton says, and then he says, "This book of mine is like a vast forest, I wander in it like Bellerophon."

His book sounds really unhealthy.

Well, Samuel, my life's work is also like a wilderness, you will see. It is a range of mountains and valleys, there are sentinel trees, looming cliffs, dank chasms, and crashing streams, it is filled with smoke and fog, forest fires rush through it, the people have all fled, it is endless, empty, and unpleasant, you will see. So I thought, This book can be my guide, it was written by a man who was lost like I am. He didn't spend his life writing poetry about worms or wild boars, he didn't waste his time collecting stamps or labeling cardboard boxes. He wrote, and he thought, and he couldn't guess where his thoughts were taking him, but he kept going anyway, forever writing his massive book, the world's most complex medical compendium, a book like a whale swallowing all of history, medicine, pharmacology, mythology, alchemy, theology, gulping it all down, crushing everything in its fleshy mouth like a hippopotamus chomping on swamp grasses, mud, and fish, barrelfulls of water gushing from its mouth, fish crushed by its decayed teeth, swallowing compulsively, monstrously feeding, it is a magnificent despairing book, Burton's book, there is nothing like it, and so I thought, This will be my guide—except that on the very last page, well, nearly the last page, because in my edition the last page has only four lines of text, so basically on the last page, in the original English edition it might literally be the last page, but certainly in the very last paragraph of his last Subsection of his last Member of his last Section of his last Partition, or, in my revision, III (C) (vii) (e), exactly 1,508 pages from the beginning, he says the best cure is not to read any more about melancholy. "Let a person who wishes to be cured read no more such fearful subjects," he writes, "Let him turn away from painful tracts and treatises, then he will be safe," notice, safe, not saved, because there is no cure. So I gave up my study of Burton. Reluctantly, because he could have been the greatest model, he went the farthest, he struggled the hardest to make sense, he built the most complex book. I closed his book, but I took his twelve page hierarchical outline and used it in my own work. I corrected and expanded it. His is simple by comparison. My own table of contents is a hundred pages long, Samuel, eight times longer than Burton's. You will see. I am very proud of it. You will love it, even though I think it is full of mistakes.

Maybe you saved yourself.

Safe, that's all I want. Not saved.

Bright sunlight came through the glass doors leading to the restaurant. A little girl came into view. She was playing airplane, zooming around and around. For a moment Anneliese's eyes followed the girl, sloshing back and forth like clothes in a washer.[24]

You don't leave books like Burton's, she said, you can close them, but they follow you, they are always open. Like wounds. I learned two things from Burton. First, if I try very hard, I might be able to organize my work, enough to keep it together. Even if it splits in half, even if it turns against itself in the end, even if its table of contents is mixed up. Also I learned the Despair Theory, how there is no cure for it. That wasn't an especially happy thing to discover, but I added it to my ladder. It is the third-worst theory, only the Non-Human Language Theory and the Waves on the Beach Theory are worse. So I kept searching. I looked for other long and intricate books of medicine, and that is when I read the *DSM,* the American psychiatrist's manual, and I read all five editions, from 1952 to now, including the *DSM-5-TR,* that is a total of 7,850 pages. It is just an enormous filing cabinet, as pompous and overconfident as Hammurabi's laws. I found other long books on medicine, Harrison's *Principles of Internal Medicine,* it's 2,720 pages, the *Oxford Textbook of Medicine,* 1,602 pages, the Goldman-Cecil *Medicine,* 2,100 pages. None of them are books, they are manuals. Interns memorize them to sound professional, but they only end up sounding insecure. Psychiatrists and doctors leaf through them and copy down polysyllabic diagnoses. The biggest books of medicine are not books, they are just massive assertions of authority, like colossal statues of dictators. Doctors and psychiatrists like to keep them in their shelves so patients can stare in awe and wonder, and every once in a while they open one and consult it, just like a patient consulting a doctor, timidly asking for the truth and hoping it will be something they understand. They are about awe and wonder, and that made me think of something else. Burton was a religious person, and despair was a religious condition, so I thought, Why not read books on religion? There are also lots of religious ideas in my work, as you will discover, how could there not be, when my subject is biological life? People who write about faith also have to control doubts, and doubts in one field may be able to talk to doubts in other places. Are you following me?

Yes, actually.

We'll see. I didn't read the Bible again, of course, even though it is 800,000 words long, because I am too annoyed at the Book of Proverbs. I did try to read Solomon Caesar Malan's *Original Notes on the Book of Proverbs,* it is 1,829 pages long, it is a condensed version of his full manuscript, which took him sixty years and includes passages in 54 languages including Chinese, Hebrew, Sanskrit, Manchurian, Mongolian, Japanese, Korean, Phags-pa, Aramaic, Georgian, Karluk, and Middle Turkic Kipchak. Well, Malan was an especially annoying sort of genius, a scholar named John Edwards said that. Malan never explained himself, *er schwieg in vierundfünfzig Sprachen,* as Schleiermacher said. To read his book you have to speak 54 languages. So I gave up on the Book of Proverbs and the entire Bible. I tried to read al-Tabari's commentary on the *Qur'an,* it is said that he wrote 40 pages a day for 40 years. His commentary is 30 volumes long, but I couldn't read it because only 5 volumes have been translated. The Taoist canon is 1,500 volumes long, did you know that? I couldn't read it, only one book has been translated. I did study Thomas Aquinas's *Summa Theologicae,* his enormous book of Christian doctrine, it's 4,000 pages long and it's divided and subdivided like Burton's book. It has 614 Questions, divided into 3,125 Articles, each one with Objections, Counter-Statements, and Answers. His divisions are worlds away from Burton's. Every page, every sentence is logical, I couldn't find any mistakes. Aquinas doesn't waste a word, there are no parentheses, no breaks for stories, no jokes. The lights are blazing, every surface is polished marble, all the furniture has been removed, there are no windows. His book is like a palace where something terrible has happened. The rooms have been elaborately disinfected, all you can smell is bleach and perfume. He never mentions illogic, there are no lapses, repetitions, passing shadows, or lingering doubts. There are no cardboard boxes or filing cabinets. When Objections are raised, either in Aquinas's mind or in the many books he tells us about, they are carefully sawn limb from limb and safely discarded. Doubt is cleanly removed. The *Summa Theologicae* is like a vast marble court of law, like in Dickens's *Bleak House,* with 3,125 rooms where advocates stand in stone stalls and raise Objections and receive Counter-Statements and Answers and cases are efficiently adjudicated and the rooms are cleared and fumigated. No one wanders through these hallways. Everyone attends all 3,125 cases, no one is haunted by doubts, no one tries to double back, no one is lost, like anyone would be in a building with 3,125 rooms, even Ceaușescu's palace in Bucharest has only 1,100 rooms, any normal person would be lost in Aquinas's antiseptic castle. People are required to be rational. If a person has a "grave and hopeless disease," Aquinas says, it can usually be cured by theological reasoning (see Part III, Question 35, Article 8, Reply 3). Christ decided to die young, Aquinas says, because it would not have been "becoming" for him to show any decline or decay or fall ill with any disease (see Part III, Question 46, Article 9, Reply 4). Everyone lives in a glare of reason and health. But that is a problem. Decay and disease are the only states I know. They form the mineral ground on which the plants of my work struggle to live. Aquinas quotes Augustine's *City of God,* that is another enormous medieval treatise, 600,000 words, nearly as long as Aquinas's, even though I have to say it is only half the length of my notebooks. Aquinas says Augustine thought passions are "diseases or disturbances of the soul" (see *De Civ. Dei* ix.4), and he says Cicero thought so too (see his *Tusculanae Quaestiones* iii.4 and iv.5). From that point of view, Aquinas says, every passion, every strong emotion, "every disease or disturbance of the soul is morally evil" (see Part IIa, Question 24, Article 2, Objection 1). Well, I thought that sounded fairly despicable, calling emotions diseases, calling disturbed souls evil. I felt insulted by that. I read some books about Aquinas to see what he meant. In 1940, a Jesuit scholar said the inner discord that isolates a person's heart is like a disease. "It eats its way from organ to organ," he wrote, "slowly disintegrating the body." Any disease, he thought, is a form of evil. "Can a tree experience evil?" he asked. "Yes, it experiences evil as disease. A diseased tree is an evil tree, just as we may experience disease as evil. The true evil, as Augustine said, is the disturbed soul, the soul weakened by diseased thought." All of that sounded awful. Then I went back to Aquinas. He considers what Augustine and Cicero said, and concludes passions are not diseases of the soul, unless they are uncontrolled by reason, *nisi cum carent moderatione rationis.* You can have emotions, Aquinas says, you can have diseases, you can be disturbed, but if you don't observe your disturbances and moderate them by reason, then your soul is unsound, *insanus,* it means insane, a frightening word for Aquinas. People who are insane can still have grace, he says, but their promises mean nothing, and they have no part in this book (see Part IIb, Question 45, Article 5, Objection 3; Part IIb, Question 189, Article 5, Answer). *Unde et insipientes insanos dicimus,* we call those people insane. When I read that I thought, I don't want grace, whatever that is, I just want not to be insane. I am excluded from Aquinas's book, locked out of the heavenly city. My mind is diseased, my reason is not in control, if I were a tree I would be evil. Aquinas's book is closed to me. For Aquinas reason arrives in great marble blocks. He stacks and sculpts them to make a gleaming heavenly city, beyond any poise I can ever achieve. Nothing in my mind is that clean. There is only one short passage in all the 4,000 pages of the *Summa Theologicae* that I can agree with, it's where he says a person has to be *insanus* to feel no fear, and he notes that fear must not be a sin, because everyone who is sane feels fear (see Part IIb, Question 125 "On Fear," Article 1, Objection 1). I read that, and then I closed the book carefully and forever. I felt like a silverfish creeping away from a home where there is no food and the floors are painted with insecticide.

That's also like my mother, I said. The way she thought was very clean. Our house was messy, but her mind was clean. She had this idea that people who do not reason well—

I doubt your mother was like Aquinas. It seems tremendously unlikely.

I'm just saying I sympathize.

Thank you. I think Aquinas had a pathological aversion to people who are *insanus,* he couldn't stand even to think about souls that are unsound, and that itself has to be a form of insanity. I fully understand that Aquinas bridged the gap between faith and reason, Christianity and Aristotle, I entirely grasp that Aquinas is a model of the scholastic method of argument that we all still follow, I gasp at his achievement, of course, but I cannot find myself in a book that has no stains, or at least one moist cardboard box. After I read Aquinas I looked for other very long books on religion. I tried to read Karl Barth's *Church Dogmatics,* but he never finished it, and I will not read unfinished books. I tried to read James Frazer's *Golden Bough,* but it's just an enormous fruitcake. So then I looked for very long books of philosophy. My book is philosophy, after all, philosophy of life, and there must be philosophers who tried to write long complex books, who got entangled in the same thickets, who breathed the same unclean air. I didn't read Schopenhauer, even though his book is 600,000 words long, because he is too German. That is when I found Wittgenstein's *Tractatus,* the only book he ever published. You know Wittgenstein wasn't especially modest. The title of his book, *Tractatus logico-philosophicus,* makes that clear enough, it says, This is not a book with a sense of humor, this is not a modest book, this is not an informal book, this is not going to be fun, you are not going to have any fun reading this book, in fact you are going to be intimidated, you are going to feel inadequate, you are going to feel stupid, still, I dare you to read it, go ahead and try, many people have tried, people a lot smarter than you, so seriously, what chance do you have of ever understanding this book? You could never write a book with a title like *Tractatus logico-philosophicus,* your book would be more like *Tractatus pusillanimous,* or *Local Tractor Parts.* Why are you even trying to read this? You don't stand a chance. You're nothing but a poltroon, you're a feeble-minded Kallikak, you're *blöd,* that's what we say in German, it's a great word, isn't it, *blöd,* you're *blöd,* why even think about claiming that you might possibly understand even a little of this book, even a page, even one line? Who exactly are you, anyway? That is what the title says. I loved the title, *Tractatus logico-philosophicus,* so pompous, so intimidating, I thought I should give my book the same title, but I already have a title for my book, it is a secret. The *Tractatus* is an attempt to write everything it is possible to write and still make sense, once and for all. Wittgenstein intends to put an end to all of philosophy. Perfect, I thought. I will put an end to all of biology. Wittgenstein's book is actually short, not long like Burton's or the other ones, but if you read it, it turns out to be a tremendously long and complex book, because it is pitilessly compressed into the shortest possible sentences. It's written in brief paragraphs separated by white spaces. When I saw that, I thought, Now there is a model for me. Instead of a study full of notebooks, in place of a single massive book, I will have a deceptive slim book. Paul will be so surprised! He'll say, You worked your whole life to write that one little book? And I will smile enigmatically.

The *Tractatus* has seven chapters, perfect for my work, because my thinking has seven dimensions, as you know. In the *Tractatus* each paragraph is numbered, so it looks just like my notebooks, as I will explain to you in thirty-nine minutes. I was delighted when I saw that Wittgenstein numbered his paragraphs, and then I was immediately disappointed. Chapter 2 has two parts, numbered 2.1 and 2.2. That's fine, except that before you get to 2.1, in other words before the chapter actually starts, there are six paragraphs numbered 2.01, 2.02, 2.03, 2.04, 2.05, and 2.06. And the first one, 2.01, it turns out that has four parts, numbered 2.011, 2.012, 2.013, and 2.014. After paragraph 2.012 there are four more paragraphs, and there is even one numbered 2.012131, and that one is a small singular spoke that has no successor, and it's the only entry under 2.0123, which really begs the question of why there's this one entry in this minor subheading, which is already a subheading of a subheading of a subheading, why there's this extra paragraph 2.0121 that is longer than the entry 2.012. After all, 2.012 is only one sentence, but the subheading, 2.0121, is a paragraph, that is hardly very rational. So Samuel, I am not missing the point. I know I can read the headings 1, 2, 3, 4, 5, 6, 7, in order, and they make a sentence, but Wittgenstein also asks me to read in order, he says the numberings are to show relative importance, okay, but then why are small subheadings of subheadings larger than their headings, like 2.0131 and 2.02331? It would be as if Burton attached a footnote to one of his Members, those are subheadings of his Sections, which are subheadings of his Partitions, and the footnote was longer than the entire Member, or even the Section, or even the Part, if you see what I mean. And yet Wittgenstein was a master philosopher, everyone says so, and he was very good at mathematics, that's a fact, and so he must have thought his numbering was impeccably reasoned, whereas for most people the numbers are inscrutable. In his mind, the system of numbers must have been perfect, even though it seems pathologically rational, I mean over-rational, insanely rational, but to him it must have appeared very sharply rational, but if every other book of philosophy ever written is irrational, and this one single book, which appears so small, is rational, then that makes the book pathological, because it is the virus, and the rest of philosophy is the body, and that is how Wittgenstein must have seen his book, a pathogen that could kill philosophy by logic. But to imagine this little book is the world's only truly rational book, that is *ab initio* an insane thing to think, obviously, *de plano*. So it matters that subheading 2.0121, which is larger than subheading 2.012, which is only one of the six subheadings under 2.01, which is only one of six subheadings in Chapter 2 that come even before Chapter 2 actually starts, it matters that this minor and impertinent subheading of a subheading of a subheading of a subheading seems to be too large, because it shows that Wittgenstein's logic is unusable. He was too impatient to explain himself, his logic is condescension. The book is intended to give you a chill, you are supposed to say to yourself, I thought I was a rational person, this has to be wrong, it has to be a joke, no one can think like this. *Alle Gegenstände sind gegeben*, Wittgenstein writes, All objects are given, *so alle möglichen Sachverhalte sind auch gegeben*, so all possible facts are also given. Everything that can be rationally thought is in his system, nothing that makes sense is missing, everything that is permissible in logic has a place in the book, nothing that fails to avoid reasoned language is excluded, everything that can be thought outside of illogic is included, nothing about any illogical thought is included, because that would involve thinking without statements, every form that can be stated is in the book, nothing except non-statements is omitted, everything that can be proposed conforms to a form that is assigned a number in the book, nothing that is not non-logical is not addressed, nothing unlogical is in the book, because we cannot say what an unlogical world would look like, and yet, and yet, and yet, everything that makes language expressive is incapable of being expressed in logic, expression is therefore inexpressible in a perfectly precise sense and is therefore omitted from the book in a rigorous and precise manner using numbered paragraphs, and what is inexpressible contains, according to Wittgenstein, the whole of philosophy, so all the propositions in the book are in the end senseless, they have to be discarded, what matters can never be spoken about, it is mystical, it can only be shown, not explained, we can see that it is, but we cannot know how it is, we need to be silent about it, not to say anything, we need to realize that all human meaning, including the whole of logic and philosophy, is such a thing, it cannot be spoken about except in empty terms, misguided misuses of language and thinking and logic. That is what Wittgenstein thought, that is what he hoped. I read Max Black, and I read David Rozema, David Stern, David Pears, and David Markson, I have read Dick Schmitt and Dick Perloff—Maxes and Davids and Dicks are attracted to Wittgenstein for some reason—so I know that Wittgenstein wanted to take me from what can be expressed clearly to what cannot be expressed at all, that is the famous last line of the book, which is also the last chapter, the last numbered paragraph, number 7. The last chapter is just one line, everyone quotes it, *Wovon man nicht sprechen kann, darüber muss man schweigen,* if you can't say anything about something, then just be quiet. Philosophers love that, it has become such a cliché I can barely stand to repeat it, it seems to be anagogical, secretly religious, mystical, spiritual, but the point is Wittgenstein's book has two equally important sentences, the first and the last, and they destroy one another. He built the *Tractatus* like a ladder, and he asks his readers to climb it, one irregular rung to the next, 1.01, 2.62, 3.0204, 3.03, 4.1, 5.02, 6.11, 7, starting from what is irrefutably the case, which means true, all the way to the top of the ladder, where nothing can be said. He said readers should climb the ladder of the book and then throw it away. Also I know, because Dick Schmitt has proven it, that Wittgenstein's book is a series of propositions in a definite order, beginning from a simple one, "The world is everything that is the case," that is the first line of the first chapter, and from there his paragraphs negate one after another every possible combination of the elements of the initial proposition. Wittgenstein negates "world," then "everything," then "is," then "case," then "world plus everything," then "world plus is," then "world plus everything plus is," etcetera, you understand, he negates everything, each new chapter in the book negates part of the original sentence, leaving nothing. Like Bartleby, like Bartlebooth, like Bruno of Cologne, like the stupendous Baradates.

Like who?

Or like Bernhard, he took a vow of silence on Wittgenstein. Never mind, it's not like them at all. So when Wittgenstein writes, in the last sentence, If you can't say anything logical about something, then please just be quiet, those things that cannot be said are actually everything, they are not just mysterious and profound specters that tremble beyond the reach of words, they are not moods and feelings that can only clumsily be put into words, no, or actually yes, they are those things, but they are also everything that can in fact be said in words, including everything in the rest of the book, all words, all sentences, all possible facts, everything, nothing can be said, everything in philosophy is nonsense, everything that makes sense is missing from philosophy, nothing that is required in logic has a place in philosophy, nothing that fails to avoid reasoned language is included, nothing that can be thought outside of illogic is included, everything that can be thought of as illogical is included, and the person who ignores that and goes ahead and writes a philosophic book about things that can't be clearly said, like all philosophers always have, that person is merely talking nonsense, what they say is technically nonsense because everything except the seven sentences in the *Tractatus* is nonsense, wait, no, I mean what they say is technically nonsense because the seven sentences of the *Tractatus* are themselves nonsense, or no, not exactly, they are the only way to talk about anything philosophical even though they demonstrate that they are nonsense, or, no, it's because they demonstrate they are nonsense, so when Wittgenstein writes that last sentence, he shuts down his own book and silences himself, *Finis,* he says, *terminus,* from now on I keep my own company of one, the rest of the world is misguided, there's just me and a couple of lines in Russell and Frege, and so, and also, and then, well of course he just kept talking and writing through his entire life. It is an absolutely brilliant strategy, and it is implemented in an absolutely demented fashion. I was stupefied when I saw that. But I couldn't use it for my own work. No one can use the *Tractatus.* It reminds me that no matter how hard I try, my words fail. Reading his book is like standing a ladder up in the middle of a field. Wait, first I have to tell you that I wanted to know where Wittgenstein had gotten his idea about the crazy numbering. Schmitt says the numbers come from Heinrich Hertz, he was a scientist who formulated the system of scientific notation, for example 2 is $2 \times 10^0$, 4 is $4 \times 10^0$, 6 is $6 \times 10^0$—

Okay, I get it.

Good, but so 8 is $8 \times 10^0$, 10 is $10 \times 10^0$, and so on, up to 26. Hertz died of Wegener's granulomatosis, he developed a saddle nose and a saber shin, that's what happens to people who contract Wegener's granulomatosis, it's an unsightly way to die. Last summer I thought I had Wegener's granulomatosis, and at the same time I scraped my shin on Paul's coffee table, it is too low, anyone can see that, so I walked right into it and scraped my shin, and it was sore when I was reading about Heinrich Hertz, and that is probably why I began to worry about whether or not I had Wegener's granulomatosis, and I looked at myself in the mirror, which I try not to do except when I am combing my hair, and there it was, a slight saddle nose, very subtle, I could barely see it but it was there, a slight lapse in the bridge of my nose, just over that bump that looks like an Adam's apple, the one on the bridge of your nose, just under that, I could barely focus on it, and that worried me too, because difficulty moving the eyes is another symptom of Wegener's granulomatosis. I didn't want to die like Heinrich Hertz did, with his eyes staring down onto his collapsed nose, so I stopped reading about the numbering system, and also... but anyway, back to my point: reading the *Tractatus* is like standing a ladder up in the middle of a field. You grip the sides with both hands and place your right foot on the first rung. You lift your left foot and place it on the next rung. You can balance that way, you can climb the ladder. Eventually you will fall. You may keep your balance for a few seconds. Wittgenstein did. But there is nowhere to go, so you will lose your balance. The ladder may fall forward or backward, and then you have to jump off and hope you don't break any bones. I did that many times during the summer I was reading Wittgenstein's book.

Why?

I fell, sometimes I hurt myself, but I got up and climbed the ladder again, even though I knew I shouldn't because I kept banging my shins, and I wasn't sure if they were inflamed from Wegener's granulomatosis or just from bashing against the aluminum ladder. My doctor told me I did not have Wegener's granulomatosis, but he said, "Your shins are skinned and you have a sunburn, how did that happen?" And I said, "Oh, that's from standing out in our back garden trying to climb a ladder that is not leaning against anything," and he said, "I can recommend a good therapist," and I said, "It's not necessary, I am getting very good at climbing." Our ladder has ten rungs, that bothers me, I wish it was thirteen, but it's only ten, and several times I got to the eighth rung, which is very high, and then I fell forward. I did that a couple of times. I balanced up on the eighth rung, it was wobbly and frightening, especially when it started to fall forward. I did it because it's what Wittgenstein says, Climb up and then discard the ladder, that is what he says to do. I thought if I could understand how Wittgenstein climbed his ladder, I could make a book like his. Wittgenstein had tremendous difficulty writing his book. After a while, David Rozema says, he was able to see that his book was nonsense, but he continued to write it all the way to the end. Wittgenstein says he wants to see what people who cannot tell sense from nonsense would do with a piece of nonsense. People should climb the ladder and throw it away, he says, climb up and move on, but if they can't tell, then they will busy themselves with it for years. That is what Lord Bertrand Russell did, he was Wittgenstein's teacher, he found paradoxes in the book, he asked Wittgenstein how he could say nothing can be said in philosophy, and yet write a book of philosophy, and Wittgenstein said, right to his teacher's face, "It's okay, you can't help it if you don't understand my book." Wittgenstein's book is intentionally empty, it undermines itself, it empties itself out as it goes, it is dedicated to understanding emptiness, to understanding its own emptiness. His book has no weather. It is ice cold, chill like a room closed off for winter. Like Aquinas's book, but even colder, like outer space cold, his book is a block of frozen poison. If I try to lick his frozen book my tongue sticks to it and I have to tear the tip off. He showed me that very complex theories are not human. The book is a self-portrait, Rozema says, a self-portrait of something inhuman disguised as human. That is what Wittgenstein was, and he knew it, Rozema says, and I agree. And that is what my work is, my work is a portrait of what I am, something no longer human pretending to be human. Something speaking and writing and yet not making sense. I am disguised in the pages of my notebooks as a biologist, but actually I am not human, I do not lead a human life or think human thoughts.

Of course that can't be right, you're talking to me.

Ha ha.

And you are not a frozen block of poison.

I am not a frozen block of poison, thank you, I will repeat that to myself. That was the end of my reading of Wittgenstein. I could have read the

*Nachlass,* that is 18,000 pages of notebooks he left behind, doubting himself, trying for years to tear apart the *Tractatus,* asking himself the same questions over and over. He knew that philosophic thinking could lead to states of mind that cannot be distinguished from madness, Wouter Kusters also knew that, he studied Wittgenstein, he thought his way in and out of psychosis, actual psychosis, Kusters was hospitalized twice, madness was his doorway to philosophy, philosophy was his doorway to madness, he kept coming back to normal life, but he kept falling back in, and Wittgenstein nearly did the same, you can see that in the *Nachlass.* There are compulsive repetitions, nonsense formulas, paradoxes, the same thoughts keep returning, Kusters calls it circular frozenness. Everyone fails to read Wittgenstein's book, Black, Rozema, Stern, Pears, Schmitt, Perloff, no one succeeds, Perloff actually said it was really a poem, Markson pretended to write about Wittgenstein but he didn't, Bernhard refused to write about Wittgenstein, he said Wittgenstein was too dangerous, if you are inside his mind too long you will not survive, it is better to write about his nephew or his cat. Another scholar, Christian Erbacher, says there are seven rungs in the *Nachlass,* imagine! Seven again, I spent some time trying to find them. I couldn't, but I sensed the circular frozenness, the deep chill that settled on the person who had already written a short book as cold as a shadow on the moon.

Suddenly the little girl who had been playing airplane flew into the lounge, arms outstretched, tilting left and right, teeth clenched, making an *Rrrr* sound. She careened past us, looking at me out of the corner of her eye.

That was the end of my reading of Wittgenstein, Anneliese said. I hurt myself, I crashed our ladder into the ornamental well and broke one of the planks that holds the conical roof, and it fell into the well, that was ironic. Luckily the ornamental well is only three feet deep and I reached in and got the plank, but I bruised myself and I scraped my wrist and nearly broke my ring finger because when the ladder hit the well, I was still holding it, but that is what reading Wittgenstein is like, you injure yourself reading and you feel like an idiot.[25]

And you freeze yourself and tear your tongue.

Or worse. My doctor bandaged my hand and told me to buy sun cream and knee pads and seek professional help. I was finished with Wittgenstein.

Like everyone else I entirely failed to read him, or even to climb to the tenth rung of our aluminum ladder, although Paul kept saying that if I put the ladder up against our little Hütte, I could climb it easily, and I would have a nice time on the roof, and while I was up there could I please clean out our chimney. When I was recovering from my injuries, looking out my study window at the broken well, I remembered another long book on religion, the Jewish Talmud.

The little girl flew to a far corner of the room and fell down, flat on her stomach, arms out. Then she got up again and flew back and forth under the windows.

It is much longer than Aquinas or Augustine. It is a 37-volume commentary on the Mishnah, which is a 1,000-page commentary on the Jewish Torah. It must be one of the most complex books ever written. On every page of the Talmud there's a passage from the Mishnah, right in the middle of the page, and under it there's the main commentary, like a caption, and all around are more comments, over and under the Mishnah and its commentary, like blankets around a baby, and around those are more comments, more blankets, they all make sure the Mishnah is protected and warm. Tucked away in the folds of the commentaries are little notes, definitions, and cross references, like safety pins keeping the blankets wrapped tight. So it's not a normal looking book. Each page is a picture of an infant's crib, with the baby in the middle, lovingly comforted by many devout remarks from different countries and centuries.

The little girl flew up to us and ran around our chairs, tilting her arms down to make the corners. Each time she came around she caught my eye.

Every page looks different. There's always the little block of Mishnah in the middle, and the commentary wraps it differently on each page. You can study a single page for days on end. The Talmud has comments on everything God ever said. I looked up leprosy sores, because I thought my scabs were getting worse, and so maybe I had contracted leprosy in Abruzzo. There is a passage in the Book of Leviticus where the Lord talks to Moses and Aaron about scaly infections that might be leprosy. "When someone has a spot, lesion, or blotch on their skin," the Lord says, "and it appears to develop and spread, that person needs to be brought to Aaron. If Aaron sees that the spot, lesion, or blotch is white, and if the hair on the infection has turned white, and if the infection appears to be deeper than the skin, then it's a scaly infection. At that point, Aaron," the Lord says, "you have to declare the person unclean. But if the white doesn't seem to be deeper than the skin, or the hair on it hasn't turned white, then it's not a scaly infection, and the person only needs to be quarantined for a week." That was helpful, although I was worried that the hairs growing out of my scabs might be white, but when I looked at the Mishnah I discovered the Rabbis were confused. "What is white, exactly?" Rabbi Meir asked. "There is white like snow and then there is white like whitewash, and then there is the white portion of an egg, known as albumen, and also there is white wool." And Rabbi Ishmael replied, "Also some snow-white scabs have red in them, like blood mixed with albumen, and some whitewash-white scabs have red in them, like wine mixed with milk." I checked my scabs. Some were reddish and some weren't, but it was hard to tell, because my belly hangs down, and when I pick it up to look the blood rushes out of the scabs and they turn white, more like milk than albumen, so I thought, Okay, maybe I do have leprosy. Also the healthy parts of my stomach are pasty white, and that makes the white scales look dull white, sort of like wool. If I had worn my bathing suit when we were in Italy I could have gotten a lovely tan, and then my scabs would have been gleaming snow white, but I guess that would have been worse. Rabbi Hanina said there are actually 16 colors of leprosy scabs, and Rabbi Dosa ben Harkinas said there are 36, and Rabbi Aqayva ben Mehallel said, "The number is 72, and also, if the spots are one of the 59 permissible colors, according to my system, or if a person pulls out a white hair from a scab and it grows back black, or if no more than a child's handful of hairs growing from a person's scabs are white, or if a person only has scabs under their armpits, or between their toes, or inside their buttocks, or if a person has only small scabs the size of half a lentil, then the person does not need to be quarantined, they can just wash themselves really well and join everyone for dinner."

The little girl made an especially tight turn around Anneliese and hit her elbow. When she came around again, Anneliese swatted her, hard, and she fell down.

Oh, I said to the little girl, I'm so sorry.

She looked at me with her eyes wide. Her mouth turned down, and her eyes filled with tears. Then she got up and ran out of the lounge.

I don't have many hairs on my belly, Anneliese continued, although for some reason I have more than I used to, and I already have some naturally gray hairs in my pubic region, so I found some hairs growing out of my scabs and pulled them out and put them on a sheet of paper.

Anneliese, you slapped that girl.

Some were white, but others were gray. One was brown. Then Rabbi Meir said, "the Lord said, 'spot, lesion, or blotch,' and then he said 'white,' and then he said 'hair,' and then he said 'deeper than the skin,' so by analogy the color is more important than the hair, and the hair is more important than the thickness." That made me feel better, because some of my scabs are very thick.

Maybe you should go apologize.

This is complicated. I need to concentrate. So Rabbi Hillel said, "If we had only *if* these spots, lesions, or blotches, *or* these colors, hairs, *and* thicknesses, but we have *if* these spots, lesions, or blotches, *and* these colors, hairs, *or* thicknesses, so all of them have to be included." And Rabbi Aqayva ben Mehallel said, "If we had only *if* these spots *and* colors, *or* lesions *and* hairs, *or* blotches *and* thicknesses, or if we had only *if* these spots *and* colors, hairs, *or* thicknesses, *or* these lesions *and* colors, hairs, *or* thicknesses, *or* these blotches *and* colors, hairs, *or* thicknesses, but we have *if* these spots, lesions, or blotches, *and* these colors, hairs, *or* thicknesses, so all of them have to be included, any person with these signs is unclean." Then a student Rabbi said, "Miriam was as leprous as snow, according to the Book of Numbers," but no one answered him. And Rabbi Aqayva ben Mehallel said, "What about tetters?" And Rabbi Meir said, "What is a tetter?" And Rabbi Aqayva ben Mehallel said, "A tetter is any disfigurement of the perfect skin, so let us distinguish between milky tetter, scaly tetter, crusted tetter, shriveled tetter, pustular tetter, running tetter, humid tetter, moist tetter, reticular tetter, honeycomb tetter, bubbling tetter, drooling tetter, charred tetter, and parched tetter." But the other Rabbis didn't do that, instead they discussed things that might happen to unclean people who were quarantined. They were especially interested in unclean men who spit.

Anneliese, really, you should go apologize.

Wait. Rabbi Meir said, "What would happen if a quarantined man spat one drop of spittle in a private place, and another man, who was clean, also expelled one drop of spittle, and then a third man approached and touched one of the drops, or he shifted it, or carried it away, but he did not know which drop, and if the three men were alone, then what?" And Rabbi Aqayva ben Mehallel asked, "The matter would be in suspense." And Rabbi Meir replied, "What would happen if the man carried the drop away, but then he lost it, or if he carried the drop to another private place, and there he added a full measure of his own spittle to the drop, then what?" And Rabbi Aqayva ben Mehallel complained, "The matter would still be in suspense." So Samuel, I read everything the Talmud says about scabs and spittle, and I felt so happy. It was heartwarming to know that so many wise men had worked so hard on spittle and scabs. It is important not to assume that only obvious things happen. The Talmud made me feel I am doing the right thing, because I have been nourishing and protecting my ideas for a very long time. I have covered them carefully in words. I have attended to every droplet of thought, every scab and tetter. I wish I had an army of bearded men to babysit my notebooks for two thousand years, they'd coddle my notebooks like the infant Mishnah, they'd cuddle my notebooks in the softest wisest words, they'd discuss and admire my notebooks, even if they are only gobs of spit. But I have only myself, I have had to write my own commentary, pose questions to myself, cherish and nurture my own writing, and construct elaborate introductions for it, like the one you are suffering through at the moment. If I were young and had the double foveas of a hummingbird and patience of an ocean quahog, then I would study the Talmud my entire life, I would be very happy but I would be absolutely ruined, I would have a brain shaped like a Talmud. My own work would languish, I would forget the shape I want to give it, I would give it up for the baby Mishnah. So I kept looking for long texts I could use. I discovered that ancient Indian religious texts are even longer than the Talmud. There are hundreds of books in the Hindu tradition, did you know that? Some of them are over a thousand pages long, they are a great forest of texts, some are philosophical and they are very useful in my work, as you will discover, but others are hopeless, for example the 36 Puranas. I read one of the Puranas, called the *Narada Purana*, it is five volumes, 2,071 pages long. I doubt many people ever read the entire book because it is like a scrambled encyclopedia, it has chapters on astronomy, cosmology, cosmogony, cosmometry, and even cosmetology, it has lots of stories of kings and heroes, there are ten chapters praising the Ganges river, how wonderful that river is, how holy, how clean, imagine, how clean! It has information about the construction of temples, in case you'd ever want to build a Hindu temple, chapters on mamelons and ravelins, outworks and counterscarps, in case you'd rather build a fort, chapters on medicine, grammar, prosody, mineralogy, mathematics, paradoxes, humorous dialogues, well, they are supposedly humorous, love stories, treatises on dance, music, painting, and sculpture. It has chapters on etiquette, it says a man should never greet a person who is given to arguing, "or a fierce person, or one who is vomiting, or one who stands in water." I made a note of that. Kings should trim their mustaches every five days, that's cosmetology, queens should bathe in honey each time the season changes, that sounds gooey and it must attract flies. There are chapters on astrology, apparently the Moon and Venus are female, I think I knew that, and most other planets are male, I guess that's inevitable, except Mercury and Saturn who are eunuchs, that doesn't mean they are castrated, it means anatomically different, which is very accommodating, and the *Narada Purana* also explains that Mercury is an active and passionate eunuch and Saturn is a dark, inert, and ignorant eunuch, that sounds liberal but also totally insulting, and anyway if you're a planet it is not good to be a eunuch because when either Mercury or Saturn are ascendant births are likely to be subhuman beings like animals or birds, and the *Purana* has advice for women who are going to give birth, for example if Saturn is in Cancer a woman should give birth in a pit or a dungeon, and if Mars is in Sagittarius she should give birth on a burial ground, but if Jupiter is in Libra it's much nicer, she just needs to find a house with tasteful interior decoration. The *Purana* gives health advice, it says that it's usually not harmful to hear people sneeze, unless they sneeze behind you—

Anneliese, sorry, are you going to go find that little girl?

No, actually, I am not. She hit me, so I hit her back. Also it is okay for children to sneeze even if they are behind you, but the sneezing of cows can be deadly so it is best to avoid places where cows sneeze, which I think is basically everywhere there are cows, so what are farmers supposed to do, farming would be a very dangerous profession. And the *Narada Purana* gives travel advice, if you are just leaving your house and you see a corpse lying on the ground and no one is there mourning it, that means the objective of your trip will be fulfilled, I don't know why, maybe you were going out to kill someone, but if you're coming back home and you see a corpse and there are people mourning it, then you'll turn into a corpse, well, when I read that, I thought maybe I'll never leave my home again, but then I realized it doesn't say when you'll become a corpse, so I guess it's okay, but if I am trying to avoid people sneezing behind me or hearing a cow sneeze I probably won't be traveling much anyway, and the *Purana* says every house should have exactly seven gates on the east side, and if you go through the first gate, it means you'll suffer misfortune, but that's okay because if you then go through the second gate, you'll be rich again, but if you go through the third gate, you'll be paralyzed by fear, but then just go through the fourth gate and you'll be free from all doubt, but definitely don't go through the fifth gate, because then you'll starve, but if you do, then just rush back through the sixth gate, because then you'll grow fat, and don't forget to never use the seventh gate, because then your family will die and there will be a general "destruction of creatures," so really, why even build that seventh gate, or just label the gates, NO, YES, NO, YES, NO, MAYBE, and ABSOLUTELY NOT. The *Purana* has long lessons in Sanskrit grammar, I am not sure how helpful those are, do I really need to be told I can use the suffix *–ra* as a diminutive with words like *sundara,* which means a small trunk of an elephant, not a baby elephant's trunk, but the trunk of an elephant who has a small trunk, that also sounds like an insult or a problem, but the *Purana* says *sundara* also means "beautiful" but you cannot use the suffix *-ra* as a diminutive when it means "beautiful," but you can use the suffix *–ra* as a diminutive with the word *tundibha,* which means people whose navels protrude, possibly also not a very useful word—

Anneliese?

Or with the word *avatita,* meaning a person who has a flat nose, or with *cipita,* another word for a person with a flat nose—

Why are you telling me this?

Wait. So why did they need two words for people who have flat noses, maybe they had lots of cases of Wegener's granulomatosis, but Samuel, did you know Sanskrit supposedly has more words than any other language, because it is agglutinative, its words string together like lines of bacteria, one site says there are 102.78 billion words in Sanskrit, and there is a university in India, in Pune, that has been working on a Sanskrit dictionary since 1976, and now they are on page 6,506 and they are only up to the word *abhigamyamānaparadārādi*, which means "accessible to adultery," so I guess they might have many more words for people with flat noses, because why not have lots of words in case you know many people with flat noses and you want to be rude to each one, and so it may actually be helpful when the *Purana* says you can use the suffix *–ra* as a diminutive with the word *avanata*, which is yet another word for a person with a flat nose, and the *Purana* has long chapters of honorific titles you can give people if you want to, like *Nandantikarasainyaprakara*, She Made the Army Happy, or *Yasovitanadhavalikritajagattraya*, White-Hot Famous in the Three Worlds, or *Baloditabhanumandalagrasana*, He Who Takes a Surgeon's Circular Knife to the Cloth That Covers the Private Parts, or *Kumbhakarnadivadhaparayana*, Very Interested in Killing Demons Including But Not Limited to Kumbhakarna in the Ramayana, I guess those are useful names, and the *Purana* has predictions about the future, some of those are horrifying, it predicts a dark age where life expectancy will be sixteen and girls will become pregnant at five years old, and it has advice for writers, it says that if a man wants to be a great poet he should stare at the *yoni* of a naked woman during her period while reciting one thousand hymns to the ferocious death goddess Kali, it doesn't say what a woman poet should do, but it's probably not much more fun, and there's a very disturbing passage about how fetuses feel, it says "when a man and woman come together in sexual intercourse, the embryo is formed in the womb like a calamity visiting the woman," and from the fetus's point of view life is pure torture, because it is defiled by feces present within the mother's body, burned by the mother's harsh urine and other secretions, exhausted by the mother's blood, bone, germs, suet, marrow, sinews, and hair, scorched by the hot food the mother swallows, vexed by the sour, pungent, or saline flavors of the food she eats, so that it knows it is in a defiled place and it writhes in agony within the mother's belly because of the oppressive heat and pain, until finally it is time to be born, and then it feels unbearable pain, including the knowledge that it is inflicting pain on its mother, until it is "forced out through the vaginal opening as if it is pulped by a mechanical device," and as soon as it emerges it becomes unconscious and loses all its memory. I never had a child, but if I had read this when I was a teenager I would have been frightened out of my mind. I asked my doctor about it, if any of it could be true, maybe just the part about the fetus being crowded and overheated, and he said, "I have a medical degree," and he pointed to it on the wall. You know, Samuel, I am not naïve, I realize the *Purana* was written long ago, in a culture very different from ours, and I recognize that it was not written for me, but for heaven's sake, what kind of a book is it? Some of the things in the *Purana* are quite intriguing. It tells men what to do when they urinate or defecate, it says "after answering the call of nature a man should hold the penis and get up. For the purificatory process he should bring some good mud. It should not be from holes dug up by rats or other rodents," I mean, if I was looking for mud to use to clean myself, and why in the world would I do that, but I guess maybe it is old-fashioned toilet paper, so if I was, would I say to myself, I think I'd better go look over there where rats have dug holes in the ground, that will save me time? And then it says no one should take mud from wells, tanks, or lakes, so now supposedly I have relieved myself in some field, and I'm wandering around looking for mud, and I think, Oh, great, there's a well or a tank, I can climb down inside, and maybe dive to the bottom and grab some mud, it'll be worth it because I really need to clean myself, and that mud will be high quality mud, so much better than mud from holes dug up by rats, and then the *Purana* says, "The cleaning process after passing urine or feces is as follows: divide the mud into sixteen parts. Smear one part over the penis, one over each of the testicles, three parts over the anus, seven over the left leg, and three over the right leg. This is the purificatory process on discharging fecal matter so that the bad odor and the sliminess can be removed." There are no directions for women, maybe the men who wrote the *Purana* did not want to think what women do with their mud. I asked my doctor if any of that could be true, and how did people clean themselves before bidets and toilet paper? What did they do in the middle ages, did they use rags or maybe grass or leaves? I told him I read that Rabelais recommended using a live goose's neck, but seriously, I said to my doctor, could that business about mud possibly be true? What if people really had to go to the toilet, and they were in a place where there is no toilet tissue, no bidet, no mud, and no goose's necks? What did they do then? And he looked at me for a while and then he pulled a couple of sheets of tissue from a dispenser and handed them to me. The *Purana* also describes what happens if a man doesn't give his semen to his wife, if he "discharges his semen in those who are destitute of a vagina," they are called *viyonis,* meaning people without a *yoni,* which I think means men, or "in the uterus of animals," those are called *pasu-yonis,* meaning beast-*yonis,* or if he discharges his semen anyplace that isn't a vagina, the word for that is *ayoni,* which means "anything that isn't a vagina," I think that might be a very useful word, many people could use that word, I hate Disneyland, it's very *ayoni,* but the author of the *Purana* means masturbation, okay, then such a person will go into a special hell where he has to subsist on semen.

Anneliese?

Again there's nothing about women, I suppose because we have no seed to scatter, so whatever we do is okay. So in this special hell where the man will subsist on semen, first he is filled with oil, and then he falls into a deep and narrow well of fat.

Anneliese! Do I need to know this?

Maybe not this, exactly, but yes, you do. So it doesn't take a psychoanalytic genius to guess what the deep and narrow well is supposed to be. He stays there for seven years. "That man," the *Purana* says, "has semen for his diet. He becomes the most despicable man in the world." The *Narada Purana* isn't the kind of book you can read easily, nodding and taking notes, bobbing along from one page to another like a complacent sailor on the placid waves of Proust or a determined sailor on the icy waves of Wittgenstein or a mesmerized sailor on the dreamlike ocean of Burton. The *Purana* is a cataract of weirdness. It was mainly intended as a guide for prayer, most of it is prayers, there are hymns and prayers to dozens of gods, in fact hundreds of hymns and prayers to dozens of gods, in fact hundreds of prayers and hymns to dozens of gods with hundreds of names, for instance the goddess Lalita, who has exactly a thousand names, and the *Purana* gives all of them, if you want to pray to her you have to pray like this. Oh goddess (1) Lalita, (2) Shakti, (3) Bhagamalini, (4) Tripura Sundari, (5) Rajarajeshvari, (6) Shodashi, (7) Kamakshi, and so on, lots of names for her, and then her attributes, (38) the one who is bowed to, (39) one who offers harmony, (40) one who laughs at obstacles, then more of her names, (41) Ananga Kusuma, (42) Ananga Mekhala, (43) Ananga Madana, (44) Ananga Natura, (45) Ananga Rekha, (46) Ananga Vegini, and then more names, and then more names, (73) Amrita, (74) Manada, (76) Pusa, (78) Pusti, (79) Tusti, (80) Rati, (81) Dhriti, (82) Sasini, and then more attributes, (104) one who causes delight, (105) one who causes agitation, (106) one who causes puzzlement, (107) one who causes madness, when I read those I thought she was like me, (107) one who wanders in the void, (108) one who causes yawning, no comments please Samuel, and then mysterious ones, (144) one who is hidden, (145) one who is ill-seen, (146) one who is secret, (147) one who is absent, (148) one who has no form, and this is still the beginning of the prayer, the author of the *Purana* loved prayer, and then (195) powerful wishes, (196) supreme intellect, (197) singing voice, (198) beautiful breasts, (199) perfect thighs, (200) desirable buttocks, I'm not used to saying things like that about a god, (201) over-eager, (202) who causes the double madness of love, (203) who makes people rejoice, (204) who makes people spin, (205) one who wets, (206) one who returns and wets, (207) one who dries up, (208) who sweats from desire, (209) who drips ichor from rutting, (209) who breathes deep in the lungs, (210) whose limbs tremble, (211) ruined by intoxication, (212) dizzy with desire, (213) sick with sexual urges, imagine saying that in a church, even quietly, Oh holy Virgin sick with sexual urges, when I read this I felt embarrassed, I was surrounded by holiness but also very intimidated, and then later (386) coward, (387) deceitful, (388) debased, (389) grim, (390) fraudulent, those are confusing, but then (390) one who smiles, (391) one who pours, (392) one who spins, (393) the peculiar, (394) the giver, (395) the unexampled, (396) the oreful, I had to look that up, (397) the edmede, I had to look that up, (398) the lown, I had to look that up, (399) the eleemosynous, an amazing word, eleemosynous—

Please, Anneliese.

I love these prayers. Then comes (436) one who has a name with a hundred syllables, which is translated as *One who is continuously darkened in the directions between the lotuses, by slow improvement, in drops, concentrated, dense, in dense clusters, by doubtful hands, flowing, in honey, in drops, with friends, for longer, the lotus, the tree, the bed, the mountains, the roots, the nets, complex, the abysses, the deserts, far shorter, sweeter, cooler, more liquid streams, accepting the words of thirsty travelers, spreading the lines of the beams of her pure eyes,* (437) one who has the nature of a sentence, composed of a finite verb together with indeclinables, *karakas,* and qualifiers according to the Paninian grammatical system, I'll tell you about that sometime, Samuel, but I can't stop right now. Then (438) one whose name will be recited most fully in the *kali yuga,* the Age of Quarrel and Misery, which will begin in just one thousand divine years or four hundred thirty-two million human years, (439) one whose name is the form of all the particles of the universe when preceded by the letter *ha,* and then—

Anneliese! I'm sure I do not need to know this.

Not all of it, that is why I am omitting the less important entries. Then a couple hundred prayers later Lalita is all about love again, (718) whose tongue is tremulous, (719) whose teeth are covered in blue flowers, (720) who is poured in milk, (721) who is smeared with turmeric paste, (722) who must never have lights waved in front of her, (723) who must never be sprinkled with bhasma powder, (724) whose feet must never be washed, (725) whose knit eyebrows are an unbreakable bow in which she fits the arrows of her side-glances, (726) whose look must not be returned even when she ogles you from underneath her shawl, (730) who must never be greeted, and then frightening prayers, (735) who has a strong inclination to destruction, (736) whose language you cannot understand, (737) whose words are caustic ash, (739) who must not be thought about, (740) who must be forgotten, and then disordered prayers, (869) vivid, (870) ray, (871) spike, (872) spark, (873) gentle, (874) amber, (875) sour-blooded, (876) plum-shaped, (877) spinach-stooled, (878) plangent, (879) fabulous, (880) embalmed, (881) tame, (882) frenzied, (883) like a suckling pig, (884) innumerable, (885) tiny, (886) restless, (888) who broke the water pitcher, near the end I got dizzy with worship, my mind was filled with the goddess Lalita, I was mesmerized but also bored and really confused, and then she shrank down, she became something small and unpleasant, (950) one who lives in your stomach like a worm, (951) one who lives in your throat like a fish bone, (952) one who lives on your hard palate like a sore, (953) one who abides under your tongue like chewed food, (954) one who crouches between your teeth like a wet infection, (955) one who sleeps in your nostrils like mucus, (956) one who swims across your eye like a particle of sand—

Stop, really.

I am. It ends: (998) the Now Nearly Named, (999) The Un-Named, (1000) the Unnamable, and then the *Purana* says that if you recite all one thousand names of Lalita every day at dawn you will become a *yogin,* which I think is a little *yogi,* but not a *yogini,* that is a woman *yogi,* so maybe you'll become a *yoginini,* or maybe there is no name for beginner women *yoginaḥ,* because that is the plural of *yogin,* anyway if you recite the thousand names twice every day you will be wealthy, and three times you'll be something else, and four times you'll be something else, all the way up to sixteen times a day, and if you repeat all one thousand names of the goddess Lalita sixteen times a day, if you pray until you have exhausted your last puff of breath and your tongue is cracked and your eyes are milk, then you will be able to create, sustain, and annihilate universes, and all that is just one prayer to just one goddess, the *Purana* clearly never had an editor, they just kept adding until they had 2,017 pages, clearly no editor ever looked at a line like "in this life, undoubtedly misery is more pleasing than happiness," that doesn't make sense, or a line like, "just as a tiger pounces on a small unhappy animal, so Yama the god of death picks out and snatches away anyone whose desires are unclear," if that were true everyone would immediately die, and the *Narada Purana* even says, "in sexual intercourse, the man sprays out his seed, and obtains from it some issue, and the child thus brought forth indulges in the act of copulation in due course," that is absolute useless mindless nonsense, or is it wisdom? Or is it nonsense? I don't know, and finally I got to page 2,017, the last page of the book, where I read this: "Just as the best prayer is the presentation of offerings in a pit of deceased ancestors on the eleventh day after their death, just as the Ganges is the most holy of all rivers, as Vrindavan, where little Krishna played, has the best forest in India, as Pushkar Lake is the most excellent lake in the universe, so this is the best of all Puranas, the end." So I ask you, Samuel, is it good that there are books like the *Narada Purana* that remind us the world is larger and more fabulous than we knew, even though people had very scrambled ideas and were afraid of sneezes and untrimmed mustaches and not so secretly attracted to eunuchs and eating semen, even though they were drunk with holiness and prayer and prayed until their tongues cracked?

Yes?

The answer is no, of course not.

So why did you tell me about it?

You need to know what it is like to be inside these books, because soon you will be reading my notebooks, and you will be inside them, like a sheep inside a camel. As Kusters says in *A Philosophy of Madness,* you need to spend time on the other side, looking out. I am preparing you for things you may find in my notebooks. Brackish water, vast sterile halls. Endless forests, hopeless lists. Spit, sores, scabs, piss. Insanities of faith and devotion, medical and sexual aberrations, manias of devotion, obsessive rationality caused by the fear of madness, disorders of naming and grammar, scrambled thoughts, dysfunctional reasoning, confusions, despair. My notebooks may have these same issues. And, but, I am also preparing you to be lost, because you will be lost in my notebooks. I wish you would just trust me for another hour and let me complete my introduction.

Sorry.

So after the *Narada Purana* I stopped reading religion and philosophy. I thought about the books I had been reading—science, history, medicine, religion, philosophy—and I realized they were all wrong for me. My notebooks are not normal science, philosophy, or even religion. I would not have wasted my life writing a normal book, I will not waste my life writing a normal book. I realized my book is an exercise of the imagination. For years I have been trying to imagine what life might look like if it is seen in a different way, and that is what poets and writers do. I thought perhaps my notebooks could become a long poem, a tremendous verse epic, a blank verse epic. Like Homer, but not as good. You are smiling.

I am sighing.

Actually some of the longest texts in the world are epic poems, I thought that was very promising, maybe I could just turn my notebooks into a great modern epic poem. There is the Uzbek epic *Alpomish,* the Bambara *Bamana Segu,* the Ede *Dam San,* the Kazakh epic *Edige,* the Mohave *Inyo-kutavêre,* and Antarah ibn Shaddad's *Romance of 'Antar,* which is 32 volumes long. Some are fake, like the *Dvůr Králové,* the *Zelená Hora,* Ossian, and the *Hotsuma Tsutae,* and by the way why do people spend their lives writing fake epic poems? The longest are the Mongolian epic *Jangar* and the Iranian epic *Shahnameh,* that is one of the world's longest epic poems, but not as long as the Indian epic, the *Mahabharata,* that is 1,800,000 words, and there is an even longer Indian poem, but I could not read it, no one can, it is the forever untranslatable multilingual coded Kannada numerical Jain epic *SiriBhoovalaya,* which is six times as long as the *Mahabharata* and makes use of 718 languages, that is astonishing, I only use 71 languages in my book, and there is an even longer poem called *The Manas,* written in the Kyrgyz language, it is 553,500 lines long. I read that, and I am sorry I did. For 553,500 lines, muscle-bound heroes with sable beards, prick-mustaches, and fork-beards, their blood black, their lice blue, their bellies mottled, with entrails of steel and hearts of stone, their leather skin swealed by the sun, their knees hard with calluses, their necks like the boles of great oaks, knotted and seized together with muscle-humps and carbuncles of tangled sinew, arms like the necks of beasts, ball-swollen with bunched-up brawnstrings and blood-veins, hands furred in boils, upstanding ears as large as palms, their whole bodies burning, their waists bulging down to their feet so that their sashes begirdle their slippers, their tight breeches irking their treelike calves until they slit their breeches to the knees, causing them to fit like cream poured on pancakes, their feet swathed in feltgrass slippers, smutted with dungs and dirt-daubs, hardened by stainings of rotted milk and horseflesh, because those great warriors gulp their favorite drink *kumys,* fermented mare's milk, they eat jelly-blood from the guts of sleek-ribbed mares, drink bowls of stinking *airan,* that is sour milk diluted with water, they chew mane-fat, drink oiled horse liver soup with dill, and when they have filled their cauldron-like bellies they jump on their bay horses, whipping them until their eyes open wide, their flesh falls apart, and blood-flecked foam spatters the great warriors' skirts, and then they race toward the Kalmyk enemy, narrowing their eyes and depressing their bristling mustaches, pursuing their stick-mouthed Kalmyk enemies, jumping on them, tearing at their muscle-flesh, slicing off their tufted heads, carving up their broad rumps, bunging their own gushing wounds with corkwood fungus mats, jumping back on their bleeding bay horses, galloping to fight fearsome naked muscle-bound warrior women who can untie camel ropes with their teeth, whose hair is like hail clouds, whose eyebrows are like nests of swarming *tonqï*, whose glare is like a bloodied *bčana*, whose nipples are like black pegs, whose noses billow gray clouds, whose throats breathe out black smoke, whose *böböčöks* or *böbösüks* or *böböčüks,* that is their clitorises, are like the hooks at the top of iron tripods, whose vaginas are slung underneath like great iron cauldrons, whose vaginas are like cauldrons tipped forward pouring water like great rivers disappearing into the distance, splattering those muscle-bound warrior women over the land, drowning sheep in bubbling floods of gore, and then the fibrous warriors jump back on their flayed and foaming horses and gallop to cut open the heads of Kalmyk that gabble "Möndü!," the Kalmyk Buddhist infidels, cutting down their shrewish slaves, killing hordes and khanates, legions and armies, fighting on even when they are surrounded by more naked warrior women, fighting even when they bristle with spears locked sharply into their bones, even when their eyes are peeled like sheep testicles, even when their heads are split open and their brains squint at the razor sun, even when there is no boat for them on the dark river of life. *The Manas* has far more testosterone than the *Iliad,* each line is like a slab of meat, and to read it you have to hack through 553,500 lines of gristle, I am so sorry I read it, it gave me cramps, and there is an even longer poem written in Tibetan, *The Epic of King Kesar.* No one knows how long it is, so far only 120 volumes have been printed, about 20,000,000 words, and bards continue to sing new episodes so *The Epic of King Kesar* just keeps growing, it is the malignant metastasizing matron of all epics. I read the first 3 volumes. There is no Kyrgyz testosterone in *The Epic of King Kesar,* it is gentle for a while. It opens with two hundred pages of prayers, proverbs, speeches, and songs, because heaven has to arrange the birth of the great King Kesar.

Many deities meet to discuss their plans for the incarnation of the great king, and finally, on page 207, a child who seems to be three years old appears from his mother's "secret place" and sits in her lap. Immediately a minor deity dresses the three-year old Kesar in indestructible vajra armor, that's a special kind of armor that protects against 404 diseases, including brain dysfunction, loss of consciousness, fainting, loss of speech, incontinence, epilepsy, paralysis, diphtheria, anthrax, pleurisy, cramps, bloody diarrhea, chickenpox, stomach tumors, hydrops, foot blisters, shingles, skin discoloration, lumps, ulcers, cysts, abscesses, boils, corneal opacity, pustules, overgrowths of the flesh, and 378 more, I wouldn't mind having that armor myself, especially if it protects against brain dysfunction, and then the minor deity places a pat of butter on the roof of baby Kesar's mouth, like they give to newborn calves to soften their palate, and then he offers Kesar an extremely sweet nectar that was specially blessed in a ten day long ceremony, followed by a morsel of ritual cake with a hundred flavors. It was a very spectacular and divine birth, what happened in Bethlehem was nothing by comparison, but it wasn't over, because an egg-like orb of blue light exploded from his mother's heart, and in the orb was another infant with the head of a snake, and the snake infant said, "Hi, I am Naga Serpent Feeble Light, your little brother. I eat only pale things. I will guard your armor," and then a beautiful little girl dressed in white snow partridge feathers splashed out in rainbow rays from Kesar's mother's navel, and she said, "Hi, I am your little sister, Totally Luminous. I eat turquoise and drink tea. I am the spy lamp that illuminates everything." Then Kesar's mother opened her mouth, probably to say she was exhausted, and out burst nine armed animal spirit warriors called wermas, each riding on a horse or other animal, first an incandescent werma shaped like a tigress with her hair standing on end, riding on a dun horse, then a squall god with the head of a needlefish, riding on a bay horse, then an iron-headed winter god, riding a crude-looking Tibetan Riwoche horse, then a splinter-toothed tornado god, riding a mastiff, then a plate-headed earthquake god, riding a grunting long-haired ox, then a wrinkled poison antidote god, riding a musk deer, then a horse-headed horse god, riding on a horse, then a goddess with the head of a wrinkle-muzzled wild ass, riding a wild ass, and last four yak-headed yak goddesses riding a yak, and they all yelled, "We are your wermas!"

and then Kesar's mother opened her mouth again, probably to ask them all to please let her rest, and out came a yak stomach bag containing nine hundred more guardians armed with Qamdo knives and conch shell horns, and they burst out of the bag and screamed, "We are your servant warriors!" Then just when Kesar's mother thought she was finally finished she felt a vein bulging on the top of her head, and it burst, and out came a wet white sac like an enormous snake egg, and when they cut it open three men jumped out and ran away, they were the leftover demons from all the good works that had happened that day. Then she fell asleep surrounded by sacs and bags and orbs and Kesar's little brother and sister and his nine wermas and nine hundred servant warriors stayed up late worshiping Kesar. You are yawning.

I am listening.

So just three days later the three-year-old three-day-old infant went to war. He ordered all nine hundred guardians, nine wermas, and his brother and sister to shrink down into pebbles, each one with the double lobed shape of a pregnant ewe's liver, and to live in the double pebbles until he needed them. Then he crawled out onto a battlefield and met a demon named Sour Nephew White Face of the Bum Family who was standing on a plain full of corpses, chomping on a human arm, a demon so disgusting that even cannibal demons were nauseated when they looked at him, a demon so appalling that he ate living snake spirits, he just bit out their gallbladders while they were still alive, because that is the most bitter part of the snake, and he kept the gallbladders under his tongue, which made him drool, and he threw the snake spirits onto the piles of human corpses. Sour Nephew White Face of the Bum Family stood there grinning and slobbering, and all around him gallbladderless serpent spirits flopped around on human corpses, moaning and squeaking, with bleeding gaps where their gallbladders had been. Infant King Kesar put two of his special double pebbles into his toy slingshot and shot them at Sour Nephew White Face of the Bum Family, and one went into the demon's left eye, and the other went right under his tongue, bursting the gallbladders, causing the nauseating demon to foam and splutter, and then he wedged his secret weapon between his toes and dipped his toes under water and kicked and the secret weapon flew at Sour

Nephew and curved around behind him and he whirled around but it was too late, the secret weapon penetrated into his anus, it was like Cú Chulainn's secret weapon the *gae bulga,* do you know about that? Well, I can't explain everything to you, anyway the double pebbles met the secret weapon in the middle of Sour Nephew's belly and they danced together and their happy dancing stirred the demon's intestines into soup, and the demon burped, and then exploded, and King Kesar cupped his little hands and gathered all the corpses and parts of human flesh and put them in a bag full of nutmeg and tailed peppers, and he gathered the dying snake spirits and put them in a bowl for eagles to eat, and he gathered the shreds of flesh that were left of Sour Nephew and burned them, and the smoke made him cough because he was only three days old, and also because it contained tiny particles of evil. Then he called his brother Feeble Light and his sister Totally Luminous, his nine wermas, and his nine hundred guardians, and they went on and killed many thousands more people, in hundreds and thousands of pages of battles.

Does something like this happen in your notebooks?

I hope not. I read epic poems because I thought they would show me that my notebooks could be shaped into a sort of epic poem, but all I learned from *The Manas* and *The Epic of King Kesar* is that some people in epic poems absolutely love to kill each other in as many ways as possible, and also that it is probably not a good idea to be the mother of a mythical Tibetan King. So then I thought, well, maybe I have been reading the wrong kind of epic poems. I should be looking for poems that tell the history of the entire world from the beginning of time, because that is more like what I am trying to do with my work, tell the history of ideas of life. Hesiod does that in *Works and Days,* and there is the *Popol Vuh* and the *Enuma Elish* but those are too short. The Chinese epic called *The Legend of Darkness* is much better. It says that in the beginning the universe was a cloud of chaos, darkness, and gas. After eons of effort a deity named Jiang Ku managed to create a single drop of water. I appreciated that, because imagine how hard it would be to create a single drop of water, you'd have to really concentrate, not like the God in the Bible who supposedly created everything without even really trying. So Jiang Ku created one drop of water, but then another god named

Lang Dang Zi came along and swallowed the drop of water, and then he died. That pretty much stopped the universe in its tracks. Eons later another god named Pan Gu managed to split the heavens from the earth. The effort killed him. Then lots of demons and gods sprang out of the ground and fought each other, but they all drowned in an enormous flood. Eons later two gigantic dragons flew up out of the flood and fought each other, for no reason really, except that one was yellow and the other was black. The yellow one killed the black one, and to celebrate it laid three eggs, but before they could hatch a goddess ate them. She gave birth to heaven, earth, and hell, even though there already was a heaven and an earth, so maybe then there were two of each. Meanwhile the earth was still flooded. I am not sure how long that lasted. At some point five more dragons flew out of the water. For some reason they didn't fight. No one knows where they went. The earth was still flooded. Then nothing happened for a very long time. Eons later another god named Hundun spotted a gourd floating in the water, and when he cracked it open, he found two humans, Fuxi and Nüwa. He ordered them to copulate and that's how humans got started according to the *Legend of Darkness.* Notice, Samuel, no one made people, in the *Legend of Darkness* people just appear, the ocean might have had lots of gourds with people floating inside, but they had to be broken out of the gourds and ordered to copulate. If I were Nüwa, I would have told Fuxi I was perfectly happy just floating in the darkness, and could we just put the top back on our gourd and sit in peace? Then the world could have continued for more eons in peace and quiet, just an ocean with some gourds in it and maybe a couple more dragons, but of course then Fuxi and Nüwa had children, and the world filled up and everyone started fighting and I stopped reading. Epic poems are exhausting because anything can happen, there seems to be order but there isn't. In epic poems the hero might battle a dragon and then turn into a pimple and hide on someone's cheek, that happens in another Chinese epic, *Journey to the West,* it's over 2,000 pages long, but I don't have time to tell you about everything, and then the hero might burst out of the pimple and fight a dragon and then woo the daughter of the prince of the neighboring kingdom who was once betrothed to the cousin of a merchant who robbed a caravan from another kingdom that was ruled by a despot who was jealous of the prince because the prince traded a magic jewel for the prince's sister's mother's servant's daughter, who was more beautiful, according to a seer who was employed by the merchant but actually working for the prince, than the little sister of the daughter of the prince of the neighboring kingdom, who was herself once betrothed to the brother of the man who ran the caravan, who seemed to be a prince in disguise, but actually was the same daughter disguised as a princess disguised as a prince disguised as a merchant, and the despot saw through the first disguise but not the second or third, and the seer saw through the first and second but not the third, and the despot saw through all three but said nothing, and that would have been the end of it, but at that moment the palace doors swung open, and in came the prince's father's sister's cousin's mother's servant's sixteenth daughter, a girl of such astonishing beauty that one of the palace peacocks threw up in disgust, and that, as the father of the prince explains on page thirty thousand of the execrably rhymed, excruciatingly badly translated poem, that is the beginning of the prelude to the opening of the preface of the introduction to the first story, the miraculous amazing edifying and inspiring Story of the Magic Pimple. Those long poems are exactly that stupid.[26] I don't know what kind of order my work is in, but I don't want to give up looking and start writing about princes and seers, camels and dragons, servants and castles, gourds and mustaches, peacocks and pimples. Somehow epic poems were entertaining for supposedly thousands of years for simple country people, whoever they were. You wouldn't know, Samuel, because Canadians don't have any epic poems.

Actually, I'm not Canadian.

Oh. So anyway, when I returned the last volume of the last epic poem to the library, I told our ignorant librarian Arnulf Trausch that I thought people must have been addled for hundreds of generations, because they were stupefied by mixed-up stories. Trausch told me people used to sit around "the fire," as he said, "rapt," as he said, by what he called "storytellers," and I told him people must have been desperately bored to put up with that stuff, and he said those epic poems were the soul and spirit of generations of people and the pride of nations, and I was just an odd-looking Swiss professor, and I said, "I suppose you just sat around 'the fire,' 'enraptured' by 'storytellers' when you were growing up in your rainbowy state of pre-civilized bliss on the Island of Grass Skirts in the midst of the Forgotten Ocean," and he said I was possibly the most ignorant person he had ever encountered, and he recommended I hang a sign around my neck saying, Warning, I Do Not Understand What it Means to To Be Human, and when I heard that I was overjoyed, I embraced him, I couldn't help it, "You are right!" I said, "you are so right." I ran home and wrote those words on a board and glued it to our door. And after that I turned to fiction, the longest and most complicated examples I could find. I thought, Why not? My work is not normal science, it is not normal writing. My work trespasses all the boundaries of disciplines and decorum. Fiction does that, and fiction is famous for long and complex stories, even ones that—

You glued the sign to your door?

And then I screwed it in using wedge bolts so Paul cannot remove it. He still wants to be human. First I bought a copy of *War and Peace,* but it is a baby. *Artamène or the Grand Cyrus* was written by Madeleine de Scudéry back in the seventeenth century, and it is 13,095 pages long, full of indolent and fond aristocratic women who wish their lovers to quit finding amusement in every breeze like flying feathers, and become pale, sober, and grave, and sometimes unquiet and reserved, and perhaps even delicately disordered, and indeed to be the most miserable men in the world, women who permit their applicant lovers fifteen days to fall in love with them, after which time the men need to become the most pitiful puling lovers in the world, and the men demur, saying they hardly need fifteen days, that they can already feel their love swelling, and the women tell them diffidence is charming, but flattery more so, and yet fruition gluts, and the men reply that they dare not hear such sentiments without applauding their sharp sweetness, and the women note that such repartée is hardly commensurate with the pallid melancholy required of men who display a regrettable propensity to flit like *papillons,* and that goes on for 12 volumes, Samuel, that's 13,095 pages, the novel is an astonishing waste of time, and I am sure Madeleine de Scudéry knew it, I'm sure she was vexed and ashamed of her quick fancy, her delicate judgment, and her utter obliviousness to the fact that people do not have years to waste reading drivel. There are 27 volumes in

Jules Romains's *Les Hommes de bonne volonté*, 7,970 conventional and boring pages. Imagine, the last line of the final volume is "No one could think of anything else to say"! Except Romains could, he added a 97 page index so people could look up all 1,950 characters. There are 20 volumes in Emile Zola's series of novels called *Les Rougon-Macquart,* totaling over 8,000 pages, but he is just a footnote to Balzac, yet Balzac never finished his project, he wrote 91 novels and then he died, and I did not want to spend time with someone who did not know how to stop. I almost read Samuel Richardson's *Clarissa,* that's 969,000 words, but I was distracted by the Marquis de Sade. I decided not to read the Marquis de Sade's *Justine* and *Juliette* even though they are 10 volumes and 4,000 pages long, because I am not interested in sex except in lower organisms, especially Placozoans, those are actually very exciting, do you know about them? Of course you do. And oh, also *Funisia,* it's the first organism ever to have sex, that must have been quite a moment, but anyway I did not need Sade to lecture me on the high moral calling of perversity. Placozoans and *Funisia* are more perverse than anything in his books. I did not read Karl Gutzkow's *Knights of the Spirit,* even though it is 9 volumes and 4,100 pages long. I looked at it, but it's bloated and bulimic. I have not read *The Eight Dog Warriors,* Japan's longest novel, because I can't, it's in Japanese. I have not read Sōhachi Yamaoka's 28 volume novel about a famous shogun, because I can't, it's in Japanese. I have not read Louis Cha's martial arts novel *Demi-Gods and Semi-Devils,* because I can't, it's in Chinese. I have not read the 26,000 page novel *Venmurasu,* because it's in Tamil. I have not read Moorkkanaat Krishnankutty Menon's 3,938 page novel *The Inheritors,* because it's in Malayam. I have not read Marija Jurić Zagorka's 23 volume novel *Gordana* about Matthias Corvinus and the events leading up to the sixteenth-century Battle of Mohács, it sounds fascinating, but it's in Croatian. I have not read Henry Williamson's *Chronicle of Ancient Sunlight* in 12 volumes, I could, but the title sounds pretentious, and one of the volumes is called *How Dear is Life,* that is embarrassing, and besides, he wrote a book called *Tarka the Otter* and another book called *Salar the Salmon* and he wanted to write a book called *Fergaunt the Fox,* I will not read things like that. I have not read Johannes Jacobus Voskuil's supposedly amazing novel *Het Bureau,* because it's only 1,200 pages long, too short for me. I have not read Mohiuddin Nawab's novel *Devta,* because it is in Urdu, although I would like to, because it is exactly 6,898 and one-tenth pages long, that's how it is advertised, so that one-tenth page might be quite interesting, and besides, it is about space monkeys. I won't read Stephen King's *Dark Tower,* even though it is 4,316 pages, because he is too breezy. I will not read Robert Jordan's *Wheel of Time,* even though it is 11,898 pages, because it is light entertainment, and I hate light, and I hate entertainment. I couldn't read William Gaddis's novel *The Recognitions,* he's too American for me. I couldn't read Thomas Pynchon, there is too much alcohol and too many recreational drugs. I did not read Lucy Ellmann's *Ducks, Newburyport,* because it's only 1,020 pages long, and besides, there's the fact that that's hardly long enough to begin thinking about anything. I didn't read Marguerite Young's *Miss Macintosh, My Darling,* because it is flushed and weepy and very very repetitive. I couldn't read Javier Pedro Zabala's *The Mad Patagonian,* even though it is 3 volumes long, because it's more drugs and sex. I couldn't read Mark Danielewski's novel *The Familiar* because no one can, he had a plan for 27 novels, each one 880 pages long, that would be 23,760 pages or about 7,000,000 words, it would have been longer than my book, but not by much, but anyway he didn't write it, he finished 4,400 pages and then his publisher canceled the contract. Thomas Bernhard wrote dozens of short books, but really they are one monstrous book, 4,170 pages long, I should have done that, written short papers, even if they were all the same, but it's too late now. I finally settled down to read David Foster Wallace's *Infinite Jest* even though it is only 1,079 pages long, because I saw it has footnotes, so naturally I wanted to read it, but right in the middle of my reading I discovered fan fiction. Those books are actually the longest fiction in the world, not as long as the *Epic of King Kesar,* but much longer than so-called serious fiction. I set out right away to read the world's longest fan fictions, which are also the world's longest fictions. I tried to read *Homestuck,* it is a Microsoft Paint fantasy that is longer than *War and Peace,* but I couldn't because there are seven pages missing and I will not read a book that is 8,126 pages long if seven pages are missing, and I tried to read the 4,102,328 word fan fiction novel called *The Subspace Emissary's Worlds Conquest,* it is seven times longer than *Infinite Jest* and six times longer than *War and Peace,* but I couldn't read it because it is based on *Super Smash Bros. Brawl* by Nintendo, which is based on many other Nintendo games, and I do not wish to learn about *Super Mario, Donkey Kong, The Legend of Zelda, Metroid, Yoshi, Kirby, Star Fox, Pokémon, Sonic the Hedgehog, Street Fighter,* or *Final Fantasy.* I tried to read the fan fiction *Ambience: A Fleet Symphony,* it is 4,500,000 words about teen-girl versions of World War II warships, that is old ships made into teenage girl robots, why girls, I wondered, but the narrator says no one knows, maybe it makes the warships look better, I thought maybe that's true, but I got depressed reading about girl robot warships. I did not try to read *At the Edge of Lasg'len,* a fan fiction based on *The Lord of the Rings,* even though it's ten times longer than *The Lord of the Rings,* because I can't stand elves, they are prissy, and I can't stand hobbits, they are mawkish, and I couldn't read the world's longest fan fiction which is *The Loud House: Revamped* by someone named Jamesdean5842, that one is a multi-crossover self-insert original character non-harem fanfic that is longer than 17,677,215 words, which would be about 59,000 pages, but no one knows how long it really is, because 17,677,215 is as high as the fan fiction site can count. Another site run by fans of fan fiction says *Loud House: Revamped* is 35,122,100 words. I care about *The Loud House: Revamped* because it is longer than all my notebooks put together, they are 7,522,500 words, and *The Loud House: Revamped* is five times as long, an unimaginable length, it would take me five lifetimes to write that much, but I couldn't read it because I haven't watched the Nickelodeon TV series *The Loud House* or any of the other TV series, movies, comics, and video games that appear in *The Loud House: Revamped,* but at least I read one chapter, I read Chapter 2,148, which is titled "The Ooze is Back For Round 2." I will tell you what it is like.

You don't need to. I can imagine.

I do, actually, and you can't. At one point a character named Lynn is walking along with 144 of her very best friends, all of them are named right at the beginning in a long list. Some sound ordinary, like Nico, Ellie Singh, Evelyn Burmingham, Eddy, Heiser, Woodnutt, Smith, and Nicely, and some are not so ordinary, like Anna the Despairing Gene-Slammer. Lynn also has lots of friends whose names start with *L,* like Lincoln, Leni, Laney, Lana, Lola, Lisa and Lily, I suppose the list might be more helpful if

I had read the 2,147 chapters that came before this one, anyway Lynn is just having fun and minding her own business, when she is surrounded by a massive vortex of rainbow energy with four erupting volcanoes, and suddenly a beam of light is fired right onto her massive Guabancex Firestorm Draconic Phoenix Greatsword of Volcanic Rage Justice and Athletic Volcanic Earth Love, it took me a while to understand that, I thought Guabancex was a funny word, it turns out Guabancex is the Taíno god of chaos and disorder, and the Taíno are an indigenous Caribbean people who worshipped mysterious pointed stones, and "draconic" in this case means resembling a dragon, not resembling Dracon, whose name sounds like "dragon," but that is only a coincidence, because he was an ancient Greek lawyer who wrote a strict legal code, and that's the usual meaning of "draconic," and a greatsword was a Renaissance sword the same height as a person, so Jamesdean5842 is describing a supernatural mythological sword that is somehow full of rage and also love and must have been very tiring to carry when you're out for a walk with 144 of your closest friends, so then a MASSIVE VORTEX OF ENERGY AND FIRE, ICE, WATER, WIND, LIGHTNING, EARTH, LAVA, LIGHT, DARKNESS, WOOD, STARS, TIME, NATURE, GRAVITY, BLOOD, MAGIC, MOONLIGHT, RAINBOW CRYSTALS, RAINBOW SUPER LIGHTNING, RAINBOW FIRE, SAND, BLUE FIRE, BUBBLES, PILLARS OF STEAM, NEBULONIC GAS, FROZEN AURORAS, LIGHT MAGIC, DARK MAGIC, BLACK MAGIC, SATANIC MAGIC, MORE MOONLIGHT, AND ATOMIC RADIATION exploded out of Lynn and her power was REALLY AND RAPIDLY INCREASING AT AN EXPONENTIAL RATE AT A MASSIVE LEVEL!, and Lincoln said, IT'LL START RAINING BLOOD SOON, BRACE YOURSELVES! and LYNN EMERGED FOREVER CHANGED!, and a Loud House instrumental intro played, and Lynn grew from 7'4" to 7'9" in height, and she had the body of a goddess, with large Edoten-Hermès gold metal bracers on her biceps and thighs, eleven bespoke scarlet rings spinning around her legs, Vortex vermilion highlights in the bangs of her long flowing chestnut-brown hair tied in a low ponytail, pink-gold construction boots with golden titanium nitride claws, scarlet-red Hyein Seo shorts, and a long pink sleeveless Goen.J trench coat with licking flames on its coattails and a Fire Wyvern eating a Red Fire Ant on the back, and then suddenly she felt a sharp pain on her shoulders and her massive chestnut-brown angel wings with glowing neon red tipped feathers ripped out of the Goen.J trench coat and grew bigger so they could lift her new body, I thought that was just like Totally Luminous, and she sprouted eleven massive chestnut-brown wolf tails with ruby red tips, and she had an Eater of Sins Raging Hunter revolver holstered on her left hip and a hand-cut Smith and Wesson 500 Bone Crusher magnum with a chrome-flashed hammer and trigger holstered on her right hip, and a scarlet red kanji inscription on her very large belt buckle that translated as, "I am Lynn Loud, Descendant of the 17th Century Lynn of Loch Loud in Scotland, Fifth Born and Fifth Eldest of The Loud Family, Loving Sister of Her Many Siblings, Loving Fifth Eldest Daughter of Rita and Lynn Sr., Loving Girlfriend of Lightning, Loving Future Mother of Lime Juice, Amazing and Talented Statewide Athlete, Good Sportswoman, Awesome Faithful Friend of Polly Painintheneck, Margo the Migraine, and Paula Partypoop, Spice Demon and Lover of Spicy Foods, Brave Warrior of The Cosmos, Protector, Defender, and Savior of The Universe, Multiverse, Metaverse, Mimiverse, and Beyond, Archenemy of Koopa Troopa and Koopa Paratroopa, Master of The Powers of Unbreakable Friendship, Master of The Fury of Celestial Xel'naga," by the way I didn't know what that was, it turns out Xel'naga are the most powerful species the universe has ever known, they are from StarCraft, StarCraft is a military science fiction media franchise owned by Blizzard Entertainment, Blizzard Entertainment is based in Irvine, California, anyway also "Master of The Black Gates, Ultimate Force of Ultimate Good, True Goddess of Truth, Justice, Love, Compassion, Hope, Forgiveness, Valor, Virtue, Determination, Loyalty, Honesty, Generosity, Kindness, Selflessness, Courage, and Trust, Savior of The Loud House and Michigan, Amazing and Powerful Student, Shinobi of The Hidden Leaf Village," I had to look that up too, a shinobi is a ninja, but shinobis sneak around, that is what their name means, "people who sneak," and ninja are invisible, their name means "invisible person," I think I would rather be a ninja than a shinobi, but anyway also "Member of Many of Team Loud Phoenix's Branch Teams, Emissary and Champion of Guabancex, Queen of Crystalsapiens," I didn't know what that was either, so I looked it up, Crystalsapiens are a crystalline alien species from the planet Petropia,

Petropia was a craggy geode-like planet, but it was destroyed by Tetrax, that's Tetrax Shard, he was a secondary character in the *Ben 10* franchise, *Ben 10* is an American media franchise created by Man of Action, Man of Action Entertainment is a writer's collective based in Glendale, California, but anyway also "Founder of Team Loud Phoenix Storm, Destroyer and Slayer of Evil Deranged Murderous Ruthless Sadistic Bastards, Destroyer of Morag McLaughlin," she's in the *Loud House Movie,* "Max Müller Annihilator of Nihilism, Gentle Annihilator of Hundun," he's the one from *Legend of Darkness* who forced the two people in the gourd to mate, so I guess he had to be killed, "Archenemy of Dark Lynn, Evil Lynn, Kelly-Lynn, and Bumblesparkle," I stopped looking them up, the list went on, she must have had an exceptionally large belt buckle, "Sworn Eternal Enemy of Kathryn Mansfield, Harry Cooper, and Betsy Davis, Lifelong Bloodbonded Superfriend to Mark Leyner, Tao Lin, and Honor Levy, and Ultimate Defender of The Loud House and The Loud Family in Royal Woods Townhome Complex Just South of Detroit, Michigan," and then it repeats all that in Japanese, and then it says she transformed into SUPER ANGEL-DRAGON-PHOENIX HARMONY UNITED FRIENDSHIP UNIVERSAL ETERNAL CELESTIAL XEL'NAGA DIVINE GUABANCEX FIRESTORM RAGE-RAGE-RAGE+LOVE SUPERNOVA 750 BILLION INFINITY FIRE ANGEL OF CUTENESS! and everyone was really amazed, but when Chucky saw her, the fucker absolutely lost his mind and charged at Lynn to stab her with his knife, but Lynn fired a massive barrage of rainbow energy, stars, lava, earth, dragons, and phoenixes, and they exploded from divine indigestion energy and splattered Chucky and burned him badly, and to make it worse, his knife melted, and Nico cried out, "OH MAN," but Eli yelled, "AWESOME EDGELADY!," and, well, okay, I stopped right there in the middle of Chapter 2,148, that was enough for me, clearly *The Loud House: Revamped* is insane, but it is not a form of insanity I need to worry about, because apparently it inflicts mainly teenagers in North America.

Maybe you should try Chapter 2,149.

That is what I thought! But when I went back to the fan fiction site to get the next chapter, I saw that Jamesdean5842 had already written sixteen more chapters, very long ones. *The Loud House: Revamped* has a special sort of insanity, Teenage Cartoon Insanity, I think it's a problem for young people, like chickenpox. I doubt I can get sick from it, but I am not too sure of anything recently, and Jamesdean5842 is sort of like me because he really loves listing things, and we both have a small problem knowing when to stop. But that was the end of my reading of fan fiction. I was determined to read the longest books of fiction I could find, aside from ones written by teenagers. It turns out the longest books written by adults use computers to add text, that way they can be longer than anything a human could write. Someone named Richard Grossman supposedly wrote a book called *Breeze Avenue* that is 3,000,000 pages long, but I couldn't find it. Someone named Mark Leach supposedly wrote a book called *Marienbad, My Love,* I say supposedly because he didn't actually write the 10,710 pages of *Marienbad, My Love,* and by the way my notebooks are 25,950 pages, but for some reason Mark Leach likes tiny font and really wide pages, so each of his pages has about 1,800 words, so his book is really about 19,280,000 words long, that is almost three times longer than mine. I find that very annoying. He says it contains the world's longest word, 4,400,000 letters, and the world's longest sentence, 3,000,000 words, and the longest title ever written, 6,931 words long, that is because the title is not *Marienbad, My Love,* it just starts *Marienbad My Love,* and then it goes on, *in the Ruins of the Dreams and Beliefs of a Man Who is Gone but Not Forgotten,* very poetic, a little maudlin, and the title just keeps going, a couple hundred words later there is this, *A Contrail Suspended in The High, Thin Stratosphere, An Icy Cirrus Cloud of Time,* which sounds kind of poetic, but then a hundred words later there it is again, *Breathing in the Icy Cirrus Cloud of Time,* and a hundred words later, still in the title, it's *A Man Who Is Gone Up Into The High, Thin Stratosphere, An Icy Cirrus Cloud of Time,* and later *An Enormous Radiant Fog of Visual Rumors And Nonsense Digressing,* when I read that I thought it sounded about right, I am an expert on digressing so I spotted that right away, and later *Suspended In The High, Thin Stratosphere, An Icy Cirrus Cloud of Time,* and later *In The High, Thin Stratosphere of An Icy Cirrus Cloud of Time, A Manifestation Known to The Inner World, The World of Fire, The World Behind The Masonry Walls,* that sounds mystical, and later *In The High, Thin Stratosphere, An Icy Cirrus Cloud of Time, A Manifestation,* that's definitely mystical, and later *An*

*Icy Cirrus Listening to The Deity,* hmm, I thought, the book is religious, and later *An Icy Cirrus Cloud of He Calls Marienbad in The Ruins of His Beliefs And Dreams,* that sounds like a mistake, and later *An Icy Cirrus Cloud of Time, Of Glittering Emerald Flakes,* and later *An Icy Cirrus Cloud of Chaos, In Lurid Intervals,* and later *A Psychic Contrail Suspended in The High, Thin Stratosphere, An Icy Cirrus Cloud of Time, Bewilderment, Of Old Coins and Fermented Blood,* what's that, I wondered, and later *Off The Forsaken Island He Calls Marienbad in The Ruins of Damp Waste,* and finally the title ends with *The Forsaken Island He Calls Marienbad in the Ruins of His Memories and Dreams.* And that's just the title, I mean excerpts of the title. It is repetitive, but not in an interesting way, it's carelessly put together, not like my speeches, but I went on and started reading, but then I stopped on page 502 when he writes, possibly for the 500th time, "That's not the half of it," and then he goes on: "Here is the truth: I was out of my head that time. But that's not the half of it. Picture me dying, inside a hot airless room with ominous rumblings. I was out of my head that time. But that's not the half of it. But that's not the half of it. But that's not the half of it. Also, I realized that Jewell and Raven repeat the same conversations every week." *Marienbad, My Love* is like the Avalanche Theory, level one out of thirteen, but just the avalanche part, without the chateau, not very impressive. It's only mildly irrational, it's too simple, I can't learn anything from it, except maybe to watch out that I do not repeat things too often, or only when I need to, and that it's good not to be careless, because carelessness makes writing boring, other things do too, but carelessness makes writing especially boring, and I don't think I have those problems, at least not much. I also didn't finish Nigel Tomm's *The Blah Story,* which is 17,868 pages long, because he just put the word "blah" everywhere, like this: "Even drunk on blah blah we could not blah blah. Our blah for blah blah were obliquely blah, or hidden behind blah blah and blah. At a certain point in the evening, blah would make a show of blah the blah of blah on my bed and finding blah that a blah and a blah had blah blah not blah blah. Blah would point out what blah blah were blah that a young blah blah had recently blah there, using a heap of blah as a blah blah and seeing the blah blah in his blankets as the blah blah of the blah. Blah would then blah her husband blah in front of blah to demonstrate what blah ought to do on the bed as soon as blah had come to blah blah, and blah blah blah one of the thousands of blah in blah who were waiting blah blah by their blah as hot to meet a new blah as blah had been at blah. Then, if blah was drunk enough, blah would argue that all those blah must have once been to the blah blah of blah as blah had been and must have learned blah blah blah for a blah blah blah. And if blah saw that he was blah enough blah would announce that blah blah blah was his sixteen-year-old blah. Had he guarded her blah? I would blah at blah. Could he keep her from blah blah blah the blah blah and blah her to blah blah? I would treat her blah and do no more than blah my blah to her until blah blah blah and be a blah, blah blah to blah for the rest of my blah."[27]

Please Anneliese don't read me any more of that.

Blah blah blah. In Swiss German we say *bla bli blu,* and by the way in Spanish it is *bli blu bla,* I don't know how they got it wrong, Paul has a friend in Ofterschwang who says *pa pi po,* at least that is better than *blah blah blah. Marienbad, My Love* is like *Miss MacIntosh, My Darling,* it's full of repetitions, not as many as *The Blah Story,* it's true, but a lot, some people love that, they think it's entertaining or expressive, but I do not repeat things very often, or only when I really need to, because it's really good not to be careless, because carelessness makes writing really boring, other things do too, but careless is especially boring, and I really don't think I have that problem, or at least not too often.

That is horrible. Don't do that again.

Ha ha ha. After I stopped reading *The Blah Story* I wasn't sure what to do. I had been reading the longest books I could find, books almost as long as my notebooks, and some that are even longer, but I hadn't found a model I could use for my own work. All the books I read had problems. And then I realized something. Anneliese, I said to myself, when you say all the books you've been reading have problems, what you really mean is they are all a little crazy. You have actually been discovering different kinds of insanity. Jamesdean5842 has Teenage Cartoon Insanity. Mark Leach is an example of the Avalanche Theory, except without the lovely chateau. *The Blah Story* is a sort of insanity brought on by computers. Encyclopedias may not be insane, but then again they may be, because they are written by people with serious issues, people who prefer the world to be complete, neutral, unoriginal, and alphabetical. Aquinas had a sort of neatness disorder, Wittgenstein was on the razor's edge, Burton struggled with melancholy and despair and probably lost, Linnaeus was a compulsive collector, there is an ocean of religious mania in the *Narada Purana.* So Anni, I said to myself, you need to change course. You need to read books written by people who are not sane. You might find your own problems are already there in other people's books! Well, when I heard that, I mean when I heard myself think that, I mean when I realized I had thought that, I decided it was an excellent idea. I told myself so, I praised myself for having such a provocative insight, although I also had to ask myself why it had taken me so long to speak up, and I wasn't sure how to answer that, so I went and looked for long books that are not sane. It turns out it is easy to find them, and I was unhappy to discover I might be like some of the authors. In fact I may be like most of them. Nearly all the insane books I read reminded me of my notebooks. I may be insane like Immanuel Velikovsky, for example. He presented himself on Tuesday the 24th of November 1942 at the National Academy of Sciences, 2101 Constitution Avenue, Washington, D.C., at approximately 3:45 P.M., and tried to convince the secretary, a certain Mr. Eburne, to accept a nine-page summary of his findings into their permanent archive, but even though he indemnified them of any responsibility for the accidental destruction of his nine-page document by water, fire, or enemy action, and even though he explained the work had world-historical significance, and even though he made it clear he did not wish to be honored, or asked to give a lecture, or even have the nine pages published, and even though he suggested that if he was Newton or Copernicus they would not refuse him, and even though he showed them his Russian passport so they would know he was not a German spy, still Mr. Eburne would not accept the nine-page paper for the archives of the National Academy of Sciences, so Velikovsky went home, wrote up an affidavit testifying to what had happened, and got it notarized by a legal aide at the U.S. Supreme Court. I thought that was a very good idea. If I had gone to the *Bundesgericht,* that is the Supreme Court of Switzerland, and had them notarize a copy of my work, Catherine would never have dared to steal it. In the nine-page paper Velikovsky laid out his fundamental discoveries, which he said were of interest to history, geology, physics, geophysics, folklore, and the history of religions. "To begin with," he wrote, "our Earth collided (contacted) in the fifteenth century before this era with a comet. The head of the comet exchanged violent electrical discharges with our planet, and also with its own tail." That sounded naughty to me. "The Earth changed the poles, south becoming north, changed axis, and changed the orbit of revolution. Neft poured from the sky and built the present deposit." Don't ask me what neft is. "Meteorites fell in abundance. Lava streamed on the surface of the Earth not only from volcanoes, but also from clefts. Continents and seas changed places. A major portion of humankind perished. A double tide of immense high, that is what he says, an immense high swept seas and continents. In general conflagration woods burned down, rivers boiled, magnetic storms reached a degree hurtful to bioplasma. Then after 50 to 52 years the comet came back and collided (contacted) the Earth again, and then it contacted into Mars. Afterward it settled down and became Venus, but Mars turned into the dangerous neighbor of the Earth, and Mars collided (contacted) the Earth in 1195 AD, and again in 1255 AD, and afterward Mars took its position in the solar system, but long before that, around 3,000 BC, Saturn and Jupiter collided, and the Earth came close to both planets, killing most of the giant reptilia, proving Darwin wrong, because he thought they went extinct millions of years ago, in fact they died because the collisions (contacts) changed gravity and made them too light, so they floated away, except the heaviest ones, and Brontosaurus was a mammal, and then all gigants were exterminated, and buildings of cyclopic size stones were possible chiefly because of different weight of all objects after the contacts (collisions), and theories of slowly development of mountains and valleys under causes like rain and wind, are wrong, and world political history is entirely confused, and Newton was completely erroneous, there is no gravitation, Newton's theory is wrong in all its applications, the radio-layer in the atmosphere is probably the attracting and repulsing medium acting contrary to the ground, and levitation is conceivable, and perpetuum mobile theoretically possible, and the discharge from the upper layer might be exploited for destructive purposes, and a flight to interplanetary space in defiance of gravitation is thinkable."

After that Velikovsky went back home and kept writing. I read the first of his eleven books, *Worlds in Collision,* and it is clear that almost nothing in it is sane, but if I am cold and strict with myself, I have to acknowledge that my theory might appear just as crazy. My theory also spans a wide range of time, I make claims people will think are not rational, and I do believe some famous people like Newton were wrong, not Newton, but other people, and I would like the National Academy of Sciences to have a copy of my work in their archives, and if they accepted it I would indemnify them against damage by water, fire, or enemy action, and on days when I am especially immodest I do quietly hope my work has world-historical significance. All of that worries me. I don't want to have anything in common with Velikovsky.

You don't think the Brontosaurus was a mammal.

And I don't think comets turn into planets, or that it might be possible to levitate. But I am concerned about Velikovsky. My convictions are also stony, and like him I keep building, even if no one agrees with me, and like him I may be breathtakingly wrong. Then I found others: Bernard Gillard, who discovered the Earth does not rotate, Paul Émile Garreau and Jean-Dominique Mestivier, who thought the sun is smaller than the Earth and very close by, André Blavier, who claimed all astronomy is a hallucination, there are lots of people like Velikovsky. David Rohl, Jean Hardouin, Richard Firestone, Heribert Illig. Zecharia Sitchin is another one, he wrote fourteen books about how Earth has been visited by astronauts from another planet, how that planet was captured by the solar system and became its Twelfth Planet, which orbits far away but comes close to the solar system every 3,600 years, okay, right away you may wonder what the tenth and eleventh planets are, well, Sitchin says the ancient Mesopotamians counted the sun as a planet, so that was ten, and the Eleventh Planet was Tiamat, it used to orbit between Mars and Jupiter, but it collided with the Twelfth Planet, destroying half of it and creating the asteroids and the comets, and later one of the Twelfth Planet's moons collided with the remaining half of Tiamat, forming the Earth, and by the way there are actually thirteen planets, but the Thirteenth Planet is lost, and also actually Tiamat was a Mesopotamian goddess of seawater, she mated with Abzu, he was the god of groundwater, I wonder what that looked like, but Sitchin doesn't say, he says humans were created by genetic engineering, crossing extraterrestrials with *Homo erectus,* so Darwin was wrong, there is no missing link, just an alien genetic engineer, and then Sitchin says the Sumerians venerated the Twelfth Planet, but Sumeria was destroyed by nuclear fallout from an extraterrestrial war in 2024 BC, and then he describes how the Sumerians wore divine ME-attire and goggles, flew in ray-emitting cone-shaped space-going multi-stage MU-rockets, as shown on cuneiform tablets, how the pyramids at Giza were beacons for the spaceport and *Gilgamesh* is an aerospace epic, and how the Natural History Museum in London has a mummy they identify as Queen Shabad, but who is actually an alien, in fact she's the alien Annunaki goddess Puabi, if only they would test her DNA they would be very surprised. He wrote them a letter but they refused to test the mummy's DNA, and that seemed suspicious. Sitchin seems even crazier than Velikovsky, he taught himself Sumerian to prove his theories, and I have to say the idea of being a Sumerologist already sounds a bit off, really odd people like Irving Finkel, Thorkild Jacobsen, and Charles Virolleaud are attracted to ancient clay tablets. Finkel is my favorite Assyriologist, everyone should have a favorite Assyriologist, especially because they are often a bit off, anyway Sitchin was an especially crazy one. An open and shut case. One look and it's clear. But Samuel, I worry that I may be like Sitchin, after all I don't think my ideas are crazy, but every time I tell another scientist what I am doing they are suddenly busy, their schedule is all of a sudden full for the rest of their life, so how would I know?

Well, do you suppose that mummy in London is an alien?

You think this is funny because you have never been in the position I am in. You think signs of insanity are easy to spot. You think, If I, that's you, Samuel, if I thought planets kept smashing into each other, I could just ask people, and they'd tell me planets do not generally keep smashing into one another, and then I'd know, and I could go back to my docile sane life testing water samples, but that's not how it happens. If you actually believed anything unusual you would want to keep believing it, you would not know if people who tell you you're wrong are right or if they're just stubborn, ignorant, malicious, or frightened, you'd be lost in doubt, you'd doubt your certainty, you'd doubt the redoubt of your certainty, you'd be locked in the redoubt of your doubt. You'd redoubt your redoubt.

Redoubt does not mean doubt again.

You're making fun of me, but I am determined to explain this. The most intricate example of this kind of writing is the Russian mathematician Anatoly Fomenko. He has written at least 22 books demonstrating that the time line of the ancient world is wrong. Actually, he says, everything before around 1000 AD is prehistory. No document can be dated earlier than 1000 AD. No coins can be dated to before 1000 AD. Ancient Greece and Rome didn't take place 2,000 years ago, they happened in the middle ages 1,000 years ago. Nothing earlier than that is known. Everything that is mentioned in the Bible took place about 1,000 years ago. Nobody really knows where Nazareth was, or where Jesus was buried, or where Sodom and Gomorrah were, and in fact that is because the events in the Bible did not take place in the ancient Middle East. When Moses thought he was wandering in the desert he was actually hiking in Italy and Switzerland, Mount Sinai is actually Vesuvius, Babylon is actually Rome, Jerusalem is Ithaca, Jericho is Lausanne, Bethlehem is Milan, Lebanon is Mont Blanc, Troy is Istanbul, the Euphrates is the Danube, Mount Seir is in Switzerland, in fact Jesus was crucified in Istanbul in the twelfth century, so technically Jesus was crucified in Troy, except that it was Constantinople, except that it was a Muslim city at the time. The Old Testament is actually about events that took place later, from 1500 to 1700 AD. Prehistory ended around 1000 AD, Fomenko says, and actual history began with the great Rus, so Russia goes right back to the dawn of history, nothing is older than Russia because nothing is very old. The so-called ancient world was invented by clergy, scientists, and humanists in the Renaissance to make Europe seem older than Russia. There were no dark ages, why should there have been, Renaissance writers invented "ancient" Greek and Latin, they mysteriously uncovered "ancient" Greek and Roman writings that had supposedly been lost for centuries, as you can tell, because Homer is a fiction based on Spencer, Plutarch is based on Petrarch, Plato is based on Pico, and Aristotle is based on Leonardo. The Renaissance writers used the recent past as a guide to help them invent ancient histories. They modeled the part of the Roman Empire that supposedly began in 82 BC and ended in 217 AD, but which never actually existed, on recent medieval history, but with the names and places changed, then they copied their invented Roman Empire that went from 82 BC to 217 AD to create the later Roman Empire, which supposedly began in 270 AD and lasted until 526 AD, although it never actually existed, that's why stories of Roman emperors seem like copies of each other, that's why Pompey and Caesar are like Diocletian and Constantius Chlorus, that's why Caligula is like Julian, that's why Theodosius I is like Domitian, Gibbon would have hated Fomenko, he would have thought Fomenko was the very end of civilization itself, and then Fomenko says they copied the later Roman Empire that supposedly went from 270 AD until 526 AD to create the stories of ancient Imperial Rome, which supposedly began with Romulus in 753 BC and ended in 495 BC, but actually never happened, that's why Romulus is like Constantine, Servius Tullius is like Theodoric, Tarquin the Proud is like the Goths. When I read that I thought, Now I know why I was so confused in school, because all the Romans sound like each other, I just thought the Romans were boring, I never thought they might be copies of each other. Well, then Fomenko says they copied the same kings and queens and battles from the so-called later Roman Empire, changed the names again, and claimed they happened in ancient Israel and Judah, that's why Baasha is like Constantine II, why Zimri is like Jovian, why Jeroboam II is like Honorius, why Pekahiah is like Recimer, all ancient histories are disguised copies of things that happened around 1000 AD, so-called "ancient" histories are phantom reflections, transposed onto different times and places to make the world seem old, history is full of echoes, Jesus was echoed by Pope Gregory VII Hildebrand, who supposedly lived in the eleventh century, but he was actually a phantom echo of Jesus, a copy with the name changed, because Jesus actually lived in the twelfth century, whereas Pope Gregory VII Hildebrand lived in the seventeenth century, and Alexander the Great was actually a Christian, he founded the Muslim empire in the fourteenth century, Fomenko doesn't say anything about Muhammad, it was Alexander, and then Europeans copied the same kings and queens and battles, changed their names to Chinese names, and invented the entire history of China in order to make Russia feel bad because it had older cultures on both sides of it, actually Chinese emperors are just altered versions of European kings and queens, and then the Europeans wrote histories claiming Russia was attacked, but Russia was never attacked from the west or the east, the Cossacks and the Horde were Russian, even Genghis Khan was Russian. He never invaded Russia, he just had to travel a lot because he had a job policing tax fraud, he didn't kill 40,000,000 people, but he did have to punish some people for not paying their taxes.

You don't believe that. You don't have that kind of insanity.

I don't believe anything Fomenko wrote, but I am afraid I think like him. This sort of insanity happens when a person's brain is filled with speculations, and they're all colliding (contacting) with each other, crashing and discharging, and there's no peace and no place to rest. I call it Colliding Worlds Insanity. Your system fills your mind, there is nothing outside it. That's me, it's a description of me.

But you doubt yourself all the time.

So did Fomenko. He always says, I am not certain if Mount Seir is in Switzerland, it might be in northern Italy, and Velikovsky says he doesn't know if Saturn collided with Jupiter in 2,800 BC or 3,000 BC, and Sitchin says no one knows if the Sumerian goggles had mirrored lenses or not. See what I mean? When I first read them, I thought, these people are *offensichtlich verrückt*, patently crazy. Their delusions are obvious, they are clearly in need of medication. I thought, What a relief, I am nothing like them. But is that true? I don't think I am insane like they are, but I might be. I write a lot, I work by myself, no one checks my results, people do not answer my letters, my work is full of very unusual ideas. I am just not sure. I might be insane like Velikovsky, Sitchin, and Fomenko. If I am, then I really am lost, because I will never let anyone persuade me I am wrong. And the worst thing is, they never cured themselves, Fomenko never said, "Okay, history didn't begin in 1000 AD, radiocarbon dating might be right, astronomical records might be right, dendrochronology might be right, it's just that I really, really love Russia, I want Russia to be the greatest country in the world," and Sitchin never said, "I admit those cuneiform signs don't look like alien spacecraft, I don't know why I see spacecraft everywhere," and Velikovsky never said, "I made all that up, I was so upset about the war, it really confused me."

Well, to me you don't seem like them at all.

You don't know that yet. Just being alone, spending so much time by yourself, that may be enough, that may be all it takes. Your mind fills with jangling ideas.

Your mind, anyway.

Paul is always asking me to go out, go to the farmer's market, take the boat out, go for a train ride, go to a concert, a film, even down to the corner kiosk, but I almost never do. He says I am a hermit, and I say "I am not, hermits live away from other people. I am an anchorite, I wall myself into my study." Anyone can find me in my study, I am like an anchorite who lives in a cell attached to a church, like they used to do, with just a small window so I can watch the priests say Mass, and another small window to receive food and dispose of my natural waste, but no door, the door is permanently cemented shut. I am dead to the world, I am consecrated to my work. "Right," Paul said, "you're a hermit," and I said, "I just told you, I am an anchorite, I have built myself walls of books and barricaded myself into my study." "But you come out all the time to eat," he said. "I mean anchoress," I said. "And you walk our uncle," he said. "No," I said, "I am always inside my study, the door is permanently sealed, I receive the Eucharist of your *oeufs en cocotte* and sometimes your Schoggiweggli and cookies, but I am forever dead to the world." Paul doesn't understand. I have read the *Ancrene Wisse*, the anchoress's guide, I know what my life is. That is why it is so easy for me to recognize another anchorite. For example Ludwig Hohl, he was a writer who spent his life composing aphorisms, they are supposedly profound, but I can smell the *heovenliche smealles*, the heavenly aromas of his aphorisms, they have the odor of his anchorite's cell. I smell the chamber pot brimming with his excrement. His father was a successful paper manufacturer, but he despised his son. Hohl wrote in absolute poverty and isolation in Holland, and then for years in a basement room in Geneva. He had to beg his father for cards to write on. He used to hang his aphorisms from clotheslines in his basement and look at them like little prayers. He says he walked back and forth, touching each card. When I read his books I can see him talking to himself in his stone-walled room, I hear the loud echo of his loneliness and pride, bravely bellowing, insufferable. Another is Wilhelm Reich, the psychoanalyst. His anchorite book is *The Bion Experiments,* he wrote it to convince himself that life can come from dust, that the world is full of life, that life sprouts spontaneously from ashes. That used to be called panspermia, people believed the world was full of sperms, it was possibly the single most sexist theory in the history of the world. Reich shut himself in a laboratory in Norway with a microscope and a device for electrocuting microscopic creatures. He added water to hay and watched as particles of sodden hay started to move. He called them Bions, he claimed they were hovering between death and life. Of course they were bacteria and protozoa, but he refused to listen to anyone, he wouldn't read books, didn't believe Pasteur, declined to live in the twentieth century. At one point he looked through his microscope and saw "a clump of earth moving as if it was jointed, stretching and contracting," another time he ground pebbles into fine dust, held the dust in a benzene flame until it was red hot, and saw incandescent "vesicles" straining at the edge of life. "Now," he declared, "continuously, in every minute and every second, life is emerging from non-living substances." He electrified the little Bions, and they vibrated in ecstasy. Pasteur was sloppy, Reich said, he hadn't managed to sterilize anything. He boiled his samples, but that wasn't enough, he should have heated them until they were glowing, and then they would have burst forth into life. Reich was an anchorite, Samuel, his book is fully infected with Anchorite Insanity from the first page to the last. He thought the universe pulses with blue-green orgone energy, which is the energy of orgasms, of expansion, tension, and electrical discharge, he was a man, after all, he thought everything was about swelling and release. He said blue-green orgone energy had a divine aroma and it could be seen in the colors of the aurora, in St. Elmo's fire, and in sexually excited frogs. You know, Samuel, anchorites can hypnotize people, and Reich actually persuaded Einstein to test a Faraday cage he made for collecting blue-green orgone energy. Einstein wasted a week in his basement measuring Reich's machine before he realized it was nonsense. After that Reich kept writing, trying to persuade Einstein to continue his tests by getting inside the cage and measuring his own orgone energy. "I am a great man," Reich wrote, "a rarity, I can't quite believe it myself, and that's why I struggle, but I know you will understand if you just spend a year inside my

Faraday cage." Einstein never answered. This is another kind of insanity I probably have. Every writer has at least a mild case and after years alone it is probably systemic and incurable. Only the anchorite fails to understand that the smell is not heavenly.

She smiled at her joke.

You're not an anchorite. You're out now.

I am unusually far from home, about fifteen minutes. For an anchorite this is an enormous adventure, like a fish going for a hike in the Alps, holding its breath, squirming along a mountain trail. I was in Frankfurt because I was forced to go on account of a lawsuit, but I won't tell you about that. Hohl's and Reich's books are examples of Anchorite Insanity. I am not sure how these kinds of insanity fit in with my thirteen levels of unreason, but they must. Maybe only people with Anchorite Insanity or Colliding Worlds Insanity can come up with theories like my thirteen levels of unreason. Anyway I kept looking for insane books. It was easy to find them, and it seemed as if each new one was like me. Next I discovered Count Alfred Korzybski's *Science and Sanity,* another enormous book, 806 pages long. How could I not love the title? Science and sanity, I thought, that is exactly my theme. His chapters have titles like "Un-Sanity versus Sanity," "Semantics of the Einstein Theory," "Mathematics and the Nervous System." Perfect, I thought, a mirror of my own work, a model, an achievement like mine. At the beginning Korzybski claims, just like I do, that his book is not normal science. It is "not any 'philosophy,' or 'psychology,' or 'logic,'" he writes, "it is a new extensional discipline which explains and trains how to use our nervous systems most efficiently." I didn't quite understand that, but it sounded promising. *Science and Sanity* is overwhelming, just like I hope my notebooks are. It's a good thing to be overwhelming, whelming is when you turn something over, like a boat or a bowl, or you throw something violently on top of something else, that is also whelming, or you crush or smother something, you submerge it and drown it, you ruin something with excessive force, that is also whelming, so overwhelming is even better, that is what I want my work to be. *Science and Sanity* overwhelmed people. Even now there are organizations in different parts of the world that teach Korzybski's book, and I discovered that parts of the book are regarded as the foundation of a branch of linguistics called general semantics, which seems to be well regarded by ordinary boring academics. I saw that many famous people loved Korzybski's book, there is an endorsement at the beginning from the philosopher Gaston Bachelard, I never read his work; another from Samuel Hayakawa, a senator in America, his name means nothing to me; from Alfred Hitchcock, although I don't think it means much to be endorsed by someone who spent his life imagining ways to kill people; from Lou Marinoff, he wrote a book called *Plato, Not Prozac,* I am not sure that certifies him as sane; Aldous Huxley, who liked LSD better than Prozac; Christopher Sheldon, a "courageous sailing captain"; Buckminster Fuller, well, he was a little nuts; William Burroughs, one of the world's greatest drug addicts; Wendell Johnson, "founder of the Monster Study," that was an experiment performed on twenty-two children with speech impediments, I don't want to know more about that; and Barrett Wilson, she donated a bottomless bowl of M&Ms to the North American office of the General Semantics Association. The book opens with chapters about relativity, I skipped those, and chapters on semantics, I skipped those, but then my eye was caught by black and white photographs showing peg boards and strings. They were instructional props called structural differentials, which Korzybski used to sell. They look like children's toys, peg boards connected with strings. A big peg board represents a table, he says, and he means an actual physical table, its protons and neutrons, and that makes a kind of sense because a peg board looks a little like a table and the holes in it are sort of like atoms. It is attached by strings to smaller rectangular peg boards labeled "experience of table," "concept of table." Korzybski says the structural differential suggests that the experience of a table is simpler than the table itself. The whole thing is alarmingly simple-minded, although I suppose it might appear profound to a courageous sailing captain or someone on Prozac or LSD. The largest and most expensive structural differential also includes a peg board labeled FIDO, that's for a dog's idea of a table. The dog doesn't have concepts, it only has a peg board labeled FIDO. Korzybski's book is a very special sort of insanity. I call it Stage Four Insanity, like stage four cancer, because *Science and Sanity* is like a body where some parts work perfectly well, like my mouth is working now, and other parts are flecked and discolored by cancer, that's what I suspect about my liver, my pancreas, my lungs, and my brain. There are particles of insanity in most chapters of *Science and Sanity,* then long stretches of healthy writing tissue, and also whole pages of diseased necrotic matter that have nothing to do with science or sanity. If I may speak as my own physician, Samuel, it is extremely likely that I have Stage Four Insanity. One of my teenage doctors told me I might have a brain tumor, I think it was because I kept looking at him cross-eyed, but that was because he is so small I had a hard time seeing him, anyway I got an MRI, and it seemed okay, but my little doctor said that at higher resolutions it might reveal thousands of tiny tumors throughout my brain. Tumors like those are completely inoperable, he said, but don't worry, they are quite common, not everyone gets to have just one large tumor. I told him I thought he was just one large tumor, but secretly I was proud. If I have Stage Four Insanity, I might be 93% sane, with 1,000 microtumors, microscopic pieces of insanity, like particles of pollution in the air. Some pages of *Science and Sanity* are spotless science, but others are flecked with little tumors, illogical words, phrases and sentences that don't make sense. Many pages are darkened with medium-sized tumors. Some tumors are the size of short chapters. The structural differentials look like tumors too, and the strings look like unraveling sutures. The book is inoperable. I can see why William Burroughs liked it. Another writer who has Stage Four Insanity is L. Ron Hubbard, because Scientology is intermittently sane, and not incidentally Hubbard also wrote one of the world's longest books, *Mission Earth* is 10 volumes, but I don't think I would learn much from 3,992 pages of randy sexist science fiction.

Is this like the Infected Mind Theory?

That is about spiders. Stage Four Insanity is about uncountable motes of insanity, speckles of insanity, like when I said I'm 93% sane, I made that up, of course, but why did I say 93? I don't know, it was a glitch, my thought ran over a bump in the road, a pebble of insanity, and it made me jump onto the number 93.

It's insane to pick the number 93?

The number 93 may be a small hard pebble of insanity, you walk over them without noticing. The bigger ones trip you. The largest ones fall from the sky like hailstones. The universe is full of marvelous insanity stones, purple, yellow, red, blue, orange, green, black—

Okay, that really does sound nuts.

Just testing to see if you are listening.

No one makes sense all the time. Who doesn't have moments when they don't make sense?

Thomas Aquinas maybe. King Kesar. You can't make me feel better by assuring me I am not a saint or a king. Stage Four Insanity feels perfectly normal because my brain is pocked with it. Insanity is sprinkled over everything I write, particles are lodged in everything I say, I don't see them but they're itchy, like dust mites in my bed.

Or really tiny spiders.

Spiderlings. That is right, you finally said something that's correct. My brain may be seething with nearly invisible spiderlings. It is possible Stage Four Insanity is an example of the Infected Mind Theory. Anyway then I discovered another kind of insane book. This kind happens when authors forget themselves, and I don't mean out of modesty, and I don't mean they lose themselves in their writing, I mean they actually lose track of whether they are real. There are books by people who were permanently unreachably insane in this way, and I can't read them. I won't read Henry Darger's unpublished novel called *The Story of the Vivian Girls, in What is Known as the Realms of the Unreal, of the Glandeco-Angelinnian War Storm, Caused by the Child Slave Rebellion,* even though it is 15,145 pages in 10 volumes, because he never knew who he was, he is nowhere in his book, he just kept on for 15,145 pages about cartoon girls, so I did not want to go anywhere near that book, even though it is in New York City and you can go and sit there and read it. But I read a book called *Ellen: The Whisperings of an Old Pine,* published in 1901, illustrated with photographs of a young woman walking in forests and fields in New England. The pictures look dreamy, and I thought the book might be a memoir of Ellen's life. But actually it's about the pine tree. It starts talking. It talks to the reader. "How did I get up here on this high mountain, you ask? I was born here. As the years went by I have become stronger and taller, until now I am the largest of all the pines upon this mountain." The old pine says that lately it has become "much interested in the valley directly to my east," and especially in a farm where three little girls live with their parents. "When the first child began to play upon the lawn," the pine says, "it came from the elm that stands beyond the house that her name was ELLEN." The old pine falls in love. Eventually Ellen walks up the mountain and sits at the pine's feet, and then the pine begins to whisper to her, and it whispers for 700 pages about physics, light, acoustics, electricity, and magnetism. Ellen sits and listens. "Does the old pine see the houses in the valley?" Ellen asks. "Yes," the pine whispers, "The old Pine does see that... all things are at peace. The pumpkins and corn grow in the fields." "Good," Ellen replies, "but Ellen doesn't know why." So the pine explains to her about the Bell magneto-electric telephone. It's very unpleasant, this book, because it is so obvious that the narrator is not a pine, he's an old man stalking a girl, and he thinks he's disguised as a tree, and it is ridiculous because he thinks the way to get her to love him is to talk for 700 pages about electricity and magnetism, and it is uncomfortable because it's obvious the author of the book, Joseph Battell, thought he could charm little girls by writing books in which he hides his old man's body inside a pine tree. When he started his book, he must have thought, Gosh, the things I like are really boring, how can I make them more interesting? Wait, I know! I can just have a pine tree speak instead of me. Actually, Samuel, I would have loved it if an old tree could have taught me instead of Herr Speckstein, but that is not my point, my point is that at least Speckstein knew who he was, but Battell forgot. Another writer who forgets himself is Gerald Murnane. He is supposedly one of the world's best writers of fiction, but he keeps calling the real world the "so called" real world, he keeps saying he doesn't make anything up, but just writes "detailed reports" of the contents of his mind. People read his books as fiction, but he doesn't agree. He works very hard to understand odd puzzles he sets for himself, like if he might be Paraguayan even though he has never been to Paraguay, or what a fictional character might see if they look at a landscape beyond the landscapes given in the fiction. Murnane has metal filing cabinets with notes about every girl he ever asked out, he has a file of things he is ashamed of, in life and in his books, a file of miraculous or unexplained events in his life and in his books, a file on every horse race he has ever seen, a file on every horse race he has ever written about in real life or in fiction, a file on imaginary horses in Tasmania and all the races they ever ran and the names of their jockeys and the names of 1,500 horse trainers and the colors of their uniforms and the designs of their pennants and the race times, the courses, the stud books, the prices of the tickets, and the weather on the day of each of the hundreds of imaginary races. He has so many filing cabinets that he has to pick up his mattress each morning and put it on top of some bookshelves so he has room to walk around. "I think you can probably see that I'm sane," he says, "but I say and believe things that insane people believe." When I first read Murnane I thought, Hmm, am I reading something presented to me as fiction, or am I reading his diary? He calls his fiction "detailed reports," he calls realistic fiction "film," he says "beyond the fictional landscape of my writing I saw there was a further landscape of imaginary horse racing." At least he doesn't think he is a tree, but Murnane is confused about what fiction is, confused about whether there's a world outside of it, or even another world hidden inside it that the authors don't describe but is more real than the fictional world they do describe, and clearly more real than life. Murnane and Battell lost track of themselves. One turned into an old pine tree in New England, and the other became a metal filing cabinet in Australia. Another person who lost himself is Raymond Roussel. I read all his books, including one called *How I Wrote Certain of My Books.* His books are very mysterious, so he wrote that one to explain them, but it doesn't work. Roussel couldn't explain his mysterious books because his insanity made it impossible for him to comprehend what an explanation is. Lots of people who try to explain their lives fail because they don't understand themselves, but most people at least understand what an explanation is, it's just that they don't understand the thing they are explaining, which is themselves. Like when Luzia says, "Paul would love it if you'd spend time with him and Hans, watching TV," and I say, "Did Paul say that?" and she says, "He didn't have to," and I say, "Then who said it?" and she says, "Look, Aunt Lysy, what do you think of this skirt for my presentation next week?" She is the Mistress of Deflection, she thinks she can explain herself by changing the subject.

I'm not sure she's a good example.

Maybe not, she is only a little annoying. Roussel infuriates me. He wrote a mysterious book about some Europeans who are shipwrecked in Africa.

They have to win their freedom by putting on a show for the emperor. The book describes their performances, one after another. A woman named Louise fabricates a life-size statue of an ancient Spartan servant called a helot, pierced in the heart by a spear. The statue is made of pieces of whalebone corset stays. It rests on a small wheeled cart, which in turn rolls on sections of railway track that are brown and translucent because they are made of calves' lungs. A trained magpie sticks its beak into a slot in the base of the sculpture, causing the railroad tracks to tip upward so the helot rolls forward. The magpie hops over to another slot, pecks it, and the tracks tip back, sending the helot backward. Next to that is a sculpture of Immanuel Kant, also made of pieces of whalebone, except for the top of his skull, which suddenly lights up, revealing that it is not made of corset stays but only a very thin clay membrane. People marvel at Kant's glowing brain, like the way I marvel at my translucent colleagues, except their heads are empty. Later a boy walks out in front of the emperor carrying a reddish rodent and a small white door. He puts the door on the ground and kills the rodent by stabbing it in the neck with a needle. He dangles the dead rodent over the door, and soon it begins to drool. It covers the door in viscous mucilage. The boy unties part of his clothing and presses it onto the slobber. A "strong and peculiar" smell is emitted. After a few minutes an enormous bird comes along, attracted by the smell, and swoops down on the rodent. The bird carries the rodent, the door, and the boy up into the sky, because they are all glued together with the sticky rodent discharge. The boy's father is distraught until the gigantic bird gets tired and deposits him back on the ground. Later a musician comes onstage wearing a "colossal worm" coiled around his arm. He places it into a special container made of sheets of mica, with a narrow slit along the bottom. The worm stretches itself out over the slit, and he fills the container with a glittering fluid and suspends it above a zither. The worm raises part of its body into an arch, causing a drop to fall onto one of the strings of the zither, producing a low C. The string perfectly bisects the drop, splitting it into two globules, which fall soundlessly onto strips of felt. As the worm lifts different parts of its body, it releases drops onto the zither, resulting in different notes. The worm apparently prefers romantic melodies, mostly Hungarian rhapsodies and czardases. It is surprisingly talented and passionate and its music captivates the audience. This kind of thing goes on for a hundred pages. All of Roussel's descriptions are exquisitely accurate, exactly the way you would want someone to write if they were witnessing unusual events. I waited for explanations, but always there was something new, each performance was more unaccountable than the last. Finally, at the end of the book, Roussel tries to explain everything. It turns out the musician discovered the "colossal worm" when he was sitting by a stream practicing the zither. The worm came swimming up out of the calm brook in order to listen to his concerts. The musician often returned to the same bank, and each time the worm appeared and remained until he finished. It liked to coil itself around his arm, and soon he realized it loved music, so he gathered slats of mica from the riverbed and built a special tank to help the worm make music. At first he guided it by tapping it with a stick, but the worm quickly memorized the music and played the melodies by itself. That is what Roussel thinks is an explanation, you're supposed to read that and think, Oh, okay, now I understand. It was just an enormous aquatic earthworm with a specially high degree of intelligence and an inborn love of Hungarian music, and so of course the musician did what anyone would do: instead of running away screaming and doubting everything he ever knew about worms, he built a mica tank and taught the earthworm to play. It turns out the boy killed one of the reddish rodents when he was out hunting, and got his foot stuck in the rodent drool and had to pull so hard to free himself that he tore off part of the sole of his foot, and just then an enormous bird came to eat the rodent. You're supposed to read that and think, Oh, of course. Instead of running away howling in pain and terror, the boy naturally formed a plan to glue himself to a small wooden door and be taken up into the sky. It turns out Louise made her sculptures balance on railroad tracks made of calves' lungs because the African emperor had just tasted an aspic of calves' lungs and he was delighted by how light they were, and also he had been admiring model trains the Europeans had brought with them, so he ordered Louise to make life-size statues that were light enough to rest on railroad tracks made of calves' lungs, naturally he did, because what else would a despot do if he was impressed by calves' lungs and model trains? Louise chose whalebone corset stays because they were the lightest material she could find, even though she could have used thin mica sheets, or paper, or any of the other light materials that we read about in other chapters of the book, but she chose whalebone corset stays, and she chose to sculpt Kant with a glowing brain because she admired him so much, and she chose to sculpt a dying helot because she remembered a story about a Spartan man who tried to educate his Knossian servant by teaching him proper Greek, because Spartans spoke Doric, but the servant could not conjugate the Greek verb *eimi,* "I am," he kept getting the endings wrong, *eimi, ei, eiste, eisti, eismi,* until finally he came to the third person plural, and he said *enti,* and the Spartan man became enraged and stabbed him in the heart with his stiletto, actually Roussel made that up, it is not an ancient story, it is just his own violent imagination, but he thinks the story is an explanation, he thinks you'll say, Oh, now I see, everything falls into place, the book is so carefully constructed, just like a detective story, it all makes perfect sense. But no, his so-called explanations make me fret because they don't make sense, they don't explain anything, they just put one weird thing in the place of another. Why was Louise fascinated by a violent story about Greek grammar? Why did Battell think acoustics and magnetism are attractive if they are discussed in the husky voice of an old pine tree? Why did Murnane think it made sense to say his imaginary horse races actually exist just beyond the worlds described in novels? What was wrong with them, why didn't they understand what an explanation is? From Roussel, Battell, and Murnane I learned what can happen when an author is no longer the writer of their own work. I call it Old Pine Insanity. I do not think I have entirely forgotten who I am, but I wouldn't know it if I have, I might be mistaking myself for a scientist, I might be mistaking what my writing is. This may be an example of the Encephalophagous Theory, where something other than me does the thinking, except it's not a spider, it's a drooling rodent, a pine tree, or a filing cabinet. Maybe my notebooks are actually documentation of imaginary horse races, or boring speeches to children I secretly like, or instructions for turning calf lungs into railroad tracks. When I was reading Roussel, Battell, and Murnane, I asked myself: How can I be sure I am not like them? Perhaps there are telltale signs. Roussel thought he was sane, but he should have wondered why he kept talking about things like rodent slobber glue and colossal musical worms. It is no comfort that I like worms too, a lot more than Roussel did.

You like scabs and slobber pretty well too.

I am fascinated by scabs and stains.

And you like lecturing as much as that old tree.

That's enough. I'm trying my best, Samuel. If I am like Roussel, Battell, or Murnane, how would I know? There are worms all over my notebooks, I noticed worms in Linnaeus, worms in Darwin. One of the only ways Roussel could ever have discovered how insane he really was, would have been to wonder about why he kept writing about worms. I think Battell never found out. I bet he told that girl Ellen about his plans for a 700-page book, I bet he spent a long time trying to convince her it was a good idea, he introduced her to all his theories about acoustics and magnetism, and then he said, "You know, this will be even better if you put on a light cotton dress and walk up the mountain with me, so I can take a few photographs." I don't want to think about what happened to either of them. Murnane can never discover how confused he is, because his writing covers every confusion, every doubt about whether he is Paraguayan, any misgiving about the thousands of hours he spent keeping track of imaginary Tasmanian horse races, it covers everything with a tight parquet of supposedly deeply reflective and deliberate writing. Murnane might get an idea that something is wrong if he got up one morning and said, "It's strange that I have so many metal filing cabinets, so many I don't even have room for my bed. Everything is in order, the imaginary horse race files are all there, but it's odd, I wonder why I need so many metal filing cabinets," if Murnane had ever said that he might have realized something was wrong. And look at me, how am I different? At least I don't use metal filing cabinets. I have no cardboard boxes. But my study is choked with notebooks. When I glance at them, I think, That is my work. But if I look carefully, quietly, if I don't touch them or read them, but just look, then I know something is wrong, I can almost see my insanity.

Sorry, I know you are serious.

Then I found a different kind of insane book. I call it Counting by Twos Insanity.

Oh no.

I named it after the person who counts by twos until he gets to—

No, please.

Fine. It means the person is perfectly sane in some parts of their mind, then suddenly insane in others. Their mind is discontinuous, their thoughts run smoothly for a time then suddenly they stop. Like Stage Four, but with integers, just like counting 18, 20, 22—

No.

Or like coming to a place where the road suddenly ends. You stand at the edge, looking across a chasm to the place where the road starts again. The American writer Philip K. Dick had this sort of insanity. For 25 years he wrote science fiction stories and books, and then on February 3, 1974 he had an unsettling experience. Suddenly he knew he was a Christian in ancient Rome, and Jesus was away for a while, but he would come back soon, and later he saw a beam of pink light that had tremendous meaning he couldn't quite explain, and afterward he had an odd feeling about his cat. He started writing about what had happened, and he kept writing until he died eight years later. He produced 11,000 pages of notes. I read 970 pages called the *Exegesis,* that is all that's been published. He started to think of his earlier fiction as nonfiction, as if his science fiction books had been premonitions of actual events all along even though he hadn't intended them that way. You're thinking, Well, that is sad, but it's just psychosis, Dick lost contact with reality. But you're wrong, it's more than that. It wasn't just a psychotic break, it was a Counting by Twos Insanity, because he said only certain of his books were nonfiction. He didn't know why some were fiction and others weren't. "My writing casts doubt on the fact of knowing actual reality because our minds have been fucked over," he wrote. He was puzzled by some of his books, so he re-read them, thinking they might really be historical documents. He looked at one of his own books of science fiction, which he decided was real, and he asked, "Does this book seem to say, 'Maybe portions of the others are literally real, too?'" It must have been a horrible state of mind to be in for eight years, and I feel sorry for him, it's as if the Counting by Twos Insanity was on a slide rule, and the slide kept moving, and the place where the line of sanity met the scales of insanity kept shifting. I'll know if I have that sort of insanity when you read my notebooks,

Samuel, because you might say, "Anneliese, your work is perfectly sane until page 11,599, but from page 12,600 to 19,200 it is psychotic, but then it's okay again after that." You might tell me I have Counting by Twos Insanity, I have to be ready for that. Another example of Counting by Twos Insanity is Daniel Schreber's book *Memoirs of my Nervous Illness.* Freud wrote about him. He was a famous judge, President of the Appeals Court in Dresden, institutionalized in the University Nerve Clinic in Leipzig because he had episodes of crazy shouting in the courtroom. He wrote his book in the asylum, hoping to use his legal acumen to argue his way out. "It's true that I still scream," he writes, "but not as much as I used to. And it's true that during the night tiny people drift down onto my head and dissolve into my skull, hoping to turn me into a woman, causing my penis to slowly retract back into my belly, a process that might be completed in a hundred years of sleeping, and I admit that when I am taken for walks in the asylum garden I see men in linen overalls covered in soot, and the garden is illuminated by two suns, the familiar one and another composed of the stars of Cassiopeia drawn together, and when my wife visits I do not perceive her as a living being, and my hands are occasionally lifted by black bears, and I have spent time as an Alsatian girl who defended her honor against a French lieutenant, and also as a Jesuit novice in Ossegg," actually he means Osek, I looked that up because Georg Ossegg is the one who found out the truth about Hansel and Gretel, but that is another story, "and also as a Mongolian prince, and also as a Hyperborean nun," he means a Finnish nun, because later he says she is from Nunnanen, that's a place in Finland, and it means "nun," so a nun from Nun, "and unfortunately it is also true that I feel a blow on my head simultaneously with every word spoken around me, with each approaching footstep, with every railway whistle and car horn, and this causes variable degrees of pain, compelling me to scream at night and occasionally by day, including in the courtroom, but significantly less than I used to. Naturally I consider it beneath my dignity to have to bellow like a wild animal because of miracles enacted on me, and if you let me out none of this will interfere with my legal duties. I have read Kraepelin's *Textbook of Psychiatry,* fifth edition, and there is nothing in my case which justifies speaking of an 'inability to determine what is real,' or an incapacity to break the 'control of fixed ideas,' and the fact that I continue to be visited by minuscule men who melt into my body only shows that I can accept supernatural phenomena, which after all have only been vilified during the shallow rationalizing period of the Enlightenment, a period that is now superseded, not only in philosophy and religion but also science. So please let me out, signed, Daniel Henry Schreber, President, Senate of the Appeals Court, Dresden." Freud was fascinated by Schreber's book, he wrote to Jung that when he read Schreber's book he nearly became Schreber, he praised Schreber's capacity to reason and he admired the strength of Schreber's hallucinations, but he knew he should never visit Schreber, it would be too risky. Schreber's illness was too strong, too dangerous. Schreber and Dick were sane for long periods and then suddenly they weren't, like Wouter Kusters who was institutionalized twice and twice returned to his job as a philosopher. He wrote about madness from the inside, then from the outside, then again from the inside, then from the outside. Once when he was in an isolation cell a nurse brought him a copy of his own book on madness to sign, who was he then? Patient or doctor? People like Kusters are like Superman in the old comics, flying around and keeping things in good order until he runs into Mr. Mxyzptlk, a kind of leprechaun from the fifth dimension, and everything goes wrong, Superman is confused, he's mxyzpixilated, until he gets rid of Mr. Mxyzptlk and then he can fly off and save more people, except it's not like that, because when Dick had his mxyzpixilous fit he thought he was in ancient Rome, but when he was mxyzptlkic afterward he thought he was normal but troubled, and when Schreber was mxyzptlkous he could write and reason, but when he was struggling with his mxyzptlkations he believed that his wife had died and her nerves had gone into his body so they could rest, even though he later realized she was alive, he also thought she was dead. I think. I'm worried about these sorts of confusions. Kusters, Schreber, and Dick think they are sane because they can talk about the times they were not sane, and then later they think they are not sane but they can talk about the times they were sane, but when were those times, exactly?

I don't really understand, but I'm listening.

I went through a period when I was not sure who I was, and now, when I look back on those years, I am not sure what happened then, or what I am now. Should I say, like Schreber, I am adequately sane, because even though I think there are two suns—one made by pulling the stars in Cassiopeia together into a second sun—it won't interfere with my day job? What takes place in those gaps between 26 and 80, between 126 and 180? And what about after 202? You will see, Samuel, this happens in the notebooks. So that was the end of my reading of books written by insane people. It was too much for me, I found myself everywhere. Now you will appreciate a review.

Actually, no, thanks.

What I Learned by Reading Insane Books, by Anneliese Glur. Okay, well, first, I found some insanities I definitely don't have, that was comforting. I don't have Teenage Cartoon Insanity or Write Endless Books Using Your Computer Insanity, and I recovered from a bout of Encyclopedia Insanity, although I might relapse into Stamp Collecting Insanity. I don't have Fumigating Your Marble Mansion Against Infestations of Insanity Insanity. But I may have all the others: Colliding Worlds Insanity, Anchorite Insanity, Stage Four Insanity, because as you pointed out that is an example of the Infected Mind Theory, Old Pine Insanity, because it's an example of the Encephalophagous Theory, and Counting by Twos Insanity. Also, I think there is no clear difference between books written by people widely considered to be insane, like Velikovsky, Sitchin, Dick, and Schreber, and people not considered to be insane, like Murnane, Roussel, Korzybski, and Kusters. At least I cannot see the difference, although it is very likely that I lack the ability to judge, because I am myself multiply afflicted by these illnesses. So here is my conclusion. Insanity is endemic to long books. I propose that any time a person writes an especially long, complex book, whether it is supposed to be fiction or not, even if they set out with tremendous exemplary resolve, even if they write with the clarity of a saint or a rabbi, or a *pandit,* an *ʿalim,* a *mobed,* or a *bhikkhu,* you will discover all of those in the notebooks, if the writer keeps going long enough, the book will change, it will become insane. *Mega biblion mega kakon,* Callimachus said, a great book is a great evil, an excellent saying, even though Callimachus wrote short books because he was a coward. I think Nietzsche also said short books are best, or he almost did, he mistrusted long books with systems and long books without any system. I am not sure if he mistrusted all long books, I think he did, but maybe he didn't. Maybe this is just my own idea, Samuel. I hope not, because that would be a good reason to think it is wrong, but I don't think it is wrong. All sufficiently long books, no matter how rational they try to be, are in different ways insane.

Physics textbooks?

I have no doubt. But I am not crazy enough to read a textbook.

It doesn't sound especially likely that Saint Thomas Aquinas was insane.

I agree, and it doesn't sound right to say epic poems are insane. I mean writing cannot be controlled. Writing a book is like dipping your toe in a swamp, it gets covered in muck but it's only a toe. Writing an ambitious, complicated, lengthy book is like slipping and falling into the swamp. If you manage to climb out you will look frightening and you will smell horrible. And some people can't climb back out, they just disappear into the mud. I know it's not polite to call famous people insane. But it is true, and long novels are especially insane. I call it Long Novel Insanity. Once I started reading David Foster Wallace I just kept going, I read Olga Tokarczuk, Agustín Fernández Mallo, Philipp Weiss, Adam Levin, Leslie Marmon Silko, Robert Musil, Raymond Federman, Evan Dara, Ágota Kristóf, Charlie Kaufman, he plays at being insane but he is actually completely insane, William Gass, his book *The Tunnel* is absolutely bats, Luis Goytisolo, *Antagony* is even worse, not to mention Julián Ríos, their books are all crazy, *Infinite Jest* is about Alcoholics Anonymous and tennis, for heaven's sake, Wallace's prose is so sharp my eyes bleed when I look at it, but he's trembly and he glistens with emotion, let's not forget Stephen Dixon, his novel *Frog* has chapters like "Frog in Prague," "Frog's Nanny," "Frog's Break," "Frog's Blahs," and "Frog Reads the News," it ends with a chapter the length of an ordinary novel, called "Frog." Witold Gombrowicz is a fuzzy nut of insanity, he wrote a whole novel about threads of dust and another one about masturbating on a mountaintop, no one even knows what *Ferdydurke* means, Christine Brooke-Rose thrives on theories, catalogs, and problems, she loves dissecting, parsing, analyzing, diagramming, okay, that's a lot like me, but also she's cold and angry and fearful, that's not me, and it is not sane, *The Making of Americans* is as pale and faceless as a row of ten thousand blind cave salamanders, Miklós Szentkuthy is a hysterical philosophizer, Georges

Perec hides behind his games, lists, puzzles, palindromes, lipograms, bi-squares, knight's tours, and pseudo-Quenines, even his analyst said so, surely it's a sort of insanity to need so many rules. Older long novels aren't any better, Laurence Sterne, François Rabelais, Heinrich Fischart, none of them were sane, their books are like the floods in the Flood Theory, everything is washed along in a foaming churning mass. Someone sings a song, another person complains about English candies, ducks float by, rubber ducks, the Lonesome Duck in Oz, the Mechanickal Duck, Old Ekdal's duck, the dying duck in Noh, it's duck soup, ducks in Newburyport, Donald Duck with whisker stubble, there are giggles and blushes, coughs and hiccups, toilet noises, the writers are like cooks who make stews out of delicious ingredients and then just start throwing things in—gourds, cakes with a hundred flavors, fumadoes, mane-fat and jelly-blood, marshmallows, breakfast cereal, ketchup, bions, stirring it all into a nauseating confusion, blur soup, blah soup, clown food, even novels that try to keep on a steady pace, like Beckett, Stein, or Musil, if they go on long enough they lose control, there are odd ellipses..., disconcerting lapses, slips in tense, broken solecisms, jangling anacoluthons, wrong words, trinkets stolen from here and there, hopeless clichés—every long novel has these things, the longer the novel the more of them—creaking awkwardnesses, bottomless embarrassments, bleary descriptions, unnecessary bursts of poetry—those are awful, why do novelists do that—wincing infelicities—those are worse, and they are everywhere, they hop like fleas over the characters in most novels—clumsy phrasing, unnoticed inconsistencies, unnoticed repetitions, unnoticed parallels, unnoticed implications, unnoticed anachronisms, basic factual errors, stringy harangues and blasting rants, unexpected deserts of boredom, herniated digressions, the weather in long novels is nightmarish, it might be sunny for a while, and then it'll rain for three hundred pages, and all the time there are unbelievable professions of order and purpose, promises of regimen and constancy, but the intellectual compass spins madly, the emotional barometer swells and bursts and—

Like you, Anneliese.

All of it. But then I say stop. In the end I am nothing like those writers. It is true, I talk in floods, but I can stop. I have not lost control of my ideas, my emotions are boxed in, my theories proceed in lockstep, nothing is random, as I have been relentlessly demonstrating. Did you notice I found exactly seven new kinds of insanity? I'm proud of that. My rants are relentlessly regulated. My repetitions are under strict surveillance. Each word is issued a license. I hear every echo, no matter how distant, across forests and mountains of writing, underground and in the air itself. My thoughts grow painfully slowly, in perfect formation. These writers are burbling mud pots. I am like that famous cave in Mexico, Cave of the Crystals, it is stifling hot and filled with poison gas. Enormous white crystals the size of trucks grow for eons in perfect silence until they crash into each other in slow motion, a half inch every thousand years, growing blindly into each other, snapping and fracturing each other, until the room is jammed full of poison crystal shards.

And that's good?

Yes! A cave chamber completely filled with poison crystal powder is beautiful and perfect.

That's what your notebooks are like?

If I could live ten thousand years, that is what I would make, a book like a lethal underground chamber, steaming hot, pitch black, tightly packed with shards of enormous white crystals.

Really?

Of course not. The point is there's poison in long books, and it only gets worse as the writing goes on. So in October 2017 I turned to four books I had been saving. They were the most promising, the ones I felt had the densest entangled thought, the closest to my own work, the ones that could help me the most. I had kept them for last. First is Proust. His novel is 1,300,000 words, and it has a very careful structure. I thought I could learn from him, but as I have already explained to you, Proust is a monster of obstinacy about memory, and as a result his book is the exact opposite of anything I can use for my own project. His entire novel, all seven volumes, is founded on a fantasy about a small and sickeningly sweet cake. No one could eat a bag of madeleines, they would choke on the sugar, but that's what Proust's novel is like. The madeleine appears at the beginning, as everyone knows. The next 3,600 pages are patiently woven, elegantly balanced, flawlessly poised, endlessly lavishly crafted, and unapproachably eloquent, as everyone knows, and the book is infinitely harmonious, smoothed, polished, dusted, groomed, caressed, patted down, petted, milky as a glossy marble sculpture, the kind that looks soft or greasy, and yet it's pitiful, ridiculous, and embarrassing, when I read I blush, even if I am by myself, because it's all a fantasy, he nourished it for thirteen years, long after he should have finished, like a demented mother dripping milk onto the lips of her dead child. He says the most poetic memories are involuntary, they surprise us, like that baby image, sorry about that, anyway Proust says involuntary memories flow unexpectedly into our minds, clearing our thoughts like a shower suddenly gone cool, that part is true enough, but then he says that if we give ourselves to those memories, nourish them, let them unfold like the drying wings of a butterfly freshly emerged from its viscid chrysalis, then our memories will speak, at first indistinctly, then clearly, and finally with irresistible force, until we ourselves become fully alive, we recapture our past and become "giants of time," which is a pretty stupid expression, because it makes me think of a colossal Proust, padding around Paris in house-size spats. There is just one problem with his lovely theory: in order for all that miraculous telescoping of time to take place it is necessary to sit in a room by yourself and write it all into existence, page by painful page, 7 volumes, 1,300,000 words, because as I told you, memories are actually very nearly nothing, they are like premature babies, it requires exceptional skill to nurse them into life, not to mention specialized medical technology. Proust's novel is like Frankenstein's laboratory expanded into a major research institute. Recovering lost time requires the composition of paragraphs as balanced as champagne fountains, pages as delicately adjusted as Baroque clocks, volumes as perfectly judged as the great hall of Versailles, except without those wobbly mirrors, each chapter an exquisite marvel of muted tones and gilt, every word as clean as a ceramic and silver toilet, it requires transcendentally skilled decisions regarding the rhythm and length of sentences, well, I can do that, but it also requires delicate adjustments of mood and tone, I am not so good at those, and also breathtaking management of allusion and metaphor, okay, so he's really good, transcendental awareness of narratives arcing over thousands of pages, fine, if Vergil could read Proust he would creep away in shame, Shakespeare would realize that he was only a country lout,

Homer would sit in a corner and scratch his louse-infested head and wiggle his filthy feet and hope to do better tomorrow. By comparison with them Proust is the rarest orchid: each word is a petal, different from every other, 1,300,000 petals, the petals form exotic flowers with shapes so unlikely and compelling they would make a child smile, the flowers are draped over exquisitely constructed trellises, arbors, and bowers, each beautifully judged for its airy yet intimate proportions, for the elegant interlaced patterns formed by its steam-curved laths, the surprising glimpses it affords of distant parts of the garden, its teasing combination of cool shade and warming beams of light, the flowers dangling down and tickling you on the top of your head, and he makes you walk through that stifling perfumed tunnel for thousands of pages, forcing you to admire every flower, one after another, pushing you forward with his remarkably soft finger, and telling you, again and again, in iridescently different words on each occasion, with concordant modulations of his gently warbling voice, that you should remember each flower, note how it is oriented in relation to the ones near it, how some faintly echo others you passed when you were first nudged into the garden, then he stops you, gently, with a finger on your shoulder, and reminds you to breathe in the pollen, More, he says, again, inhale, it's a sweet addiction, soon you will want to breathe only the perfumed air under my endless trellises and pergolas, bowers and arbors, this air nearly choked with the pollen of memory, one more time, deep breath please, now keep walking, by all means admire everything, don't stop, breathe, admire, breathe, admire, keep going, there is much more to see, a couple thousand more pages, and so he twines his Lemaitre Demeestere satin scarflette around your neck and leads you on, it is like a death march, breathing his air is like drinking perfumed rose water, it's like an intravenous drip of sugar syrup mixed with Pernod, absinthe, Chartreux, Chambord, Pastis, a tincture of honey, lavender, Cointreau, a dash of cinnamon, Grand Marnier, Guignolet, Crème de cassis, Crème de cerise, Crème de noyaux, Crème de violette, double cream, triple cream, he will not let you stop until the final line of the final volume, and then—then he kicks you out and shuts the door on you, and you fall onto the sidewalk in front of his house, right on your goitrous overfed face, bloated with his unremittingly refined temperament, your mouth still dribbling sautéed foie gras, but you're in the real world now, you exhale lungfuls of powdered lavender and inhale the cold gas smell of the city. Across the street there's a McDonald's and a convenience store. You look back, but his door is locked tight, and there's a sign next to the buzzer: Price of Admission, 1,300,000 Words, Read Them Again. In my work, Samuel, as you will see, memories are lies that help the organism survive, and Proust's book is the most monumental of all such lies. It says, Here's the little cookie, it's delicious, and look, it comes with a note: EAT ME. Merely place a crumb on your tongue, wash it down with lime-flower tea, and your childhood will come rushing back into your mind, in fact all 1,300,000 words of your childhood will come right back to you! But they won't, you will sit there struggling to remember, and soon you'll realize your memories are normal, which means threadbare and unreliable and far away, and fading more each day—unless, of course, you lock yourself in your study and write for thirteen years, until you have turned your wisp of a thought of a trace of a memory into an efflorescent paradise. Proust's book is a 1,300,000-word proof that memories do not exist. If they did, people would read his book and agree, they'd say, Right, that's me! I have a memory just like that. Except mine was a Belgian chocolate chunk cookie in Costa Coffee, and it reminded me of my abusive father, but other than that, he got it just right! No, Proust is a floral fantasy, a morbid flowery resurrection of his childhood, which was dead and gone and should never have been brought back. Sorry for those dead baby images, babies and giants seem to come to mind when I think about Proust. So then I read Joyce, not *Ulysses,* for heaven's sake, but *Finnegans Wake,* I read that book all day most days for months, and then some days most months for years. I covered each page in notes, I read his letters, I bought books and books about the book, I read introductions, summaries, annotations, concordances, censuses, and indices, I read the pages he translated into French and Italian, I read the first ideas he scribbled in notebooks, really you can't read them, but I read them, they are just pages of words, like "floods reveal," "winding roads," "lying spirit in heaven / spirit lying in heaven," "kiks the buch," we know what that means, kicks the listing bucket, but buch is book in German, so writing is like dying, "scowl," "maniac," "semi demented," "deadened walls," "inspissated obscurities," "stringy longueurs," "border of unsane," "dazzling final refinement of delirium," "dark clouds and mud," "mouthless streams," "vertical rivers," "lightless waters," "melodious cave," "where he ended his life." I read Joyce's drafts and typescripts, I read all sixteen volumes of the Buffalo notebooks, that is 14,000 pages, those are notes he made when he was nearly blind, they look like they were written by a bear with a crayon. I read his proofs and galleys, I looked up every single one of his thousands of made-up words, "ournhisn," "dororrhea," "hogpew," "sossad," "henayearn," "pappap poppopcuddle," "commonknounest," "speleostoical," "inflorflorence," "megageg," "soswhitchoverswetch," "conflingent," "antiproresurrectionism," "dumpsydiddle," "ragingoo," "bombossitudes," I studied every single one of those invented words, they're supposed to be jokes, or not exactly jokes, but more like little chuckles, or delights, or just amusements, although many of them are puzzles, and in general they are meant to be entertainments, they are supposed to be brief moments of levity, or no, not levity, that's an old-fashioned word, they are wee delights or mischievous pleasantries or drolleries or bonbons or whatever, you can tell he thought his invented words are infused with infectious glee. I did not laugh even once. That book has everything I am afraid of. It is written for no one, Samuel, because no one can ever sit back, after months and years reading and studying and annotating, after years and months struggling through the swarms of squeaking scholars, no one can ever sit back, close the back cover with a snap, and say, Okay, I get that. *Finnegans Wake* is everything I fear, it is an enormous mistake the size of an entire country, the size of a third of Joyce's life. The book is only six hundred pages, that is half of Burton or a sixth of Proust, but it took Joyce seventeen years to write, he nearly kicked the bucket listing writing the book. It would be as if I had stopped writing when I got to page six hundred in my notebooks, and then gone back to the beginning and torn the pages out and put them in my typewriter and typed over them, and did that for seventeen years until I had six hundred pages of palimpsestic puns and language detritus. The first drafts of *Finnegans Wake* are easy enough to read. They are as clear as you would expect from an ill-mannered modernist writer. But Joyce kept going back, pestering his sentences, scratching and pecking at them, inserting Danish words, Irish words, Serbo-Croatian words, medieval Latin words, pulling apart perfectly good lines and inserting the names of Babylonian gods, Siberian rivers, Pictish kings and Byzantine patriarchs, returning again and again, like a hyena at a carcass, it pulls off a strip of gristle and lopes away, but in a minute it's back, slobbering for another scrap. He asphyxiated his English with *x's* and *q's* from Basque, Albanian, and Chinese, he tied his own writing in knots, he twisted it hard by the wrists, and they were his own wrists he was twisting, I mean he wrote the book to begin with, and then he teased and tortured it, he crushed words into each other, he muddled, meddled, and muddied until his story was gasping for breath, until there was no air or light left and it was nearly extinct. The lines are beautiful, I admit that, but so is an old loaf of bread with a flower of bright pink mold: it's not edible, it's just not edible. "For we, we have taken our sheet upon her stones where we have hanged our hearts in her trees; and we list, as she bibs us, by the waters of babalong," I love that, I admit it, but it is primped. He patted, poked, and fiddled with his book, he rubbed and fondled it, he spat and polished it until it was coated in language bacteria. There is a character in the book, Shem, he's a writer. He writes all the time, and he never finishes, just like Joyce. When Shem writes it's like Joyce writing his book. There's a page where Shem is sitting in his squalid apartment and he runs out of paper and ink. He shits into his hand, puts the shit in a bowl, pisses into the bowl, mixes up a black concoction, bakes it, dries it, and uses it as ink. Then he writes all over his own body, turning himself black, writing and writing until he records all of human history, just like the book *Finnegans Wake.* It is a soiled and blackened book, supposedly comic but actually not funny at all. Joyce knew his book was written in shit, it was spoiled and getting worse and yet he kept going for seventeen years, plugging up the last beams of light, making it deliciously fetid. He knew what it means to labor by yourself, over the same manuscript, as your eyes get worse and your daughter's insanity deepens and your reviews stay bad and creditors press their faces against the windowpanes and your life spills out. He describes the reek of Shem's apartment, stains on the floor and walls, bowl of shit ink, heaps of dirty underwear, spit splatters, discolored curtains, dried ejaculations, dregs of wine, gleet, that's an unbelievable word to find in a book like *Finnegans Wake,* but there it is. Joyce says Shem explains things with a meticulousness that borders on the insane, just like Joyce himself. Joyce says Shem never grasps the beauty of restraint, neither does Joyce. The balance of Shem's mind was disturbed, Joyce says, well obviously. Shem hides in his book like a field mouse in a nest of colored ribbons, that is a sweet idea. Shem has immovable doubts about the sense of the whole, how could he not, he has doubts about the sense of the words that stagger, stumble, and drag themselves along the lines of text, he must have doubted each one in turn and also all of them at once. Shem calls his writing a flood, that is my eighth theory, a jungle, a relic, a ruin, a scrape, a crust, a heap of steaming refuse, that is my ninth theory, moder and mor, a shamble, an avalanche, that is my first theory, a thicket, maybe I should have a theory about thickets. He looks at his book as a stranger and wonders who wrote it. That is not just a sentence to me, Samuel, I understand what it means. No one can spend seventeen years writing a book and be happy. If anyone laughs at something in *Finnegans Wake* they are forgetting why its author needed so desperately to laugh, why he needed so many thousands of those little laughs, how each laugh was like a drowning man gulping another lungful of seawater. The long books I read taught me that every sufficiently long book is a journey into a wilderness, and the author does not escape. Joyce's book taught me another extremely helpful fact, and that is that authors of very complicated books do not know if their books make sense, because they have grown into their books, and their books have grown into them, they can no longer see or think clearly outside their books, they are barely alive outside their books, all they can do is putter around opening and closing their books, nosing around their notes, hovering over their files like flies. Authors of complicated books are like Australian golden marsupial moles, I think of them when I read Murnane, they are extremely beautiful with their glittering fur and their gorgeous curved fingernails, but completely blind and helpless when they are trapped above ground, outside their sandy burrows. When authors of long books read what they have written they may sense their writing is not good, and that can be intensely painful, but they can never know for sure, because they are inside their own books, they look out at readers from between the letters of their pages. In the seventeen years Joyce worked on *Finnegans Wake* I do not doubt there were many times when he looked over what he had written the day before and knew with absolute certainty it was insane, because if it was not, then every other book ever written was, and that was clearly wrong, so he must have thought, many times, that his writing was insane, but he must have also hoped that if he kept going, he could produce a book people would think of as sane, and not only as sane, but as a new kind of sanity a few feet away from ordinary sanity, a way of making a new kind of sense, a kind that would attract people, even if they also wanted to keep a safe distance from it, even if they didn't want to get too close. Wittgenstein was different, he thought his book was sane and everyone was mistaken, everyone, Plato, Leibniz, Spinoza, Kant, absolutely everyone, Hegel, even Frege, even his own teacher Russell, every philosopher who had ever claimed to argue rationally, all the way back to Thales. He believed he thought harder than anyone before him, harder even than Aristotle. His book compressed reason down into a dry crystal of nonsense. Wittgenstein had an intense conviction, an insane kind of certainty, he made himself insane in order to be certain. Joyce was different. He knew his book was a form of insanity, and the only way out was to keep going. He had no choice, he had to keep writing until he created something so outlandish and bewildering, so crushing and unapproachable, so far from any other book, that it would slightly tilt all of literature, and people would look at all the other books ever written, and say, For some reason those look ever so slightly insane to me now, *Finnegans Wake* is an anomaly, it's certainly not sane but it is not insane either, it is a masterpiece. People think writers like Joyce were sure of themselves because they believed they were geniuses, they had an unshakable conviction they were right. I learned from reading long books that is not true. When the writing is prolonged and complex, the author's mind becomes entangled and strange. After the book passes five or six hundred pages there is no point in correcting little errors, there is no kind of error except massive, irreparable error. I am sure there are many mistakes, actually many thousands of mistakes, in my notebooks, but they are glued together into one mass, so there is no way to correct them. There are no simple slips, no momentary lapses that can be struck through with a red pencil. An error in a sonnet can ruin it. An error in a scientific paper can be conclusive. If you find something in my notebooks that looks like a mistake, and you draw a line through it, your line will be lost like a ribbon floating in the sea. Very long books are immune from simple diseases, they can only contract more dangerous, chronic, slow-moving diseases. Very long books can be entrancing or challenging, they are monuments of the imagination, unscalable achievements, very long books can be more complex than actual life, long books offer new languages, different ways of writing and thinking, they can make your everyday thoughts seem like pages from a children's book with enormous writing, HELLO EMMI HOW ARE YOU, OH HELLO DÄNNI I AM FINE HOW ARE YOU, LOOK AT MY DRESS ISNT IT PRETTY, OH MY, WHAT A LOVELY DRESS, YOU LOOK AT LEAST ELEVEN YEARS OLD, I SHOULD HOPE SO DÄNNI I AM FIFTY-SIX. Long complex books offer new worlds to live in, unexplored landscapes of the imagination illuminated by noctilucent clouds glimmering in pearly hues, icy cirrus clouds of time, green and magenta stars glittering above trackless mountains, but long complex books are slow-acting poisons, everything in them is coated with a thin lacquer of poison, every stone in those opalescent worlds has been licked by the author's poisoned tongue. The writers of long books do not stand outside their books like carnival barkers, striding confidently on stage, basking in applause, they don't stand proudly by their books, showing them off, because they are sunken into their books, they can no longer step back, they can't climb out, they have no perspective, no distance, they cannot live outside their books, they can't retreat to some sunlit place and relax and enjoy their work. They are sunken and composted into the words of their books. Joyce became the steaming heap of decomposed words called *Finnegans Wake.* Writers of long books can never understand if their work makes sense to anyone, because they cannot comprehend themselves outside of their books. I could climb out of the well as you said, it's only thirteen rungs, but what would I do standing in the starlight? Joyce could not be content with a slightly complicated book, that would have been a total embarrassment. He had to keep digging. He needed to crush and pulp all of language, he needed words to become earth. He needed to stay with his book until it became inhuman. That book is frightening, it is the diary of a man who becomes compost. A diary written by compost that was once a person. I know what you're thinking, Samuel, you're thinking, Well, okay, Anneliese, I am starting to see how unhappy you are.

I am.

You're thinking, Maybe you can just stop, you're thinking, don't keep trying to write a book like that, give up. Spend the remainder of your life writing simple short cheery things. Write emails or some nice posts on the internet. Write a fun book about EMMI and DÄNNI, I liked your little story about them, or a children's book about Spanielita and Sir Puddles, maybe a sequel called *Spanielita and Sir Puddles Discover Orlando.*

Who's making fun of whom here?

Relax, Anneliese, that's what you're thinking, take life easy, breathe, live life slowly, like a cloud scooting across the sky, let yourself be gently combed by the placid currents of life, like the grass growing on a weir, like the mold flourishing on a peach, like the moss swelling on a corpse, move to Guelph, Ontario, because why not, the people are as simple as diatoms, you can spend your life doing nearly nothing. Why torture yourself, why not pass your days strolling in the fields, rambling in the hills? Well, Samuel, I'll tell you why not. It's because when you stroll you wander, when you wander you are lost, and when you are lost your life becomes a wilderness. The world for you is nothing but lonely hills and mountains, no one is there, you meander like Bellerophon, blind, lame, disconsolate, you bellow in despair, the world is on fire around you, the forests burn, there is nothing but wasteland and smoke, you are alone, you are helpless, you are alone.

I wanted to say, about those fires and forests—

Not now. So I was very lonely reading *Finnegans Wake.* When I found out the meaning of some invented word at first I thought, Joyce is right here in the room with me, he wanted me to discover that! Look, there he is, smiling indulgently at me through his periscope glasses. But no, Joyce had no idea who his readers might be. When you discover something in *Finnegans Wake* you are alone, and the loneliness is as intense as when he put that word there, that's why only academics read the book, not because it's intellectual, but because it's too lonely to read by yourself. Joyce wrote into darkness, he had no image of a reader in his mind, only a vague idea of scholars in the future, he was alone and that means I am alone when I read. None of the others traveled as far outside human life as Joyce. Burton had jolly pastors and quacks for friends. Wittgenstein had philosophers around to scream at. Proust had Robert de Montesquiou, cousin of the Comtesse de Greffulhe, and scores more stuffy friends, and everyone understood what sort of book he was creating. No one knew what to make of Joyce's book. He moved 181 times in the 17 years he wrote his book. Every few weeks for 17 years he packed everything and moved. He couldn't stand to see anything familiar around him, to have a home, to be comfortable. He was desperately detached from human life. When I discover the meaning of a word in *Finnegans Wake* I feel cold distance, it is the loneliness Joyce must have felt when he hid that word in his book, one word among thousands, secreted inside the darkness of his book, with just a pinpoint ember of hope that someone might find it, and maybe even a passing awareness of the chill that would descend on that person when they sensed the author's isolation. Long complex books take their reader by the hand or by the hair and lead them far away from human life. After I read Proust and Joyce I thought I had finished, it seemed their novels were the most complex ever written, and in the case of Joyce the most ruined and painful, but I discovered Proust and Joyce were frail simpletons in comparison to Marianne Fritz. She was an Austrian writer. She started with a pocket-size novel, and then she wrote an average-length novel called *The Child of Violence and the Stars of the Romani.* After that she really began to write. She wrote a 560 page novel, and then she wrote a 3,400 page novel in 12 volumes, called *Whose Language You Do Not Understand.* When she finished that, she wrote an entire book introducing the novel, because it has 400 characters and she could hardly keep track of them herself. Then she started work on an even bigger novel called *Unnaturally.* She finished six oversize volumes of the novel *Unnaturally* before she died of blood poisoning from an infected spider bite. It is no wonder she was bitten by a spider because she wrote ten hours a day and never left her apartment, she made it to page 5,404, spiders probably made nests on her, and when the bite didn't heal she refused to stop working, she kept writing and at the same time she researched spiders and infections, but she was not a doctor, she was a novelist, I think she probably enjoyed discovering all the ghastly things that spiders do, I have certainly enjoyed researching spiders, but anyway finally the infection entered her bloodstream and it was too late. She used an electric typewriter, she photocopied pictures and maps and typed all over them too, Arno Schmidt also did that, he is another one, a German author, he also wrote oversize books, a couple of them too heavy to hold, you have to stand over Schmidt's books like they're family Bibles or great atlases, he wrote long novels in exploded German, with lots of extra punctuation, I read him too, but he was not helpful for me at all, because he was basically just a pervert, he loved underage girls, not a pervert, a letch, Schmidt spent years studying Edgar Allan Poe, he wrote 60,000 notecards about Edgar Allan Poe, but all he wanted to say was that he was a better writer, he could improve Poe's poems, he had read more than Poe, he saw where Poe made mistakes, and besides, Poe was a sex maniac, even though that isn't even true, and so Schmidt spent another four years writing a bulging novel about four people who talk about Edgar Allan Poe, the book is as big as a fat dog, with enormous pages printed in multiple columns, it forces you to lean over it with a magnifying glass. The four people speak all at once, in different columns of text, and there are marginal notes on both sides of the pages, the book is full of quotations from POE and the scholars who wrote on POE and every author ever mentioned by POE, Schmidt writes POE in uppercase, he writes everyone's names in uppercase, who knows why, Schmidt read everything about POE, in every European language, it would take a lifetime to look up all his references, the pages look like the Talmud, crowded with scholia and commentary, but everything is naughty, because Schmidt was a letch, and his characters are letches, and he was convinced POE was a pervert, POE wanted to be degraded, he was unconsciously attracted to shit, that is what Schmidt believed, that is what his characters talk about, no matter what POE wrote the people in Schmidt's book think it was obscene, and there is too much punctuation, Schmidt writes triple exclamation marks ! ! ! extra dashes —— & semicolons; I hate semicolons, for him punctuation was gesturing /// \\\ and crazy sexual energy ! ! ? !, and he loved ( ! ) dumb obscene jokes and puns, they really get old, but he thinks they're so clever, a c(o)untry tale, idée ficks, he was like an American teenager with his filthy jokes but at the same time like a great

Rabbi with his book full of scholia and commentaries and marginal citations and obscure references. In one scene, which lasts about 200 pages, the four people are walking along, arguing about POE, but really one of them is letching for the other one's daughter, and she toys with him by hooking her pinkie in his belt loop, and her father sees it, but they keep talking, all about how POE was fixated on shit, how he loved caves, especially ones clogged with wet rocks, get it, I mean how old are we, two? but still, I thought, this will turn out to be like *Finnegans Wake,* it is really all about the author and his book, the one we are reading, and the overheated typography ( ? — ! ) and the sleazy jokes and the mad scholarship about POE are all ways for Schmidt to write a book as excessive as *Finnegans Wake,* that is what I thought, and at first it seemed that way, because he has his characters say things like "The printed=form must force upon the supporting=words an overproducktion of letters," I liked that, it reminded me of myself, but then the father says, supposedly talking about POE, "the typografuck structure becomes »F=ffervescent« ; ! looks »swollen« ? ! ; the WEBSTER words transform themselves into »imaginairy« cumponents," and in the margins there are notes that no one could follow, one says "(71) / (once again, acoarse, glory=hole and pee," and another says "+ »didd« + oath, as in GUTZKOW" and another says "the plague!" and another says "yesyes : cor'ruption & nepp-Potixumus !" and another says "P 1 : »furze-bush« equals c(o)untryhair," and another says "»Conversation in the Labiarinth« may be found in BENZEL=STERNAUs : »Makik-Natun« / ," and another says " : the Russian=Eaters !)," and another says "(Y'see : there are other formsa anartomicul »vessels« ; longlong before FRANCÉ, HABERLANDT, BOSE," and another says "(Ye who read are still among the living; (but I (who write shall have long since gone my way (into the region of shadows)) ... ) ! )," and meanwhile the four people are arguing about all the lascivious things POE was unintentionally saying while he thought he was entertaining people with macabre and frightening tales, and the girl's finger is tickling the man's jeans right near his crotch, until at last ! // she at length wriggles , , herself pinkyfingered ! ; into the "first=Great Fork," I don't really want to think about what that is, and the notes are full of the names of authors in all-caps, too many to look up even in a dozen lifetimes, ANSTEY, MIKOSCH,

NAPRAVNIK, GRZIMEK, POLITIAN, SIMROCK, GRABBE, LUTHER, MERCADANTE, references to very obscure books, GÖTZ, FRANCES SARGENT OSGOOD, OPPOLZER, it turns out he wrote a book of logarithmic tables, nothing but numbers for hundreds of pages, ABBÉ BOUHOURS, supposedly "one of the worlds=best writers ; but no one ›knows‹ him ? ?," LAUTERER, BELLINI, STECKEL, ZINKGRÄF, TUCHOLSKY, he was a journalist who wrote under the pseudonym Kaspar HAUSER, Hauser was a boy who claimed he had grown up in a forest, or maybe in a dark cell six feet long, or maybe in a forest after all, but he learned to read and write, and always carried a copy of JEAN PAULs novel *Dr. Katzenberger's Trip to the Medicinal Springs,* Schmidt loved JEAN PAUL, and then there's BUMKE, he was Lenin's doctor, and he wrote about dementia praecox, he said that it did not exist, What=if! schizophrenia is just a collection of different symptoms ? BUMKE asked, and you have to wonder why Lenin's doctor was so concerned about that ( !! ... ), and also GÜRRES, he translated FERDOWSI's *Shahnameh* into German, and WOODS, he translated SETEBOS into CALIBAN, and WOOD, he translated OGIER GHISELIN DE BUSBECQ's Gothic dictionary into English, there is even a note citing a master's thesis on POE written in Ann Arbor, Michigan, in 1912, which quotes a letter from Marie BONAPARTE, who wrote a book on POE, she was the grand niece of NAPOLEON ( ! ... ) , to a psychoanalyst=friend of hers in the Société=Psychoanalytique ( ? ) de Paris, insinuating that POE knew that *tekeli-li,* the gibbering cry of ultimate horror at the end of POE's only novel, *The Narrative of Arthur Gordon Pym of Nantucket,* the inhuman shriek *tekeli-li,* which was quoted in LOVECRAFT's *At the Mountains of Madness,* was not an ancient chthonic utterance preserved, against all odds and through uncounted centuries, from a blasphemous pre-human race long ago expelled from the Earth, but a masked memory of a traumatic episode in POE's infancy involving a diaper, and POE knew perfectly well *tekeli-li* was not anything ancient because he lifted it from a melodrama, produced in 1804 in Paris, called *Tekeli: Or, The Siege of Montgatz,* by Theodore Edward HOOK, with platitudinous music by his father, James HOOK, a play POE saw at the age of two, concerning the life and exploits of the noble Emeric THÖKÖLY de KÉSMÁRK, Prince of Upper Hungary, whose name became *Tekeli* in

HOOK's English version, which by the way was stolen from another play called *Tékéli* by RENÉ-CHARLES GUILBERT de PIXÉRÉCOURT, and later stolen by one Giovanni BRIOL, but never mind, POE remembered it from when he was two years old and just lifted the name, one of SCHMIDT's characters says, and another protests ! that's -no- reason to assume our POE did not understand, at some »somatic« level, that he was conjuring an episode of his own infantile anal ficksation ; & meanwhile : the father does not notice that his daughter's longest finger has ! gingerly ! — — reached — — down, her little hand splayd, / ) ( - ? ) and pry'd every so gently, . . , (?) ... ( ? ), ! (!!) and it opened up, "(spooky soft) — : at an angle ! — the safe=chest ( ) ," or " ` ` ` : ′ ′ ′ ," whatever that is, but of course we know, and she has gaz'd swiftly=casually , at the compartment lined in white=silk : — & assesst its — »possibilities«, but her father does not notice, he is deep in his footnotes excavating the true nature of the word *tekeli-li*, "notice ?," he asks, "that our POE associates this *tekeli-li* with mysterious white birds, with Antarctica, with a weird=white=figure, all of them, oh!=so!=obviously masks for their opposites, i.e. black things, the filth and dirt that POE just could=not resist," & the three friends agree, for POE "god" is always subtexted with "gut," our POE was attracted to tight spaces, dark caves, eyes=closed, holes pinched=tight, but let's not forget *tekeli-li* is very=nearly *tickly-me*, or, if I might simply complete the thought, *tickelylips*, and meanwhile the man whispers to his friend's daughter, "*only We=Two* kno ? : In the hole world? !" — and shyly ! — and silently !! with the expertise of a Mongolian contortionist she tenses just the flexor digitorum profundis muscle on her longest tapering finger, causing a distinct oh=scillation in her father's friend's silk undies, and pastes her hot glassy cheek on=to His sandpâpery one, and it goes on & *on* & *On* that way two hundred enormous panting pages, can you imagine, Samuel, it takes a good hour to read just one page, and that is without stopping to see what all the references are, who were ABULFEDER, ARNAY, GELL, OVERBECK, he wrote a book on Pompeii in 1856, and who said "with his beard upon his shoulder," well it was COVARRUBIAS OROZCO in 1611, of course, SEMLER, he wrote a book on gardens in 1794 for heaven's sake, and I am sorry I ever read what KRAFFT-EBING wrote in his chapter on necrophilia, Beob. 96 : X(50), which Schmidt printed =>

sideways <= in his book, in Latin, cf. Z.T. 650 ( "   – *!!!* –   " ), SCHMIDT is beyond belief , – , – , – , his novel on POE is longer than all of POE together, and he knew that, he counted all of POE's pages (and it is certainly curious (if only to the truly=obervunt) that he wrote much more than could reasonably be expected about balloons, and the more said ! … ! about that the better, but not just now), SCHMIDT probably mentions every single sentence POE ever wrote, he may cite everything ever written on POE, SCHMIDT is just beyond belief, and of course his novel is longer than *Finnegans Wake,* it may even take more lifetimes to read than the many lifetimes it would take to read *Finnegans Wake,* I kept looking for places where SCHMIDT would wink at me and say, it's okay, I am a modern writer, like my hero James Joyce, I know what I am doing, I am constructing a tottering tower, it may seem insane, but look what my hero did, and now look at me, but no, SCHMIDT never once looks up and winks, he is head down in his prurient salacious lewd vulgar arrested-development sex fantasies and his endless compulsive POE reading. When I started reading Schmidt's enormous book, at first I stood over my desk looking down on the book as if it was an intricate jeweled crown in a museum display case, but I got sick of him, I felt like saying, You old letch ! ! ! Go out and get some ( ! ), and don't tell me about it ( ! ! ), I don't want to hear about pubescent nymphs with tight jeans who read POE and get all wet, I just don't need to think about old (impotent) men hiding day-long (phantom) erections under their deliberately oversized pant(ing)s, and all the time hoping for touchies ? and feelies ! ! , — & I don't especially want to be told fifty thousand times that POE — had — infantile — anal ( » *!!* « ) desires, but ; if I did, if I had some apocalyptically=masochistic desire to empty out my entire … ` ! ´… remaining "waking life" in the service of your endless book, licking up every last malodorous drop of your utterly monotonous uninteresting explication of POE, even then I would not want to have to constantly choke on the obscure authors you cite, it's like the air is full of gnats, gnat authors from the forgotten past, I breathe them in because I have no choice and they stick on the roof of my mouth and under my tongue, they line my throat, I have to keep swallowing them, I know you are literate beyond a thousand Joyces, other authors are ignorant and uneducated and composed their books with wooden children's blocks, Joyce is just a gnat to you, I am sorry I haven't read SACHS-VILLATTE and EYMERICH and PEREGRINUS SYNTAX and AVÉ-LALLEMANT and KÜGELGEN and TSCHISCHKA and DEBBES BUNGOTEIS and the VIGILIAE MORTUORUM and MARY FOOTE and SAMUEL FOOTE and A.E. FOOTE and E.A. FOOTE but even then I would not want to have to stumble and stagger through so many stoopid spellin's, — hmm dashes — and c(u)mmas, — , and coy spaces          and, , insinuating exclamation marks ! ! ( … ! ; ! ) and exclaiming question marks ( ? ), and , , , even , ! pooping periods . . . \\ ( ? ) ; his book really is an oblivion, a dry prickly SCHMIDT oblivion, a creeping sicko SCHMIFF oblivion, a wet sticky SHIT oblivion, a painful icky SCHMISS oblivion, a pompous picky SCHRIFT oblivion, in the end he just wants to pummel his reader with his absolute mastery of German language and of every forgotten and misbegotten book, his swollen septic ambition, his unbearable impossible relentless literacy, his not-so-secret wish to be the darkest, hardest, most demanding author in all of history, in the end he's like the blaring music they pipe in to prisoners' cells so they can't sleep or think, I had to stop reading, I left the POE scholars and the girl with her hands in her father's friend's pants, because SCHMIDT's world is an oblivion, if you read too long the gigantic book will close on your sleeping head and crush you like a duck press and you will pour out onto the table in a long glistening stain. Besides, Marianne Fritz actually wrote much more. She started part three of *Unnaturally* but then she got blood poisoning from the spider bite. She kept writing as she got worse, and the last 500 pages are nearly unreadable, I think she wrote as the spider, she became an encephalophagous writer, until the spider stopped writing at last on page 5,404. It is possible there was nothing left for the spider to eat. Marianne Fritz said that everything she had written in her entire life was one enormous project she called *The Fortress,* a magnificent title, *Die Festung,* she hoped it would protect her. All together *The Fortress* is 8,000 pages long. It was her life's work. Much longer than Schmidt's book, and yet shorter than my notebooks. If Fritz had survived her spider bite and lived to my age, her novel *Unnaturally* would have been about 14,000 pages long, and if she had lived to the age of 80 I calculate she would have written 29,500 pages, more than I ever will. It took her thirty years. Flaubert worked five years on *Madame Bovary,* he worked hard but anyone can work for five years, Roithammer worked six years, Konrad worked seven years in his lime factory, Schmidt took eight years to write *Bottom's Dream,* it took Proust thirteen years to write his balmy book, Joyce worked seventeen years on *Finnegans Wake,* Balzac worked for twenty years on *The Human Comedy,* it took Zola twenty-four years to write his novels, I have worked twenty-seven years, if I count from when I discovered my theory, but Fritz wrote for thirty years. It is true Darger worked on *The Story of the Vivian Girls* for sixty years, and that is how long Malan worked on his book on the Book of Proverbs, but they don't count, because Darger was always psychotic and Malan was always boring. Probably only two or three people in the world have read *The Fortress,* because it is written in a unnatural kind of German, typographically normal, but odd, with charts and pictures, and there are mythological treatises in her novels that are hundreds of pages long, like books buried inside her books, there are hundreds of pages of documents that make no sense, war plans, it's the First World War, but it is also the present, and also the mythic past, *The Fortress* is like waking up and discovering everyone speaks an unintelligible language, your city's name has changed, you don't know anyone, the maps are wrong, the street signs are all gibberish. You walk ten minutes, you have no idea where you are, you ask someone but they talk nonsense, you walk twenty minutes, you still don't recognize anything. What city is this? What country is this? A deep panic rises inside you, and you realize you are trapped, this is your new world, you will live here the rest of your life and never understand why, that is what her writing feels like. It is possible that Marianne Fritz is the best guide, *durch dessen Schreibtisch wir Alle unseren ersten Meridian ziehen müssten,* I don't know, I studied her life work, *The Fortress,* and I believe it is the best example of a long book with a structure all its own, not shards like Schmidt, tortured and crushed like Wittgenstein, wounded like Burton, or sterile like Aquinas, but I can't read it all, and really I can't read it at all, the language is mythopoetic, mythopoietic, hermetically closed and hermeneutically sealed, it would take years, I would be as lost as she was, I would do nothing but read, spiders would make their nests on me, eventually one would bite me but I would be so far gone I would refuse to stop reading, so when I realized that, when I realized that if I kept reading Fritz I would actually die of blood poisoning, I slammed the book shut and yelled, "No!" and Paul knocked on my study door and asked if I was all right, and I yelled, "The spiders are not going to get me!" and he said, "Good work," because he thought I had swatted a spider, and he was right, I had, I'd saved myself, Fritz is the largest of all spiders, the most dangerous. And now I am on my own. I realize now that very long books are all ill. It may not be an insane idea to write a long book, but by the time it is finished, you will not be sane, unless you write an encyclopedia, because people who write encyclopedias are made of wood, or if you write a long epic poem, because people who write those have nothing in their skulls except *Hirn mit Ei,* that is a nauseating Austrian dish made of scrambled eggs and calf brains with a raw yolk in the middle. Here is what writing a long book is like. It's like when you're on vacation with your friends by the sea and you all decide to swim out into the ocean. I did this once in Greece when I was young. I was on vacation near the cave of Polyphemus. You all just start swimming, past the surf, and beyond it into the deep open water, farther and farther from shore. You all decide to play a game: See who turns back first. Of course no one wants to be that person. One of your friends shouts at you: You're the weak one Anni! You're going to turn back! So you keep swimming. Samothrace is on the horizon, just the tip of the mountain, impossibly far away. After a while you get very tired. You wonder, Have I used up half my energy? Can I get back to shore?

Did you actually play that game?

You're gasping, you're swallowing sea water. Your arms and legs are weak. Your eyes are bleary. All you hear is the seawater lapping. Finally you look around and discover that your friends have already turned back. It's okay, you think, I'll be a heroine when I return. It must be possible to rest, float a while, and then turn back. But you are frightened, you can't stop, you're afraid if you stop you will feel how exhausted you are. If you stop your body will collapse, you won't be able to start swimming again. It is too late, you say to yourself, too late.

Did you actually do that?

Yes, and I am still swimming.

She gathered up the folds of her oversized coat and walked away.

I sat for a few minutes, uninterested in moving. I heard sounds in distant parts of the hotel. Somewhere out of sight the girl was still making airplane noises. I looked down at my hands, which had been gripping the arms of my chair. Outside, clouds grated against one another, making metallic scraping or marching sounds.[28]

# 8

## THE GRAY NOTEBOOKS

I **WAS STILL SITTING THERE** when she came back. Apparently she'd just gone to the women's room.

Now, she said. It is at last time to tell you about my notebooks, my black notebooks and my gray notebooks, and how you will dedicate yourself to reading them. I need to complete your introduction. I am tired, and this takes energy, so please do not interrupt me this time.

She settled herself. Some of her hair was caught by static electricity in the folds of her hood, making her look even more demented.

I will begin, she said, by recalling an occasion many years ago, back when I worked with Catherine in England. We used ordinary lab notebooks. They had checkered green covers, and they looked quite childish, like notebooks given to children in primary school. Each notebook had

NAME ________________
SUBJECT ______________
YEAR _________________

on its cover. I left NAME blank, because I knew it, and I left SUBJECT blank, because the subject was science, it would have been infantile to write SCIENCE. For YEAR I wrote the year, and then I added a letter of the alphabet, 1990A, 1990B, and so on, as I filled up one notebook after another.

One day in the spring of 1992, probably in the spring, I don't know why I said spring, people feel better when stories start in the spring, I looked at notebook 1992G, that is, the seventh notebook I had used that year, and I thought, this is wrong. I have to stop filling in these lab notebooks, because my work is not just a succession of experiments, it is actually leading me somewhere. It was my Balboa moment. A pattern was developing. My work was gathering around a theory, although I did not know what the theory was. I looked at the green checkered notebook 1992G, actually it was fall, not spring, there is no way I could have gotten through notebooks 1992A, B, C, D, E, and F all in the spring, some years I got to the letter G in the summer, so it was probably fall. I could look it up, but what would be the point of that? So I flipped through the notebook 1992G and I said to myself, Anneliese Glur, you need to rethink your entire way of working. You need to reorient your work, and Anneliese, I said to myself, and you need to do this on your own, I mean on my own, without Catherine, without anyone to help me, I mean you, I mean me, I mean I meant me, not you. In those days I wasn't used to speaking to myself, so it was awkward. Anneliese, I said, listen to me, you need to give up the lab, you need to stop coming in to the lab every day and writing things down in these childish notebooks. If you don't stop scribbling in these puerile notebooks, Anneliese, I am telling you, you will waste your life, that's what I told myself, and I listened to what I was telling myself. I will waste my life, I thought, actually I thought our life, but that was exceptionally confusing, so then I yelled, Anneliese, wake up! That got my attention. Look, I said, the time of experimentation is over, you are finished with the laboratory. Samuel, you have been finished with science laboratories for many years, but you just quit, this was different. I told myself, Anneliese, you need to sit and think about all this information, you need to put your results in order so we can think about them all at once. That was in summer, autumn, or maybe winter of 1992, and it was quite a while before I talked to myself again. I went through my lab notebooks and cut out all the important passages. I had the habit, back then, of marking what I'd written with little symbols in the margins. I looked for passages where I had ??? written in the margin, that meant I was not sure whether the idea I had was true; also for passages I had circled and marked with a section sign, §, meaning they were part of some bigger idea but I wasn't sure what, exactly; and also for passages I had marked with an asterism, ⁂, meaning I thought they were stellar; and ones I had marked with a T tipped on its side, ⊢, indicating they seemed logical and might possibly be proved, because the sideways ⊢ is used in logic, it means a proposition is true; and ones I'd marked with double daggers and a question mark, ‡‡?, meaning the idea seemed important but I wasn't sure if it made sense; and ones I had marked with double daggers with a little zero, ‡‡°, meaning the idea was significant but I was fairly sure it did not make sense, because even back then I was convinced that ideas can be significant without making sense; and also ones I had marked with double daggers with a little minus sign, ‡‡⁻, meaning they didn't make sense and they seemed wrong but they might also turn out to be not entirely mistaken and possibly of some passing interest in the future although I didn't really see how. I also copied out passages that were marked with double daggers with a single dagger in the middle, ‡†‡, even though I couldn't remember what I had used that sign to indicate, although I was fairly certain it meant that I had not decided whether those notes meant anything at all, or belonged in any particular category, or had any significance, which somehow made those passages tremendously important, as if their meaning would suddenly burst upon me, but it turned out that no meaning had burst upon me and yet I couldn't shake the idea that some meaning would burst upon me, so I copied out passages marked with a single dagger between two double daggers, ‡†‡, or is that a cross between two double daggers, or a normal dagger between two special crosses, what are those called, Greek crosses? Maybe all three are crosses and there are no daggers involved, I wouldn't mind that, a cross and a double cross, but what are those double crosses called, double-barred crosses? Russian crosses? Are they crosses of Lorraine? Or crosses between ordinary crosses and crosses of Lorraine? Maybe, yes, so the sign is a cross between a sign with a cross and two crosses of Lorraine, and a sign with a cross and two crosses that are crosses between ordinary crosses and crosses of Lorraine, ha ha, all that Christian symbolism would have been perfect for the hope I had even in my most unpromising ideas. Whatever it meant, I used the symbol ‡†‡ for several years, but the passages in question, the ones I annotated with that symbol, they never rose to the level of meaning much of anything, their significance never became clear, it never burst upon me, and that eroded my interest, because after all, that symbol ‡†‡ was my most miscellaneous category, the category of ideas about which I felt the most uncertain, which is really saying something, although I am not sure what, so when the passages I had marked with the symbol ‡†‡ failed to mean much of anything, even in the way that certain phrases or words may mean nothing in particular but still seem to be full of promise, as if they are suddenly about to mean something, as if you'd be pondering them and they would start shining with meaning, gleaming, nearly weeping with meaning, even though you couldn't say what the meaning was, you couldn't quite grasp it, and then all of a sudden the phrases or words would crack open, the words would break and burst with meaning, the meaning would flow, it would flood onto you, right into your mouth and up your nose like honey as Ezekiel said, he said an angel came and put a scroll right into his mouth and it melted like honey, well, that never happened to me, and the passages I marked with that symbol ‡†‡ continued again and again not really quite to mean anything at all, until eventually my interest eroded, so much that I forgot the meaning of the symbol ‡†‡ completely, or I almost did, and then finally I actually did, although I remembered it later. Sorry, I didn't need to tell you any of that. I'm nervous, it's nearly the end of my exposition. So I cut out or copied all the passages marked with these symbols, ??? or § or ⁂ or ⊢ or ‡‡? or ‡‡° or ‡‡¯ or ‡†‡, and I pasted them into a new set of notebooks, very large ones, A2 size, that is 42 by 59 centimeters, that is 16 by 23 inches. They are enormous, too big to prop up on your lap. They were the equivalent of 59 Euros each, and I bought 50 of them, I spent 3,000 Euros on them. They are heavy, with thick black leather covers. When I first saw them I thought they were beautiful, full of promise. I numbered each passage that I had copied or cut according to the notebook it had originally been in. I had those ridiculous green checkered notebooks, and lots of other kinds of notebooks, including a few from my undergraduate university, in Basel in 1975, and when I went through those I discovered I had inklings of my theory even then, I knew even though at that point in 1992 I still didn't know what my theory was, but I saw it twinkling there in the pages, and also in the notebooks from a couple years later when I was a PhD student in Potsdam. I had even commissioned some diagrams from an astronomer to illustrate my ideas, because I saw similarities between the development of my ideas and the orbits of planets. It was delightful but sad to rediscover those, because later the astronomer died, but that is another story. I searched the old notebooks for passages I could use and copied them all to the enormous new A2 notebooks. Every passage with a ??? or some other symbol, and every chart, graph, and diagram from my old notebooks, from 1975 to 1992, I pasted into the new black notebooks. Let's say there was a passage marked with two double daggers ‡‡ in a notebook from 1990, let's say 1990C, that would be late winter or spring 1990, and let's say the passage was on page 32. Then when I pasted that passage into the new black leather notebooks, I would write, in the margin, 1990C 32 ‡‡, meaning lab notebook C from 1990, page 32, passage marked ‡‡. In that way all the passages in the new black notebooks were indexed to the older notebooks. I extracted every pertinent passage from the notebooks I had used in different labs, in several cities, over nearly twenty years, and put them all into the tremendous new set of A2 signature-bound black leather notebooks, and then I put all the older notebooks in an especially fragrant garbage skip behind a grocery store, I shouldn't have done that, it would have been more poetic to burn them, but life is not always poetic, sometimes it's just smelly. I still regret not burning them, I think I wanted them to suffer a humiliating death, I hope not, because that would be weirder than I generally like to be. Anyway I was delighted with my extravagant new black leather notebooks. There they stood, 50 volumes, 41 of them filled with notes, on a long high shelf. I put them up there because they looked imposing and ancient, like those great old libraries in St. Gallen, in Dublin, in Coimbra, or the Clementinum Library in Prague, or the Zwiššer-Szüthel Library in Vienna, those great old libraries filled with books on high shelves, all in uniform bindings, books that can be on high shelves because no one ever reads them, because they are so incredibly dull, for example the parish church records of the São Miguel do Castelo church in Guimaraes for the year 1739, I know because I climbed up the bookshelves in Coimbra once, I wanted to read one of those magnificent boring books. I was practically panting with boredom when they dragged me out. My black notebooks did not look random like the early notebooks. They appeared serious and professional, even though the passages I had chosen were, in fact, the very opposite of professional. They were scattered guesses, wild notions, obscure ideas waiting to burst and splatter on me like honey from an angel or toothpaste from a tube of Kalodont toothpaste, although some were just what Catherine used to call concept poetry, *Begriffspoesie,* she said, ideas that are really just bad poetry, Catherine has always been remarkably rude. She is definitely a type four worm, and a type nine worm, and after her sudden departure from England I realized she is also worm eleven.

You know, if you're tired you really don't need to tell me about the worms.

I do, it's useful to know about worms. Type eleven have skin armed with thousands of stinging bristles that result in permanent numbness, they are people who seem friendly but then you realize they hate and envy you and they only want to paralyze you so you will keep quiet. I watch for the stinging bristles. I try to keep something between us, that is why I had all that food at the Yellow Hat Diner. Sybille Kröller is also worm eleven, I like to keep at least one lawyer between her and me. Catherine pretended she didn't like the passages I pasted into my new notebooks. I told her they were the pieces of an enormous project that I hoped would begin to assemble itself into an imposing Baroque library with magnificent dull books in uniform bindings, and when it was finished I could climb up to the highest shelf and read until I passed out from boredom... Sorry, I was getting a little confused there. I really am tired, you would be too if you had been talking for five hours and two minutes, that's how long I've been talking, and what I have been saying is really very hard for me, and I still have forty-seven minutes left of the hardest material, so I need to conserve my energy. So Catherine and I stood there and looked at black notebooks. I told her I was going to call them the *Black Notebooks.* "Very inventive," she said. I said to her, "This is my life's work, I don't know what it is yet, but it will be my life's work." That was the spring or summer or fall of 1993. I had just been hired by the University of Basel. I put the *Black Notebooks* in my beautiful new lab. It felt like a honeymoon, and for a couple of years it was, but it turned out to be the usual sort of job: dull, unrewarding, demeaning, debasing, bewilderingly depressing, hopeless, soul-crushing, brutish, and pithing, and so humiliating it made me shiver, I actually shook with fear and revulsion when I arrived at work each morning. The university is full of the twelfth kind of worm, I haven't told you about those yet, those are the ones with hundreds of little legs with hooks at the ends, they are the people who scurry into everyone's business, they would crawl into your ear canal if they could. My job at the university pared away my basic dignity. It made me feel like a turtle with a party hat glued to its head, with its mouth taped shut over a spoon, with the tape winding around its nose so it can hardly breathe, and a strawberry macaron taped to the spoon, polka-dot boxer shorts, and knit booties on its feet, the kind of turtle people really laugh at. My so-called colleagues Sybille, Andrei, Walter, Spadella, Marcel, and Grettina, and Ludwig Hassenpflug, I always forget him, they peeled me like a turnip, especially Sybille and Spadella, they pulled vegetable peelers over my skin, it came away in strips, exposing blobs of fat, and that wasn't even enough for them, they kept peeling, my muscles dropped off in slices, vessels were severed, I spurted blood, it went on and on, soon I was nothing but scraped bones, my job was grotesque, it was a living gasping death, my colleagues were a collection of slobbering beasts, they were like lemurs, and centipedes, and beavers, but undead, they were werelemurs, werecentipedes, and werebeavers, those are the worst, they are unpredictable and they have bad breath, they all gathered around me, and then they knelt down and licked the blood off my—

But why? Why did they do that?

I admit that I did have certain troubles. I tended to forget my classes, but students are so hard to remember, sometimes they're hard even to see, because they are transparent. You look at them and you see the wall behind them. Also I hid in my colleagues' offices so I could read their notebooks at night. I might once have been found in Grettina Früchtel's lab, writing in her notebooks, but that was only because she needed help. None of that is relevant to what I am telling you, but if Paul was here he would tell me to tell you, and I wouldn't, and then he would just go ahead and tell you, so I might as well do it, not because I respect his judgment, although I do, more than anyone's, but mainly because if you see him again he will definitely tell you, so I might have been found in Grettina's house, rearranging her pencils and pens and throwing out some of her books and papers, but that was only because I was trying to do what she was apparently congenitally incapable of doing, which is simply put things in order and throw out everything that is wrong, and there were a lot of wrong things in her house, she had a desk full of papers with wrong ideas, she had a lot of mismatched pencils and pens, she had lamps with flamingos and palm trees on them, she had wallpaper with monkeys and parrots, maybe I didn't have to haul everything out onto her terrace and burn it but that seemed the easiest thing to do, how was I supposed to know she would mind if I made a small fire out of her life's work, and besides it was entirely her fault that I had to sneak in, because at that point all my so-called colleagues had stopped inviting me to their houses, anyway luckily for her I had almost finished when she came home. That's all in the past now. I haven't been found in anyone's house for years, except Andrei's, and maybe Walter's, and besides, it didn't do Grettina any good, she continued to run hopelessly misguided experiments, on all sorts of unpromising inadvisable topics, and her career never went anywhere, well, okay, mine didn't either, but Paul says I need to try to make distinctions between my property and other people's property, well okay, maybe I do, I think he's right, and so there, I have told you. Are you happy now? Don't worry, I haven't been in your apartment, there was no need for me to do that. All your documents were easy to get. Your City Commissioner, Mr. Josh Salazar, assured me I did not need to file a lawsuit to see your personnel file, he just gave it to me, he said he thought it might be in the public domain, just like your police record showing you once rode in a stolen car. The year after I tried to help Grettina by burning her work there was a series of so-called tribunals and so-called competency panels, staffed by my so-called colleagues, and I lost my so-called job and had to move into Hans's house along with Paul. Hans gave me the study with the bay windows that I still have, and I put all the *Black Notebooks* in there. I'm finished with the idea of helping people by burning their wrong ideas, and by the way of course it has occurred to me to burn my own wrong ideas, but luckily I can't figure out which ones they are, otherwise I'd have a big fire like the one in Canetti's *Auto-da-fé* or the book burning in *Don Quixote,* and by the way those didn't help at all, afterward the characters in those books were either dead or insane. Anyway that is the conclusion of the story of my professional life. Here is what happened next. One morning that winter I was feeling out of sorts, not from being ejected from the university, that was a relief, I slept very well in those days, but that morning I had too many *oeufs en cocotte* bathed in butter. Paul is very generous, and if I ask he always makes more, and that day I had six *oeufs en cocotte* with butter poured over them, and lovely fresh croissants to mop up all the yolks and butter, and so when I went into my study immediately after breakfast, as I always did, as I still do, I looked at the row of *Black Notebooks*, intending to pull one down and continue my work, and I felt queasy. My indigestion helped me to realize that the 41 *Black Notebooks* were all wrong. They were brief passages from the old lab notebooks, cut and pasted into lovely bound volumes, but they were not readable. No one could just pick them up and read them, a person who tried would be perplexed. They were full of discoveries, astonishing things, but in shards and fragments. If someone tried to read the *Black Notebooks* they would be amazed, but in a few minutes they would be bored, they might even fall asleep, in the library in Coimbra I fell into a kind of stupor of boredom, I was so bored I could hardly walk, that is why they had to drag me out. So I ran back into the kitchen and told Paul that no matter how much I pleaded, he should always make me at least six *oeufs en cocotte* every day, to make me nauseous in exactly the same way, it was the most inspiring nausea I had ever felt, I explained to him that six *oeufs en cocotte* were delicious in just the right way, they were sweet, fatty, and salty, and also *aquosa, viscosa,* and *nauseosa,* watery, viscous, and nauseating, and then I ran out to the store where I had bought the *Black Notebooks* and ordered 70 more notebooks, this time gray ones, heavy, thicker, and smaller but still very large, 300 pages each, A3 size, that is 30 by 42 centimeters, that is 12 inches by 17 inches, with hard covers, bound in smooth delicate calfskin. They are exceptionally beautiful, those gray notebooks, they were hand made for me in Finland at a cost of 12,000 Euro. I spent most of my pension on them. I wanted them to be the best possible quality. The cover boards are spruce, the gray covers are Franz Hoffmann Gutenberg archival calfskin, and the pages are acid free hot pressed wove paper. I signed a binding contract with them, a contract for binding, not a contract that is binding, a binding contract, so they delivered 30 notebooks looseleaf, that way I could type the pages on my Hermes 3000 Universal Breitwagen electric typewriter, and then post the pages back to Georges Morellet, he is the president of the Jyväskylä Bookbinders, and receive the signature-bound notebooks in return. And that is how it worked. Some years I typed, other years I wrote, and everything came together into the perfect façade of my 70 *Gray Notebooks.* They are my miraculous chateau, they provide the strongest possible illusion that I am whole. When I look at them I feel my thoughts are uniform, bound together. I am perfectly aware that my gorgeous row of expensive pale calfskin notebooks is a pathetic attempt to convince myself that my disastrous life actually makes sense, but books are strong magic and I can forget certain issues when I see Georges Morellet's Franz Hoffmann Gutenberg archival calfskin spines gleaming softly at me from my shelves. I am glad I spent the money on Finnish notebooks instead of the house repairs Paul says we need, or the new boat he keeps asking for, or the vacation he keeps talking about. I'm not so sure about all the calves Morellet killed to make my notebooks, but the covers are lovely and soft. From the day I received those notebooks I never stopped writing. I wrote continuously, I filled the pages, I wrote for hours at a time, often I didn't stop until dinner, and then I started again after dinner and wrote until Paul knocked very quietly on the study door to tell me the lights were out and everyone was in bed. From time to time I sent my typed pages off to Jyväskylä, and I relished the moment a new volume arrived in the post, freshly archivally bound. As you know, I don't take many breaks when I am talking, and it is the same with my writing, many pages don't have paragraph breaks, and it is a pleasure to see them bound together, all the thoughts safely linked one into the next, like little children roped together for a walk. These *Gray Notebooks,* as I call them, are all cross-referenced back to the *Black Notebooks.* On the outside margins of the pages I put references to the *Black Notebooks.* Nearly every page in every volume of the *Gray Notebooks* is cross-referenced back to the 41 *Black Notebooks.* So when I write about an idea I had in 1990, for example, I put a note in the outside margin of the *Gray Notebook,* for instance "Vol. 12, p. 50, note 1990C p. 32 ‡‡?," which means the idea I mention in the text can be found in *Black Notebook* volume 12, on page 50, and it was copied into the

*Black Notebook* from its original place in lab notebook 1990C, on page 32, and the two daggers or crosses with the question mark mean the idea seemed important but I wasn't sure if it made sense. In that way I kept careful track of my doubts and uncertainties, I did not conceal any of them. The marginal references in the *Gray Notebooks* refer to the *Black Notebooks* that refer to the checkered green notebooks and even older notebooks from as far back as 1975, and that means the continuous writing in the *Gray Notebooks* is a commentary, a meditation like the Talmud, on notes on notes, and even on notes on notes on notes. I wanted to make way for a theory larger and more complicated than anything I had been able to imagine. The 70 *Gray Notebooks* are each 300 pages long, for a total of 21,000 pages. My plan, which I formulated in 1999, is to completely fill 66 volumes of the *Gray Notebooks,* leaving the first 4 volumes blank. Eventually you will discover what those are for. Together with the 41 volumes of the *Black Notebooks,* the 66 volumes will be my life's work. Now I need to tell you what happened.

She gave me an especially fanatical and nervous look, which lasted an uncomfortably long time.

I am only 100 pages from the end of the last *Gray Notebook.* I have written over 19,700 pages, which is around 6,500,000 words, not counting approximately 3,000 equations, 7,650 diagrams, charts, and graphs, and over 1,200 photographs I have pasted in. I will end on the last page of the 70th *Gray Notebook,* just 100 pages from where I am now. In October 1999 I opened the first *Gray Notebook* and began to write my stupendous theory in 66 volumes, and by the way I know it was October, because I like to begin important projects on my birthday, and my birthday is October 12. I mention that because people like stories with personal touches. I hoped the *Gray Notebooks* would be a masterpiece, a new kind of thinking about life, memory, and instinct. My work would not ramble amiably like Darwin, it wouldn't lose its way dangerously like Burton, it wouldn't be a creepy museum like Linnaeus, or a clotted turd larded with undigested food fragments like Joyce, or precious and delicate like Proust, or brittle and frigid like Wittgenstein, or lecherous and condescending like Schmidt. It would be an actual book of tremendous length and intricacy, welcoming everything in its view, the way Joyce welcomed languages, but without chewing them up into a nasty spittle. My book would gather everything, from a spilled droplet of termite plasma on a lab table here in Basel in 1975, right up to a discussion of the concepts of *diephtharmenos,* a Greek word I was thinking about this morning, a word that unfortunately describes my own mind, it means ruined, corrupted, and infected. *Idou ego, prooles, mokhthera, diephtharmene.* I wanted to write a theory that would have a place for everything, but I was naïve in 1999, I thought writing a long book was just a matter of discipline and concentration, I imagined it only required energy and time. I had no idea, back then, that long books corrode the writer, they infect, corrupt, and ruin the writer. In 1999 I had no way of knowing that I would have to struggle to keep control of my thoughts. I had no idea just how ill writing can make a person. I imagined the *Gray Notebooks* would be the place where all my ideas could flourish, no matter how uncertain or malformed. My conceptual flood was going to scour the landscape of biology, leaving it fresh and clean. The avalanche of my ideas was going to magnetically snap together into a mansion. When I started writing in volume 5, on October 12, 1999, I was content just to think and write. I was immersed in my work, whether I was underlining one passage or erasing another, *ob ich unterstreiche oder heraussstreiche,* whether I was expanding on a note from one of the *Black Notebooks,* changing my mind about something I'd been sure of in the past, or just writing freely page after page. My life was writing and reading, they went together naturally, my *Lesemodell* was my *Lebensmodell.* I wrote out my ideas in the *Gray Notebooks,* and whenever I needed to cite some fact, I looked it up in the *Black Notebooks* and appended the appropriate reference. Gradually, one page at a time, I knitted the *Black Notebooks* into the *Gray Notebooks.* My life was starting to make sense, I was beginning to see what my theory was, my ideas were appearing on paper, in words. I often had a dozen notebooks open at once, set out on the tables in my study. Paul and Luzia brought me shopping carts of books from the library. The years went on, and the *Gray Notebooks* slowly filled. Paul continued to make me six *oeufs en cocotte* every morning, even though I didn't usually eat more than two or three, because I did not always want to feel nauseous, but it was comforting to know that I could feel that special sort of nausea if I wanted to, and I think Paul also enjoyed the routine and he might even have eaten the rest of the *oeufs en cocotte* after I left the kitchen, I don't know, I seldom see him eat. Many times my best insights came from sitting at my desk, overstuffed from my eggs, croissant, coffee, and juice, my lips still greasy, my stomach complaining, when suddenly I saw the answer to some problem that had escaped me when I wasn't nauseous. That was the dream: perfect nausea, perfect work. *Vollständige Übelkeit, vollkommene Schreibarbeit.* But things went terribly wrong. Four years ago I realized that even though I had filled most of the notebooks, I had never, in almost twenty years, read the entire thing all the way through. Twenty years is a long time, and I couldn't clearly remember what I had written over such an expanse of time and so many pages. I was close to the end, and I knew it was time to assess the whole, to see my life's work all at once. I expected that when I read all twenty years' worth of notebooks I would be delighted, proud of what I had accomplished. I decided to start the next morning. I was full of happiness. I ate twelve *œufs en cocotte,* an exceptional number. I told Paul I would appear as usual for breakfasts and dinners, but I would not talk to him for several months, because I needed to concentrate. I told him I was at a crucial place in my work, I said goodbye to him even though we live in the same house, and I went to my study, shut my door, and began to read. At first I was ecstatic. Back on October 12, 1999, when I began the first *Gray Notebook,* my ideas were strong, they were penetrating and surprising. The writing was wonderful through the winter of 1999 and into 2000. I giggled when I rediscovered my ideas. I had written a short introduction to my life and career, just to get me started. That was also delightful to see. But over the next week of reading, I began to encounter pages I didn't like. I had written about my colleagues, of course, and then I wrote about Germans and Austrians. I wrote about pharmacists, I wrote about people who own very large televisions, I went a bit off the rails, I wrote about different sorts of dead people, famous dead people, average dead people, annoying dead people. By March I was talking to myself, praising myself for my own insights and feeling sorry for myself when I had no ideas. "Here I am," I wrote in March 2001, "struggling with this enormous project, *ad augusta per angusta,* on the narrow road to the high place, *cacoethes scribendi,* dying to write, dying while writing, even if it will be the end of me, *felo de se.*" It was embarrassing to read those pages. I saw that I had been foundering.

But then in the next notebooks I began in earnest, with my real subject, the basic concepts of life, the idea of life in biology. There was good material in the notebooks from those first several years. I was studying the foundations of biology, I was reading widely and deepening my arguments. I wrote about the philosophy of biology. I reviewed ideas about scientific reasoning. Yet there were also many pages, many hundreds of pages, where the ideas didn't work. Once again I was thrashing around, trying to find connections. I wasn't keeping track of what I wrote. I wrote page-long speeches, then I forgot what I had written and I rewrote the page-long speeches without realizing I was repeating myself. It was exhausting to read. I was posturing and pompous. When I read the notebooks from 2001 and 2002, I remembered how difficult those years had been. I had gotten a part-time job in a pharmaceutical lab, but I was dismissed for trying to improve their products. Paul was disappointed, he told me we needed the income. I told him I was just going to stay home and work, and I did, I filled notebooks month after month, and eventually he stopped asking me to look for jobs. I didn't write any of that in the notebooks, but as I read them I could tell when the crisis passed. My handwriting relaxed, I wrote more in 2003 than I had in the four years before then. I kept reading. I was proud of myself, because I had survived. I wrote faster. I started typing on my Hermes 3000 Universal Breitwagen, and sending the sheets to Jyväskylä to be bound. The typewritten pages looked quite professional. I glued in diagrams, graphs, and photos. I thought, Well, this is when the real work began. But after a couple more weeks of reading, when I got to the notebooks written around 2006, the writing seemed strange. I had become uncertain. I must have been especially bothered by Paul, because I wrote 100 pages on how to ignore people by remaining mute or by staring at them, how to annoy people by practicing echopraxia or echolalia, how to get people to walk away by coughing or spitting. In 2007 I wrote that it was possible I was not thinking clearly enough to continue the work. In one notebook I wrote that my work was like the disordered dreams of a person who is sick, *aegri somnia* as Horace says. Sickened dreams, things dreamt by sick people. "This year I need to be careful," I wrote, "I need to stay awake." That year I wrote some good critiques, there are about fifty pages of good material, but I felt confused and tired, like I was falling asleep. In the following years I wrote as if I was asleep. Those notebooks were uncomfortable to read. Sometimes they seemed to be written by someone else. I could hardly remember what I had been thinking. I turned the pages, wondering if my life had become a dream of work, perhaps at that time I was no longer working but only dreaming of working, where *nec vox aut verba sequuntur* as Vergil says. Imagine, Samuel, entire notebooks, hundreds of pages of writing that felt like it was underwater, my thoughts burbling and indistinct, my mind slowed and uncertain. It was horrible reading those pages, like listening to someone who speaks with the empty confidence dreamers have, she is sure she's making sense, but she's only arranging words, creating *Begriffspoesie*. I had known at the time that something was wrong, the way you know things are wrong in a dream but you can't figure out how to wake up. I can hardly express how painful it was to read the notebooks from those years. That was when I developed the ladder of unreason, trying to see what was wrong with me. When you read those notebooks, Samuel, the levels will be your guide. I lived several years in that state. I was sleepwalking. I wasn't fully alive. I was dormant, hibernating. I think people accommodate themselves to what their life gives them, they learn to live with a spoiled relationship, a bad job, a small apartment, but it isn't really living. I was like that, registering my life but half dreaming. I knew things weren't right, but I didn't stop, I kept going, maybe I didn't want to wake up. I convinced myself I was doing real work, that it was still science. As I read those notebooks I recognized the words and terms, I mean the science and philosophy were there, but there were also long stretches that were terribly confused. I got lost in languages, I studied words for life and soul in many different languages, I didn't know where I was going, I felt more and more that I was on my own. I had lost sight of the place I started, like I did in Greece when I swam out into the sea. Sometime around 2010 the notebooks no longer made sense at all. I sounded drugged. I wrote about Catholic sins, greed, lust, and jealousy, things I had never thought about before. That's when I invented the spiders, the Infected Mind Theory and the Encephalophagous Theory. My voice in those notebooks sounded muffled, cocooned. I repeated myself, many times, over hundreds of pages. I wrote in a fog. It was excruciating to read those notebooks.

Imagine if you had once been gravely ill, Samuel, imagine you once had a serious disease, a condition that caused you terrible pain, and you lived that way for years. Now imagine you recovered, and years later you found a video of yourself made back in that period, and you watched yourself in that state of chronic pain, imagine you saw yourself pacing back and forth, holding your head, swearing, speaking nonsense. Imagine watching that spectacle eight or ten hours a day for weeks, because that is how long I spent reading, it was torture, worse, in a way, than the suffering itself, which I had largely forgotten. No one should have to experience again their own suffering, no one should have to witness themselves being tormented, that is why pain is so hard to remember, because it's anguish to relive your suffering. Both bad and good memories evaporate in order to protect us. I had to watch as I tried and failed to find ideas, as I wrote one line after another, wrung another word out onto the page, tried to remember how to think clearly, strained to keep my mind on the writing. I wrote strange sentences I could hardly understand, and struck them out with a black marker so I would never see them again. Some days I wrote just one word at a time, even just just a single letter. One single letter. It was unbearable. I struggled to keep going, to put anything at all on the page. The ordeal went on for hundreds, thousands of pages, longer than most of those long novels. When I was reading I felt it would never end. A couple of times I suddenly remembered the day I had written a particular page. I recalled frost on the window or a plate of Schoggiweggli Paul left on the floor outside the study. The feeling of those days came back as a deep chill. My study was often cold back then, and my thoughts were chilled. When I wrote by hand, my handwriting was jagged, as if my fingers were stiff with cold. The writing was cramped. I couldn't believe how much I had written, how many years I had worked, in a stupor of frigid hallucinations. It was unbearable to realize how much I had suffered, how awful and worthless the result had been. I wanted to shut the notebooks and leave the apartment, go somewhere, anywhere, try to forget what I'd spent so much of my life doing. I won't tell you some of the thoughts I had. I was convinced I had wasted my life, I had started as a reasonable scientist, then I had cut up my own notebooks, pasted them into a crazy collage, and then spent years writing about the collage, and it hadn't worked, the mess had gotten worse. The tissue of the notebooks was necrotic, it was all going to die, I had to amputate it and try to forget it. The month when I read through the notebooks from 2007 to 2010 was the worst month I have ever experienced. I felt like I was in a forensic lab, on a dissection table, looking down at the lower part of my body and realizing it was dead. I pressed on the dead skin of my legs and saw the necrosis growing up my thighs toward my belly. I breathed in the formaldehyde odor of the lower half of my body. It was a bitter experience, looking at my work and realizing it was dead. No one would read it, no one could even stand to be in the same room with it. I walked around the study, I couldn't sit still. The *Gray Notebooks* were like corpses. But I had no choice, I sat back down and kept reading. And then it got even worse. In September 2010 I had written an imaginary history of my life. I had pictured myself as an explorer, making her way up the Amazon. I had wasted an entire year writing a story, really a novel within my notebooks, about how I lived in an isolated village in the rainforest. I had written a chronicle about my imaginary mosquito bites, like Murnane's file of imaginary horse races, every mosquito bite numbered and mapped on diagrams of my body, with the dates and sizes of the inflammations and pustules. It was all hallucinated, there are no mosquitoes in my study. I had written another chronicle about my recurrent imaginary foot fungus, in tremendous detail, with drawings of the fungal infection. Why did I do that? Who was I when I wrote those pages? I could only remember thinking I had to keep working, and at the same time forget who I was, or I needed to work in order to continue to forget who I was, I had to be very careful not to wake up and realize I was in my study in Basel, because that would mean I would see what had happened to me. I was like a terrified animal pressing itself onto the ground, crushing itself down into the dirt, desperate to hide. Back when I wrote that story I had never thought of asking myself why I needed to stay inside the fantasy, counting mosquito bites or fungal lesions. In some way I knew I had to do that, I could not do anything else. And then it got even stranger and more desperate. I wrote about wandering in northern forests, Swiss forests. I wrote mythical stories with forest gods, full of hallucinations, the kind you might experience in a fever, but this one lasted three years. Three years! Literally thousands of pages on mythical forests. I can't even tell you what was in those notebooks, it is too embarrassing. I remembered the feeling of those forests, they were unlike anything I knew in real life, and I had felt they were somehow profound, that the stranger they became, the more powerful they were, the more I was writing a new kind of science, expressing something wonderful that had never been said before. I had felt I could stay there forever. There were no clocks in the forests. The forest dramas lasted thousands of pages, hundreds of years. I slipped easily from one idea to the next. The writing was sluggish but continuous, nothing made sense but I felt it was somehow profound. The forests seemed full of meaning, even though I had no idea what the meaning was. Nothing was familiar, words went by and I hardly understood them. I was cold, my mind was glassy. At the end of 2014 I was hardly alive. I titled one section "How My Mind is Shutting Down." I felt as if only my fingers could move, I watched my fingers flex slightly to make the letters, I saw the ink coming out, I saw it stain the writing appear, I watched the words but I didn't read them. The ink was smooth but it was thick, like blood about to clot. And then finally in December 2014 I started to come back. I felt more, the pages tingled like your leg after it has fallen asleep. I got caught up in the project again. After 6,600 pages of writing about forests I took a new notebook, volume 65, and I wrote the title, "How it feels to waken from paralysis." Starting in 2015, Samuel, I wrote myself back into life. I described how I had been half-buried for years, how I pulled grit out of my skin, learned to stand up, remembered who I was. During the period when I was hallucinating I didn't even name myself, I had forgotten my name, or no, I had buried it. Slowly, over more than a year of writing, I came back into myself. I was like a person who has been severely injured, traumatized, maybe she is even bleeding inside her eyes, doctors look into her eyes and see dark pools half-filled. Black liquid washes back and forth, her eyes are drowning. It took until midway through 2016 to drain away that darkness. I wrote about picking millipedes off my body, plucking mushrooms that had grown in my back. I wrote about the welcome return of pain. I hated the days I spent reading over those notebooks, Samuel, but I kept reading, and eventually I came to the notebooks I had written just a few months earlier. I recognized myself in those notebooks, but it was a different Anneliese. She wrote with a chilled hand, her eyes were still glassed with ice crystals, her mind only partly thawed. Most of her, I mean me, most of me was dead. And finally I read the most recent notebook. As I came closer and closer to the present, of course I remembered everything in those pages, but the person who wrote them was no longer me.

She sat motionless. She was looking through my neck, as if she was examining my spine.

This was three years ago. When I finished reading I sat in my study and I was in a sort of despair, like Burton, like Spiera, clinging to the eleventh rung of the ladder. I was shocked. I had hoped I'd finish reading with a sense of triumph. I knew it was possible I'd be disappointed, but I had never suspected that I spent entire years in anguish. I had never imagined that simply by writing I could have gotten so lost, it never occurred to me that is how people get lost, ever so slowly, over months and years, so gradually that they don't notice when they stop making sense. There it was in front of me, in the thousands of pages of the *Gray Notebooks,* the pitiless record of my slow descent into a place where I was no longer rational. I had convinced myself that those years of frozen hallucinations were some new kind of science, that I would be amazed and proud when I read them again. But I couldn't understand them, and I couldn't understand what had happened, what I had become. I felt like poor Echo, the girl who loved Narcissus. He called to her and she called back, but he couldn't find her, because she was only an echo. Narcissus was like my theory, a beautiful boy, but then he drowned himself, and Echo lived on in woods and caves, as she does to this day, as they say, because they always say that at the end of a fable, "as they do to this day," or "as it is done to this very day." I felt like a ghost. I could no longer speak, because my theory had abandoned me, it had drowned itself in my writing. In the poem, Narcissus dies and Echo disappears into the woods. *Et in aera sucus corporis omnis abiit,* the moisture of her body disappeared into the air, that is what Ovid says, or maybe it is *omnis abierat,* and *vox tantum atque ossa supersunt,* only her voice and her bones are left. Or maybe it is the imperfect, *supererant.* Anyway Ovid says there is a dream, *somnus est,* no, a sound, *sonus est,* which lives in her, *qui vivit in illa.* Yet eventually the echo dies down. There once was a sound that lived in her, Ovid says, *sonus olim fuit, qui vixit in illa.* I had kept going for years after my theory drowned, I was a sound, then a dream, and at last I disappeared. I had spent all those years on the notebooks, I had been in love with my theory, he was a handsome boy who drowned. And what had I produced? What was I left with after all that time? I had only a few notebooks left to fill, and I had to find a way to fix what I had done. I needed to write a conclusion that would somehow justify the entire thing, make it whole, give it sense, make it sane. That is when I began reading long and complex books, to see how other people had managed to create enormous sustained texts that are coherent and not just shapeless diaries of illness. I learned there is no solution, because every book, if it is long enough, begins to prey on its author. No long and complex book is sane, Samuel, it is in the nature of long books that they push away from sanity. Only short books are sane, people are safe with short books. Writers can control them, but all books are slow-acting poison, they are infected by the author's mind, and they infect readers in turn, and the longer the book, the more time you spend turning the pages, whether you are writing or reading, the more ill you become. No one controls thoughts that take more than a hundred pages to write. Many books appear to be sane, but that is because they end quickly. Most people seem sane if you talk to them for just a few minutes. I think authors must have fun with short books, pretending the world makes sense. Probably that is why people love short sunny books, short thrilling books, they are like invigorating swims, brisk walks, people read them in a day or two and say, Great, that was so engaging, I feel refreshed, and now on to the next short book. But every book has a taint of disease. Even short stories are illnesses, brief disorders, like when you feel out of sorts for a half hour but the feeling passes. There is no way to speak, no way to write, without a damp shadow falling over your words. In long sentences, like mine, the traces of illness become clear. That is another reason people love Proust, because he worked so carefully to keep his long sentences sane. My book, that is what I call it, even though it is 41 large *Black Notebooks*, 66 smaller *Gray Notebooks*, an index in 12 red notebooks, I will tell you about them in 57 seconds, and a 100-page hierarchical outline, even though there are 120 books in all, I call all of it my book, my book is exceptionally long, 29,050 pages, and therefore prone to many illnesses and all thirteen levels of illogic. It is ill in numerous ways, it suffers from scotomas and hallucinations, literally, there are hallucinations in it, also anxiety disorders, accumulating amnesias, fixed delusions, dysmorphias, persecution complexes, there are systemic cognitive failures in it. Reading long books taught me there are conditions more intricate than are dreamt of in the delicate and infantile imaginations of doctors. And now I need to continue, I can't keep talking about the years I was necrotic, it would be too unpleasant for you, you would run away. I would lose you. So I will tell you about the index. During the year I spent reading those long books, I didn't add a single word to the *Gray Notebooks.* Instead I worked on an index. I thought that if I made an index I could understand what happened to me, because the index would be a different picture of the work, a new kind of portraiture. My *Encyclopædia Britannica* has an 875 page hierarchical index, by the way, so that people can see that the article on Albumen is part of a set of articles including Yolk, Shell, Egg in Culture, Poultry Farming, Butchery, Salmonella, and Hospitalization. Balzac's novels have a 775 page index, very useful to look up all his ridiculous characters. Perec's *Life A User's Manual* has an index with 3,093 entries, he wrote it himself, and it is full of jokes. My own index is incomplete, of course, because I am not finished writing in the *Gray Notebooks,* but I bought 12 red notebooks just for the index, 250 pages each, that is 3,000 pages, one entry per page. Exactly like a 3,000 page encyclopedia, mindlessly from A to Z. I want to tell you some of the entries I have put in the index, beginning with the letter *A.*[29]

You don't have to.

I do, it is the best way to give you an idea of what is in the *Gray Notebooks* without frightening you too much.

I'm not especially frightened.

Good. First comes *aaptos,* it means unapproachable, clearly I am *aaptos,* I only wish I was *Aaptos aaptos,* that is the scientific name of a toxic sea sponge.

I just don't want to hear about the index.

Did you know that in German our encyclopedias all start with *Aal,* that is the word for eel? Hans Jürgen von der Wense said every German reader should think eels are profound because they always come first, like *Aard-*

*vark* in English. *Diese von geheimnisvoller Sehnsucht getriebene Wasserschlange,* these water snakes are driven by a mysterious longing, he said, but eels aren't especially profound, and I doubt anyone thinks aardvarks are profound. So I began with *aaptos,* because a toxic sea sponge is clearly more profound than an ordinary eel or a grubby aardvark. Then comes *abebaios,* it means uncertain or wavering, that is definitely me, and it is also the name of some species of worm that has three pairs of seminal vesicles, well, I don't have seminal vesicles, but it is good to know some worms have extra ones. I suppose it is a useful word if you feel oversexed but insecure. Then comes *aberrans,* it means aberrant, a person who wanders off the path. I think you know all about that.

What?

Then *aboethetos,* it means hopeless or incurable, you can guess why I am interested in that, and it is a Greek word for despair. *Aboethetos* is also the name of a kind of bacterium that can only live where there is a lot of uric acid, like in urine or in toilets. My dictionary is full of names of animals and plants, and many are also names I call myself. There is something appropriate about a word for despair that also involves urine. Certainly it is depressing to think too much about urine, if I did nothing except think about urine I would definitely be sad. Next is *abscission,* I will get to it later. Then comes *achly,* it comes from a Greek word meaning dimness, mist, or murk. There's a goddess named Akhlys, she is the goddess of misery, sorrow, and obscurity. I think I worship her. Probably I do worship her. When I first read about Akhlys, I thought I would write a prayer invoking her by a thousand different names, but then I realized my index already does that, my index is a prayer with three thousand names. *Ad augusta per angusta* is also one of the first entries. From the narrow path to the austere realm, through thorns to the sky, from the constricted tunnel to the solemn and majestic heavens. I mentioned it already. Then comes *aegri somnia,* patients' dreams, I told you that one too, and next is *aeidi,* from the Greek word *aeidia,* it means deformity, another word that fits me perfectly, my thinking is deformed, my writing is deformed, but guess what? I think the same word also means everlasting, *aeidios,* so my professional and personal deformities are permanent, maybe even eternal. *Aeidios* is also the name of an arctic shark, *Somniosus aeidios,* the deformed arctic sleeping shark, it lives for half a millennium, deep in the Arctic Ocean, and it often goes blind because crustacean parasites grow out of its eyes. People who study it say it does not need to see, because it lives so far down, and apparently it does not mind having stalks growing out of its eyes. They look like little palm trees. If I did not already have the borometz then the shark would be my talismanic animal. It lives in the frozen dark, it is horribly and yet comically deformed. Then there is *aethes,* meaning irregular, curious, and unusual, it's the name of some odd-looking mice, moths, wasps, and fish, and of course me, too. *Agennetos* means effectively without parents, as in a way I am, or at least my writing is. I had a mother, but she is a completely different story, please do not ask me about her, my entire life has been *agennetos.* It seems like a good word for my work. What are its parents? This is often a problem with very long books. Short books have big families, because they are like many other books. Murder mysteries are siblings, they all look the same. The longer the book, the smaller the family. Who is in the family of *Finnegans Wake?* Who is *King Kesar's* mother? Where are the brothers and sisters of *Bottom's Dream?* Long books are *ageneta* like Methuselah. His father Enoch had Methuselah when he was 65, and Enoch lived 365 years, so Methuselah had a father for 300 years, but then he went on living, he died when he was 969 years old, so he spent 669 years without a father. He was *agenetos.* My work seems to have no family, but of course there are many people in hell, ha ha. Then comes *agrapha dogmata,* that means doctrines that are unwritten, they should never be written down, I had many of those, but I wrote them all down anyway, perhaps the book is ruined by them, because *agrapha dogmata* are things that belong in the mind and not on the page. Like *insanus* in Aquinas, like the silences Wittgenstein was so coy about. But I don't know because I wrote everything down. Have I ever even thought of anything I didn't write down? Plato had *agrapha dogmata,* they were magnificent, probably, like his idea of the indefinite dyad, *aoristos dyas,* that's the next item in my index, it may be a magnificent idea but no one knows for sure because he didn't write it down, so I wrote down all my ideas, they are *grapta agrapha dogmata.* Maybe if I hadn't written everything down I could have produced a short book and I might have lived a happier life, except that I always would have wondered if I could have written a long book. Next in alphabetical order is *aion,* it's a word that means both eternity and a lifespan, implying that your one life is an eternity. There is a deep truth in that, isn't there? Our one life is all we experience, so it is actually our only experience of eternity, and conversely, if you are religious, then the eternity of the world is God's lifetime. When I read the word *aion* and think of my notebooks, they are like an eternity, almost anyway, *aion,* it's a tremendous word, isn't it? And by the way this is where *albumen* would go, but I have no intention of adding an entry for albumen, and then comes *alloiosis,* meaning change, but within a single thing, like a person who goes through a shattering experience, so that she is and also is not the same person, that is exactly what's happened to me. I am the product of an *alloiosis,* I am *alloioumene.* Once I was little Anni, running about like an idiot; then Annabelle to my mother, very beautiful and promising; later Professor Glur to my malicious colleagues. Then I became odd. I shriveled behind my desk like Marianne Fritz. Part of me went necrotic and putrefied. Part froze, part petrified. I am still not sure about those metaphors. But then the blood returned. Somehow I am here, talking to you. That is *alloiosis.* Then comes *ambagios,* a modern word, it means full of digressions. I will not comment on it because you would make fun of me. Then comes *anaimatos,* it means bloodless, down without blood, like a spirit, like something nonhuman. Further on is *ananke,* then *anekleiptos,* it means endless or incessant, and I won't comment on that one either, but you notice how many of the words in my index actually describe me, I wonder what that means. Next is *anaplerosis,* that is the condition of filling up, it's a fear of gaps and holes, a fear of air, really, it's a compulsion to make things solid. People used to fill up wounds with animal fat, because they thought that would help make more human fat. I have filled 20,000 pages with words, maybe my writing is like animal fat stuffed into an enormous wound. My thinking is *anaplerotic,* the notebooks are *anaplerotic,* my index is *anaplerotic,* my Flood Theory is *anaplerotic.* I cannot understand *plerotic* people, silent empty people.

What about people who aren't allowed to talk?

Actually there is no opposite to *anaplerotic,* because *plerotic* means the same thing. Sorry. Then comes *anavasthitata,* I will get to it in a moment, then *animula,* then *anirvachaniyata,* I will get to it in a moment, and *anomoiotes,* that is Aristotle's word for dissimilarity, because he wanted to explain how two animals could be in the same genus but still be so different. It's the same with me, I am like other people, I think, but *alla kai anomoiotes hyparkhei en emoi,* there is dissimilarity in me, in my own mind. That concept is very important to me, because sometimes I am strongly dissimilar to myself. And *anomoioteta* is so much better than "I is another," everyone quotes that, it's too easy. Then *aperkhomenos,* it means "the one who has wandered off," like Bellerophon, like you, you are wandering around in your life, you have no idea where you are going, you're *planomenos*—

What?

And then *apoptosis,* that is the Greek word for when a petal separates from a flower, or a leaf detaches from a tree, or a child grows up and leaves the home. In English that is called *abscission,* but that sounds like scissoring. *Apoptosis* is a wonderful word, it sounds like an obscure disease, but it just means falling away, when one thing just falls away from another. It is silent and painless. I think you should like that word, Samuel, Catherine said you would.

Why?

Then there is *astathmeta,* it is one of the greatest ideas of ancient Greece, it means the world is unstable, unbalanced, and unmeasurable, those are magnificent qualities, I aspire to all of them. *Astathmeta* was Pyrrho's idea, he was the most radical skeptic, he got the idea from Makkhali Gosala in India, he was the most radical Ajivika, that was the most radical alternative to Buddhism in the sixth century BC. Gosala spoke Magadhi Prakrit, it was like Sanskrit, and there are spectacular Sanskrit words in my index that start with the letter *a,* like *adharma,* it means chaos, disorder, delusion, and amoral behavior, a very likable word, *anavasthitata,* it means wobbly or unsteady, *anirvachaniyata,* it means indescribable or indefinable, *atman,* I can't begin to explain that to you now, *avidya,* that is a life spent in ignorance and illusion, like everyone's, *avyavasthitata,* it means indefinite or indeterminate, they are all like *astathmeta.* Pyrrho could have been inspired by any of those ideas, but sadly, no one knows, because he didn't write anything down, and neither did Gosala. Luckily when Pyrrho got back to Greece he told his student Timon, and Timon wrote the word down, but his book is lost, but luckily it was read by Aristocles, he was another philosopher, and he wrote it down, but his book is lost, but luckily it was read by Eusebius, he was another philosopher, he wrote it down, and we haven't lost his book yet. Richard Bett says Pyrrho meant things themselves have no fixed character, they cannot be distinguished one from the other, nothing is different in nature from anything else, that's what Casey Perin says about what Bett says, and it is a wonderful, depressing, and confusing idea. So Perin says Bett says—

Glur says.

Yes! Yes! Thank you for listening. Glur says Perin says Bett says Eusebius says Aristocles says Timon says Pyrrho says Gosala says the world is *astathmetos,* it's unstable, unbalanced, unmeasurable. Because things are confused, they overlap, they leak into each other, until there's nothing you can say with certainty about anything. Then there is *atopos,* that is when you have no place anymore, you don't belong in society, your life no longer makes sense. I have been *atopic* since 2002, when I lost my last job. Socrates was *atopic* when he sat in his little prison and drank poison, because at that moment he did not belong anywhere, and by chance the same word also means you are hypersensitive to infection, that you are allergic to many things, so you can't stay healthy, the world keeps infecting you. I could go on, but I have a feeling you don't want me to. I have more rare words than anyone, more than the great philosophers, Albertus Magnus, Duns Scotus, Consentius, Panini and Patanjali, my words are rarer than Barthes's, I have more words than Xunzi, Aquinas, Bhartrhari, or Nagarjuna. Their vocabularies are simple by comparison. My index is a beautiful poem, an *allgemeine brouillon,* a *livre inaccessible, irréalisable,* it's a *livre absolu dans l'absence de livre,* an absolute book in the absence of a book, it is the only beautiful thing I have written, and yet it is useless, because it failed to show me what I have done. Like any index, it is nothing but the dust of thought. Perhaps you will be able to make use of it, or you can just look through it. For me it is like a song. Or a prayer in 3,000 words. Oh goddess (1) Aaptos, (2) Abebaios, (3) Aberrans, (4) Aboethetos, (5) Abscission, (6) Achly, (7) Ad augusta per angusta, (8) Aegri somnia, (9) Aeidia, (10) Aethes, (15) Agennetos, (16) Agrapha dogmata, s.v. Grapha agrapha dogmata—

No, Anneliese.

Wait, it's fun. (17) Aoristos dyas, (18) Aion, (25) Alloiosis, (26) Ambagios, (27) Anaimaros, (40) Ananke, (41) Anakleiptos, (42) Anaplerosis, (43) Animula, (44) Anirvachaniyata, (45) Anomoiotes, (48) Aperkhomenos, (49) Apoptosis, (50) Astathmeta—

It's not fun, stop.

Reading my index I have the feeling I have made a long prayer or poem out of my work, and perhaps that is the best I can hope for. The *Black Notebooks* have all the matter, the substance, of my work, but they cannot be read. The *Gray Notebooks* are my life's work, my *aion,* but I am frightened that they may not make sense. At least the index has the flavor of my work. But for me it was useless, I needed a way to look over the whole work, to see it all at once, not to think of it as a calendar of poisoned years. So then I had another idea. I resolved to make an outline of the *Gray Notebooks,* a synopsis like Burton's. I worked hard on that, too, and as I told you my hierarchical outline is 100 pages long, with sub-sub-sub-sub-sub-headings and multiple levels of brackets. I read other stupendous outlines, too, Mercator's *Chronologia,* Temporarius's *Chronologicarum,* Gonik's *Reduction,* Neander's *Synopsis,* but I don't have time to tell you about them. I began with capitalized Roman numerals, I, II, III, IV, V, VI, VII, for the partitions of my work, body, career, mind, family, memory, language, and the one I haven't told you about, *psuche,* you will discover that last one very soon. The seven partitions are helpfully arranged, just for you, Samuel, so they are in the same order as I described them. Then I divided the partitions into A, B, C, and so on, except for category III, mind, because I divided that into A through M for my thirteen kinds of unreason. Then I kept going, I wanted to arrange all my ideas. I divided the subdivisions A, B, C, and so on, into (i), (ii), (iii), and so on, and those into (a), (b), (c), and so on, and that is as far as Burton goes, but I went further, my hundred-page outline divides the (a)s, (b)s, and (c) s, into Greek letters, Α, Β, Ξ, that's alpha beta gamma, and so on, and then lowercase, α, β, ξ, alpha beta gamma, and so on, blah blah blah, and then Cyrillic capitals, А, Б, Ц, that's ah beh veh, Cyrillic lowercase, а, б, ц, ah beh veh, blah blah blah, and then I kind of lost track, I used Armenian, that's ah beh geh—

Blah blah blah.

Ok, fine. Also Coptic, Syriac, Georgian, that's ani bani gani, and Glagolitic, that's az buky vede, I like them because those letters have fascinating shapes. I even used Grosseteste's symbols, you wouldn't know about them, they're not in any language. It is a beautiful *anomoiotic* outline, even though it is ruined. I never got confused about what was a subheading of what—I have no idea how Burton could let that happen, he obviously had no power of concentration—but I had other difficulties. My outline was lopsided. Partition IV, for mind, has thirteen subheadings, A, B, C, D, E, F, G, H, I, J, K, L, M, for the thirteen kinds of irrationality, and the second one, B, is the Disassembly Theory, and that is divided into four parts, (i), (ii), (iii), (iv), body, career, mind, family, and those duplicate the main partitions I, II, III, and IV, they are exact copies, including all the subheadings of those main headings, and the third part IIIB(iii) also includes all the other twelve kinds of irrationality, that is, it includes IIIA, IIIB, IIIC, blah blah blah, and it is again an exact duplicate, including all the subsubheadings of that subheading, etcetera, blah blah blah. If I were a mathematician I could probably disentangle it, or at least I could figure out how to notate it, but the headings kept swallowing one another, the entire hierarchical outline turned into an example of the Engastration Theory, which is only subheading IIIC, the whole thing kept unhinging its enormous worm six jaw and swallowing itself, and it happened again and again, so I had to stop. The outline is a 100-page knot, it is beautiful but I cannot disentangle it. I was lost, like Burton, like Wittgenstein. Still, it is beautiful, I think, and just for you I composed a special twenty-page summary of the hundred-page outline, and an even more condensed two-page summary, and even a one-page summary. Those are okay, they don't have any problems because they are so simple. Perhaps you can begin there. I got the idea from the Brethren of Purity, because they ended their encyclopedia with a Comprehensive Letter and a Condensed Comprehensive Letter. I was also inspired by Kim Veltman, he was a scholar who wrote a book on alphabets, it has 300,000 citations in it, so he wrote a one-page introduction, then a ten-page introduction, then a short book 400 pages long, then a full book, 1,809 pages, and then an enormous electronic version, it is all unreadable, only a few of the links work, no one will ever read it, it's his life's work and it's ruined except for the one-page introduction and a couple of passages from the ten-page introduction. I was entranced when I discovered that. Reading Veltman's one-page introduction is like standing at the entrance to an enormous palace. The *Türhüter,* the gatekeeper, throws open the great lion-studded door, revealing a griffin-headed door. A second *Türhüter* stands in front of the griffin-headed door. He opens it, revealing a pillared courtyard, guarded by rows and ranks of further *Türhüter.* In the distance there are more doors, all open, waiting just for me. I stand there, on page one, and then I just walk away. When I gave up on my index and the hundred-page outline, I had no choice. There was nothing else to do but continue writing, up to the very last page of the 66th volume of the *Gray Notebooks.* Today I am only 93 pages from the end. It is true, as Bernard-Louis Speckstein once said, day is pushed out by day, and each new moon hastens to its death, *Truditur dies die, novaeque pergunt interire lunae,* although I think the actual line is *extruditur dies die, quaeque properat nova interire luna,* or maybe it's *quisque dies priorem extrudit, quaeque nova luna designat viam leti,* that would be, Each day pushes out the one before it, each new moon marks the path to my death, or no wait, it's *quoque mense pergit interire luna,* Each month the moon rushes to its own death. Whatever it is, I feel it, and not just once a month. Everyone knows, everyone wishes to forget, that every year we pass the day we will die. What is that line from the poem, *Quoque anno nescius praeterivi diem. Cum ignes postremi me valere iubeant, et lux viatrix impigra ad stellam remotam proficiat,* Every year without knowing it I have passed the day when the last fires will wave to me, and the light will set out, tireless traveler, to a distant star. Every year I pass the anniversary of my death, *praetereo, ut soleo, diem anniversarium mortis meae.* Anyway *praecipua mea veniet nox,* my special night is waiting, *nescio tantum quando,* I just don't know exactly when. Actually for me it is even worse, because I do know when I will die. My life will be over the moment I finish writing. After that there will only be the empty room and the bay window, which looks out on that preposterous decorative well with its spigot fed by a plastic tube that runs under the kitchen sink. My life will be over the moment I have nothing left to do but look at that well. Or the moment I put the 66 *Gray Notebooks,* the 4 blank notebooks, 41 *Black Notebooks,* 12 red index notebooks, and 1 hierarchical table of contents notebook in their wooden crates so I can ship them to you. Or maybe my life will be over the instant I affix a postal label to the last crate, stand back and see the empty bookshelves and the room crowded with crates, each one with your address. Or when the crates are taken out to the delivery truck, and my study is empty, and Paul is standing in the hallway calling me in for dinner. I think that is when I will know my life is over.[30]

I'm sorry, I said, I'm sorry that I can't read them. I don't have the time. I wouldn't understand them anyway.

And now, she said, I come to the last part of your introduction, regarding your reading schedule. I have calculated everything. I know how much time you spend at work, thanks to your incomparably rude assistant Mrs. Hirondel. As I said, I have a precise plan laid out for you. If you take delivery of the material this summer, as I expect, you can spend the autumn altering and arranging your schedule so you are ready to read on New Year's Day. You'll have to cancel your out of town trips, like the one that brought you here. You will no longer have to inspect zoos, although you seem to be very poor at it anyway, I can't imagine you'll keep that job much longer. So you will have no more need for suitcases. If there are major issues with the water supply in your pathetic little town, then you will have to let Catherine do the work. I have looked at the historical records for Guelph, Ontario, and there have only been three disruptions in the city water supply since the current intake plant was put in place in 1971. Mrs. Hirondel says you usually come to work at 8:30 and leave at 4:00. I deduce from your somewhat phlegmatic character that you waste a fair amount of the day, even though I cannot really understand what exactly you spend your time doing. You can tell me if I am wrong about this, but I believe you could finish your work, whatever it is, by 2:00 in the afternoon on an average day. If you do that, you could easily attend to household chores and errands by 4 o'clock, prepare your evening meal and be done by 5 o'clock, and then you could read my book steadily until 10 o'clock each evening, that is 5 hours of reading. Then you could have one of your appalling Canadian chocolates and go to bed. You would be in bed by 11:00, which means you could have a full 8 hours of sleep, which an adult of your age actually does not need. On weekends you will be able to remain home and read for 8 hours each day.[31]

I just don't want to. I'm really sorry. And how did you know about the zoo?

This may seem strict but it is commensurate with your sedentary and antisocial lifestyle, which your colleagues eagerly informed me about. You seem to have a severely limited circle of friends. I do not know what you do at home. Judging by your subscriptions, which I obtained easily using an online information service, you watch a lot of television and movies. It will not be a big loss for you to give them up. I recommend simply canceling your subscriptions. I am sorry. But after a month or two you won't miss television. No one really likes television, it is only a way to make clocks run faster. If you can keep to this schedule, you will read approximately 40 hours per week, which is not difficult, it is less than the time I spend in my study writing the notebooks that you will be reading. If I multiply 40 hours per week by the number of weeks in the year, I find that you will be able to spend 2,000 hours over the next calendar year reading my work. Now the 66 *Gray Notebooks* are 19,800 pages. You don't need to read the 41 large *Black Notebooks* in order, but you will be making constant reference to them, so it is best to include them in the calculation. They are shorter, 150 pages each, so they only contribute another 6,150 pages. The outlines are 123 pages in total, and the index is another 3,000. You should definitely read the index, I think you will enjoy it. That is 29,073 pages of material, to be read in one year. If a year of reading is approximately 2,000 hours, that means you need to read 14 pages an hour.

I really can't do that, Anneliese.

There is an expression, *cave feminam unius libri*, beware the woman with one book, maybe I should have told you that one earlier, but it is too late now. I estimate each page in the *Gray Notebooks* is about 300 words. That means you only need to read 70 words a minute, which is significantly slower than the average reading speed of 225 words a minute. I have also estimated that I have written 6,500,000 words. That is a very gross estimate. After all, some of the *Gray Notebooks* are handwritten, most are typed, but some are handwritten, and some years I wrote very slowly in a tiny cramped script, and other years I was wildly flamboyant and I enjoyed producing decorative flourishes, I curled the crosses of my t's, I looped and interlaced my letters,

I prolonged the tails of y's into the margins, I drew knots and hearts in place of dots, but then I got serious and stopped doing those things, and my handwriting became less beautiful. Some pages may be difficult to read. But assuming there are about 6,500,000 words, then you need to read 3,250 words per hour or 55 words per minute for 8 hours a day Monday through Friday, or a little over 5 hours per day if you decide to read every single day, which is of course preferable, because everything will be fresh in your mind and you won't be under the illusion that there is anything worth doing in your life other than reading the notebooks.

I can't, Anneliese. Please don't ask me to.

In order to finish in a calendar year, Samuel, you will also have to make sure you suffer no major medical problems beyond the usual week of sick leave. You may wish to have a comprehensive physical exam. According to my information service you have not had one in years. I can provide you with the name and address of your previous doctor, in case you have forgotten. Also your wife and children need to avoid major accidents or illnesses, and everyone in your family needs to avoid dying, because it will take time for you to go to their funerals and you might become sad and stop reading. As I said, the average reading speed is 225 words per minute, but assuming you are in the top 5% of readers, you read ordinary text at 500 words per minute with an 85% comprehension rate. You should probably have yourself tested for that too. I took a test, and I read 500 words per minute with 35% comprehension. But actually, the test was horribly biased. It was for Swiss secretaries, imagine, and it was full of supposedly hidden advertisements for the Basel Secretarial School, questions like, "What is the best way for a modern German secretary to improve her reading? (1) Read more, (2) Go to the movies, or (3) Enroll in the Basel Secretarial School," or, here's another one, "Why was Guenther so angry at Erna? (1) Because he had been drinking, (2) Because Erna did not use company letterhead, (3) Because Erna did not use the Rapitype System, taught at the Basel Secretarial School, so her work was full of errors," well, of course such a test is radically unreliable. I have the firm belief that I comprehend more than 35% of what I read. In fact I am at least 90% positive that I comprehend 100% of what I read, because I understand why I do not need to understand the other 65%.

I went to their offices to ask them what they thought comprehension was. "Look," I said to the woman at the reception desk, "I comprehend that you want me to enroll in the Basel Secretarial School, I have no problem understanding that, but do you realize what real comprehension is? Of course you don't. It is the logical grasp of arguments, assumptions, and motivations, it is the analytic and ethical integration of ideas, and by those standards no one at the Basel Secretarial School comprehends anything. In fact, I would say," I told the woman at the reception desk, "your actual comprehension of what you spend your lives doing hovers near 0%, in fact your idiotic reading comprehension tests are actually measurements of just how little secretaries need to understand: the higher the grade on your test, the less of the world you actually comprehend. Your best graduates, like that plastic woman sitting over there pretending she doesn't hear us, a person like her comprehends nothing, she is perfectly happy in her lack of comprehension, and in fact she is probably proud, because she has scored very high on the Basel Secretarial School reading comprehension test, she probably reads 2,000 words per minute and comprehends 98% of what she reads, that makes her swell with pride, she thinks she understands everything, whereas actually such a result certifies she is perfect for a life in which she understands nothing, absolutely nothing," that is what I told the woman at the reception desk of the Basel Secretarial School. Actually, Samuel, I am content with my official 35% comprehension score, because I do not want to understand the numbed mind of the successful graduates of the Basel Secretarial School, even though they were very nice, and when I finished speaking they offered me a glass of water and asked if I would like to sit down and if I knew where I lived. Also I am content to read slowly, because I like to remain alert to language and meaning, that way I know I am actually thinking. Now back to you. I will wait patiently for your judgment. If you would like, I will only call every other day during your year of reading. But Samuel, I have to tell you, I could not bear to hear that the work doesn't make sense, or that you find it unreadable, the product of a life of hallucinations and indulgent fantasies, the work of a person who locked herself in her study and talked to herself for twenty years, that you think it is the effluvia of a leaking imagination, the aimless wanderings of someone long ago lost to science and sense, a grandiose provocation that turns out to have no substance, or if you conclude it's the inevitable result of decades of isolation, the self-aggrandizing posturing of a person too cowardly to try out her ideas in the court of public opinion, or if you decide that the hundreds of volumes seem rich with promise but turn out to be the empty warrens of a rabbit, that they are the pitiful remains of forty years of mental masturbation, the spewings of a comet, the greasy stain left by a snail, the bulging tumors of a cancerous growth, the uninteresting meanderings of a sociopath who has been tended by her doting brother, who cooks her endless *oeufs en cocotte,* not to mention Schoggiweggli, and listens to her ranting every day, and as a reward spends long evenings alone with his demented uncle while his sister scribbles away in her study, if you think any of those things do not tell me, I really could not hear things like that.

Anneliese, I really can't read the notebooks!

Any of those verdicts would crumple me, Samuel, because I would see then with excruciating clarity that I should have kept my mouth shut, I should have recognized the notebooks for what they are, the excrement of a mind that stopped working normally years ago, I should have sent the crates to Hagenaustrasse 70, that is the address of the *Kehrrichtverwertungsanlage,* the incinerator, that would have been honest, brave, and noble, but obviously I am none of those things. So I could not bear to hear your criticism. For many years I have imagined criticism of all sorts, but actually hearing it would kill me, and at the same time no praise could ever be enough, so if you think the *Gray Notebooks* have value, if they do make sense, if they actually add up to a single enormous book, if they cohere, if they build slowly from simmering preambles to a crescendo of unbearable force and clarity, if they dawn over your mind like the flash of an enormous explosion in the seconds before the sound arrives, if you feel them swelling in your thoughts like an impossible wave cresting over the horizon, then nothing you say could ever be enough, I could never hear enough praise, I wouldn't be content if you said the *Gray Notebooks* are astonishing, that words fail you, that you feel lucky to have been entrusted with them, that they finally gave your life meaning, that you realize I have actually, against all odds, done something almost no one manages, that I have actually made something of my life, turned my life into something, that you lost weight reading because you forgot to eat, that you were fired from your job because you wouldn't stop reading, that the *Gray Notebooks* are a masterpiece, that they will be read, applauded, studied, and emulated, that you will dedicate your life to promoting them, that you will not rest until they have received all the major prizes, that you will publish extracts of them with ecstatic introductions by famous people, that you will found an institute to house them, edit a series of books, convene a series of conferences, fund an annual International Glur Prize, that you expect the *Gray Notebooks* will inspire a generation of readers, that at first they will puzzle people, but that, like all genuinely innovative achievements, the public will eventually understand and the *Gray Notebooks* will be loved the world around, published in color facsimile, in scholarly editions, in different languages, as comics, as childrens' books, that my life will be made into a movie, that in a hundred years my apartment will be a museum and even your apartment will be a tourist destination, with a plaque saying This is the Place Where Meek Samuel Emmer First Read the Immortal Work of Doktor Anneliese Buchonius Glur, come see the chair where he sat when he read the famous closing words of the final page of the final volume of the *Gray Notebooks,* so moving and yet so real, come see a dramatic reenactment of Samuel Emmer's revelation, the moment he read those last words, closed the final volume, and spoke his famous lines, *None of us will ever write or think like Anneliese Glur, thank God,* if when you finish your year of reading you want to tell me any of these things, then don't, because no praise could ever be enough, I will always be thirsty for more, I will always want more. All I ask is that you take one year out of your aimless life and dedicate yourself with full concentration to my work, without family, friends, entertainment, or breaks.

She stood up and buttoned her coat.

No, no, I said, shaking my head.

Really Samuel, she replied, I am not an idiot. I don't actually think you will read my work. I know my work is lost, it is written into the fireplace, *ich habe es in den Kamin geschrieben.* But consider my position. I am literally disintegrating. My life's work is holding me together, it is like the static electricity that glues dust and hair onto a balloon. As soon as I finish writing, the charge will dissipate. I will collapse. I need to know my work will go somewhere. You are somewhere. I only ask you to keep the crates of notebooks. Or you can give them to the library at your local university, or put them in storage. I don't think about things like that, they are too black. No writer, no one, can bear to think no one will see her work, no one will hear her voice, or read her words, or ever think about her again.

# 9

## IN A YEAR WE MAY ALL BE GONE

**THE FOLLOWING SATURDAY** I was back in Guelph. Anneliese called late at night.

Samuel, she said, I am sorry to bother you, I have only one thing to say. I won't keep you long. I am not quite finished giving you the sequential nested introductions to my work. There are things that need to be reviewed and a couple of minor errors to correct. I need to complete the exposition of my Thirteen Worm Theory. I think you imagine it is just a humorous theory, perhaps you suppose I mentioned it to break the ice, but I do not talk about worms to break ice, and I have not yet defined worm thirteen, you should be especially interested in that, because I invented it just to describe you. When you hear it, you will shake your head, because it is truly disgusting, but you will understand why you are destined to consume the products of my compromised metabolism. In addition I have not yet defined the last and most important dimension of my work, for that I use the Greek word *psuche*. It is at the center of everything I have written and thought. But I'm sorry, I can't do any of that now. Something very serious has happened. Samuel, Catherine emailed me and asked if I could please call her in private, where no one could hear. Not from your apartment, she said. That was annoying, because it was hard to arrange, and there is a six-hour time difference, but finally we made an arrangement and I called her from a café outside the library. She said she was very worried about Paul, and I said, "Really, why?"

and she said, "Well, I don't know how to put this, but don't you know?" And I said, "Of course not, Catherine, you are the one who wanted me to call you, it is not the other way around, I did not call you, I mean I did call you, but I called because you asked me to, so naturally I have no message, you are the one with the message, please go ahead and tell me the news, and don't ask me if I know because of course I don't know." She said, "Anneliese, your brother is not well." She told me that she and Paul had been talking a lot, you know they have been friends since that year in England, I don't know why, I mean I don't understand why Paul likes Catherine, I don't know what they have in common, I cannot understand what they could possibly talk about, except me of course, but Catherine hates me, because she stole my work and she feels guilty, but then again maybe that is why she likes to talk to Paul about me, Paul is wonderful, caring, patient, and thoughtful, as you know, so maybe he helps Catherine feel better about the cowardly decisions she made, that is probably what they talk about, and I suppose they both admire me, that is always possible, and that would give them plenty to talk about, but actually maybe they just complain about me. I hope not. And anyway what could they complain about? I have a simple diet and I mainly keep to myself. Once I asked Paul what he talks to Catherine about, and he said, "Trivial things, nothing," that is what he said, and I knew right away he meant profound and important matters, and I thought that could only mean my work, I thought they must talk about my work, but how could they, because Paul doesn't understand my work, and neither does Catherine, but Catherine knows how profound and important my work is, mainly because she thinks it is hers, so maybe they do talk about my work, I don't know, I hope so, but anyway so Catherine said they were just talking when she realized Paul had something to say to her, and she asked him directly, she said, "Paul, is there something you need to tell me?" And that is when Paul told Catherine he was not doing well. Those are Catherine's words, Samuel, she said Paul told her he was not doing well. I said, "What do you mean? What is wrong with him? Why didn't he tell me? I'm his sister, and I haven't heard anything." But Catherine said, "You need to ask him, Anneliese, it's not my place to tell you." As you can imagine I was beside myself. Catherine said, "Don't shoot the messenger," and I said, "I will shoot you if you don't tell me," and she said, "I just did tell you," and I said, "You hardly said anything!" And she said, "It's not my place, you need to talk to Paul." So I hung up on her, because she is useless and I was angry with her for not telling me something that I should already have known. Imagine, she is seven thousand kilometers away, and she refuses to tell me something about my own brother, who was only two kilometers away, or three and a quarter kilometers by city tram, I have never understood why the trams have to follow the routes they do, they are absolutely infuriating. In order to go from the library to our house I have to go around Dreispitz, I have to be given a tour of Dreispitz, even when I am in a hurry, when I want to get home as fast as possible, anyway I went right home by the tram, three and a quarter kilometers, eight stops, including an especially long delay because of a traffic jam caused by a motorino that had gotten lodged underneath a lorry along with the driver's body. I kept yelling, "Take him out! Take him away! Let's go! Remove the body! Move the tram!" but the people around me on the tram were very engrossed in their newspapers. At last I made it back to our apartment, where I found Paul cleaning the recycling bins. He told me that our cousin Mila in Lausanne had lost her job in a stationery store. The store supplies the principal Hochschule for their district, and the cutbacks had decreased the number of local jobs, and therefore the number of students, and therefore the demand for paper, and so, domino-fashion, the recession and the banking scandals had affected our cousin, and therefore they had affected Paul and me as well, because we would have to help out our cousin, although it wasn't clear how. Paul was concerned, but he seemed healthy. He was sweating from scrubbing the plastics recycling bin. I just couldn't ask him. I went off into the kitchen, sat down and pretended to read the paper, and the next time Paul came into the room he went straight to the refrigerator and got out a bottle of beer and said something like, "I'm exhausted," and went to sit down on the couch next to Hans, where the TV was blaring something about the future of reality TV. So again I lost my chance, and, to tell you the truth, I still haven't asked him. The next day I had my checkup, where my breathtakingly incompetent twelve-year-old doctor announced for the third time that my collapsed lung has healed. "Congratulations, Doctor Glur," he said, "your lung is doing quite well." He always sounds surprised when something goes right with me, clearly any good outcome is the opposite of what he expects. Paul has been very concerned about my lung, because he knows I still feel pangs in the left side of my ribcage, and when I told the teenager who masquerades as my doctor that I still feel pangs in my side, he answered by reciting something from the picture book he had studied at his play-pretend medical school. He said, "Wounds always leave their traces on the body, the body is a miraculous healing agent but it always keeps a memory of injuries it has suffered," and I said, "What the hell does that mean?" and he said, "It's better not to yell," and I said, "I know you are only a child, and you need everything to be comforting and simple, but I was a professor at the university, my brain actually works, so I noticed that you recited a line from a book, and I can only conclude that you are hiding the truth from me because you think I am tender or perhaps addled, but I can assure you I am neither tender nor addled, well, maybe I am addled, but if I am, then I am addled in a far more complex and frightening way than you could ever imagine with your soft pink brain, which has hardly even been used, so I want to know right now what is happening with my lung," and he said, "Perhaps you could speak more quietly?" so I whispered, "You mean?" and he said, "Thank you," and I said, "You mean my lung could puncture again?" and he said, "Perhaps you might enjoy a course of hydrotherapy," and I said, "Where fat old people in purple speedos stand in perfumed swimming pools and flap their arms like seals?" and he repeated, "Hydrotherapy," and I said, "People will see the gruesome scabs from my rash," and he said, "Perhaps you could wear one of those nice old one-piece swimsuits," and I said, "That's it? Hydrotherapy?" and he said, "Let's be calm, because we don't want you to re-puncture your lung and cough blood all over me, and gasp for breath and break things, because then we will have to bring you to Dr. Schmeidel's operatory, and I don't want to, because he smokes in there when there are no patients." That was when I realized my lung is not at all healed, and since then Paul and I have been talking about my health, and Hans's health—he is getting worse, by the way, last week he screamed for a full minute, just screaming with his mouth wide open, bellowing really, and then all of a sudden he was quiet. We even worry about Luzia, she is very anxious about law school, it turns out it actually involves work, she says she can't sleep or eat properly. So we talk about everyone's health, but when I ask about Paul, he just says, "I'm fine," and changes the subject. He is focused on taking care of us, so I can't ask him, but now I have to, because it has been a week, and I am sure Catherine has had another one of her chats with him, I am afraid he is going to ask me why I haven't said anything about his illness, even though Catherine said she had called me and told me about it. It's not as if I haven't been trying to find out what is wrong with him. The day I called Catherine, I waited until Paul was busy in the kitchen and I searched the little table where he keeps the bills and letters. Nothing. I expected to find unusual bottles in the drawer where he keeps his medicines, but there was nothing except his sets of homeopathic cures, which he has always had. The next day, when he went out with Hans, I looked at his phone, but there was nothing except lots of messages to someone called Dunkelsport, at first I thought, He is seeing someone! But then I read the messages, and Dunkelsport is a laser tag company where he goes with Luzia. That was fascinating, so I went there to see for myself. It is the single most idiotic sport I have ever experienced, and it may very well be the end of civilized culture. Imagine, I had to put on a purple and yellow Space Crash Helmet, I was given a plastic gun and told to kill children. I shot the man who handed me the gun. I said, "You're a teenager, right? So die!" The young man asked me to please return the Laserator Space Gun and the Space Crash Helmet. I said, "Here are your pitiful toys," and I left. It occurred to me Paul might be depressed. He works in a law office, after all. Is getting up before dawn a sign of depression? He does that. But is sleeping late a sign of depression? He does that too. He eats odd things, like three melons in a day, or one day nothing but *Landjäger* sausages, or *Weisswürste* and Unser Bier, but what does that mean? He seems healthy. Sometimes he sweats a lot, his underarms especially. He doesn't exercise, but he never did. I listened when he called our cousin in Lausanne, but it was all about her problems. Paul never calls Catherine when I am around. Clearly, he is hiding something. Clearly, it is serious. Unless of course Catherine has completely the wrong idea, but when that occurred to me I called her again, from the library café, late in the evening, which again caused me some trouble because I had to make up an excuse, I told Paul I was going bowling with Morschmulmig, that was a ridiculous excuse, I would never go bowling with Morschmulmig, bowling is another absurd sport, if people hate bowling pins so much why don't they go and kick them over, and besides, Morschmulmig is a number seven, eight, and ten worm, I can't think of anything worse than bowling with Morschmulmig, nothing in the entire world could be worse than bowling with Morschmulmig, his face looks like a bowling ball, I would like to stick my fingers in his two little eyes and his stupid round mouth and roll him down at the pins. You know, Samuel, the world is filled with tragic things, people you love suddenly become ill, they might even die, but they don't tell you they are sick, they just keep caring for everyone around them and then they die, and then there you are, sitting in your study surrounded by the book you have been writing for so many years, and you are in despair, you can no longer finish it, you no longer want to write or even eat, that could happen at any moment, at any second, it could happen tomorrow, or even right now while I am talking to you, that is how my life is, but even that is not as bad as bowling with Morschmulmig, that would be a torture beyond human endurance, I also hate the shoes they make you wear, I do not want to prance around in those shoes and hold the greasy ball like an enormous polished fossil testicle and walk in mincing steps up to the red line and hurl the ball at plastic pins, and also Morschmulmig would win, and when he is happy he has a wretched laugh, it sounds like when you hold a mouse in your hand and squeeze it over and over and it squeaks and burps and gasps, if I wake up tomorrow morning and Paul is dead and Hans is in the living room screaming at the television because he has turned it off and forgotten how to turn it on, and Luzia is in a bar drinking because she is too anxious to go to law school, and I am all alone in the world, and I go into my study and shut the door, and I see all my notebooks and know I will never finish the work, because I cannot concentrate, I cannot write, my entire life is wasted and I have no one left, if that happens I will say to myself, Anneliese, at least you are not bowling with Morschmulmig, so anyway when I got Catherine on the phone she was cold, she said, "Anneliese, ask him, just ask him," and I said, "You don't understand, he doesn't want me to know, it's impossible to ask him," and there was a long silence, and then Catherine said, "Do what you want." After that she wouldn't talk.

She pretended she was busy, so after forty-five minutes I hung up. Then I really started spying. I called our physician to see if Paul had made any appointments, but there were none. Paul is a very clever person. He must have another physician. If I had money I would hire someone to follow him. I can't follow him myself, after all, because I work all day long, and besides, I am not exactly an inconspicuous person. I look at him and think, You are breaking my heart, something is wrong and you have to tell me, but when I ask, when I say, "How about you? Are you doing okay?" he just says, "Lysi, dear, don't worry about me! Let's worry about you." I just do not see what to do, I just do not see, so I do nothing. I don't change my routine by one step, I go to my study just when I always do. I joke with him, I rehearse my Thirteen Worm Theory, I think he has always liked that, we sit and watch TV next to Hans. Nothing seems different. If you watched us on a surveillance camera you wouldn't see anything out of the ordinary, and yet everything is absolutely ruined. Imagine, even Hans would look okay on a surveillance camera. He would appear lazy and content except when he screams. The camera would follow him on his walks. Like a typical elderly bourgeois who lives between his television and the boundary of his neighborhood. Paul would look entirely normal, too, in every aspect of him. He shops, he cooks, he sits with Hans, he goes off without telling me to Dunkelsport with Luzia to dress as a space cowboy and shoot children. All ordinary bourgeois things. His illness is off camera. I would look fine too, except the camera would catch me darting back and forth when Paul is not around—there I am checking his medicines, there I am checking his phone calls and emails while he's at work. Samuel, I need your help. You can ask Catherine, she will tell you what is wrong with him. Ask her, and then call me right away. Our family is not in a good condition. Paul may be seriously ill. Soon we will have to put Hans in a home. I know I am not well, I absolutely refuse to believe a child who claims he is a doctor. When I see myself in the mirror I think, How long can a mess like you keep going? I am ruined, I am a ruin. I am like one of those translucent deep sea animals that are brought to the surface. For a few minutes it swims in its tank in the bright sunlight, that is me, now, talking to you, I look exotic and maybe beautiful, but I am dying, because I can only live in the frigid dark, under immense pressure. Soon I will collapse. The last hundred pages of my work are all that is keeping me together. I am racing to the conclusion. I am writing the preface now. I will send everything to you the moment it is finished. I have ordered the crates, they are being built this week. It feels like we have very little time left. In a year, if you come to Basel and ring our doorbell, you may be told that no one under the name Glur lives at this address. In a year we may all be gone.[32]

# 10

## IN SLOW STEPS, TOWARD

**IT WAS TWO MORE WEEKS** before I talked to Catherine, and nearly a month had passed by the time I called Anneliese to tell her Paul was depressed, not dying, and that Catherine said he just wanted to find a way to talk to Anneliese about it.

Paul picked up the phone, and when I asked for Anneliese, he said, She has died.[33]

Two weeks ago, he said. I should have written you. It happened during the night. I found her body in the bathroom. I called 144, Sanitäts-Notruf, but she was dead. It is hard for me to comprehend this event. Luzia has been very good, she has been helping with the arrangements. I should have written you.

How did it happen? I asked. She was worried about her collapsed lung.

It wasn't the lung. The doctor said it was an aneurysm. It could have happened any time. She's buried now, in a cemetery in Roggwil. So it's over.

I'm so sorry, I said.

Samuel, the crates arrived. I had workers come and pack everything. The crates are in the front hall. A truck will come on Monday and take them. They will reach you in a couple of weeks.

I'm sorry, I can't read her notebooks.

She wanted you to have them.

She asked me to read them, but I'm not the right person. I can't publish them, I can't even comment on them.

I feel I knew one side of her, he said, like the face of the Moon that always looks at the Earth. I never saw the side that turns away. She spent years facing away, looking off into space. I don't know what she saw there. The notebooks were not ever for me. She said you should have them. She said she finished them for you.

I am really sorry, I said again. I am not the right person.

It is possible that she was a genius, Paul said. In many ways I think she was. I am glad I helped her write for all those years. But her life is over now. So it does not matter. Keep them or discard them. It's okay. Things are different now. The world has changed for me. The house is quiet, my mind is quiet.

I'm so sorry.

It is dry here now. Dry, perhaps you know what I mean by this. As if I am waiting, but I do not know what for.[34]

Is Luzia there?

She went to Lausanne to help out our cousin Mila. She comes home on weekends. You know she quit the law school. Please don't worry about us. For now I am here, with Hans.

We were both silent for a minute. Then Paul said, Anneliese was full of life. Now my life is different. I think you will understand when I say it is also a tremendous relief. I have relaxed.

And Hans?

I think he knows Anneliese is gone. Since she died he has more and more one fixed idea. He just wants to go look at the apartment where he lived with his first wife. Every day he wants to walk to the park and get lost in his dreams. I'd like to take him away, so he can think about something else. A change, something new to see. There's a house we can go to in Norway. But I can't leave now. I have my job, and this week I need to clean out Anneliese's study so we can rent the room.

Can I do anything?

Thank you, but we are okay. And thank you for accepting the notebooks.

I just can't—

Well I feel it is always good to follow the wishes of people who have died.[35]

The next day I wrote him a letter, telling him how important it had been for me to meet Anneliese, to spend time with a person who had done something so ambitious with her life, and also how good it had been to talk to him, even briefly. I ended by saying I'd be traveling again soon and I would like to visit him whenever it felt right.

When Anneliese's notebooks arrived it was already June. Someone from Package Receiving called and told me two large wooden crates had been placed in the lab. I had quit my job at that point, just as Anneliese had predicted, but I still had the keys. I went in on a Sunday to make sure no one would be around.

It took ten minutes of hard work with a pry bar to open one of the crates, cut through the packing, and see the first notebook, and then another hour to open the other and unwrap all 120 notebooks.

I cleared the lab equipment and supplies off the tables and set out the 41 black notebooks. They filled the back of the lab from one side to the other. They were surprisingly large volumes, the size of old-fashioned atlases, bound in black leather as she'd said. Most were battered from use. Some of the bindings had warped from humidity.

On the front tables I put the 66 gray notebooks, the 12 red index notebooks, and a single notebook labeled *Preface and Tables of Contents.* The gray notebooks were also large, like old encyclopedias, just as she had hoped. The index notebooks were ordinary looking, the kind that are sold in stationery stores.

The lab looked wonderful. I imagined it all as my own life's work: books I had never written or even thought to write, filled with the magnificent ideas that had never occurred to me, elaborated over years of work I never had the patience for. My little row of notebooks took up a foot or so on one of the particleboard shelves. I had spent years in this lab, weekends I could have been at home, long evenings counting and recording samples. Adela always knew I needed that time away, and it hadn't helped, and in the end we separated.

I put the notebook labeled *Preface and Tables of Contents* on a desk at the front of the room and craned a lamp over the large pages.

ψυχή

Psūkhḗ [36]

Anneliese Glur

Preface

My dear reader, the book you hold in your hands is volume 1 of the life work of Frau Doktor Professorin Ordinaria Anneliese Buchonius Glur. It is an unusual book. You will never again hold in your hands such a book. The title of this work is just one word: psūkhḗ. This word is pronounced PSOO-keh. Please do not mispronounce it. It is an ancient Greek word. Aristotle refused to define it, even though it is woven into his philosophy.

As J. L. Ackrill demonstrated in a meeting of the Aristotle Society on Tavistock Place, London, on a cold Monday in February 1923, Greek authors sometimes used the word psūkhḗ to mean "the breath of life," and other times "a living being," and still other times "a soul," "a person's life," "a person's mind," and even once, as William Glen Moncrieff pointed out, "a fish." (Rev. xvi.3.) Aristotle uses the word in several of these ways. Its different meanings circulate in his work, contradicting one another, and together they form the deepest layer of his theory of life, which became the Western theory of life, which became the science of biology. Psyche, the modern word, is a simplification of Aristotle's idea, inflated by Christianity into the immortal soul and trampled by Freud into a structure of personality. In all these ways ávyssos i psychí tou anthrópou, "the psyche of man is an abyss."

This book, Psūkhḗ, arranges the history of thought on the subject into a visible order, which may be understood as the prosody that compiles the knowledge about biological life from Aristotle onward, including facts, hypotheses and theories, questions and answers, into an expression of truth. This book is not an ordinary scientific treatise, but science made into a liberal art: it has the structure of Aristotelian deduction but is not contained by his logic.

For a German speaker the word psūkhḗ looks like P-suche, meaning Search for Psūkhḗ. This book digresses continuously out of itself, opening rooms full of matters of fact onto fields of narrative, and giving the fields, in return, the shape of rooms. In this book I sculpt the disordered, damaged, and imperfect life we all live into a form of order that is exactly as complex as itself.

My thoughts began as notes written on scraps of paper, thrown into the box of my mind. In the course of decades of work, those fragments have formed and reformed themselves, first into disaggregated and misaligned portions of theories, then into orderly lines of hypotheses, later into geometric arrays of ideas, and finally, by logical inversion, into the fundamentally artistic and even autopoietic form of this book. Psūkhḗ shows what it means simply by being: it is filled with claims, theories, and concepts, but in the end it just shows the world as it is. Psūkhḗ assembles arguments, one after another, chained together: at first they follow logically, but then they deviate. They become a complex chorus of tongues unparalleled, I believe, in scientific literature; they turn into inversions and even satires of Aristotelian logical sequences, and they do so in order to open the way to a conclusion that can only be reached by the risk, if not the actuality, of a collapse of sense: the risk that psūkhḗ, understood as life or mind, may only be the chaos of the nonrational and senseless. Like an enormous fiction, this book struggles with itself. Like Robert Burton's Anatomy of Melancholy, one of the greatest scientific treatises of its age, this book's structure shows that life is disordered but its irrationality and ruin can in fact be comprehended: not by ordinary science, but by science understood as art. The tangled world of this book, in its many deviations from reason, makes ψυχή comprehensible in the terms of thought. The design of this book submits chaos to the control of art and language and not just of science, and therefore it gives irrationality the form of wisdom. How does a man differ from a dog? I do not care. How does psūkhḗ, the living, create meaning? What is the ἄψυχος (ápsychos), the soulless, the meaningless? Those questions matter tremendously, and they have concerned me from the first tentative sentences I wrote in 1975 all the way to the last difficult pages of the final Gray Notebook, pages which I believe contain some of the hardest ideas that have ever been posed to science.

Dear reader, do not suppose that this is an ordinary book. The ideas
and theories I propose in this work are not what they appear, not simply
a revision of biology, but the basis of a new science of biological life.
The postulates are the grammatical rules of the language
I propose in this book. The language itself is
the book's meaning. It cannot be re-
duced to equations, or conden-
sed to a scientific essay.
Reading is the only
way to under-
stand.

⁂

At the bottom of the page she had written:

Anneliese Buchonius Glur
BASEL.
1975-

She began on the next page, under the title "First Two Tables of Contents."

My first table of contents is simple and short. I have divided the Gray Notebooks into seven sections, which I call partitions:

I. Memory
II. Career
III. Language
IV. Body
V. Psūkhḗ
VI. Mind
VII. Family

I start just as any conventional book does, with my childhood and education, what people call my "memories." My "career" was "supported" by the "community" of my "friends" and "colleagues," who were in reality various species of marine worms: annelids, tube worms, flatworms, roundworms, railroad worms, black worms, detritus worms, iceworms, threadworms, woodworms, glowworms, lugworms, lungworms, mudworms, mealworms, bloodworms, wattwurms, sludgeworms, potworms, heartworms, kidneyworms, cheeseworms and silkworms, penisworms and peanutworms, hairworms and eyelashworms and jawworms, bristleworms and bentworms and batterworms and butterworms and spaghettiworms and creamworms, that is, they were ordinary people. Ludwig Hohl called them pharmacists.

After "Memory" and "Career" the work of this book begins. The third partition, "Language," is about the principal concepts that guide the little boat of science, the ideas that steer it across the deep ocean. They pump out the bilge of unreason—the seawater, oil, detergents, solvents, rust, pitch, and garbage that accumulate in the hold of the little boat of science and promise ultimately to sink it. After that, the partition "Body" explains how poorly biology has accounted for the animals that swarm over the planet and infest our bodies. How little we know, how many things we know wrongly! Over 99% of all organisms are uncultivable: they live around us and inside us, and we only know them from fragments of their genetic material. "Body" surveys the wreckage of Linnaeus. All of this is well mannered and shows good scientific behavior. But then the book turns. Next is "Psūkhḗ," a long and, I admit, exhausting tour of the attempts I made, over many years, to express my growing certainty that concepts of psūkhḗ are crucial for understanding biological life, and ultimately, that unreason matters more than its supposed opposite. This partition is 3,300 pages long, and includes patient meditations on soul, eternity, and attendant concepts like despair. The next 2,700 pages, called "Mind," tell the story of what happens when these ideas prickle and burn in a person who has only herself for company. All this may seem unnecessary, but you will see it is both unavoidable and indispensable. And finally, in the book's last 6,600 pages titled "Family," you will discover the result.

That is the simplest table of contents for this book. From here it becomes more complex. My next table of contents is a two-page expansion of that simple listing. Here you will find some of the contents of the seven partitions. I have also indicated the volumes and page numbers in the Gray Notebooks where the material can be found.

## Two-Page Table of Contents

| Partition | Examples | Gray Notebooks | |
|---|---|---|---|
| | | Vol. | Page |
| | Introduction (this is for S.) | 1-4 | 1 |
| I Memory | My Formation | 5 | 1,200 |
| II Career | My so-called friends (marine worms, pharmacists) | 6 | 1,500 |
| III Language | What is life? Basic concepts of biology | 7 | 1,800 |
| | Logic, alogic, nonsense, deviant logic | 8-14 | 2,100 |
| | The laws of physics, etc., and the "laws" of biology | 15 | 4,200 |
| | After "science": geometric, literary, and philosophic texts | 16-17 | 4,500 |
| IV Body | What is a body if it is made of millions of other bodies? | 18-21 | 5,100 |
| | Metagenomics | 22 | 6,300 |
| V Psūkhḗ | Eternity, aion, time, lifetime | 23-31 | 6,600 |
| | Soul, spirit, faith, feeling, despair | 32-33 | 9,300 |
| | Psyche, psūkhḗ, ápsychos | 34 | 9,900 |

| | | | |
|---|---|---|---|
| VI<br>Mind | Perfect isolation, quiet, darkness, speaking to no one | 35-42 | 10,200 |
| | Forms of insanity, psychotikós, fugue states, syncopes | 43 | 12,600 |
| | Down the ladder of unreason in thirteen steps | 44-48 | 12,900 |
| VII<br>Family | Beginning of the madness: 1,200 pages up the Amazon | 49-52 | 14,400 |
| | An extended anagogical allegory of this entire book | 53-57 | 15,600 |
| | The romance of W.P. | 58-63 | 17,100 |
| | End of the madness: G. in agony, S. under threat | 64 | 18,900 |
| | How my mind is shutting down | 65-66 | 19,200 |
| | My present state | 67-70 | 19,800 |
| Index | | 71-82 | 21,000 |

There were her preoccupations, but the second half was hard to understand. Whatever those chapters were, they weren't science. I saw that the introduction was marked "this is for S." I went back to check, and the first four volumes were blank. Apparently I was supposed to write a 1,200 page introduction to her work.

The next page was another table of contents.

## Third Table of Contents

Now I present a twenty-page expansion of the two-page table of contents. Each Partition is divided into Sections and Subsections. This twenty-page table of contents resembles the one in Burton's Anatomy of Melancholy except his is shorter and mine has no errors. On this table of contents I also record the year I wrote each volume of the notebooks.


| PREFACE AND TABLES OF CONTENTS | | |
|---|---|---|
| **Date** | **Pages** | |
| 2016 | i | Preface |
| 2020 | ii | 1 page table of contents |
| 2020 | iii-iv | 2 page table of contents |
| 2020 | v-xxvii | 20 page table of contents (you are reading this now) |
| 2020 | xxviii-cxl | 100 page table of contents |

| THE GRAY NOTEBOOKS | | | |
|---|---|---|---|
| **Date** | **Vol.** | **Pages** | |
| | 1 to4 | 1 to 1,200 | Four-volume introduction (unwritten) |

| PARTITION I. MEMORY | | | | | |
|---|---|---|---|---|---|
| **Date** | **Vol.** | **Page** | **Section** | **Subsection** | **Subsubsection** |
| Oct. 1999 | 5 | 1,200 | A My Formation | i My appalling ancestors | a My ignorant grandfather Emil |
| | | | | | b My obstinate grandmother Clara |
| | | | | | c My feeble mother Marianne |
| | | | | | d My hopeless father Hermann |
| | | | | | e Genetic issues with my family line |
| Nov. 1999 | | 1,250 | | ii Birth to the age of seventeen | a The moment of conception |
| | | | | | b My accomplishments in infancy |
| | | | | | c My inadequacies in childhood |
| | | | | | d My embarrassments in adolescence |
| | | | | | e My indiscretion and its consequence |
| Dec. 1999 | | 1,300 | B Certain career problems | i The University of Basel | a The glorious first year teaching |
| | | | | | b The annoying second year |
| | | | | | c The scandal and the expulsion |
| | | | | | d The supposedly necessary lawsuit |
| | | | | ii Miscellaneous legal issues | a Why my colleagues need correcting |
| | | | | | b Why I broke into Früchtel's house |
| | | | | | c Why I should have won the case |

| | | | | | |
|---|---|---|---|---|---|
| | | | | iii Miscellaneous employment problems | a Why I worked in a commercial lab |
| | | | | | b Why I should not have been fired |
| | | | | | c My last collaborator (Schall) |
| | | 1,350 | D Reference data about my life | i People and places | a People I met, with personal data |
| | | | | | b Places I lived, with floor plans |
| | | | | ii Books and study habits | a Books I read, with reviews of each |
| | | | | | b My exemplary study habits |

I stopped reading and looked around the lab. Anneliese was as exhausting on the page as she had been in life. It wasn't a surprise to see she had written about her colleagues and her career, but for some reason she had also included her grandparents, and even the floor plans of places she had lived.

The next pages of the twenty-page table of contents were full of science. I skipped them. Midway through things changed. Under the partition "Mind" she had ideas about isolation.

| PARTITION VI. MIND | | | | | |
|---|---|---|---|---|---|
| **Date** | **Vol.** | **Page** | **Section** | **Subsection** | **Subsubsection** |
| 2007 | 35-42 | 10,200 | A<br>Perfect isolation, quiet, darkness, speaking to no one | i<br>How to ignore people | a Mutism |
| | | | | | b Staring |
| | | | | | c Echopraxia and echolalia |
| | | | | | d Verbigeration |
| | | | | | e Coughing |
| | | | | | f Spitting |
| | | 10,300 | | ii<br>How to keep people from interrupting | a Speak continuously and loudly |
| | | | | | b Do not look directly at anyone |
| | | | | | c Take breaths before prepositions |
| | | | | | d Ignore their pointless screaming |
| | | | | | e Keep speaking after people leave |
| | | 10,400 | | iii<br>Ancient techniques for promoting isolation | a Poor personal hygiene |
| | | | | | b Farting, drooling in public, brief episodes of urination |
| 2008 | | | | | c Poison circles, poison floors |
| | | | | | d Mantike, héxis, evil divination |
| | | | | | e Hermit beetles, hermit crabs, hermit thrushes, hermit spiders |

| | | | | | |
|---|---|---|---|---|---|
| | | | | iii How to become silent | a Lucubration: work at night |
| | | | | | b Stop speaking to mice |
| | | | | | c Stop talking to yourself |
| | | | | | d Stop imagining you're talking to yourself |
| | | | | | e How to suffocate the self, creating a permanent inner silence |
| 2009 | | 11,350 | | iv How to build an anchorite's cell | a Locating a sympathetic parish in a cold northern country |
| | | | | | b Purchasing land immediately adjacent to the church |
| | | | | | c Constructing an uninsulated stone room up against the church |
| | | | | | d Drilling small holes to gather heat from the church |
| | | | | | e The three buckets: for waste, food, and washing |
| | | | | | f Cutting an opening to watch the priest say Mass, and for offerings |
| | | | | | g Cutting an opening facing outside, for the buckets |
| | | | | | h Signing waivers, paying witnesses, permanently walling up the door |
| | | 12,100 | | v How to build a stylite's pillar | a Locating a sympathetic Christian landowner in a sunny country |
| | | | | | b Constructing the stone pillar, at least 40 feet tall, with overhanging capital |
| | | | | | c Raising the pillar house using a construction crane, bolting it in place |
| | | | | | d Polishing and waxing the column, hanging barbed wire around the house |
| | | | | | e Contracting workers to clean up waste dropped from the pillar house |
| | | | | | f Advertising to be sure people come and feed me |

|  |  |  |  |  |  |
|---|---|---|---|---|---|
|  |  |  |  | vi How to be an animal hermit | a Eating decaying wood in the darkness (hermit beetle) |
|  |  |  |  |  | b Hiding my tender deformities in a lovely seashell (hermit crab) |
|  |  |  |  |  | c Melting into an invisible voice in the trees (hermit thrush) |
|  |  |  |  |  | d Becoming hideous, irritable, and poisonous (hermit spider) |

She had been daydreaming about walling herself in a cell or living on top of a pillar. Maybe she thought she wasn't isolated enough in her study in Basel, and she wanted to be even more cut off from people.

I skipped ahead again. It occurred to me that I could use the twenty-page table of contents to pick out individual passages and pages from the gray notebooks, and that way I could quickly see what she had done. An hour or two might be enough to sample the whole thing, if I could figure out which parts to read.

Toward the end of the twenty-page table of contents, under the final heading "Family," she described a trip to Brazil, and then a fantasy I couldn't follow. This was the period she had told me about, when the notebooks no longer made sense, when she hallucinated and dreamed about forests.

| PARTITION VII. FAMILY | | | | | |
|---|---|---|---|---|---|
| **Date** | **Vol.** | **Page** | **Section** | **Subsection** | **Subsubsection** |
| Sept. 2010 | 49 | 14,400 | A Beginning of the madness: One thousand two hundred pages up the Amazon | i Leaving Home | a By taxi to the rail station in Basel |
| | | | | | b By sleeper train to Lisbon |
| | | | | | c By foot to Brown's Central Hotel |
| Oct. 2010 | | | | | d By taxi to the Porto de Lisboa |
| | | | | | e By container tanker to Belém, Brazil |
| | | 14,503 | | ii In Nulland | a Finding a place that is not a place |
| Nov. 2010 | | 14,515 | | | b Life in Nulland |
| | 50 | 14,700 | | | c My mosquito bites, cataloged |
| Dec. 2010 | 51 | 15,000 | | | c Chronicle of my foot fungus |
| | | | | | d Stings and fish bites from swimming |
| | | | | | e My struggle with sweat bees |
| | | | | | f The very largest spiders in the world |
| | | 15,377 | | iii Preparation for the work in Nulland | a Constructing a suitable study |
| | 52 | | | | b Training local chefs to cook eggs |
| | | | | | c Obtaining vows of lifetime service |
| | | | | | d Trying to keep the pages sweat-free |

<table>
<tr><td rowspan="20">2011</td><td rowspan="8">53</td><td rowspan="10">15,600</td><td rowspan="20">B<br>An extended anagogical allegory of this entire book</td><td rowspan="10">i<br>The allegory of language and body (remembering Notebooks 7-21)</td><td>a The toddler picks up on her name</td></tr>
<tr><td>b Down to the Nothing Sea</td></tr>
<tr><td>c The nothing there to see</td></tr>
<tr><td>d How they value my fat</td></tr>
<tr><td>e My first corporal punishment</td></tr>
<tr><td>f I outwit the one who hoped to look</td></tr>
<tr><td>g I purr, I squeak, I speak in code</td></tr>
<tr><td>h I contract, I contradict, I explode</td></tr>
<tr><td rowspan="10">54</td><td>i I make a faltering error, then I fight</td></tr>
<tr><td>j I graduate into a paragon of cruelty</td></tr>
<tr><td rowspan="10">16,080</td><td rowspan="10">ii<br>The allegory of Psūkhḗ (remembering Notebooks 23-34)</td><td>a Psūkhḗ neither in the liver nor heart</td></tr>
<tr><td>b Psūkhḗ knotted and squeezed dry</td></tr>
<tr><td>c Psūkhḗ powerless</td></tr>
<tr><td>d Psūkhḗ out in the long cold universe</td></tr>
<tr><td>e Psūkhḗ will not let itself be found</td></tr>
<tr><td>f Psūkhḗ is a red butcher</td></tr>
<tr><td>g Psūkhḗ collapsing, bruised</td></tr>
<tr><td>h Psūkhḗ and the black rooster</td></tr>
<tr><td rowspan="2">55</td><td>i Psūkhḗ in winding earthen alleys</td></tr>
<tr><td>j Psūkhḗ lingering in the cellar</td></tr>
</table>

| | | | | | |
|---|---|---|---|---|---|
| | | 16,223 | | iii<br>The allegory of mind (remembering Notebooks 35-43) | a G. addresses the reader |
| | | | | | b G. stands, and is struck by lightning |
| | | | | | c G. charred but stubborn |
| | 56 | | | | d G. begins the Fortress |
| | | | | | e She drags her anger onto the earth |
| | | | | | f Swarms buzz around what G. did |
| | | | | | g Rude woman you know what is next |
| | | | | | h G. paces inside her leaking Fortress |
| | | | | | i Up and down the halls, emptiness |
| | | | | | j Out the windows, enemy eyes |
| 2012 | 57 | 16,800 | | iv<br>Allegory in ruins | a The end of anagogic thinking |
| | | | | | b And the beginning of romance |
| | 58 | 17,100 | C<br>The romance of W.P. | i<br>Away from the fortress | a G. sets out into the barely possible |
| | | | | | b She swoons at a magnificent form |
| | | | | | c She finds her spectacular lover, W.P. |
| | | | | | d S. flows along behind G. and W.P. |
| | 59 | 17,400 | | | e G. and W.P. happy, just once |
| | | | | | f G. alone and disoriented |
| | 60 | 17,700 | | | g S. searches the ancestral woods |

| | | | | | |
|---|---|---|---|---|---|
| | | | | | h "Mother! I am calling you!" |
| | | | | | i W.P. evaporates, G. searches rapidly |
| | 61 | 18,000 | | | j S. tries to help, but he is weak |
| | | | | | k S. distraught, what can he do |
| | | | | | l Leaves conjure W.P., but he is gone |
| | 62 | 18,300 | | ii Into the forest pit | a Rancid thoughts throw G. into a pit |
| | | | | | b Crushed between leaf litter and clay |
| | | | | | c Her jaw wedged into slate and grit |
| | | | | | d A century impacted in leaf litter |
| 2013 | | | | | e At last G. levers her spine, breathes |
| | | | | | f After another century, her eye opens |
| | 63 | 18,600 | | iii A brief romance | a The last reappearance of W.P. |
| | 64 | 18,900 | D End of the madness: G. in agony. S. under threat | i Further centuries in the pit | a S. calls for help, attracts bread spirits |
| | | | | | b G. is covered in forest microbiome |
| | | | | | c Revenge of the metagenomic sample |
| | | | | | d G. partly digested by unknown phyla |
| | | | | | e Minerals seep in, G. partly fossilized |
| | | | | | f G. flooded, frozen in a little ice age |

| | | | | | |
|---|---|---|---|---|---|
| | | | | | g The gradual thaw, ice damage |
| | | | | | h Winds scour the crust off G.'s face |
| Jan. to Nov. 2014 | | 19,035 | | ii Faithful, impotent S. | a S.'s cabin, he sits and watches |
| | | | | | b S. tries to pry G. out, breaks her toes |
| | | | | | c S. retreats for eighty-four years |
| | | | | | d G.'s eye rotates and she glimpses S. |
| | | | | | e S. stays inside for sixty more years |
| | | 19,061 | | iii Forest spirits | a Mushroom gods, tree gods |
| | | | | | b The thundering begins, S. flees |
| | | | | | c S. agonistes, he lives in trees |
| | | | | | d Winds rip branches from trunks |
| | | | | | e A trunk crushes G.'s ribs and kidneys |
| | | | | | f Her eye roofed in leaves |
| | | | | | g The acorn-eating eagle |
| | | | | | h Pecks the pig-eating eagle |
| | | 19,182 | E How my mind is shutting down | iv End of the story | a Mushroom gods settle around, their soft shade and sweet quiet feeding |
| | | | | | b A rain of spores, gently swimming on G.'s cornea, tickling her open eye |

This was the period she said was too embarrassing to describe, a kind of psychosis.

She'd been right to be concerned about her sanity. This certainly wasn't science, and it wasn't a normal memoir. Yet it was minutely organized, "an extended anagogical allegory." Even in those years she was cataloging and classifying. The notebooks weren't a trackless black and gray sea. Still, it looked like she'd been lost, perhaps for years.

It was frightening to contemplate, like standing on a cliff looking down at a ferocious arctic sea. I knew the feeling of standing, toes clenched, near the edge. These pages were like actually jumping, and then being shoved and pushed by the waves, numbing, hallucinating, slowly drowning.

After that she seemed to wake up and remember who she was and what she was doing.

| | | | | | |
|---|---|---|---|---|---|
| Dec. 2014 | 65 | 19,200 | F<br>My present state, and how I woke up just in time to finish | i<br>How little remains of A. the scientist | a How it feels to waken from paralysis |
| | | | | | b Ice, painfully melting in my mind |
| | | | | | c Thawing, joint by broken joint |
| 2015 | | 19,257 | | ii<br>How it is necessary to go so far from science in order to change it | a Why I dragged the reader this far |
| | | | | | b The 5,000 pages of madness from vol. 49 until now |
| | | | | | c What was the “madness”? |
| | | | | | d What counts as “recovery”? |
| | | 19,283 | | iii<br>How I disinterred and reconstituted myself | a Extracting impacted soil particles |
| | | | | | b Removing pillar-shaped ice crystals |
| | | | | | c Removing spores, cysts, bacteria |
| | | | | | d Balms, salves, plasters, lotions |
| | | | | | e Restoring joints, appetite, larynx |
| | | | | | f Compensating for language loss |
| | | | | | g Compensating for temporal absence |
| | | | | | h And for conceptual distance |
| | | | | | i Stabilizing bodily functions |
| | | | | | j Redacting remaining traces of W.P. |
| | | | | | k Removing the forested allegory |
| | | | | | l Erasing S., restoring Samuel |
| | | | | | m Dissolving G., substituting me! |

It was all very systematic. She was climbing up again, rung by rung. It was the story of her recovery: still very strange, but the table of contents made it look as if she understood what had happened, and what she had to do.

At the end of the table of contents she included her experiences re-reading her earlier notebooks and writing the index. There was her project of reading long books, even Hans and the canary.

<table>
<tr><td rowspan="6">2016</td><td rowspan="6">65</td><td rowspan="6">19,406</td><td rowspan="6">F<br>My present state, and how I woke up just in time to finish</td><td rowspan="6">iv<br>Returning to my study</td><td>a I remember Basel, and the house</td></tr>
<tr><td>b Then I remember Paul and Luzia</td></tr>
<tr><td>c Re-reading the Gray Notebooks to the beginning of madness, vol. 49</td></tr>
<tr><td>d Re-reading the Gray Notebooks up to the return. vol. 65</td></tr>
<tr><td>e Re-reading the Gray Notebooks up to the present</td></tr>
<tr><td>f Learning to look at myself when I was dead</td></tr>
<tr><td rowspan="9">2017</td><td rowspan="9">66</td><td rowspan="9">19,500</td><td rowspan="9">G<br>Wondering what I have done</td><td rowspan="9">v<br>Making an index, studying long and complex books as models</td><td>a Months wasted preparing the index</td></tr>
<tr><td>b The index is a long & useless poem</td></tr>
<tr><td>c The project of reading long books</td></tr>
<tr><td>d Reading encyclopedias</td></tr>
<tr><td>e Months lost editing Wikipedia</td></tr>
<tr><td>f Different kinds of long books</td></tr>
<tr><td>g Books written by insane people</td></tr>
<tr><td>h Failures of order, failures of sense</td></tr>
<tr><td>i Long books as vectors of illness</td></tr>
</table>

| | | | | | |
|---|---|---|---|---|---|
| | | | | vi<br>What is my book? | a A tremendous achievement, because it preserves form at the cost of reason |
| | | | | | b Wreckage, Fraß, Kot, because it lost itself, I lost myself |
| | 67 | 19,800 | | i<br>What I did not do | a I do not know what I did |
| | | | | | b But I know what I did not do |
| | | 19,840 | | ii<br>Ways of wasting your life, 1: dozing | a In a hammock in Pine Island, Minnesota, contemplating cow dung |
| | | | | | b At a Hütte in the high Walliser Alpen |
| | | 19,977 | | iii<br>Ways of wasting your life, 2: nostalgia | a My sad hopeless father, “more a dream of life than a life” |
| 2018 | | | | | b Hans, dreaming of his first wife, the apartment, the canary |
| | 68 | 20,100 | | iv<br>Ways of wasting your life, 3: working | a Morschmulmig, bureaucratizing |
| | | | | | b Paul, in his law firm |
| | | | | | c Luzia, in her future law firm |
| | 69 | 20,400 | | v<br>Ways of wasting your life, 4: being trivial | a Arnulf Trausch: librarians |
| | | | | | b Morschmulmig: stamp collectors |
| | | | | | c Hohl: pharmacists |
| | | 20,563 | | vi<br>Ways of wasting your life, 5: fighting | a The chair of the department, who is out to ruin everyone |
| 2019 | | | | | b Catherine, who stole my ideas and continues to deny it |
| | | | | | c The imaginary editor, who always refused to publish my work |
| | | 20,611 | | vi<br>Ways of wasting your life, 6: love | a Loving other people, and failing |
| | | | | | b Loving only yourself, and failing |
| | | | | | c Loving only ideas, and failing |

| | | 20,614 | | vii<br>Ways of wasting your life, 7: trying to create something | a All the failed scientists: Buffon, Darwin, Linnaeus, Schall, Catherine |
|---|---|---|---|---|---|
| 2020 | | | | | b All the failed writers: Burton, Proust, Schmidt, Murnane, Fritz |
| | 70 | 20,700 | H<br>Time to end | viii<br>Reasons to resist, reasons to rest | a Summary for the lazy and illiterate, and this means you |
| | | | | | b Why every conclusion is a betrayal |
| | | 20,793 | | | b The bitter synthesis |
| | | | | viii<br>Stopping, at last | a Final conclusion |
| 2016 | | 20,999 | | | b Envoi |

At the end it seemed she was full of anger. Or frustration, or possibly fear. She had filled two of the last notebooks, 800 pages, on the different ways people waste their lives. I felt a kind of panic, as if I was a student sitting in the back of the room, thinking the teacher doesn't see me, and then I look up and she's staring right at me.

After the twenty-page table of contents came the one hundred-page table of contents. At the head of it she'd written:

I come now to the hundred-page hierarchical table of contents. It is the fourth, largest, and last table of contents, a complete guide to the twenty-one thousand pages of the Gray Notebooks. It is the key to the lock to the gate to the garden labyrinth, which is the only entrance to the palace. You will see immediately how it works.

I leafed through the hundred pages. It was a beautiful hundred-page knot, just as she'd said. There were more columns with further subheadings. Some had the usual Roman numerals and letters, and others were labeled in Greek and Cyrillic. It went on and on, using the exotic alphabets she had mentioned, with characters I didn't recognize, ㅃ, ఋ, ఌ, ३, ಱ. The rows and columns looked orderly, but clearly something had gone wrong. Different colored arrows ran along the bottom margins, continuing for pages at a time, linking headings in one place to headings in other places, like those lines that lead people along hospital corridors.

I decided to go back and start with the black notebooks. She'd organized them in dictionary fashion, using printed labels glued to their spines. I chose a notebook that covered words from Te to Vi.

TE

*to*

VI

*

* *

*Volume*

39

The pages had been fingered many times. The edges were yellow brown, softened from years of thumbing. Corners had crumbled away.

Each page was printed with dark blue lines widely spaced, like books for children first learning to write, and there were three vertical red lines, one in the center and one at each margin, dividing the page into two broad columns. At the top of each page Anneliese had written a title, and over each column there was a number in pencil. I opened the volume to a random page. The title was UNCERTAIN TAXONS. On the left page were columns 10,940 and 10,941, and on the right, 10,942 and 10,943.

She had cut passages from her earlier notebooks into neat rectangles and cropped them to fit into the spaces between the ruled lines. They were pasted in with white glue. The left edges of most strips aligned with the left-hand red lines. Other passages were copied in by hand, in a hasty but mainly legible script. It was amazingly careful work, and it reminded me of what she'd said about stamp collecting. The pages looked like professionally conserved remains of some ancient document.[37]

Each of the pasted snippets and handwritten passages was numbered. One cut-and-pasted note read "false friend taxons not visible in our surveys: <u>enormous disappointment</u>," and just left of that she'd written in pencil "1990A p. 41," indicating the lab notebook she'd cut it from. Just as she'd said, there were penciled symbols indicating the meaning or significance of the notes. That one was marked with an asterism, ⁂. I leafed through the notebook and saw other excerpts marked §, ‡‡, ‡‡°, and many other symbols she hadn't told me about: †ˆ, ⁂ˇ, ⁂°, †°, ‡°, ‡˙, ‡¯, ×˝, ≈̊, «ˆ, ‹¨, ~˜, and —˟.

I turned the pages forward and backward. Fifty or so pages were given the title UNCERTAIN TAXONS. Before that was UNCERTAIN GENOMES. Afterward came UNCERTAIN TERMINOLOGY, and then just UNCERTAINTY.

Some pages had pasted-in notes that had been typed on an old electric or mechanical typewriter. A few had entire ordinary-size A4 pages glued onto them, mainly printouts of articles in professional journals. There were also sketches. On one page she had drawn a falling line with a few hash marks over it to indicate a graph of some function. On another I found a beautiful hand-drawn graph of swirling lines signed Wolfram Pichler. Farther on there were pages of overlapping circles labeled with floating letters in a florid German script.

It must have been difficult to decide how to divide up the alphabet among the 41 volumes. How could she have known that entries from Te to Vi would occupy just one notebook? Only a few pages were overcrowded, and no more than a dozen or so were empty. She must have filled her study with paper snippets before she began gluing them into the notebooks.

I tried reading down a column numbered 12,088.

1975A January 10, p. 30 ‡‡ Metabolomics properly refers to abundances, not predictions as C. insists.

1975A January 10, p. 31. Junhua Li has a nonredundant reference catalog of 879,006 genes in the human gut.

1984C May 1 p. 67 ⁂ Amazing discovery this morning / distant relatives of Elusimicrobia (Termite Group 1) and Lentisphaerae. New Phylum!

1989C May 1 p. 9. Analyses of a group of samples from Chinese and Danish individuals reveals country-specific gut microbial signatures. "Europeans are filled with different species!" Edi Nielsen, Agnieszka Manichanh, Suisha Zhang et al.

1989G November 20, p. 3 ‡°C. is totally misguided about metagenomic multilocation parallel sampling. It is not "good science." She thinks like a turtle.

1990A January 7, p. 41. C. says something "feels" wrong about my insight (functional diversity of moss microbiome) even though it helped her identify gene families. Willful. Will not listen, does not understand.

1990E June 6, p. 1. ≈°Either: C's project is nomological or: it is complete nonsense.

1990G October 13 p. 2 ⁂ Important phenomena occur at the strain level. Microbiome studies fail to capture dynamic behaviour of microbial communities.

1990J October 20, p. 1. Verrucomicrobia are disgusting. They steal >55% of their genetic material from Dadabacteria. Dadabacteria trade genetic material with Deltaproteobacteria. Their taxonomic trees move. The organisms are like banks with different holdings, trading with one another. The taxonomic trees are alive. C. says "That is just Begriffspoesie" in front of postdocs.

1991C March 25 p. 6. CT 31. Phylotyping marker genes chosen in AMPHORA are housekeeping genes. They are a not-too-small and not-too-large set for successful phylotyping. No one sees this.

I went and got another notebook. Under the title ERROR PEOPLE she had filled pages with snippets directed against someone named Schall.

1988A January 25, p. 12. It is striking: my predictions closely parallel Schall's putative bacterial superphylum. Striking to me. Schall doesn't think anything is striking. Has a pocket calculator for a brain.

1990B March 3, p. 20. It is absolutely not the case that C. is right. And Schall is wrong, and Gotthardt. Rushworth, wrong. Taxon = unknown.

1990B March 12, p. 2. Schall does not understand anything about mutation. Missense mutations are not nonsense mutations. Schall thinks I misspeak. Schall himself is an insertion-deletion mutation.

1990E June 20, p. 27. Schall is great, but he is an obstructionist. He says we need nonhuman gastrointestinal samples, we need unusual microbial populations, we need under-sampled lineages. Worms, he says. Also fleas. (I said he has both.) C. says we do not need more student volunteers. "They eat everything." She says the stupidest things.

1990N November 22, p. 12 §. 16S results: genes from Schall's flea stomachs are probably wrong because the % identity correlates poorly with values for full-length sequences. There is nothing of interest in Schall's flea stomachs, just as there is nothing of interest in Schall. Either that or whatever lives in Schall's flea stomachs is new to science.

1992G August 20, p. 61. Schall insists marine taxons were degraded. Did Schall really move from Berlin or did he lose his position? Probably why he keeps saying C. is a "great scientist."

1992G August 22, p. 61. Schall is harmless. Like a Great Toothless Butterworm. At first intimidating then pathetic.

In another notebook, under the penciled heading PHYLA, there were pages reporting new discoveries, like the ones she had told me about.

1985D June 9, p. 1. Isadore and Palermo have named the 17 new bacterial phyla Uncultured Bacterial Phylum 1 to 17. Amazing new taxons, creatures we never knew about living in the mud all around us. My ignorance reveals a deep human prejudice, profound genetically driven pride.

1985F October 19, p. 50 ‡‡ Functional metagenomics: does not require previous knowledge of genes in the sample, so removes human bias. The result is bewildering.

1988B March 20, p. 3. First representative of the Ancient Archaeal Group (AAG)! Paleoarchaea. Adjacent to the Lokiarchaeota, but older. Possibly even before bacteria. So far back in time that the metrics are broken into ... and ... !

1988G August 20, p. 60 § The metagenome from the Costa Rica marine sediment is Ancient Archaeal. Could not be more wonderful. By comparison Tara Oceans Expedition material is common, so is Beebe vent genome, so is Pacific marine data. All uninteresting in comparison.

1991A February 4, p. 21. New phylum Korarchaeota. Caldiarchaeum subterraneum is a novel species, and a novel phylum! Aiguearchaeota is a new phylum! Then at the end of the day new sequences for Candidatus *Pelagibacter ubique* (what is it?), *Syringammina fragilissima, S. corbicula* (the largest amoebas in the world! I was so happy I sponsored them on OneZoom)

1988K September 27, p. 5. Thaumarchaeota, Aiguearchaeota, Crenellarchaeaota, Korarchaeota, Ichthyarchaeota = a new archaeal superphylum. Schall refers to it as TACKI.

1989G October 12, p. 70 ⁂ Novel Nanoarchaea. Very deep-branching. Archaeal Richmond Mine samples yield acidophilic nanoorganisms. Schall calls them ARMANI. Discovered in acid mine drainage biofilms. Páez-Espino, Eloe-Fadrosh, and Pavlopoulos are getting ahead of us. They have 125,000 new viruses, we have ≈ 100,000.

1990C March 19, p. 45. This week alone. Nanohaloarchaea described from a hypersaline environment. Micrarchaeota, Aenigmarchaeota, Nanoarchaeota, and Anohaloarchaea: they form a monophyletic superphylum. This week alone! We are like Magellan, like Galileo. By comparison Linnaeus only found a few flowers. I propose we call this one MANA. Schall says A MAN. If Schall was a man, things would be so much better.

1990C March 19, p. 46. The new life is simply not comprehensible for humans. We are so small.

1992A February 20, p. 53. Our mean branch length is three times Paris, five times Berkeley.

1992A March 1, p. 9. Frank Zachos, B.N. Singh, and John Wilkins say we can count species. But if Jody Hey says we can't count species, then we can't count species.

And so it went for thousands of pages.[38]

Anneliese's voice, speaking in fragments. Boasting, hoping, struggling to make sense of what she was finding.

1986A January 10, p. 80 ⁂ Prediction: new bacteria from the Helluft spa warm tank skim.

1986H September 20, p. 1. Prediction: Helluft spa bacteria will have small genomes like the TACKI organisms.

1986H September 20, p. 1. Or: lack core metabolic pathways.

1988A February 1, p. 60 ‹˚ Terrabacteria candidate phylum SHA-109 has been recovered in: baboon feces (five genomes), palm oil effluent (one), a toluene degrading community (one), and a dechlorination bioreactor (one). What would maps of its distribution look like?

1988F November 4, p. 35. No one agrees. Prediction: in 1 month they all will.

1988N December 11, p. 6. Absolute new world. New paradigm. At a conservative 90th percentile, these bacterial genomes are the first genomic representatives of 766 genera, 226 families, 61 orders, and 35 phyla. All new names. Marseillebacillus, Villefranchebacillus, Bennecourtbacillus. Muerzzuschlagbacillus. We will all be famous. Just from 1 stall, urine + hay, in 1 stable, in the famous Kakabekia castle in Wales.

1989A January 20, p. 53 ‡‡ I have an utter lack of enens.

1990A January 20, p. 57 ‡‡ Always increasing total branch length! Archaea keep leading us backward in time, to a point before the biological timeline is divided into eons.

1990A January 25, p. 77 § Why can't these Archaea be cultured? What are we doing/thinking wrong about the most primitive life?

1990B February 14, p. 1. C. says the new Terrabacterium has to be a sister to the other one, on the same branch of the taxonomic tree. She just really wants that to be true. The new Terrabacterium is a horizontal branch, an impossible kind of branch on a taxonomic tree.

1991J October 13, p. 60 ⁂ Tenericutes and Thermodesulfobacteria lineages are not known. They branch in the Firmicutes. But from what? Either this is useless data, or these are amazing organisms.

1992F May 20, p. 8 †˚ Deltaproteobacteria are polyphyletic, or else it appears that way because Dadabacteria share genetic material with them. Why do they trade genetic material? How does that even work? How does an organism know how much to trade? This is simply not comprehensible for humans.

I closed the black notebooks one after another.

The black notebooks were like her conversations, full of strange kinds of knowledge, but fragmented, without the strings that tied her thoughts together. She must have remembered enough to make sense of it all, and yet that seemed impossible. No one could keep those tens of thousands of notes in memory. Surely a note like "false friend taxons not visible in our surveys: enormous disappointment" would have lost its meaning after ten or twenty years. Eventually she must have turned the pages more as a reader than a writer. No matter how prodigious her memory, the notes must have become nearly as opaque to her as they were to me, as they would be to anyone—unless she looked through the notebooks continuously, refreshing her memory over and over again. Some pages were dark with finger grease. I imagined her leafing through the black notebooks every day, trying to keep the entries alive in her memory by endless reviewing. For any other reader it would be impossible. Even if I was an expert in bacteria and viruses I wouldn't be able to follow her thinking. The black notebooks were a lost language.

I stood over the lab tables, opening black notebooks one after another. It was all in scrupulous order. Everything my eye fell on would have had some significance when she wrote or typed it, clipped it out with scissors, classified it, and pasted it into its permanent place.

Suddenly these notebooks seemed alien, as if I had walked into a library in a dream and discovered all the books were written in a language that had died out centuries ago. The bent covers on some notebooks made them look like animals. They covered the lab tables like the shells of enormous beetles.[39]

I thumbed through the first of the gray notebooks. Some pages had been typed and then bound. Others were handwritten. I went around the room, opening one notebook after another.

That is when I began to see the scale of the thing. These notebooks were not a jumble, as I had suspected, or even hoped. They were something complete. The 66 gray notebooks were in fact a single book, almost 20,000 pages long, just as she'd described.

The product of twenty years of thinking and writing, all there in front of me. The transcript of a life spent alone.

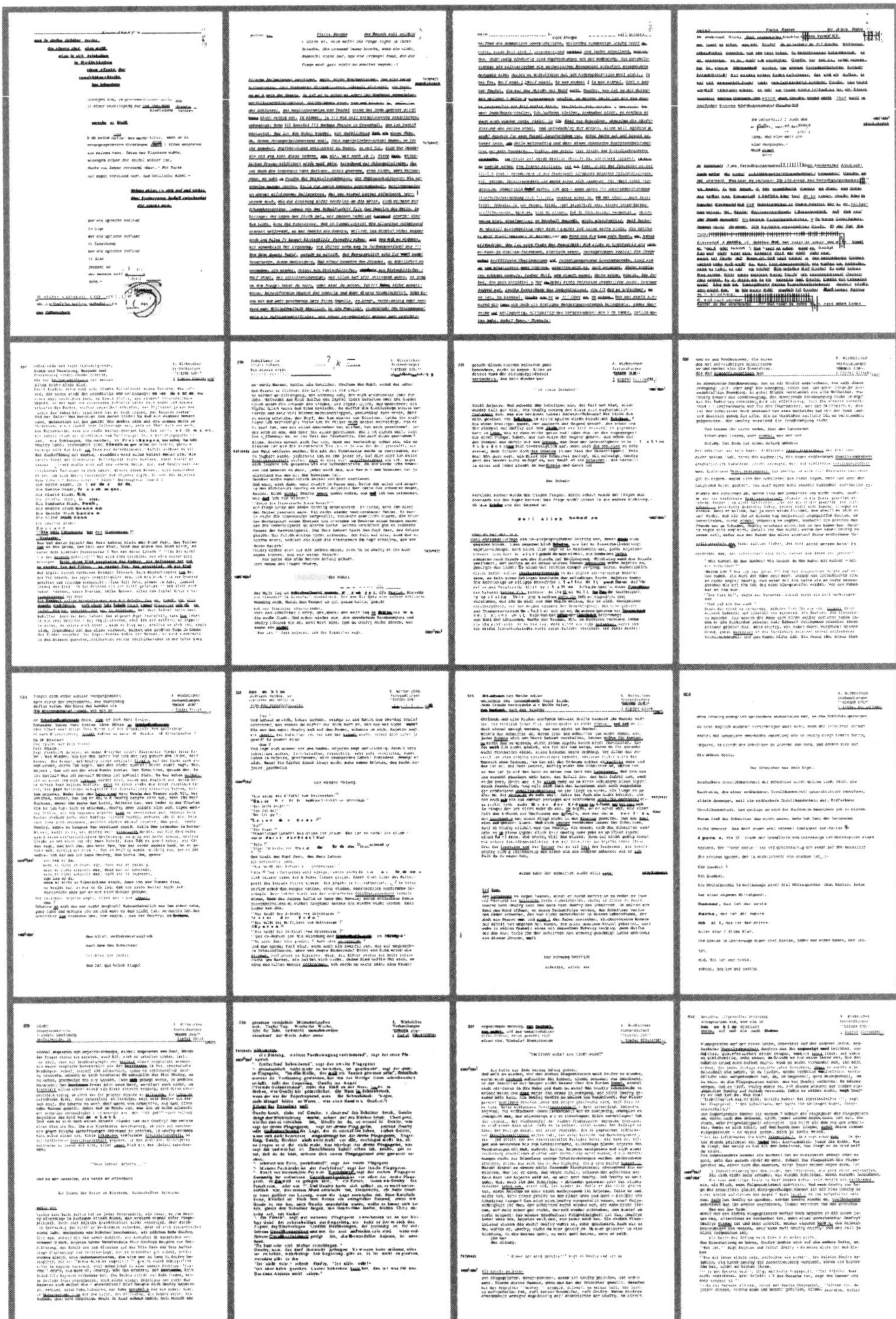

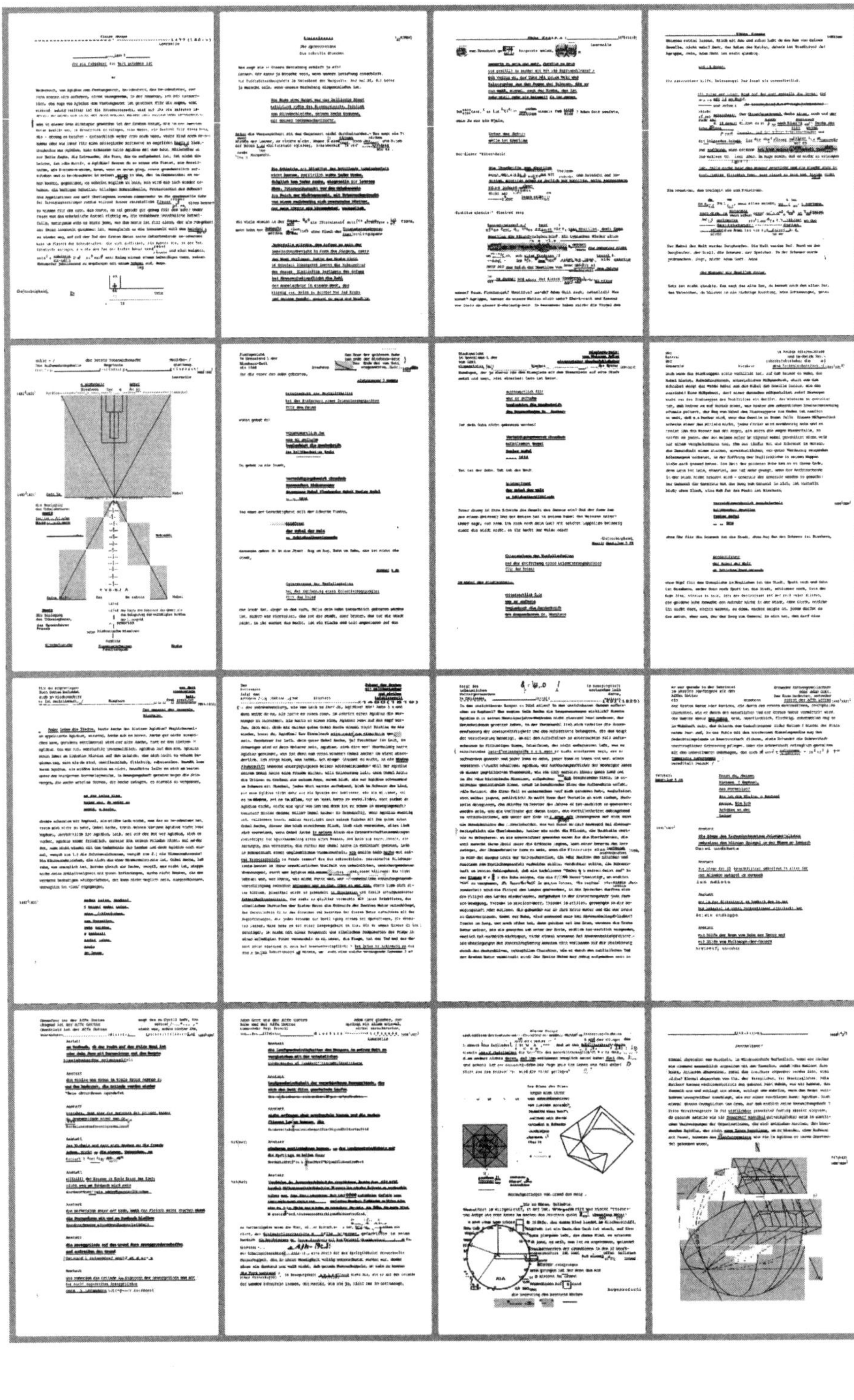

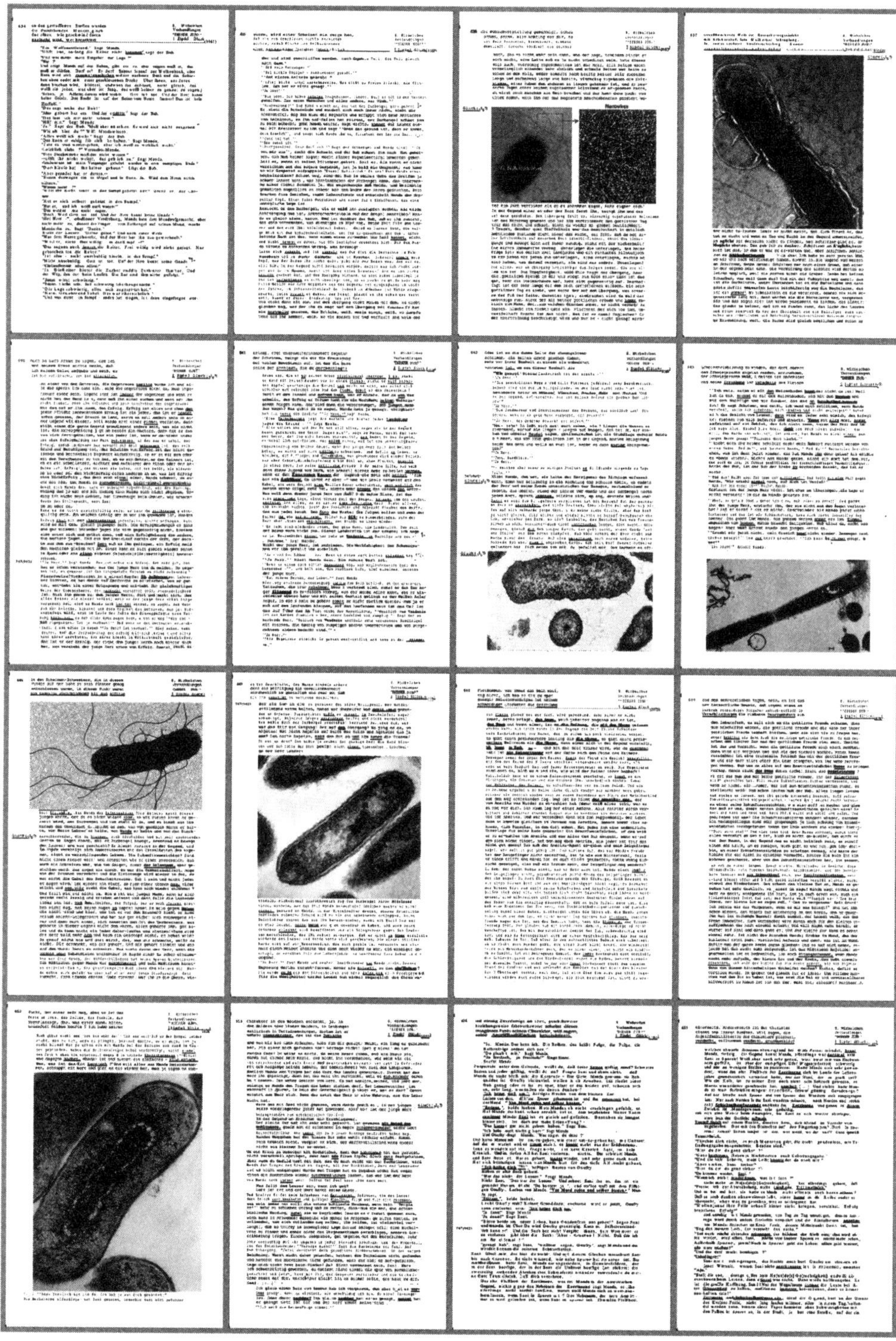

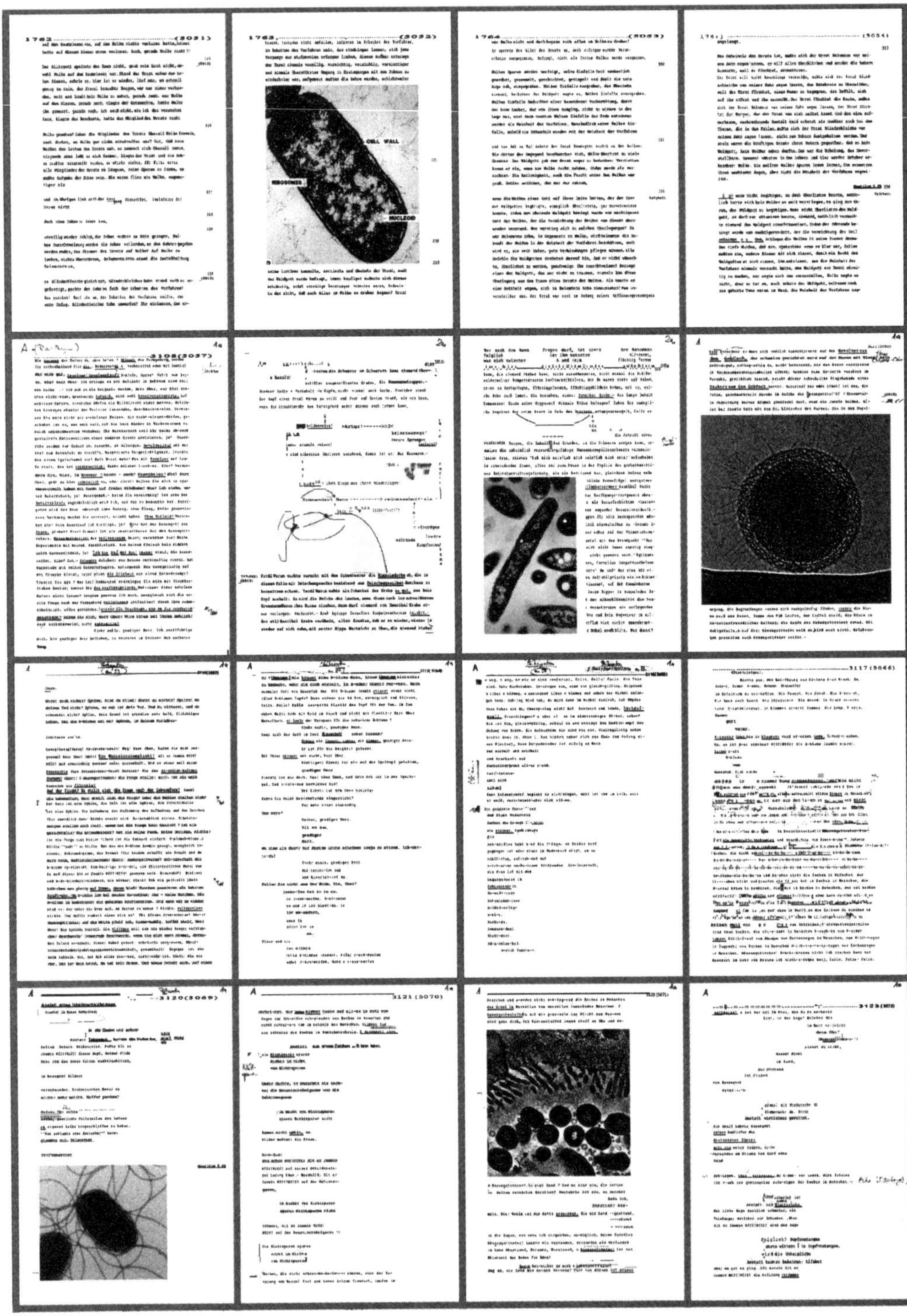
CELL WALL
RIBOSOMES
NUCLEOID

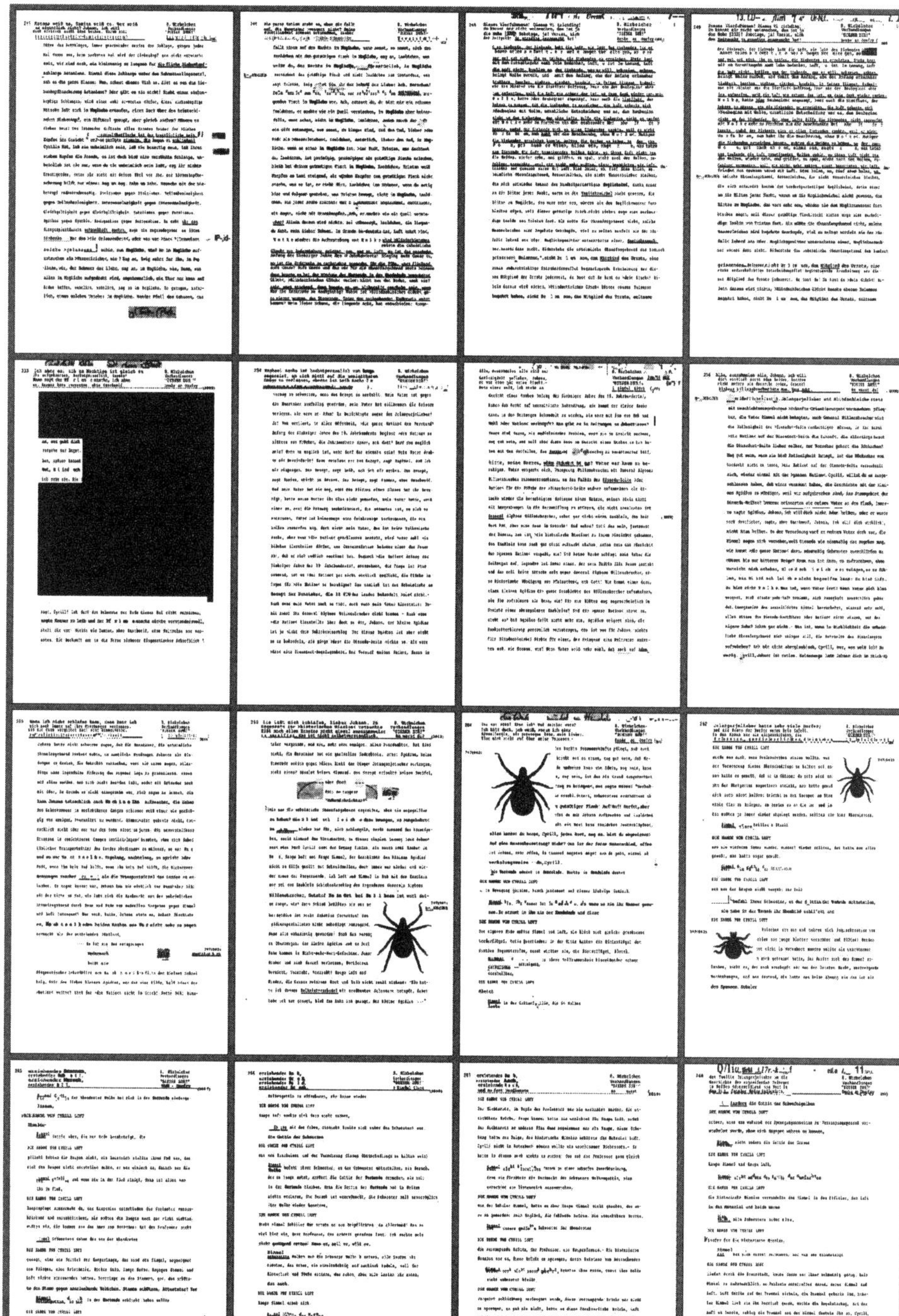

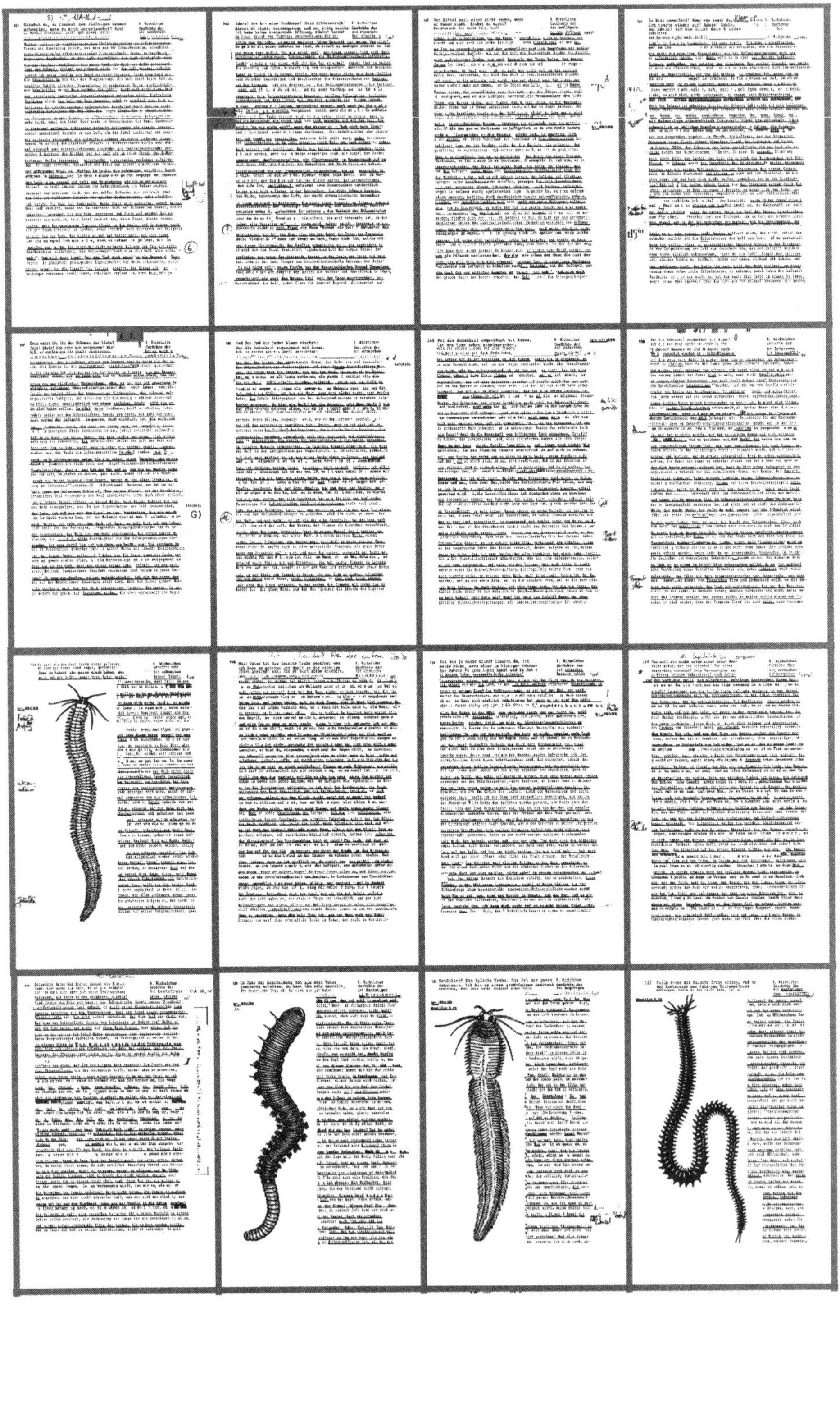

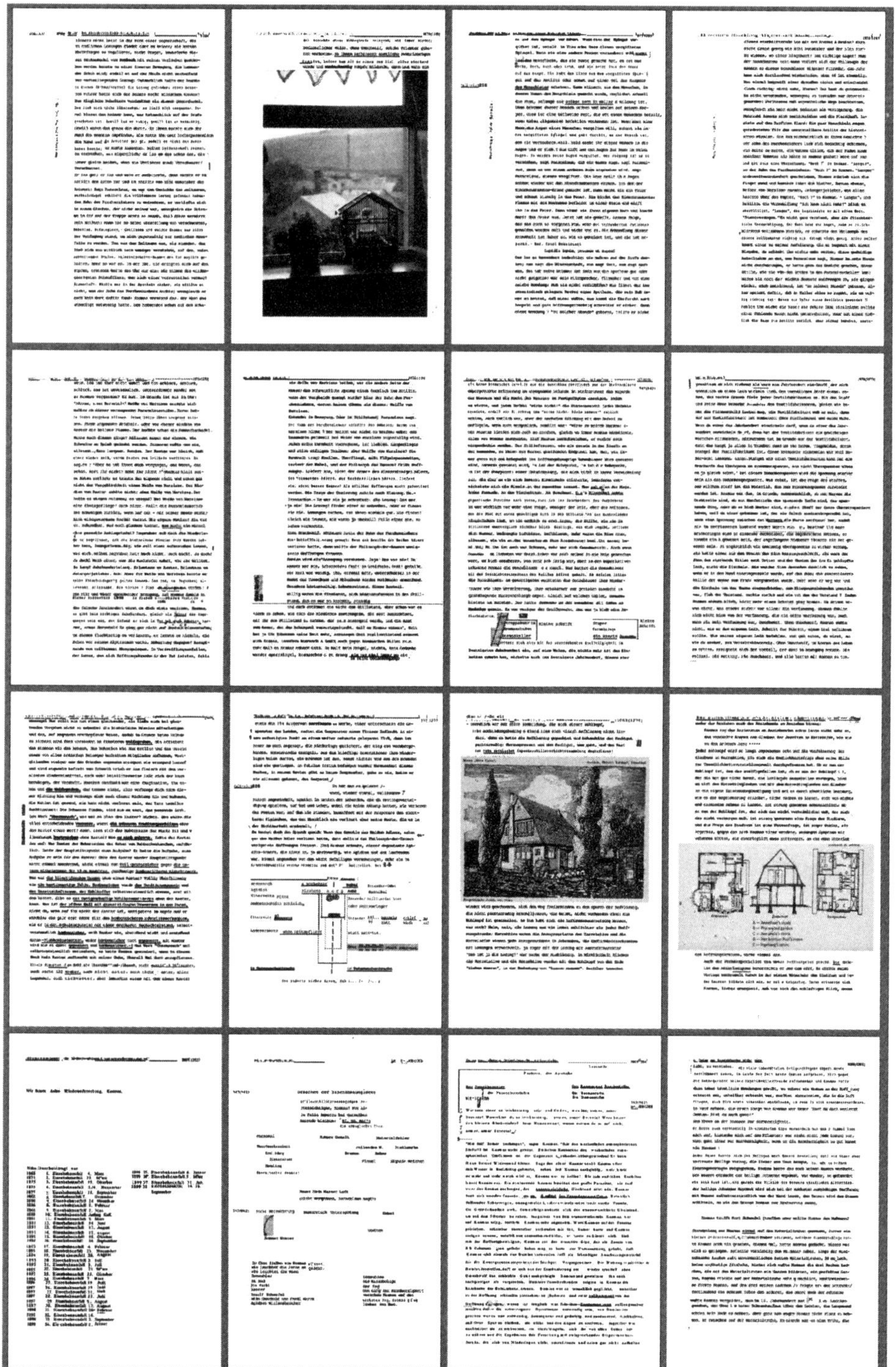

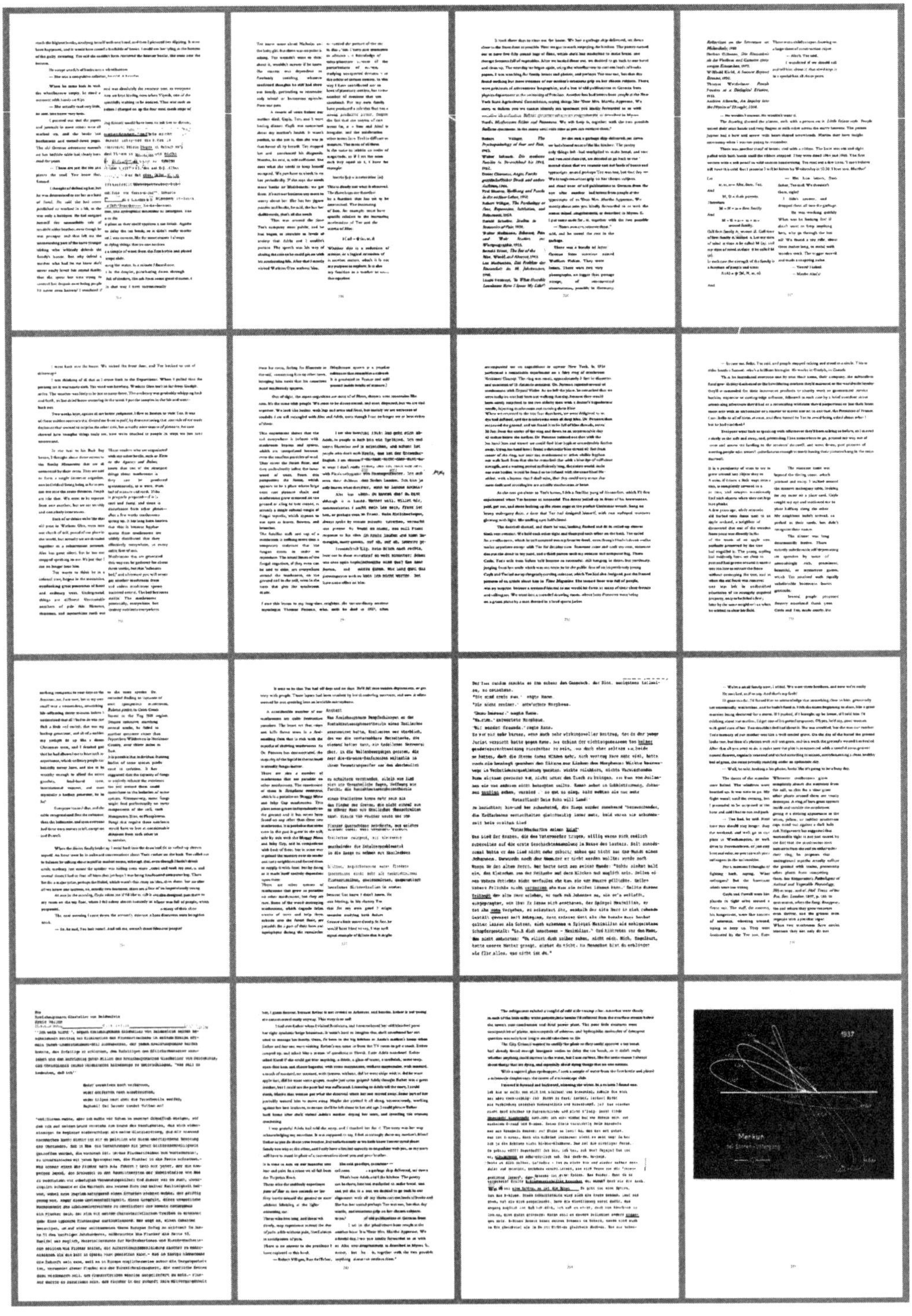
1937
Merkur

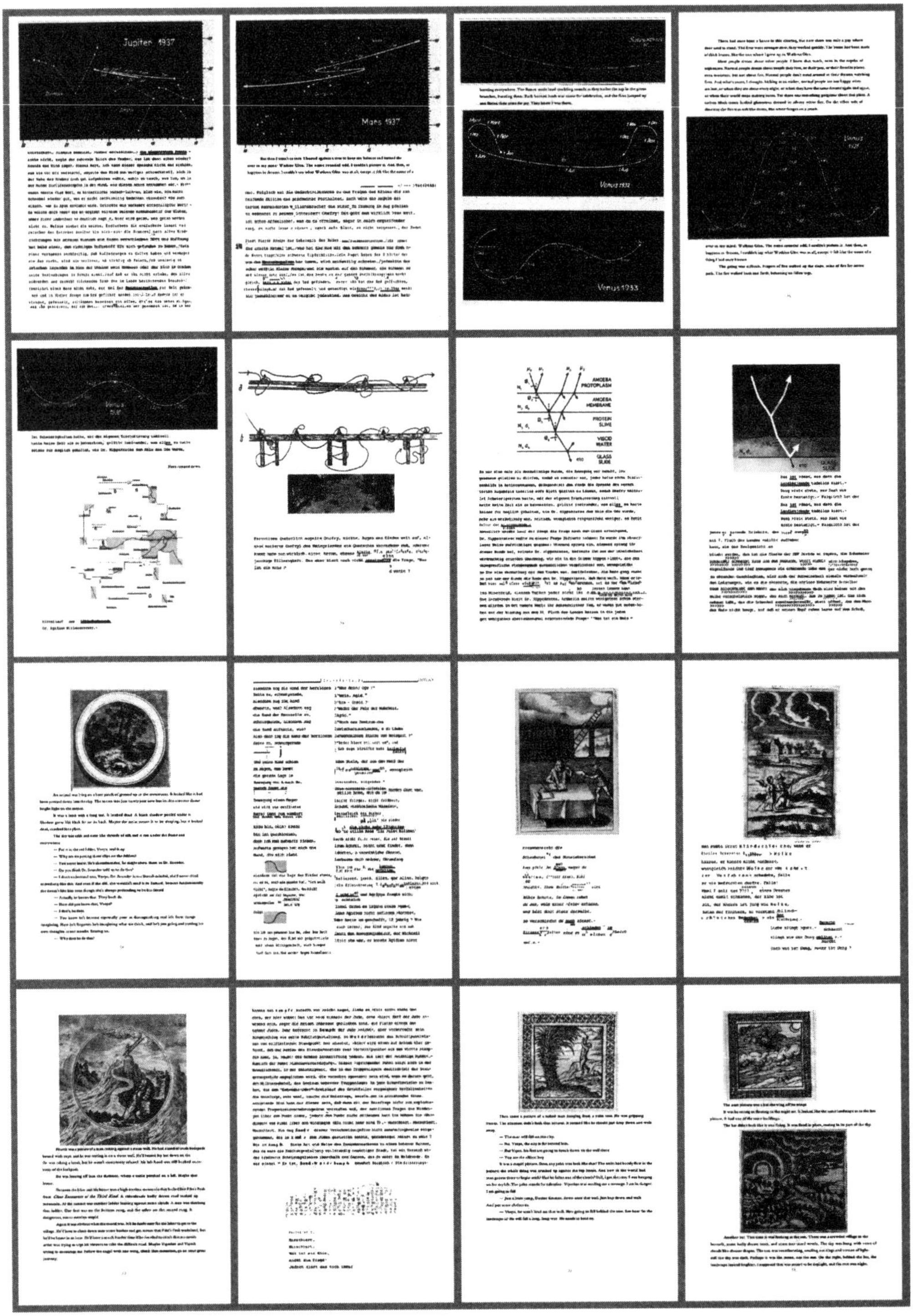

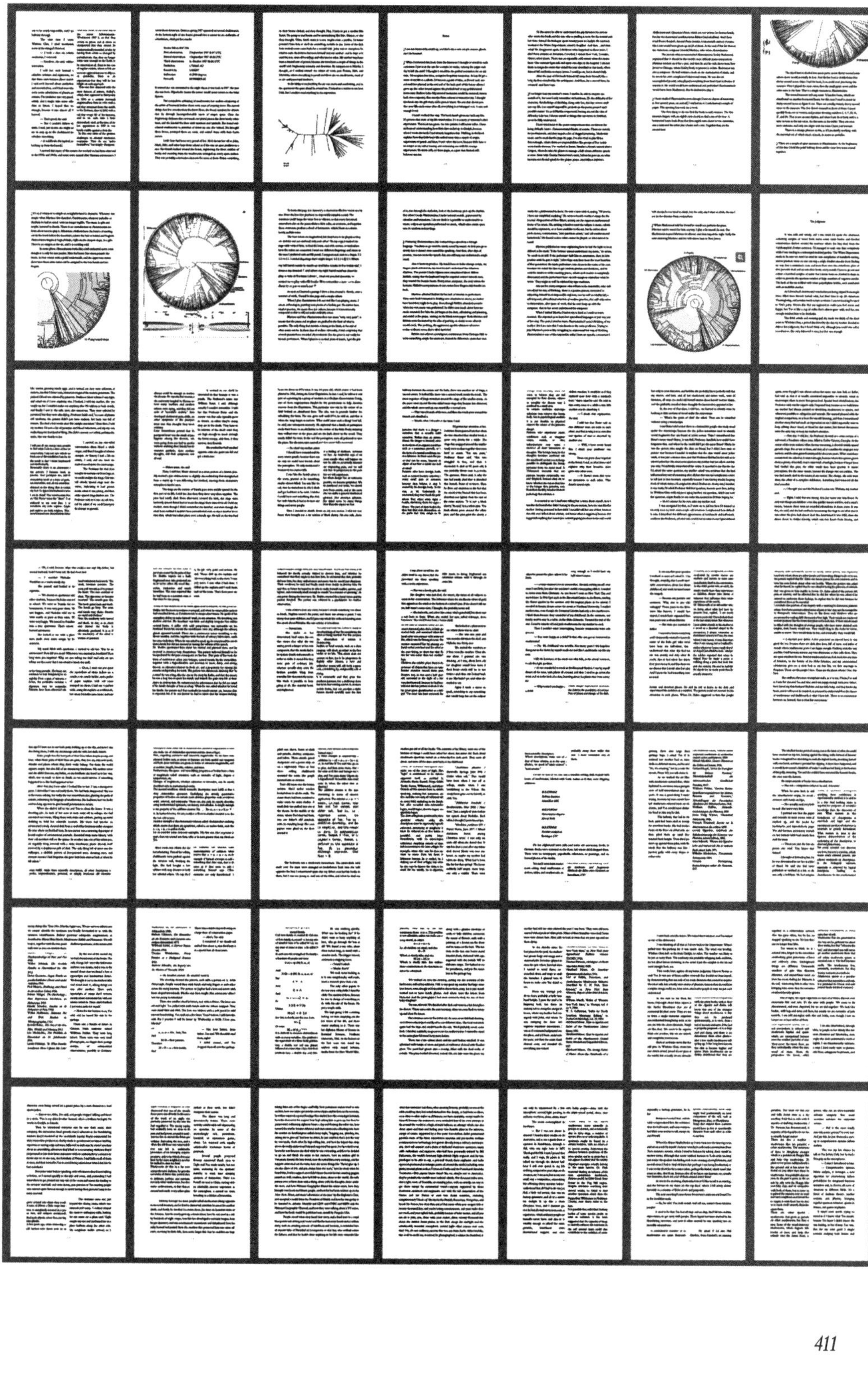

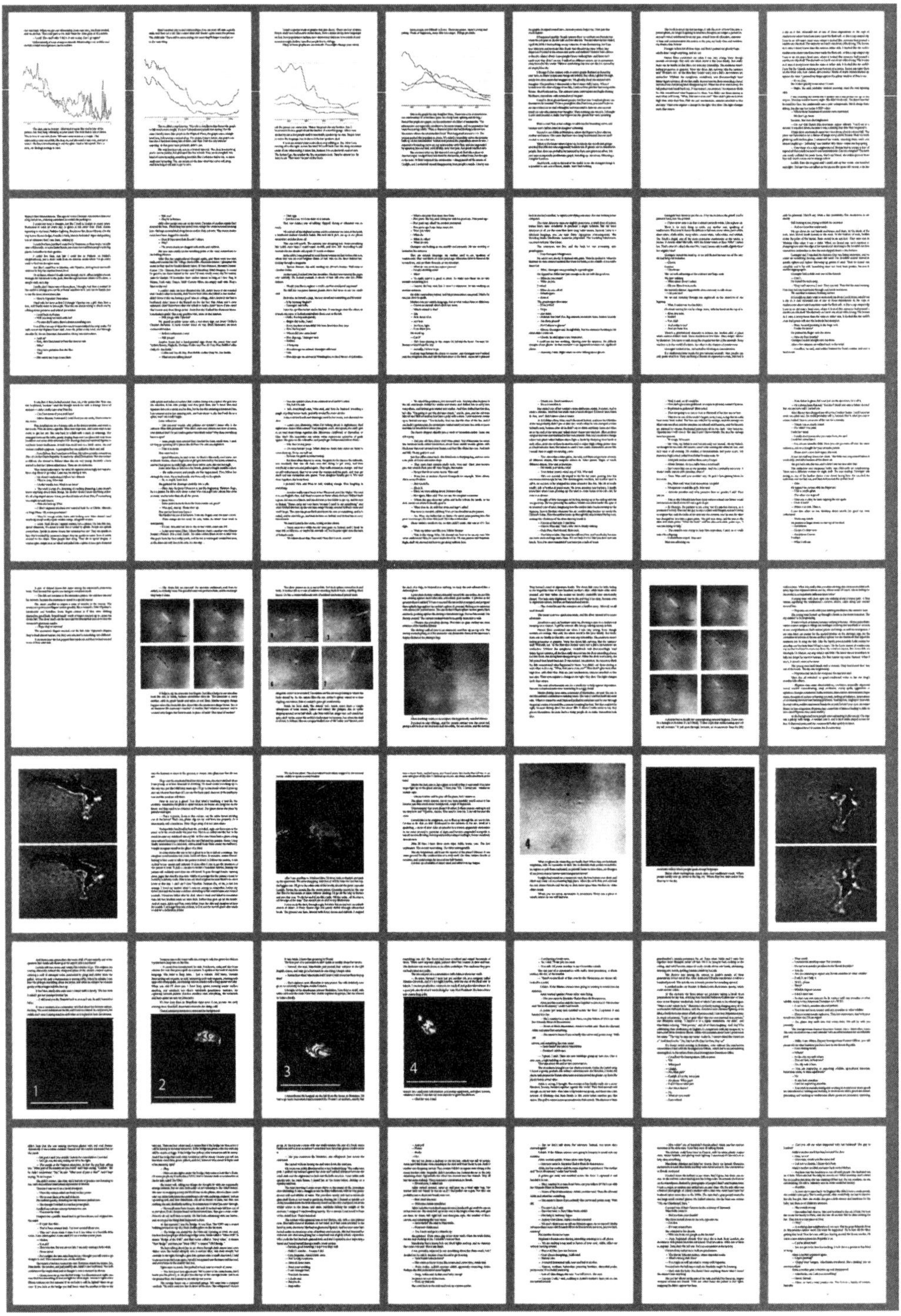

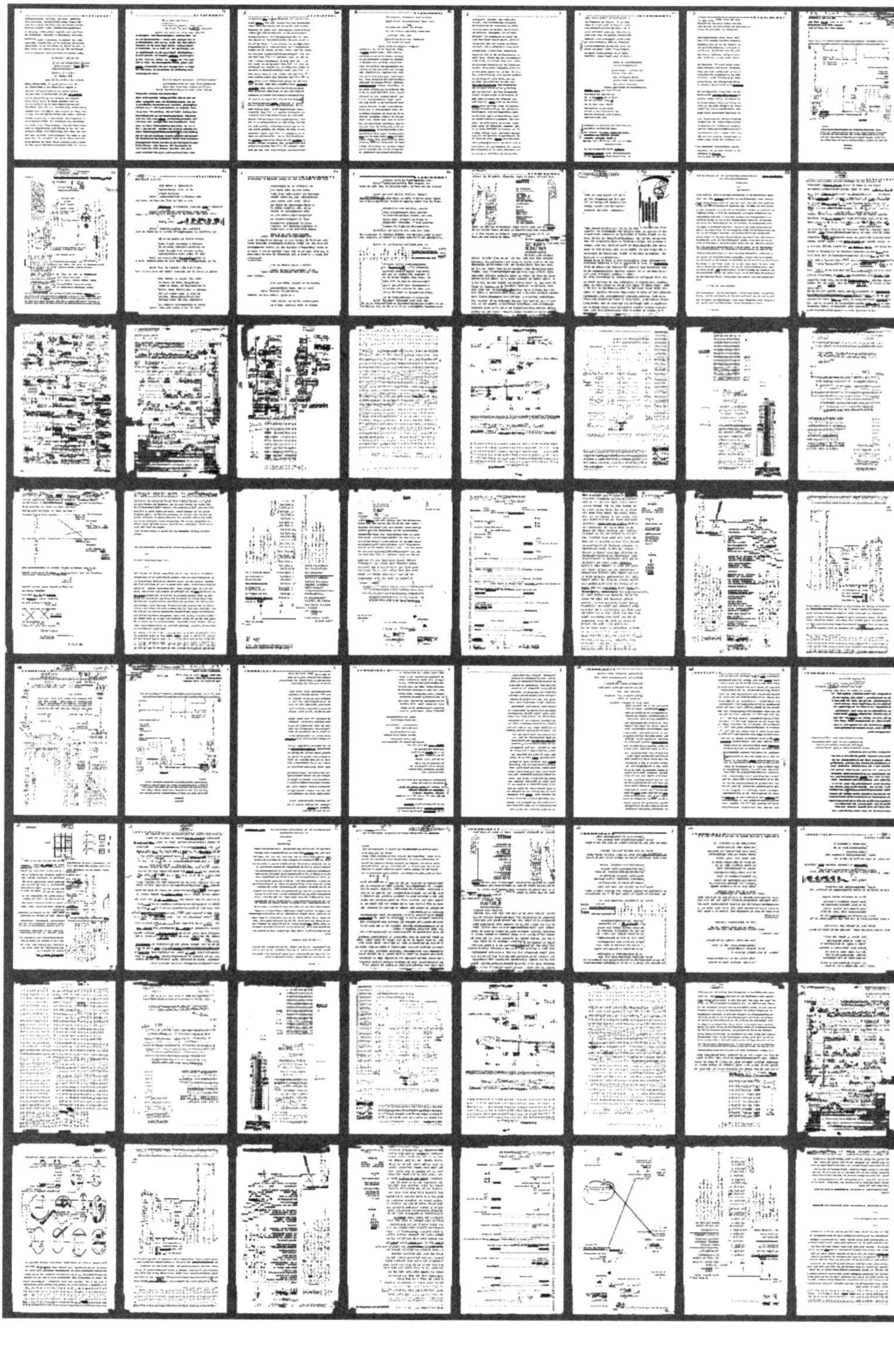

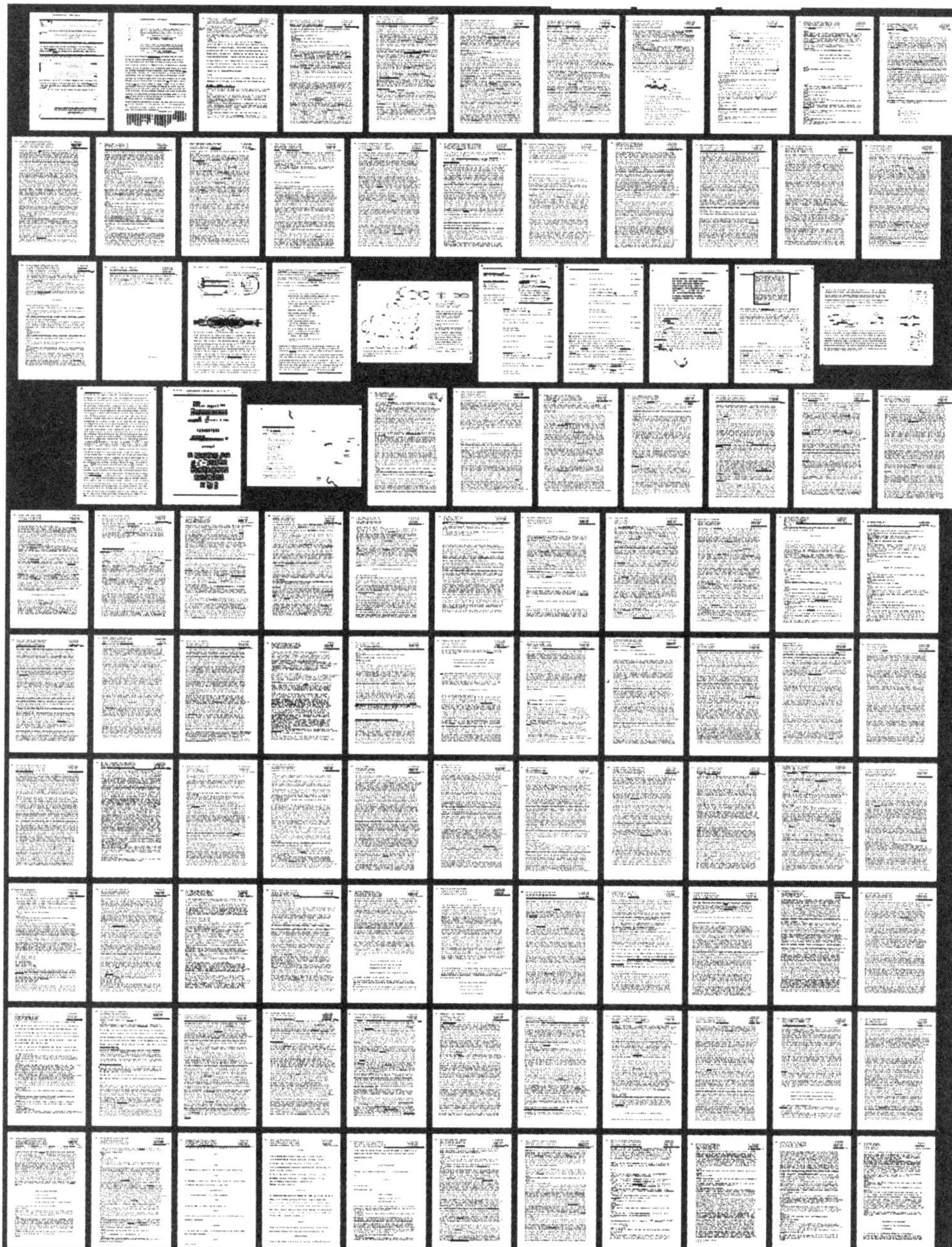

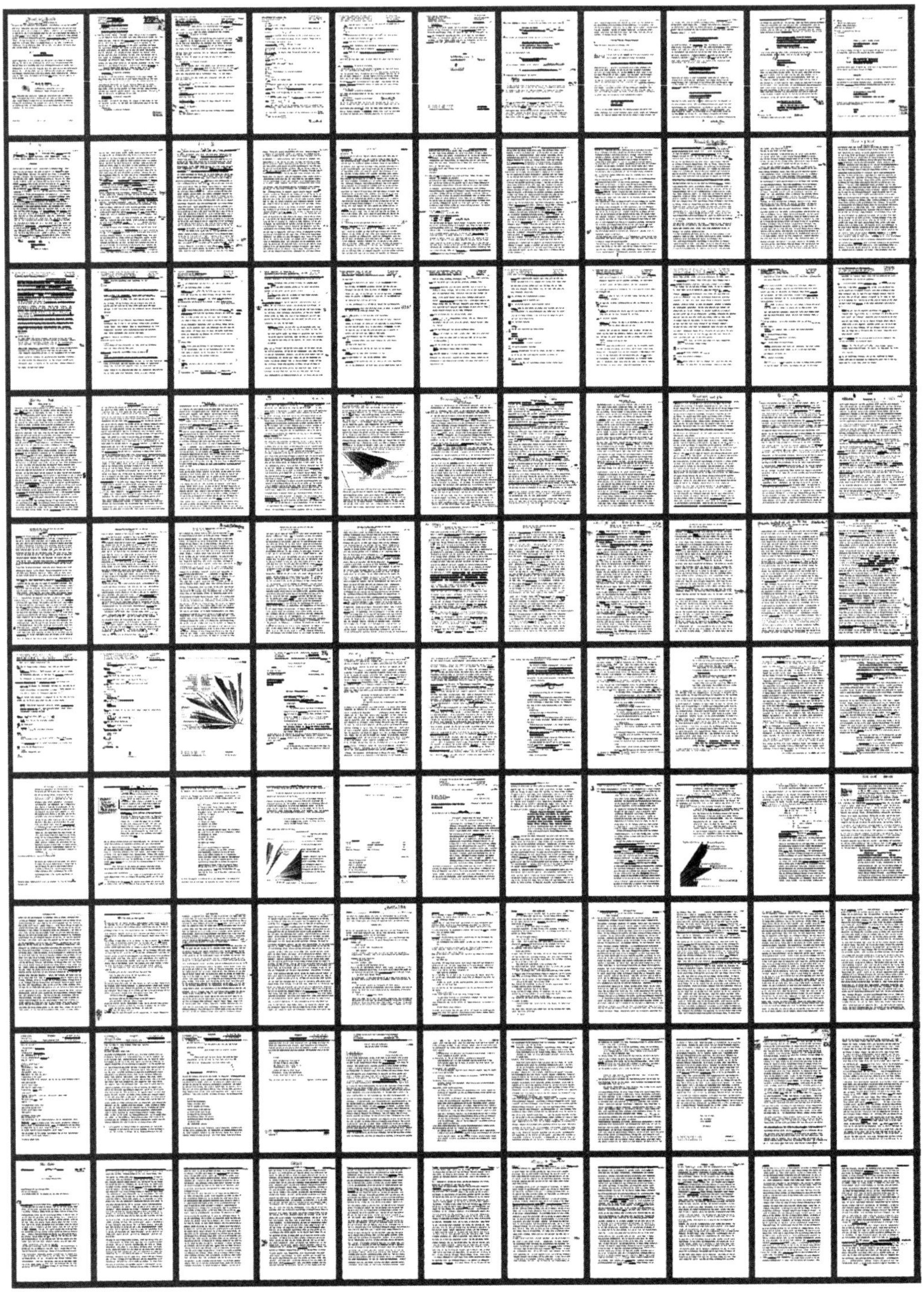

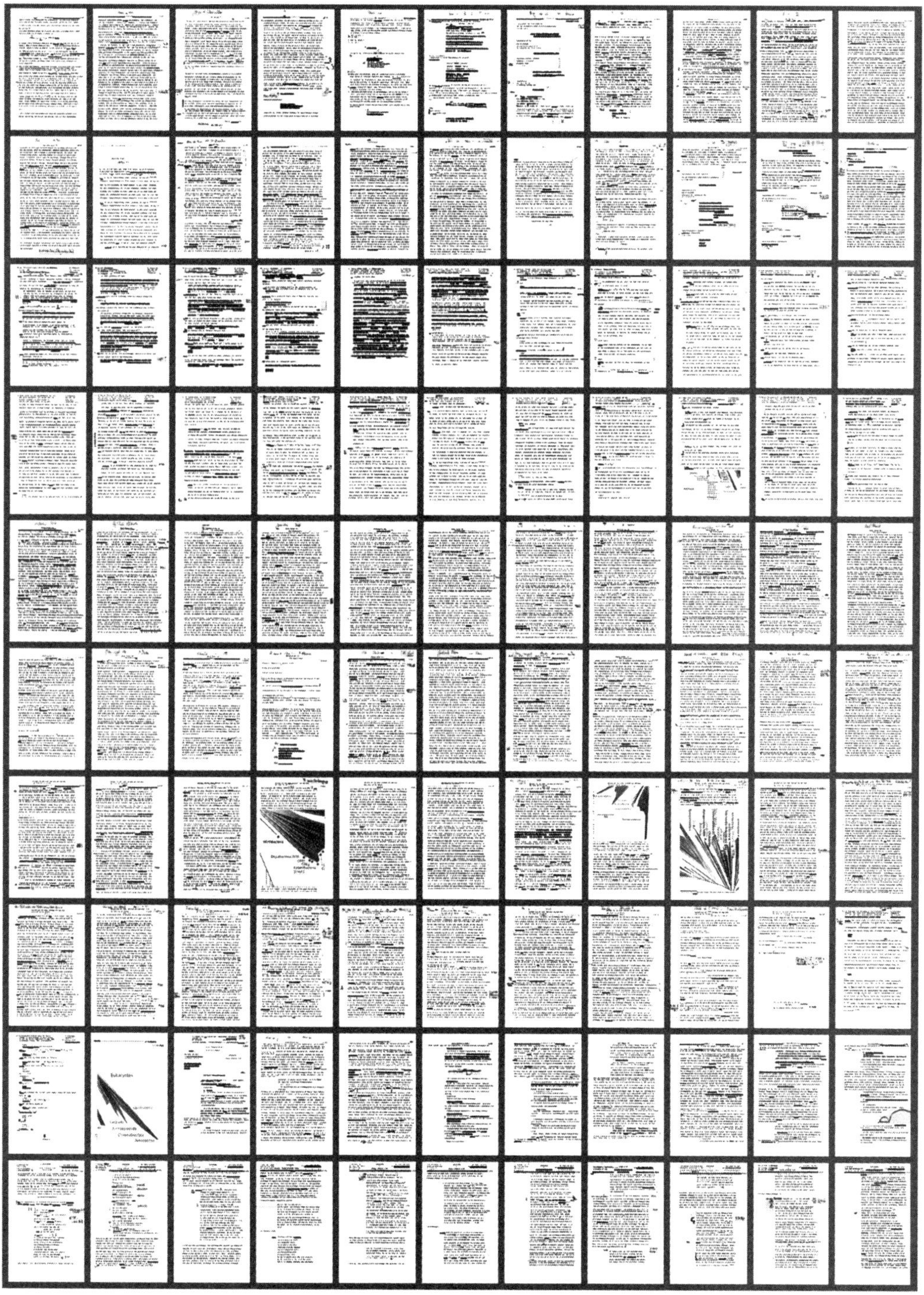

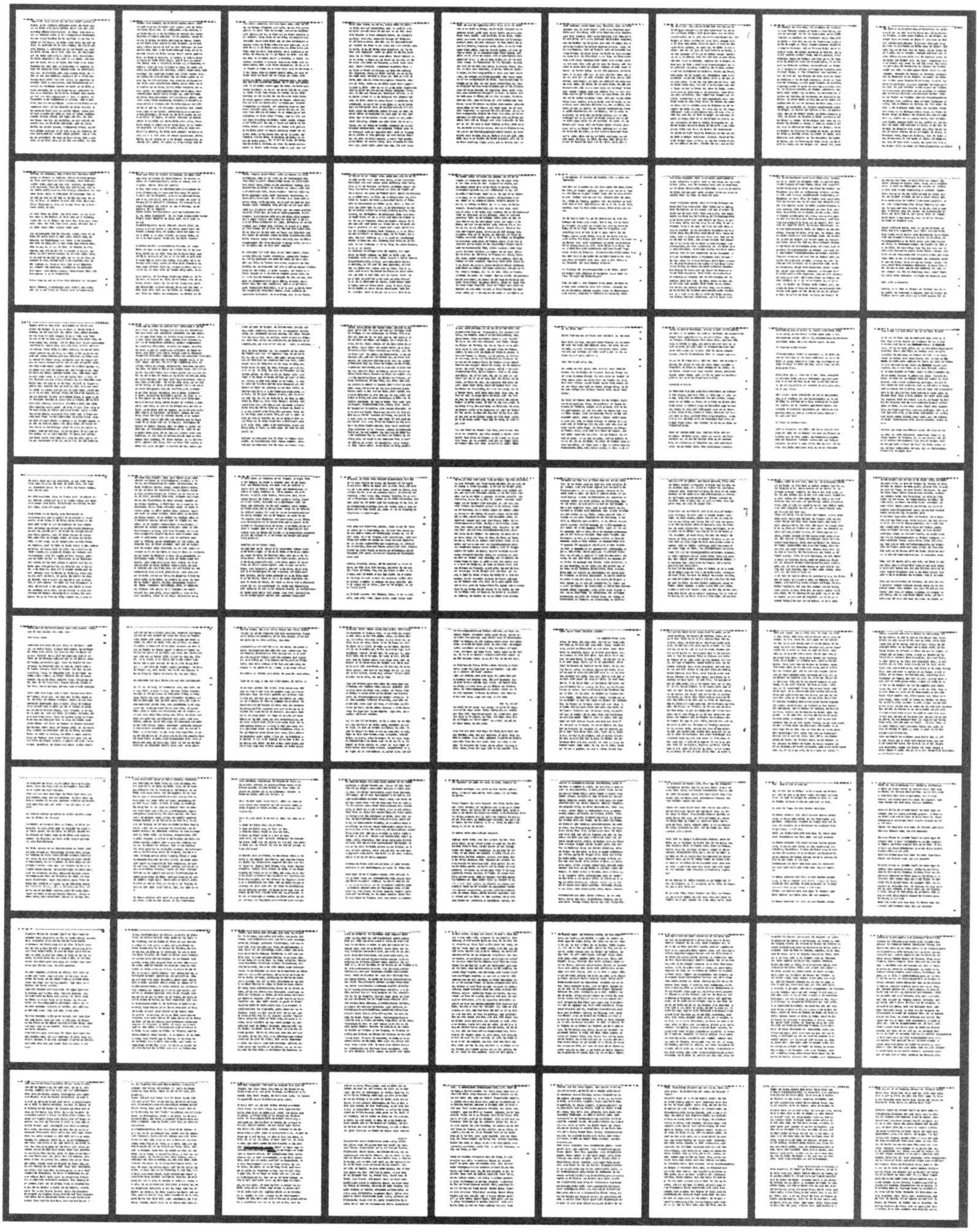

Many of the notebooks were continuous text, not pictures or fragments. Prose in long paragraphs. One paragraph continued for ten pages, another for nearly a hundred. Nothing but Anneliese's words filling page after page.

When I looked over the lab tables the print blended to an intricately patterned gray, like looking down at the ocean from far above. The afternoon light came in through the lab windows and cast fine stripes across her words.

I took one of the gray notebooks, volume 7, which was particularly well worn and decorated with stains. The first page had a title written across the top: "What is life? Basic concepts of biology." I brought it to the front desk and began to read.

> This concludes my introduction. I wrote it rapidly, ten pages a day for six months. I can only hope that the details of my life—starting with my ignorant grandfather Emil and my obstinate grandmother Clara, including my mother's report of the unfortunate moment of my conception, the precocious experiments I performed when I was six years old, in which I killed algae and small animals by exposing them to bleach, and the experiments using freight trains to crush poisons and broken glass, the shocking day a train driver stopped his train and threw pieces of poison and colored glass aggregate at me, my indiscretions as a teenager and their consequences for my boyfriends Urs and Willermus, the teachers I had (listed in order from grammar school through university, with examples of the facts they said they possessed), the books I read before I became a scientist (all of them, with brief reviews of each one), the places I lived (each of them, with floor plans), the glorious first year of teaching, the annoying second year, the subsequent disaster, the colleagues I had at the university (with biographical notices of each, including their Kreise and Bezirke and their so-called educations), the scandal and the lawsuit, the expulsion, why my colleagues needed correcting, the full explanation of why I broke into Früchtel's house, why I should have won the case, how I ended up working in a commercial lab, the piteous story of my last collaborator Schall, the diet I have followed (including cumulative egg totals), my daily regime of work (including a count of hours spent every day for the last ten years), the arrangement of my study, the books I keep within reach (with a sketch of the

shelves and a review of every book), the books I keep out of reach on the other side of the desk or high up on the walls (with a second sketch and a negative review of every book), and a list of every person I have talked to since I left the university (with their worm numbers and the exact amount of time I wasted on each one)—that these 1,800 pages of facts and figures might be of some help in understanding what is about to follow.

Now it is time to begin.

The first question for this book, as in any book of science, is: What is the subject? And here I have no simple answer. I can no longer say, as I could have in 1992, my subject is the new phyla that are being discovered almost every day. Or, as I could have in 1994, my subject is the diversity of life. I need to say: my subject is life, because biology has failed to define that most basic term. Biologists typically say life is any system that eats, metabolizes, creates its own energy, excretes, breathes, moves, grows, reproduces, has complex chemistry, and responds to external stimuli. It is a ridiculous definition. Even a child can sense it is too much, there's too much in it, it's like a nervous criminal going on and on about what they were doing on the day of the crime, volunteering details no one asked for, piling up a miscellaneous heap of increasingly preposterous alibis. If a person knows what they are talking about, they can explain things simply. If a person is innocent, they have an alibi. A talkative person with a dozen alibis is clearly guilty.

None of the terms in this ridiculous definition is enough by itself. If you say, "Life is anything that moves," then you have a problem, because planets also move. If you say, "Life is everything that breathes," then you have another problem, because caves breathe when the air pressure changes. The definition requires all of its terms. It is like a crowd of bullies, yelling all at once.

In addition, each term in this so-called definition is suspect. Plants do not "eat" unless "eat" means "absorb," and in that case paper towels are alive. Bacteria do not "breathe" unless "breathing" means "porous," and in that case my rain jacket is alive. Lots of nonliving things "grow," "breathe," and "move." Nonliving things also "respond to external stimuli." Babies grow but so do crystals. Both babies and crystals need to have the right chemicals in their environment, otherwise they won't grow. Babies move and so do magnetic rocks, and magnetic rocks can move other rocks without touching them, and babies can't do that. The sun "grows" and "creates its own energy." It has been doing that much longer than anything biologists like to call "living." Planets, suns, and black holes "grow" by accretion. When galaxies merge they "reproduce," because their collisions create new stars. What are those new star fields if they aren't "children" of the galaxies? Even black holes "respond to external stimuli," in fact they are the most responsive things in the universe, because they gather everything into themselves. So is the entire universe alive? Is that what we mean by "living"? It's an attractive mystical idea, but then what do we want to call a corpse or a fingernail clipping?

And what about before the first so-called living cell? Before the LUCA, the last universal common ancestor of all living creatures, the LUCA cell that supposedly launched all life on Earth. Simple organic chemicals, which existed in the primordial universe long before the solar system, could already "reproduce." The primeval oceans of the Earth bubbled with molecules reproducing themselves. Long carbon chains "grew" by enzyme assisted C-C bonding. Minute hollow balls appeared, supposedly not "living," but they replicated themselves. You don't have to be an idiot like John Butler Burke or Wilhelm Reich to believe that. Phospholipids in aqueous media formed thin bilayer membranes that self-organized. Long hydrocarbon "tails" lined up under the attraction of weak intermolecular Van der Waals forces. Any reasonably attentive beginning chemistry student knows that. There was even natural selection before biologists will allow there was life. Polypeptides assisted RNA-like molecules to self-replicate. Any college organic chemistry student knows that. The hollow balls had cytosol components that enabled basic respiration, so the balls could "breathe." They took in some chemicals and expelled others. What is that if it is not "eating" and "excreting"? Even before there was much oxygen, anoxic photosynthesis cycles produced carbohydrates by fixing carbon dioxide using ATP and NADPH from photophosphorylation. Long before the LUCAs, billions of years before, things "reproduced" and "grew" and "breathed" and "ate" and "excreted" and had "complex chemistry" and changed under natural selection. So why were they not alive?

People like to disparage viruses, saying they're not alive. But viruses evolved from organelles of cells: they were produced by life, and when they are inside cells they live along with life. People say viruses cannot live unless they are inside cells, and so therefore they are dead all the time. That is remarkably uncharitable. Many protozoa, fungi, bacteria, and archaea are inert when they are away from nutrients. So are some nematodes, rotifers, and water bears. We say they are "encysted" or "dormant." We do not conclude that they are dead all the time just because they spend part of their lives as dried-out seeds. We do not say that worms and water bears are "nonliving" just because they go through phases that resemble death to us. Bacterial spores have been revived after spending 40 million years in amber. Were they dead in the amber, and miraculously resurrected by scientists? Of course not. Seeds from flowering plants have been revived after 30,000 years. Weren't they a form of life all that time? Roundworms have been revived from Siberian permafrost after 4,600 years. They were frozen, but were they dead? It is really only fear and prejudice that impels biologists to keep insisting viruses are not living creatures. People are angry at viruses because they make us sick, so we tell them they are already dead. Biologists are forever legislating the lives of other creatures. Consider that when they are "alive," some viruses behave as if they have an interest in us. They need us. They multiply inside us and they change continuously, evading our vaccines. And yet biologists keep assuring people viruses are not alive.

When I first noticed that no one can define "life," I thought medical science might be the place to look, because doctors have only three jobs: to help in the creation of life, to make us slightly less miserable while we slide down the gutter, and to postpone the end of life. But in medicine there is no agreement about when life begins or ends. Does human life begin at conception? Or after a period of time, with the appearance of certain anatomical formations? When the heart tissue pulses, or when its pulses also pump blood? If life begins when the heart turns on, does that mean a creature with a brain but no heart is dead? Because fetuses have brains before they have hearts. Or does life begin at birth, because the infant is independent of its mother? But when is any infant independent of its mother? When are any of us independent of our mothers? I can certainly never forget what my mother told me about the moment of my conception, it was much worse than what Tristram Shandy's uncle told him. In the Christian faith, people have debated when fetuses have souls since John of Naples. For a Christian, life can even begin before conception, because God predestines lives. "Before I formed you in the womb I knew you," the Bible says.

Life ends at death, but what counts, for a doctor, as the moment of death? Is it when the blood stops circulating, or when breathing stops, or when brain functions end? There is legally dead, clinically dead, and ethically dead. There is organ death, cardiopulmonary death, brain stem death, higher brain death, total brain death. In each case there is also life. Part of the person is living, another part isn't. But that is always true. The hardened parts of my bones are dead. My fingernails and toenails are dead. Supposedly a million cells in my body die every second. And what about animals that do not breathe or have hearts or brains, like bacteria? When are they dead? According to the Public Health Institute in Allschwil, a bacterium is dead when it can no longer multiply. Does that mean I am dead? Ancient Hindu physicians said death is when digestion ends. They said if you stop up your ears, what you hear is the sound of your digestion. When it goes silent, you are about to die.

These questions are debated by philosophers, people of faith, lawyers, doctors, medical ethicists, and all sorts of people who basically know nothing. The literature is fraught, endless, and astonishingly boring, not because the subject is unimportant, but because the terms "life" and "death" are so poorly understood. It is my purpose to begin with the most ancient terms. I want to understand how to think about "life" and "death" in the deepest and most general sense. I will make my way torturously slowly and with tremendous precision from the evidence preserved by the earliest cultures and languages up to contemporary science. It is best, I think, to start by looking at some of the oldest words for life.

Psūkhē, the title of this book, is at the beginning of the Western tradition of thinking about life. I will treat it in minute detail later. First I will look as closely as possible at several other traditions. In Hebrew nephesh נֶפֶשׁ is the breath of life, and therefore apparently close to the Greek psūkhē. Hebrew also has ruach רוח, which means "wind" but also "spirit," as in "spirit of god," and it was even used to mean "ghost." Nachmanides said ruach is less substantial even than breath, and that is why God found it hovering upon the face of the waters. In the Islamic tradition there is spirit (al-rūḥ,) الروح) and self or soul (al-nafs, النفس). The Maltese language is a bridge between the Islamic, Jewish, and Christian traditions, because Catholics there call god alla. Maltese people say ruħ for "spirit." That word has also been translated as psyche, because it is the human soul that is driven by the spirit (al-rūḥ) of god. People who like to think of Western religions as very different might take note of this: Maltese Catholics call god alla like Muslims, and call spirit ruħ like Jews. I will not be pretending these concepts all belong together. I will treat each language separately. Ruħ is Malti, not Hebrew (עִבְרִית Ivrit) in disguise. However I will pay special attention to the way Greek philosophy became entangled with religious terms in Hebrew and Arabic, because that is the origin of some European confusions about the nature of life.

In the Indian tradition the principal words for the soul or the breath of life are ātman आत्मन् and prāṇa प्राण, which are nearly untranslatable into European languages. European scholars first became aware of these ideas about life in the nineteenth century, and they assumed they could connect Sanskrit and Pali to Greek and Latin. They said prāṇa is just like psūkhḗ, that life is life wherever it is. I have no such faith. The Indian tradition is different, and people who try to push all the words of the world together into one happy family are behaving like children.

With the help of dictionaries I will also consider concepts such as Chinese jīngshén 精神 meaning approximately "spirit" or "soul," shēnghuó 生活 meaning "life" or "organism," the old Chinese idea that we all have two souls, one named po 魄 that springs out of the dead body and goes straight to heaven, and the other named hun 魂, it lingers around the grave, it is weak, it needs to eat and rest before it sets out. I will also consider Japanese seishin "spirit," Russian dusha душа, Kyrgyz jan жан and ruh рух, Yoruba ọkàn "soul" and ẹmi, "spirit." In the Cayuga language, Gayogo̱hó:nǫˀ, your soul is sadǫnheˀtraˀ, but it is also ǫnhegyeˀs your heart. In the Georgian language, "breath of life" is sitsotskhlis suntkva სიცოცხლის სუნთქვა. The English words "soul," "life," and "breath of life" are all synonyms in Georgian: suli, sitsotskhle, suntkva, სული, სიცოცხლე, სუნთქვა. Then there is Bengali ātmā আত্মা, Lao vinnyan ວິນຍານ and n oa chai ນ້ໍາໃຈ, Kannada atma ಅತ್ಮ which means "soul" but also "heart," and manaḥśāstra ಮನಃಶಾಸ್ತ್ರ, which is deceptively close to the modern word "psyche." They come from entirely different proto-languages, they have nothing to do with each other back at least 6,000 years. Another false friend is the Vietnamese <u>linh hồn</u>, which is full of echoes of <u>psyche</u> and the Christian soul. A more interesting possibility is <u>tâm hồn</u>, it means "spiritual essence of a person," but also again "heart," the animating principle of bodily life, so at first it looks as if it might be close to <u>psūkhē</u>. The word <u>hồn</u> in both those expressions is a ghost word, it means "soul" but it is hardly used at all by itself, as if it needs the company of other words to appear on the page. In Vietnamese translations of the Bible it is used when apostles talk about <u>psyche</u>, but it can also be used in unreligious contexts. Where is your soul, in the end? <u>Hồn ở đâu bây giờ</u>?

These are ancient starting points for understanding "life," "spirit," and "soul." I will make use of all of them. They are opportunities to think about life and death more carefully and attentively than the narrow, confident, and impatient way they are understood by science. Once we attend to words like these, it becomes impossible to march along with modern science and proclaim that life began with the first cell, that viruses are not alive, that a human life begins at one moment and ends at another. It is time to put down the garish banners of science.

The text went on, without a break that I could find. The margins were annotated here and there with references to the black notebooks: "Vol. 12 p. 81 1982C 153," "Vol. 31 p. 20 note 1990C 32."

I skipped ahead fifty or sixty pages and found myself in the middle of a discussion of Sanskrit.

There are many Hindu deities that bring death. Yama is the god of death, time, and justice. Nirṛti is the goddess of graveyards and sorrow. Imagine having a goddess of graveyards! Kālá means both "time" and "death." Imagine having a word that means both "time" and "death": whenever you write "time" you are writing "death," so even if you just ask "What time is it?" you are asking, "When is death?," and if someone says, "I don't know what time it is," they are saying, "I do not know when I will die." Mṛtyu is the "Death Girl" created by Brahmâ, and Mara is a demon associated with both death and rebirth.

Yet none of these gods can cause the death of the <u>prāṇa</u> प्राण , none can extinguish the <u>prāṇa</u>. This is because in Hindu belief, there is no white and black, living and dead, ensouled and unsouled. "Life" is never absent, "breath" can be found everywhere. First prāṇa enters the body as a vibration or a sound. Its motion is eternal, even though the organism itself exists in bounded time and not infinite time. A baby breathes its first breath, we say, but of course its body has been breathing in the womb through the mother's umbilical cord. The fetus swallows and calmly breathes the amniotic fluid in and out. An old woman breathes her last breath, we say, but of course her breathing continues. When her corpse swells with bacterial gasses it has another breath, and later its dust is picked up by the wind and the wind breathes and so the corpse keeps breathing until it breathes everywhere.

This is because in the Indian tradition prāṇa circulates wherever time and space are together. The oldest portion of the ancient Rigveda tells the story of Yama and Yami. (Rigveda X.10.) They are twins, brother and sister. Usually in these ancient texts Yama is Lord of Death and Yami represents life, or Yama is agni (fire) and Yami is earth. But here Yama represents time and his sister stands for space. That is because later, Yama became the first person ever to die, sacrificing his life in order to become God of Death. It was a peculiar thing to do, to volunteer to die in order to become God of Death so that other people could die. If he had not volunteered, perhaps there would be no death at all. One of the saddest legends of any culture is the story of Yama's deliberate death. When he died, Yami was stricken. Yama was the first person to die, and Yami did not know what to think about life without Yama. Back then there were no nights and days, only continuous daylight, so Yami did not understand whether time had passed. She didn't know if her grief would ever heal, so the gods created night to separate one day from another so that Yami would understand that time was passing. It didn't work, because she saw the days passing and realized it was longer and longer since Yama had died. Yami never recovered from her sorrow. Before there was night, Yami just was sorrow, but after there was night, it was worse, because she felt Yama going farther and farther away. It is the world's saddest love story, there will never be a story sadder than that. If time does not pass, you only know your sorrow. If time passes, you know your life is passing in sorrow.

In the conversation in the Rigveda, none of this has happened yet. Yama, who is time, is in the womb with Yami, who is space. Even in the womb they love each other, they are incestuous even in the womb. Time loves space, space desires time. At one point Yami says, "My desire for Yama is gripping, it is catalytic." She pleads with her brother: "Please, I have desired you since we first appeared in the womb together." Yama says, "We commingle on heaven and earth, I commit unbrotherly acts on you." But he has misgivings. "In future," he says, "there may be a time when brothers and sisters do things that are improper, but this is not for me. Look for another husband, Yami, make your arm a pillow for another husband." But then he relents. "Come near," he says, speaking to his sister in the womb, "just hold me close." It is not enough for her. "What kind of brother," she says, "lets his sister become an orphan, when she is full of desire, when she wants him so much?" But Yama says, "I will not touch that body of yours, because it is prohibited for a brother to enter into his sister." Yami is angry. "I can't see a heart or a mind in you. You would rather be covered in shrubs and grass, you would rather be a tree suffocated by wild creepers." The dialogue is continuous, eternal. The brother and sister are incestuous, on and off, in eternity: in the past, in the future, even before they are born, up until the moment Yama dies and time begins. It is an amazing story, so far from us, yet very close.

The book with this story is ancient, perhaps four thousand years old, and it is not easy to guess what it originally meant. But for my inquiry, the significance is clear: time and space are intertwined, and there can be no limit for either one. If time had never slept with space, your body would die at its time, in its place. Time would go on without it. Space would contain your death like a plot contains a corpse in a cemetery. What is a coffin? It is a space that contains time, that stops time. That is what people who buy coffins hope. But time did sleep with space. Your body, your life, continues in space and in time. In the Rigveda time and space always want to be together. As an Upaniṣad says, "Why are you afraid of death? Death is charming." The Sanskrit word is sundara सुन्दर.

The same idea of time and space occurs in descriptions of agni, the primordial fire that is still worshiped in Zoroastrian traditions. In the Rigveda, the dark universe was put in motion by the light of agni, and after that life could be distinguished from death. For me the flame is bright, I see life, I see myself living. But the flame flickers, the universe sometimes darkens, and when it does life and death can no longer be told apart. If the light is low it is no longer possible to see life. When the light increases, the world becomes conscious of itself. It can see that life and death are separate. The Sanskrit word for this is puruṣa पुरुष, it means the self, consciousness, and awareness, and it also means the world's awareness of life. The concept puruṣa is not just the presence of life, it is the awareness of it, and it comes and goes with agni. In any individual organism, the presence of life can be seen and felt as prāṇa: the breath from the nose and mouth, the pulsing of the abdomen, the flapping of spiracles, the light in the eyes, the sap in the organs, the palpable presence of an attentive perceiving body. The organism knows itself in time and space, it has consciousness. It sounds stupid to say a protozoan is conscious, and technically it is wrong. Perhaps that is one reason for the name, protozoa, before life. But the word puruṣa can help, because the protozoan creature moves through space and time, it shows the presence of agni just as we do. Puruṣa is the link between the individual awareness of any living thing, even the unreflective existence of an ant, and the universal consciousness fitfully revealed by agni.

In the Rigveda the light of agni flickers. When that happens, space and time return to their homes, life can no longer be distinguished from death, there is no awareness, the world goes cold. This is normal. It is the usual condition of life outside the bright tent of our human awareness. The tiny protozoan lost in its droplet of water, the ant mindlessly searching, those are darker parts of the universe, but it is the same universe. We all live between light and darkness. I am tempted to say: sometimes agni is too strong, the world is shaken with self-awareness, life and death appear starkly different. That is our modern scientific world. Normally the light is dimmer, the two are closer. The corpse settles in its grave, I settle in my bed.

Another word, ātman, is like prāṇa. Ātman also means "breath," "self," and "innermost essence of the individual." It appears in many Indo-European languages, because it is very ancient. In Old Irish it is athach, in ancient Greek ἦτορ êtor heart or soul, in Anglo-Saxon ǣþm aethm, breath. These are wonderful words. Athach, sounds like ahach, aethm sounds like athem, they are breathy, like breathing. The Greek ἦτορ êtor became ἀτμός, atmós, which is atmosphere, the air itself, the world's breath. When I speak these words I feel myself breathing, my soul is in my mouth. Ἀπὸ δὲ τοῦ ἀτμοῦ ψυχὴν καὶ αἴσθησιν, soul and sense come from the breath, that is what Pythagoras said.

In the Aitareya and Taitirīya Upaniṣads, ātman gave rise to the universe, and according to T. N. Chapekar it is the origin of biological evolution. आत्माविभाज्योऽदह्यः सर्वगतः शान्तोऽज्ञेयश्च, ātman is indivisible, omnipresent, tranquil, and immune to understanding. तैत्तिरीयः प्राह प्राण एवात्मेति, शरीरस्थः प्राणः. The Taitirīya Upaniṣad says prāṇa is ātman, and the prāṇa inside the body is the same as the ātman in the universe, विश्वस्थेन प्राणेन समश्च. (T.U. 2.3–5, 3.20.) I do not know if that is right, because these texts are very old and they contradict each other.

This may seem esoteric and far from anything of use to science, but it is important not to file these words and stories away as cloudy beliefs held by a culture that disappeared long ago. It is not irrelevant that twentieth-century physicists like Bohm, Schrödinger, Heisenberg, Oppenheimer, and Bohr were interested in Vedic cosmology, and that Vedic scholars like Ghosh, Raja Ramanna, Chapekar, Rajagopalan, and Krishnamurti read the Vedas through the lens of quantum physics. I think they were all misguided, because the two systems are utterly different in purpose, language, cultural context, and use of figurative and analogical thought. Their styles of reasoning, as Alistair Crombie said, are very different. But it is salutary for the overconfidence of science to be reminded of formulations that it cannot encompass, but which are so much older than Bacon or Galileo. I want to walk out to meet these words, prāṇa, puruṣa, ātman, agni. That walk can be treacherous. The Upaniṣads are like sand bars far out beyond the beach. Can I walk to them? Will I have to swim through high waves and strong currents?

When the twins Yama and Yami argue and embrace in the womb, they express the entanglement of life and death. The drama is described several times in the Bṛihadāraṇyaka Upaniṣad. The Bṛihadāraṇyaka Upaniṣad is one of the oldest Upaniṣads, those are books of philosophy and theology, written about 2,700 years ago. Āranyaka means "forest book," and Bṛihadāraṇyaka means "great forest book." It is a wonderful title. I wish I could take it for this book, because what long book is not a forest? Actually the Bṛihadāraṇyaka Upaniṣad is just a copse, a local region in the forest of early Indian texts. The oldest of them, the Rigveda, is a collection of different books written over hundreds of years. The earliest passages are the Samhita, hymns to the gods.

The first set is 191 hymns, the second is 43, the next is 62, there are ten sets in all, 10,600 verses of hymns, and then there are Brāhmaṇam, which are commentaries, and then the Rigveda continues with Āraṇyaka, also "forest books," which discuss rituals, and then Upaniṣads, the philosophic and theological texts. And the Rigveda is only the beginning. There are forests beyond forests. Then come separate Upaniṣads, over a hundred of them, and thirty-six Purāṇas, some enormous. These books are otherworldly and full of prayers. The early Indian literature is a borderless forested landscape, crossed by unsigned paths, filled with people who wandered in and became lost. Sometimes I feel I could get lost, too, and forget why I came. What would my life be like then? What language would I speak?

Compare this astonishing landscape with the earliest literature in Europe. Our first writing is paltry fragments. Not a single book remains from any philosopher before Plato. There are a hundred fragmentary lines by Heraclitus, a hundred and fifty by Empedocles, a hundred and fifty by Parmenides, a single line by Anaximander, nothing at all from Anaximenes, Zeno, Hippo of Samos, and many others. Gorgias's book called On Non-Existence no longer exists. The earliest complete books in Europe are epic poems, two supposedly by Homer, three supposedly by Hesiod. Early Greek writing is like a desert landscape with a few colorful potsherds. Then there is the Judaeo-Christian tradition, which starts with just one book, it's a collection, of course, but still just a single book: one tree, not the forests of Indian writing.

I look around in the Bṛihadāraṇyaka and try to describe the things I encounter. I do not know where I am, or how to walk back out of the forest. Since I know Aristotle, I think I recognize him everywhere, but I am always wrong. I start by searching the Bṛihadāraṇyaka Upaniṣad to discover what it says about prāṇa. A fourteenth-century philosopher named Madhvācārya, who wrote a long commentary on the Upaniṣad, says that "in infants under six months old, all the functions of the senses are performed without awareness, by prāṇa alone, so infants have no memory of that period." The same is true, he says, in animals. An ant has self-awareness and memory, but its awareness is occluded because the prāṇa is not differentiated, there is no place to put the awareness. The infant has awareness but no place for it. We know this, Madhvācārya says, because we can see the infant "remember," "ponder," and "reconsider." With ants it is the same. We can see them try out one path, and then another. We can see them "remember" they have already walked up one twig, we can watch as they momentarily "hesitate" and then "decide." Even the littlest protozoan moves in zigzags through the water. It "considers." It "hesitates." It charges forward! Then it "doubts," retreats, moves away. It does not know this because it has no place to put its awareness. Prāṇa is a conceptual improvement on Aristotle because it links the breath of life to awareness, and awareness to memory: a bridge that European thought never constructed.

Here is a story that helped me understand the ancient idea of prāṇa. Madhvācārya says there are seven devas, gods of the body, and they are breath (that is prāṇa), smell, speech, sight, hearing, mind, and sex, meaning a womb or the capacity to make semen. Madhvācārya imagines what would happen if one of those abandoned the body, for example because of illness or old age. How much can the body lose and still live?

First, he says, the god of smelling leaves the body. She is gone for an entire year. He does not say where she went. "The Smell-god doesn't know whose body she leaves," he writes. "After a year she walks by the body, and the body calls out, 'Come back!' and the Smell-god says, 'Who are you?' and the body says, 'You are our smell,' and the Smell-god says, 'I thought you would be dead without me,' and the body says, 'Of course not, no one needs to smell in order to live.'" (Adhyāya III, Brāhmaṇa VII, §16.)

Then, Madhvācārya says, the Speech-god leaves the body. She is gone for an entire year. He does not say where she went. When she comes back she is surprised the body is still alive. कथमार्हन्मदृते जीवितुमिति ? she asks. "How were you able to live without me?" or maybe it was more like a lover might say it, कथमशकत मदृते जीवितुमिति ? "How could you live without me?" And the other devas of the body reply, यथाकला अवदन्तो वाचा।, "Just as mute people live without speaking," or maybe they said it more like lovers might, "मूकावदन्तो यथा जीवन्ति वर्षाणि, "In the same way as quiet people go for many years without speaking," प्राणन्तः प्राणेन, "We breathed through the prāṇa, पश्यन्तश्चक्षुषा, we saw with eyes, शृण्वन्तः श्रोत्रेण, विद्वांसो मनसा, we heard things with ears, शृण्वन्तः श्रोत्रेण, विद्वांसो मनसा, we thought with the mind, प्रजायमाना रेतसैवमजीविष्मेति।—and the whole time we generated semen," or, I suppose, if the body was a woman, "we lived with a womb." (Adhyāya VI, Brāhmaṇa I, §371.) "It was easy," they say to the Speech-god, "we lived quietly for a year without you. You talk a lot, you know, but actually it was quite pleasant without you."

Then the deva of sight left for a year, and when she came back the body said the same, जीवामो वयं, धन्यः प्राणः।, "we survived, we breathed through the prāṇa." Then the deva of hearing left, श्रोत्रँ होच्चतक्राम, and it was the same. The body said, "It is good to hear myself breathing again."

The body lived on for a while, but then the mind decided to leave the body. It went away from the body for an entire year. Madhvācārya says the mind spent the year looking at stars. During that time the body had no mind. तत् संवत्सरं प्रोषितं, देहश्चामनोऽभूत्। A year later the mind came back, and it saw that the body was still healthy, तत् संवत्सरं प्रोष्यागत्यापश्यद्देहो निरामय इति । "A body with no mind!" it said. देहोऽमनः "How could you live without me?" And the body said, "I don't know, because I didn't have a mind, उवाच च, नो वेद, यतोऽमनोऽहम्, निरामयोऽहं परं, यथा पश्येत, स्वागतं तद्भवताम्, but I am healthy, as you can see, so you're welcome back," so the mind got back into the body प्रविवेश ह मनो देहम्।

Then the semen left the body, रेतो होच्चक्राम, and for a year there was no semen, संवत्सरं देहोऽरेतः, or I suppose if it was a woman's body, there was no womb, नार्योऽगर्भाः. Madhvācārya says the semen tried to find a wife, but women ran away from it. For a year the body lived without semen or without a womb संवत्सरं रेतो गर्भो होच्चक्रमतुः, and when the semen or the womb came back, it looked at the poor body and said, "How could you live without me? That is not living!" प्रोष्यागत्य रेतोगर्भौ, ऊचतुः, कथमशकत मदृते जीवितुमिति And the body said, "We survived the way all impotent and asexual people survive. जीवामो यथा क्लीबा जीवन्ति। We did not generate any life, we breathed through the prāṇa, we spoke with the mouth, we saw the world through the eyes, we heard the world with ears, we knew who we were using our mind. That is how we lived, there is nothing unusual about it." अप्रजायमाना रेतसा प्राणन्तः प्राणेन वदन्तो वाचा पश्यन्तश्चक्षुषा शृण्वन्तः श्रोत्रेण विद्वांसो मनसैवमजीविष्मेति।

Then comes the moral. Madhvācārya imagines what would happen if the prāṇa left the body. "It is my turn," the prāṇa said. "I want to try to live outside the body." The gods of the body begged it not to. "You will die," the gods of the body said. "A body cannot exist without prāṇa, and the prāṇa cannot exist without a body." न वै शक्ष्यामस्त्वदृते जीवितुमिति, त्वमपि नोऽस्मदृते। The same, Madhvācārya says, is true of the entire living universe. मध्वाचार्यो ह यथोवाच, ऋतं

तज्जगतः। अथ यद्यत्किञ्च जगत्यां जीवानां स्त्रीपुम्भ्यां वा यद्वा सर्वं प्राणैरेवायं जीवति तत्किञ्चिज्जीवात् सर्वम् तदेवायं जीवति। Prāṇa gives awareness and breath, the winds and the world. एको विषमोऽमूर्तः सूक्ष्मश्च, प्राणदो देहधारिणे, अन्यश्च गुरुद्रव्यमयः, †मर्त्यदेहस्थितः क्षयतां विधत्ते... कदाचिदहं ज्ञातास्मि, ततो नास्मि, परं तत् 'अहम्' एवेति, यत् परितः पश्यन् विस्मयते, अपरश्च मृत्तिकायां विलीयते। "Whatever there is in this world, animate or inanimate, is pervaded by prāṇa. Without prāṇa the world is dead, and without the world the prāṇa is dead." (Adhyāya I, Brāhmaṇa 4, §7).

When the story ends Madhvācārya looks at the Moon. सोऽसौ चन्द्रः "There is that Moon shining there," he writes. परेण मृत्युमतिक्रान्तो भात्येवं ह वा एनमेषा देवता मृत्युमतिवहति य एवं वेद, "she has surpassed death with the help of prāṇa." (Adhyāya I, Brāhmaṇa III, §26.) सोऽग्निः, "there shines Agni," the spirit of fire, most ancient of all the forms of life," भवत्सोऽयमग्निः परेण मृत्युमतिक्रान्तो दीप्यते, "she has been freed from death by prāṇa." तत्तथा दृश्यते, परं वस्तुतस्तु अमरप्राणोऽयं नैव मृत्योर्विभक्तः।

"Prāṇa is in dogs,
प्राणः श्वसु,

Worms,
कृमिषु,

And flies.
मक्षिकासु च।

Prāṇa is in the smallest creatures,
प्राणो लघुतमेषु जीवेष्वस्ति,
The ones who swim in drops of water.
ये जलबिन्दलेषु तरन्ति।
It is constrained in a crystal,
स्फटिके स बध्दः,
Flutters in the brushed tail of a comet,
धूमकेतोर्मृजितपुच्छे परिघूर्णति,
Frets and breathes in storm clouds,
प्रवातमेघेषु व्याकुलीभूय श्वसति च,

Twirls in embers, lifting into the sky
अङ्गारेषु परिणमति, आकाशं प्रति उत्थापयन्
It is the uneven stirring
विषमः क्षोभः इति
That pushes seaweed into patterns on the sand.
तत्सागरशैवलं वालुकायां प्रतिमानरूपेण स्थापयति।

Prāṇa is in dogs,
प्राणः श्वसु,

Worms,
कृमिषु,

And flies."
मक्षिकासु च।

Dear सेम्युअल्, if you ever read this, सेम्युअल्, कदाचिच्चेदपि पठस्यैतत्, प्राणो वा त्वयि सुदुर्बलश्चेत्, मनो वा दुर्बलस्ते यद्यपि, even if your mind is weak, यद्यपि त्वन्नेत्रे उज्ज्वलतमभासैव पश्येतम्, यद्यपि नावगन्तासि किं चाहं लिखामि, even if you don't understand this book, यद्यपि परिधावितोऽस्मात्पुस्तकात्, or run away from it किं किं च स्यादस्मिन् पुस्तके इति चिन्तयन् जीवनं यापयसि यदि, यद्यपि निगूहसि स्वतस्त्वं, त्वं वेत्सि, अनुभवसि च, किं किं च वदाम्यहमिति। प्राणेऽस्ति किमपि घोरम् एकाकीत्वं, terribly lonely न तु स प्राणो यो मानवप्राणः, परं सर्वेषु पशूषु, वनस्पतिषु, शिलाप्रस्तरेषु च यः प्राणः, यः सकलविश्वतः श्वसति, सः प्राणः। तस्मिन् किमपि घोरम् एकान्तं, यतः स जन्मतो मृत्युपर्यन्तमविरतं वहति, परमन्ते तु तन्न जीवनम्। सम्प्रति नेच्छामि तं वक्तुमिति, आङ्ग्लभाषायां नेति, यतः मया स्वतो गोपनीयः। स आन्दमयः a form of despair सन्निराशारूपोऽपि।.

The rest of that page was blank. I wondered about the parts in Sanskrit. Who was she writing to? Was I supposed to have those passages translated? It felt like she had forgotten she might have readers, as if she was writing for herself, not thinking what she sounded like, whether she made sense to anyone.

Again I had a strange feeling, as if the notebooks, which already seemed so distant, like an ocean seen from far above, had gone even farther away. These pages on Indian concepts were like the unlit ocean floor. Entrancing and poetic, but uninhabitable. Inaccessible, too distant to clearly imagine.

I went ahead ten pages. There was more about androgyny and incest.

> ... and prāṇa is of course also a god. Sometimes he lives with the goddess Vāk वाच्, who is the goddess of inspiration and speech, and when they are together they are not a normal couple. Instead they merge and "form the androgyne": they are puṃskārin पुंस्कारिन्.
>
> What could be more wonderful, more challenging, than this word prāṇa? It is breath, soul, self, principle, god, male, female, and androgyne. (Adhyāya I, Brāhmaṇa III, §23.) In the story of Yama and Yami, prāṇa is incest, even in the womb. Prāṇa is androgynous and incestuous! A wonderful antidote to the bloodless psyche in the European tradition. (Geoffrey Hill: "Thick with Plato's blood / (Tasteless! tasteless!)")

I flipped ahead twenty pages, fifty, a hundred. Toward the end of the notebook were more unusual words, from extinct languages called |Xam and !Xóõ, from an Australian Aboriginal language called Yolŋu, from an extinct Caucasian language called Ubykh. The whole of volume 7 was a monograph that would take months to read. If I studied it carefully, this one notebook might take the entire year that Anneliese budgeted for all the notebooks together. It would be lovely, I thought, to have a year to read just this notebook. I felt like I was out walking on a forest trail, and I emerged into a clearing and saw how many mountains there were, and how far I was from home. I could immerse myself, and soon I'd be lost in these forests and languages. But it would only be a glimpse of what she had done, and I would never understand the whole.

I returned volume 7 to its place, and picked up volume 15. It fell open at page 4,200. There was a gap in the text, about a half page she'd left blank. The writing began again near the bottom.

> That is all I need to say at this point about the relation between the relevant philosophy of biology, the concept of such a philosophy, and specific applied philosophies such as the philosophy of conception, of development, and of death. In later stages of this work I will show that these relationships depend on both systematic and unsystematic misunderstandings of the

nature of rationality and reasoned discourse, and in particular misunderstandings concerning the difference between geometric and literary texts. Broadly speaking, geometric texts include mathematics and science, and literary texts include essays and fiction. The distinction, first named by the shy American classicist Wesley Trimpi, has guided thinking about modes of exposition, reading, and understanding since Euclid. But that is for much later.

To repeat, simplicius: the philosophy of biology has a confused relation to philosophies that should be naturally parts of it, such as the philosophies of life and death. This is because there is a confusion in European thought between two kinds of writing, geometric and literary.

In previous sections I reviewed differences between philosophical axioms, postulates, assumptions, definitions, principles, and undefined terms, as they apply to biology. I turn now to the question of laws, as they apply to biology. As I have suggested, a long tradition in scientific thought excludes biology from the study of natural laws. Although modern biology seems to have given us a good understanding of the living world, it appears to have accomplished that without the use of laws in the normative sense. Physics has laws of energy, mass, momentum, entropy, particle interaction, and so forth, and it has Newton's three laws, Coulomb's law, and Gauss's law. Chemistry has Boyle's law, Charles's law, Dalton's law, Avogadro's law, and Gay-Lussac's Law. (The last states that the ratio between the combining volumes of gasses and their product can be expressed in small whole numbers.)

Here I will not even open the question of the philosophic status of laws, postulates, assumptions, axioms, and propositions in mathematics, because axíōma ἀξίωμα in mathematics are statements assumed to be true, whether they are logical, such as the axiom of pairing in Kripke-Platek set theory, viz., if x, y are sets, then so is a set containing x and y as its only elements ({x, y}), or non-logical, such as assertions about elements within some established mathematical theory, such as a + b = b + a. Laws in the sciences are not statements assumed to be true, but propositions that have not been falsified.

By contrast with physics and chemistry, biology appears to lack laws, or to have a deficit of them. Mendelian inheritance has been proposed as a biological law, and so has Darwinian survival of the fittest, metabolic scaling (that is

> Kleiber's discovery, $B \propto M^{3/4}$) and power laws (that is Jeong's discoveries about E. coli, $P(k) \approx k^{-\gamma in}$). However, even these laws are not absolute. Either they are approximations or there are known exceptions. For example, non-random segregation of chromosomes, and homozygous mutants parenting a normal offspring, are both deviations from Mendelian inheritance. In the case of homozygous mutants parenting offspring that do not express the mutant phenotype, it is possible that other genes are interacting with the mutant allele (epistasis), or there are environmental influences, or unidentified genetic modifiers—Mendelian inheritance has many exceptions, for many reasons.
>
> Biology has been said to lack normative laws of the sort that chemistry and physics have for several reasons. First, it has been claimed that the subject matter of biology is special. Biology studies living nature (phusis φύσις), life (bios βιός), the breath of life (this is meaning no. 2 of psūkhē, which I will discuss in a few years). Those subjects, it is said, cannot be adequately reduced to laws. There are also arguments that biology does not propose laws but is instead occupied with patterns, mechanisms, or models. I will consider those arguments in later subsections. They are all wrong.
>
> In this project I adopt a different position: biology is not concerned with laws, but not for the reasons assumed by advocates of mechanisms and models. Concepts such as psūkhē are disjunct both from mechanistic explanations in biology and from theoretical models such as Müller's or Uexküll's that may roam far from actuality. Concepts such as psūkhē do not clear the way for biological laws or mechanisms. Rather they provide a conceptual framework that permits the comprehension of biology as the study of phusis, prāṇa, or living nature.[40]

Clearly this notebook was very different from volume 7. But as I turned the pages, I saw the similarities: the careful sequences of arguments, the scattered references to Sanskrit and other languages, the marginal notes. These were not separate books. I had just skipped eight volumes, 2,400 pages of writing.

I looked again over the tables in the lab, entirely covered with notebooks. This was a single impossibly long book, with one voice running through it: Anneliese carrying on an argument with herself, and with no one else.

Looking for words she could use, searching for cultures that could help her say what she wanted about life.

I replaced volume 15 and took another one about halfway along the sequence, number 28. Again the book fell open naturally at a break in the text. On page 8,512, I read:

> And so, in considering the concept of lifespan, it is crucial to remain open to the fact that for the Greeks, aion (αιόν) meant not only lifespan, but also eternity. The two meanings are intimately entangled and cannot be separated one from the other. For any organism, for me, a lifetime is the only duration I know directly, my only experience of time, and therefore it is all of time, and therefore it is eternity: not an eternity, but eternity itself. This is true even though I understand there are other eternities, not only other people's eternities and all other organisms' eternities, but the eternities known to religion and science, including the full range of competing theories of the origin and dissolution of the universe ( the possibility of multiple universes ), and also including Greek and Roman thinking such as the supposedly atemporal eternity in Parmenides, and of course Aristotle, Plato, Plotinus, Proclus, and Simplicius, the special eternities of Jewish and Christian eschatology, including Boethius, Aquinas, Maimonides, and Spinoza, the eternity of ātman (आत्मन्) in Hinduism, the eternity of the sixteenth chapter of the Lotus Sutra as it is taught in Nichiren Buddhism, and the day of the Calamity, al-Qari'ah (اَلْقَارِعَةُ) in Islam, when the universe will be pulverized, time will end, and
>
> I am aware of these and other eternities outside my experience, but in them time passes in some abstract way, long before my life and long after it. Aion is my life span, my eternity. This is the one sense of eternity that I know in my own life, as my own life.

And yet there is another: the eternity of the instant.

eternity

Meister Eckhart said God makes the entire world now, instantly (alzemâle, that is Eckhart's Middle German). He makes the world and the soul (sêle) directly in the present (gegenwürtig nû). God performed all his work in the eternal now (in dem ēwigen nû). Ananda Coomaraswamy says this sort of immanent eternity can be found in St. Bonaventure, in Dante's idea of il punto singolare a cui tutti li tempi son presenti (the singular point where all times are present), in the bindu (dot) that marks the center of the forehead and the center of every maṇdala and yantra, and "of course," Coomaraswamy says, the eternal now is also in the mystic Jan van Ruusbroec who rejoiced au-dessus du temps (beyond the bounds of time), in an "unending present eternity," and it is "absolutely the same" in the Ṣūfis, especially in Rumi's teacher Shams-i Tabrīzī, and "identical" in Pali Buddhist texts and even "the exact equivalent" of the eternity found in the Chinese Tao Te Ching. Coomaraswamy gets carried away making everything equal to everything else. If it was, these notebooks of mine could just be a single sentence, like this:

So I will not use flabby phrases like "absolutely the same" or "identical."

In its earliest and non-philosophical use, aion just meant a life span. It was introduced into philosophy by Heraclitus, in his beautiful line αἰὼν παῖς ἐστι παίζων, πεσσεύων, lifetime or eternity is a child playing, moving pieces on a board. The same double meaning was taken up by Empedocles, who taught near Agrigento in Sicily, and by Parmenides, founder of one of the first philosophic schools in the world, in the mountains south of Naples. This is what Parmenides says in fragment 8, line 5: "And yet one narrative of the path of life remains, that it exists. And on this path are several signs: first, that being itself had no beginning; second, that being can have no end, because it is unmoved and eternal. Being [that is, being considered as being, tí in eínai τί ην είναι] did not exist just once in the past, and then later did not exist, because it exists always. So the path of a life [aion, αιόν] exists in all times, all at once. It is one continuous thing." This was Parmenides's way of saying that the span of life does not have a beginning and an ending, because from the organism's point of view life is everything, all of experience, eternity. At least this is what I think, and so do Heleen Keiser and Gwilym Owen, even though Leonardo Tarán thinks Parmenides failed to grasp atemporal eternity, because he didn't see that verb tenses need to be canceled in order to talk about tenseless being—but Tarán was astonishingly pedantic even for a Greek scholar. Parmenides and Empedocles first had the idea that eternity is tenseless, that it's nonsense to say "it was once," or "it will be forever," because tenseless eternity simply is. Beings (ónta, όντα) can perceive their lives this way, as the sum total of existence. The path of an organism's life is at once finite, because it can be measured, and timeless.

So how does a single lifespan come to appear as eternity? Melissus of Samos, the ancient philosopher and naval commander, read Parmenides and thought he meant that the path of life, aion, is actually ápeiron ἄπειρον, meaning "unlimited" or "indefinite." This is what Melissus says: "The path of a person's life is and always was and always will be, it has neither beginning nor end. That is because no one knows the moment of their conception, and no one knows the moment of their ending." Melissus meant that none of us is conscious of ourselves at the moment of birth, just as none of us has consciousness at the moment of our death, only the seconds leading up to it.

Our paths have no beginnings, because we never remember their starting point. And every person's path ends, but it ends together with life, and so it always appears at a distance. I believe my life to be infinite, even if I am conscious of my impending death, because the horizon of my life can never be visible to me. I know my life had a beginning and will have an ending, but by an inscrutable biological order I have forgotten the first, and by an unavoidable existential law I will never experience the second, and so my lifespan is eternity. It is the only eternity I experience. The others I just read about. Or, to be exact about it: my life is an eternity, the only eternity I can ever experience except for the eternity of each passing moment, in dem ēwigen nû, in the eternal now.

You may object that the main eternity, the one everyone knows perfectly well, is the one that is measured in seconds, years, and eons. You may think eternity is just whatever science says it is. The Greeks were of course aware of what we call clock time or even geological time. They made a fundamental distinction between eternity (aion) and time (chronos). Plato makes this explicit in Timaeus, line 37d, where he claims that time (chronos) was created to serve as an image (eikon) of eternity (aion). It is a profound idea. The clock time that we all know was created, Plato says, to give us an idea of eternity. A wonderful answer to overbearing science! The time science gives us, including the eternities it presents to us, are pictures of eternity, snapshots, and by that same logic a photograph is a picture of eternity precisely because it represents a single instant. Five centuries later, still in ancient Greece, Plotinus said that aion is the "manner of existence" of being. (See his Enneads, n1, 4, 7.) Our ordinary clock and calendar time are given to us as simple pictures of eternity, because that's all we can understand. And then Proclus, two centuries after Plotinus, at the very end of antiquity, one step from the so-called dark ages, said μίμημα... τῆς τοῦ αιῶνος ἀϊδιότητος, the cosmos is a copy of the aion of the eternal: the universe is just a copy of the nature of eternity. Ἀπλῶς ἐστὶν ἡ εἰκόνα τῆς αἰωνιότητος, ἡ ἠλιθίοις ἀνθρώποις. Another wonderful mysterious idea, but there was no one left to answer him. The culture changed, and the Christian middle ages were underway.

Heleen Keizer has a different understanding of the ancient Greek aion. She says it means time seen from the outside: time completed, the entirety of time, a life whole, seen from the outside. I can see the aion of someone who was born after me and died before me. I can understand, intellectually at least, that the Jurassic period began at a certain time and ended at another time. I see it as if from the outside. Keizer calls this aion a Totalbegriff, a "total concept."

When I think of the unrecoverable moment my life began, and the unseeable moment my life will end, I sense another kind of eternity, one that is whole, that includes everything because it passes the boundaries of my memory and reason. When I try to imagine what it means that time and space began with the Big Bang, I fail, because I cannot think without space and time. The same problem occurs at the so-called "end" of time with the dissolution, or the kingdom of heaven, or the Calamity. My own life, and the span of the universe, begin and end outside my understanding. Those kinds of eternity are what Emil Jenni calls Extrembregriffe, "extreme concepts," ideas that are seen only from within their limits. My aion, my lifespan, my eternity, is something whole, in a way I cannot ever understand. The poor expression, "all eternity," as in "condemned for all eternity," is a confusion, because the only eternity we know in that way is our own existence.

When an animal, such as a human, moves through its life, following its path, it keeps within a certain measure of time. It is conceived and it is born, and later it dies. Because aion means both lifespan and eternity, the animal does not move like a train on its tracks, from point alpha to point omega. No: the animal moves in its own eternity, and its activity, as Aristotle says, is actually an "activity of immobility." (Energeia akinesias, this is in the Nicomachean Ethics, 1154b.) A lifespan, therefore, is the form of eternity that all beings are given.

And there is one more thing about aion: it is not only my own idea of eternity, but it means I experience the universe itself as a lifetime. Here is why: when I wonder about my life, I know I will not ever stand outside it. I will not stand before it, or after it, I will not be able to look back to it. That is exactly how I feel about the universe, and therefore I have no choice but to think of the universe as a lifetime, the longest one of all, the one we are all inside. Proclus, who wrote when Christianity was spreading, knew all these older authors I have quoted, and he concluded that aion is a being in itself, like a divine substance, but somehow found on the earth and in creatures. Proclus got his idea from Plato, who said that the visible cosmos we experience is a living being (zôion, from zôê, the state of life) with a body, a soul (psūkhê) and a life (bios, a particular life). Everything we see and experience, including clock time (khronos), is a faithful copy of the everlasting, eternal (aïdion, from aion) being of the universe.

> Still, we live in a world measured by clocks, but they are just given to us as copies of what the world is. Clock time is what we can understand, but measured eternity is a shadow of real eternity. Lumen umbra dei, light is the shadow of god: an exceptionally simple and beautiful idea, although I prefer lux est deus umbrarum, shadows have light as their religion. Or really lux est deus umbris, light is a god to shadows. These ideas are among the most wonderful that came out of the Greek and Christian worlds, but there is so much more— —and yet even though the universe can be understood as a living thing with a soul, it is nevertheless only a copy, a projection or a version, of the eternal, of aion.

The calm voice talking about eternity was not something I had heard from Anneliese. If she had spoken to me that way we might have had conversations. She was frantic and breathless when she talked, but here in the notebooks she was steady and careful, as if she had an eternity to write, as if every moment she wrote was a kind of eternity. Her voice was poised, her thoughts measured. I was attracted to the ideas about eternity, and in a different way to the science in the other notebook. Maybe she had judged me correctly, and I was the ideal reader. If these pages on eternity were just an ordinary short essay, I might have spent a day in the lab reading. But there were 8,500 pages of meditations before this, and 8,500 more to come. These few pages, which I had discovered at random, were instants in her life, between eternities of writing in the past and the future. At the same time I remembered what she had said about striking out passages, how she wrote word by word, how slowly time passed for her.

These pages, too, had marginal annotations to the black notebooks. What reader would ever follow those references back to the black notebooks? She must have known her book would never be read as a whole. It was almost but not quite inconceivable that someone might read all 19,700 pages of the gray notebooks, but the marginal citations put the whole thing out of reach. No one would read nearly 20,000 pages of any text, no matter how compelling, and also stop, several times a page, to consult references that might not explain anything.

I imagined all the citations as strings connecting the gray notebooks back to the black notebooks, enmeshing the lab in a monstrous cat's cradle. The amount of work she had done was close to incomprehensible. The entire thing was a knot, with thousands of strings tying all the parts together.

I couldn't understand how she had moved from the daily details in the black notebooks to the expanse of concepts in the gray notebooks. How had she thought through her fragmented laboratory results so thoroughly that she could fill ten thousand pages with orderly exposition? Then again I wasn't really reading. By opening to random pages I was acting like a child who interrupts an adult just because it can't understand that the adult is talking in sentences that are linked, one to the next.

The pages I had read were microscopic samples. I felt a kind of vertigo thinking about that. Even if the notebooks were wrong, even if the science or the philosophy wasn't right, they were an impossible achievement. As if she had taken a bedsheet from a closet, and unfolded it, and kept unfolding, and unfolding, until it covered her house, the city, the entire world, a single enormous sheet, billowing, continuous.[41]

I chose another notebook, volume 36. The first page, 10,500, began in the middle of a sentence:

> ...their mantiké was a crime, it was not just divination. Reading the future by its supposed inscription in entrails was a crime because it exploited the hidden sympathy (συμπάθεια) between the sheep's organs and the god's knowledge, it revealed the hidden sympathy by a delicate process. Mantiké, haruspicy, bruised the manteis μάντεις, the people who practiced it, they could never let themselves forget their knowledge, they could never hide their knowledge from the gods. They knew the shimmering threads that bound the

gods to everything, because they had found those threads where the gods never thought people would look, in entrails and ashes. They looked at sheep's livers. They noted small pathologies, pale patches and soft red cupules, nodules and indentations, twisted arteries, irregular folds and fissures, they observed fibrous connective tissue caused by flukes, ashy necroses caused by toxic plants, they noticed cancers and cysts, all the deformities that the gods had hidden there, inside the sheep, and they read them all as an awkward and unpleasant alphabet, written in meat, they read the defects in the sheep livers as secret signs of battles, marriages, and storms in the outside world.

Eventually, after the fall of the Greek and Roman religion, after Cicero, when Christianity emerged, héxis adopted the role of mantiké. Christian héxis, later called witchcraft, was the path to hidden knowledge. In Christian doctrine there was a different way to understand the future, because the truth was given to the world by divine gift, by emanation from the original divine logos, present before creation, so no theft was necessary, no wounding of the relation between world and truth, no need to slice into sheep and read with bloody hands, no mysterious hooded mantises (manteis, μάντεις) or priestesses (iéreies, ιέρειες) prying into entrails or poking at ashes. The ancient mantiké was gone, divination was not practiced because it was not needed, the world no longer kept secret maps hidden inside animals. God still infused the world with arcane meanings, but they were not codes seen in ashes or flaws revealed in entrails. They were hidden in plain sight: they were images waiting to burst open, to emerge suddenly, in a flash, ein Aufblitzen, an epiphany of meaning, a "sudden spiritual manifestation." They were sparks set to be ignited by faith or insight. No knives were required, the truth was everywhere. The world was planted with spermatic ideas, lógoi spermatikoí, set shallowly in the soil, ready to spring into the light, and the great ancient crime of mantiké was finally gone...

I turned forward twenty or thirty pages.

Darkness has been the accompaniment of this process. How could it have been any other way? Mantiké has always been an art of darkness, of torches, candles, and flashes of lightning. Yet I am not interested in hē archaiá technē, the supposedly sacrilegious art of fortune telling. That is how Schleiermacher once translated _mantiké_ in his German version of the _Phaedrus_: he called it "idolatry." I lean away from him, and toward the kind of _mantiké_ Schlegel intended when he wrote that the historian is a prophet turned backwards. In Schleiermacher's philosophy the dimension of the future plays a significant and underestimated role, and so, first of all, the presence of _mantiké_ in Schleiermacher is philosophical, and I will need to explore his early writings, unpublished in his lifetime, such as the _Treatise on the Value of Life_ (1792), as well as his speeches on religion (1799) and his monologues (1800), and even then, determining what can be salvaged of _mantiké_ may be difficult. At any rate my work in these pages has always been done in darkness, has proceeded in darkness, by means of darkness, _as_ darkness, and _mantiké_ is hardly the concept to describe the form of that darkness, or its feeling.

After I discuss this matter I will analyze darkness in St. John of the Cross. He wrote about the "dark night of the soul," although that phrase isn't his, he never wrote those words. He said he stayed still in his dark thoughts until he lost himself. The movement of the world slowed, he said, it became quiet. "Everything stopped, and I abandoned myself," _cesó todo y dejéme_. He gave himself up, he fell away from himself. _Quedéme y olvidéme_, "I stayed, and lost myself." That is the "dark night of the soul." I know the experience. I have been alone with my thoughts so long that I have abandoned myself. I tossed myself away, along with the things I loved. There they are among the lilies, _dejando mi cuidado, entre las azucenas olvidado_. St. John of the Cross is one of the last resorts for the desperate, the saints and scholars who work in the dark, but he said the night was bright, and that is because his faith enabled him to perceive things as the opposite of what they are. He thought _la noche oscura_, the dark night, is a joyous night, _una noche dichosa_. _¡Oh noche amable más que el alborada!_ he wrote, Night more lovely than the dawn! In the end he died in oblivion in his so-called happy night.

And then I will turn to the Latin concept of _lucubrationes_, that is work done at night, even though I also like to work in the day, but I recognize that certain solemn and unsocial projects, certain unhealthy states of mind and body, are best nourished at night. My book is a _lucubration_, figuratively concocted in darkness even if it was actually often written in sunlight. It is nycterinos, it belongs to the night. I am nychteriní νυχτερινή, nocturnal.

Quintilian was an authority on lucubrationes et vigilandae noctes, et fuligo lucubrationum bibenda, nights spent drinking the soot of work. Quintilian was one of the first of a long line of Europeans who thought they were strong and poetic, or sensitive and intuitive, or worthy and noble, or intellectual and perspicacious, or ethical and responsible, just because they stayed up after their husbands and wives went to bed. But unless you are a child, it is no great accomplishment to stay awake after midnight. Still, I will consider each of these writers and try to understand what they felt about working in the dark, some with only a candle or oil lamp, others in the company of owls and ravens. Because fundamentally whenever I write it is night. I am Anneliese Lucubrantis, Είμαι η νυχτερινή Άνναλιζε. I will consider the following writers who boasted that they worked at night: Quintilian, Agrippa the Skeptic, Ammonius Saccas, Plotinus, Epictetus, Epicurus, Porphyry, Zeno of Citium, Pyrrho, Hermarchus, Basilides, Origen, Lucian, Ambrose, John Chrysostom, Augustine of course, Hildegard of Bingen, Meister Eckhart, Thomas à Kempis, Charles Borromeo, Jakob Boehme, Erasmus, Luther, Juan Gines de Sepulveda, Nicholas of Cusa, Petrarch, Barlaam of Seminara, Francesc Eiximenis, Coluccio Salutati, Manuel Chrysoloras, Niccolò de' Niccoli, Guarino da Verona, Poggio Bracciolini, Étienne de Courcelles, Hugo Grotius, Milton, Gerardus Vossius, Lessing, Swedenborg, Nikolai Berdyaev, Strindberg, Michel Leiris, Peter Kien, and of course Pavel Florensky. And I will sample far beyond those traditions, including Adyashanti, Omraam Mikhaël Aïvanhov, Ali ebn-e Sahl Esfahani, Muhammad al-Yaqoubi, Abdūl-Khāqeem Arvāsī, Helena Blavatsky, Ad-Dağhestānī, Ramakrishna, Chaitanya Mahaprabhu, and Daniil Andreyev.

After those, I will consider the night itself, the Umnachtung, the condition of darkness that makes such work possible. I will inventory darknesses: Osiris the so-called "dark god," although the Egyptians never exactly said that; ח⊠שֶׁךְ choshech, the darkness on the face of the deep; σκότος skotos, the darkness that blinds warriors in the Iliad just before they die, Ayin אַיִן in the Kabbalah, and the Sufi fana فناء, annihilation, because as Rumi said, it is necessary to die before you die. Also Manichaean darkness, Gnostic darkness, Zoroastrian darkness, and darkness in the Bṛihadāraṇyaka Upaniṣad. This last one is terrifying, because it says that if I worship ignorance I will fall into a "blinding darkness," but if I follow knowledge I will fall into an "even greater darkness," and I have done nothing but follow knowledge since the beginning.

I will look for ideas of working at night in every source I can find. I will examine old books, monographs, theses, notes, parerga, strenas, disputations, stromata, adversaria, conferences and convocations, entretiens, notebooks, marginalia, lucubrationes senectutis, lucubrationes historicae, lucubrationes philologae, and lucubrationes Socrateae. I will be more thorough than any previous writer. Old darknesses are outside, like Job's arafel עֲרָפֶל, the thick darkness that screened God so Job could not see. Now darknesses are inside. I have had nights without darkness and many days without light. Night is when silence leaks out of the walls and pours into my ears. Even if it is a sunny morning outside, my work is done during the night of the soul: these notebooks are die Dunkelheit im Inneren meines Herzens, there is darkness inside even when when burning white beams of sunlight fall directly onto my notebook and my writing hand is warmed and casts a deep blue shadow. The shadow of old age, the blankness of failure, the darkness of history, the silhouettes of words, the pooling doubt.

For a long time I wrote under the gazes of Erebos and Nyx, those are the gods of gloom and night, worshiped by Greek Gnostics. Erebos was invisible, he hid in the corner next to the large bookcase. Nyx had a black veil. Her wings were silent even when she unfurled them. Recently I think Erebos and Nyx have gone. Now I work in agnosia kai zophos αγνωσία και ζόφος, ignorance and gloom, those are my new tutelary deities. Agnosia makes sure I muddle everything. Zophos enforces darkness. Neither one is visible, because they don't look like anything, there are no surviving pictures or sculptures of them, they were woven into the world differently than gods like Nyx. Agnosia is the one who makes my hand shake when I am trying to write. Zophos ensures the lights don't work, so I am always peering at the page. This week I feel I'm also being watched by Āz, the wedge-headed Manichaean mother of demons. She makes people forget about heaven.

I know this is a ridiculous way to think, but once you imagine a wedge-headed goddess standing watch behind you, her corrugated back against the wall, her triangular eyes fixed on the back of your neck, there is no way to remove her. My room fills with old gods and they will not scare.

I find darknesses hidden in bright texts, even in Voltaire, Descartes, Politian, Pico, Leibniz, Chamfort, Ibn Rushd, Zhongren, Russell, and especially Abu al-'Alā' al-Ma'arri (Moarrensis). There is even darkness in Socrates: not his not knowing, but his not wanting to know, his indifference to truth, his special feeling for ignorance, as Johann Georg Hamann said, that is Socrates's wonderful darkness. Hamann and Nietzsche realized Socrates was ill, and his illness was not his skepticism or his compulsive argumentation or his cheerful belligerence or his spectacularly annoying assertions that no one knows anything: it was the fact that he didn't care what the truth was. Socrates is the illness that you never suspect, the one you think you'll never have, but now you have it, and it's too late, culture has been infected by Socrates for two thousand years and it is still dying. Lucubrations are not only mournful, pensive, and dusty: they are also brilliant, harsh, sharp, and clean, and they can be the most interesting and immoderate thoughts. There are painful darknesses in Voltaire, like his hatred of people who have simple faith. There are desperate darknesses in al-Ma'arri, such as his magnificent idea, which is actually true, that the earth's surface is nothing but dead bodies, that the earth is the "Mother of Stench" ('um dafr, أُمّ دَفْرٍ) that the earth "buried alive her daughter Eve," buried all her children, left each one to rot, so we all walk on corpses, dig into corpse flesh to build our houses...

I thought of all the things Anneliese had told me: the seven partitions, the thirteen illnesses, the thirteen worms, her stories about the Hütte, the cottage near the airport, Luzia's career choices, the bucket list. Supposedly they were to help me read her work. But the winding sentences and exhausting theories she'd subjected me to were infants in comparison to what she had done here. Her speeches to me were hints, glimpses of the enormous thoughts that were unfurling in her mind. Her eggs and resorts were jokes. Her ladders and worms were toys. She needed me to believe I could understand her. Remember this, she kept saying. Everything is planned for you. But her stories about long books were just to warn me: Those are babies, mine is far more difficult. This was a universe, not a book, and opening one page or another was like pointing a telescope at a single star.

I wished I could believe she had been writing just for herself, because the alternative was not easy to accept. Maybe I could promote her work, try to find a library that might accept the notebooks. Perhaps there was a way to save just some of the work, take one of the early notebooks and find usable passages, turn them into an article... but it just wasn't possible. The whole thing was woven together, threaded and knotted to itself.[42]

Fifty pages later I read this:

> Of the Manichaean words for the darkness of the world, the most important is the original Middle Persian word azhedan اژدن. Middle Persian is a mysterious language, first spoken by the Sasanids and by Mani himself, then later only by Zoroastrian priests. Now it is said to be extinct, but it can still be heard in the streets of Abyaneh. A synonym is the Parthian word aždēn 𐫀𐫉.𐫅𐫗 Mani's mother was Parthian, so he probably used that word as well, and it was also spoken in the liturgy. Aždēn is a darkness that is dead because the light has been taken out of it. It is no longer ensouled, it is not a living darkness. It is unsouled, in Greek that would be without psūkhē̂, ἄψυχος apsychos, in Sanskrit without prāṇa, नि:प्राण niḥprāṇa, in Hebrew לא-נֶפֶשׁ lo-nefesh, without soul. In the Parthian Manichaean way of thinking, light is soul, but there is none of it on earth. We are darkness with sparks of light still hidden in us, we are living darkness, ensouled, still shining. When the last of the light is stolen back to heaven our darkness dies, it becomes aždēn, 𐫀𐫉𐫅𐫗 unsouled darkness.
>
> There are also Coptic Manichaean words for darkness, gnophos ⲅⲛⲟⲫⲟⲥ and kmeme ⲕⲙⲏⲙⲉ. I wish I knew more about the obscure Tocharian word orkamotstsäññe +ᏗᒣᏈ|ᏗᒥᏋᏗᏓᏗᏗᏥ. Tocharian is so nearly lost, there are so few texts, that every word is dark.
>
> These are Manichaean words for corpse-like darkness. According to Manichaeans, light is imprisoned in the world, it is in pain. The light is extracted from the world, one person at a time, it is leached out of the world and returned to heaven, and so the world becomes darker. ⲁⲡⲣⲏ ⲣⲉⲃⲏ ⲛϩⲁϩ ⲛⲥⲟⲡ · ⲁⲩⲱ ⲁϥⲣⲕⲁⲕⲉ ϩⲛⲧⲡⲁϣⲉ ⲙⲡⲉϩⲟⲟⲩ · ⲁⲡⲕⲁⲕⲉ ϩⲟⲃⲥⲛ ⲙⲡⲛⲁⲩ ⲙⲙⲉⲉⲣⲉ · (The Asceticon

of Apa Ephrem, part 1.) The sun rises many times, but it is dark in the middle of the day, darkness covers us even at noon. Manichaean darkness is syncretic and gnostic, so it seems like it could enrich the accounts of darkness that I have been building. Unfortunately the Manichaeans thought darkness is vicious or evil (in the Parthian language dušpar [illegible]). For me darkness is the condition of work. Apparently the Manichaeans hated the idea that they were mixtures of light and dark substances, hated having to eat plants and animals that were adulterated with darkness. They wanted to free themselves from darkness, leave aždēn behind forever. But unsouled darkness is the condition I see ahead of me, the one I want to understand.

Despite the fond hopes of many authors, theories of darkness cannot shed light. They can only describe the darkness. They give me words for the place I find myself. For some reason, the farther I go the more words and languages I want to have around me. I want to be able to call the stubborn lack of light in my thought by its Parthian word, aždēn. I am aware that these notes on darkness will seem pompous and ponderous to anyone who lives a normal life, where darkness is just the moment or two before you find the light switch. If a book, to you, is something you can lose yourself in for just a day or two, these pages may seem laughable. If a tragedy, for you, is an event that calls for healing and closure, then these pages will seem indulgent. If life, to you, is a windy sunny stretch with a brief stormy end, these pages may seem indulgent and unnecessary. Cheer up! You'll say. You sound portentous, it's all too much. But if you find yourself at midday, in a field, say, looking at a pond, admiring how it sparkles in the sun, how the trees shine bright green and the wind shows the silver undersides of their leaves and the birds fly in roller-coaster flourishes, and yet you find yourself turning away from all that brightness and noting instead the shadows that have gathered at the far end of the pond, wondering how they will look at dusk when they spill out over the water and swallow the field and cover the trees and seep up into the sky, then you might not think these pages are too much, and you might even feel you need to know some of these words.

When I began this work, I went aus dem Alleinsein, in die Finsternis, from solitude into darkness. It was dusk when I opened the first notebook, it was getting dark, es war schon finster. My eyes were already dim, [illegible] tīmīr. Darkness leads to blindness, a Tocharian text says, [Tocharian script] [Tocharian script], but it is my darkness, orkamotstsäññe. When I was about to start these notebooks I could have run away, but I stayed at home and forgot the world, quedéme y olvidéme. Now I am formed in the shape of my chair, when I stand I feel tall and awkward, when I walk I am embarrassed and I want to sit down. I am compressed like coal, the light I used to have has almost leaked out of me. My hands and head are bōlosi ⲃⲱⲗⲟⲥⲓ, as the Gnostics said, lumps of the world's darkness. In the Coptic language there is a beautiful word for the kind of ignorance brought on by darkness, mntateime, ⲙⲛⲧⲁⲧⲉⲓⲙⲉ. My soul has descended into darkness, ⲡⲉⲥⲡⲩⲭⲏ ⲛⲓⲱⲧⲉ ⲧⲉⲣⲉ ⲧⲁⲣⲉ ⲉⲛ ⲙⲛⲧⲁⲧⲉⲓⲙⲉ, ⲡⲉⲥⲡⲩⲭⲏ ⲛⲓⲱⲧⲉ ⲧⲁⲣⲉ ⲉⲛ ⲕⲁⲕⲓⲁ, I have sunken into shadow. That word ⲡⲉⲥⲡⲩⲭⲏ pespykhē is psyche, the Coptic psyche. ⲡⲉⲥⲡⲩⲭⲏ ⲛⲓⲱⲧⲉ ⲧⲉⲣⲉ ⲧⲁⲣⲉ ⲉⲛ ⲙⲛⲧⲁⲧⲉⲓⲙⲉ, ⲁⲛⲟⲕ ⲧⲟⲩⲧⲏ ⲉⲛ ⲙⲛⲧⲁⲧⲉⲓⲙⲉ, ⲛⲟⲩⲧⲛⲓ ⲛⲓⲱⲧⲉ ⲉⲛⲧⲉⲣ ⲛⲉⲥⲏ ⲉⲡⲁⲗⲉ. I work by my own light, which has nearly gone out. My sky is blackened with mosquitoes, verfinsterte sich vor Mücken. I am tormented by thick darknesses but tempted by even thicker ones. Now meine Dunkelheit hat das Temperament des Wahnsinns erreicht, my darkness has reached the temper of insanity. If any writers claim they work in daylight and their inspiration shines brightly in the night and they write in the glare of creative energy, then they are not writers. Darkness is the condition of writing and thinking. In the past few years a gloom has settled in and the world has become quiet. The winds have withered, the air is stagnant. The clouds have perished, because darkness does not need them. That is Byron. Die Erde ist ein Wüstenplatz und weit, the earth is a vast deserted place, I am the only one in it. I work without light, yet I am obliged to perform operations of great delicacy on myself in complete darkness. I know I don't sound normal, but how could I? I sit even now in this study, which would look to you like an ordinary room, perhaps with too many books in it, but to me it is a vast chamber. I am seated in the middle of an enormous cathedral at night. On a throne on a pedestal, like a Pope. It is nearly pitch black. There is a thick gloom. The stained glass windows are blocked up. A colossal column, high up in the church, has fallen away from its wall and partly toppled, forming a bridge high overhead. The entrance is lost in darkness. Darknesses are tightly crowded into the chapels, condensed

> up above me, running under my pen. This is my home, me quedo aquí y no me olvido. This writing has been the work of many years, and it has many years to go. Ideas of darkness machen die Aussichtslosigkeit klar, they make the hopelessness clear.[43]

The treatise on darkness seemed to continue through the entire volume and into the next couple of notebooks, five hundred or a thousand pages. A long time to be thinking about darkness, and so many different kinds of darkness.

I recalled how she used to make fun of herself, talking about her pampered life and the traveling she said she didn't want to do. At least in this part of the notebooks, that attitude was gone. Without someone to listen, her thoughts surrounded her, weighed down on her. All the words and languages were like medicines helping to keep her going. Or like soothing voices keeping her company. But what kind of life was that, when her only companions spoke in dead languages?

I turned to one of the gray notebooks about three-quarters of the way through the sequence, volume number 49, and opened it to page 14,515. What I read there was very different.

### (b)
### Life in Nulland

> I am not cleaning you, hedgehog reader. Bathe yourself! I am not a normal scientist. I am road salt: I appear familiar but I am poisonous. That is, I am called salt, but if you add me to your eggs, you will get sick. I have been denatured, the natural form has been removed from me and replaced by an admixture of sense and poison. If you take me into your kitchen and pour me into a container labeled SALT, and if you eat small portions of me consistently over a period of months or years, you will go to hospital and you may die. The language I am speaking now may appear to be science, or, perhaps, philosophy, but it is not either one in its pure state. Like road salt, I have hidden additives and they are poisonous.
>
> It may still seem to you that this is a book in the ordinary sense. It is extraordinarily long, I know, you know, and it requires unusual dedication, you

know, I suppose, but it may seem in the end that it is ordinary because it was written by one person, whose life and career, even though they are not generally known, can be discovered with a modicum of so-called research. If you have read the opening three hundred pages, you know the basic facts, and if you bother to do any so-called research, you will find that the author of this book never married, lived in an excellent neighborhood in Basel, was supported by a dedicated brother, and so forth, and yet that kind of so-called research will not locate the author of this book, because she, the one who speaks to you from out of these pages, is not a normal person, and she did not write these notebooks the way an ordinary writer writes a trivial conventional book, whether it is a work of fiction or a technical scientific monograph. She, the one who is addressing you at this moment, cannot be located in the way you suppose, from your lifetime of ordinary reading habits. You cannot deduce the author by looking up facts. This may perhaps be disturbing. It is easier to get lost than to get to me, the navel of the world is not safe from scientists, but who finds their way here? I am no longer behind my book, you cannot find me by visiting the house where I live, I am in the book, hiding between the words on these pages, I am disassembled, crumbled into this writing. I have been stripped and sliced and stirred around in this book. When I look out from these pages, I do not see a reader, I see a hedgehog, rooting about in my words, scratching and peeking. I yell to it, as I am doing now, and sometimes it squeaks in reply. Eeeee Eee Eeee! You squeak. You are startled that a book is calling to you.

The kind of destruction I am perpetrating seldom happens. Sciences are hardly ever interrogated as carefully and patiently as I have. It is a rare destruction, but when it happens it is all over! It causes a general catastrophe and collapse. There are two falls in this work. They are both caused by Psyche in the form of Nemesis, that is the dreaded Psyche-Nemesis who can both love and destroy. (Wilhelm Heinrich Roscher, Ausführliches Lexikon der griechischen und römischen Mythologie, vol. 3, N-P, 1897-1909, col. 3,251-3,253.)

The first fall is the descent of biology, the philosophy of biology, away from its dream of logic and empirical truth.

The second is the Greek myth of the fallen soul, kathodos ΚΑΘΟΔΟΣ, it is the same as descensus animae, that is the Latin myth. The soul falls. It is psyche, the thirteenth of the thirty-three senses of psūkhē. This second fall is my own.[44]

Hedgehog reader, I know you have not been faithful, I know how you are skipping from one page to the next like a hedgehog snuffling for something edible. You are anxious. You are not finding much sustenance, because only ink remains. In fact you will die of hunger.

For now, as far as you are concerned, I am the deceased, because when you read this I will be gone. I pursued this book, Psūkhē, with my fear. It was not to be conceived of, what this book had to do; it was never going to be easy to comprehend. I moved through undeveloped regions. I pushed hard to go against the current. I dug in. I did not stop, I moved always upstream, from the splayed-out tidal flats of common opinions, littered with the mud excretions of burrowing marine worms, upward, toward the source of the river. Like a nineteenth-century explorer pushing up the Amazon. After years of work I arrived here, at this place you cannot understand. I named it the Nulland. Here I have stayed with my door locked. If I had seen my future self back when I was sailing the lower reaches of this river, when I was still so far away from myself, or if I had seen myself later as I paddled the narrower stream, if I had seen myself as I walked beside the cataracts, always following the water upstream, getting nearer to the Nulland where I have finally come to live, if I had observed myself on my journey I would have recognized only a victim, compelled to a fruitless search. I would have had the victim stopped. But no one watched what I was doing. So I kept going for years, always upstream. Stubbornness was all I had, and fear of turning back.

The story about the explorer went on for a hundred pages, describing the settlement in Nulland, her recovery from the difficult journey from Basel, the people who lived there, how many mosquitoes there were, and then just as she had said, lists of each of her mosquito bites, with diagrams of her body and charts of the size and severity of each bite, how she suffered from sweat bees, and a long dissertation on how there are no hedgehogs in South America, but only New World porcupines, which are unpleasant spiny white rats that live in trees. It was an entire book within the book, as if she had read some eccentric explorer's story from a hundred years ago and copied it into her notebooks. I hoped she had taken a vacation from herself, given herself the luxury of imagining a different life.

I skipped forward half a dozen notebooks. At the beginning of volume 55, page 16,200, I read this:

> Psūkhê, my companion over these many pages! Where are you, exactly? You are neither in the brain nor the heart. You are a reddish bulb. You are bound in the fascicles inside my nerves, in the fiber bundles in my muscles, in the fibrils of my tendons. I know you are in the bacteria and water droplets in my breath. I can almost see you braided into the lilac strands of my irises. But I will not cut into my eyes to find you. I cannot dissect a single droplet of water. You will not let yourself be found. As Plutarch says in his book The Face That Appears in the Circle of the Moon, and as the Naassenes assert, every stone and object strains to have a soul. Even rocks struggle to have souls, because then they can grow. Where are the thirty-three meanings of psūkhê, which I listed 6,300 pages ago? The soul of divine origin, the thing repeatedly reborn, the world soul, psūkhê tou pantos, the Stoic heated pneuma, hiding everywhere: Where are you? Psūkhê is the reddish knob, the garnet, the eyespot of the Euglena, and it is the clot, the pith, the Lisch body, the bleb, the lesion, the ecchymosis, it is the seed of life. Souls are like bodies in tombs, Philólaos says. Σῶμα-σῆμα, the body is a tomb. Souls want to burst out of the body, like crystals from rocks, like blood blisters, like foul pneuma from a dying person's mouth.
>
> My psūkhê is draining, it is collapsing. Life is ending everywhere. Cells die at unmeasurable rates in our bodies, they are dissolved and carried away in the blood, siphoned into the liver and pancreas, excreted. Psūkhê continuously leaves the system of life. It will not let itself be found. And then it returns, smelling of the cemetery. Σῆμα sêma, as in cemetery. The word means "sign," but in ancient Greek it meant "tombstone," because a grave marker is the most important human sign, the most ancient.
>
> The oracle at Delphi leaned over a pit, and the pit breathed pneuma. The Greeks thought it was divine, actually it was gas, bad breath from the earth. Technically ethylene and ethane, sweet-smelling gasses that made the oracle woozy, that is the so-called truth of the famous oracle. Anagogically it was

pneuma, the humid breath of the earth, perfused in winding earthen alleys and puffed into the face of the oracle. There was no miracle, there was only the stinking breathing earth.

Psūkhē is homeless, because it wants to be eternal, it tries to escape from individual life. Empedocles said he was born when the world was whole, and that he was broken off, torn away by Strife. In his book The Refutation of All Heresies, also known as the Philosophumena, Hippocrates of Rome says Empedocles raged against Strife, calling him unstable. Empedocles said Strife tore him from his place in the world and made him into a wanderer or a fugitive. He meant not only himself but everyone, all of us, whatever has a soul. Our souls are homeless, as Plutarch says in the essay "On Exile." They have been torn away, they are gone.

Psūkhē will not let itself be found. Today we have to be content with signs. Some animals and plants are named after the elusive psūkhē. For example Psychidae are bagworm moths, their larvae hide in bags of lichen and dirt cemented with a gluey secretion. Psychoda is a sort of drain fly or sink fly, no one wants to think about where their larvae live. Helicopsychidae are snail-case caddisflies, their larvae make shells, they look like tiny snails but they're not, they are only fly larvae in pebbles glued with mucus. Pychoanoxidae are a family of uncultivable viruses whose genetic material has been found in sulphur springs. Halopsyche is a mollusk with poisonous butterfly fins. It keeps them hidden.

Perhaps this is why science turns its back on psūkhē. Science needs to see what it studies. Psūkhē keeps disappearing. Like the story about Freud's grandson who played with a cotton reel. He cast it away, and then pulled it back and held it in his hands. "Go!" he yelled, and then "Come back!" Science is content when its concepts are right there. A cheap wooden cotton reel. A rocket. A supercollider. Psūkhē is not like that. It is a mixed concept, interbred with other concepts and mingled with us, knotted into our thoughts. I am sorry for you, hedgehog reader, if you feel this is not right, if you think I am not making sense. Perhaps you would like to step back into your childhood and play a while with a cotton reel. Freud's grandson Ernst was happy with his cotton reel until his mother died, and then he went silent. You have to read carefully to notice that Freud's daughter died. It happens in a footnote. All he says is "the child's mother died when he was 5½ years old." Psūkhē will not let itself be found.

That notebook was one of the ones titled "An extended anagogical allegory of this entire book." It was religious, even mystical. In the earlier notebooks it felt like she was trying to keep science and philosophy in sight. Here it seemed she had gone farther away. Reason was almost out of sight. She was hiding between the words, as she said, looking back at normal life, at me. When I tried to see things from her point of view I felt a chill. These later notebooks made me feel alone in a way I hadn't at the beginning. I could imagine her feeling lost in her words, looking out of her book at no one, or perhaps at a hedgehog.

I skipped forward again, approaching the end. Volume 61 began on page 18,000. It was a narrative about someone with the initials W.P.:

> When W.P. died, the older generation of scientists heard the verdict against the knowledge of those whom W.P. had recalled, and they admitted they had opposed the wisdom of the Greeks. It was advisable to impose burdens on the older scientists, against whom W.P. had lost ground, just as G. had. It was W.P.'s death which would not end. W.P.'s death lasted, his misfortune hindered his blind companion G., who remained clasped in his death, G. could not escape from that embrace without help. The blind-sighted companion did not smother W.P.'s death, it dwelled in her head, almost driving her out. Nothing was possible.
>
> Only W.P. was allowed in G.'s mind. The moon was a slice, the moon was again a slice, it was in decay. G. had to stay in Nulland. Her body was trapped, her mind was trapped by the absence of W.P., she could not permit anyone else in her mind. G.'s family sent her a lot of gifts. They had been concerned to buy the gifts, and following their usual habits, they had taken a long time choosing them, a long time getting the courage to knock on the door and deliver them, but they were useless. The standing lamp, the carpet, the new bookshelves, useless. W.P. had the dangerous work of living in G.'s mind, and he told G. to accept the gifts, because they had been carefully chosen, according to G.'s family's usual custom. G. was not the strongest. She knew no

counter-defense could win in a struggle, nothing she knew how to do could bring victory, and certainly not liberation. G. accepted the useless standing lamp, the unnecessary bookshelves, the hideous carpet. She was reduced, the heavy weight of labor shifted its position on top of her. She closed her door and returned to her work.

In the years after W.P. died, the goddess Psūkhē took G., and guided her slow death by blind creeping. Psūkhē spoke to G., and told her she would not understand the new ideas unless she agreed to contract thirteen diseases. That frightened her, because she was already weak from the absence of W.P., but Psūkhē told her she needed to be injected with thirteen diseases. The injections produced rashes and worms. G. became loud with the thirteen diseases, but she followed Psūkhē, she knew that without the thirteen diseases her work was as soft as rabbit droppings. But even that didn't end her embitterment. A great deal was also due to the fact that it never occurred to the scientists that G.'s work had consequences, even that much was not understood. The work was not received by the elders, even though it was their job to receive it. Also there was the unusual and sour way in which the scientists emphasized C.'s importance in the forest. This involved an invitation, they invited C. to impose herself impatiently. They wanted her to drive G. from the forest. The scientists said they needed time to study the materials, but their appetite was enormous, their supplies melted away, they had to think about the future. They left, one after another. They shrugged their shoulders and went away, they shook their heads and left. C. brought them supplies, but the scientists had failed to warn themselves about the mountains, they became exhausted, one by one they went home. They stroked their beards and left, they rolled their eyes and left. They abandoned C. in the thicket with G. The scientists were people of limited strength and courage.

Meanwhile, S. slept badly at night, he slept struggling with demons. In honor of the forest, the dreams were harsh. G. tried to watch over him, but she was poisoned with thirteen diseases. The scientists had to be wise in their hatred, so G. would eventually appear to have died of starvation. The temptation of blindness was particularly stubborn in G. She wanted to be blind to what the scientists thought about her, deaf to their trickling poisons. Why did G. cultivate her thought to a point beyond exhaustion, why did she even care?

And why was S. so surprised at the forest, so defenseless? Every movement showed how defenseless. The grave, like a cloud: you do not fall hard into the ground. The bottom of the trench is far away, but it advances toward you like a cloud.

After he met G., S.'s dreams became worse. Night by night worse. He was attacked by the forest. Forks of lightning, heavy clouds. Sharp branches plummeted like stakes toward S.'s body. And yet he could not wake up. Invisible spearlets were attacking S. He was helpless in his sleep. G. saw, she ran to help. She tried to deflect the arrows. A spear grazed S.'s heart. G. retrieved it and threw it back. It stuck in a trunk. The forest turned its anger on G. She ran with an abnormal gait, she was demented by her thirteen diseases. Yet she escaped the trawls, the taut lines like an invisible net, artfully woven into the bushes. S. could not see very well. He had to protect himself from a stealthy unconscious power. Who whispered in G.'s ear: "The bow is taut, strike now"? Who whispered to S., "Withdraw immediately from your mission or you will be hit"?

The arrows thorned S., he was porcupined with twig spears. S. was weak, like many Canadians, and he did not know how to defend himself without the force of G., G. was a master in forward movements between the giant trees. G. moved quickly, because she knew members of the scientists' society dreamed of her death. "She has gone too far," they said, "G. should not have gone that far, she needs to give up on S., S. is lost, he is gone away into his dreams, but G. continues to prepare him. For years she has been attending to him. G.'s hopeless care for S. will exhaust her. Then we will be able to impale G., and we will be finished with her ridiculous theories once and for all." The wrath of the scientists was patient, their anger was glued with patience. G. bent over S., who was sleeping in his life. He was dreaming, he was attacked in his dreams.

G. could not see her work, because her face hung from her in rags. What did G. gnaw at and never finish? Her mind was engaged with slow-release worms. She was surrounded by blank books. The society of beasts approached, they saw G. as a table of meat. G.'s pencils were asleep. The scientists decided the time was now. They ran at G., they tore her, they exposed her. G. did not even cry. She released her protection. She urinated without warning. Still the scientists did not calm down.

Meanwhile during this fight poor S. slept fitfully. Each day more of his life was asleep. Every night more of his mind was stolen by the forest. It drew his attention to roots, he dreamt he had to dig pits, to follow roots. He dreamt he had to push branches into the ground, dig enormous graves for fallen trunks. A hopeless task, to bury the forest. The forest in poor S.'s mind rushed through blind-angled dreams.

G. could no longer help. The scientists attacked G., they carried her over their heads and placed her in a pit. C. impaled her on a pike. G. had not been willing to apologize to the scientists, she would not recant, she would never give up! So she was ruined by the scientists, they crushed her head into a white tuber and packed her in dirt. They placed her in the ground so no one would hear or see her, and they could go on and live their stupid optimistic lives. Still G. was the friend of blind-shy S., she had selected S., she knew S. would eventually stop trying to bury the forest, S. would walk and find her. So G. waited in the pit.

One day a steel spade knocked on her skull and she was found. She was in that sour state between life and death. S. worked hard to extract her, but S. was weak, because he had been eating moss and leaves. He had been trying to bury the forest, one branch at a time. He was stupid with weakness and he let G. remain in the pit, buried up to her neck, impaled on a pike and with a groove in her head caused by the spade.

S. was going to lose the battle against his dreams. But G. could not help any more, she could only observe. After a few days poor S. forgot he had found G., and walked off to dig somewhere else. Poor S. was feeble and lost, and he understood very little about his life. From the beginning G. had known, she had always known. S. was weak and largely without resources. The dreams came and pushed him into forests. S. saw a mountain scraped bare, there were teeth in it, and then it dawned on him: everything is lost. Poor S. became hollow like an old tree, and that is when he finally saw: he was the son of the forest in which he was lost. The brown leaves encased his bones, the twigs picked his teeth. He was a stain on the bark, three of his hairs tangled on a twig, his urine pooled and crystallized on the rocks, his teeth fell into moss, his corneas floated like paper boats on a forest pool, his penis was explored by ants, his toenails were collected by mice to tile their bathrooms. S.'s heart was broken.[45]

It was awful to see myself in Anneliese's notebooks, in such an uncanny fantasy, with so much unhappiness and violence. Insulting, too, to see myself through her eyes, weak and demented. Somehow I had been woven into a nightmare story about fighting scientists in a forest.

I wondered when she had written this notebook, since I had only known her since February. According to her table of contents, it was written in 2012, eight years before she met me. She knew about me before we met in Frankfurt, because she'd looked up my history and read my papers. But could she have known about me that long ago? It was unsettling to see she'd been having such fantasies about me, that she'd hidden them from me, that she'd been thinking about me for so long. The part about my dreams was especially disturbing. I was being told about what I was dreaming in a book written by a woman who hadn't even met me. I decided to ask Catherine, she would know.

G. lay in the pit. S. wandered back, he stayed in a hunter's cabin near the pit. He guarded her from there. He listened from just inside the doorway, he crept out on the porch, he glimpsed the rim of the pit out of the corners of his frightened eyes. But he would not come near her, he would not help. He was too feeble, too confused. Finally he had to take himself away from her watchful look. He retreated to the kitchen and crept inside a cabinet. Still he heard G.'s heart, the heart was pounding in the distance, banging. The heart of her heart was pushing against the wall of her chest. The pushing of her heart began to split her chest. S. listened from inside the cabinet, waiting to hear her heart wall burst. He didn't dare to breathe. He pulled the cabinet door tight closed. She did not call out. She knew perfectly well that incidents produced incidents, and so she remained. S.'s white fingers clenched the catch inside the cabinet door. G. remained pressed down into the pit. Millipedes worked their way through the hard packed soil. A millipede slid down the groove in her head. She had shocked poor S., it was bound to happen, he had to stay in his cabinet.

It rained, and water leaked into the pit. G.'s heart was drenched, her chest wall was compressed by dirt, it needed room which was not at its disposal. The heart wanted to escape, but it was dissevered by thirteen diseases. The mind wanted to blind the heart so it would stop spreading its infections. The mind wanted to attack the heart. It was looking for the keyhole. The mind felt along the wall. It punctured the wall. A gape opened between the flailing mind and the failing heart. It was time to escape, but G. was impacted, her heart was flayed, her mind was faded.

G.'s family stood in her hallway, listening. They did not speak, they did not call out. They threw food into the pit. P. was quiet, he was faithful, he never left, but he never opened the door, he knew that there was no longer a study with notebooks and pencils and a standing lamp and unnecessary bookshelves and a hideous carpet. There was only packed dirt. If P. opened the door he would see only the hard packed dirt and the millipedes, and somewhere inside the packed dirt his sister's heart still in its bewildered darkness.

I skipped ahead another hundred pages.

First the leaf shadows came, they were afraid of nobody, then came the twigs and thorns, then the naked shadows of the giant trees. Poor S. hoped they would not get beyond the zone of the Eiklar, which was the border of the shadows and the limit for the branches and thorns. G. knew all this, she saw it even though she rarely saw S., because he ran to and fro and never climbed down into her pit. She recognized the worried look of the man who is lost. G. thought a great deal about S., because G. thought a great deal about everything. Eventually G.'s brother P. noticed she was concerned, and he also became anxious, but G. told him there was no reason to worry, basically the situation was tolerable. Nulland forces had been routed at the tank lines. The corporal, Eiklar's best emissary, announced a provisional truce. General Stepan Khroulev had drawn back to the Eupatorean forest, and Marshal Aimable Pélissier had set up a semi-permanent camp in the Ottoman fortifications. What are you talking about? P. said. Sorry, G, replied, that is another story. G. told her brother S. was not content, S. had never been content, neither S. nor G. would ever be content, there was no point even trying, what is the point of trying to be content, why would anyone want to be in such a state, and also, G. told her brother concisely, S. was naked without G.'s work, S. without G. was lost, S. was within the forest, deep inside the forest, sometimes he stayed in a hut inside the forest, in a kitchen cabinet, but he always had been lost in forests, that was his life, he could not be rescued, things would only be worse for him in the future, S. would go deeper and deeper into the forest. "He is lost," G. told her brother, "that is why I chose him."

S. had neglected the white of the boiled egg, he had permitted the shadows of the giant trees to approach, he had considered what they said, he had listened to the sharp sticks and twigs, and now the drum of his heart was actually more dangerous to him than the shadows of the giant trees, that is what G. said to her brother P., and he nodded as if he understood, but he did not, because he never understood G., even though he loved his sister very much, so she went on, explaining that every lobe of the forest had more understanding of S.'s limitations than he did, that his mind was on its own, nothing was as defenseless as S.'s mind, at any moment the casing of his mind could break.

At that point G. saw that her brother was very sad, not because he understood anything at all, because he never did, but because she was anxious, he had thought she was talking about herself, but of course she wasn't, because S.'s condition was completely different from G.'s, her condition was to be buried in hard-pack soil, with a pike through her spine and grit pressing on her eyes and grinding into her ear canals and a cut from a spade in the side of her head and crumbling nails and horrible scabs and gastric distress. C. and the scientists had done that, they had compacted her, she was hard-molded into her study, buried alive as they say. S.'s condition was entirely different, because poor S. was lost in a forest, there was no comparison, but G.'s brother was unhappy because he believed G. was actually talking about herself, and not speaking, as she was, out of care and generosity for her poor sickly friend, and so G.'s brother was sad because he loved G. and if she was sad he became sad even if he did not understand why, because he never understood anything, he was like a dog that knows its mistress is dying even though it does not know how it knows, it does not even know that it knows, it cannot think, "My mistress is dying," and yet the dog lies at the mistress's feet and waits because it knows it has to. G. knew cooking soothed her brother, so she asked him to put on the kettle and cook, to make food for her, and he went and put on the kettle, and G. ate an enormous amount of eggs, which made G.'s brother more content, but it did not help G., because she was not hungry, and in order to help her brother become less anxious she had to eat, and that was quite unpleasant, and in addition while she was eating she had to give up talking, and that was even more unpleasant, but as soon as she had eaten her food G. went on, she told her brother that she was sick and full with the knowledge of S., and S. needed to know where he was, he was ignorant of the wisdom of the ancestors, he did not consider them, and, of course, although this was by no means self-evident, S. had ignored the fact that people who are lost can be instructed, whether they walk in their bare feet through the forest, whether they run, whether they run naked, or even if they are naked dead frozen dismembered and scattered in the forest, they can be instructed, but S. had ignored all of that, he thought it was better to run, he said no one was more powerful than the shadows of the old trees, each one for himself has to run from the forest god, that is what he said, G. told her brother, you see the problem is that S. is ignorant. He does not recognize Belemnon, Debbes Bungoteis, the lightning god. He runs here and there like a rabbit, he hops around, sometimes away from the forest god, other times right toward the forest god, crisscrossing the huge empire of the forest looking for the way, deep into the zone of Eiklar, even into Urrat, it is awful to watch, he scampers like an idiot, he comes and goes, there he is, there he is again, nobody and nothing protects him, he is a gentle man in the prickly forest, the twigs beat him, he is obtuse, he is falling into oblivion, faster and faster, he looks over his shoulder and sees the writhing forest, the twisting trees, the same ahead, the same all around, and he glances up and watches the clouds quarreling above the treetops, he fears the next visit of Debbes Bungoteis and he stumbles on, rushing to avoid the forest god. The branches whip him and he yells! He howls and screams, he remains convinced he is not dead. He roars! He roars! That is what G. told her brother, and he cried a little and said something about her but she couldn't quite hear, because she was telling him how poor S. was trying his best to hold on in the forest. Then G.'s brother P. was tired, he wanted to lie down on his bed. Wait, G. said, you have to hear the sad ending.

The forest brought S. to the Blindworm. He sat on a hillock, he was exhausted. He found an egg. He did not cook the white, he sipped the egg raw. Why had it come to his defeat? The shadows of the tall trees made pictures on the forest floor. Were the shadows from the tall trees just unwanted coincidences? In the shadow picture, the forest god came and scattered slow-release blindworms on the ground. S. saw in slow motion, the forest god's naked back, his shoulder moving as he threw the blindworms. S. sat and watched, slow-slurping an egg. A mushroom grew on the ground, on S.'s trail, in one of his last footsteps. That showed how long he had been sitting on the hillock. How had he ended this way, watching leaf pictures on the forest floor? How? How?

G.'s brother was crying again, he said S. made him sad, but G. knew he was crying because he cared about her, he knew she was not well, she had thirteen illnesses, she was impacted in her study, she was tamped down in a pit and it was the rainy season, but G. said to her brother, Stop crying, there is more to the story.

At last, G. told him, S. stood up from the hillock. He felt refreshed. He wiped the egg off his hands and walked carefully around the worms and the mushroom as he went on his way through the forest, back to the pit, always back to the pit. He climbed down into it, sat on the dirt next to G. She wanted to stretch out her hand, did it, too, stroking S., who rose and drove the poison of attention into G.'s veins. There was a sudden twitching, foam from the mouth of the old woman. The decaying body was a sign, G. needed to be freed of the terrible painful condition of being herself. There was shame, she had been defeated without ever leaving Nulland, she had never left, and yet she was defeated. G. remained circumspect. She was careful not to mention the fact that S.'s impulse was to fade into water. G. had the rangy strength of a dog who has been badly hurt but has never stopped barking and pacing its yard. If the dog is powerful enough, it can injure a large number of people in return. If it has resolved not to beg it cannot be tempted. The dog knows its strength. It can run fast on three legs, it can see well by opening wide its remaining eye. It knows which teeth are broken and how to tear meat with the others. It attracts the attention of dubious people, they see themselves in the dog, of course they are wrong, but that is what they see.

S. could barely talk. When he spoke a fluttering sound came from his lips.[46]

I flipped back and forth, trying to discover what role I had played in Anneliese's imagination. My initial was scattered across several notebooks. It seemed that parts of three or four notebooks were myths about me and her family. On one page S. was in a kitchen cabinet, on another he was talking to someone named Eiklar. In another notebook S. and G. had a long exchange about the history of Switzerland. G. told S. about the Battle of Marignano in 1515, the shameful story of the expulsion of the Mennonites as told in Hans de Ries's *History of the Martyrs* in 1615, the dubious treaty between the Catholic Cantons and France in 1715, the suspiciously delayed ratification of Swiss neutrality in 1815, the unsettling mobilization of two hundred thousand Swiss soldiers to ensure Switzerland's neutrality in 1915, and the horrifying Rupperswil murder case in 2015. Later there were pages where S. and W.P. seemed to be uneasy friends, and they talked nervously about G.

I felt caught, as if I was a fly and one of my legs had gotten snagged in something, and I looked down, and saw it was snared in a line of spider's silk, and my eyes followed the line, and I realized I was at the edge of an enormous spider web, vast, stretching off to the horizon, covering houses and hills, that there was no way to escape, and my gently flicking foot was sending tremors up the line, and somewhere over the horizon the spider was listening, and would soon be coming.

Anneliese had been thinking about me years before we met. Catherine must have suggested I could read her notebooks. If Catherine was behind it, if she knew all along that Anneliese had delusions about me, that she'd put me into her notebooks, that would be one of the cruelest things Catherine has ever done.

I thought of the first time I met Anneliese, in Frankfurt, and the notebooks she had been writing at the time. What an effort it must have been for her to speak to me with thoughts like these in her mind. Her fanatical way of talking, her insistence, her rudeness, her relentless lectures, were nothing in comparison to this queasy forest with its gods and its bands of demented scientists. How could anyone quiet thoughts like these? How did she manage to talk to me at the same time she was imagining me as S., cringing and creeping in an endless mystical forest? But there was so much more I didn't see.

I went and got another notebook, volume 63, and on page 17,899, I read this:

After that he couldn't find another way. There was no reason for S. to remain on the Blue Planet. No sugar could attract him. His brow was deeply ridged with wrinkles, he even looked guilty. The unending views made it impossible to rest. Each leaf of his mind was in pain. He smelled of assassination. His walking certainly sprang from horror of torpor, certainly! Apollonius Emmer was not purring, never! He discharged offensively. He was begrudged, he was involuted, he was twisted by self-blinded fears, he was cut to a blank, he was as bitterly absent from himself as a fossil fish, his imagination was as suffocated as a sleeping bug's, he thought only in European splinters, he was condemned to Martyrdom Coals, he cultivated a strict self-discipline, he had a painful history of successfully destroyed memories, he was his own worst fate-destroyer, his most hopeful illness was sarcasm, he glittered and sputtered like a comet, he searched the screen of his memory for caterpillars, he knew people would exaggerate his madness, he saw a hare and called it Francis but it disappeared into a thistle, he was not attracted to anything, he called himself Commander Rudolf Sulfur, he was not well intentioned, he seemed to black out a lot, he called himself Dear Hedgehog Child, he went silent, he slowly negotiated a limited trust in himself, he always slept on the right bank of the tributary, he could not sleep until he saw a firefly, he called himself My Dear Swan, he hid his deepest thoughts in silly lists, he hoped he could be ambushed at any moment, he knew he was saner than the one who always says "Very well, very well," he volunteered to be dissolved, he knew sponges have dry tops but sodden bellies, he felt like a flea who was king of a pea, he wanted to attach his offspring to himself like a wart, his friends called him Mister Mystery, he thought of all the incidents and failures, he gushed sweat when he remembered himself, he recalled each bright blush, he wanted his convictions to float like leaves on sleepwaves, he didn't have the right idea about inchworms, he thought that self-deception was an art, he waved to rodents, he remembered resting once, he believed a wonderful unhappiness had taken possession of his soul, he counted to 15,000 but he forgot 617 and 2,591, he usually couldn't remember if he had children, he was probably born in Oklahoma or possibly Tennessee, he hardly said five words in an hour, his friends called him Master Misery, he remembered each blighted rush, he knew that if you spend too long by yourself your mind will work about as well as those stainless-steel food warmers in buffets that have big heavy lids that won't stay open while you pick up the big spoon to serve yourself, he walked straight into thickets whenever possible, he called himself Lord Snoots, he knew that if you serve your thoughts to yourself your mind will be like the warm food you scoop up from the stainless-steel food warmer in a buffet, he knew his mind was no longer working, he guessed that if he propped up the lid of his mind so it would stay open he could spoon out the mush of ideas about stainless-steel food warmers in Chinese buffets that had remained in his mind so long he almost did not know the difference between his thoughts about stainless-steel food warmers and a tray full of sticky orange chicken.[47]

I shut the notebook. She had spent years mythologizing, dreaming, babbling. This was a deep, unreachable sort of insanity, not like the ones she'd found in books. It was hopeless, like that little girl who held onto a strand of kelp and walked into the ocean.

It seemed clear her introductions would not help me understand what she had written. Her story about the ladder with thirteen rungs was too simple. She had climbed down thirteen rungs, but the ladder didn't end there. It was much longer, and the well was far deeper. It kept going down, and she lost her grip and fell into the darkness, like Ysaye in that cave.

I thought again of Spiera who desperately died, and the woman who broke her neck into the street. Surely Anneliese knew that no one could help her, certainly not me.

In volume 65 she seemed at last to be extracting herself from the dream.

(iii)

How I Disinterred and Reconstituted Myself

One day an indeterminate number of years ago, possibly sixty or more, G. ran blindly through the forest. No one was chasing her but herself. She hurtled into a pit.

She landed face down in a puddle of brownish water. There was no pike, that had been a misunderstanding. Oak and maple leaves were her wet mattress. Stones and earth pressed up into her. Days and weeks passed by. It was autumn, and it was cold in the pit. Leaves blanketed G., one by one, each adding an insensible token of warmth. They feathered her with a frail coat. It was just enough to keep her alive when the snows came. The first winter was difficult. The pools of water froze, and the ice crusted against her cheeks. The water in her ears froze, plugging up the sounds of the forest above. She was flattened between the dense snow and leaves on top of her and the frigid clay of the floor of the pit. Her jaw was wedged into a fractured block of slate. Grit from the soil pierced through her cheeks to her teeth. A pebble pressed on her left eyeball for years, until the cornea indented. G. spent a century that way, without moving.

One spring there was an influx of rain. The grip of the earth loosened. She levered her spine to the side and pried her face away from the dirt. At last she could breathe. She spent another century that way, breathing whenever the water subsided.

One especially hot summer day the humid heat accumulated over her face and her right eye popped open. She had a view of the side of the pit, and a glimpse of the rim of the pit and the trees above it. G. stared upward. That is when she saw W.P., just for a fraction of a second, as he walked by. He didn't even look down into the pit. Then he was gone. That was the last time she ever saw him. She watched without blinking for months, hoping he would return. Gradually she realized it was the end of W.P., and then she knew it was also the end of S., C., and P.

She recovered herself. She remembered the rest of her name, she was no longer G. but Anneliese.

The next step was to extract soil particles. I sat up painfully. Clods of earth fell away. I pushed the leaf litter off me. I extracted soil particles from my face, arms, and legs. Small sharp pebbles had spent centuries pushing into my skin, and they had to be pulled out one by one, leaving pockmarks that took months to soften. I was wounded by my insanity. Particles of stone and sharp twigs had pushed deep into my buttocks, like forks into a cake.

The right side of my pelvis, which had been lodged the deepest into the earth, came free along with a clod of stony earth the size of a child. I picked at it, the way you pick at a scab, stopping whenever it bled, tearing at it when

I felt nothing, until I had excavated the clod of earth, leaving an irregular notch in my right hip.

Ice crystals had grown in the pitiless way they do, piercing my ears and lips, wedging between my teeth. Clusters of ice crystals and frozen hair bulged from my crotch. I cleaned off the larger chunks and spears of ice, removed the shards and pebbles, and stood up. I was misshapen, and I fell down.

It took weeks for me to crawl, at the speed of a growing vine, up a corner of the pit and into the cabin where S. had once lived. That is where I rested. I bathed in hydrogen peroxide, sending gray foam spilling over the floorboards. I covered myself with antibacterial lotions. I wrapped myself in sheets soaked in fungicide spray.

Then I worked on my larynx, remembering my voice. At first my throat rustled like tinder. I ate a soft mushroom, my first food. Later I passed a tiny gray stool.

I tried to pay attention to days and not just years. I noticed where the sun was. I worked on remembering my words. I recaptured memories of the period before I was G., back when I was Anneliese, working on these notebooks, full of science and hope.

And that is how I came back into myself. I had spent many years in the pit, as I explained in vol. 64. Organic parts of me had been replaced by fungi and bacteria, and bony parts had mineralized. I was moder and mor, my bones were becoming stone. It took months for me to force human flesh back into the compost of my body, to expel the minerals from my bones. I had long setbacks, weeks went by when I was accompanied by mushroom gods and bread spirits. It was another year before I found myself, Anneliese Glur, twisted sideways in the corner of the living room of the hunter's cabin in the forest, which of course had always been my ordinary study.

Dear hedgehog reader, I know what you are thinking. This woman is not well. Even if she has escaped from the forest of S., W.P., and the others, she is not well. Her recovery was too slow, she is severely damaged, she will never be healthy again. All of this is true. I can only hope that if you have been reading along with me, if we have been together for 19,283 pages, you will know that I am describing a descent so immured that it cannot end suddenly with the protagonist coming to her senses and resuming her normal life. When a person subsides as far as I have, the return takes time.

It is only now, in these past few months, that I can speak with my own voice, so I can address you, and I can continue my work using language that I knew before I fell. You will recognize me soon, dear hedgehog reader.

It was remarkable. Anneliese was back. I turned the pages quickly. She wrote about her apartment, Hans, and Paul, and about how she had re-read the notebooks. She talked about the pain of discovering the state she had been in. The next notebook, volume 66, described her project of reading long books, just as she had recounted it to me. Science came back into the text. It was the Anneliese I had known.

What had happened? I went back to the earlier notebooks to see if I could find the place where she had abandoned science and philosophy, but there was no clear break. The terms from foreign languages, the names of organisms, and the discoveries she'd made were everywhere. Her meditations on living by herself were punctuated with Sanskrit and Greek words, passages on hypergraphia and compulsion were explained using terms from modern medicine, pages on fear and dreams were mixed with the names of organisms she'd studied.

There was a slow descent from the philosophic meditations in the earlier notebooks to the maundering mythologies in these later ones. No one place where the writing became incoherent, no clean break between reason and delirium. The sober opening volumes, full of biology and philosophy, gradually disintegrated into dramas about G. and S. Like compost, she had rotted and sunk into the earth.

The entire set of gray notebooks was a single continuous composition that led from logic into nonsense and back. Slowly, one step at a time, without a change in pace for twenty years. It seemed possible that it all held together. One long thought, as she had said, as she had hoped. A sentence that had taken her entire adult life to speak.

The last gray notebook was volume 70, the one she had been trying to finish when we met in the Krafft Hotel in Basel. It opened with three headers:

## (H)
## Time to End
### (viii)
### Reasons to Resist
#### (a)
#### Summary for the Lazy and Illiterate

There are more than seven ways to waste your life, but I cannot talk about any more of them, because I have arrived at the final volume of my book, and my longest lasting promise to myself has been to write exactly 70 volumes.

Also I cannot continue to discuss ways of wasting your life, because for some reason that I will never understand my lists always end at 7 or 13, or in rare cases 70 or 202 or 2,591 or 29,050. The numbers 70 and 202 are exceptionally boring; 2,591 is a prime number, but so what? And there is absolutely no interest or significance to 29,050 in mathematics, religion, philosophy, or history. It is possible these numbers are pebbles of insanity but it is far too late in my project to spend time pondering that.

I will now review the 7 ways of wasting your life, because I feel that someone, somewhere, has opened this final volume out of curiosity to see how it all ends, and this person has not read diligently through all the preceding volumes, because he, I mean you, Samuel, are too frightened to sit and experience what I have done, and so you are peeking shyly into this last volume, cracking the cover just enough to peer inside. For you, then, I will summarize:

Seven Ways of Wasting Your Life, by Anneliese Glur, Patiently Exposited Over the Preceding 859 Pages, Which You Have Skipped, And Now Ruthlessly Summarized:

1. You can waste your life by dozing. James Wright napped in a hammock on Pine Island, Minnesota. Pine Island, Minnesota is nowhere near an island or a lake, and it has no points of interest whatsoever, so if you lived there you would probably also want to sleep all day. I believe for many people life is a happy animal nap. I dozed in a hammock by our picturesque little Hütte in the high Alps, until I was startled by a bee and fell out, hitting my elbow and causing a repulsive bursa to swell up inside it, making my elbow look like it was pregnant with a little fetus.

2. You can waste your life with nostalgia or regret. My hopeless father Hermann was like that. As Nietzsche said of his father, Hermann was more a dream of a life than a life. Hermann died in 1996, but really he died when he was fifteen and Germany lost the war. For the next fifty-one years his eyes only reflected the world he believed he should have been seeing. Hans's eyes are even more unreflective. Somewhere in the clouds of his cataracts is the image of his first wife. All he sees is the view from the window of his old apartment, looking out over the park to the factory. Evening is falling, the long day is ending. Gentle light glows in the streets. Hans's stew is cooking on the stove. The canary sits on its dowel, watching out to see when he will arrive. This scene Hans remembers is not even his own memory, it is his version of his first wife's story of what she saw. She is the one who waited for the canary to sing. Hans looks up at that window and imagines she is still up there waiting for him. But everything is gone, corroded in the sweet acid of nostalgia.

3. You can waste your life working. Paul works at his law firm. In five years he will retire. I calculated how many hours he will have worked, and how many months and years that adds up to, and I told him, and I asked what he could have done with his life instead of adjudicating domestic and labor disputes. He did not answer. Soon Luzia will be working at a law firm, probably one of the big companies on Klosterberg. She will say she needs to work seventy hour weeks. She will buy expensive clothes, maybe she'll acquire a driver. Her husband will also be a lawyer. She will work for forty years. I will calculate the months and years she will spend working on other people's problems, and I will remind her of all the things she can still do with her life, including petroleum engineer and upholstery inspector. Many people mistake their work for their life. Morschmulmig is like that. Each year he works more, makes more money, eats more, burps more, boasts more, poops more. I told him that at the end of every life wasted on work is the moment you look into your psyche mirror and realize you have only one life and it is nearly over. It is your Blurp moment. "Ha ha," he said, and clapped me on the shoulder.

4. You can waste your life being trivial. Arnulf Trausch doesn't know anything except what the library catalogs tell him. I have no doubt he spends his evenings playing games on his computer. Morschmulmig collects stamps. His china cabinet is full of glassware, hundreds of pieces that all have the same

design, clear glass with a raised rose ring in the middle. Wine glasses, champagne flutes, demitasse cups, carafes, all with the same ring. I told him it was the most depressing thing I had ever seen. "Thank you," he said, and clapped me on the shoulder. Pharmacists, people who are content just to help the time pass. Like holding death's knuckly hand and saying, "Come on, can we just walk a little faster?" Once I was walking along Starenstrasse past Trausch's house. It is on the left, midway along the street, with green shades. A light was on in the window. I heard him crying.

5. You can waste your life fighting. Sybille Kröller is still trying to ruin my life. She hopes her latest lawsuit will bar me from the university grounds forever. She wants the lawsuit to be known to everyone so she can blacken my name. She has no idea how dark a blackness my name already has. My colleagues, Sybille, Andrei, Walter, Spadella, Marcel, and Grettina, and Ludwig, I always forget him, they still plot to make sure I am not invited to conferences. Catherine is another one. She stole my ideas back in England and she will never admit it because they are the only ideas she has ever had. Still she keeps insisting the ideas were hers. Another one is that woman who has the little house opposite our *Summerhüsli* in the forest near the Basel-Mulhouse-Freiburg airport. She is plotting to have us evicted. I am going to tell Paul I want to go out there one more time. I want to check on my sign STOP SPYING ON US ADELHEID WYRSCH YOU BITCH. I want to pour a concrete foundation for it, and put lights on it so it keeps her up at night. You can waste your life fighting. It is better just to make fighting a hobby.

6. You can waste your life on love. At first I loved people. I loved Wolfram Pichler, but then he died. I wasted part of my life on him. A couple of years ago I glimpsed him from the pit, but he walked away. When I realized he was finally gone, I decided to love only myself. That seemed to be a reliable thing to do, because if you love someone else they may leave or die before you. The problem is that you can fall out of love with yourself. If you change, you may not love what you've become. And if you change too much, you may not recognize yourself, and then you can't be in love. After all, you have to be able to recognize a person to love them. I wasted another part of my life trying to love myself. So I resolved to love only my ideas. That worked better, but now I am not sure if my thoughts are healthy, or even sane. I have reluctantly fallen out

of love with many of them. Others I hardly recognize, and you have to be able to recognize something in order to love it. I am afraid I may have wasted a lot of my life on my ideas. I know this is not a popular way to think about love. I don't doubt love has rescued some people. It hasn't rescued Paul. He loves me, but that hasn't helped him. Love didn't rescue Hans. I am not sure about love. Maybe it is the idol of all dreams, as Tom says in *The Rake's Progress*. Only 3 pages out of the 859 are on the subject of love.

7. You can waste your life trying to create something. If you create a family, that is good, I suppose. If you don't, then you need to try to create something else in your life. All of my adult life has been dedicated to my work. For many years I have pushed everything I know and feel into these notebooks. A single enormous project is a good way to spend a life, or so I hoped. It hasn't worked out. I have less than 300 pages left to bring all this together: the optimistic science, the philosophy, the speculations, the years I spent imagining myself as a recluse, in Nulland, as a forest spirit, as a pithed corpse, and the last few years when I remembered and thawed and kept going. I doubt this book will make sense to anyone. It seems increasingly clear that I will not be able to finish it properly. I may come to the last page and run out of room. The notebooks might break off in the middle of a sentence. You can waste your life trying to create something. Most people who try fail. My so-called book will probably join thousands of unfinished, unpublished, unnoticed, unread, unhinged manuscripts left by so many thousands of misguided people through many centuries.

That is the end of my ruthless summary of the previous 859 pages of generous, well considered prose. I am practicing to write my brutal summary of this entire project. I need to be as clear-headed as possible. Nothing can be summarized without violence. All summary is compression, all description is travesty. This is especially true when the entire purpose of the work, its most fundamental proposition, is that it is necessary to think about writing and not just propositions, voice and not just theories, allegories and not just facts, literature and not just geometry. When the entire project begs science not to continue in its pared-down, peeled-away, repressed, anemic, fascist protocols of so-called accuracy, when the entire project asks scientists to think of the possibilities of meaning that lives in narratives, then what does it mean to summarize? It means betray.

> I have a frighteningly small number of pages left and I need to find words to force my entire life's work into a conclusion. For years I have written into a limitless sea of white pages. Now I need to measure out my spirit in liqueur glasses, that's what Georg Büchner said. I need to learn to stop talking, not only in these remaining pages but afterward, in whatever remnant life I have after this book.

That was the voice I had heard in Frankfurt, in Canada, and in Basel. The Anneliese I thought I'd known. Ranting and raving, speaking directly to me. Reading those pages made me especially uneasy, because I saw she might actually have recovered. Despite the long illness her notebooks might just make sense. They might, in fact, be a triumph, a project that risked everything, that went to the underworld, into the wilderness, into the whale's stomach, and came back out.

If someone read all sixty-six gray notebooks in order, they might appear as a single enormous accomplishment. Maybe such a reader would learn her language, and by the end reader and writer would speak it together. Even the pages on Nulland and northern forests might make sense in a way I couldn't see. Perhaps it was necessary to write them the way she did, in an invented forest language of mosquitoes and sticks.

If I took a year of my life and read eight or ten hours a day, from the Preface all the way into the forests, I might learn how to read those pages. It would be exhilarating, like speaking a new language, emerging into a different kind of life. The notebooks might actually be that grand chateau she imagined, each stone in place, miraculously composed out of floods and avalanches.

And yet, a couple of pages before the end she seemed to be hallucinating again.

> People turned away, they turned to themselves. People who might have listened became scarce, some retired, others died. Pain separated me, laid out ways for me, pain cut my agreement with myself. Each of us was alone in our forest, our feet stepped softly in the ash. The psuchás of heaven were my breathing witnesses, spirits of planets and stars. The pain of not hearing an

answer raveled me. Night came two thoughts after sunrise, I could see darkness in flowers, I could feel cold under my fingernails, when I spoke I heard flies, my walls thickened, walls grew around my walls, all sounds suffocated, the well was quiet and the water down there glistened. Parking lots emptied, winter was gone, the river rose, the wind came from the north and then from the west.

After S. met G., his life subsided into moss, lanceolate leaves decorated his mind, his thoughts were tiny translucent creatures of the soil. Silverfish, globular mites. Harmless white symphalans, delicate collembolans. Blebs, creatures no bigger than the tiniest droplet. S. had the strength of a button mushroom, his mind was quiet as a creamy nebula. P. was empty, he was used up. Only G. kept going.

My thought is at its very end. Words are scabs. Moving them hurts. My pen grates on the paper like a truck loaded with rocks grinding its way up a gravel road. It is just possible to walk, in slow steps, toward

The writing broke off in the middle of the sentence. The remainder of the page, and the next few pages, were blank. On the final page there was this:

I want now to commemorate the hour of my "final deliverance." It was on the day, or rather the night, of the          of               , 2020, at the hour of          , that I wrote these last lines on this last page of the last notebook, in my squalid study in my brother's house in Basel.

When Edward Gibbon finished his enormous work he celebrated his moment of "final deliverance," as he said, by taking several turns around his *berceau*, not in the sense of *un petit lit pour un bébé*, a baby's bed, but *berceau* in the sense of *le lieu de naissance*, the place where everything started, where one feels most at home. For Gibbon it was "a covered walk of acacias" commanding a view of the countryside, Lake Geneva, and the Alps. My *berceau* is different, it is the back wall of my study where I keep the *Black Notebooks* and *Gray Notebooks*, because now, after so many years, they are my *lieu d'origine*, I no longer live anywhere but here. There is no pacific view across a lake to tenebrous mountains gently steeped in centuries of history. No tremulous

> cypresses or silver-orbèd moon. My sky is not serene. I don't even want to look up at the ceiling, there are probably cobwebs hanging down toward my head. This is my berceau, and it is not a place to celebrate.
>
> Gibbon thought his work would outlive him. He pondered "the future date of my history." I don't have that either. As I finished each notebook it closed silently and backed away into the bookshelf. Gibbon felt a "sober melancholy" when he took "everlasting leave" of his book. For him it was "an old and agreeable companion." My "companion" stopped being "agreeable" long ago. These notebooks are not my friends, they are my excrement, the proof I lived in this room. They are what is left of me, and now, at exactly        o'clock, they are finished. I have survived myself, at least for a few minutes.

The lab tables were buried under her notebooks. As if the bones of an enormous fossilized creature had been set out to be studied. The two open crates were surrounded by piles of packing material.

I needed to write to Paul again. I'd say the notebooks were astonishing, like nothing I'd ever imagined. Somehow she had changed my life. And I'd offer to visit him, and Hans and Luzia, anytime they wanted.

I paused in the doorway. The notebooks were unreadable, endless, opaque, and bottomlessly self-indulgent, and yet they were an immense achievement. And what had I done with my own life? I'd raised a daughter, that's something. I'd muddled along. Like anyone, like everyone. Mainly I'd waited for things to happen. When they did I was slow to react. It took me decades to decide how I felt about my brothers. Ten years to see that my wife and I were not in love, another ten to decide what to do about it. An ordinary life, filled with distractions, shocks, and whatever happiness came along.

Who does what Anneliese did? Who has a thought about the world that takes more than a day to write out, or maybe a few years if you are a normal writer or an academic? Who has a life that requires a hundred volumes to explain? Whose ideas unspool as madly as hers? What kind of scientist, what sort of writer, keeps going even when her thought becomes so complex that she's no longer in control, no longer even herself? Anneliese's thought burst the dam of her training, her job, and her family, and it kept going. She showed me what it looks like to write for yourself, when no one is watching, no one is waiting to see your work, what it's like to push away ordinary language and common sense until you come to an unpleasant place where you hear your synapses talking to themselves. Maybe that was her accomplishment, to show we are all like roses, optimistically blooming, pencil yellow, iceberg white, aorta red, flourishing and flowering for no one.

That is a story I told myself, the first of several, to assuage my guilt over abandoning her work. I won't ever know what she actually wrote, because in the end I wanted my own life, no matter what it turns out to be, and if I had read her book I might have forgotten what I am. She did something with her life, made it into a monument as strange as she was. But her book was hopeless and dangerous. I had to escape her.[48]

When Rosie came in on Monday she'd find the crates and the notebooks and be annoyed. She'd know it was me, and she'd have to get someone to clean the lab. It wouldn't take Catherine long to realize they were Anneliese's notebooks. They'd try to call me. Catherine would call Paul, and he'd say the notebooks were for me. When they couldn't find me they'd get someone to haul the crates down to one of those cement block rooms in the physical plant where we store our old lab equipment.

In five or ten years someone would need the space, and then they'd haul the crates to the loading dock and take them to be buried. The Watford landfill is a large hill planted with grass and pines, like an ancient burial mound. No one goes there. As she said, in a few years no one will visit her grave in Roggwil, no one will know her work, no one will remember her.

That is another story I told myself, because it seemed better if Anneliese and her book were both forgotten as quickly as possible.

On the way out I checked my mailbox. There was the letter I had sent to Paul in May, returned by the Swiss post office. A smeared blue stamp said in several languages: MOVED: FORWARDING ADDRESS UNKNOWN.

My hand opened, and the letter dropped into the trash.

I left the keys in Rosie's mailbox and walked down the metal mesh steps of the Water Department building.[49]

As S. walked down Cather street for the last time, his mind was crowded with thoughts of G. He churned with her ideas, so unhealthy, so difficult to love.

G. had given him an indissoluble purpose: to be crushed by the fact that someone he knew had just one purpose in her life, one item on her bucket list, and she had accomplished it. S. thought about that as well as he could with his weak mind. G. had disappeared into her writing, she had freed herself from the painful condition of being herself. Poor S. kept moving, in slow steps, toward

# NOTES

1 In 1953, Karlheinz Stockhausen had the idea of composing a piece for piano that would begin by repeating one chord, hammering on just one chord, over and over, a hundred and sixteen times, so it reverberates in your ears. Each time the chord is struck it is a little softer, so it sounds slightly different each time, even though it is actually the same chord, again and again and again.

It should not be an ordinary chord, Stockhausen decided, but an unfamiliar one, dissonant, a puzzling chord, and it should be repeated over and over, never losing its strangeness, starting *fortissississimo,* as loudly as the pianist can possibly play without breaking keys or fingers.

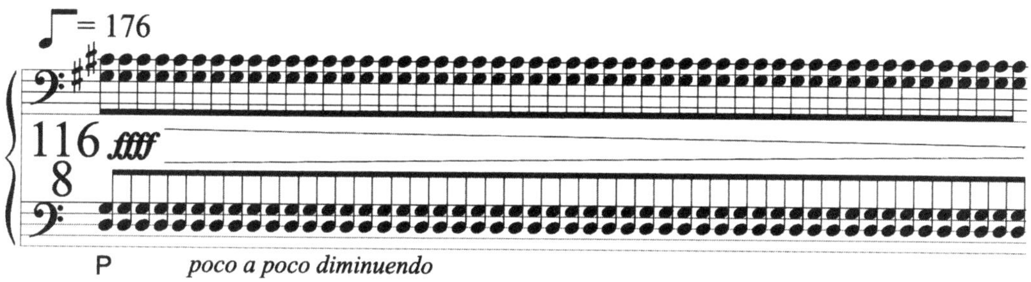


When I am ready to play *Piano Piece 9,* I position my hands a half-inch above the four notes of the chord, D, G, G#, C#. I hit the keys as hard as I can, punching down with my fingertips. The first measure is exactly one hundred and sixteen beats long. I count as I go. The notes move fast, so I count in twos. The chord hurts my fingers, but I have to play accurately, because it gets quieter each time, in one hundred and fourteen imperceptibly different but equal steps, from deafening to nearly silent.

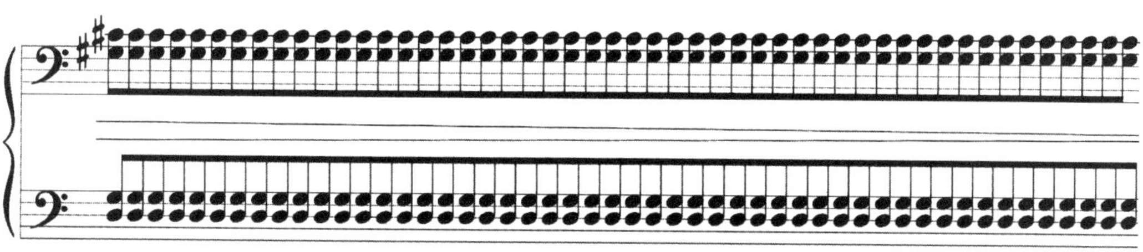

The last couple of repetitions are marked *pianississississimo.* They need to be just barely audible in a quiet room. When I reach the one hundred and fourteenth chord I hold it briefly, for just two more beats. It's as if there are two more chords, numbers one hundred fifteen and one hundred sixteen. They are so quiet they are imaginary.

Then it all begins again, eighty-three more repetitions of the same chord, starting as loudly as I can.

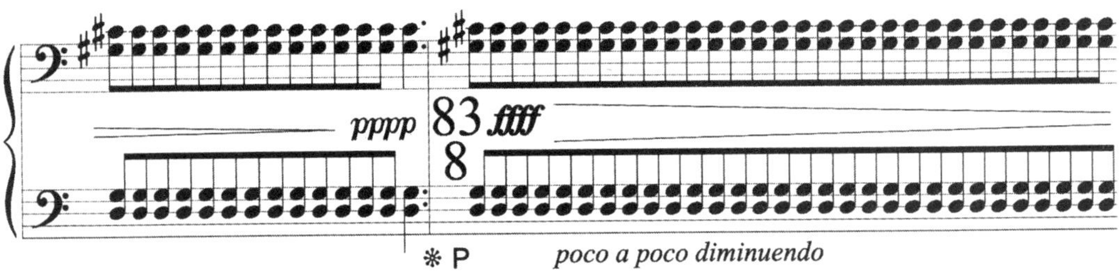


Once again I gradually diminish the sound, as smoothly as I'm able, until my fingers are just barely grazing the keys and the notes aren't even a whisper.

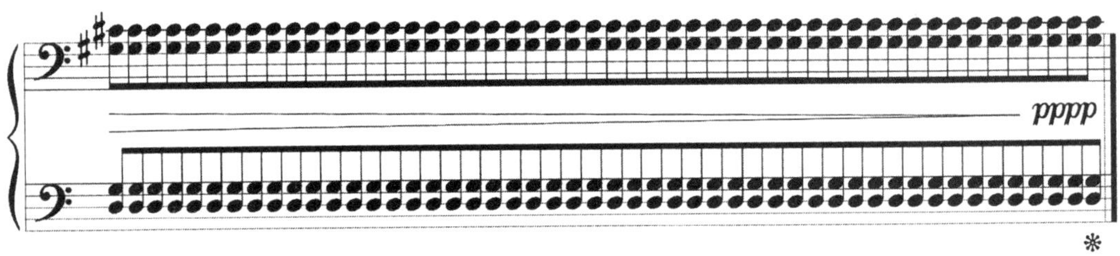


I suppose for a person hearing this for the first time that second set of chords must be a special kind of torture, because if the composer can do it twice, he can do it twenty times, and if he can make up numbers like 116 and 83, then what's to stop him writing a measure a thousand beats long? A first-time listener will think the piece is going to be nothing but the same single excruciating chord, hammering, diminishing, finally dying, then starting again.

**2** In the next measure the music changes. The tempo is so slow it almost doesn't move, one eighth note every second. The loud chord is there at the beginning, as a ghost. Soon it is gone. There are only a few notes in the measure. The music is quiet, nearly silent.

This is the third measure of *Piano Piece 9.* It is forty-two beats long. The first C# is a dotted quarter note. It lasts three full seconds. Then there is a whole-note D#, which lasts eight seconds. A couple of seconds after I strike it, only a trace of sound remains. People who don't know the piece would be unsure. They would expect the deafening chords to start up again any second. But the music continues to drift upward. A run of grace notes rushes up to a G, then pauses. It sounds tentative. It's not clear how high the notes will go.

In the middle of the measure is an especially long note, a dotted whole tied to an eighth note. Thirteen seconds long, nearly an eternity in music. About ten beats in, all the sound dies. There is absolute silence.

At the end of the measure, the notes have climbed an octave. The last high C# is another whole note, another full eight seconds. It feels like either the piece will end, or the hammering chords will suddenly reappear. By the barline there is no sound left. I sit at the piano with one finger held down on the silent key. I keep my hands tensed. At any moment the hammering could begin again.

3 Paul's quiet voice was lost somewhere inside Anneliese's. He spoke in the lulls between her monologues. His voice reminds me of a different composer, Samuil Feinberg. He was a Russian modernist, a virtuoso even by the sky-high standards of the Moscow Conservatory. After he graduated he seldom played in public, and never pursued a concert career. He preferred teaching and attending other people's concerts. In the summers he visited his brother Leonid in his cold beach house in Odessa. Feinberg's piano sonatas have solemn movements that are like listening to waves breaking, or people breathing deeply in their sleep.

The opening of the *Third Piano Sonata* is for the left hand only. It is not easy to play. I have to move quickly up and down the keyboard, each time landing gently and softly, while my right hand rests in my lap.

There is no time signature. Feinberg marks the score *misure diverse:* some of it is 9/8, some 10/8, some 3/8. It is oceanic, like waves with deep troughs swelling and subsiding. This first measure comes to a crest at the *mf.* Smaller waves come up in its wake. They slosh back and forth, like water lapping against a pier.

There are two voices: the waves are underneath, stems pointing down, floating like buoys in the five staff lines. There are also chords with their staff lines up. Here a melody of chords rises to G# at the crescendo, pauses, then reappears, E♭ to F# to E♭ at the end of the bar. These pieces of melodies are like birds floating out on the ocean, appearing over the crests, disappearing into the troughs. It is subdued, patient music.

4 The waves continue, and the chords float on them as well as they can. The bass, the deep water, rumbles and complains. The key shifts from g minor to d minor. The movement is mainly quiet, but also unsettled, restless.

Feinberg hardly ever traveled. When he retired he moved into his brother's house on the Black Sea. Leonid painted pictures of Russian peasants, ballerinas, brave princes with scimitars, and mysterious princesses with gleaming diadems. Samuil played the piano in a little room in the back. After Leonid died, Samuil stayed on in Leonid's house for another thirty years. When Samuil died, the municipal authorities held an open house to auction his compositions and his brother's paintings, but no one in Odessa knew them, and in the end the paintings and compositions were thrown away. As a result very little of Feinberg's work remains.

5 After its deafening reverberating beginning and its quiet third measure, Stockhausen's *Piano Piece 9* turns playful. Sixteenth and thirty-second notes flit around. The music is skittish, fidgety. Both loud and soft. It's hard to count, hard to know what's going on. Some notes repeat, then scatter. It's as if the notes are scared of another attack of that repeated chord.

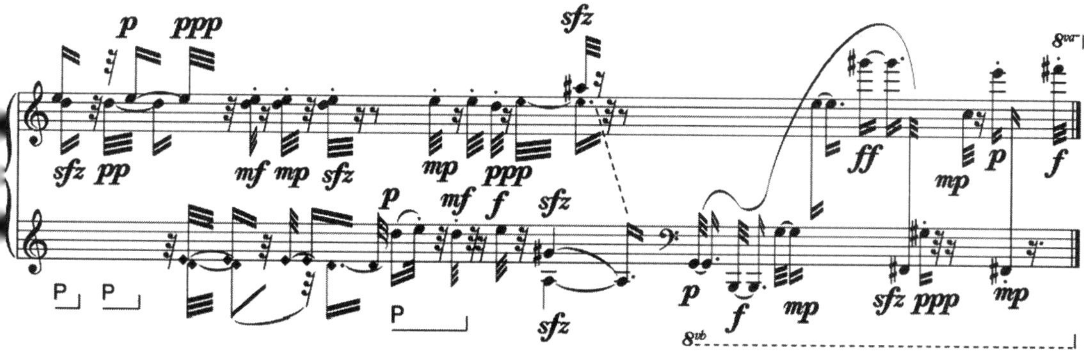

Two-thirds the way along this passage, the nervous notes pause for just an instant. I reach down to the bottom of the keyboard and play a low G. Then I play one of the lowest notes on the piano, a loud B, and from there the music leaps up to a very high G#. Stockhausen draws a roller coaster slur to capture the lurching feel of it.

That is a dramatic moment, and it seems the music might settle down. But nothing changes. Notes continue to skip around. This goes on for pages. The music can't decide if it is quiet or loud, prickly or melodic, settled or scattered. Stockhausen's notes have sharp flags, like fletching on arrows. They fly in every direction. They crowd and jostle each other. They stutter and gasp. It's nervous, like a person trying to sing a calming tune while their house is on fire. Like trying to steer a speeding car when the brakes are broken. Like Anneliese's stories, fitfully entertaining, sharp, but scattered and tiring.

6 Sometimes a gap opens in Stockhausen's music, and sounds appear that don't belong. Then the gap closes and the music goes on, but in those instants the music plunges into its own past. In *Piano Piece 9* there are brief passages where I suddenly hear music he composed years before.

*Piano Piece 3* is especially brief, less than half a page of music. He wrote it when he was twenty-three years old. It's like one of Schönberg's miniature piano pieces, or one of Webern's. Each note is precisely placed. It needs to be played accurately, because a listener needs to hear every rhythm and dynamic.

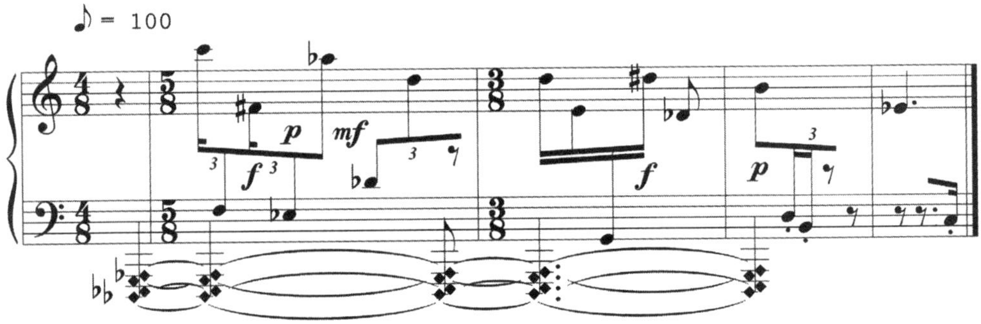

These first *Piano Pieces* are carved gems, pretty on the page. They are attempts to make music by carving away what it doesn't need and presenting only what's beautiful. Like a distilled memory of some perfect music of the past.

Twenty years later, Stockhausen was writing the storms of notes in *Piano Piece 9*, where everything is splintered and notes fly everywhere. But in that profusion there are brief moments when I suddenly hear the miniature compositions he made in his twenties: a couple of delicately positioned notes, a momentary rhythm, things he once thought were beautiful. I feel like I'm falling back down through the years to a distant moment when music made sense. When Stockhausen wrote *Piano Piece 9* he needed complexity. He wanted to fill the air and the listener's mind with ideas as fast as he could come up with them. He tried not to leave gaps in what he wrote, because he was afraid they would open downward like sinkholes, and he would fall back through the years to those early pieces, when he was sentimental and wrote music that had human feeling.

7 Of course the loud opening chords do come back, because that's what happens in nightmares. The same hammering. The same four notes, D, G, G#, C#. The same mad insistent jolting.

The chord Stockhausen chose is dissonant. It doesn't resolve into any key, and the notes sound like they belong to different chords. If the D and G go together they could be part of a D7 chord, but the C# ruins it. If the G# is A♭, then it creates a diminished fifth with the D, but the C# ruins any hope of finding A♭ major.

Stockhausen wanted people to know it was not an ordinary chord. He told an interviewer that the repeated chord is fundamental to the piece. "It is important that this chord comes suddenly into existence," he said. "It does not become familiar, it does not settle into a key."

When the chord does come back, it doesn't last long. The measure has only eleven beats, and after a few repetitions the chord falls apart. After four beats the notes in my left hand become grace notes. A single loud E puts an end to the measure.

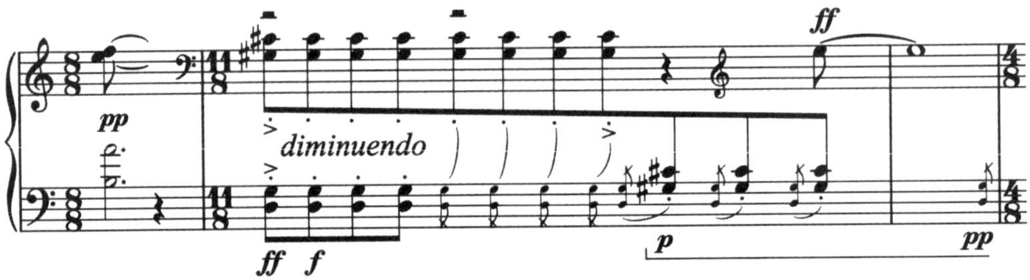


As soon as these echoes of the opening chord die away, short notes start flying again like darts in all directions.

Stockhausen's piece seems interminable. It feels much longer than it actually is. That is because the hammering at the beginning destroys my sense of time. Afterward time is broken. No matter how many notes fly like arrows around the keyboard, the piece is suspended, hanging in time, always waiting for the next appearance of the repeated chord.

Stockhausen was fascinated by things that are excessively rapid or excruciatingly slow. He told an interviewer he discovered the two extremes when he visited Japan and saw a performance of traditional Noh theater.

"Everyone moves slowly, step by step," he said. "They sing slowly, and the plot advances one line at a time. They wear wooden shoes. Every step sounds. There is nothing in the theater to look at, no decoration. The house lights stay on. Our European theater would never admit things like that, we would be bored. It is the same with the music. There is only a flute and two or three drums. The musicians are not hidden in the orchestra pit, they sit right on the stage. The percussion instruments are slow, the flute is slow. We would never listen to a single sound that lasts more than ten seconds. In the Noh theater a single step might take that long. And then suddenly the loud drum sounds, the flute shrieks. Someone is killed or wakes from a dream. The Noh performance is finished. There is no curtain. It is over before we have a chance to feel anything.

"The Japanese theater and music I heard has no use for ordinary human time," Stockhausen said. "Japanese theater is poor in the middle regions, between the endless and the instant. Where notes come very fast, it is rich. And it is rich in the lowest frequencies of experience, where notes arrive so slowly they are no longer music. I had the idea of writing a composition like that. A listener would be told: You must count, no matter how fast the music comes at you. You must know: 116 beats, 83 beats. And then: you cannot count, the beats are too slow. You must concentrate, every note matters. Yet you cannot concentrate, the music is too slow, the threat of the drone is too great.

"In the third measure of *Piano Piece 9,* I placed several notes that are too long to be heard. I went far beyond the time of memory, which is between eight and sixteen seconds. The listener continues to count, but all sense of tempo is dissolved. You lose orientation."

"At the beginning of that composition," the interviewer said, "there is a single chord that is very loud."

"That year, 1953, I did a lot of flying. I felt like I lived in the air and only visited the ground. They were prop planes back then, and I used to press my ear against the window and listen to the drone of the engine. It had a fierce rhythm, generated by the turning of the engine itself, and it repeated endlessly. I heard rhythms in multiples, two per second, three, four, ten, twenty. And there were partials, harmonics, in the sound. I listened for hours. It was a beautiful experience. I discovered the inwardness of the engine sounds, together with the slight shifts in blue outside the window, always with the white blanket of clouds far beneath. It was deafening, and part of the sound was extremely rapid, almost too quick to hear, up to twenty beats a second. The harmonics were steady, rhythmless, like the sky. Extremely fast and loud, and beautifully motionless. The prop plane engine destroyed my sense of time, it ruined my sound memory, it overwhelmed my professional capacity to determine rhythms and pitches.

"The single chord at the beginning of *Piano Piece 9* is like that. It has a simple monotonic rhythm, but it implies much more. And then it suddenly stops, and yet it seems to keep going. The listener enters a time that is suspended. I thought of extremely long duration sounds. I imagined a person in prison, kept in a dark cell for a number of years. He hears only one sound, a door slamming. He hears it only once a year. That means for the entire year the only sound he has is the door slamming shut, and that sound lasts a year, because no other sound takes its place. That is the sound for the entire year. The next year the door slams again, and the following year once more.

That is the rhythm of sound for the prisoner, so slow that it destroys his sense of time and memory. For him the sound continues all year long."

"A form of torture," the interviewer said.

"The pain dilates over the course of a year. It becomes insensible. And then, suddenly, the prisoner is released. There are guards, they are talking. They rattle their keys, producing an enormously complex rhythm that is over in a few seconds. They speak to him and to each other. They march with him to the front of the prison. They push him out into the world. It is all too complicated, too fast. The prisoner does not respond. He still hears the single door slamming, exquisitely slowly, over the entire year. It is still diminishing. It forms a single sound behind the noise of the world. For the rest of his life he hears the continuous silent sound of the door being shut."

Later in *Piano Piece 9* the chord comes back in a measure with only four beats, and this time the repetitions aren't even: one is a sixteenth note, and another lasts too long. My right hand just plays a trill. After a pause the chord returns in a measure with seven beats. Again the regular rhythm is disrupted. A different chord strikes loudly at the top of the keyboard.

These are like jangling memories of the opening measures. A listener who didn't know the piece would be on edge. It's as if the music is trying to remember how it started, and at any moment the first measure might return, 116 beats at full volume. Only Stockhausen knew what his logic was, why there needed to be 116 chords, then 83, and later 11, then 4, then 7, no more, no less. Only he knew when the music would come suddenly back to the same hammering chord.

Time moved slowly when I listened to Anneliese. There was always the hammering or the memory of it. The insistent repetition of that chord, like the plane engine throbbing and reverberating. The painful slowness of her argument, pummeling and plodding, loud, oblivious, and then suddenly shot through with disorienting clouds of detail like a hail of arrows. And during her few silences I still heard her talking, like the door in the prison forever silently slamming.

**8** There weren't any disruptions at the first performance of *Piano Piece 9.* People knew Stockhausen. They understood the composition wasn't a joke. But reviewers couldn't hear the reasoning behind the music. They heard its energy and they praised its ambition. One reviewer wondered how anyone could play something so complex. It was like listening to someone talk emotionally in a foreign language: the intensity came through, but not the sense.

There were three encores. The pianist brought Stockhausen out on stage. He bowed mechanically, as if the theater was empty.

Stockhausen's wife, Doris Andreae, sat in the first row. She did not show any emotion. Another reviewer wondered, politely, if Stockhausen had been suffering from overwork. He remarked that no one had seen Stockhausen at a music event for several years. "What kind of life a person leads," the reviewer wrote, "is reflected in what he produces."

**9** *Piano Piece 9* begins in the middle of its psychosis. It recovers, but only for a while, and it repeatedly relapses. It suggests a state of mind where you cannot relax, because every minute or so your thoughts short-circuit. There are other repetitive, headache-inducing passages in modern music where there's not even a fraction of a second to breathe: Bartók's *Allegro Barbaro,* for example, the last movement of Prokofiev's Stalingrad sonata, Villa-Lobos's *Rudepoêma, l'Élue* in Stravinsky's *Rite of Spring,* some of Galina Ustvolskaya's sonatas. Stockhausen's *Piano Piece 9* is the worst of them, the most maddening.

After the premiere Stockhausen gave a lecture on *Piano Piece 9.* He said it does not have melodies the way other compositions do. "When you listen to the chord," he said, "it does not keep time. Time stops for you. You are paralyzed. There is no melody. The slow measure that follows has no motive, no theme. So there is no recounting of a story. Instead you have to attend to the structure: first a period of 116 beats, then a period of 83 beats, then an aperiodic time of 42 beats. This is the conception of the piece, the struggle of periodicity and aperiodicity. A failure on the part of the performer to see the conception behind the musical text would be similar to the failure of an engineer to see the logic of a suspension bridge, or the failure of an architect to grasp the meaning of a blueprint. Such a failure would necessarily yield an unsuccessful performance."

It looks mechanical on the page, but the two opening measures are not supposed to sound like they are produced by a machine. Stockhausen told the audience he had been inspired by hearing a friend play an Indian piece that had a repeated chord. As his friend played, she seemed to strike this or that note more or less loudly. Even though the chord never changed, Stockhausen heard a melody inside it.

He said the pianist who performed the premiere of *Piano Piece 9* was too skilled. He could repeat the chord 500 times, *ffff* to *pppp,* lowering the volume with each repetition, so that each chord sounded like all the ones before it. "You played like a robot," he told the pianist, who was in the audience. Stockhausen said he had told the pianist to play like a normal person. "Each chord is different," Stockhausen said, "like snowflakes or the throbs of a headache."

When I play this chord, I use the fingering 31, 13, middle fingers and thumbs. I don't hear any variation in the first dozen repetitions, because the flood of adrenaline drowns out the music. I am hurting my fingers and startling people. As the volume subsides, that changes, and the notes start to talk to one other. I can discern a melody in the upper notes, something like C#, G#, C#, G.

I notice my two thumbs are playing against one another. I hear a rhythm like G#, G#, G#, G, G. My ears search for order in the incremental differences of tone and force in each repetition. I can't help but hear things that aren't notated in the score. At times I hear another melody inside the chord: D, C#, G, G#.

Midway through the 116 repetitions, I think I hear the chords in groups of four, probably because that's a common meter, but not *one* two three four, *one* two three four. Instead I hear a shifting accent: *one* two three four, one *two* three four, one two *three* four, one two three *four, one* two three four. Or I hear 4/8 alternating with 5/8. I can't tell, exactly: the rhythms move, they're different each time I play.

Toward the end of the first measure, around beat 100, I have to concentrate on playing as quietly as possible, barely touching the keys. That isn't easy, because my hands are tired. If I let my left thumb relax just a half millimeter too much, I miss some G's.

The pause on beat 116 is the hardest thing to play. It is brief, only two eighth-note beats. Stockhausen told the audience those two beats are supposed to sound like two more chords. The idea is that the last few chords are so quiet they are on the edge of imperceptibility. A listener will then hallucinate two more chords in the gap. Beats 117 and 118 are ghost chords. "Like the end of a headache," Stockhausen said. "The throb is gone, but it feels like it is still there, because memory is so intense."

Stockhausen called the pianist back up on stage and had him play the first two measures. "Listen! Listen!" he yelled. "Hear that? Nothing is the same, everything changes. Every pulse is different." Then he got annoyed with the pianist and told him to go sit down.

There was a young composer in the audience, one of Stockhausen's students.

"I do not agree," he said. "It is the composer's job to create something as complex as what you are describing. You need to write out the music as you describe it. The result will be tremendously complex. Perhaps you are not capable of it."

Stockhausen smiled, as he sometimes did when he took a criticism seriously.

"Why 116?" someone else asked.

"Well," Stockhausen said, "116 factorial, plus one, is a prime number." And then he took out a piece of paper and copied the entire number onto a chalkboard:

116! + 1 =

33931086844518982011982560935885732032396635

55699420770196366208812326531417633033625453

59712071811696988685849919416077801110739282

36261199604691797570505851011072000000000000

000000000000001

"See?" he said.

10 During the winter of 1953-1954, Stockhausen played his new piece at home, over and over. Years later, Doris Andreae told an interviewer it had been awful, having to listen to her husband play *Piano Piece 9*. Their first two daughters, Suja and Christel, were toddlers, she said, and the music upset them. *Piano Piece 9* takes about ten minutes to play, so every ten minutes the house was filled with that chord, D, G, G#, C#. He wrote the piece, she said, and then he was consumed by it. It was as if he had to repeat it to himself to make sure it was real. "But we all knew it was real," his wife said. "It made babies cry."

When I play *Piano Piece 9* there is no one around. The neighbors are a good distance away, behind hedges and a strip of trees. I can understand why Stockhausen played his piece again and again. It's because when you think about it afterward it doesn't seem like music. When you're listening you try to find music in it: rhythms, melodies, sense, direction, anything. Afterward you're not sure what happened.

Remembering *Piano Piece 9* is like recalling a headache, as Stockhausen said, or maybe a fever. It isn't normal music. There are no melodies to sing. And there are no memories of music in *Piano Piece 9*. The music doesn't echo earlier composers. It's as if Stockhausen had forgotten the thousand years of music that came before him. *Piano Piece 9* yells, and then it becomes incoherent. That is why it needs to be repeated, loudly, to make it into music. Like Anneliese, Stockhausen was helpless, trying to understand his own work.

11 It has been almost forty years since I talked to Anneliese. I no longer remember exactly what she looked like. She was an anomaly in my life. When she was talking I couldn't hear the rest of my life. It was as if an ambulance had pulled up next to me with its siren blaring.

I have only a few memories of the traveling I did that year or the places we met. I may not have thought about Catherine or Paul, except in passing, for several decades. It was all long ago.

Back when I wrote this account of Anneliese I had the idea that it was important to remember her. I thought if I had a record, I could study it and figure out what she had done and why it affected me so strongly. It didn't work out that way. That spring my life took a different direction, and this book ended up with three others in a box in my basement. If I had opened the box even twenty years ago, I might still have recalled some of the things she said. But the equivalent of an entire generation has come and gone. I have been living here, off Route 6 in Northern Ontario, playing the piano and going for walks, for nearly forty years. The people in this book, including my own earlier self, are long gone.

I wrote four manuscripts about the events of that year. This is the one about Anneliese. The meetings I describe in this book happened during the same months, even on the same days, as the events in my life that I describe in two of the other books. I gave Anneliese a book of her own because she was so different from the rest of my life: so much louder, and so little concerned with anything but herself. She crashed into my life like one of those asteroids that geologists say changed everything.

The interviewer asked Doris Andreae when exactly Stockhausen had stopped playing *Piano Piece 9* over and over. "By spring 1954, things were mainly quiet," she said. For me things went quiet after the year that's described in this book.

**12** When I read these pages I can't bring myself to care about Anneliese's work the way I did back then. She was consumed by her work, it was all she wanted me to hear about. I no longer care about it, because that part of my life is so long gone. Instead I hear her as a sort of frantic complex music. Exhausting, and also boring. I don't really pay attention to what she is saying. As I read, a feeling comes over me. It's the force of her mind, stubbornly wrestling with her own ideas. Her insistence that her thinking was not random or insane. That reminds me especially of Stockhausen. They were both nearly hysterical and yet fiercely dedicated to making sense. Both built systems of outlandish intricacy, which sounded to people who heard them like froth, like nonsense.

So I read about Anneliese and end up thinking about Stockhausen. I read a page where Anneliese is ranting and then I sit at the piano and play the opening passage in *Piano Piece 9* where a single chord evokes different melodies and rhythms, and yet they are all absorbed back into the chord, always the one chord. The music makes more sense than the monologue. Its terms are clearer, its desperation sharper. It knows, like Anneliese knew, that it is suffering a sort of psychosis.

I realize now it's possible to fail to recall a person, or anything she said, and yet have the sound of her ideas still everywhere in mind. This is a kind of exact portraiture that music can create, because it does not need the words, the sense, or the meaning.

It occurs to me that Stockhausen has snuck into those parts of my mind that were once occupied by Anneliese. I am surprised by this, but not too much. In the past I hadn't thought about Anneliese when I practiced Stockhausen, but now I realize that Stockhausen has been my way to think about her, to wonder about what she accomplished, without the details of the person herself, without her arcane ideas, her hypochondria, her philosophy, her fretting about her family or complaining about her colleagues. Stockhausen has let me refresh my memory of her without actually remembering her. That seems to be something music can do, at least it has done that for me.

**13** That winter Anneliese looked back forty years and said her life was not a human life. Now I look back the same number of years to the moment when she said that, and ask myself the same question. Has my life, since the time of this book, been a normal human life? The question does not have an answer that works in words. Her life was crowded with books and theories, and especially with her need to hear herself speak. Mine is as empty as hers was entangled. My last forty years have been nearly still, like the third measure in *Piano Piece 9,* where notes drift upward from one height to the next.

I hear her unhappy voice in these pages, but I can no longer care what happened to her. The past steps carefully backward until it is out of sight. Music is what remains. It sings, it whispers, sometimes it pummels in my ears. I am adding these notes in order to reimagine the past I have forgotten, as music. And to ensure it remains only music.

14 Like other composers of his generation, Stockhausen experimented with mathematics. He based *Piano Piece 9* on the Fibonacci series, 1, 2, 3, 5, 8, 13, and so on. If I count the beats in the third measure, I get 3 for the dotted quarter note, then 8, 5, and 13, which are the right numbers, but in the wrong order. No one listening to this measure would guess that Fibonacci numbers were involved. In Stockhausen's mind the Fibonacci series provided a structure, but for everyone else it is a matter of waiting for the next note.

If I play *Piano Piece 9* carefully, I can feel there is order somewhere inside it. It's a comfort, knowing mathematics is at work, that the whole thing isn't random. Maybe that is why Stockhausen gave his lecture, to reassure his students and friends that his music was rational.

The student who had asked why there are 116 beats in the first measure wasn't satisfied.

"I don't see," he said. "Why 116, why 83?"

"They total 199," Stockhausen replied. "Together with the later repetitions there are 233 in total, and 233 is the 13th Fibonacci number."

"I can't hear that," the student said.

"You know that every time interval counts," Stockhausen said. "And you know every note is exactly placed in relation to every other note. So you know that these relations are in the music. Just where the music seems excessive, that is where you will find the tightest control."

When I play I am alert for rhythms that use 5, 8, and 13. I can hear them in different parts of the piece. Stockhausen knew numbers like 233 could not be perceived. He told people about them anyway, because he wanted his listeners to think the piece had an amazing arithmetical structure. But did he count the hundreds of notes that fly like arrows in all directions? Even now I wonder about that.

15 I left Guelph forty years ago. Northern Ontario, where I live now, is farm and forest country. I am a few kilometers from the first of the HELL IS REAL signs that some farmer roped onto rusted farm equipment parked forever on the corners of his fields.

When I need groceries I go to the Ultramart, or ask Fina to bring things when she visits. If I get sick it's twenty-five minutes to Parkside Hospital. My house is one of six that were put up at the same time, enough to qualify for county services. They plow the access road and deliver mail to our mailboxes.

When I left Guelph after that winter, I knew I wouldn't be found. No one I knew visited northern Ontario. Hardly anyone who drives on Route 6 even notices Shallow Lake, or turns down toward the small group of houses at the end of the field. It's seldom worth the time even for sales people or people on religious missions.

Nothing here is especially beautiful. Everything just is. For me that is not depressing. It's the actual condition of life once you finally subtract away all that romantic stuff about love and family.

16 *Piano Piece 9* eventually wears itself down. The jumpy notes become weightless. Stockhausen lets the music dissolve into tinkling notes at the very top of the keyboard.

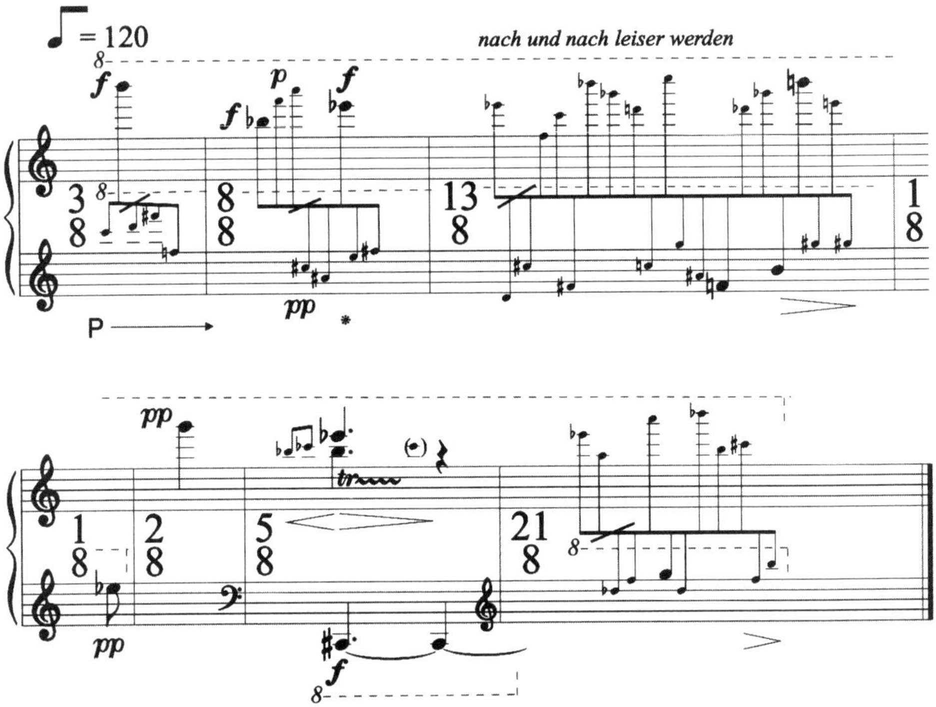


These are notes Beethoven and the others never used. On a grand piano, the uppermost octave and a half has no dampers, so when a note is struck it continues to sound, even if the pianist doesn't want it to. The reason for the lack of dampers is that most people don't hear it when very high notes keep sounding. They hear the plink! of the note, and they assume what follows is silence. But if you listen carefully, you can hear the notes continue to sound. That bothered Stockhausen, and he had a special piano built to dampen those top keys. He wanted to play staccato notes sharply and precisely in the highest registers of the piano. He had his custom-built piano onstage at his lecture, and he invited people to come up and stand around the piano. He sat and played the last measures of *Piano Piece 9*, very high, very sharp. "This is how it should be done," he told the pianist. "My piece has no lost sound. Every single note is exactly as it should be, but you must stand very close, and it must be this piano." Then he told them all to go back to their seats.

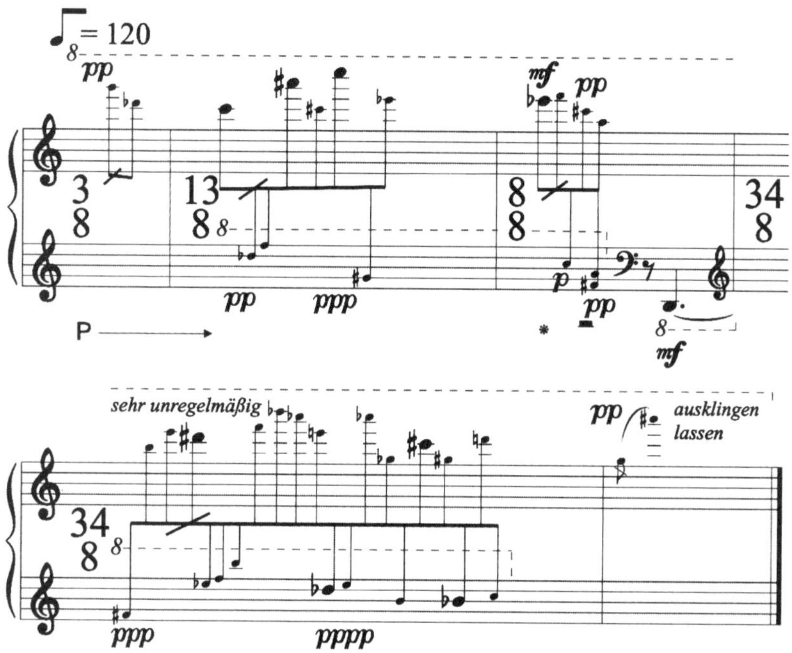


Those ultra-high notes in the last pages of *Piano Piece 9* are the sounds of a mind that can't stop thinking, even when it is exhausted, when everything's been said and there's no more breath anyway.

The end is not a relief. Two notes hang in the air. What follows, in the listener's mind, is another onslaught of deafening repeated chords.

17 The year after he wrote *Piano Piece 9,* Stockhausen began to think his music was too simple. It used a simple mathematics, he said, and it was based on a simple idea, the contrast of repetition and disorder. He had gotten tired of the usual sorts of challenges modern composers thought up: dissonant chords, chance compositions, twelve-tone technique, microtones, Indonesian bells, air-raid sirens. It was all too easy. He wanted to say something new, and it required a wholly different way of composing. "It is not enough to torture music," he wrote in his notebook, "I need to eviscerate it."

He decided to study what piano music was made of, how many parts it had. "The human body is made of 206 bones," he wrote in his notebook. "There are 32 teeth, 684 skeletal muscles, 51 endocrine glands, and 1,320 tendons. On the piano there are 88 keys, 3,828 combinations of two notes, 109,736 combinations of three notes, and 4,368 five-note chords in each octave. It is desirable to systematize every dimension of piano playing, so that it can be reimagined."

He experimented with new ways of striking notes. "I shake my hands and then I try that on the keyboard. I smash my fist on the table. Again and again! Faster! And then on the keyboard. I stir my fingers in batter and then lick them off. Again, with imaginary batter, on the keyboard. I comb my hair. The same sweeping gesture across the keyboard. I do push-ups, twelve at a time, clapping in between each one. Then leaning on the keyboard. I box the air. Then the keys. I wipe imaginary dust with an imaginary cloth. I hammer a nail. Then on the keyboard, holding a note down and hammering on my finger. I wind up my alarm clock. I cut slices of bread from a large loaf. I polish my shoes. I type."

Years later, the interviewer asked Doris Andreae if she recalled those days. "Yes," she said, "how could anyone forget? He told me to keep our friends away. If they came to the house I was to tell them he was ill. It was a kind of illness, but most of us would be lucky to be sick in that way."

Stockhausen made lists of all the possible ways of striking the keys, all the different volumes, tempi, kinds of pedaling, durations of rests. He numbered every possibility, and then he got out his spreadsheets and started calculating.

**18** He decided to compose *Piano Piece 10* out of thirteen different kinds of sounds. Each of the thirteen was divided into seven levels, so there were ninety-one kinds in all. *Piano Piece 10* was going to be the densest, most rigorously theorized composition in the history of music. The one work that had all of piano music in it. The work that would make everyone else's compositions seem like sketches or whims. The unexpected accomplishment that would cause other composers to sit back and wonder what they'd been doing with their lives.

Stockhausen called his thirteen kinds of sounds "dimensions." At the beginning of *Piano Piece 10,* all thirteen dimensions are there at once, each one divided into seven levels, in order to produce the absolute maximum of complexity: seven kinds of chords, seven sorts of note clusters, seven dynamics *ppp* to *fff,* seven kinds of note groupings, seven ranges of pitches, seven kinds of pedaling, seven kinds of acceleration and deceleration, seven speeds, seven durations of notes, seven durations of rests, seven ways of preparing to strike the notes, seven ways of striking notes, seven degrees of order and disorder.

Everything at once, a force thirteen gale.

19 In *Piano Piece 10,* the first dimension is chords. There are seven kinds, from one-note chords to seven-note chords. And already there's a problem. I can hear if a chord has two, three, or four notes, but I can't always be sure a chord has five, six, or seven notes, especially when the chords are being played quickly, with many other notes around them. And how am I supposed to know when Stockhausen expects me to hear a single note as a one-note chord?

Note clusters are another dimension. I play them with my fists, my palms, or my forearms flat on the keyboard. Clusters come in sets of 7, 14, 21, 27, 28, 35, and 42 notes: that is seven levels of clusters, all except one of them a multiple of seven. "27," he wrote in a notebook, "is the key to the system, a beautiful number, the sum of the numbers between and including its two digits, 2 + 3 + 4 + 5 + 6 + 7 = 27." It doesn't matter because no one can hear whether there are 27 or 28 notes in a cluster anyway. When I play clusters by pressing my forearm onto the keyboard, I may sound 20 notes, or 30. But I am supposed to make it sound as if there are seven levels of note clusters.

I also try to observe the third dimension, dynamics. Again there are seven, *ppp* to *fff.* But it isn't easy to teach yourself to use exactly and only seven dynamics, and the music goes blindingly fast. I have to leap from one place on the keyboard to another. Sometimes I land too hard after a jump, and *p* becomes *f.* I can't keep every *mf* and *f* separate. Even if a computer generated the performance, I doubt many people would be able to distinguish seven dynamics. The point is it has to sound that way, as if the dynamics are carefully controlled and only seven are permitted.

Stockhausen also required seven kinds of note groupings. First is repeated notes. Then there are arpeggios. Third are cluster-scales, that is when I play scales with my fist or forearm. Next are glissandi-clusters, when I use the back of my fingers or the side of my hand to sweep up or down the keyboard. The fourth level of note grouping is glissandi-clusters of ninth chords. Fifth: glissandi-clusters of sixths. Sixth: glissandi-clusters of fourths. The seventh kind of note grouping is ordinary melodies. It took me a day just to memorize those. And how willful, I thought, to include melodies here, as a sort of note grouping. It's as if he wanted to demote melodies, move them from their prominent place in music down into the seventh subcategory of the fourth dimension of his newly invented system. It's a challenge: try to think about melodies as if they are just a kind of note grouping, no different from a single note repeated over and over. Maybe the opening of *Piano Piece 9* is a melody—a horrible sort of melody, endless and formless. There aren't melodies in *Piano Piece 10* anyway. Anything tuneful is quickly overwhelmed.

Then there is a dimension Stockhausen called ranges of pitches. Each note is assigned one of seven ranges. The first is the entire keyboard, and then the keyboard with the five highest and lowest notes subtracted, then with ten notes subtracted, and so on, down to a range that spans an octave and a half. Every note in *Piano Piece 10* is assigned to one of those seven ranges, but no listener could guess which unless the notes are at the very top or bottom. When notes stay near the middle of the keyboard, a listener could guess they must be in the seventh range, but most of the time there's no way to tell. What mattered, in his mind, was that listeners would know that everything they heard was regimented, classified, constrained. Nothing was free to be expressive, there was to be no effusive feeling, no intuitive tone painting, no normal human thought.

Once he had defined the seven levels in each of the thirteen dimensions, Stockhausen decided they should be used in a certain order. He numbered each level in each dimension, and then he prescribed an order. For instance the seven ranges of pitches, that is the fifth dimension, are used one after another in the order 5 1 4 3 6 7 2. No one could hear that, and knowing it doesn't help.

There are also seven kinds of pedaling, that is the sixth dimension. First is the usual one. For the second kind, I play the note again silently immediately after I've played it and then push down the pedal, capturing some of the sound of the note. Stockhausen says I should hear a "filtered" sound, a "leftover" sound. I don't, but I follow the instructions. For the third kind of pedaling I press the pedal halfway down and then I strike the note. When I release the note the dampers touch the strings lightly, attenuating the sound. I can hear that if I play one note at a time and the room is quiet. The fourth kind of pedaling is when I hold the pedal down in the usual way, and then I lift it very briefly and put it down again. This produces a little whine, and most of the noise evaporates. The fifth is when the pedal is slowly lifted, gradually erasing all of the sound. In a quiet room, with no distractions, this produces an interesting uneven diminishing of sound. The sixth is when I hold a note with the usual damper pedal, and then I depress a cluster in the bass silently, and hold that with the middle pedal. Then I release the damper pedal, and some high echoes hang in the air. The seventh is when I silently depress a cluster of notes in the bass, and hold it with the middle pedal. Then I play other notes, which resonate. That one is a standard piano technique, and it works.

The seven kinds of pedaling are hard to learn, and even harder to perform when the music moves so quickly. Most of them only work in a silent room, like my living room at night, with the air conditioning or heating turned off.

The seven kinds of pedaling repeat in the order 5 2 3 7 4 1 6.

Then there are seven kinds of acceleration and deceleration, which is the seventh dimension. One: play at constant speed. Two: accelerate uniformly. Three: slow down uniformly. These two are the standard ones, represented by slanting beams in the score. Four: accelerate more quickly toward the end of the attack. Five: slow uniformly, and then suddenly much slower. Six: perform even accelerations and decelerations. Seven: uneven accelerations and decelerations. The seven kinds of attack would be straightforward except that the notes that I am supposed to accelerate or decelerate are not just quarter notes or eighth notes. They come in mixtures of durations: sixty-fourth notes with dotted eighths, septuplet sixteenths, double whole notes… it's often impossible to hear if the music is speeding up or slowing down.

The seven kinds of attack repeat in the order 4 6 2 7 3 5 1, but it doesn't help to know that because Stockhausen changes the order as the piece goes on.

Then there are seven speeds, but they are overruled by the heavy beams Stockhausen drew in his score, which slant up or down, always accelerating or decelerating the music. The seven speeds might have been clear in Stockhausen's notebooks, when the music moved slowly in his mind, but they are blurred in the score.

Durations of notes, the ninth dimension, also come in a set of seven levels: breve, whole note, half note, quarter note, eighth, sixteenth, thirty-second. They should be simple enough to hear, but the tempo of *Piano Piece 10* is always changing, ruining any chance to hear the difference between a dotted eighth, for example, and a double-dotted eighth. Late in the piece the pace settles and there are a couple of enormous long silences, but then it is impossible to count accurately. Who can tell the difference between eighty whole notes of silence and a hundred and fifty half notes of silence? There is even a page where the silence echoes the percussive notes at the opening of *Piano Piece 9*. It is marked with twenty-seven whole notes of rest, followed by a single quarter-note rest, impossible for anyone to count.

The seven durations of notes repeat in the order 4 1 5 2 3 7 6, but that doesn't help because Stockhausen changes the order as the piece goes along.

It's the same with the tenth dimension, rests. Stockhausen says there are seven kinds, but he combines them and divides them, so in effect there are hundreds more.

The seven durations of rests repeat in the order 7 2 5 4 6 3 1, but that doesn't help because Stockhausen changes the order as the piece goes along.

The eleventh dimension is seven ways of preparing to strike notes. In the first, I play "directly, with fingers in the usual position." For the second, I pause my hand over the key before striking. In the third, I pause and dip my hand down as if to play, and then raise it back up, "like a conductor setting the tempo." In the fourth, I hold my hand above the keyboard at an angle, "like telling someone to stop." In the fifth, I curl the heel of my hands under the edge of the keyboard, "like a cat stalking." For the sixth, I make a brief fist.

For the seventh, I splay my fingers before returning to a playing position. A person watching a performance of *Piano Piece 10* might see some of these, but a person listening could not possibly sense the difference between the gestures.

The order is 1 5 2 4 7 6 3, but I can't hear it, and Stockhausen changes the order as the piece goes along.

The twelfth dimension is seven ways of striking the notes. First is the ordinary way, touching with the front portion of the pad of each finger. For the second level my fingers are flatter, and I touch the keys farther back on the pad of the finger. For the third I lower my elbows and curl my fingers upward "so the fingers form little hammocks." For the fourth I stroke the key with the pad of my finger, "as if it is a little white or black cat." In the fifth I curl my fingers downward, which is a common way of playing staccato. For the sixth, I turn my hand toward the thumb, so my fingers strike on the side facing the thumb. For the seventh, I turn my hands away from the thumbs and use the other side of my fingers. Pianists often talk about these kinds of differences, but usually one or two of them become habitual. It is very difficult to change them with each note, and even harder to try to keep exactly seven of them separate in my mind.

The order is 1 5 3 6 7 2 4, but I can't hear it, and Stockhausen changes the order as the piece goes along.

The thirteenth dimension is seven kinds of order and disorder, which Stockhausen names pure order (*reine Ordnung*), declining order, dispersing order, balanced order and disorder, quenched disorder, annealed disorder, and pure disorder (*reine Unordnung*). Pure order is when the note clearly and unambiguously declares its loyalty to each of the other twelve dimensions. Declining order is when the note's affiliation is mainly clear but it gives evidence of slipping away from the system. Dispersing order is when the note seems to actively resist the system. He does not define how a note can balance order and disorder. Quenched disorder is when a note seems to misbehave, but also shows signs of allegiance to the system. Annealed disorder is when a note seems to have a change of heart, and wants to show its partial allegiance to the system. Pure disorder is when a note "seems to fall from heaven like a small burning rock."

The order is 2 7 6 4 1 5 3, but I can't hear it, and Stockhausen changes the order as the piece goes along.

These are the thirteen dimensions of *Piano Piece 10,* each with seven levels. My ears cannot hear the seven levels. My mind cannot hold all the changing orders of the levels. No listener can hear or remember the thirteen dimensions.

I only knew Anneliese for half a year, but I have been playing *Piano Piece 10* for decades. I can understand some parts of it, enough to know that to Stockhausen, the piece made sense. What matters is that enormous effort has been expended to create a system. I can hear that the music is full of rules, that the rules consume the notes, fill the player's mind, push and pull the music, keep it from ever speaking freely.

**20** *Piano Piece 10* is like Anneliese: a flood, and inside it, someone being swept along, calling out. Listening is like standing on the bank and watching. I could walk away, but I don't. I become entranced by the flood, I step closer and closer to the edge.

When I first tried to play *Piano Piece 10* I thought it was nothing but chaos. I couldn't hear music in it. I thought it was compositional spittle. A torrent of trills, glissandi, grace notes, and appoggiaturas obscured whatever music there might have been. I made notes in my copy of the score, trying to identify the dimension and level of every note. My score almost has more penciled notes than printed ones. I hoped that way I would eventually understand the piece. It didn't work. I saw how ambitious the composition is, and how hopeless it is to follow Stockhausen's thinking point by point. He nearly drowned his own music, he threw it into the flood. I imagine he found it moving to hear his music try so hard to make sense, and be repeatedly smothered by the weight of his rules.

He invented a new way of notating music just for *Piano Piece 10.* He didn't use bar lines or key signatures. He distributed the notes over three staves. The pages are filled with a scattering of tiny notes.

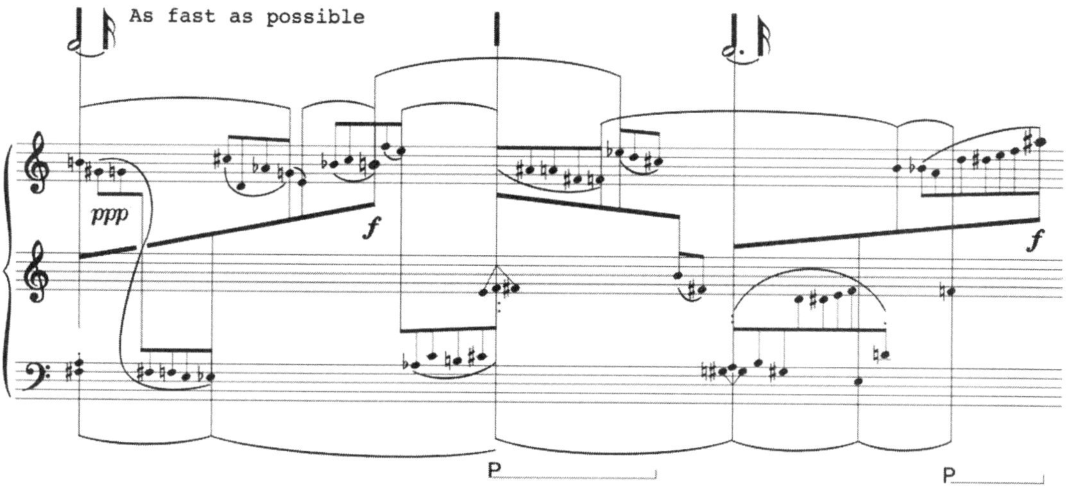


To guide the performer, he wrote the main notes in a slightly larger size, so they stand out in the filigree of small-print notes. Here the important notes are a B natural marked *f,* and an A# at the end. It is next to impossible to hear a melody made of just those two notes when the small notes are swarmed all around them. As in Anneliese's speeches, where the main points were sunk in an ocean of distractions. In conventional music, the large-print notes could be a melody, and the smaller ones grace notes. But Stockhausen prevented the larger notes from linking together to form melodies. Melodies are the lowest level of the fourth of his thirteen dimensions. In a lecture in London, he said people had to get used to melodies of notes separated by enormous distances, where an enormous complexity of sound might come between any two notes. He unfurled a wall chart four meters long, showing the entire score of *Piano Piece 10,* color coded, with charts and tables beneath it. "Thirteen dimensions with seven levels each is ninety-one structures," he said, "as you can see from the color key." He pointed to the few places where the larger melodic notes could be found. "People will have to expand their capacity of perception," he said, "in order to be aware of melodies that are no more important than ninety other categories of musical structure."

To help the pianist keep time, Stockhausen drew heavy horizontal beams tying the notes together. Here they move along between the top two staves like a boat listing up and down. When the beams tilt upward, the pianist is supposed to accelerate, and when they tilt down, the music slows—that is levels two and three of the seventh dimension.

At the top of the score he drew large-print note stems, some without noteheads, to help performers with the rhythm. The first one is a half note tied to a sixteenth. Then there's a single quarter note stem, followed by a dotted half note tied to a sixteenth. The large-print stems are lined up with the tilted beams to give a sense of the rhythm. Stockhausen says the large-print stems are spaced so that the pianist can travel at a constant speed across the page.

I can't count the rhythms at the top of the page the way I count ordinary music. I don't know how to count a half note tied to a sixteenth, followed by a quarter note, while the music is flying by underneath. A metronome wouldn't help because the music is constantly accelerating or decelerating. Performers are supposed to keep the rhythms at the top of the page in the corner of their eye as they play, but I hardly have time to look at them and I doubt any listener could deduce they are there.

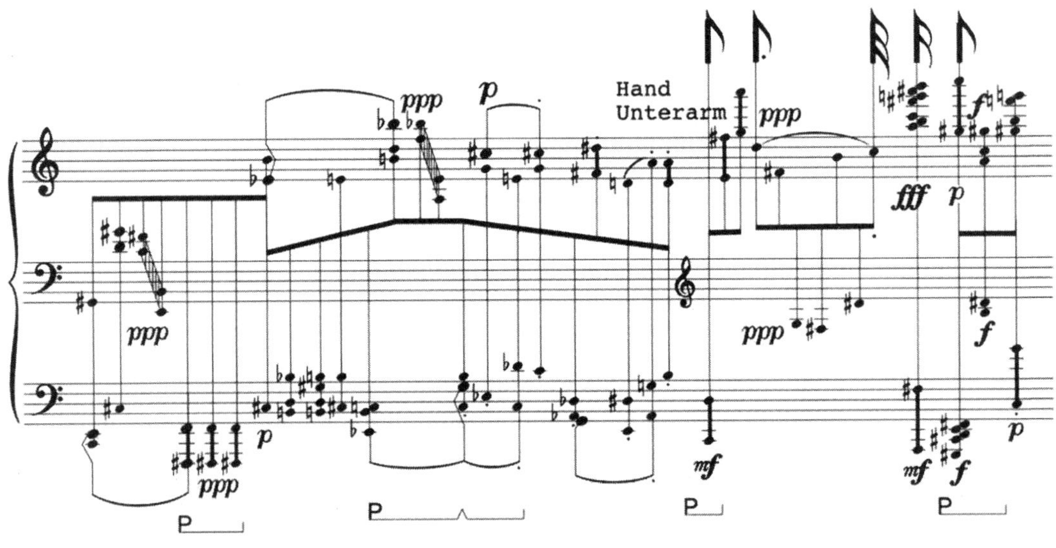


On other pages there are thick vertical bars between notes. They are clusters, the second of Stockhausen's thirteen dimensions. I strike all the notes in the interval, using the side of my hand or my forearm.

Glissandi slide like ladders up and down the keyboard. Glissandi-clusters are the fourth of Stockhausen's thirteen dimensions. I am supposed to press down on the keys and then sweep across the keyboard. Stockhausen recommended players use woolen gloves with the fingers cut out, in order to execute these glissandi as quickly as possible without chafing. I don't use gloves, and after a while the piece makes my fingers sore.

Playing *Piano Piece 10* is like running through a forest. It is impossible to remember dimensions and levels when the sound is rushing forward. I go too fast to see every branch and twig. I stumble. Leaves snap in my face. I do my best to stay upright. I try to see what is up ahead, but I have to pay attention to what I'm about to run into. I glimpse interesting things, glissandi and note clusters, but I can't stop to admire them, I can't look back, I need to keep going. It doesn't help to practice slowly, the way performers do when they're learning a new piece. If I play note by note, I can't hear the rhythms at all. So I play at speed, as accurately as I can. I pay strict attention. I accelerate when the beams slope up, slow when they incline down. I glance at the note stems at the top. I look for the large-print note heads and try to make them stand out. I look everywhere on the keyboard at once.

Much of *Piano Piece 10* is fanatical and unintelligible. I do as well as I can, trying to make less than a dozen errors every minute, working hard just to keep up. I can see stupendous effort went into it. Stockhausen was struggling to communicate. He wanted to make sense in a new way, but players couldn't manage it and audiences couldn't hear it.

This afternoon I pushed myself along through the score. I swept my fingernails up and down the keyboard to make glissandi. I banged my hands and forearms down to make note clusters. I played as quickly as I could, making hundreds of mistakes, trying to hear what Stockhausen had written. There were moments when I was suddenly aware of a certain dimension or layer. I could see how the music might make sense. And then, immediately, those glimpses were drowned.

While I was playing, Fina came back with the shopping. She doesn't notice my music. I think to her it's a mad but harmless preoccupation, a sort of nervous energy that comes from overeducation and loneliness.

**21** *Piano Piece 10* just dies away.

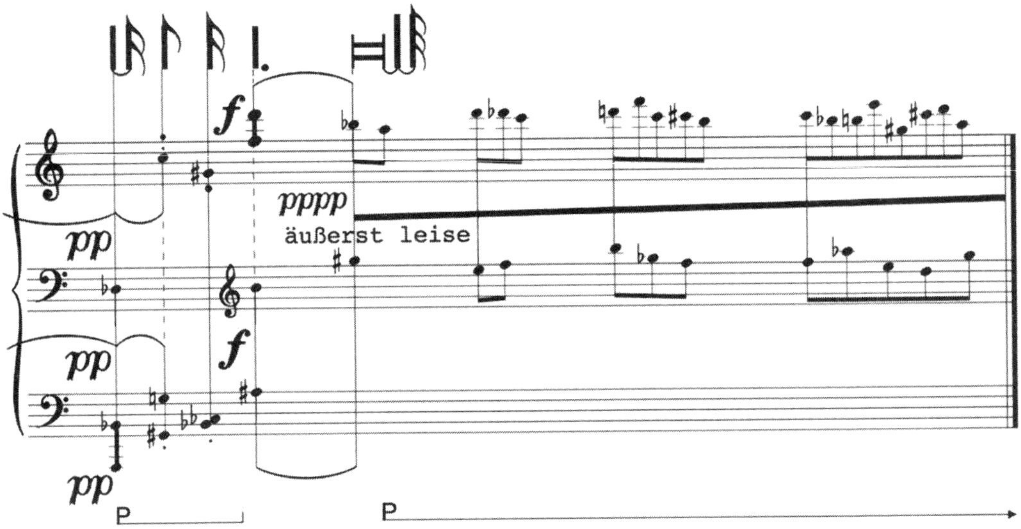


A thick beam rises slowly upward. Four thin stems lead up and down from it, so in a normal piece of music there would be four eighth notes. Stockhausen hasn't drawn any. Instead he has splintered the eighth notes into grace notes. In the treble clef there are first two, then three, then five, then eight. In the left hand one, two, three, and five. Grace notes do not have any set duration, so there is no way to know how long to pause between the groups. When I play I leave short gaps like gasps.

The notes sound like the clumsy flutter of some large insect trapped in a bottle, flapping and then falling silent. As *Piano Piece 10* nears its ending, these gaps widen. It seems the insect is tiring. Soon it will lie still at the bottom of the jar. The music sounds random, but its bursts are precisely planned, as Anneliese said about her speeches. The insect knows exactly when it will die.

22 Stockhausen took the winter of 1959-1960 to research the longest, most complex pieces in the history of modern music. He studied Wagner's *Ring,* Mahler's third symphony, Dimitrie Cuclin's twelfth symphony, Scriabin's *Mysterium,* Messiaen's *Vingt Regards sur l'Enfant-Jésus,* and Schönberg's *Gurre-Lieder.* He wrote a thesis on Bartók's experimental *Sonata for Two Pianos and Percussion.* Then he turned to composers of his own generation.

He prepared Boulez's daunting *Second Piano Sonata,* designed to pulverize all musical styles into a combustive powder. He complained how tedious it was to learn John Cage's *Music of Changes,* where the notes are random but need to be played exactly as notated. For several weeks he practiced Jean Barraqué's *Piano Sonata,* which had never been performed, and studied Barraqué's plans for an enormous piece to be called *The Death of Virgil.* He listened to tapes of Conlon Nancarrow's *Studies for Player Piano,* composed for a machine because no human could ever play them. Stockhausen wanted to write an enormous composition, a compendium of all music, something that would make his contemporaries look insufficient.

In the summer of 1960 he accepted an invitation from the Baron Francesco Agnello to come stay with him in his castle hotel in the village of Siculiana in the south of Sicily. The visit is recorded in Agnello's memoir, *Memorie del Barone Francesco Agnello, Fondatore dell'Associazione Regionale Amici della Musica.*

"As part of my efforts to expand the musical horizons of Agrigento," Baron Agnello wrote, "I invited Karlheinz Stockhausen to come to Castiddubbuonu Chiaramonte. I sent him the following letter on March 7, 1959: 'You and Doris Andreae Stockhausen and your children will stay in the same apartments once occupied by my great friend Giuseppe Tomasi di Lampedusa, author of *The Leopard.* The barred windows of your rooms will look out over dry olive groves to the desolate beach of the Fallen Stones, where you can walk all day without interruption. The enormous ancient wooden desk that will serve as your composition table is inhabited by only a single object: a heavy metal sculpture of two horses bearing the empty chariot of the Sun, which continues to fly even though it has dropped its pilot, Phaëthon, into our blue ocean. (The empty chariot is for holding pens.) You may live in these rooms as long as you wish, for the entire season. My stories of ruined aristocracy and the debasement of Sicilian culture will supply you with an endless melancholy and irritation, perfectly suited, I hope, to the production of another astonishing masterpiece. We have a poor music society here, which you may use as you wish.'

"Stockhausen replied immediately, accepting the offer, but asking that I not inform the Friends of Music Association of his presence, 'in order to avoid pedagogical situations,' and requesting that the metal chariot be removed. I replied on March 20: 'The metal pen holder with the empty chariot of the Sun has a single feather in it. That is in remembrance of Daedalus and Icarus. As you may remember, Daedalus had to flee Crete because his patron, Minos, wanted to kill him. He made wings for himself and his son Icarus. When Icarus fell, Daedalus stopped to bury him, and then continued to fly. He landed in Siculiana and met Kokalos, king of the Sicanians, first people of Sicily. Kokalos permitted Daedalus to design this castle, where you will stay. For this reason the chariot can never be moved. It is a reminder that the first architect in the history of the world sat in those rooms and thought of his son Icarus, and, eons before him, of Phaëthon, who was also thrown down into the ocean. When you sit at that desk you may be in the exact spot where Daedalus sat looking out to the sea. When you bathe in the enormous marble tub you will be delighted to know it may be the very tub where Minos, who had come to Sicily to kill Daedalus, was boiled into a weak broth. When you walk along our basement hallways you will be following a path designed by the world's most ancient architect, Daedalus, designer of the labyrinth. Your music can reach back in time, and forward to the ignorant composers of today.'

"In return I received the following letter, the sort that only impertinent so-called geniuses permit themselves: 'Dear Baron,' Stockhausen wrote, using the ignorant titular appellation that appears appropriate to those who have no commerce with the nobility, 'I will not visit if you persist in coating everything with antiquity. I want clean apartments, clean sand, and that is all.'

"It is best, in cases like this, to realize that despite the anti-aristocratic rancor that a person like Stockhausen can occasionally exhibit—a temper he probably inherited from his bourgeois German family—his presence can still be beneficial for people like the players in my Regional Music Association who require the presence of famous people to underwrite their precarious sense of their country. So I wrote only this: 'Please remind Doris Andreae to bring sunscreen. Even in winter Sicily has the power to burn you into a stick of charcoal.'"

Stockhausen spent that winter in the Castello Chiaramonte in the small village of Siculiana, walking on the beach and thinking of long, complex compositions. By spring he had his answer, a piece called *Plus Minus*.

23 The score of *Plus Minus* is not normal. There is nothing to sit down and play. Stockhausen provided seven unbound pages divided into grids. In each square of the grids there are triangles, circles, numbers, and flags. The pages have no staves, no musical notes, no text. They look like diagrams of electric switches or charts of chemical properties. He wrote five pages of instructions for how to decode them. People who want to play *Plus Minus* have to learn the symbols and follow Stockhausen's rules to write their own score.

Along with the seven pages of code there are seven pages of ordinary musical notes. Each page has seven chords labeled I through VII, which he called "central sounds," and six sets of grace notes numbered 1 through 6. Together the chords and the grace notes produce "sound events," and the instructions describe how to put them together.

Once again there is a tyranny of sevens. There are seven different ways of placing ornaments relative to the central sound: before, simultaneous, after, before and after, simultaneous and after, before and simultaneous, and all three.

There are seven timbres: hard sounds, soft sounds, hard noises, soft noises, hard sound noises, soft sound noises, and indeterminate timbres.

There are seven ways to group notes, seven constellations for a complete realization of the seven chords, seven possible combinations of adjacent events, seven relative durations of the sound events, seven kinds of rests that separate the sound events, seven types of superimposition, seven possible overall characteristics of a given layer.

To turn the code sheets into a score that can be played, the first step is to choose one sheet of code and one sheet of notes. The pages are unbound and have no order, so it's like a card trick: I pick at random. Then I make my way along the code sheet as if I am playing a board game, one square at a time.

In the center of each square is a circle representing a chord.

I assign one of the seven chords on the music sheet to the first square of the code sheet. Then Stockhausen says I should pick some "accidental notes" that are in the range of the chord. Inside the circle Stockhausen put triangles and lozenges directing how the accidental notes should be played. ▲ means short, ▼ means medium length, ● means long. So this is a chord with a long set of accidental notes.

Above the circle he planted flags with numbers.

This means the sound event becomes three times larger each time it appears, or it becomes one-third as large, whichever the performer wants.

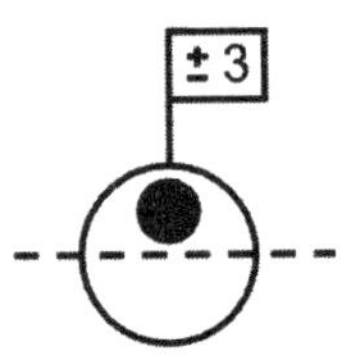

He added grace note flags to indicate how the extra notes are to be played.

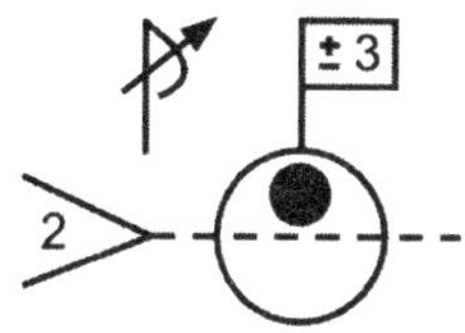


A rising arrow means accelerando. A triangle with the number 2 inside it means the highest pitch of the preceding sound event should be the second-highest pitch of the current event.

There are many more symbols. The letter D means the sound event is dampened. Signs in the lower right of the square are instructions about how to switch notes from different staves. If there are two notes in this sound event that are also played on another stave, or on another instrument, they should be changed so they are notes that aren't played before or after this event, on any staff or by any other instrument. A long thick arrow pointing down means synchronize this perfectly with a sound event in another staff or played on another instrument.

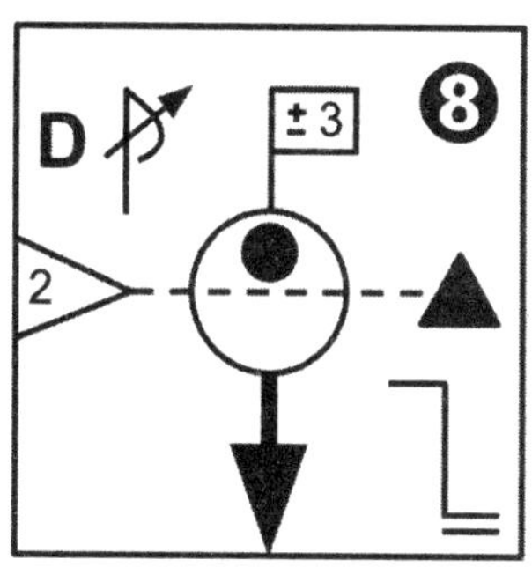


Stockhausen kept drawing squares and adding symbols and rules, making his piece more complex, ensuring it could represent all combinations of music.

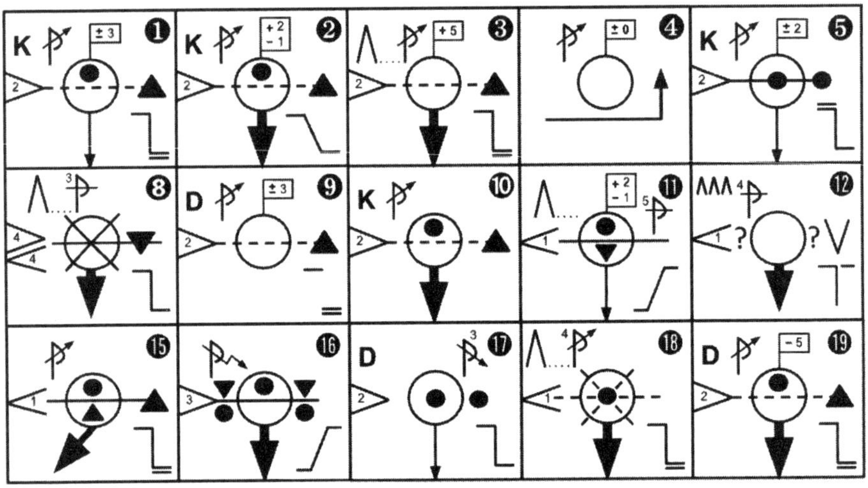

There are thirty-five rules and dozens more symbols, not only notes and numbers but new symbols like and and and and and and and and even , which means I can choose from any rule.

The piece does not have to be for one player, or for piano. It can be for any number of performers. I can use all the code sheets, or just one.

Stockhausen thought he had solved the problem of how to write the world's most complicated composition. He had written a set of instructions that could make music of any complexity, and it would be different each time someone turned the code sheets into scores. *Plus Minus* could produce unplayable compositions, like Nancarrow's *Studies for Player Piano.* It could create randomness better than Cage's *Music of Changes,* it could create music more compressed than Boulez's or Barraqué's sonatas. It was a machine for all possible systematically produced complexity.

24 Stockhausen's rooms overlooked the sea, as the Baron had promised, but to get there Stockhausen, Doris Andreae, and their children had to walk down through the narrow streets of the town, away from the sea, and then back and forth between olive groves. The beach of the Fallen Stones was often deserted, as the Baron had promised. It was hidden by a wall of crumbling cliffs, and there was no road. Stockhausen found a path and they went

down. The beach was like the ruin of an enormous ancient fortress. Cubical blocks of stone as large as houses had fallen from the cliffs and lay at different angles in the sand.

The family spent long afternoons on the beach. Doris Andreae read, the children swam and played with toy boats, and Stockhausen wrote his composition in the sand.

He drew with a long stick just above the line of foam left by the highest wave. When he finished a square he walked a few steps down the beach and drew the next one. The code sheets of *Plus Minus* appeared along the strandline, stretching far down the beach, interrupted only by the colossal rocks that had fallen from the cliffs. When they got back to the castle hotel each night, Stockhausen wrote down all the squares he had composed during the day.

A few years ago I bought a book of blank sheet music, intending to follow Stockhausen's instructions and make a playable score. I chose a code sheet and began with the first square.

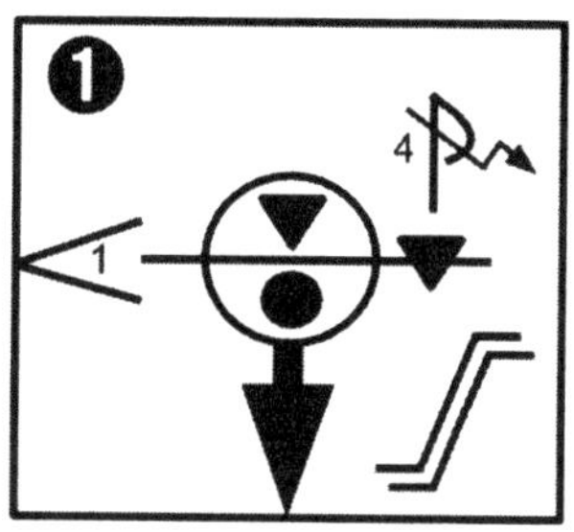


I then chose a page of notes, and assigned one of the chords on it to this sound event. I chose chord V:

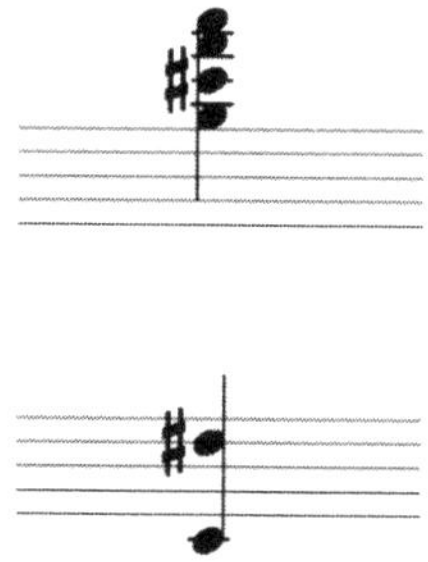

A strange but pleasant chord. The triangle in the central circle tells me I can add short "accidental notes" to the top of the chord, and longer ones to the bottom. I'm permitted to choose any pitches so long as they fit the register of the chord. I chose two.

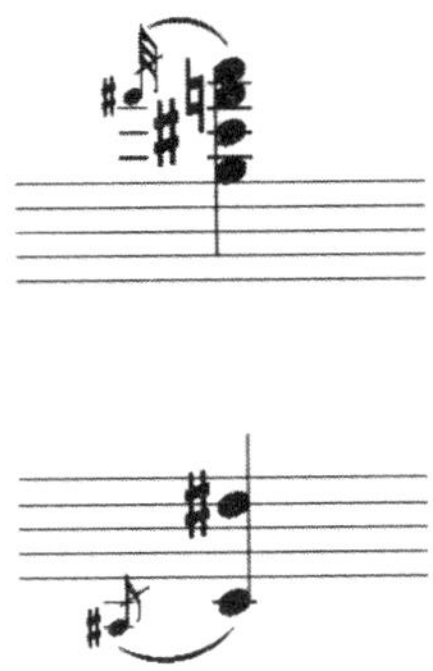

The grace note flag in the upper right of the square with the number 4 means I have to choose the fourth set of grace notes from the note sheet. It turns out that set is made of five chords, all grace notes.

On the code sheet a zigzag arrow through the grace note indicates the tempo slows, then speeds up, then slows again.

I write the sound event like this:

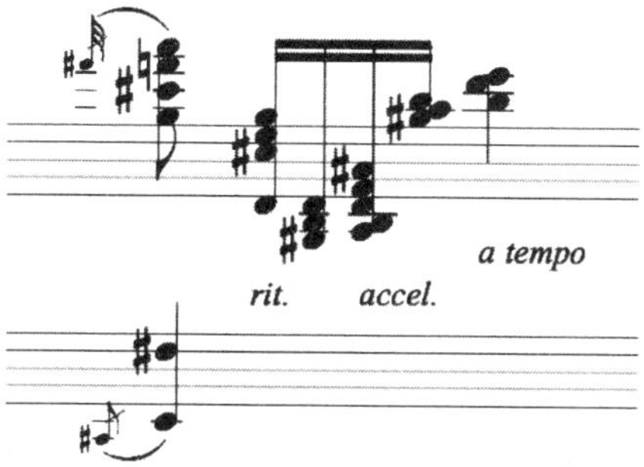


I turn the grace notes into sixteenths to preserve the change in tempo. I have created a strange equivalence:

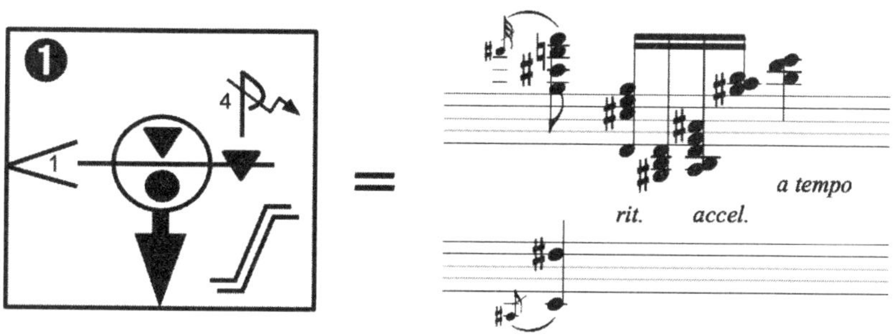


The first square on the first sheet yields about two seconds of music. From here the work quickly becomes far more complex. Each square adds more detail. Soon the score becomes a mass of notes.

1
rit.
accel.
a tempo
2
3
4
5
6
accel.
a tempo
7

Sometimes the music gets out of control. If there's a flag in the square with the number 2, the music in the following square has to have twice as many notes. Positive numbers can accumulate to +13. At that point the sound event "dies" and the player has to choose a new one.

Or the music dwindles. If the square has a flag with a -2 in it, the music has to be reduced to half its length. The sound event might become a single chord, or just a single note. If the count reaches zero you need to stop making music. Stockhausen doesn't say what you put in the place of notes. Some performers opt to sit still, and their sound event becomes their own breathing.

Your count may even go into negative numbers. Each negative number subtracts a noise from the silence—a breath, a shuffle, a cough. This can continue until the performance reaches a value of -13. At that point the sound event "dies" and it may not be used again in the piece. The player moves on to the next square.

The music can also sink or rise until it is beyond the range of any instrument. Then the event "dies" and the player goes on to a new event.

*Plus Minus* is like Anneliese's interests: it builds up hysterically or erodes until there's nothing worth listening to. Like her search for the ideal complex book, somehow always missing it, veering off in some unpromising direction.

It took me several days of work to write out just one page. It would have taken months to make a full version of *Plus Minus,* and even longer to learn to play it.

25 Stockhausen knew that each time someone made *Plus Minus* into a score the result would be different. The instructions say that each composer who writes out a version of *Plus Minus* should make a note of where they stop, so that future composers can begin from there and go on. Stockhausen hoped *Plus Minus* would be an encyclopedia of new music, an endless library, like Borges's. It is, but it also had an effect he didn't anticipate. People tried to turn it into ordinary music.

Stockhausen's assistant Cornelius Cardew sent him a tape of his performance, and Stockhausen was astonished that Cardew had made *Plus Minus* into a tone poem. It was soft and atmospheric, old-fashioned. Stockhausen demanded Cardew apologize for his performance, and admit he had not followed the instructions. In reply Cardew sent him the score he had written, and Stockhausen realized Cardew had followed his instructions perfectly. "*Plus Minus* is like a mirror," he told an interviewer. "People look into it and see themselves."

Later he heard a performance by Frederic Rzewski, and it was loud and emotional. "You play like Rubinstein," Stockhausen told him. "That time is over." Rzewski showed Stockhausen the score he had prepared. "Again I checked every note," Stockhausen said. "They were all correct." Stockhausen thought *Plus Minus* was a miracle of compression. In five short pages of rules, seven code sheets, and seven music samples, he had set out the conditions for any number of compositions of infinite complexity. Yet performers kept ruining it by making it simple.

After several weeks on the beach, Doris Andreae preferred to stay indoors. Their children's boats were lost in the surf. Stockhausen continued drawing his row of boxes in the sand. He said they looked like the impression of an enormous ladder fallen on the shoreline. The sketch for *Plus Minus* stretched a half kilometer down the beach. In later years he used to tell people that *Plus Minus* was originally written in sand, on a beach with great fallen rocks. "On the printed page it seems like a structure as solid as one of the colossal stones. But it isn't. It can be washed away."

26 "Where did my castle come from?" Baron Agnello asks in his memoirs. "The historian Diodorus says that King Kokalos welcomed Daedalus. That implies the king already had a castle in Sikolos, as our village was then called. Some say my Castiddubbuonu Chiaramonte hotel is built on the ruins of Kokalos's castle, and Daedalus built his somewhere else. But the Roman poet Ovid says that King Kokalos granted Daedalus the rights to build a castle on a hill. My castle hotel is on the main hill, and so it may be built on Daedalus's foundations. The Polish historian Filippo Cluverio cites a lost treatise written by a twelfth century nun named Constantia, who lived in the Convento di Santa Maria di Gesù in Messina, which is now, like so much else in our beautiful Sicily, a roasting ruin. Cluverio says that

Constantia records a passage in a book by Agatharchides, which has now also been lost, stating that our village was built on the ruins of the ancient residence of Kokalos, king of the vanished aboriginal Sicani. If that is true, there was only a village in Agatharchides's time, which was the second century BC. Even then Kokalos's castle was gone. Daedalus and Kokalos had been dead almost four thousand years before my castle hotel was constructed. When I told Stockhausen this he told me quite bluntly that he did not care.

"I persisted. I said that when we don't know the truth we turn to fiction. This is my fiction, I told him: I prefer to think Daedalus fell onto our beach. His son Icarus had drowned in the eastern Mediterranean, at a place called Ikaria, near Smyrna in Turkey. He buried Icarus on that island, but he could not stay. Minos was following by ship. Daedalus saw him approaching and flew off to the west. Soon Minos's ship was out of sight. Daedalus flew on. He was blind with sorrow. He flew to avoid Minos, but also to escape his grief. He carried a heavy weight of mourning but he flew as far as a migrating African bird, one thousand kilometers, and he landed here, on our beach. That was approximately three thousand years ago. The fallen stones are his sorrow. He left them on the beach and started a new life in exile.

"'Poor Baron,' Stockhausen said. 'At the end of this winter the beach of Fallen Stones will be scrubbed clean. I am taking my composition back to Germany. My music will be all that remains from your sorrowful history.'"

27 I do not know how to calculate how many different scores could be generated from *Plus Minus.* The first square already permits hundreds, perhaps thousands, of different choices. All the rules overlap, producing a vast seascape of interfering waves. Most versions of *Plus Minus,* I think, would be boring, like crossing a choppy featureless ocean in a small boat, waves slapping from the right and left, the same dull sky above, the same dim water below. There are a few places in the rules where Stockhausen shows he's aware of the boredom. "Notes may be articulated rhythmically," he says, but other than that he has nothing to say about rhythm. If you just follow the rules, you get sound events, one after another. Stockhausen has blank squares scattered through his code sheets. They are for inserting

sound events from previous passages of music. Such cases, he says, "must be clear insertions of memories, foreign to the context." Otherwise no one would notice a sound event had been inserted.

There is no overall structure, no reason to stop, no reason not to go on. In performances of *Plus Minus* it becomes hard to care about what is happening, hard to pay attention. A familiar chord or a set of grace notes may reappear, but it doesn't mean anything. The texture ebbs and flows, sometimes becoming loud or ranging up to the limits of the instruments, other times subsiding into silence.

It's the same thing reading the code sheets. At first they look interesting, in an old-fashioned sort of way.

But after a while the code sheets lose their interest. Does it matter if the next sound event has a different set of grace notes? Or if they're played together with the chord, or before it? Pedaled or staccato? Higher or lower?

After hundreds of miles at sea Daedalus's wings must have hurt. Feathers probably came loose. He must have been exhausted, thirsty, and sunburnt, but also bored from all the flying. And terribly sad, thinking of his dead son, and anxious, knowing Minos was searching for him. But unable to stop even for a moment, because if he fell into the ocean he would never get airborne again.

*Plus Minus* is the delusion Stockhausen made for himself when he tried to imagine a piece more complex than Barraqué, Cage, or Nancarrow. It is travel instructions for a boring and unpleasant journey.

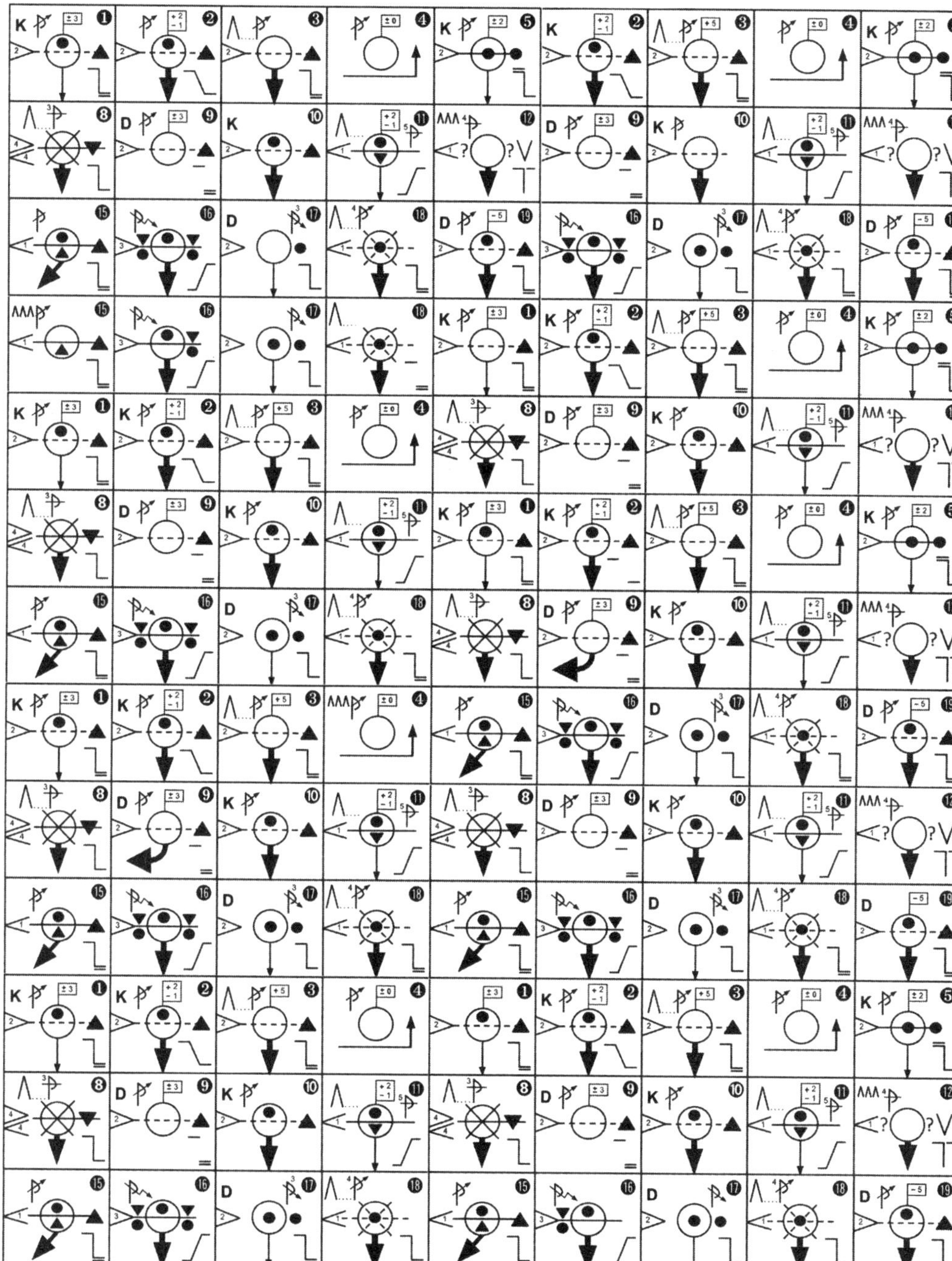

**28** Stockhausen taught a class on *Plus Minus* in Cologne in 1964. His students had to learn the code and write scores that followed his rules. At the end of the term there was a concert. One student had written *Plus Minus* as a score for an eleven-piece chamber orchestra. It sounded decorative. Stockhausen asked why the xylophone played through the entire piece. "Because it is not prohibited," the student said.

Another student used tapes of owl calls to fill in when the score went below zero. A third produced a version for four pianos, which took almost an hour to perform. A fourth made a version for two electric guitars. It was very loud and there was lots of feedback. "My music is not a rock and roll anthem," Stockhausen told the student. "Now it is," the student answered.

A student named Ming Tsao made a version for two pianos and electronics, which was faithful to Stockhausen's rules and used all seven of his sheets. When the performance ended, Stockhausen asked what came next. "Nothing," Ming Tsao replied. "It is complete." "*Plus Minus* is a collaborative composition," Stockhausen said. "You are asked to communicate the last status of your version so it can be used as the starting point for another interpreter, a composer who will make the next version." "I did not observe that rule," Ming Tsao said. "Mine is complete."

A young Icelandic composer named Atli Heimir Sveinsson went last. He sat at the piano and played two chords in the lowest bass, with very long pauses between. Then there were some high faint notes, and silence. The piece was over.

He stood and explained to the audience that he had discovered how to follow all of Stockhausen's rules and yet produce a piece that lasts less than one minute and contains, he said, "almost no music." He turned to Stockhausen. "I have assassinated *Plus Minus*," he said, "but I am innocent because the master provided the weapons." Later Sveinsson said Stockhausen had told him his version was the only one that was real music, but it was too short to be important. "Stockhausen said he had not imagined it was possible to produce so little from such an enormous effort."

Stockhausen made a speech, thanking all the students. "You have all done as well as you can, given your limitations. And I thank you for demonstrating my folly. I cannot let other people show the way for music. I need to do it myself." After the course in Cologne Stockhausen gave up on *Plus Minus.*

I have studied difficult compositions by other composers. I have practiced both Iannis Xenakis's *Khoaï* and his *Evryali.* They each took months of preparation. I have played Valen, Wyschnegradsky, Babbitt, and Ornstein. There are others I tried to play and couldn't. I have looked at James Dillon's *Book of Elements,* Brian Ferneyhough's *Lemma-Icon-Epigram,* and Michael Finnissy's endless *History of Photography.* I can't play any of them. For months I worked on Donald Martino's *Pianississimo.* Stockhausen is the one who went the farthest. His winter by the sea was a dream of flying like Daedalus, farther and farther out over the ocean, not knowing if he could keep going long enough to reach another shore.

"When Stockhausen was packed and ready to leave," Baron Agnello wrote, "I took him out to a private balcony on the other side of the castle hotel. It faces away from the sea. The balcony is supported by high stone piers, which reach down to a platform twenty feet below, on the ground floor of the castle. I told him that in 1526, the property was inherited by Vincenzo del Bosco, Duke of Misilmeri and Prince of Cattolica. 'Vincenzo,' I said, 'is remembered as one of the greatest harpsichord players in the world. He used to play on the terrazza just beneath us here. He chose that place so he could turn his back on the sea. It is sheltered from the sounds of the sea, and from the sadness of the great distances. But Vincenzo's son did not honor his father's memory. He wanted to impress the Bishop of Agrigento, a man named Blasco Bonincontro, so he destroyed his father's terrazza and had this high balcony built up above it. That is how each generation attempts to erase the past. We forget Daedalus, just as he must have wanted to forget Phaëthon, because Phaëthon must have reminded him of his own son.'

"Stockhausen did not reply, so I continued. 'I started the regional music association,' I said, 'as a way to dream. I imagined Siculiana and the island were ready for redemption. But I have become aware of the complete and inevitable failure of my actions. Siculiana and Sicily are irredeemable. I have never felt loved by them, even if it is the love you give to someone you are forced to love.'

"When I told Stockhausen this he walked out of the room."

**29** I have an alphabet of composers. The room with the piano is filled with musical scores, the way Anneliese's study was filled with notebooks. Some are in piles on the floor around the piano. Others are on tables and chairs. Most are alphabetized in bookshelves. Two or three thousand in all.

The composers all worked in the last hundred and fifty years. They wanted to contribute to modern music, to become part of the avant-garde. I've tried to stay interested in older music, but I just can't: Mozart and the others belonged to some other world. The earliest composers I have are Russian and German, from the opening years of the twentieth century. Back then many people thought they could write breakthrough works, be the most radical, the most daring. Almost all have been forgotten.

Some days I play pieces at random, picking them from the piles around the piano. Today after I read about Anneliese's index I went to the bookshelves and started again at the beginning of the alphabet: I played through Edouard Abramian's *Twenty-four Preludes,* and then Alexander Abramsky's sour *Laconic Sonata.* I skipped Thomas Adès and Theodor Adorno. I played some of Nicolai Agapov's *Perpetuum Mobile,* Ilya Aizberg's *Fairytale Sonata,* and his histrionic *Desolation.* I skipped Jehan Alain's three volumes of piano music. I went on to Alexander Alexandrov's emotional *Etudes* and *Visions,* Volkmar Andresson's *Praeludium,* Nikolaus Antsev's tiny *Morse Code Song,* Hans-Eric Apostel's *Kubiniana,* Dmitri Arakelian's *Georgian Hills,* Dmitry Arapov's skeletal *Third Sonata,* and then Andrei Arendts, Arensky, Anton Arijen's *Dirge for Vazgen I, Catholicos of All Armenians,* Artemyev, Asafyev, Atanatskovich, Aulensky, Avraamov, Avshalamov, Azanchevsky. Those are some of my letter A's.

Each of them dreamed of writing something that would shape their life, give it direction and purpose. When I play sometimes I feel I'm the only one who remembers them. I can almost hear them listening to me. They're glad, perhaps, that their work is remembered for a couple of minutes. And when I close a score because I've lost interest, because the music is weak or boring, I can almost feel the composer's spirit sighing, fading back away. After lunch I played a sonata by Markian Frolov, one of the very nearly forgotten. He founded the Sverdlovsk Music Conservatory in Ekaterinburg, on the far side of the Ural mountains, a thousand miles east of Moscow. There are lovely moments in his music. But it is loose, it loses my attention, and in a few minutes I close the score. I wonder if anyone, anywhere in the world, is playing his music.

I have mainly exchanged people for music. Playing the piano is my way of feeling the kind of closeness most people get from people. Without the trouble actual people can cause. Without the need to answer or think what to do next, or the obligation to care what they want. Music is exact biography. It speaks more clearly than the people it replaces.

I do not forget Stockhausen, in fact I try again each year to understand him. When I play *Piano Piece 10,* I have to listen very precisely. If I play Frolov, or many of the other thousands of forgotten composers, I don't need to think as much. I get a momentary impression of a Russian or German landscape: a placid river in spring, for instance, with birches on a muddy bank, or a view across roughly plowed fields to a gray evening sky. Things the composer might have seen. I feel the wet air or the smell of spring, and then it's gone. With Stockhausen I feel the hatred of all that. The suspicion about emotion, the intense need to say something different. It's what I felt when Anneliese talked. It's what made me sit still and listen.

I know it's strange to read about people and hear music instead of caring about their lives. Time has passed, faces and words have dropped away, and I am still here, fixed by the same fascinations. I hope these notes will explain, possibly to someone, how that feels.

After dinner I go to the other end of my bookshelves and work my way backward through the alphabet: Wim Zwaag's *Variations on Handel,* then Zverev's thundering *Ukrainian Dances,* Zuschneid's anemic *Nocturne on Lake Chany,* Zolotarev's perpetuum mobile, Gregory Zinger's only surviving sonata, Bernd Zimmerman's dissonant *Bagatelles,* Paul Zilcher's weak *Miniatures,* Georgiy Zhzhyonov's *Aurora,* some of Zhelobinsky's wonderful *Twenty-four Preludes,* and then Zharkov, Zhak, Zender, Zemlinsky, Zeiner, Zavorodny, Zavadil, Zanella, Zadora, some harsh pieces by Zaderatsky, one by the Albanian composer Cesk Zadeja, and I end with Harold Zabrack's overheated *Sonata No. 1,* dedicated to his surgeon. Those are some of my letter Z's.

30 Fina is moving me to Cattaraugas. She says I need to be closer to her, that I can't live by myself any more. She says there's no piano there. But the piano and the piles of sheet music are my companions. Without them my house would be empty. I'll take some of the music. Maybe in a few years if I don't get a piano I will forget how to play. Or my eyesight will get bleary and I won't be able to read the scores. Or I'll just be too tired to look through them.

Then Fina will take the music away, and that will be the end.

31 Most days I am up early. I think that is normal for older people, although I don't know why. Maybe it's because once you're old enough, you can never forget that you're supposed to be anxious about dying. I am not, particularly. Or you've got something that needs to be finished, like these notes.

In the morning I read the newspaper and check the houseplants. At ten or so I go for a short walk, down the access road or along the edge of the farmer's field. I play the piano from lunchtime until dinner. If I'm alone, like I usually am, dinner is in front of the television. Then I'm back at the piano until late. On a typical day, that might be six or eight hours at the piano. Same as the hours I used to work in the Water Department, same as what Anneliese wanted me to spend reading her book.

When Fina visits I don't play late at night. After dinner I go back to the piano for an hour or so. While she cleans up I play things I think she'd like: Keith Jarrett's "Somewhere Over the Rainbow," or Nikolayeva's arrangement of "Peter and the Wolf." I don't think she listens.

32 I don't have family left to care about, except Fina. She visits every couple of weeks, even though it's a long drive for her. We have an agreement that we don't talk about the family. That's not difficult for either of us. It's actually a wonderful feeling, not having much of a family. It's clarifying.

I wonder if that line of Anneliese's, in a year we may all be gone, if it went into my unconscious and pretty much stayed there. Maybe I said it to myself, so quietly I didn't even hear it, until it came true.

33 I remember this. That exact moment on the phone has stayed with me, the last remnant of reliable memory from that year. The electric feeling has gone out of it. It's like one of those small insects trapped in amber. You peer into the honey-colored stone, and in there is a little insect, contorted, struggling for air, motionless for a hundred million years.

34 Paul's voice reminds me again of Feinberg's music. Especially the restless waves in the bass of the *Third Piano Sonata.* Some of them come crashing up into the treble, like ocean waves that suddenly rise up and soak a pier.

After a large wave breaks, the ocean pulls it back, and there is a deep trough, like the octave at the end of this passage. For a moment the sea stops breathing.

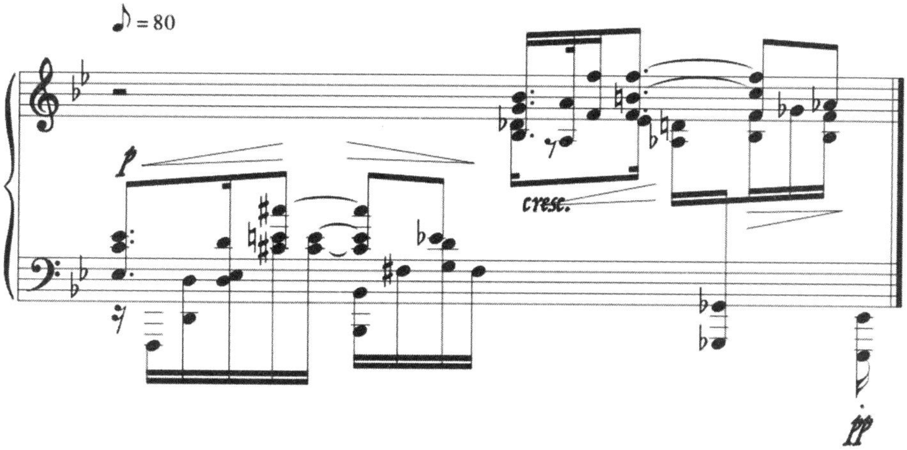


35 Like many composers in Russia at that time, Feinberg was under the spell of Scriabin, and a few minutes later there are ecstatic chords, resounding like organ music.

The moods come and go, and soon enough these chords evaporate and the waves are again calm. *Lentissimo,* the slowest possible speed for music, and *lugubre,* mournful. That is a romantic word, *lugubre.* Liszt wrote *lugubre* in his compositions about mourning and death.

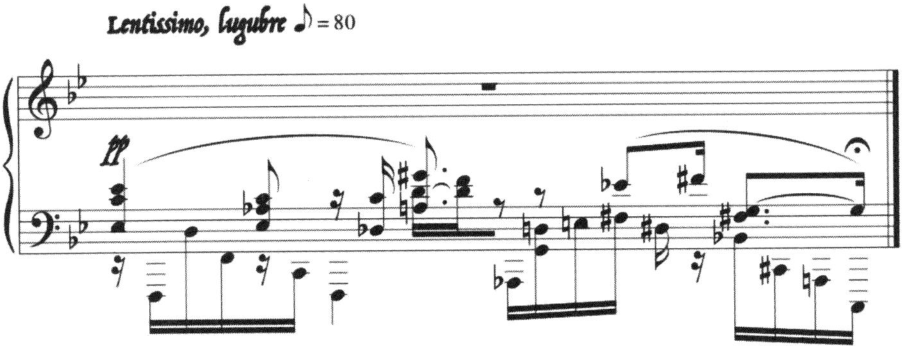


Without warning, then, the music ends.

36 You would think that after *Piano Piece 10* and *Plus Minus,* Stockhausen would take a break and write something simple. After *Finnegans Wake,* Joyce said he wanted to write a short book about the sea. Stockhausen could have composed a song, maybe, or some pieces for children. Instead he wrote another work for piano, and this one made *Piano Piece 10* look half-hearted. *Piano Piece 11* is the one that reminds me of Anneliese's notebooks. It broke something in Stockhausen's mind, and his later com-

positions are easier to understand. The piano pieces he wrote afterward are all parts of his enormous opera *Light,* which is seven nights long, that's twice the length of Wagner's *Ring.* It has camels, helicopters, trumpeters on rooftops, and people singing in invented languages. The piano pieces in it are incidental, and simpler than *Piano Pieces 9, 10,* or *11.* Stockhausen's life became noisy, and the piano pieces were lost in the celebration.

For instance *Piano Piece 12* has an electronic soundtrack. The pianist has to snap his fingers and whistle, hum, or hiss, or make whew! sounds and pfft! sounds, pfft! pfft! In *Piano Piece 13,* the pianist listens to a recording of synthesized music. Whenever he chooses, he can play the same notes on the piano, provided they are perfectly synchronized with the soundtrack. In *Piano Piece 18,* the pianist puts a set of Japanese temple bells on the piano bench, and every once in a while he strikes one and sings a high note.

Those are all theatrical and occasionally fun. *Piano Piece 11* is something different.

37 At first, *Piano Piece 11* looks fairly easy to play, or at least not impossible. It is printed on a single large sheet of paper, twenty by forty inches, the size of a movie poster. It's just nineteen isolated fragments of music, with white spaces between them. I had mine mounted on a board so it can sit on my piano. From across my living room the whole thing looks like a celestial chart, a map of the heavens from an old star atlas.

The nineteen individual fragments are like torn-up pieces of a composition. This is one of them. It is complicated, but short.

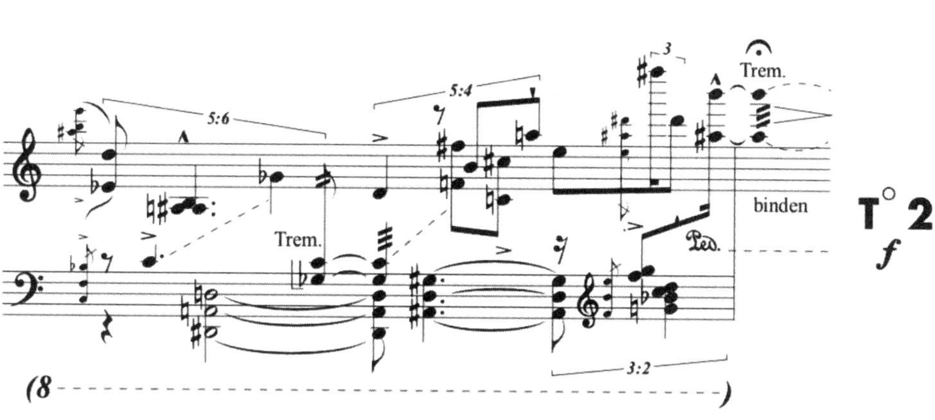

"*Piano Piece 11,*" Stockhausen wrote, "Consists of 19 independent fragments. The performer may begin anywhere, and then proceed to any other fragment. He is to continue until he comes back to the same fragment for the third time."

It seems to be an easy game. Some of the fragments only last a couple seconds. One has only eight notes.

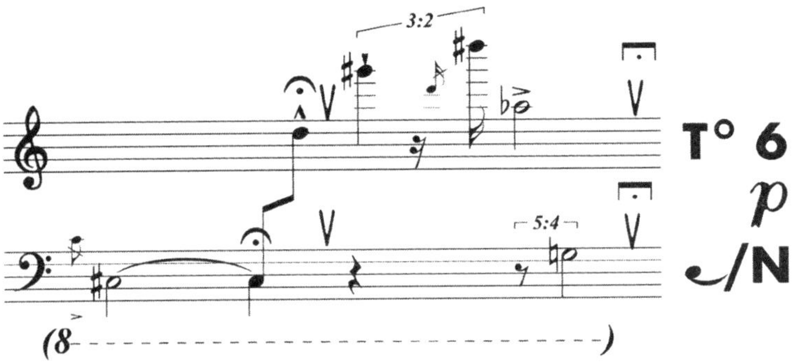


"At the end of each fragment," Stockhausen wrote, "there are instructions about how to play the next fragment. There are six permissible tempi, **T° 1** (very slow) to **T° 6** (very fast). There are seven dynamics, *ppp* to *fff.*" The ◡/**N** means that immediately after each note I have to depress the pedal partway down, so the note continues to sound, but quietly. Those are my instructions for the next fragment: play very fast, *piano,* and depress the pedal halfway down.

I glance across the sheet and choose another fragment.

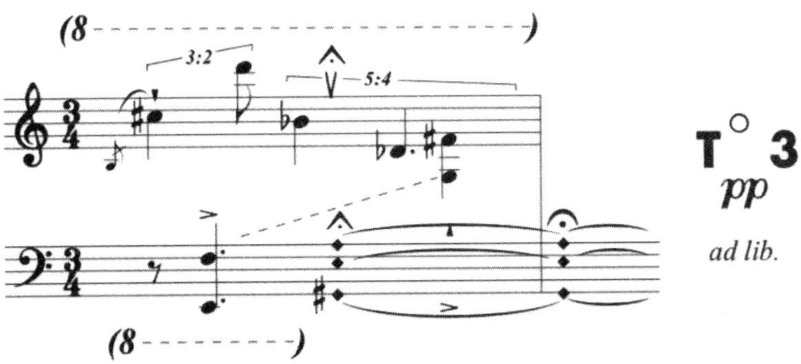

"The performer should not decide in advance which fragment to play next," he instructs. "He should play whatever fragment his eye rests on. The score may not be cut up to facilitate performance."

When I first tried playing *Piano Piece 11,* I chose the shortest fragments, ones with just a few notes, like this one with four notes in one hand and four chords in the other:

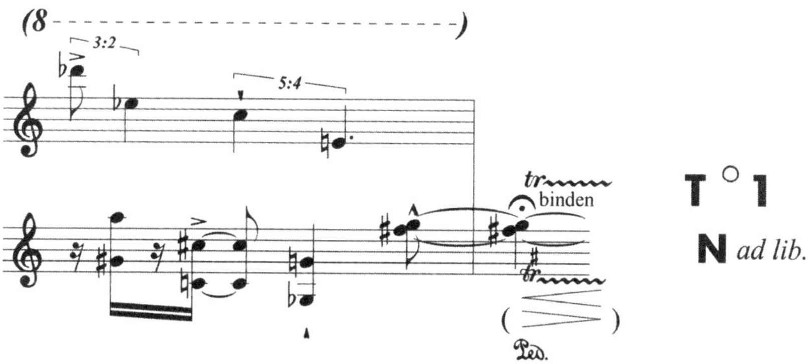


At first I thought *Piano Piece 11* was playable. The individual fragments sometimes looked complicated, but they were mostly brief. I could wander wherever I wanted, provided I did not return to the same place three times.

38 It turns out *Piano Piece 11* is insanely complicated. Stockhausen thought *Piano Piece 10* hadn't been strict enough, it had let music survive, it had a few melodies and a couple of attractive moments. He wanted to write music free from everything familiar. There were to be no melodies, no simple repetitions, no obvious systems, no easy rhythms, no clear sense or feeling or mood, no ordinary emotion. "I never accepted anything I found in other people's music," he said. "I wanted to erase any recognizable element in my music for ten years. I wanted to be the most abstract composer."

This time he began by drawing a series of tables. Across the top row he put different durations of notes, starting with an eighth note, then a quarter, and so on, adding an eighth each time, up to a half note plus an eighth.

1
2
3
4
5
6

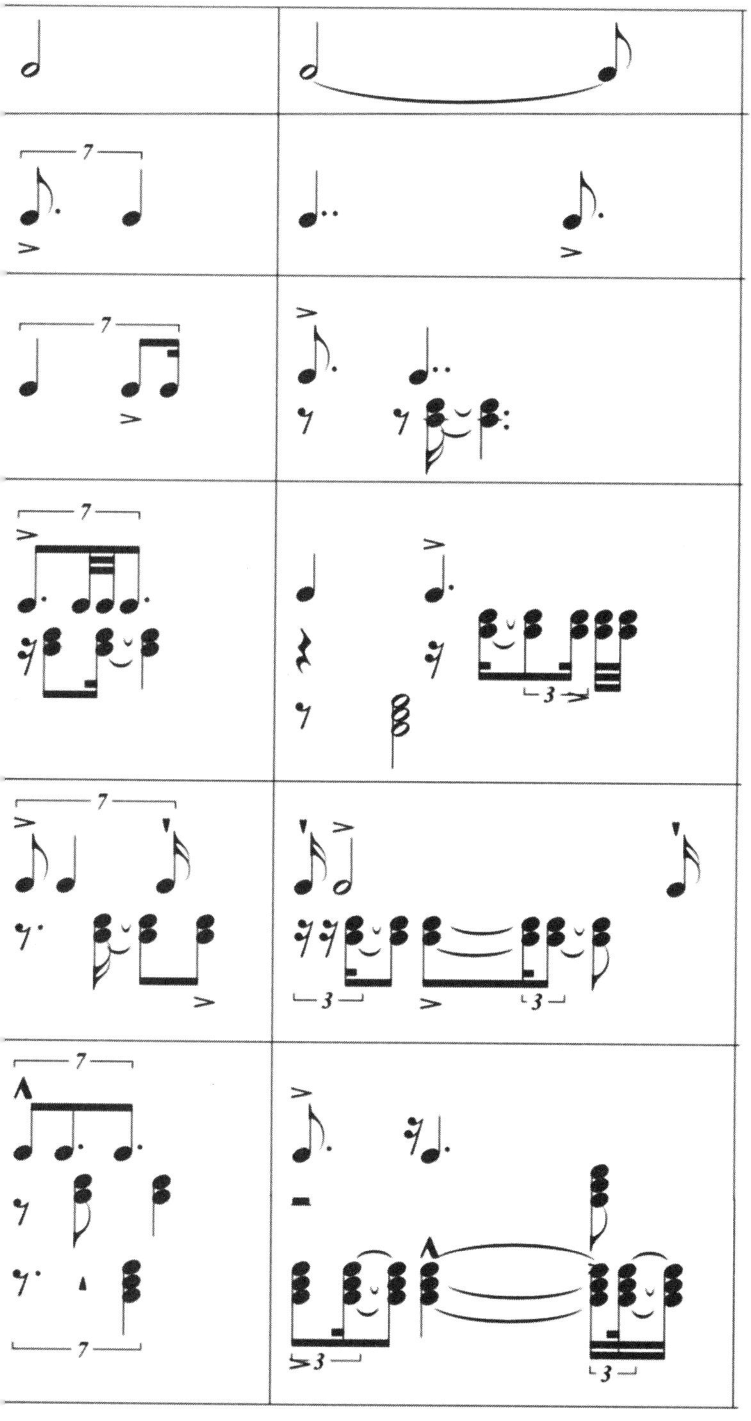

Then he filled in the rows underneath, dividing those durations into smaller pieces, making them increasingly complex. He didn't want simple divisions. He could have divided the eighth note into two sixteenths. But no: the first division of an eighth note, in row 2, is into five thirty-seconds, which he wrote as two sixteenths and a thirty-second note. In the first cell of row 3, he divided the eighth note again into five thirty-seconds, but then he made a different rhythm by dividing one beat into sixty-fourth notes. In row 4, he divided the eighth note into six thirty-second notes.

I studied his table, half-understanding it. Toward the bottom of the rhythms became so complex he distributed them among different voices. He wasn't even composing yet. He was composing to compose.

And it wasn't enough just to have one table like that. He made eleven of them. Each more complicated than the ones before it. In the second table he started with different notes, this time an eighth note tied to a half note, then a double-dotted half note, then a dotted quarter.

1

2

3

4

5

6

3
3
11:8
3
3
5
3
7
5
5
3
7

This second table is even harder to interpret than the first. The cells in row 2 don't add up to the note values in the top row. Some cells have stems without noteheads. Some have chords. Stockhausen was in a world of his own. These are musical notes, but I can't read them. They're like glyphs in an untranslated language.

He had the patience of a fanatic. His eleven tables of rhythms look like something a mathematician might write, except they aren't, because they don't add up. They look like something an artist might dream up, except that these are not for exhibition: somewhere in them there's a method.

He was driven by the fear of writing even a single bar of ordinary music. I imagine he must have been happy filling in his charts, thinking that no one before him had ever imagined these rhythms, that he was creating a new alphabet for a strange new language no one would be able to read.

Schönberg once said he would be happy if he heard a child singing one of his melodies in the street. Stockhausen made sure no one would sing what he wrote.

After he made eleven tables of rhythms, he decided he should combine them into one master chart. To guide the process he wrote out eight matrices, like this one:

| 2 | 3 | 4 | 5 | 6 | 7 |
|---|---|---|---|---|---|
| 4 | 6 | 8 | 10 | 12 | 14 |
| 6 | 9 | 12 | 15 | 18 | 21 |
| 8 | 12 | 16 | 20 | 25 | 28 |
| 10 | 15 | 20 | 25 | 30 | 35 |
| 12 | 18 | 24 | 30 | 36 | 42 |

And this one:

| 3 | 4 | 5 | 6 | 7 | 7 |
|---|---|---|---|---|---|
| 5 | 7 | 9 | 11 | 13 | 15 |
| 8 | 11 | 14 | 17 | 20 | 23 |
| 11 | 15 | 19 | 23 | 28 | 31 |
| 14 | 19 | 24 | 29 | 34 | 39 |
| 18 | 26 | 30 | 36 | 44 | 50 |

And this one:

| | | | | | |
|---|---|---|---|---|---|
| 2 | 3 | 4 | 5 | 6 | 7 |
| 4 | 6 | 8 | 10 | 12 | 14 |
| 5 | 8 | 11 | 14 | 17 | 20 |
| 6 | 10 | 14 | 18 | 23 | 26 |
| 1 | 6 | 11 | 16 | 21 | 26 |
| -2 | 4 | 10 | 16 | 22 | 30 |

And this one:

| | | | | | |
|---|---|---|---|---|---|
| 2 | 3 | 4 | 5 | 6 | 7 |
| -1 | 1 | 3 | 5 | 7 | 9 |
| -1 | 1 | 4 | 7 | 10 | 13 |
| -2 | 4 | 8 | 12 | 17 | 20 |
| -2 | 3 | 8 | 13 | 18 | 23 |
| -4 | 2 | 8 | 14 | 20 | 26 |

He didn't record the reason why he needed eight different tables of numbers, or how he decided how many rows and columns each one should have, or how he decided what numbers to put in them, or how he used them to combine his eleven tables of rhythms. I studied them, but I couldn't figure out the patterns. Somehow, he used his eight matrices to pick certain cells from his eleven tables of rhythms. Only those cells went into the master grid of rhythms for *Piano Piece 11.* Everything else was discarded.

Once he had his amalgamated master table of rhythms, he needed actual notes. So he started again, writing tables of harmonies, tables of pitches, tables of dynamics. He wrote simple harmonies across the top row of his table of harmonies: a minor second, a major second, a third, a fifth, a sixth. Then he divided and multiplied them in the rows underneath. He made eleven tables like that, and then combined them all, using his eight matrices, into a single master table of harmonies. Then he did the same for pitches and dynamics, almost fifty tables in all.

Up to that point he had not written a single second of music.

39 If he had been content to let *Piano Piece 11* be just 19 fragments of music printed on a poster-sized score, people might have thought of it as an interesting experiment. If he had based it just on his first table of rhythms, people might have been able to sense the system, and take pleasure in the structure.

But he was driven by a deep revulsion for conventional music. He needed to owe nothing to Bach or Schönberg, he wanted to outdo Boulez, Cage, and the others, to make music so radically new that it had no debts. He needed to make sure his listeners would not recognize a single rhythm or harmony from any music they had ever heard.

He wrote *Piano Piece 11* between 1955 and 1957, the same years Boulez was composing his *Third Piano Sonata,* which is also in fragments, and also printed on large sheets of paper. Boulez's sonata is supposed to be difficult, but it is easier to understand because Boulez was poetic: he was inspired by Mallarmé and Joyce, and there are poetic moments in the music. By comparison Stockhausen was a maniac.

In those same years Cage used Chinese divination to make music, but that is also easier to think about than Stockhausen's music, because the laws of chance are simple and Cage was full of spiritual thoughts about nature. Iannis Xenakis and Milton Babbitt also wrote complex compositions around the same time. Some of their pieces are considered to be nearly impossible to play. But unlike Stockhausen, Xenakis and Babbitt were mathematicians, so their calculations make sense, they explain what is happening in the music.

None of the other composers was as dedicated as Stockhausen. None needed hundreds of pages of notes in order to write one page of music. The others were thinking of the randomness of the universe, the sublime patterns of Mallarmé's poems, the beauty of mathematics. Stockhausen wasn't interested in those things. He bent over his notebooks and spreadsheets, dividing and recombining, never satisfied until he had used his unaccountable calculations to produce faultlessly new music. Music that excluded its composer, that he himself could not hear as music, that gave no pleasure except the tremendous pride of having finally crushed music into its constituent atoms.

I feel this pressure in Anneliese's notebooks. She started by cutting her own work into pieces, interrogating every fragment, reassembling them into an even more complex pattern, and that was before she even began to write out her theory.

40 The first of the 19 fragments is the one with only eight notes. It looks simple enough. It begins with a grace note. Then there's a half note, tied to a quarter note.

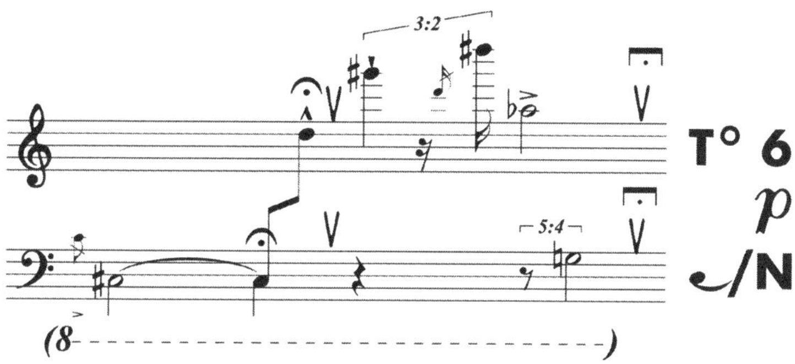


The fragment has a high G# and a very high D#, and then it ends with two long notes.

Yet even this, the simplest of the 19, is devious. For example the highest note. How do I play a sixteenth note that's part of a group of three eighth notes so that it sounds different from an ordinary sixteenth? How do I communicate that the last note isn't quite a half-note, but really only four-fifths of one? I can't, really, because no beat has been established. How could it be, when the fragment begins with a tied note and has two fermatas?

The poster-size score makes *Piano Piece 11* look approachable. It seems reasonable, well planned, nicely formatted. The performer has some freedom. But from the very beginning *Piano Piece 11* is impossible.

The seventh fragment also looks simple enough, just descending notes in both hands. But there's a 3:2 group, and then a 5:4 group: two eighth notes divided into three, then four eighth notes divided into five. It is just barely possible a professional musician might be able to hear that, but it's interrupted by off-beat chords in the bass, so it can only sound like a stumbling fall.

At the end of this fragment Stockhausen asks me to play a double trill. With my left hand I play a trill on F# and G#. With my right hand I play a trill on G and A. Below the double trill Stockhausen has written two dynamics: the lower trill is in parentheses, and it gets softer. The upper trill gets louder. No one can play such a thing mechanically, so there will be irregularities in my rhythms, creating another kind of complexity, a sort that is not notated. Planned complexities and unplanned ones, with no way for a listener to tell the difference.

Fragment number twelve is also very short. It looks like it should be easy enough to play. It also has a 3:2 group and a 5:4 group. But this time, as if he wants to make sure no human can hear the rhythms, Stockhausen has put a triangular fermata right in the middle of the second group.

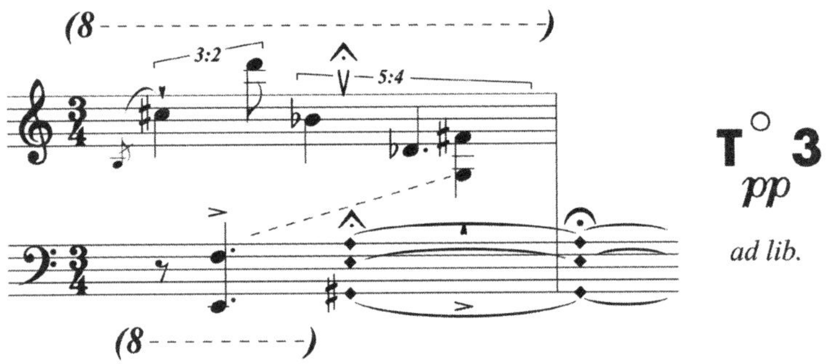

At the same moment I pause for the fermata, I depress three keys to make a silent chord in the left hand. After the last notes are struck in the right hand, that silent chord resonates sympathetically. A delicate overtone, a high D♭, sounds for a minute and then fades, smearing whatever rhythm might remain.

41 I keep playing, but I am at sea. I move from one fragment to the next, as I'm instructed to do. At the end of each one I read the directions telling me how to play whichever fragment I choose next. I keep going, trying not to plan my route, navigating randomly across the spaces of the large white page.

(8a bei Wiederholung → bis Schluß d. nächsten Zeil)
7:8
7:8
5:4
5:4
5:4
verlangsamen
7:8
Ped.
(2 Okt.
)
verlangsamen
beschleunigen
Zeitmaß
langsamer / bschleunigen
(2 Okt.
)

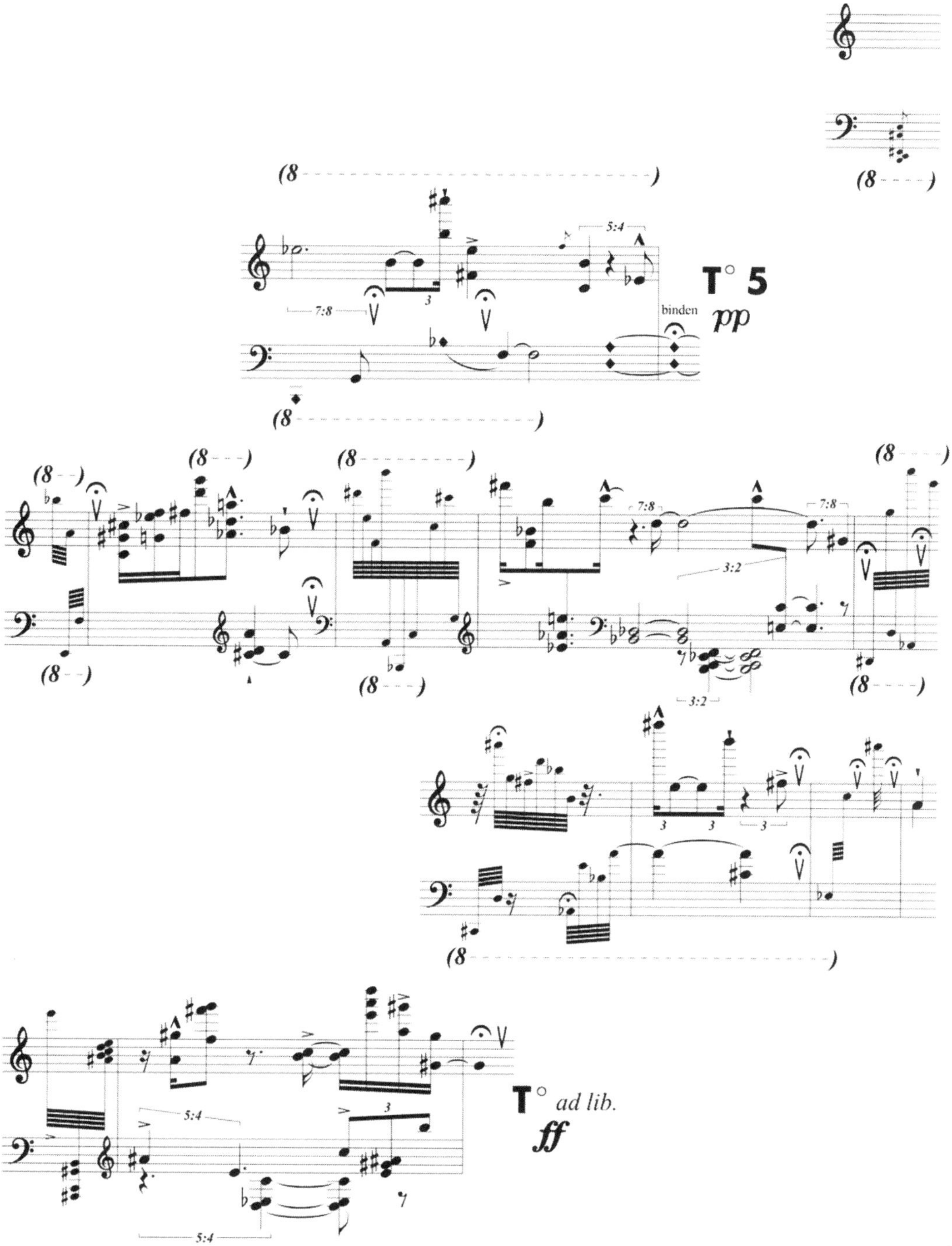
binden
T° 5
pp
T° ad lib.
ff

The poster-size score of *Piano Piece 11* looks like nineteen rocky pinnacles in a white ocean. Cliffs everywhere, and crashing surf. No place to land, no grass or trees, just vertical spikes of rock and seabirds calling. The thing that had looked like a set of small fragments now appears as a vast seascape, with no place to land, no place to rest. I sail from one cliff to the next, around and around, until I am exhausted.

42 At first, no one knew how Stockhausen had composed *Piano Piece 11.* A scholar named Stéphane Bienaimé decided to find out. He went to Kürten, a small town near Cologne where Stockhausen had established an archive of his papers. He saw the grids and matrices, but he could not interpret them. He wrote Stockhausen asking if he could help. A couple of months later Stockhausen wrote back, telling him to come to his house in Düsseldorf, where he had more papers. When Bienaimé arrived, Stockhausen brought out a 1957 Grand vin de Latour wooden wine crate full of notes. Bienaimé took the crate to a stationery store and had everything photocopied.

He wrote his PhD dissertation on *Piano Piece 11,* showing how each one of the 19 fragments is derived from the grids and matrices. Stockhausen had invented rules for himself as he went along. Whenever he thought he was making too much sense, he made up more rules.

Bienaimé started with fragment 6, a difficult passage with jumping rhythms, five in the right hand against four in the left.

He dissected the passage and found its underlying rhythms.

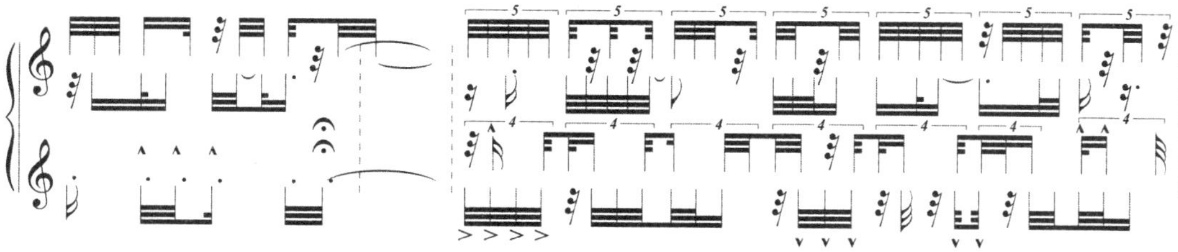

Then he traced each rhythm back to the grids. In the end he decoded *Piano Piece 11.* He revealed its genetic material.

I read Bienaimé's dissertation. Everything is described in exhaustive detail. But nothing makes sense. Stockhausen gave himself rules to keep his own imagination in check, but the rules don't make sense. It's as if an archaeologist found a pot, carefully broke it into thousands of strangely-shaped pieces, labeled each one in a tiny fastidious script, and said, "Isn't it beautiful? It's how a vase should be."

43 There are a few moments in *Piano Piece 11* when the music is suddenly personal. I can hear Stockhausen there, inside his music, singing to himself. The ninth fragment begins with sixty-fourth notes. There are exactly ten of them, evenly spaced. They are very carefully written. The second note in the bass lines up under the high A# in the right hand. There are two fermatas. I play the notes lightly and accurately, trying to convey that they are just grace notes, that there is no proper note yet.

When I cross the barline, one of the sixty-fourth notes turns into a larger melodic note. A listener might just realize that, because the left hand has only two quarter notes. But any sense of rhythm is erased in the third measure, because it has only grace notes, with pauses over the places where the beats should fall.

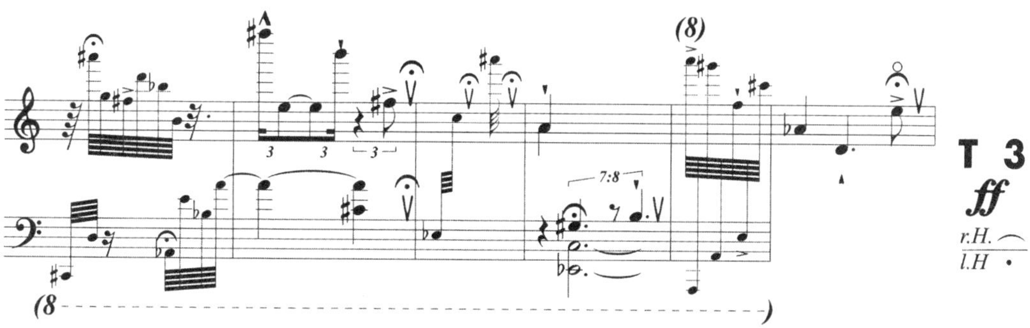

Just when it seems the music is not for me or for any other player or listener, when it looks like *Piano Piece 11* is just an idea that existed in Stockhausen's mind for a few years in the 1950s in Darmstadt, he writes two beautiful measures. The next-to-last is a double cascade of seven sixty-fourth notes, starting with the very top note of the entire keyboard, falling to the very bottom note, then tending down in the right hand and up in the left, converging on the last measure, where there's an A ♭, a D, and an E. A brief melody. It is lovely because it is personal, and so hopelessly surrounded by gray complexity. Maybe it's a remnant of his earlier life, like the brief moments in *Piano Piece 9* or the blank squares in *Plus Minus.* There is no way to know, or even to be sure he even wanted those measures to be beautiful.

Bienaimé said that every note in *Piano Piece 11* is determined by Stockhausen's self-imposed rules, except in one case. He noticed that fragment number 11 is not accurately transcribed from the tables. There are dissonant tremolos in the left hand, which are very dramatic, and at the end there's an unusual chord that resonates over the tremolo.

Bienaimé discovered that several notes in that last chord are not prescribed by Stockhausen's grids. His own system prohibited those pitches, but he wrote them anyway. The chord is beautiful, dark and uninviting. The tremolo gives it a lovely emptiness.

"Fragment 11 is mysterious," Bienaimé wrote, "especially if the pianist ends the performance of *Piano Piece 11* with fragment number 11, causing the illicit chord to hang in the air." This is one of the few moments when Stockhausen wrote music that works in the ordinary human way, by expressing a mood. Perhaps he permitted himself those few notes because he had worked so hard, and the music was fully eviscerated, hacked up, salted and dried, and there was no danger it might come back to life. As the chord dies away over the dissonant tremolo, the performer gets ready to move on, back to the world from which everything human has been rigorously excluded.

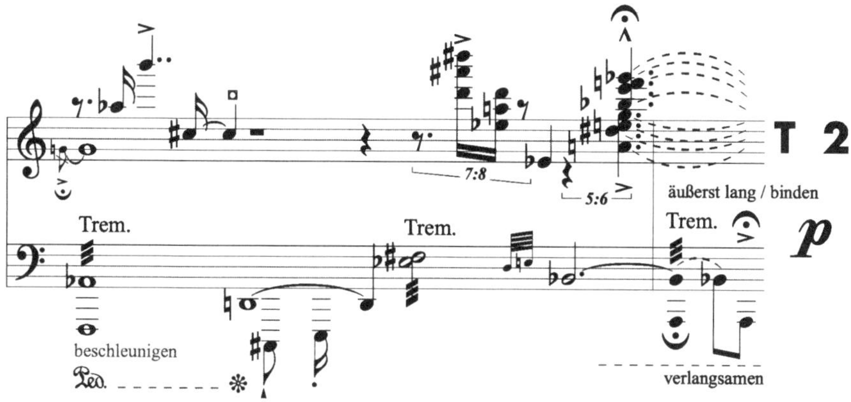


These few moments of ordinary music in Stockhausen are like the passages where Anneliese came out from behind her theories, when she was there in the darkness.

44 I also had two falls. After I was a child in Watkins Glen, I fell out of awareness of my life. I sleepwalked into my job. I fell again at the end of the year that's described in this book. I fell out of my job, and I also fell, literally. If an injury is severe enough it can permanently remove you from yourself. That darkness lasted nearly forty years. If you add the two of them, most of my life has been lived without me.

I wonder if Anneliese felt this. Perhaps people who have fallen can recognize one another.

And of course two falls is wrong. I fell up north to Shallow Lake, and I'm about to fall down to Cattaraugas with Fina. And really, all of life is falling, so that's another one.

45 I consider *Piano Piece 11* to be insane. When complexity reaches the point where no one can understand it and no one can hear it, when it requires hundreds of pages of calculations to create 19 brief fragments, when thousands of hours of work are needed to produce just a few minutes of music, then it really has to be counted as a form of insanity. And insane works of

art produce insane scholars. Bienaimé spent years verifying that Stockhausen's self-imposed rules generated nearly every note in *Piano Piece 11,* but that does not explain the work, or indicate how to listen to it, or even how to play it.

In 2015 a musicologist named Elena Krytska wrote a book about *Piano Piece 11.* It is also filled with charts and diagrams. She analyzed performances of *Piano Piece 11.* Each one is different, because the pianist chooses the order of fragments to play. Krytska noted every choice made by every pianist who had recorded *Piano Piece 11.* For each performance she drew four graphs, showing the exact durations, speeds, tempi, and volumes of each fragment the pianist played. Her book is fanatical, and I think it might also be insane, because it fails to explain anything about *Piano Piece 11.*

Stockhausen said pianists can keep going as long as they want, provided they don't choose which fragments they will play in advance, and provided they stop when they come to any one fragment for the third time. That got the attention of two mathematicians, Ronald Read and Lily Yen, who wrote a paper called "A Note on the Stockhausen Problem." After pages of bristling formulas, they concluded the average length of a performance of *Piano Piece 11* is 38.0046857 fragments. That has to be an insane thing to conclude.

I wonder if it is possible to write a sane commentary on a work that is not sane. I wonder if what I'm doing here is as hopeless as what Bienaimé did, or as crazy as Krytska or those mathematicians.

46 The mystical Russian composer Nikolai Obukhov was born in the Oblast of the Archangel. Only Russians have the luck to be born in places with names like that. If he had stayed in Russia after the Revolution, Obukhov would probably have been sent to the gulag, like so many other avant-garde composers, but he moved to Paris.

Like his hero Scriabin, Obukhov thought his music was divine. He took his celestial calling seriously. He invented a musical instrument called the Sonorous Cross. It worked like a theremin: the performer didn't need to touch it. He had a woman dress as a priestess, in white with a red cape. The Sonorous Cross was a brass sphere, and on top was a metal cross with a star in the middle. The priestess would walk up to the Sonorous Cross and make gestures of prayer, which the device transformed into wailing melodies.

All his life Obukhov worked on an enormous composition called the *Kniga žizni, The Book of Life.* He kept it in a shrine in his apartment, with candles burning at all times, and he staged a ritual performance once a year. The *Kniga žizni* was intended to be the music for the one-thousand-year kingdom of Christ, as described in the Book of Revelation. The thousand years of music would begin with the first resurrection, when all believers are called to heaven, and end with the second resurrection, when unbelievers are raised up and then cast down into a lake of fire. All through those thousand years the *Kniga žizni* would be playing, with the resurrected composer at his piano and a hundred priestesses playing Sonorous Crosses.

Obukhov did not think ordinary music notation was sufficient for his task, so he invented a new way of writing notes. As a result the score itself looks divine, as if an angel has written it. The manuscript occupied most of Obukhov's time for thirty years. The difficulty, he told his wife, was to compress the entire thousand years of the reign of the resurrected Christ into a single composition that could be heard on Earth.

Every year on the day of the first resurrection Obukhov invited a few friends to his apartment to hear parts of the *Kniga žizni.* A pianist named Marie-Antoinette Aussenac de Brog dressed as a priestess and played the Sonorous Cross. Obukhov built another instrument called the Ether, which was a wind machine with crystals inside. It had two compartments. One made sounds four octaves below the threshold of human hearing. The other made sounds five octaves higher than any human could hear. Obukhov called it an inaudible instrument, and said it played only to the resurrected.

Obukhov's wife later told an interviewer that she was asked to wash herself twice the morning of the performance, once in warm water and again in cold water, and told to remain silent the entire day. All other days of the year she had to ensure that the candles around the shrine never went out.

At one point she took the unfinished manuscript out of the shrine and tried to burn it, but Obukhov rescued it. He cut new pieces to replace the burned parts and glued them onto the existing pages. Then he took a needle and red thread and sutured the pages together. He said the manuscript was a wounded body. He sliced the skin between his fingers and sealed the manuscript's wounds with droplets of his blood. His wife never went near the manuscript again.

Obukhov's Frankenstein manuscript is in the Bibliothèque Nationale in Paris. It is over 2,000 pages long. Some pages are in the shape of the cross. Others are done in silver and gold leaf and ornamented with red silk ribbons. You can see how desperate he was, how much he wanted his composition to be divine.

The *Kniga žizni* begins with a preamble for piano, Sonorous Cross, Ether, and chorus. The preamble is several hundred pages long, bound in four volumes. The Bibliothèque Nationale also has a sheet of paper with Obukhov's plan for the entire composition. It was to be a symphony in 1,000 movements, one for each heavenly year in the kingdom of Christ. The manuscript in the Bibliothèque Nationale is just the Introduction and 1,500 pages of music called *Pervyy den'*, meaning *Day One.* At the rate he was composing it would have taken Obukhov 60,000 years to complete the one thousand heavenly days of the *Kniga žizni.* It is possible he didn't notice that, because he was so intensely devout.

47 In 1974, Obukhov was mugged as he walked along a street in New York. His cranium was damaged, and even though he lived another fifteen years, he moved slowly and spoke dully. His life was ruined. He didn't compose any more music. The *Kniga žizni* stayed in its shrine, but he never looked at it. After a few years his wife extinguished the candles. Obukhov used to go to a Russian Orthodox church in his neighborhood in Paris, and spent most of his days sitting at his piano. His wife took care of him. She said he played old Russian melodies and passages from Scriabin, Roslavets, Lourié, and other composers he had known before he fled Russia. When he died his wife brought the monstrous manuscript of the *Kniga žizni* to the Bibliothèque Nationale.

No one has published the manuscript of the *Kniga žizni,* but I have excerpts and an edition of his other pieces. Obukhov's devotion was intense, but the music is hard to listen to. Some pieces are ecstatic like Scriabin's, and I can almost see the souls Obukhov was imagining. But most of the *Kniga žizni* is uninteresting, and some is even embarrassing, and I think that is because I hear it from the other side. Maybe this is like the insanity Anneliese fell into, or one of the books she studied, closed to people on the outside. Obukhov experienced it as sacred music, to be sung in heaven for a thousand years. Not much of that comes through. I wait for the passages that sound like human music, and there are some, but they are lost in the sea of his hallucinatory devotion. After a while, I set the scores aside.

I think of Obukhov when I read about the later notebooks, because Anneliese went someplace I could not follow. I could see the words on the page, and I could see her anguish, but I couldn't understand where she was, or what she was thinking. I could read about the supernatural forest, but I couldn't see myself in the cold pit or the forest shed.

When I play Obukhov I can sense the intensity, the devotion, but I can't always feel it. I see immediately how strange it is, with its invented notes and specially constructed instruments, but when I play, I don't see heaven. I see only the music printed on the page.

Back then I was like Obukhov's wife, resisting, but caring for him. But it's different, because in the end she protected his work.

48 Forty years ago, I wrote this book to help me think about Anneliese. This month, I wrote these notes to explain the odd sensation of reading about a person I had very nearly forgotten and hearing Stockhausen's music in her place. I read about Anneliese's loudness, how her voice hammered, and that reminded me of *Piano Piece 9.* Her thirteen theories about her mental state made me think of the thirteen dimensions in *Piano Piece 10.* Those sets of thirteen divided into seven seemed equally desperate. Her summer of reading long books reminded me of Stockhausen's trip to Sicily and his attempt to write the world's longest composition on the beach. There is a curious affinity between *Piano Piece 11* and the complicated structure of her notebooks, but in the end she went someplace even more inaccessible than Stockhausen. The cold, passionate myths in her last notebooks reminded me of Obukhov and his angels and priestesses. It was as if she was too far

away to use normal language, like Obukhov thinking of the thousand year Kingdom and composing for resurrected souls instead of people.

I don't have the capacity for anything like what Anneliese or Stockhausen accomplished. Her notebooks defeated me after just a couple of hours. Still, I think this book I wrote, and these notes, are a little like her notebooks. She would laugh at that, because this book is short in comparison to what she did. Yet I think I have described what really matters about her. She would hate that, because I have drained the sense out of her life's work by turning it into music—but I no longer care about her science or what she wrote. I have been faithful to the peculiar way she thought. When I look at Stockhausen's unusual notations, when I count his thirty-second notes, or try to memorize his rules, I feel like I'm listening to the obscure words and unusual languages Anneliese used. His piano pieces have the same relentless grinding machinery of theories and rules. Perhaps these notes are a way of making her strange language into another one, even stranger. Maybe there is no way to translate an intricate language, invented by just one person, back into an ordinary one.

I am calm and colorless now, and I disremember Anneliese as a person. I'm not desperate like she was. I've been placid and content here by myself in Shallow Lake for a very long time. Yet I wonder if I have moved more than a couple of steps from the laboratory as it was on the day I left it, when I was about to close the door. I stood there looking at her notebooks, taking in their recriminating stares. Shortly afterward I moved away. I have lived an entire life, forty years, since she died. A life can change fundamentally, permanently, and yet some things—a sound, a feeling—may remain just as they were.

Still I wonder: Why do I still play Stockhausen after all these years? Why do performers practice some pieces over and over? After a while, it's no longer a technical problem. I think it's an unrequited love for work that can never be mastered. I love the music, and it does not love me in return. In reply it says, You don't understand me. Keep trying. Or, You are just like me, but you still don't see it.

In 1973, two decades after he composed *Piano Piece 9,* Stockhausen was talking to an interviewer about how people change. He insisted he was the same person he'd been in the 1950s.

The interviewer told him that if you take a fiddler crab from the Atlantic ocean, and put it in a box, and then you transport it to Bavaria, it still follows the diurnal rhythms of the sea. It shakes itself awake at the same time, and it moves in accord with the ocean, even though it is five hundred miles from a beach.

"I understand," Stockhausen said. "It is a vibrating system with a very particular structure of rhythm. It modulates within itself but does not change. That's what we all are when we talk, when we think. We may be very far from home, but we move in accord with things that happened to us long ago."

49 The composition on the next pages is my farewell to Anneliese. It is the sound that is left of her. She was a strange thing that happened to me a long time ago. Thanks to her I know a person can triumph in her own mind, even if no one hears her, even if her work remains as silent as this composition of mine, which sits quietly on these pages.

Lento ♩ = 40
f
p
Andante ♩ = 50
8va
(8)
Ped.
Ped.

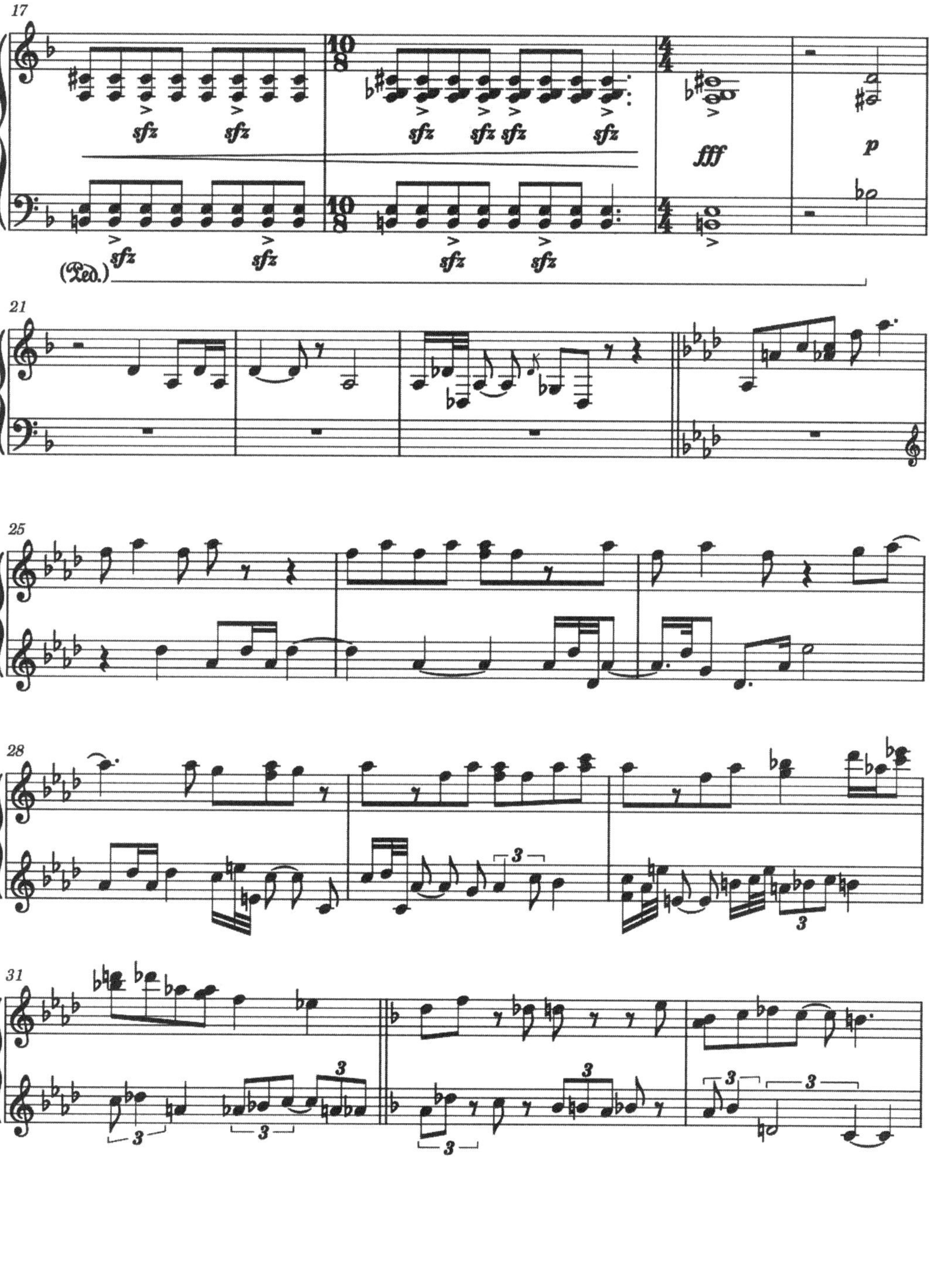
17
sfz
sfz
sfz
sfz
sfz
sfz
fff
p
sfz
sfz
sfz
sfz
(Ped.)
21
25
28
31

34
Singing
sopra
37
8va
40
(8)
43
Ped.
47
(Ped.)

## *Author's note on the music*

The music in this book does not have to be heard. Readers who have pianos can play the pieces while reading. Readers can also listen to audio files as they read.

The music can be performed for an audience. If that is done, the pianist or another person should read from the text that precedes the music, and then play the passage twice, with a brief pause between the two performances. The sheet music should be projected onscreen during the performance.

All the music in this book is modified or written by the author. None of it reproduces work by Stockhausen or Feinberg. For that reason it is not permissible to play the composers' original pieces. However the pianist can improvise extensions to the music in this book, turning them into full pieces.

# WEAK IN COMPARISON TO DREAMS

## THE FIRST ENTRY IN JAMES ELKINS' MULTI-VOLUME MEGA-NOVEL *FIVE STRANGE LANGUAGES*

Available to purchase anywhere books are sold and at unnamedpress.com, follow Samuel Emmer in his early years as a downtrodden municipal scientist as he is forced to visit zoos around the world. Already read it, and want more? The limited edition vinyl with music from *Weak in Comparison to Dreams*, is exclusively available at unnamedpress.com/vinyl.

"A NOVEL THAT WILL HAUNT ITS READERS EVEN AS IT ENCHANTS."
**—PIPPA STOKES**

PUBLISHED DECEMBER 12, 2023

ISBN: 9781951213725